Hickory Flat Public Library
2740 East Cherokee Drive
Canton, Georgia 30115

American Crimes

Edited by Martin H. Greenberg

BARNES & NOBLE

NEW YORK

This edition published by Barnes & Noble Publishing Inc, by arrangement with Tekno Books.

Designed by Lundquist Design, NY

ISBN 13: 978-0-7607-7971-2
ISBN 10: 0-7607-7971-6

Printed in the United States of America

05 06 07 08 9 8 7 6 5 4 3 2 1

Table of Contents

Copyrights

JOHN HELFERS

Introduction to
American Crimes

THERE IS A GENERAL CONSENSUS that the United States of America has contributed only two things to world culture; the iconic cowboy of the Wild West, and jazz. Both very notable achievements in their own right, but I would like to put forth the idea that there is a third, somewhat more dubious accomplishment that America has given the world, for better or for worse. That is, the packaging of crime as entertainment.

Bear in mind that I'm not just talking through fiction; as that has been done for hundreds of years by many authors around the world, including William Godwin (*Caleb Williams*), Edward Bulwer Lytton (*Pelham*), Charles Dickens (*Bleak House*), and others. However, even in those books, the crime and mystery was often a subplot, and it took an American, Edgar Allan Poe, to present the solving of a crime on center stage with his stories "The Purloined Letter" and "The Murders in the Rue Morgue."

Fictionalized "police procedural" books have also been around for about 150 years, with detective casebooks written and sold in Great Britain, Australia, and France back in the mid-19th century, and continuing into the 20th with *In Cold Blood*, Truman Capote's infamous blurring of the line between truth and fiction. As the reign of Ann Rule and others similar authors indicate, the only difference today is that authors can now make their career writing nonfiction books that exhaustively examine every angle of a particular crime.

A far greater change has happened in the modern-day packaging of crime for entertainment, which has transformed the recreation and imagining of once-shocking acts into something that is completely accepted—as long as it is happening to someone else, or distanced from the participant by other media. Today, it is hard to think of another country in the world that has most entertainment resources devoted to the creation and display of crime-tainment. From fictional television series (*CSI, NCIS, Without a Trace, Law & Order*) to documentary crime shows (*Cold Case Files, The First 48, City Confidential, Forensic Case Files, Dr. G: Medical Examiner*) to entire networks based around the criminal justice system (Court TV, large blocks of A&E and the Discovery Channel) to video games (the *Grand Theft Auto* series, *True Crime; Streets of L.A.*, etc.), America has made the packaging and selling of crime entertainment a part of our everyday life.

Is this a bad thing? Not necessarily. According to 2003 Department of Justice statistics, crime across all age groups and genders decreased over the previous 10 years, particularly among teens and young adults. Crime rates in many major metropolitan areas have dropped by double digits. Has the influx of crime in our daily media actually tempered our society's fascination with it? Perhaps, although Americans' interest in crime entertainment in all forms shows no sign of slowing down, particularly in fiction. However, it may be that being able to participate in the vicarious thrill of "crime" through video games, television—and yes, literature—may actually have sated America's desire to actually go out and walk on the wrong side of the law.

And it is in fiction where, once again, America (as our country has so many times before) has taken a position at the forefront of crime and mystery novels and short stories. Authors like Thomas Harris, Patricia Cornwell, Jeffery Deaver, Michael Connelly, Elizabeth George, Mary Higgins Clark, and others have perched atop bestseller lists regularly for years. Other authors, such as Donald Westlake, Edward D. Hoch, Ed Gorman, John Lutz, and Clark Howard, have enjoyed commercial and critical success in both short and long fiction over their long and distinguished careers. But it is unlikely that this would have happened with the existence of America in the first place. Our nation is like no other place on earth—a place where people from all around the world can come together in pursuit of whatever they think will make them happy—even if that happens to be committing a crime.

Even in the 21st century, America is still a melting pot, in some ways now more than ever. Yet, far from being a homogenized nation and "indivisible," regions, cultures, and races still maintain their own identities. And nowhere is that more evident than in regional fiction, no matter what the genre.

Mystery fiction in general seems particularly suited to adapting the patterns and rhythms of a particular area, whether that be the hustle and bustle of New York City, the insular, folksy small-town life of the rural South, the independent frontier spirit that still lives on in the west, the glitz and glamour of neon-coated Las Vegas, the sun-drenched beach culture of Hawaii, or the awesome majesty of the Alaskan wilderness. America encapsulates a world of different regions in one country, a world vividly rendered in the short crime fiction that has been published over the last few decades. Although mystery and crime—like food or speech or clothes—takes on different aspects in different parts of the nation, it remains never less than fascinating.

To this end, we've assembled a star-studded list of mystery stories from around the great nation of ours, from New England to the Deep South to the Southwest to the West, and Alaska and Hawaii, just for good measure. Featuring crimes and criminals as varied as one would expect—from their motives and methods to the sleuths that capture them—*American Crimes* truly represents the best mystery fiction that our nation has to offer. I hope you enjoy this larcenous tour of our nation, featuring criminals, cops, and everything in between.

ISAAC ASIMOV

The Good Samaritan

THE BLACK WIDOWERS HAD LEARNED by hard experience that when Mario Gonzalo took his turn as host of the monthly banquet, they had to expect the unusual. They had reached the point where they steeled themselves, quite automatically, for disaster. When his guest arrived there was a lightening of spirit if it turned out he had the usual quota of heads and could speak at least broken English.

When the last of the Black Widowers arrived, therefore, and when Henry's efficient setting of the table was nearly complete, Geoffrey Avalon, standing, as always, straight and tall, sounded almost light-hearted as he said, "I see that your guest has not arrived yet, Mario."

Gonzalo, whose crimson velvet jacket and lightly striped blue pants reduced everything else in the room to monochrome, said, "Well—"

Avalon said, "What's more, a quick count of the settings placed at the table by our inestimable Henry shows that people and no more are to be seated. And since all six of us are here, I can only conclude that you have not brought a guest."

"Thank Anacreon," said Emmanuel Rubin, raising his drink, "or whatever spirit it is that presides over convivial banquets of kindred souls."

Thomas Trumbull scowled and brushed back his crisply waved white hair with one hand. "What are you doing, Mario? Saving money?"

"Well—" said Gonzalo again, staring at his own drink with a totally spurious concentration.

Roger Halsted said, "I don't know that this is so good. I like the grilling sessions."

"It won't hurt us," said Avalon, in his deepest voice, have a quiet conversation once in a while. If we can't amuse each other without a guest, then the Black Widowers are not what once they were and we should prepare, sorrowing, for oblivion. Shall we offer Mario a vote of thanks for his unwonted discretion?"

"Well—" said Gonzalo a third time.

James Drake interposed, stubbing out a cigarette and clearing his throat. "It seems to me, gentlemen, that Mario is trying to say something and is amazingly bashful about it. If he has something he hesitates to say, I fear we are not going to like it. May I suggest we all keep quiet and let him talk."

"Well—" said Gonzalo, and stopped. This time, though, there was a prolonged silence.

"Well—" said Gonzalo again, "I do have a guest," and once more he stopped.

Rubin said, "Then where the hell is he?"

"Downstairs in the main dining room—ordering dinner—at my expense, of course."

Gonzalo received five blank stares. Then Trumbull said, "May I ask what dunderheaded reason you can possibly advance for that?"

"Aside," said Rubin, "from being a congenital dunderhead."

Gonzalo put his drink down, took a deep breath, and said firmly, "Because I thought she would be more comfortable down there."

Rubin managed to get out an "And why—" before the significance of the pronoun became plain. He seized the lapels of Gonzalo's jacket, "Did you say 'she'?"

Gonzalo caught at the other's wrists, "Hands off, Manny. If you want to talk, use your lips, not your hands. Yes, I said 'she.'"

Henry, his sixtyish, unlined face showing a little concern, raised his voice a diplomatic notch and said, "Gentlemen! Dinner is served!"

Rubin, having released Gonzalo, waved imperiously at Henry and said, "Sorry, Henry, there may be no banquet.— Mario, you damned jackass, *no woman can attend these meetings.*"

There was, in fact, a general uproar. While no one quite achieved the anger and decibels of Rubin, Gonzalo found himself at bay with the five others around him in a semicircle. Their individual comments were lost in the general explosion of anger.

Gonzalo, waving his arms madly, leaped onto a chair and shouted, "Let me speak!" over and over until out of exhaustion, it seemed, the opposition died off into a low growl.

Gonzalo said, "She is not our guest at the banquet. She's just a woman with a problem, an old woman, and it won't do us any harm if we see her *after* dinner."

There was no immediate response and Gonzalo said, "She needn't sit at the table. She can sit in the doorway."

Rubin said, "Mario, if she comes in here, I go, and if I go, damn it, I may not ever come back."

Gonzalo said, "Are you saying you'll break up the Black Widowers rather than listen to an old woman in trouble?"

Rubin said, "I'm saying rules are rules!"

Halsted, looking deeply troubled, said, "Manny, maybe we ought to do this. The rules weren't delivered to us from Mount Sinai."

"You, too?" said Rubin savagely. "Look, it doesn't matter what any of you say. In a matter as fundamental as this, one blackball is enough, and I cast it. Either she goes or I go and, by God, you'll never see me again. In view of that, is there anyone who wants to waste his breath?"

Henry, who still stood at the head of the table, waiting with markedly less than his usual imperturbability for the company to be seated, said, "May I have a word, Mr. Rubin?"

Rubin said, "Sorry, Henry, no one sits down till this is settled."

Gonzalo said, "Stay out, Henry. I'll fight my own battles."

It was at this point that Henry departed from his role as the epitome of all Olympian waiters and advanced on the group. His voice was firm as he said, "Mr. Rubin, I wish to take responsibility for this. Several days ago Mr. Gonzalo me to ask if I would be so kind as to listen to a woman he knew who had the kind of problem he thought I might be helpful with. I asked him if it were something close to his heart. He said that the woman was a relative of someone who was very likely to give him a commission for an important piece of work—"

"Money!" sneered Rubin.

"Professional opportunity," snapped Gonzalo. "If you understand that. And sympathy for a fellow human being, if you can understand *that*."

Henry held up his hand.

"*Please*, gentlemen! I told Mr. Gonzalo I could not help him but urged him, if he had not already arranged a guest, to bring the woman. I suggested that there might be no objection if she did not actually attend the banquet itself."

Rubin said, "And why couldn't you help her otherwise?"

Henry said, "Gentlemen, I lay no claims to superior insight. I do not compare myself, as Mr. Gonzalo occasionally does on my behalf, to Sherlock Holmes. It is only after you gentlemen have discussed a problem and eliminated what is extraneous that I seem to see what remains. Therefore—"

Drake said, "Well, look, Manny, I'm the oldest member here, and the original reason for the prohibition. We might partially waive it just this once."

"No," said Rubin flatly.

Henry said, "Mr. Rubin, it is often stated at these banquets that I am a member of the Black Widowers. If so, I wish to take the responsibility. I urged Mr. Gonzalo to do this and I spoke to the woman concerned and assured her that she would be welcomed to our deliberations after dinner. It was impulsive act based on my estimate of the characters of the gentlemen of the club.

"If the woman is now sent away, Mr. Rubin, you understand that my position here will be an impossible one and I will be forced to resign as waiter at these banquets. I would have no choice."

Almost imperceptibly the atmosphere had changed while Henry spoke and now it was Rubin who was standing at bay. He stared at the semicircle that now surrounded him and said, rather gratingly, "I appreciate your services to the club, Henry, and I do not wish to place you in a dishonorable position. Therefore, on the stipulation that this is not to set a precedent and reminding you that you must not do this again, I will withdraw my black-ball."

*   *   *

The banquet was the least comfortable in the history of the Black Widowers. Conversation was desultory and dull and Rubin maintained a stony silence throughout.

There was no need to clatter the water glass during the serving of the coffee, since there was no babble of conversation to override. Gonzalo simply said, "I'll go down and see if she's ready. Her name, by the way, is Mrs. Barbara Lindemann."

Rubin looked up and said, "Make sure she's had her coffee, or tea, or whatever, downstairs. She can't have anything up here."

Avalon looked disapproving, "The dictates of courtesy, my dear Manny—"

"She'll have all she wants downstairs at Mario's expense. Up here we'll listen to her. What more can she want?"

Gonzalo brought her up and led her to an armchair that Henry had obtained from the restaurant office and that he had placed well away from the table.

She was a rather thin woman, with blunt good-natured features, well dressed and with her white hair carefully set. She carried a black purse that looked new and she clutched it tightly. She glanced timidly at the faces of the Black Widowers and said, "Good evening."

There was a low chorused rumble in return and she said, "I apologize for.coming here with my ridiculous story. Mr. Gonzalo explained that my appearance here is out of the ordinary and I have thought, over my dinner, that I should not disturb you. I will go if you like, and thank you for the dinner and for letting me come up here."

She made as though to rise and Avalon, looking remarkably shame-faced, said, "Madame, you are entirely welcome here and we would like very much to hear what you have to say. We cannot promise that we will be able to help you, but we can try. I'm sure that we all feel the same way about this. Don't you agree, Manny?"

Rubin shot a dark look at Avalon through his thick-glasses. His sparse beard bristled and his chin lifted but he said in a remarkably mild tone, "Entirely, ma'am."

There was a short pause, and then Gonzalo said, "It's our custom, Mrs. Lindemann, to question our guests and under the circumstances, I wonder if you would mind having Henry handle that. He is our waiter, but he is a member of our group."

Henry stood motionless for a moment, then said, "Mr. Gonzalo, that—"

Gonzalo said, "You have yourself claimed the privilege membership earlier this evening, Henry. Privilege carries with it responsibility. Put down the brandy bottle, Henry, and sit down. Anyone who wants brandy can take his own. Henry, take my seat." Gonzalo rose resolutely and walked to the sideboard.

Henry sat down and said mildly to Mrs. Lindemann, "Madame, would you be willing to pretend you are on the witness stand?"

The woman looked about and her look of uneasiness dissolved into a little laugh. "I never have been and I'm not sure I know how to behave on one. I hope you won't mind if I'm nervous."

"We won't, but you needn't be. This will be very in and we are anxious only to help you. The members of the club have a tendency to speak loudly and excitably at times, they do, that is merely their way and means nothing.—First, please tell us your name."

She said, with an anxious formality, "My name is Barbara Lindemann. Mrs. Barbara Lindemann."

"And do you have any particular line of work?"

"No, sir, I am retired. I am sixty-seven years old; as you can probably tell by looking at me—and a widow. I was once a schoolteacher at a junior high school."

Halsted stirred and said, "That's my profession, Mrs. Lindemann. What subject did you teach?"

"Mostly I taught American history."

Henry said, "Now, from what Mr. Gonzalo has told me, you suffered an unpleasant experience here in New York and—"

"No, pardon me," interposed Mrs. Lindemann, "it was, on the whole, a very pleasant experience. If that weren't so, I would be only too glad to forget all about it."

"Yes, of course," said Henry, "but I am under the impression that you have forgotten some key points and would like to remember them."

"Yes," she said earnestly. "I am so ashamed at not remembering. It must make me appear senile, but it was a very unusual and frightening thing in a way—at least parts of it were—and I suppose that's my excuse."

Henry said, "I think it would be best, then, if you tell us what happened to you in as much detail as you can, and if it will not bother you, some of us may ask questions as you go along."

"It won't bother me, I assure you," said Mrs. Lindemann. "I'll welcome it as a sign of interest. I arrived in New York City nine days ago—from the West Coast. I was going to visit my niece, among other things, but I didn't want to stay with her. That would have been uncomfortable for her and confining for me, so I took a hotel room.

"I got to the hotel at about six p.m. on Wednesday and after a small dinner, which was very pleasant, although the prices were simply awful, I phoned my niece and arranged to see her the next day when her husband would be at work and the children at school. That would give us some time to ourselves and then in the evening we could have a family outing.

"Of course, I didn't intend to hang about their necks the entire two weeks I was to be in New York. I fully intended to do things on my own. In fact, that first evening after dinner, I had nothing particular to do and I certainly didn't want to sit in my room and watch television. So I thought—well, all Manhattan is just outside, Barbara, and you've read about it all your life and seen it in the movies and now's your chance to see it in real life.

"I thought I'd just step out and wander about on my own and look at the elaborate buildings and the bright lights and the people hurrying past. I just wanted to get a feel of the city, before I started taking organized tours. I've done that in other cities in these recent years when I've been traveling and I've always so enjoyed it."

Trumbull said, "You weren't afraid of getting lost, I suppose."

"Oh, no," said Mrs. Lindemann. "I have an excellent sense of direction and even if I were caught up in my sightseeing and didn't notice where I had gone, I had a map of Manhattan and the streets are all in a rectangular grid and numbered—not like Boston, London, or Paris, and I was never lost in those cities. Besides, I could always get in a taxi and give the driver the name of my hotel. Besides, I was sure anyone would me directions if I asked."

Rubin emerged from his trough of despond to deliver himself of a ringing, "In Manhattan? Hah!"

"Why, certainly," said Mrs. Lindemann, with mild reproof. "I've always heard that Manhattanites are unfriendly, but I have not found it so. I have been the recipient of many kindnesses—not the least of which is the manner in which you gentlemen have welcomed me even though I am quite a stranger to you."

Rubin found it necessary to stare intently at his fingernails.

Mrs. Lindemann said, "In any case, I did go off on an excursion and stayed out much longer than I had planned; Everything was so colorful and busy and the weather so mild and pleasant. Eventually, I realized I was terribly tired and I had reached a rather quiet street and was ready to go back. I looked in one of the outer pockets of my purse for my map—"

Halsted interrupted. "I take it, Mrs. Lindemann, you were alone on this excursion."

"Oh, yes," said Mrs. Lindemann. "I always travel alone since my husband died. To have a companion means a perpetual state of compromise as to when to arise, what to eat, where to go. No, no, I want to be my own woman."

"I didn't mean quite that, Mrs. Lindemann," said Halsted. "I mean to ask whether you were alone on this particular in a strange city—at night—with a purse."

"Yes, sir, I'm afraid so."

Halsted said, "Had no one told you that the streets of New York aren't always safe at night—particularly, excuse me, older women with purses who look, as you do, gentle and harmless?"

"Oh, dear, of course I've been told that. I've been told that of every city I've visited. My own town has districts that aren't safe. I've always felt, though, that all life is a gamble, that a no-risk situation is an impossible dream, and I wasn't going to deprive myself of pleasant experiences because of fear. And I've gone about in all sorts of places without harm."

Trumbull said, "Until that first evening in Manhattan, I take it."

Mrs. Lindemann's lips tightened and she said, "Until then. It was an experience I remember only in flashes, so to speak. I suppose that because I was so tired, and then so frightened, and the surroundings were so new to me, that much of what happened somehow didn't register properly. Little things seem to have vanished forever. That's the problem." She bit her lips and looked as though she were battling to hold back the tears.

Henry said softly, "Could you tell us what you remember?"

"Well," she said, clearing her throat and clutching at her purse, "as I said, the street was a quiet one. There were cars moving past, but no pedestrians, and I wasn't sure where I was. I was reaching for the map and looking about for a street sign when a young man seemed to appear from nowhere and said, 'Got a dollar, lady?' He couldn't have been more than fifteen years old—just a boy.

"Well, I would have been perfectly willing to let him have a dollar if I thought he needed it, but really, he seemed perfectly fit and reasonably prosperous and I didn't think it would be advisable to display my wallet, so I said, 'I'm afraid I don't, young man.'

"Of course, he didn't believe me. He came closer and said, 'Sure you do, lady. Here, let me help you look,' and he reached for my purse. Well, I wasn't going to let him have it, of course—"

Trumbull said firmly, "No 'of course' about it, Mrs. Lindemann. If it ever happens again, you surrender your purse at once. You can't save it in any case. Hoodlums think nothing of using force and there's nothing in a purse that can be worth your life."

Mrs. Lindemann sighed. "I suppose you're right, but at the time I just wasn't thinking clearly. I held on to my purse as a reflex action, I suppose, and that's when I start failing to remember. I recall engaging in a tug of war and I seem to recall other young men approaching. I don't know how many but I seemed surrounded.

"Then I heard a shout and some very bad language and the loud noise of feet. There was nothing more for a while i that my purse was gone. Then there was an anxious voice, low and polite, saying, 'Are you hurt, madam?'

"I said, 'I don't think so, but my purse is gone.' I looked about vaguely. I think I was under the impression it had fallen to the street.

"There was an older young man holding my elbow respectfully. He might have been twenty-five. He said, 'They got that, ma'am. I'd better get you out of here before they come back for some more fun. They'll probably have knives and I don't.'"

"He was hurrying me away. I didn't see him clearly in the dark, but he was tall and wore a sweater. He said, 'I live close by, ma'am. It's either go to my place or we'll have a battle.' I *think* I was aware of other young men in the distance that may have been a delusion.

"I went with the new young man quite docilely. He seemed earnest and polite and I've gotten too old to feel that I am in danger of—uh—personal harm. Besides, I was so confused and lightheaded that I lacked any will to resist.

"The next thing I remember is being at his apartment door. I remember that it was apartment 4-F. I suppose that remains in my mind because it was such a familiar combination during World War II. Then I was inside his apartment and sitting in an upholstered armchair. It was a rather run-down apartment, I noticed, but I don't remember getting to it at all.

"The man who had rescued me had put a glass into my hand; and I sipped from it. It was some kind of wine, I think. I did not particularly like the taste, but it warmed me and it seemed to make me less dizzy—rather than more dizzy, as one would suppose.

"The man appeared to be anxious about my possibly being hurt, but I reassured him. I said if he would just help me get a taxi I would get to my hotel.

"He said I had better rest a while. He offered to call the police to report the incident, but I was adamant against that. That's one of the things I remember *very* clearly. I knew the police were not likely to recover my purse and I did not *want* to become a newspaper item.

"I think I must have explained that I was from out of town because he lectured me, quite gently, on the dangers of walking on the streets of Manhattan.—I've heard so much on the subject in the last week. You should hear my niece go on and on about it.

"I remember other bits of the conversation. He wanted to know whether I'd lost much cash and I said, well, about thirty or forty dollars, but that I had traveler's checks which could, of course, be replaced. I think I had to spend some time reassuring him that I knew how to do that, and that I knew how to report my missing credit card. I had only had one in my purse.

"Finally I asked him his name so that I could speak to him properly and he laughed and said, 'Oh, first names will do for that.' He told me his and I told him mine. And I said, 'Isn't it astonishing how it all fits together, your name, and your address, and what you said back there.' I explained and he laughed and said he would never have thought of that.—So you see I knew his address.

"Then we went downstairs and it was quite late by then, at least by the clock, though, of course, it wasn't really very late by my insides. He made sure the streets were clear, then made me wait in the vestibule while he went out to hail the cab. He told me he had paid the driver to take me wherever I wanted to go and then before I could stop him he put a twenty-dollar bill in my hand because he said I mustn't be left with no money at all.

"I tried to object, but he said he loved New York, and since I had been so mistreated on my first evening there by New Yorkers, it had to be made up for by New Yorkers. So I accepted it—because I knew I would pay it back.

"The driver took me back to the hotel and he didn't try to collect any money. He even tried to give me change because he said the young man had given him a five-dollar bill, but I was pleased with his honesty and I wouldn't take the change.

"So you see although the incident began very painfully, there was the extreme kindness of the Good Samaritan young man and of the taxi driver. It was as though an act of unkindness was introduced into my life in order that I might experience other acts of kindness that would more than redress the balance. And I still experience them—yours, I mean.

"Of course, it was quite obvious that the young man was not well off and I strongly suspected that the twenty-five dollars he had expended on me was far more than he could afford to throw away. Nor did he ask my last name or the name of my hotel. It was as though he knew I would pay it back without having to be reminded. Naturally, I would.

"You see, I'm quite well-to-do really, and it's not just a matter of paying it back. The Bible says that if you cast bread upon the waters it will be returned tenfold, so I think it's only fair that if he spent twenty-five dollars, he ought to get two hundred and fifty back, and I can afford it.

"I returned to my room and slept so soundly after all that; it was quite refreshing. The next morning, I arranged my affairs with respect to the credit card and the traveler's checks then I called my niece and spent the day with her.

"I told her what had happened but just the bare essentials. After all, I had to explain why I had no bag and why I was temporarily short of cash.

She went on and on about it. I bought a new purse—this one—and it was-n't till the end of the when I was in bed again that I realized that I had not made it my business to repay the young man first thing. Being with family had just preoccupied me. And then the real tragedy struck me."

Mrs. Lindemann stopped and tried to keep her face from crumpling, but she failed. She began to weep quietly and reach desperately into her bag for a handkerchief.

Henry said softly, "Would you care to rest, Mrs. Lindemann?"

Rubin said, just as softly, "Would you like a cup of Mrs. Lindemann, or some brandy?" Then he glared about as though daring anyone to say a word.

Mrs. Lindemann said, "No, I'm all right. I apologize for behaving so, but I found I had forgotten. I don't remember the young man's address, *not at all*, though I must have known it that night because I talked about it. I don't remember his first name! I stayed awake all night trying to remember, that just made it worse. I went out the next day to try to retrace my steps, but everything looked so different by day—and at night, I was afraid to try.

"What must the young man think of me? He's never heard from me. I took his money and just vanished with it. I am worse than those terrible young hoodlums who snatched my purse. I had never been kind to *them*. They owed me no gratitude."

Gonzalo said, "It's not your fault that you can't remember. You had a rough time."

"Yes, but *he* doesn't know I can't remember. He thinks I'm an ungrate-ful thief. Finally I told my nephew about my trouble and he was just think-ing of employing Mr. Gonzalo for something and he felt that Mr. Gonzalo might have the kind of worldly wisdom that might help. Mr. Gonzalo said he would try, and in the end—well, here I am.

"But now that I've heard myself tell the story I realize how hopeless it all sounds."

*   *   *

Trumbull sighed.

"Mrs. Lindemann, please don't be offended at what I am about to ask, but we must eliminate some factors. Are you sure it all really happened?"

Mrs. Lindemann looked surprised, "Well, of *course* it really happened. My purse was *gone!*"

"No," said Henry, "what Mr. Trumbull means, I think, is that after the mugging you somehow got back to the hotel and then had a sleep that may have been filled with nightmares so that what you remember now is partly fact and partly dream—which would account for the imperfect memory."

"No," said Mrs. Lindemann firmly, "I remember what I do remember perfectly. It was not a dream."

"In that case," said Trumbull, shrugging, "we have very little to go on."

Rubin said, "Never mind, Tom. We're not giving up. If we choose the right name for your rescuer, Mrs. Lindemann, would you recognize it, even though you can't remember it now?"

"I hope so," said Mrs. Lindemann, "but I don't know. I've tried looking in a phone directory to see different first names', but none seemed familiar. I don't think it could have been a very common name."

Rubin said, "Then it couldn't have been Sam?"

"Oh, I'm certain that's not it."

"Why Sam, Manny?" asked Gonzalo.

"Well, the fellow was a Good Samaritan. Mrs. Lindemann called him that herself. Sam for Samaritan. His number and street may have represented the chapter and verse in the Bible where the tale of the Good Samaritan begins. You said his name and address fitted each other and that's the only clue we have."

"Wait," put in Avalon eagerly, "the first name might have been the much less common one of Luke. That's the gospel in which the parable is to be found."

"I'm afraid," said Mrs. Lindemann, "that doesn't sound right, either. Besides, I'm not *that* well acquainted with the Bible. I couldn't identify the chapter and verse of the parable."

Halsted said, "Let's not get off on impossible tangents. Mrs. Lindemann taught American history in school, so it's likely that what struck her concerned American history, instance, suppose the address were 1812 Madison Avenue and the young man's name was James.—James Madison was President during the War of 1812."

"Or 1492 Columbus Avenue," said Gonzalo, "and the young man was named Christopher."

"Or 1775 Lexington Avenue and the name Paul for Paul Revere," said Trumbull.

"Or 1623 Amsterdam Avenue and the name Peter," Avalon, "for Peter Minuit, or 1609 Hudson Street and the name Henry. In fact, there are many such named streets in lower Manhattan. We can never pick an appropriate one unless Mrs. Lindemann remembers."

Mrs. Lindemann clasped her hands tightly together, "Oh, dear, oh, dear, nothing sounds familiar."

Rubin said, "Of course not, if we're going to guess at random. Mrs. Lindemann, I assume you are at a midtown hotel."

"I'm at the New York Hilton. Is that midtown?"

"Yes. Sixth Avenue and 53rd Street. The chances are could not have walked more than a mile, probably less, before you grew tired. Therefore, let's stick to midtown. Hudson Street is much too far south and places like 1492 Columbus or 1812 Madison are much too far north. It would have midtown, probably West Side—and I can't think of anything."

Drake said, through a haze of cigarette smoke, "You're forgetting one item. Mrs. Lindemann said it wasn't just the name and address that fit but what the young man said back there—that is, at the site of the rescue. What did he say back there?"

"It's all so hazy," said Mrs. Lindemann.

"You said he called out roughly at the muggers. Can you repeat what he said?"

Mrs. Lindemann colored. "I could repeat some of what said, but I don't think I want to. The young man apologized for it afterward. He said that unless he used bad language the hoodlums would not have been impressed and would not have scattered. Besides, I know I couln't have referred to that at all."

Drake said thoughtfully, "That bites the dust then. Have you thought of advertising? You know, 'Will the young man who aided a woman in distress—' and so on."

"I've thought of it," said Mrs. Lindemann, "but that would be so dreadful. He might not see it and so many impostors might try to make a claim.—Really, this is so dreadful."

Avalon, looking distressed, turned to Henry and said, "Well, Henry, does anything occur to you?"

Henry said, "I'm not certain.—Mrs. Lindemann, you said that by the time you took the taxi it was late by the clock but not by your insides. Does that mean you arrived from the West Coast by plane so that your perception of time was three hours earlier?"

"Yes, I did," said Mrs. Lindemann.

"Perhaps from Portland, or not too far from there?" asked Henry.

"Why, yes, from just outside Portland. Had I mentioned that?"

"No, you hadn't," interposed Trumbull. "How did you know, Henry?"

"Because it occurred to me, sir," said Henry, "that the young man's name was Eugene, which is the name of a town only about a hundred miles south of Portland."

Mrs. Lindemann rose, eyes staring. "My goodness! The name was Eugene! But that's marvelous. How could you possibly tell?"

Henry said, "Mr. Rubin pointed out the address had to be in midtown Manhattan on the West Side. Dr. Drake pointed out your reference to what the young man had said at the scene of the rescue, and I recalled that one thing you reported him to have said was that you had better go to his place or there'd be a battle.

"Mr. Halsted pointed out that the address ought to have some significance in American history and so I thought it might be 54 West 40th Street, since there is the well-known election slogan of '54-40 or fight,' the election of 1844, I believe. It would be particularly meaningful to Mrs. Lindemann if she were from the Northwest since it pertained to our dispute with Great Britain over the Oregon Territory. When she said she was indeed from near Portland, Oregon, I guessed that the rescuer's name might be Eugene."

Mrs. Lindemann sat down, "To my dying day I will never forget this. That is the address. How could I have forgotten when you worked it out so neatly from what little I did remember?"

And then she grew excited. She said, "But it's not too I must go there *at once*. I must pay him or shove an envelope under his door or something."

Rubin said, "Will you recognize the house if you see it?"

"Oh, yes," said Mrs. Lindemann. "I'm sure of that, it's apartment 4-F. I remembered that. If I knew his last name, I would call, but, no, I want to see him and explain."

Rubin said mildly, "You certainly can't go yourself, Lindemann. Not into that neighborhood at this time of night after what you've been through. Some of us will have to go with you. At the very least, I will."

Mrs. Lindemann said, "I very much dislike inconveniencing you, sir."

"Under the circumstances, Mrs. Lindemann," said Rubin "I consider it my duty."

Henry said, "If I know the Black Widowers, I believe we will all accompany you, Mrs. Lindemann."

LINDA BARNES

Lucky Penny

L
IEUTENANT MOONEY MADE ME dish it all out for the record. He's
a good cop, if such an animal exists. We used to work the same shift
before I decided—wrongly—that there was room for a lady PI in this
town. Who knows? With this case under my belt, maybe business'll take a
180-degree spin, and I can quit driving a hack.

See, I've already written the official report for Mooney and the cops,
but the kind of stuff they wanted: date, place, and time, cold as ice and sub-
mitted in triplicate, doesn't even start to tell the tale. So I'm doing it over
again, my way.

Don't worry, Mooney. I'm not gonna file this one.

The Thayler case was still splattered across the front page of the
Boston Globe. I'd soaked it up with my midnight coffee and was puzzling it
out—my cab on automatic pilot, my mind on crime—when the mad tea
party began.

"Take your next right, sister. Then pull over, and douse the lights.
Quick!"

I heard the bastard all right, but it must have taken me thirty seconds or so to react. Something hard rapped on the cab's dividing shield. I
didn't bother turning around. I hate staring down gun barrels.

I said, "Jimmy Cagney right? No, your voice is too high. Let me
guess, don't tell me—"

"Shut up!"

"*Kill* the lights, *turn off the* lights, okay. But *douse* the lights? "You've
been tuning in too many old gangster flicks."

"I hate a mouthy broad," the guy snarled. I kid you not.

"*Broad?*" I said. "Christ! *Broad?* You trying to grow hair on your balls?"

"Look, I mean it, lady!"

"*Lady's* better. Now you wanna vacate my cab and go rob a phone booth?" My heart was beating like a tin drum, but I didn't let my voice shake, and all the time I was gabbing at him, I kept trying to catch his face in the mirror. He must have been crouching way back on the passenger side. I couldn't see a damn thing.

"I want all your dough," he said.

Who can you trust? This guy was a spiffy dresser: charcoal-gray three-piece suit and rep tie, no less. And picked up in front of the swank Copley Plaza. I looked like I needed the bucks more than he did, and I'm no charity case. A woman can make good tips driving a hack in Boston. Oh, she's gotta take precautions, all right. When you can't smell a disaster fare from thirty feet, it's time to quit. I pride myself on my judgment. I'm careful. I always know where the police checkpoints are, so I can roll my cab past and flash the old lights if a guy starts acting up. This dude fooled me cold.

I was ripped. Not only had I been conned, I had a considerable wad to give away. It was near the end of my shift, and like I said, I do all right. I've got a lot of regulars. Once you see me, you don't forget me—or my cab.

It's gorgeous. Part of my inheritance. A '59 Chevy, shiny as new, kept on blocks in a heated garage by the proverbial dotty old lady. It's the pits of the design world. Glossy blue with those giant chromium fins. Pvestrained decor: just the phone number and a few gilt curlicues on the door. I was afraid all my old pals at the police department would pull me over for minor traffic violations if I went whole hog and painted "Carlotta's Cab" in ornate script on the hood. Some do it anyway.

So where the hell were all the cops now? Where are they when you need 'em?

He told me to shove the cash through that little hole they leave for the passenger to pass the fare forward. I told him he had it backwards. He didn't laugh. I shoved bills.

"Now the change," the guy said. Can you imagine the nerve? I must have cast my eyes up to heaven. I do that a lot these days. "I mean it." He rapped the plastic shield with the shiny barrel of his gun. I checked it out this time. Funny how big a little .22 looks when it's pointed just right.

I fished in my pockets for change, emptied them. "Is that all?"

"You want the gold cap on my left front molar?" I said. "Turn around," the guy barked. "Keep both hands on the steering wheel. High."

I heard jingling, then a quick intake of breath.

"Okay," the crook said, sounding happy as a clam, "I'm gonna take my leave—"

"Good. Don't call this cab again."

"Listen!" The gun tapped. "You cool it here for ten minutes. And I mean frozen. Don't twitch. Don't blow your nose. Then take off."

"Gee, thanks."

"Thank you," he said politely. The door slammed.

At times like that, you just feel ridiculous. You know the guy isn't going to hang around, waiting to see whether you're big on insubordination. *But,* he might. And who wants to tangle with a .22 slug? I rate pretty high on insubordination. That's why I messed up as a cop. I figured I'd give him two minutes to get lost. Meantime I listened.

Not much traffic goes by those little streets on Beacon Hill at one o'clock on a Wednesday morn. Too residential. So I could hear the guy's footsteps tap along the pavement. About ten steps back, he stopped. Was he the one in a million who'd wait to see if I turned around? I heard a funny kind of whooshing noise. Not loud enough to make me jump, and anything much louder than the ticking of my watch would have put me through the roof. Then the footsteps patted on, straight back and out of hearing.

One minute more. The only saving grace of the situation was the location: District One. That's Mooney's district. Nice guy to talk to.

I took a deep breath, hoping it would have an encore, and pivoted quickly, keeping my head low. Makes you feel stupid when you do that and there's no one around.

I got out and strolled to the corner, stuck my head around a building kind of cautiously. Nothing, of course.

I backtracked. Ten steps, then *whoosh.* Along the sidewalk stood one of those new "Keep Beacon Hill Beautiful" trash cans, the kind with the swinging lid. I gave it a shove as I passed. I could just as easily have kicked it; I was in that kind of funk.

Whoosh, it said, just as pretty as could be.

Breaking into one of those trash cans is probably tougher than busting into your local bank vault. Since I didn't even have a dime left to fiddle the screws on the lid, I was forced to deface city property. I got the damn thing open and dumped the contents on somebody's front lawn, smack in the middle of a circle of light from one of those snooty Beacon Hill gas street lamps.

Halfway through the whisky bottles, wadded napkins, and beer cans, I made my discovery. I was doing a thorough search. If you're going to stink like garbage anyway, why leave anything untouched, right? So I was opening all the brown bags—you know, the good old brown lunch-and-bottle bags—looking for a clue. My most valuable find so far had been the moldy rind of a bologna sandwich. Then I hit it big: one neatly creased bag stuffed full of cash.

To say I was stunned is to entirely underestimate how I felt as I crouched there, knee-deep in garbage, my jaw hanging wide. I don't know what I'd expected to find. Maybe the guy's gloves. Or his hat, if he'd wanted to get rid of it fast in order to melt back into anonymity. I pawed through the rest of the debris. My change was gone.

I was so befuddled I left the trash right on the front lawn. There's probably still a warrant out for my arrest.

District One headquarters is off the beaten path, over on New Sudbury Street. I would have called first, if I'd had a dime.

One of the few things I'd enjoyed about being a cop was gabbing with Mooney. I like driving a cab better, but, face it, most of my fares aren't scintillating conversationalists. The Red Sox and the weather usually covers it. Talking to Mooney was so much fun, I wouldn't even consider dating him. Lots of guys are good at sex, but conversation—now there's an art form.

Mooney, all six-feet-four, 240 linebacker pounds of him, gave me the glad eye when I waltzed in. He hasn't given up trying. Keeps telling me he talks even better in bed.

"Nice hat," was all he said, his big fingers pecking at the typewriter keys.

I took it off and shook out my hair. I wear an old slouch cap when I drive to keep people from saying the inevitable. One jerk even misquoted Yeats at me: "Only God, my dear, could love you for yourself alone and not your long red hair." Since I'm seated when I drive, he missed the chance to ask me how the weather is up here. I'm six-one in my stocking feet and skinny enough to make every inch count twice. I've got a wide forehead, green eyes, and a pointy chin. If you want to be nice about my nose, you say it's got character.

Thirty's still hovering in my future. It's part of Mooney's past.

I told him I had a robbery to report and his dark eyes steered me to a chair. He leaned back and took a puff of one of his low-tar cigarettes. He can't quite give 'em up, but he feels guilty as hell about 'em.

When I got to the part about the bag in the trash, Mooney lost his sense of humor. He crushed a half-smoked butt in a crowded ashtray.

"Know why you never made it as a cop?" he said.

"Didn't brown-nose enough."

"*You* got no sense of proportion! Always going after crackpot stuff!"

"Christ, Mooney, aren't you interested? Some guy heists a cab, at gunpoint, then tosses the money. Aren't you the least bit *intrigued?*"

"I'm a cop, Ms. Carlyle. I've got to be more than intrigued. I've got murders, bank robberies, assaults—"

"Well, excuse me. I'm just a poor citizen reporting a crime. Trying to help—"

"Want to help, Carlotta? Go away." He stared at the sheet of paper in the typewriter and lit another cigarette. "Or dig me up something on the Thayler case."

"You working that sucker?"

"Wish to hell I wasn't."

I could see his point. It's tough enough trying to solve any murder, but when your victim is *the* Jennifer (Mrs. Justin) Thayler, wife of the famed Harvard Law prof, and the society reporters are breathing down your neck along with the usual crime-beat scribblers, you got a special kind of prob-lem.

"So who did it?" I asked.

Mooney put his size twelves up on his desk. "Colonel Mustard in the library with the candlestick! How the hell do I know? Some scumbag housebreaker. The lady of the house interrupted his haul. Probably didn't mean to hit her that hard. He must have freaked when he saw all the blood, 'cause he left some of the ritziest stereo equipment this side of heaven, plus enough silverware to blind your average hophead. He snatched most of old man Thayler's goddamn idiot artworks, collections, collectibles—whatever the hell you call 'em—which ought to set him up for the next few hundred years, if he's smart enough to get rid of them."

"Alarm system?"

"Yeah, they had one. Looks like Mrs. Thayler forgot to turn it on. According to the maid, she had a habit of forgetting just about anything after a martini or three."

"Think the maid's in on it?"

"Christ, Carlotta. There you go again. No witnesses. No finger-prints. Servants asleep. Husband asleep. We've got word out to all the fences here and in New York that we want this guy. The pawnbrokers know

the stuff's hot. We're checking out known art thieves and shady museums—"

"Well, don't let me keep you from your serious business," I said,
getting up to go. "I'll give you the collar when I find out who robbed my
cab."

"Sure," he said. His fingers started playing with the typewriter
again.

"Wanna bet on it?" Betting's an old custom with Mooney and me.

"I'm not gonna take the few piddling bucks you earn with that
ridiculous car."

"Right you are, boy. I'm gonna take the money the city pays you to
be unimaginative! Fifty bucks I nail him within the week."

Mooney hates to be called "boy." He hates to be called "unimaginative." I hate to hear my car called "ridiculous." We shook hands on the deal.
Hard.

Chinatown's about the only chunk of Boston that's alive after midnight. I headed over to Yee Hong's for a bowl of wonton soup.

The service was the usual low-key, slow-motion routine. I used a
newspaper as a shield; if you're really involved in the *Wall Street Journal*, the
casual male may think twice before deciding he's the answer to your
prayers. But I didn't read a single stock quote. I tugged at strands of my hair,
a bad habit of mine. Why would somebody rob me and then toss the money
away?

Solution Number One: He didn't. The trash bin was some mob
drop, and the money I'd found in the trash had absolutely nothing to do
with the money filched from my cab. Except that it was the same amount—
and that was too big a coincidence for me to swallow.

Two: The cash I'd found was counterfeit and this was a clever way
of getting it into circulation. Nah. Too baroque entirely. How the hell would
the guy know I was the pawing-through-the trash type?

Three: It was a training session. Some fool had used me to perfect
his robbery technique. Couldn't he learn from TV like the rest of the crooks?

Four: It was a frat hazing. Robbing a hack at gunpoint isn't exactly
in the same league as swallowing goldfish.

I closed my eyes.

My face came to a fortunate halt about an inch above a bowl of
steaming broth. That's when I decided to pack it in and head for home.
Wonton soup is lousy for the complexion.

I checked out the log I keep in the Chevy, totaled my fares: $4.82

missing, all in change. A very reasonable robbery.

By the time I got home, the sleepiness had passed. You know how it is: one moment you're yawning, the next your eyes won't close. Usually happens when my head hits the pillow; this time I didn't even make it that far. What woke me up was the idea that my robber hadn't meant to steal a thing. Maybe he'd left me something instead. You know, something hot, cleverly concealed. Something he could pick up in a few weeks, after things cooled off.

I went over that backseat with a vengeance, but I didn't find anything besides old Kleenex and bent paperclips. My brainstorm wasn't too clever after all. I mean, if the guy wanted to use my cab as a hiding place, why advertise by pulling a five-and-dime robbery?

I sat in the driver's seat, tugged my hair, and stewed. What did I have to go on? The memory of a nervous thief who talked like a B movie and stole only change. Maybe a mad toll-booth collector.

I live in a Cambridge dump. In any other city, I couldn't sell the damned thing if I wanted to. Here, I turn real estate agents away daily. The key to my home's value is the fact that I can hoof it to Harvard Square in five minutes. It's a seller's market for tar-paper shacks within walking distance of the Square. Under a hundred thou only if the plumbing's outside.

It took me a while to get in the door. I've got about five locks on it. Neighborhood's popular with thieves as well as gentry. I'm neither. I inherited the house from my weird Aunt Bea, all paid for. I consider the property taxes my rent, and the rent's getting steeper all the time.

I slammed my log down on the dining room table. I've got rooms galore in that old house, rent a couple of them to Harvard students. I've got my own office on the second floor, but I do most of my work at the dining room table. I like the view of the refrigerator.

I started over from square one. I called Gloria. She's the late-night dispatcher for the Independent Taxi Owners Association. I've never seen her, but her voice is as smooth as mink oil and I'll bet we get a lot of calls from guys who just want to hear her say she'll pick 'em up in five minutes.

"Gloria, it's Carlotta."

"Hi, babe. You been pretty popular today."

"Was I popular at one-thirty-five this morning?"

"Huh?"

"I picked up a fare in front of the Copley Plaza at one-thirty-five. Did you hand that one out to all comers or did you give it to me solo?"

"Just a sec." I could hear her charming the pants off some caller in the background. Then she got back to me.

"I just gave him to you, babe. He asked for the lady in the '59 Chevy. Not a lot of those on the road."

"Thanks, Gloria."

"Trouble?" she asked.

"Is mah middle name," I twanged. We both laughed and I hung up before she got a chance to cross-examine me.

So. The robber wanted my cab. I wished I'd concentrated on his face instead of his snazzy clothes. Maybe it was somebody I knew, some jokester in mid-prank. I killed that idea; I don't know anybody who'd pull a stunt like that, at gunpoint and all. I don't want to know anybody like that.

Why rob my cab, then toss the dough?

I pondered sudden religious conversion. Discarded it. Maybe some robber was some perpetual screwup who'd ditched the cash by mistake.

Or . . . Maybe he got exactly what he wanted. Maybe he desperately desired my change.

Why?

Because my change was special, valuable beyond its $4.82 replacement cost.

So how would somebody know my change was valuable?

Because he'd given it to me himself, earlier in the day.

"Not bad," I said out loud. "Not bad." It was the kind of reasoning they'd bounced me off the police force for, what my so-called superiors termed the "fevered product of an overimaginative mind." I leapt at it because it was the only explanation I could think of. I do like life to make some sort of sense.

I pored over my log. I keep pretty good notes: where I pick up a fare, where I drop him, whether he's a hailer or a radio call.

First, I ruled out all the women. That made the task slightly less impossible: sixteen suspects down from thirty-five. Then I yanked my hair and stared at the blank white porcelain of the refrigerator door. Got up and made myself a sandwich: ham, Swiss cheese, salami, lettuce and tomato, on rye. Ate it. Stared at the porcelain some more until the suspects started coming into focus.

Five of the guys were just plain fat and one was decidedly on the hefty side; I'd felt like telling them all to walk. Might do them some good, might bring on a heart attack. I crossed them all out. Making a thin person look plump is hard enough; it's damn near impossible to make a fatty look thin.

Then I considered my regulars: Jonah Ashley, a tiny blond southern gent; muscle-bound "just-call-me-Harold" at Longfellow Place; Dr. Homewood getting his daily ferry from Beth Israel to MGH; Marvin of the gay bars; and Professor Dickerman, Harvard's answer to Berkeley's sixties radicals.

I crossed them all off. I could see Dickerman holding up the First Filthy Capitalist Bank, or disobeying civilly at Seabrook, even blowing up an oil company or two. But my mind boggled at the thought of the great liberal Dickerman robbing some poor cabbie. It would be like Robin Hood joining the sheriff of Nottingham on some particularly rotten peasant swindle. Then they'd both rape Maid Marian and go off pals together.

Dickerman *was* a lousy tipper. That ought to be a crime.

So what did I leave? Eleven out of sixteen guys cleared without leaving my chair. Me and Sherlock Holmes, the famous armchair detectives.

I'm stubborn; that was one of my good cop traits. I stared at that log till my eyes bugged out. I remembered two of the five pretty easily; they were handsome and I'm far from blind. The first had one of those elegant bony faces and far-apart eyes. He was taller than my bandit. I'd ceased eye-balling him when I noticed the ring on his left hand; I never fuss with the married kind. The other one was built, a weight lifter. Not an Arnold Schwarzenegger extremist, but built. I think I'd have noticed that bod on my bandit. Like I said, I'm not blind. That left three.

Okay. I closed my eyes. Who had I picked up at the Hyatt on Memorial Drive? "Yeah, that was the salesman guy, the one who looked so uncomfortable that I'd figured he'd been hoping to ask his cabbie for a few pointers concerning the best skirt-chasing areas in our fair city. Too low a voice. Too broad in the beam.

The log said I'd picked up a hailer at Kenmore Square when I'd let out the salesman. Ah, yes, a talker. The weather, mostly. Don't you think it's dangerous for you to be driving a cab? "Yeah, I remembered him, all right: a fatherly type, clasping a briefcase, heading to the financial district. Too old.

Down to one. I was exhausted but not the least bit sleepy. All I had to do was remember who I'd picked up on Beacon near Charles. A hailer. Before five o'clock, which was fine by me because I wanted to be long gone before rush hour gridlocked the city. I'd gotten onto Storrow and taken him along the river into Newton Center. Dropped him off at the Bay Bank Middlesex, right before closing time. It was coming back. Little nervous guy. Pegged him as an accountant when I'd let him out at the bank. Measly, undernourished soul. Skinny as a rail, stooped, with pits left from teenage acne.

Shit. I let my head sink down onto the dining room table when I realized what I'd done. I'd ruled them all out, every one. So much for my brilliant deductive powers.

I retired to my bedroom, disgusted. Not only had I lost $4.82 in assorted alloy metals, I was going to lose fifty dollars to Mooney. I stared at myself in the mirror, but what I was really seeing was the round hole at the end of a .22, held in a neat, gloved hand.

Somehow, the gloves made me feel better. I'd remembered another detail about my piggy-bank robber. I consulted the mirror and kept the recall going. A hat. The guy wore a hat. Not like my cap, but like a hat out of a forties gangster flick. I had one of those: I'm a sucker for hats. I plunked it on my head, jamming my hair up underneath—and I drew in my breath sharply.

A shoulder-padded jacket, a slim build, a low slouched hat. Gloves. Boots with enough heel to click as he walked away. Voice? High. Breathy, almost whispered. Not unpleasant. Accentless. No Boston *r*.

I had a man's jacket and a couple of ties in my closet. Don't ask. They may have dated from as far back as my ex-husband, but not necessarily so. I slipped into the jacket, knotted the tie, tilted the hat down over one eye.

I'd have trouble pulling it off. I'm skinny, but my build is decidedly female. Still, I wondered—enough to traipse back downstairs, pull a chicken leg out of the fridge, go back to the log, and review the feminine possibilities. Good thing I did.

Everything clicked. One lady fit the bill exactly: mannish walk and clothes, tall for a woman. And I was in luck. While I'd picked her up in Harvard Square, I'd dropped her at a real address, a house in Brookline: 782 Mason Terrace, at the top of Corey Hill.

Jojo's garage opens at seven. That gave me a big two hours to sleep. I took my beloved car in for some repair work it really didn't need yet and sweet-talked Jojo into giving me a loaner. I needed a hack, but not mine. Only trouble with that Chevy is it's too damn conspicuous.

I figured I'd lose way more than fifty bucks staking out Mason Terrace. I also figured it would be worth it to see old Mooney's face.

She was regular as clockwork, a dream to tail. Eight-thirty-seven every morning, she got a ride to the Square with a next-door neighbor. Took a cab home at five-fifteen. A working woman. Well, she couldn't make much of a living from robbing hacks and dumping the loot in the garbage.

I was damn curious by now. I knew as soon as I looked her over that she was the one, but she seemed so blah, so *normal*. She must have been five-seven or -eight, but the way she stooped, she didn't look tall. Her hair was long and brown with a lot of blond in it, the kind of hair that would have been terrific loose and wild, like a horse's mane. She tied it back with a scarf. A brown scarf. She wore suits. Brown suits. She had a tiny nose, brown eyes under pale eyebrows, a sharp chin. I never saw her smile. Maybe what she needed was a shrink, not a session with Mooney. Maybe she'd done it for the excitement. God knows, if I had her routine, her job, I'd probably be dressing up like King Kong and assaulting skyscrapers.

See, I followed her to work. It wasn't even tricky. She trudged the same path, went in the same entrance to Harvard Yard, probably walked the same number of steps every morning. Her name was Marcia Heidegger and she was a secretary in the admissions office of the college of fine arts.

I got friendly with one of her coworkers.

There was this guy typing away like mad at a desk in her office. I could just see him from the side window. He had grad student written all over his face. Longish wispy hair. Gold-rimmed glasses. Serious. Given to deep sighs and bright velour V-necks. Probably writing his thesis on "Courtly Love and the Theories of Chretien de Troyes."

I latched onto him at Bailey's the day after I'd tracked Lady Heidegger to her Harvard lair.

Too bad Roger was so short. Most short guys find it hard to believe that I'm really trying to pick them up. They look for ulterior motives. Not the Napoleon type of short guy; he assumes I've been waiting years for a chance to dance with a guy who doesn't have to bend to stare down my cleavage. But Roger was no Napoleon. So I had to engineer things a little.

I got into line ahead of him and ordered, after long deliberation, a BLT on toast. While the guy made it up and shoved it on a plate with three measly potato chips and a sliver of pickle you could barely see, I searched through my wallet, opened my change purse, counted out silver, got to $1.60 on the last five pennies. The counterman sang out, "That'll be a buck, eighty-five." I pawed through my pockets, found a nickel, two pennies. The line was growing restive. I concentrated on looking like a damsel in need of a knight, a tough task for a woman over six feet.

Roger (I didn't know he was Roger then) smiled ruefully and passed over a quarter. I was effusive in my thanks. I sat at a table for two, and when he'd gotten his tray (ham-and-cheese and a strawberry ice cream soda), I motioned him into my extra chair.

He was a sweetie. Sitting down, he forgot the difference in our height, and decided I might be someone he could talk to. I encouraged him. I hung shamelessly on his every word. A Harvard man, imagine that. We got around slowly, ever so slowly, to his work at the admissions office. He wanted to duck it and talk about more important issues, but I persisted. I'd been thinking about getting a job at Harvard, possibly in admissions. What kind of people did he work with? Were they congenial? What was the atmosphere like? Was it a big office? How many people? Men? Women? Any soulmates? Readers? Or just, you know, office people?

According to him, every soul he worked with was brain dead. I interrupted a stream of complaint with "Gee, I know somebody who works for Harvard. I wonder if you know her."

"It's a big place," he said, hoping to avoid the whole endless business.

"I met her at a party. Always meant to look her up." I searched through my bag, found a scrap of paper and pretended to read Marcia Heidegger's name off it.

"Marcia? Geez, I work with Marcia. Same office."

"Do you think she likes her work? I mean I got some strange vibes from her," I said. I actually said "strange vibes" and he didn't laugh his head off. People in the Square say things like that and other people take them seriously.

His face got conspiratorial, of all things, and he leaned closer to me.

"You want it, I bet you could get Marcia's job."

"You mean it?" What a compliment—a place for me among the brain dead.

"She's gonna get fired if she doesn't snap out of it."

"Snap out of what?"

"It was bad enough working with her when she first came over. She's one of those crazy neat people, can't stand to see papers lying on a desktop, you know? She almost threw out the first chapter of my thesis!"

I made a suitably horrified noise and he went on.

"Well, you know, about Marcia, it's kind of tragic. She doesn't talk about it."

But he was dying to.

"Yes?" I said, as if he needed egging on.

He lowered his voice. "She used to work for Justin Thayler over at the law school, that guy in the news, whose wife got killed. You know, her work hasn't been worth shit since it happened. She's always on the phone, talking real soft, hanging up if anybody comes in the room. I mean, you'd think she was in love with the guy or something, the way she . . ."

I don't remember what I said. For all I know, I may have volunteered to type his thesis. But I got rid of him somehow and then I scooted around the corner of Church Street and found a pay phone and dialed Mooney.

"Don't tell me," he said. "Somebody mugged you, but they only took your trading stamps."

"I have just one question for you, Moon."

"I accept. A June wedding, but I'll have to break it to Mother gently."

"Tell me what kind of junk Justin Thayler collected." I could hear him breathing into the phone. "Just tell me," I said, "for curiosity's sake."

"You onto something, Carlotta?"

"I'm curious, Mooney. And you're not the only source of information in the world."

"Thayler collected Roman stuff. Antiques. And I mean old. Artifacts, statues—"

"Coins?"

"Whole mess of them."

"Thanks."

"Carlotta—"

I never did find out what he was about to say because I hung up. Rude, I know. But I had things to do. And it was better Mooney shouldn't know what they were, because they came under the heading of illegal activities.

When I knocked at the front door of the Mason Terrace house at 10:00 A.M. the next day, I was dressed in dark slacks, a white blouse, and my old police department hat. I looked very much like the guy who reads your gas meter. I've never heard of anyone being arrested for impersonating the gasman. I've never heard of anyone really giving the gasman a second look. He fades into the background and that's exactly what I wanted to do.

I knew Marcia Heidegger wouldn't be home for hours. Old reliable had left for the Square at her usual time, precise to the minute. But I wasn't 100 percent sure Marcia lived alone. Hence the gasman. I could knock on the door and check it out.

Those Brookline neighborhoods kill me. Act sneaky and the neighbors call the cops in twenty seconds, but walk right up to the front door, knock, talk to yourself while you're sticking a shim in the crack of the door, let yourself in, and nobody does a thing. Boldness is all.

The place wasn't bad. Three rooms, kitchen and bath, light and airy. Marcia was incredibly organized, obsessively neat, which meant I had to keep track of where everything was and put it back just so. There was no clutter in the woman's life. The smell of coffee and toast lingered, but if she'd eaten breakfast, she'd already washed, dried, and put away the dishes. The morning paper had been read and tossed in the trash. The mail was sorted in one of those plastic accordion files. I mean, she folded her underwear like origami.

Now coins are hard to look for. They're small; you can hide 'em anywhere. So this search took me one hell of a long time. Nine out of ten women hide things that are dear to them in the bedroom. They keep their finest jewelry closest to the bed, sometimes in the nightstand, sometimes right under the mattress. That's where I started.

Marcia had a jewelry box on top of her dresser. I felt like hiding it for her. She had some nice stuff and a burglar could have made quite a haul with no effort.

The next favorite place for women to stash valuables is the kitchen. I sifted through her flour. I removed every Kellogg's Rice Krispy from the giant economy-sized box—and returned it. I went through her place like no burglar ever will. When I say thorough, I mean thorough.

I found four odd things. A neatly squared pile of clippings from the *Globe* and the *Herald,* all the articles about the Thayler killing. A manila envelope containing five different safe-deposit-box keys. A Tupperware container full of superstitious junk, good luck charms mostly, the kind of stuff I'd never have associated with a straight-arrow like Marcia: rabbits' feet galore, a little leather bag on a string that looked like some kind of voodoo charm, a pendant in the shape of a cross surmounted by a hook, and, I swear to God, a pack of worn tarot cards. Oh, yes, and a .22 automatic, looking a lot less threatening stuck in an ice cube tray. I took the bullets; the loaded gun threatened a defenseless box of Breyers' mint chocolate-chip ice cream.

I left everything else just the way I'd found it and went home. And tugged my hair. And stewed. And brooded. And ate half the stuff in the refrigerator. I kid you not.

At about one in the morning, it all made blinding, crystal-clear sense.

The next afternoon, at five-fifteen, I made sure I was the cabbie who picked up Marcia Heidegger in Harvard Square. Now cabstands have the most rigid protocol since Queen Victoria; you do not grab a fare out of turn or your fellow cabbies are definitely not amused. There was nothing for it but bribing the ranks. This bet with Mooney was costing me plenty.

I got her. She swung open the door and gave the Mason Terrace number. I grunted, kept my face turned front, and took off.

Some people really watch where you're going in a cab, scared to death you'll take them a block out of their way and squeeze them for an extra nickel. Others just lean back and dream. She was a dreamer, thank God. I was almost at District One headquarters before she woke up.

"Excuse me," she said, polite as ever, "that's Mason Terrace in Brookline."

"Take the next right, pull over, and douse your lights," I said in a low Bogart voice. My imitation was not that good, but it got the point across. Her eyes widened and she made an instinctive grab for the door handle.

"Don't try it, lady," I Bogied on. "You think I'm dumb enough to take you in alone? There's a cop car behind us, just waiting for you to make a move."

Her hand froze. She was a sap for movie dialogue.

"Where's the cop?" was all she said on the way up to Mooney's office.

"What cop?"

"The one following us."

"You have touching faith in our law-enforcement system," I said.

She tried to bolt, I kid you not. I've had experience with runners a lot trickier than Marcia. I grabbed her in approved cop hold number three and marched her into Mooney's office.

He actually stopped typing and raised an eyebrow, an expression of great shock for Mooney.

"Citizen's arrest," I said.

"Charges?"

"Petty theft. Commission of a felony using a firearm." I rattled off a few more charges, using the numbers I remembered from cop school.

"This woman is crazy," Marcia Heidegger said with all the dignity she could muster.

"Search her," I said. "Get a matron in here. I want my four dollars and eighty-two cents back."

Mooney looked like he agreed with Marcia's opinion of my mental state. He said, "Wait up, Carlotta. "You'd have to be able to identify that four dollars and eighty-two cents as yours. Can you do that? Quarters are quarters. Dimes are dimes."

"One of the coins she took was quite unusual," I said. "I'm sure I'd be able to identify it."

"Do you have any objection to displaying the change in your purse?" Mooney said to Marcia. He got me mad the way he said it, like he was humoring an idiot.

"Of course not," old Marcia said, cool as a frozen daiquiri.

"That's because she's stashed it somewhere else, Mooney," I said patiently. "She used to keep it in her purse, see. But then she goofed. She handed it over to a cabbie in her change. She should have just let it go, but she panicked because it was worth a pile and she was just babysitting it for someone else. So when she got it back, she hid it somewhere. Like in her shoe. Didn't you ever carry your lucky penny in your shoe?"

"No," Mooney said. "Now, Miss—"

"Heidegger," I said clearly. "Marcia Heidegger. She used to work at Harvard Law School." I wanted to see if Mooney picked up on it, but he didn't. He went on: "This can be taken care of with a minimum of fuss. If you'll agree to be searched by—"

"I want to see my lawyer," she said.

"For four dollars and eighty-two cents?" he said. "It'll cost you more than that to get your lawyers up here."

"Do I get my phone call or not?"

Mooney shrugged wearily and wrote up the charge sheet. Called a cop to take her to the phone.

He got JoAnn, which was good. Under cover of our old-friend-long-time-no-see greetings, I whispered in her ear.

"You'll find it fifty well spent," I said to Mooney when we were alone. JoAnn came back, shoving Marcia slightly ahead of her. She plunked her prisoner down in one of Mooney's hard wooden chairs and turned to me, grinning from ear to ear. "Got it?" I said. "Good for you." "What's going on?" Mooney said.

"She got real clumsy on the way to the pay phone," JoAnn said. "Practically fell on the floor. Got up with her right hand clenched tight. When we got to the phone, I offered to drop her dime for her. She wanted to do it herself I insisted and she got clumsy again. Somehow this coin got kicked clear across the floor."

She held it up. The coin could have been a dime, except the color was off: warm, rosy gold instead of dead silver. How I missed it the first time around I'll never know.

"What the hell is that?" Mooney said.

"What kind of coins were in Justin Thayler's collection?" I asked. "Roman?"

Marcia jumped out of the chair, snapped her bag open, and drew out her little .22. I kid you not. She was closest to Mooney and she just stepped up to him and rested it above his left ear. He swallowed, didn't say a word. I never realized how prominent his Adam's apple was. JoAnn froze, hand on her holster. Good old reliable, methodical Marcia. Why, I said to myself, *why* pick today of all days to trot your gun out of the freezer? Did you read bad luck in your tarot cards? Then I had a truly rotten thought. What if she had two guns? What if the disarmed .22 was still staring down the mint chocolate-chip ice cream?

"Give it back," Marcia said. She held out one hand, made an impatient waving motion.

"Hey, you don't need it, Marcia," I said. "You've got plenty more. In all those safe deposit boxes."

"I'm going to count to five—" she began.

"Were you in on the murder from day one? You know, from the planning stages?" I asked. I kept my voice low, but it echoed off the walls of Mooney's tiny office. The hum of everyday activity kept going in the main room. Nobody noticed the little gun in the well-dressed lady's hand. "Or did you just do your beau a favor and hide the loot after he iced his wife? In order to back up his burglary tale? I mean, if Justin Thayler really wanted to marry you, there is such a thing as divorce. Or was old Jennifer the one with the bucks?"

"I want that coin," she said softly. "Then I want the two of you"— she motioned to JoAnn and me—"to sit down facing that wall. If you yell, or do anything before I'm out of the building, I'll shoot this gentleman. He's coming with me."

"Come on, Marcia," I said, "put it down. I mean, look at you. A week ago you just wanted Thayler's coin back. You didn't want to rob my cab, right? You just didn't know how else to get your good luck charm back with no questions asked. You didn't do it for the money, right? You did it for love. You were so straight you threw away the cash. Now here you are with a gun pointed at a cop—"

"Shut up!"

I took a deep breath and said, "You haven't got the style, Marcia. Your gun's not even loaded."

Mooney didn't relax a hair. Sometimes I think the guy hasn't ever believed a word I've said to him. But Marcia got shook. She pulled the barrel away from Mooney's skull and peered at it with a puzzled frown. JoAnn and I both tackled her before she got a chance to pull the trigger. I twisted the gun out of her hand. I was almost afraid to look inside. Mooney stared at me and I felt my mouth go dry and a trickle of sweat worm its way down my back.

I looked.

No bullets. My heart stopped fibrillating, and Mooney actually cracked a smile in my direction.

So that's all. I sure hope Mooney will spread the word around that I helped him nail Thayler. And I think he will; he's a fair kind of guy. Maybe it'll get me a case or two. Driving a cab is hard on the backside, you know?

LAWRENCE BLOCK

Keller On Horseback

A T THE AIRPORT NEWSSTAND KELLER picked up a paperback western. The cover was pretty much generic, showing a standard-issue Marlboro man, long and lean, walking down the dusty streets of a western town with a gun riding his hip. Neither the title nor the author's name meant anything to Keller. What drew him was a line that seemed to leap out from the cover.

"He rode a thousand miles," Keller read, "to kill a man he never met."

Keller paid for the book and tucked it into his carry-on bag. When the plane was in the air, he dug it out and looked at the cover, wondering why he'd bought it. He didn't read much, and when he did, he never chose westerns.

Maybe he wasn't supposed to read.this book. Maybe he was supposed to keep it for a talisman.

All for that one sentence. Imagine riding a thousand miles on a horse for any purpose, let alone the killing of a stranger. How long would it take, a thousand-mile journey on horseback? A thoroughbred got around a race-course in something like two minutes, but it couldn't go all day at that pace any more than a human being could string together twenty-six four-minute miles and call it a marathon.

What could you manage on a horse, fifty miles a day? A hundred miles in two days, a thousand miles in twenty? Three weeks, say, at the conclusion of which a man would probably be eager to kill anybody, stranger or blood kin.

Was Ol' Sweat 'n' Leather getting paid for his thousand miles? Was he in the trade? Keller turned the book over in his hands, read the paragraph on the back cover. It did not sound promising. Something about a drifter in the Arizona Territory, a saddle tramp, looking to avenge an old Civil War grievance.

Forgive and forget, Keller advised him.

Keller, riding substantially more than a thousand miles, albeit on a plane instead of a horse, was similarly charged with killing a man as yet unmet. And he was drifting into the Old West to do it, first to Denver, then to Casper, Wyoming, and finally to a town called Martingale. That had been reason enough to pick up the book, but was it reason enough to read it?

He gave it a try. He read a few pages before they came down the aisle with the drinks cart, read a couple more while he sipped his V-8 and ate the salted nuts. Then he evidently dozed off because the next thing he knew the stewardess was waking him to apologize for not having the fruit plate he'd ordered. He told her it didn't matter, he'd have the regular dinner.

"Or there's a Hindu meal that's going begging," she said.

His mind filled with a vision of an airline tray wrapped in one of those saffron-colored robes, extending itself beseechingly and demanding alms. He had the regular dinner instead and ate most of it, except for the mystery meat. He dozed off afterward and didn't wake up until they were making their descent into Stapleton Airport.

Earlier he'd tucked the book into the seat pocket in front of him, and he'd intended to let it ride off into the sunset wedged between the airsickness bag and the plastic card with the emergency exit diagrams. At the last minute he changed his mind and brought the book along.

*   *   *

He spent an hour on the ground in Denver, another hour in the air flying to Casper. The cheerful young man at the Avis counter had a car reserved for Dale Whitlock. Keller showed him a Connecticut driver's license and an American Express card, and the young man gave him a set of keys and told him to have a nice day.

The keys fit a white Chevy Caprice. Cruising north on the interstate, Keller decided he liked everything about the car but its name. There was nothing capricious about his mission. Riding a thousand miles to kill a man you hadn't met was not something one undertook on a whim.

Ideally, he thought, he'd be bouncing along on a rutted two-lane blacktop in a Mustang, say, or maybe a Bronco. Even a Pinto sounded like a better match for a rawboned, leathery desperado like Dale Whitlock than a Caprice.

It was comfortable, though, and he liked the way it handled. And the color was okay. But forget white. As far as he was concerned, the car was a palomino.

*　　*　　*

It took about an hour to drive to Martingale, a town of around ten thousand midway between Casper and Sheridan on I-25. Just looking around, you knew right away that you'd left the East Coast far behind. Mountains in the distance, a great expanse of sky overhead. And, right in front of you, frame buildings that could have been false fronts in a Randolph Scott film. A feedstore, a western wear emporium, a rundown hotel where you'd expect to find Wild Bill Hickok holding aces and eights at a table in the saloon, or Doc Holliday coughing his lungs out in a bedroom on the second floor.

Of course, there were also a couple of supermarkets and gas stations, a two-screen movie house and a Toyota dealership, a Pizza Hut and a Taco John's, so it wasn't too hard to keep track of what century you were in. He saw a man walk out of the Taco John's looking a lot like the young Randolph Scott, from his boots to his Stetson, but he spoiled the illusion by climbing into a pickup truck.

The hotel that inspired Hickok-Holliday fantasies was the Martingale, located right in the center of things on the wide main street. Keller imagined himself walking in, slapping a credit card on the counter. Then the desk clerk—Henry Jones always played him in the movie—would say that they didn't take plastic. "Or p-p-paper either," he'd say, eyes darting, looking for a place to duck when the shooting started.

And Keller would set a silver dollar spinning on the counter. "I'll be here a few days," he'd announce. "If I have any change coming, buy yourself a new pair of suspenders."

And Henry Jones would glance down at his suspenders, to see what was wrong with them.

He sighed, shook his head, and drove to the Holiday Inn near the interstate exit. It had plenty of rooms and gave him what he asked for, a non-smoking room on the third floor in the rear. The desk clerk was a woman, very young, very blond, very perky, with nothing about her to remind you of Henry Jones. She said, "Enjoy your stay with us, Mr. Whitlock." Not stammering, eyes steady.

He unpacked, showered, and went to the window to look at the sunset. It was the sort of sunset a hero would ride off into, leaving a slender blonde to bite back tears while calling after him, "I hope you enjoyed your stay with us, Mr. Whitlock."

Stop it, he told himself. Stay with reality. You've flown a couple of thousand miles to kill a man you never met. Just get it done. The sunset can wait.

*   *   *

He hadn't met the man, but he knew his name. Even if he wasn't sure how to pronounce it.

The man in White Plains had handed Keller an index card with two lines of block capitals hand-printed.

"Lyman Crowder," he read, as if it rhymed with louder. "Or should that be Crowder?" —as if it rhymed with loader.

A shrug in response.

"Martingale, WY," Keller went on. "Why indeed? And where, besides Wyoming? Is Martingale near anything?"

Another shrug, accompanied by a photograph. Or a part of one; it had apparently been cropped from a larger photo and showed the upper half of a middle-aged man who looked to have spent a lot of time outdoors. A big man, too. Keller wasn't sure how he knew that. You couldn't see the man's legs, and there was nothing else in the photo to give you an idea of scale. But somehow he could tell.

"What did he do?"

Again a shrug, but one that conveyed information to Keller. If the other man didn't know what Crowder had done, he had evidently done it to somebody else. That meant the man in White Plains had no personal interest in the matter. It was strictly business.

"So who's the client?"

A shake of the head. Meaning that he didn't know who was picking up the tab or that he knew but wasn't saying? Hard to tell. The man in White Plains was a man of few words and master of none.

"What's the time frame?"

"The time frame," the man said, evidently enjoying the phrase. "No big hurry. One week, two weeks." He leaned forward, patted Keller on the knee. "Take your time," he said. "Enjoy yourself."

On the way out he'd shown the index card to Dot. He said, "How would you pronounce this? As in 'crow' or as in 'crowd'?"

Dot shrugged.

"Jesus," he said, "you're as bad as he is."

"Nobody's as bad as he is," Dot said. "Keller, what difference does it make how Lyman pronounces his last name?"

"I just wondered."

"Well, stick around for the funeral," she suggested. "See what the minister says."

"You're a big help," Keller said.

*   *   *

There was only one Crowder listed in the Martingale phone book. Lyman Crowder, with a telephone number but no address. About a third of the book's listings were like that. Keller wondered why. Did these people assume everybody knew where they lived in a town this size? Or were they saddle tramps with cellular phones and no fixed abode?

Probably rural, he decided. Lived out of town on some unnamed road, picked up their mail at the post office, so why list an address in the phone book?

Great. His quarry lived in the boondocks outside a town that wasn't big enough to have boondocks, and Keller didn't even have an address for him. He had a phone number, but what good was that? What was he supposed to do, call him up and ask directions? "Hi, this here's Dale Whitlock, we haven't met, but I just rode a thousand miles and—"

Scratch that.

*   *   *

He drove around and ate at a downtown cafe called the Singletree. It was housed in a weathered frame building just down the street from the Martingale Hotel. The cafe's name was spelled out in rope nailed to the vertical clapboards. For Keller the name brought a vision of a solitary pine or oak set out in the middle of vast grasslands, a landmark for herdsmen, a rare bit of shade from the relentless sun.

From the menu he learned that a singletree was some kind of apparatus used in hitching up a horse, or a team of horses. It was a little unclear to him just what it was or how it functioned, but it certainly didn't spread its branches in the middle of the prairie.

Keller had the special, a chicken-fried steak and some french fries that came smothered in gravy. He was hungry enough to eat everything in spite of the way it tasted.

"You don't want to live here," he told himself.

It was a relief to know this. Driving around Martingale, Keller had found himself reminded of Roseburg, Oregon. Roseburg was larger, with none of the Old West feel of Martingale, but they both were small western towns of a sort Keller rarely got to. In Roseburg Keller had allowed his imagination to get away from him for a little while, and he wouldn't want to let that happen again.

Still, crossing the threshold of the Singletree, he had been unable to avoid remembering the little Mexican place in Roseburg. If the food and service here turned out to be on that level—

Forget it. He was safe.

*   *   *

After his meal Keller strode out through the bat-wing doors and walked up one side of the street and down the other. It seemed to him that there was something unusual about the way he was walking, that his gait was that of a man who had just climbed down from a horse.

Keller had been on a horse once in his life, and he couldn't remember how he'd walked after he got off it. So this walk he was doing now wasn't coming from his own past. It must have been something he'd learned unconsciously from movies and TV, a synthesis of all those riders of the purple sage and the silver screen.

No need to worry about yearning to settle here, he knew now. Because his fantasy now was not of someone settling in but passing through, the saddle tramp, the shootist, the flint-eyed loner who does his business and moves on.

This was a good fantasy, he decided. You wouldn't get into any trouble with a fantasy like that.

*   *   *

Back in his room Keller tried the book again but couldn't keep his mind on what he was reading. He turned on the TV and worked his way through the channels, using the remote control bolted to the nightstand. Westerns, he decided, were like cops and cabs, never around when you wanted them. It seemed to him that he never made a trip around the cable circuit without running into John Wayne or Randolph Scott or Joel McCrea or a rerun of *Gunsmoke* or *Rawhide* or one of those spaghetti westerns with Eastwood or Lee Van Cleef. Or the great villains—Jack Elam, Strother Martin, the young Lee Marvin in *The Man Who Shot Liberty Valance.*

It probably said something about you, Keller thought, when your favorite actor was Jack Elam.

He switched off the set and looked up Lyman Crowder's phone number.

He could dial it, and when someone picked up and said, "Crowder residence," he'd know how the name was pronounced. "Just checking," he could say, cradling the phone and giving them something to think about.

Of course, he wouldn't say that; he'd mutter something harmless about a wrong number, but was even that much contact a good idea? Maybe it would put Crowder on his guard. Maybe Crowder was already on his guard, as far as that went. That was the trouble with going in blind like this, knowing nothing about either the target or the client.

If he called Crowder's house from the motel, there might be a record of the call, a link between Lyman Crowder and Dale Whitlock. That wouldn't matter much to Keller, who would shed the Whitlock identity on his way out of town, but there was no reason to create more grief for the real Dale Whitlock.

Because there *was* a real Dale Whitlock, and Keller was giving him grief enough without making him a murder suspect.

It was pretty slick the way the man in White Plains worked it. He knew a man who had a machine with which he could make flawless American Express cards. He knew someone else who could obtain the names and account numbers of bona fide American Express cardholders. Then he had cards made which were essentially duplicates of existing cards. You didn't have to worry that the cardholder had reported his card stolen because it hadn't been stolen; it was still sitting in his wallet. You were off somewhere charging the earth, and he didn't have a clue until the charges turned up on his monthly statement.

The driver's license was real, too. Well, technically, it was a counterfeit, of course, and the photograph on it showed Keller, not Whitlock. But someone had managed to access the Connecticut Bureau of Motor Vehicles' computer, and thus the counterfeit license showed the same number as Whitlock's, and gave the same address.

In the old days, Keller thought, it had been a lot more straight forward. You didn't need a license to ride a horse or a credit card to rent one. You bought or stole one, and when you rode into town on it, nobody asked to see your ID. They might not even come right out and ask your name, and if they did, they wouldn't expect a detailed reply. "Call me Tex," you'd say, and that's what they'd call you as you rode off into the sunset.

"Good-bye, Tex," the blonde would call out. "I hope you enjoyed your stay with us."

* * *

The lounge downstairs turned out to be the hot spot in Martingale. Restless, Keller had gone downstairs to have a quiet drink. He walked into a thickly carpeted room with soft lighting and a good sound system. There were fifteen or twenty people in the place, all of them either having a good time or looking for one.

Keller ordered a Coors at the bar. On the jukebox Barbara Mandrell sang a song about cheating. When she was done, a duo he didn't recognize sang a song about cheating. Then came Hank Williams's oldie, "Your Cheating Heart."

A subtle pattern was beginning to emerge.

"I love this song," the blonde said.

A different blonde, not the perky young thing from the front desk. This woman was taller, older, and fuller-figured. She wore a skirt and a sort of cowgirl blouse with piping and embroidery on it.

"Old Hank," Keller said, to say something.

"I'm June."

"Call me Tex."

"Tex!" Her laughter came in a sort of yelp. "When did anybody ever call you Tex, tell me that?"

"Well, nobody has," he admitted, "but that's not to say they never will."

"Where are you from, Tex? No, I'm sorry, I can't call you that; it sticks in my throat. If you want me to call you Tex, you're going to have to start wearing boots."

"You see by my outfit that I'm not a cowboy."

"Your outfit, your accent, your haircut. If you're not an easterner, then I'm a virgin."

"I'm from Connecticut."

"I knew it."

"My name's Dale."

"Well, you could keep that. If you were fixing to be a cowboy, I mean. You'd have to change the way you dress and talk and comb your hair, but you could hang on to Dale. There another name that goes with it?"

In for a penny, in for a pound. "Whitlock," he said.

"Dale Whitlock. Shoot, that's pretty close to perfect. You tell 'em a name like that, you got credit down at the Agway in a New York minute. Wouldn't even have to fill out a form. You married, Dale?"

What was the right answer? She was wearing a ring herself, and the jukebox was now playing yet another cheating song.

"Not in Martingale," he said.

"Oh, I like that," she said, eyes sparkling. "I like the whole idea of regional marriage. I *am* married in Martingale, but we're not *in* Martingale. The town line's Front Street."

"In that case," he said, "maybe I could buy you a drink."

"You easterners," she said. "You're just so damn fast."

* * *

There had to be a catch.

Keller didn't do too badly with women. He got lucky once in a while. But he didn't have the sort of looks that made heads turn, nor had he made seduction his life's work. Some years ago he'd read a book called *How to Pick Up Girls,* filled with opening lines that were guaranteed to work. Keller thought they were silly. He was willing to believe they would work, but he was not able to believe they would work for him.

This woman, though, had hit on him before he'd had time to become aware of her presence. This sort of thing happened, especially when you were dealing with a married woman in a bar where all they played was cheating songs. Everybody knew what everybody else was there for, and nobody had time to dawdle. So this sort of thing happened, but it never seemed to happen to him, and he didn't trust it.

Something would go wrong. She'd call home and find out her kid was running a fever. Her husband would walk in the door just as the jukebox gave out with "You Picked a Fine Time to Leave Me, Lucille." She'd be overcome by conscience or rendered unconscious by the drink Keller had just bought her.

"I'd say my place or yours," she said, "but we both know the answer to that one. What's your room number?" Keller told her. "You go on up," she said. "I won't be a minute. Don't start without me."

He brushed his teeth, splashed on a little aftershave. She wouldn't show, he told himself. Or she'd expect to be paid, which would take a little of the frost off the pumpkin. Or her husband would turn up and they'd try to work some variation of the badger game.

Or she'd be sloppy drunk, or he'd be impotent. Or something.

* * *

"Whew," she said. "I don't guess you need boots after all. I'll call you Tex or Slim or any damn thing you want me to, just so you come when you're called. How long are you in town for, Dale?"

"I'm not sure. A few days."

"Business, I suppose. What sort of business are you in?"

"I work for a big corporation," he said. "They fly me over to look into situations."

"Sounds like you can't talk about it."

"Well, we do a lot of government work," he said. "So I'm really not supposed to."

"Say no more," she said. "Oh, Lord, look at the time!"

While she showered, he picked up the paperback and rewrote the blurb. He killed a thousand miles, he thought, to ride a woman he never met. Well, sometimes you got lucky. The stars were in the right place; the forces that ruled the universe decided you deserved a present. There didn't always have to be a catch to it, did there?

She turned off the shower, and he heard the last line of the song she'd been singing. "'And Margie's at the Lincoln Park Inn,'" she sang, and moments later she emerged from the bathroom and began dressing.

"What's this?" she said. "'He rode a thousand miles to kill a man he never met.' "You know, that's funny, because I just had the darnedest thought while I was runnin' the soap over my pink and tender flesh."

"Oh?"

"I just said that last to remind you what's under this here skirt and blouse. Oh, the thought I had? Well, something you said, government work. I thought maybe this man's CIA, maybe he's some old soldier of fortune, maybe he's the answer to this maiden's prayer."

"What do you mean?"

"Just that it was already a real fine evening, Dale, but it would be heaven on earth if what you came to Martingale for was to kill my damn husband."

*   *   *

Christ. Was *she* the client? Was the pickup downstairs a cute way for them to meet? Could she actually be that stupid, coming on in a public place to a man she was hiring to kill her husband?

For that matter, how had she recognized him? Only Dot and the man in White Plains had known the name he was using. They'd have kept it to themselves. And she'd made her move before she knew his name. Had she been able to recognize him? I see by your outfit that you are a hit man? Something along those lines?

"Yarnell," she was saying. "Hobart Lee Yarnell, and what he'd like is for people to call him Bart, and what everybody calls him is Hobie. Now what does that tell you about the man?"

That he's not the man I came here to kill, Keller thought. This was comforting to realize but left her waiting for an answer to her question. "That he's not used to getting his own way," Keller said.

She laughed. "He's not," she said, "but it's not for lack of trying. "You know, I like you, Dale. You're a nice fellow. But if it wasn't you tonight, it would have been somebody else."

"And here I thought it was my aftershave."

"I'll just bet you did. No, the kind of marriage I got, I come around here a lot. I've put a lot of quarters in that jukebox the last year or so."

"And played a lot of cheating songs?"

"And done a fair amount of cheating. But it doesn't really work. I still wake up the next day married to that bastard."

"Why don't you divorce him?"

"I've thought about it."

"And?"

"I was brought up not to believe in it," she said. "But I don't guess that's it. I wasn't raised to believe in cheating either." She frowned. "Money's part of it," she admitted. "I won't bore you with the details, but I'd get gored pretty bad in a divorce."

"That's a problem."

"I guess, except what do I care about money anyway? Enough's as much as a person needs, and my daddy's got pots of money. He's not about to let me starve."

"Well, then—"

"But he thinks the world of Hobie," she said, glaring at Keller as if it were his fault. "Hunts elk with him, goes after trout and salmon with him, thinks he's just the best thing ever came over the pass. And he doesn't even want to hear the word 'divorce.' You know that Tammy Wynette song where she spells it out a letter at a time? I swear he'd leave the room before you got past *R*. I say it'd about break Lyman Crowder's heart if his little girl ever got herself divorced."

*   *   *

Well, it was true. If you kept your mouth shut and your ears open, you learned things. What he had learned was that "Crowder" rhymed with "powder."

Now what?

After her departure, after his own shower, he paced back and forth, try-ing to sort it all out. In the few hours since his arrival in Martingale, he'd slept with a woman who turned out to be the loving daughter of the target and, in all likelihood, the unloving wife of the client.

Well, maybe not. Lyman Crowder was a rich man, lived north of town on a good-size ranch that he ran pretty much as a hobby. He'd made his real money in oil, and nobody ever made a small amount of money that way. You either went broke or got rich. Rich men had enemies: people they'd crossed in business, people who stood to profit from their death.

But it figured that Yarnell was the client. There was a kind of poetic inevitability about it. She picks him up in the lounge, it's not enough that she's the target's daughter. She also ought to be the client's wife. Round things out, tie up all the loose ends.

The thing to do . . . well, he knew the thing to do. The thing to do was get a few hours' sleep and then, bright and early, reverse the usual order of affairs by riding off into the sunrise. Get on a plane, get off in New York, and write off Martingale as a happy little romantic adventure. Men, after all, had been known to travel farther than that in the hope of getting laid.

He'd tell the man in White Plains to find somebody else. Sometimes you had to do that. No blame attached, as long as you didn't make a habit of it. He'd say he was blown.

As, come to think of it, he was. Quite expertly, as a matter of fact.

*   *   *

In the morning he got up and packed his carry-on. He'd call White Plains from the airport or wait until he was back in New York. He didn't want to phone from the room. When the real Dale Whitlock had a fit and called American Express, they'd look over things like the Holiday Inn state-ment. No sense leaving anything that led anywhere.

He thought about June, and the memory made him playful. He checked the time. Eight o'clock, two hours later in the East, not an uncivil time to call.

He called Whitlock's home in Rowayton, Connecticut. A woman answered. He identified himself as a representative of a political polling organization, using a name she would recognize. By asking questions that encouraged lengthy responses, he had no trouble keeping her on the phone. "Well, thank you very much," he said at length. "And have a nice day."

Now let Whitlock explain that one to American Express.

He finished packing and was almost out the door when his eye caught the paperback western. Take it along? Leave it for the maid? What?

He picked it up, read the cover line, sighed. Was this what Randolph Scott would do? Or John Wayne, or Clint Eastwood? How about Jack Elam?

No, of course not.

Because then there'd be no movie. A man rides into town, starts to have a look at the situation, meets a woman, gets it on with her, then just backs out and rides off? You put something like that on the screen, it wouldn't even play in the art houses.

Still, this wasn't a movie.

Still . . .

He looked at the book and wanted to heave it across the room. But all he heaved was a sigh. Then he unpacked.

*   *   *

He was having a cup of coffee in town when a pickup pulled up across the street and two men got out of it. One of them was Lyman Crowder. The other, not quite as tall, was twenty pounds lighter and twenty years younger. Crowder's son, by the looks of him.

His son-in-law, as it turned out. Keller followed the two men into a store where the fellow behind the counter greeted them as Lyman and Hobie. Crowder had a lengthy shopping list composed largely of items Keller would have been hard put to find a use for.

While the owner filled the order, Keller had a look at the display of hand-tooled boots. The pointed toes would be handy in New York, he thought, for killing cockroaches in corners. The heels would add better than an inch to his height. He wondered if he'd feel awkward in the boots, like a teenager in her first pair of high heels. Lyman and Hobie looked comfortable enough in their boots, as pointy in the toes and as elevated in the heels as any on display, but they also looked comfortable in their string ties and ten-gallon hats, and Keller was sure he'd feel ridiculous dressed like that.

They were a pair, he thought. They looked alike, they talked alike, they dressed alike, and they seemed uncommonly fond of each other.

Back in his room Keller stood at the window and looked down at the parking lot, then across the way at a pair of mountains. A few years ago his work had taken him to Miami, where he'd met a Cuban who'd cautioned him against ever taking a hotel room above the second floor.

"Suppose you got to leave in a hurry?" the man said. "Ground floor, no problem. Second floor, no problem. Third floor, break your fockeen leg."

The logic of this had impressed Keller, and for a while he had made a point of taking the man's advice. Then he happened to learn that the Cuban not only shunned the higher floors of hotels but also refused to enter an elevator or fly on an airplane. What had looked like tradecraft now appeared to be nothing more than phobia.

It struck Keller that he had never in his life had to leave a hotel room, or any other sort of room, by the window. This was not to say that it would never happen, but he'd decided it was a risk he was prepared to run. He liked high floors. Maybe he even liked running risks.

He picked up the phone, made a call. When she answered, he said, "This is Tex. Would you believe my business appointment canceled? Left me with the whole afternoon to myself."

"Are you where I left you?"

"I've barely moved since then."

"Well, don't move now," she said. "I'll be right on over."

*　*　*

Around nine that night Keller wanted a drink, but he didn't want to have it in the company of adulterers and their favorite music. He drove around in his palomino Caprice until he found a place on the edge of town that looked promising. It called itself Joe's Bar. Outside, it was nondescript. Inside, it smelled of stale beer and casual plumbing. The lights were low. There was sawdust on the floor and the heads of dead animals on the walls. The clientele was exclusively male, and for a moment this gave Keller pause. There were gay bars in New York that tried hard to look like this place, though it was hard for Keller to imagine why. But Joe's, he realized, was not a gay bar, not in any sense of the word.

He sat on a wobbly stool and ordered a beer. The other drinkers left him alone, even as they left one another alone. The jukebox played intermittently, with men dropping in quarters when they could no longer bear the silence.

The songs, Keller noted, ran to type. There were the tryin'-to-drink-that-woman-off-of-my-mind songs and the if-it-wasn't-for-bad-luck-I-wouldn't-have-no-luck-at-all songs. Nothing about Margie in the Lincoln Park Inn, nothing about heaven being just a sin away. These songs were for drinking and feeling really rotten about it.

"'Nother damn day," said a voice at Keller's elbow.

He knew who it was without turning. He supposed he might have recognized the voice, but he didn't think that was it. No, it was more a recognition of the inevitability of it all. Of course it would be Yarnell, making conversation with him in this bar where no one made conversation with anyone. Who else could it be?

"'Nother damn day," Keller agreed.

"Don't believe I've seen you around."

"I'm just passing through."

"Well, you got the right idea," Yarnell said. "Name's Bart."

In for a pound, in for a ton. "Dale," Keller said.

"Good to know you, Dale."

"Same here, Bart."

The bartender loomed before them. "Hey, Hobie," he said. "The usual?"

Yarnell nodded. "And another of those for Dale here." The bartender poured Yarnell's usual, which turned out to be bourbon with water back, and uncapped another beer for Keller. Somebody broke down and fed the jukebox a quarter and played "There Stands the Glass."

Yarnell said, "You hear what he called me?"

"I wasn't paying attention."

"Called me Hobie," Yarnell said. "Everybody does. You'll be doing the same, won't be able to help yourself."

"The world is a terrible place," Keller said.

"By God, you got that right," Yarnell said. "No one ever said it better. You a married man, Dale?"

"Not at the moment."

"'Not at the moment.' I swear I'd give a lot if I could say the same."

"Troubles?"

"Married to one woman and in love with another one. I guess you could call that trouble."

"I guess you could."

"Sweetest, gentlest, darlingest, lovingest creature God ever made," Yarnell said. "When she whispers 'Bart,' it don't matter if the whole rest of the world shouts 'Hobie.'"

"This isn't your wife you're talking about," Keller guessed.

"God, no! My wife's a round-heeled meanspirited hardhearted tramp. I hate my damn wife. I love my girlfriend."

They were silent for a moment, and so was the whole room. Then someone played, "The Last Word in Lonesome Is Me."

"They don't write songs like that anymore," Yarnell said.

The hell they didn't. "I'm sure I'm not the first person to suggest this," Keller said, "but have you thought about—"

"Leaving June," Yarnell said. "Running off with Edith. Getting a divorce."

"Something like that."

"Never an hour that I don't think about it, Dale. Night and goddamn day I think about it. I think about it, and I drink about it, but the one thing I can't do is do it."

"Why's that?"

"There is a man," Yarnell said, "who is a father and a best friend to me all rolled into one. Finest man I ever met in my life, and the only wrong thing he ever did in his life was have a daughter, and the biggest mistake I ever made was marrying her. And if there's one thing that man believes in, it's the sanctity of marriage. Why, he thinks divorce' is the dirtiest word in the language."

So Yarnell couldn't even let on to his father-in-law that his marriage was hell on earth, let alone take steps to end it. He had to keep his affair with Edith very much backstreet. The only person he could talk to was Edith, and she was out of town for the next week or so, leaving him dying of loneliness and ready to pour out his heart to the first stranger he could find. For which he apologized, but—

"Hey, that's all right, Bart," Keller said. "A man can't keep it all locked up inside."

"Calling me Bart, I appreciate that, I truly do. Even Lyman calls me Hobie, and he's the best friend any man ever had. Hell, he can't help it. Everybody calls me Hobie sooner or later."

"Well," Keller said, "I'll hold out as long as I can."

*　　*　　*

Alone, Keller reviewed his options.

He could kill Lyman Crowder. He'd be keeping it simple, carrying out the mission as it had been given to him. And it would solve everybody's problems. June and Hobie could get the divorce they both so desperately wanted.

On the downside, they'd both be losing the man each regarded as the greatest thing since microwave popcorn.

He could toss a coin and take out either June or her husband, thus serving as a sort of divorce court of last resort. If it came up heads, June could spend the rest of her life cheating on a ghost. If it was tails, Yarnell could have his cake and Edith, too. Only a question of time until she stopped call-ing him Bart and took to calling him Hobie, of course, and next thing you knew she would turn up at the Holiday Inn, dropping her quarter in the slot to play "Third-Rate Romance, Low-Rent Rendezvous."

It struck Keller that there ought to be some sort of solution that didn't involve lowering the population. But he knew he was the person least like-ly to come up with it.

If you had a medical problem, the treatment you got depended on the sort of person you went to. You didn't expect a surgeon to manipulate your spine, or prescribe herbs and enemas, or kneel down and pray with you. Whatever the problem was, the first thing the surgeon would do was look around for something to cut. That's how he'd been trained; that's how he saw the world; that's what he did.

Keller, too, was predisposed to a surgical approach. While others might push counseling or twelve-step programs, Keller reached for a scalpel. But sometimes it was difficult to tell where to make the incision.

Kill 'em all, he thought savagely, and let God sort 'em out. Or ride off into the sunset with your tail between your legs.

First thing in the morning Keller drove to Sheridan and caught a plane to Salt Lake City. He paid cash for his ticket and used the name John Richards. At the TWA counter in Salt Lake City he bought a one-way ticket to Las Vegas and again paid cash, this time using the name Alan Johnson.

At the Las Vegas airport he walked around the long-term parking lot as if looking for his car. He'd been doing this for five minutes or so when a balding man wearing a glen plaid sport coat parked a two-year-old Plymouth and removed several large suitcases from its trunk, affixing them to one of those aluminum luggage carriers. Wherever he was headed, he'd packed enough to stay there for a while.

As soon as he was out of sight, Keller dropped to a knee and groped the undercarriage until he found the magnetized hide-a-key. He always looked before breaking into a car, and he got lucky about one time in five. As usual, he was elated. Finding a key was a good omen. It boded well.

Keller had been to Vegas frequently over the years. He didn't like the place, but he knew his way around. He drove to Caesar's Palace and left his borrowed Plymouth for the attendant to park. He knocked on the door of an eighth-floor room until its occupant protested that she was trying to sleep.

He said, "It's news from Martingale, Miss Bodine. For Christ's sake, open the door."

She opened the door a crack but kept the chain fastened. She was about the same age as June but looked older, her black hair a mess, her eyes bleary, her face still bearing traces of yesterday's makeup.

"Crowder's dead," he said.

Keller could think of any number of things she might have said, ranging from "What happened?" to "Who cares?" This woman cut to the chase. "You idiot," she said. "What are you doing here?"

Mistake.

"Let me in," he said, and she did.

Another mistake.

*   *   *

The attendant brought Keller's Plymouth and seemed happy with the tip Keller gave him. At the airport someone else had left a Toyota Camry in the spot where the balding man had originally parked the Plymouth, and the best Keller could do was wedge it into a spot one aisle over and a dozen spaces off to the side. He figured the owner would find it and hoped he wouldn't worry that he was in the early stages of Alzheimer's.

Keller flew to Denver as Richard Hill, to Sheridan as David Edwards. En route he thought about Edith Bodine, who'd evidently slipped on a wet tile in the bathroom of her room at Caesars, cracking her skull on the side of the big tub. With the Do Not Disturb sign hanging from the doorknob and the air conditioner at its highest setting, there was no telling how long she might remain undisturbed.

He'd figured she had to be the client. It wasn't June or Hobie, both of whom thought the world revolved around Lyman Crowder, so whom did that leave? Crowder himself, turned sneakily suicidal? Some old enemy, some business rival?

No, Edith was the best prospect. A client would either want to meet Keller—not obliquely, as both Yarnells had done, but by arrangement—or would contrive to be demonstrably off the scene when it all happened. Thus the trip to Las Vegas.

Why? The Crowder fortune, of course. She had Hobie Yarnell crazy about her, but he wouldn't leave June for fear of breaking Crowder's heart, and even if he did, he'd go empty-handed. Having June killed wouldn't work, either, because she didn't have any real money of her own. But June would inherit if the old man died, and later on something could always happen to June.

Anyway, that was how he figured it. If he'd wanted to know Edith's exact reasoning, he'd have had to ask her, and that had struck him as a waste of time. More to the point, the last thing he'd wanted was a chance to get to know her. That just screwed everything up when you got to know these people.

If you were going to ride a thousand miles to kill a man you'd never met, you were really well advised to be the tight-lipped stranger every step of the way. No point in talking to anybody, not the target, not the client, and not anybody else either. If you had anything to say, you could whisper it to your horse.

* * *

He got off the fourth plane of the day at Sheridan, picked up his Caprice—the name was seeming more appropriate with every passing hour—and drove back to Martingale. He kept it right around the speed limit, then slowed down along with everyone else five miles outside Martingale. They were clearing a wreck out of the northbound lane. That shouldn't have slowed things down in the southbound lane, but of course it did; everybody had to slow down to see what everyone else was slowing down to look at.

Back in his room he had his bag packed before he realized that he couldn't go anywhere. The client was dead, but that didn't change anything; since he had no way of knowing that she was the client or that she was dead, his mission remained unchanged. He could go home and admit an inability to get the job done, waiting for the news to seep through that there was no longer any job to be done. That would get him off the hook after the fact, but he wouldn't have covered himself with glory, nor would he get paid. The client had almost certainly paid in advance, and if there'd been a middleman between the client and the man in White Plains, he had almost certainly passed the money on, and there was very little likelihood that the man in White Plains would even consider the notion of refunding a fee to a dead client, not that anyone would raise the subject. But neither would the man in White Plains pay Keller for work he'd failed to perform. The man in White Plains would just keep everything.

Keller thought about it. It looked to him as though his best course lay in playing a waiting game. How long could it take before a sneak thief or a chambermaid walked in on Edith Bodine? How long before news of her death found its way to White Plains?

The more he thought about it, the longer it seemed likely to take. If there were, as sometimes happened, a whole string of intermediaries involved, the message might very well never get to Garcia.

Maybe the simplest thing was to kill Crowder and be done with it.

No, he thought. He'd just made a side trip of, yes, more than a thousand miles—and at his own expense yet—solely to keep from having to kill this legendary Man He Never Met. Damned if he was going to kill him now, after all that.

He'd wait a while anyway. He didn't want to drive anywhere now, and he couldn't bear to look at another airplane, let alone get on board.

He stretched out on the bed, closed his eyes.

*   *   *

He had a frightful dream. In it he was walking at night out in the middle of the desert, lost, chilled, desperately alone. Then a horse came galloping out of nowhere, and on his back was a magnificent woman with a great mane of hair and eyes that flashed in the moonlight. She extended a hand, and Keller leaped up on the horse and rode behind her. She was naked. So was Keller, although he had somehow failed to notice this before.

They fell in love. Wordless, they told each other everything, knew each other like twin souls. And then, gazing into her eyes, Keller realized who she was. She was Edith Bodine, and she was dead; he'd killed her earlier without knowing she'd turn out to be the girl of his dreams. It was done, it could never be undone, and his heart was broken for eternity.

Keller woke up shaking. For five minutes he paced the room, struggling to sort out what was a dream and what was real. He hadn't been sleeping long. The sun was setting; it was still the same endless day.

God, what a hellish dream.

He couldn't get caught up in TV, and he had no luck at all with the book. He put it down, picked up the phone, and dialed June's number.

"It's Dale," he said. "I was sitting here and—"

"Oh, Dale," she cut in, "you're so thoughtful to call. Isn't it terrible? Isn't it the most awful thing?"

"Uh," he said.

"I can't talk now," she said. "I can't even think straight. I've never been so upset in my life. Thank you, Dale, for being so thoughtful."

She hung up and left him staring at the phone. Unless she was a better actress than he would have guessed, she sounded absolutely overcome. He was surprised that news of Edith Bodine's death could have reached her so soon, but far more surprised that she could be taking it so hard. Was there more to all this than met the eye? Were Hobie's wife and mistress actually close friends? Or were they—Jesus—*more* than just good friends?

Things were certainly a lot simpler for Randolph Scott.

*　　*　　*

The same bartender was on duty at Joe's. "I don't guess your friend Hobie'll be coming around tonight," he said. "I suppose you heard the news."

"Uh," Keller said. Some backstreet affair, he thought, if the whole town was ready to comfort Hobie before the body was cold.

"Hell of a thing," the man went on. "Terrible loss for this town. Martingale won't be the same without him."

"This news," Keller said carefully. "I think maybe I missed it. What happened anyway?"

*　　*　　*

He called the airlines from his motel room. The next flight out of Casper wasn't until morning. Of course, if he wanted to drive to Denver—

He didn't want to drive to Denver. He booked the first flight out in the morning, using the Whitlock name and the Whitlock credit card.

No need to stick around, not with Lyman Crowder stretched out somewhere getting pumped full of embalming fluid. Dead in a car crash on I-25 North, the very accident that had slowed Keller down on his way back from Sheridan.

He wouldn't be around for the funeral, but should he send flowers? It was quite clear that he shouldn't. Still, the impulse was there.

He dialed 1-800-FLOWERS and sent a dozen roses to Mrs. Dale Whitlock in Rowayton, charging them to Whitlock's American Express account. He asked them to enclose a card reading, "Just because I love you—Dale."

He felt it was the least he could do.

Two days later he was on Taunton Place in White Plains, making his report. Accidents were always good, the man told him. Accidents and natural causes, always the best. Oh, sometimes you needed a noisy hit to send a message, but the rest of the time you couldn't beat an accident.

"Good you could arrange it," the man said.

Would have taken a hell of an arranger, Keller thought. First you'd have had to arrange for Lyman Crowder to be speeding north in his pickup. Then you'd have had to get an unemployed sheepherder named Danny Vasco good and drunk and sent him hurtling toward Martingale, racing his own pickup—Jesus, didn't they drive anything but pickups?—racing it at ninety-plus miles an hour, and proceeding southbound in the northbound lane. Arrange for a few near misses. Arrange for Vasco to brush a school bus and sideswipe a minivan, and then let him ram Crowder head-on.

Some arrangement.

If the man in White Plains had any idea that the client was dead as well or even who the client was, he gave no sign to Keller. On the way out Dot asked him how Crowder pronounced his name.

"Rhymes with 'chowder,'" he said.

"I knew you'd find out," she said. "Keller, are you all right? You seem different."

"Just awed by the workings of fate," he said.

"Well," she said, "that'll do it."

*　　*　　*

On the train back to the city he thought about the workings of fate. Earlier he'd tried to tell himself that his side trip to Las Vegas had been a waste of time and money and human life. All he'd had to do was wait a day for Danny Vasco to take the game off the boards.

Never would have happened.

Without his trip to Vegas, there would have been no wreck on the highway. One event had opened some channel that allowed the other to happen. He couldn't explain this, couldn't make sense out of it, but somehow he knew it was true.

Everything had happened exactly the way it had had to happen. Encountering June in the Meet 'n' Cheat, running into Hobie at the Burnout Bar. He could no more have avoided those meetings than he could have kept himself from buying the paperback western novel that had set the tone for everything that followed.

He hoped Mrs. Whitlock liked the flowers.

BRIAN GARFIELD

Scrimshaw

S HE SUGGESTED LIQUID UNDULATION: a lei-draped girl in a grass
skirt under a windblown palm tree, her hands and hips expressive of
the flow of the hula. Behind her, beyond the surf, a whaling ship was
poised to approach the shore, its square-rigged sails bold against a polished
white sky.

The scene was depicted meticulously upon ivory: a white fragment of
tusk the size of a dollar bill. The etched detail was exquisite: the scrimshaw
engraving was carved of thousands of thread-like lines and the artist's knife
hadn't slipped once.

The price tag may have been designed to persuade tourists of the seri-
ousness of the art form: it was in four figures. But Brenda was unim-
pressed. She put the piece back on the display cabinet and left the shop. The
hot Lahaina sun beat against her face and she went across Front Street to
the Sea Wall, thrust her hands into the pockets of her dress and brooded
upon the anchorage.

Boats were moored around the harbor—catamarans, glass-bottom
tourist boats, marlin fishermen, pleasure sailboats, outrigger canoes,
yachts. Playthings. It's the wrong place for me, she thought.

Beyond the wide channel the islands of Lanai and Kahoolawe made
lovely horizons under their umbrellas of delicate cloud, but Brenda had lost
her eye for that sort of thing; she noticed the stagnant heat, the shabbiness
of the town, and the offensiveness of the tourists who trudged from shop to
shop in their silly hats, their sunburnt flab, their hapless T-shirts embla-
zoned with local graffiti: "Here Today, Gone to Maui."

A leggy young girl went by, drawing Brenda's brief attention: one of

those taut tan sunbleached creatures of the surfboards—gorgeous and lus-
cious and vacuous. Filled with youth and hedonism, equipped with all the
optional accessories of pleasure. Brenda watched gloomily, her eyes following the girl as far as the end of the Sea Wall, where the girl turned to cross
the street. Brenda then noticed two men in conversation there.

One of them was the wino who always seemed to be there: a stringy
unshaven tattered character who spent the days huddling in the shade sucking from a bottle in a brown bag and begging coins from tourists. At night
he seemed to prowl the alleys behind the seafood restaurants, living off
scraps like a stray dog: she had seen him once, from the window of her
flyspecked room, scrounging in the can behind the hotel's kitchen; and then
two nights ago near a garbage bin she had taken a shortcut home after a dis-
satisfying lonely dinner and she'd nearly tripped over him.

The man talking with the wino seemed familiar and yet she could not
place the man. He had the lean bearded look of one who had gone native;
but not really, for he was set apart by his fastidiousness. He wore sandals,
yet his feet seemed clean, the toenails glimmering; he wore a sandy beard
but it was neatly trimmed and his hair was expensively cut, not at all shaggy; he wore a blue denim short-sleeved shirt, fashionably faded but it had
sleeve pockets and epaulets and had come from a designer shop; and his
white sailor's trousers fit perfectly.

I know him, Brenda thought, but she couldn't summon the energy to
stir from her spot when the bearded man and the wino walked away into the
town. Vaguely and without real interest she wondered idly what those two
could possibly have to talk about together.

She found shade on the harbor front. Inertia held her there for hours
while she recounted the litany of her misfortunes. Finally hunger bestirred
her and she slouched back to her miserable little third-class hotel.

*   *   *

The next day, half drunk in the afternoon and wilting in the heat,
Brenda noticed vaguely that the wino was no longer in his usual place. In
fact, she hadn't seen the wino at all, not last night and not today.

The headache was painful and she boarded the jitney bus to go up-
island a few miles. She got off near the Kapalua headland and trudged down
to the public beach. It was cooler here because the northwest end of the
island was open to the fresh trade winds; she settled under a palm tree,
pulled off her ragged sneakers, and dug her toes into the cool sand. The toes

weren't very clean. She was going too long between baths these days. The bathroom in the hotel was at the end of the corridor and she went there as infrequently as possible because she couldn't be sure who she might encounter and anyhow, the tub was filthy and there was no shower.

Across the channel loomed the craggy mountains of Molokai, infamous island, leper colony, its dark volcanic mass shadowed by perpetual sinister rain clouds, and Brenda lost herself in gruesome speculations about exile, isolation, loneliness, and wretched despair, none of which seemed at all foreign to her.

The sun moved and took the shade with it and she moved round to the other side of the palm tree, tucking the fabric of the cheap dress under her when she sat down. The dress was gone—frayed, faded, the material ready to disintegrate. She only had two others left. Then it would be jeans and the boatneck. It didn't matter, really. There was no one to dress up for.

It wasn't that she was altogether ugly; she wasn't ugly; she wasn't even plain, really; she had studied photographs of herself over the years and she had gazed in the mirror and tried to understand, but it had eluded her. All right, perhaps she was too bony, her shoulders too big, flat in front, not enough flesh on her—but there were men who liked their women bony; that didn't explain it. She had the proper features in the proper places and, after all, Modigliani hadn't found that sort of face abominable to behold, had he?

But ever since puberty there'd been something about her gangly gracelessness that had isolated her. Invitations to go out had been infrequent. At parties no one ever initiated conversations with her. No one, in any case, until Briggs had appeared in her life.

. . . She noticed the man again: the well-dressed one with the neatly trimmed beard. A droopy brown Hawaiian youth was picking up litter on the beach and depositing it in a burlap sack he dragged along; the bearded man ambled beside the youth, talking to him. The Hawaiian said something; the bearded man nodded with evident disappointment and turned to leave the beach. His path brought him close by Brenda's palm tree and Brenda sat up abruptly. "Eric?"

*   *   *

The bearded man squinted into the shade, trying to recognize her. Brenda removed her sunglasses. She said, "Eric? Eric Morelius?"

"Brenda?" The man came closer and she contrived a wan smile. "Brenda Briggs? What the devil are you doing here? You look like a beachcomber gone to seed."

*   *   *

Over a drink in Kimo's she tried to put on a front. "Well, I thought I'd come out here on a sabbatical and, you know, loaf around the islands, recharge my batteries, take stock."

She saw that Eric wasn't buying it. She tried to smile. "And what about you?"

"Well, I live here, you know. Came out to Hawaii nine years ago on vacation and never went back." Eric had an easy relaxed attitude of confident assurance. "Come off it, duckie, you look like hell. What's happened to you?"

She contrived a shrug of indifference. "The world fell down around my ankles. Happens to most everybody sometimes, I suppose. It doesn't matter."

"Just like that? It must have been something terrible. You had more promise than anyone in the department."

"Well, we were kids then, weren't we. We were all promising young scholars. But what happens after you've broken all the promises?"

"Good Lord. The last I saw of you, you and Briggs were off to revitalize the University of what, New Mexico?"

"Arizona." She tipped her head back with the glass to her mouth; ice clinked against her teeth. "And after that a state college in Minnesota. And then a dinky jerkwater diploma mill in California. The world," she said in a quiet voice, "has little further need of second-rate Greek and Roman literature scholars—or for any sort of non-tenured Ph.D.s in the humanities. I spent last year waiting on tables in Modesto."

"Duckie," Eric said, "there's one thing you haven't mentioned. Where's Briggs?"

She hesitated. Then—what did it matter?—she told him: "He left me. Four years ago. Divorced me and married a buxom life-of-the-party girl fifteen years younger than me. She was writing advertising copy for defective radial tires or carcinogenic deodorants or something like that. We had a kid, you know. Cute little guy, we named him Geoff, with a G—you know how Briggs used to love reading Chaucer. In the original. In retrospect, you know, Briggs was a prig and a snob."

"Where's the kid, then?"

"I managed to get custody and then six months ago he went to visit his father for the weekend and all three of them, Briggs and the copy-writer and my kid Geoff—well, there was a six-car pileup on the Santa Monica Freeway and I had to pay for the funerals and it wiped me out."

Eric brought another pair of drinks and there was a properly responsive sympathy in his eyes and it had been so long since she'd talked about it that she covered her face with the table napkin and sobbed.

*   *   *

"God help me, Eric. Briggs was the only man who ever gave me a second look."

He walked her along the Sea Wall. "You'll get over it, duckie. Takes time."

"Sure," she said listlessly. "I know."

"Sure, it can be tough. Especially when you haven't got anybody. You don't have any family left, do you?"

"No. Only child. My parents died young. Why not? The old man was on the assembly line in Dearborn. We're all on the assembly line in Dearborn. What have we got to aim for? A condominium in some anthill and a bag full of golf clubs? Let's change the subject, all right? What about you, then? You look prosperous enough. Did you drop out or were you pushed too?"

"Dropped out. Saw the light and made it to the end of the tunnel. I'm a free man, duckie."

"What do you do?"

"I'm a scrimshander."

"A what?"

"A bone-ivory artist. I do scrimshaw engravings. You've probably seen my work in the shop windows around town."

*   *   *

Eric's studio, high under the eaves in the vintage whaler's house that looked more New Englandish than tropical, revealed its owner's compulsion for orderly neatness.

She had never liked him much. He and Briggs had got along all right, but she'd always found Eric an unpleasant sort. It wasn't that he was boorish; hardly anything like that. But she thought him pretentious and totally insincere. He'd always had that air of arrogant self-assurance. And the polish was all on the surface; he had the right manners but once you got to know him a little you realized he had no real understanding of courtesy or compassion. Those qualities were meaningless to people like Eric. She'd always thought him self-absorbed and egotistical to the point of solipsism; she'd felt he had cultivated Briggs's friendship simply because Eric felt Briggs could help him advance in the department.

Eric had been good at toadying up to anyone who could help him learn the arts of politics and ambition. Eric had always been very actorish: he wasn't real—everything was a role, a part, a performance: everything Eric did was done with his audience in mind. If you couldn't be any help to him he could, without a second thought, cut you dead.

He wasn't really handsome. He had a small round head and ordinary features. But he'd always kept himself trim and he'd always been a natty dresser. And the beard sharpened his face, made it longer, added polish to his appearance. Back on the mainland, she remembered, he'd tended to favor three-piece suits.

Eric's studio was spartan, dominated by a scrubbed-clean workbench under the dormer window's north light. An array of carving tools filled a wooden rack, each tool seated in its proper niche, and there were four tidy wooden bins containing pieces of white bone of graduated sizes. Antique inkwells and jars were arranged beside a tray of paintbrushes and other slender implements. In three glass display cases, each overhung by a museum light, lay examples of Eric's art. One piece, especially striking, was a large ivory cribbage board in the shape of a Polynesian outrigger canoe with intricate black-and-white scenes engraved upon its faceted surfaces.

"That's a sort of frieze," Eric explained. "If you follow those little scenes around the board, they illustrate the whole mythology of the Polynesian emigration that led to the original settlement of Hawaii a thousand years ago. I'm negotiating to sell it to the museum over in Honolulu."

"It must be pretty lucrative, this stuff."

"It can be. Do you know anything about scrimshaw?"

"No," she said, and she didn't particularly care to; but Eric had paid for the bottle and was pouring a drink for her, and she was desperate for company—anyone's, even Eric's—and so she stayed and pretended interest.

"It's a genuine American folk art. It was originated in the early 1800s by the Yankee whalers who came out to the Pacific with endless time on their hands on shipboard. They got into the habit of scrimshanding to pass the time. The early stuff was crude, of course, but pretty quickly some of them started doing quite sophisticated workmanship. They used sail needles to carve the fine lines of the engraving and then they'd trace India ink or lampblack into the carvings for contrast. About the only materials they had were whalebone and whales' teeth, so that's what they carved at first.

"The art became very popular for a while, about a century ago, and there was a period when scrimshanding became a profession in its own right. That was when they ran short of whalebone and teeth and started illustrating elephant ivory and other white bone materials. Then it all went out of fashion. But it's been coming back into favor the past few years. We've got several scrimshanders here now. The main problem today, of course, is the scarcity of ivory."

At intervals Brenda sipped his whiskey and vocalized sounds indicative of her attentiveness to his monologue. Mainly she was thinking morosely of the pointlessness of it all. Was Eric going to ask her to stay the night? If he did, would she accept? In either case, did it matter?

Watching her with bemused eyes, Eric went on, "The Endangered Species laws have made it impossible for us to obtain whalebone or elephant ivory in any quantities any more. It's a real problem."

"You seem to have a fair supply in those bins there."

"Well, some of us have been buying mastodon ivory and other fossilized bones from the Eskimos—they dig for it in the tundra up in Alaska. But that stuff's in short supply too, and the price has gone through the ceiling."

Eric took her glass and filled it from the bottle, extracting ice cubes from the half-size fridge under the workbench. She rolled the cold glass against her forehead and returned to the wicker chair, balancing herself with care. Eric smiled with the appearance of sympathy and pushed a little box across the bench. It was the size of a matchbox. The lid fit snugly. Etched into its ivory surface was a drawing of a humpback whale.

"Like it?"

"It's lovely." She tried to summon enthusiasm in her voice.

"It's nearly the real thing," he said. "Not real ivory, of course, but real bone at least. We've been experimenting with chemical processes to bleach and harden it."

She studied the tiny box and suddenly looked away. Something about it had put her in mind of little Geoff's casket.

"The bones of most animals are too rough and porous," Eric was saying. "They tend to decompose, of course, being organic. But we've had some success with chemical hardening agents. Still, there aren't many types of bone that are suitable. Of course, there are some people who're willing to make do with vegetable ivory or hard plastics, but those really aren't acceptable if you care about the artistry of the thing. The phony stuff has no grain, and anybody with a good eye can always tell."

She was thinking she really had to pull herself together. You couldn't get by indefinitely on self-pity and the liquid largess of old acquaintances, met by chance, whom you didn't even like. She'd reached a point-of-no-return: the end of this week her room rent would be due again and she had no money to cover it; the time to make up her mind was now, right now, because either she got a job or she'd end up like that whiskered wino begging for pennies and eating out of refuse bins.

Eric went on prattling about his silly hobby or whatever it was: something about the larger bones of primates—thigh bone, collarbone, "Young enough to be in good health of course—bone grows uselessly brittle as we get older . . ." But she wasn't really listening; she stood beside the workbench looking out through the dormer window at the dozens of boats in the anchorage, wondering if she could face walking into one of the tourist dives and begging for a job waiting on tables.

The drink had made her unsteady. She returned to the chair, resolving to explore the town first thing in the morning in search of employment. She *had* to snap out of it. It was time to come back to life and perhaps these beautiful islands were the place to do it: the proper setting for the resurrection of a jaded soul.

Eric's voice paused interrogatively and it made her look up. "What? Sorry."

"These two here," Eric said. She looked down at the two etched pendants. He said, "Can you tell the difference?"

"They look pretty much the same to me."

"There, see that? That one, on the left, that's a piece of whale's tooth. This other one's ordinary bone, chemically hardened and bleached to the consistency and color of true ivory. It's got the proper grain, everything."

"Fine." She set the glass down and endeavored to smile pleasantly. "That's fine, Eric. Thank you so much for the drinks. I'd better go now—" She aimed herself woozily toward the door.

"No need to rush off, is there? Here, have one more and then we'll get a bite to eat. There's a terrific little place back on the inland side of town."

"Thanks, really, but—"

"I won't take no for an answer, duckie. How often do we see each other, after all? Come on—look, I'm sorry, I've been boring you to tears with all this talk about scrimshaw and dead bones, and we haven't said a word yet about the really important things."

"What important things?"

"Well, what are we going to do about you, duckie? You seem to have a crucial problem with your life right now and I think, if you let me, maybe I can help sort it out. Sometimes all it takes is the counsel of a sympathetic old friend, you know."

By then the drink had been poured and she saw no plausible reason to refuse it. She settled back in the cane chair. Eric's smile was avuncular. "What are friends for, after all? Relax a while, duckie. You know, when I first came out here I felt a lot the way you're feeling. I guess in a way I was lucky not to've been as good a scholar as you and Briggs were. I got through the Ph.D program by the skin of my teeth but it wasn't enough. I applied for teaching jobs all over the country, you know. Not one nibble."

Then the quick smile flashed behind the neat beard. "I ran away, you see— as far as I could get without a passport. These islands are full of losers like you and me, you know. Scratch any charter-boat skipper in that marina and you'll find a bankrupt or a failed writer who couldn't get his epic novel published."

Then he lifted his glass in a gesture of toast. "But it's possible to find an antidote for our failure, you see. Sometimes it may take a certain ruthlessness, of course—a willingness to suspend the stupid values we were brought up on. So-called civilized principles are the enemies of any true individualist—you have to learn that or you're doomed to be a loser for all time. The kings and robber barons we've honored throughout history— none of them was the kind to let himself be pushed around by the imbecilic bureaucratic whims of college deans or tenure systems.

"Establishments and institutions and laws are designed by winners to keep losers in their place, that's all. You're only free when you learn there's no reason to play the game by their rules. Hell, duckie, the fun of life only comes when you discover how to make your own rules and laugh at the fools around you. Look—consider your own situation. Is there any single living soul right now who truly gives a damn whether you, Brenda Briggs, are alive or dead?"

Put that starkly it made her gape. Eric leaned forward, brandishing his glass as if it were a searchlight aimed at her face. "Well?"

"No. Nobody," she murmured reluctantly.

"There you are, then." He seemed to relax; he leaned back. "There's not a soul you need to please or impress or support, right? If you went right up Front Street here and walked into the Bank of Hawaii and robbed the place of a fortune and got killed making your escape, you'd be hurting no one but yourself. Am I right, duckie?"

"I suppose so."

"Then why not give it a try?"

"Give what a try?"

"Robbing a bank. Kidnapping a rich infant. Hijacking a yacht. Stealing a million in diamonds. Whatever you feel like, duckie—whatever appeals to you. Why not? What have you got to lose?"

She twisted her mouth into an uneven smile. "You remind me of the sophomoric sophistry we used to spout when we were undergraduates. Existentialism and nihilism galore." She put her glass down. "Well, I guess not, Eric. I don't think I'll start robbing banks just yet."

"And why not?"

"Maybe I'm just not gaited that way."

"Morality? Is that it? What's morality ever done for you?"

She steadied herself with a hand against the workbench, set her feet with care, and turned toward the door. "It's a drink too late for morbid philosophical dialectics. Thanks for the booze, though. I'll see you. . . . "

"You'd better sit down, duckie. You're a little unsteady there."

"No, I—"

"Sit down." The words came out in a harsher voice. "The door's locked anyway, duckie—you're not going anywhere."

She scowled, befuddled. "What?"

He showed her the key; then he put it away in his pocket. She looked blankly at the door, the keyhole, and—again—his face. It had gone hard; the polite mask was gone.

"I wish you'd taken the bait," he said. "Around here all they ever talk about is sunsets and surfing and the size of the marlin some fool caught. At least you've got a bigger vocabulary than that. I really wish you'd jumped at it, duckie. It would have made things easier. But you didn't, so that's that."

"What on earth are you talking about?"

She stumbled to the door then—and heard Eric's quiet laughter when she tried the knob.

She put her back to the door. Her head swam. "I don't understand. . . ."

"It's the ivory, duckie. The best material is fresh human bone. The consistency, the hardness—it takes a fine polish if it's young and healthy enough. . . ."

She stared at him and the understanding seeped into her slowly and she said, "That's where the wino went."

"Well, I have to pick and choose, don't I? I mean, I can't very well use people whose absence would be noticed."

She flattened herself against the door. She was beginning to pass out; she tried to fight it but she couldn't; in the distance, fading, she heard Eric say, "You'll make fine bones, duckie. Absolutely first-rate scrimshaw."

ED GORMAN

The Reason Why

"I'm scared."

"This was your idea, Karen."

"You scared?"

"No."

"You bastard."

"Because I'm not scared I'm a bastard?"

"You not being scared means you don't believe me."

"Well."

"See. I knew it."

"What?"

"Just the way you said 'Well.' You bastard."

I sighed and looked out at the big red brick building that sprawled over a quarter mile of spring grass turned silver by a fat June moon. Twenty-five years ago a 1950 Ford fastback had sat in the adjacent parking lot. Mine for two summers of grocery store work.

We were sitting in her car, a Volvo she'd cadged from her last marriage settlement, number four if you're interested, and sharing a pint of bourbon the way we used to in high school when we'd been more than friends but never quite lovers.

The occasion tonight was our twenty-fifth class reunion. But there was another occasion, too. In our senior year a boy named Michael Brandon had jumped off a steep clay cliff called Pierce Point to his death on the winding river road below. Suicide. That, anyway, had been the official version.

A month ago Karen Lane (she had gone back to her maiden name these days, the Karen Lane-Cummings-Todd-Browne-LeMay getting a tad too long) had called to see if I wanted to go to dinner and I said yes, if I could bring Donna along, but then Donna surprised me by saying she didn't care to go along, that by now we should be at the point in our relationship where we trusted each other ("God, Dwyer, I don't even look at other men, not for very long anyway, you know?"), and Karen and I had had dinner and she'd had many drinks, enough that I saw she had a problem, and then she'd told me about something that had troubled her for a long time . . .

In senior year she'd gone to a party and gotten sick on wine and stumbled out to somebody's backyard to throw up and it was there she'd overheard the three boys talking. They were earnestly discussing what had happened to Michael Brandon the previous week and they were even more earnestly discussing what would happen to them if "anybody ever really found out the truth."

"It's bothered me all these years," she'd said over dinner a month earlier. "They murdered him and they got away with it."

"Why didn't you tell the police?"

"I didn't think they'd believe me."

"Why not?"

She shrugged and put her lovely little face down, dark hair covering her features. Whenever she put her face down that way it meant that she didn't want to tell you a lie so she'd just as soon talk about something else.

"Why not, Karen?"

"Because of where we came from. The Highlands."

The Highlands is an area that used to ring the iron foundries and factories of this city. Way before pollution became a fashionable concern, you could stand on your front porch and see a peculiarly beautiful orange haze on the sky every dusk. The Highlands had bars where men lost ears, eyes, and fingers in just garden-variety fights, and streets where nobody sane ever walked after dark, not even cops unless they were in pairs. But it wasn't the physical violence you remembered so much as the emotional violence of poverty. You get tired of hearing your mother scream because there isn't enough money for food and hearing your father scream back because there's nothing he can do about it. Nothing.

Karen Lane and I had come from the Highlands, but we were smarter and, in her case, better looking than most of the people from the area, so when we went to Wilson High School—one of those nightmare conglomerates that shoves the poorest kids in a city in with the richest—we didn't do badly for ourselves. By senior year we found ourselves hanging out with the sons and daughters of bankers and doctors and city officials and lawyers and riding around in new Impala convertibles and attending an occasional party where you saw an actual maid. But wherever we went, we'd manage for at least a few minutes to get away from our dates and talk to each other. What we were doing, of course, was trying to comfort ourselves. We shared terrible and confusing feelings—pride that we were acceptable to those we saw as glamorous, shame that we felt disgrace for being from the Highlands and having fathers who worked in factories and mothers who went to Mass as often as nuns and brothers and sisters who were doomed to punching the clock and yelling at ragged kids in the cold factory dusk. (You never realize what a toll such shame takes till you see your father's waxen face there in the years-later casket.)

That was the big secret we shared, of course, Karen and I, that we were going to get out, leave the place once and for all. And her brown eyes never sparkled more Christmas-morning bright than at those moments when it all was ahead of us, money, sex, endless thrills, immortality. She had the kind of clean good looks brought out best by a blue cardigan with a line of white button-down shirt at the top and a brown-suede car coat over her slender shoulders and moderately tight jeans displaying her quietly artful ass. Nothing splashy about her. She had the sort of face that snuck up on you. You had the impression you were talking to a pretty but in no way spectacular girl, and then all of a sudden you saw how the eyes burned with sad humor and how wry the mouth got at certain times and how absolutely perfect that straight little nose was and how the freckles enhanced rather than detracted from her beauty and by then of course you were hopelessly entangled. Hopelessly.

This wasn't just my opinion, either. I mentioned four divorce settlements. True facts. Karen was one of those prizes that powerful and rich men like to collect with the understanding that it's only something you hold in trust, like a yachting cup. So, in her time, she'd been an ornament for a professional football player (her college beau), an orthodontist ("I think he used to have sexual fantasies about Barry Goldwater"), the owner of a large commuter airline ("I slept with half his pilots; it was kind of a company benefit"), and a sixty-nine-year-old millionaire who was dying of heart disease ("He used to have me sit next to his bedside and just hold his hand—the weird thing was that of all of them, I loved him, I really did—and his eyes would be closed and then every once in a while tears would start streaming down his cheeks as if he was remembering something that really filled him with remorse; he was really a sweetie, but then cancer got him before the heart disease and I never did find out what he regretted so much, I mean if it was about his son or his wife or what"), and now she was comfortably fixed for the rest of her life and if the crow's feet were a little more pronounced around eyes and mouth and if the slenderness was just a trifle too slender (she weighed, at five-three, maybe ninety pounds and kept a variety of diet books in her big sunny kitchen), she was a damn good-looking woman nonetheless, the world's absurdity catalogued and evaluated in a gaze that managed to be both weary and impish, with a laugh that was knowing without being cynical.

So now she wanted to play detective.

I had some more bourbon from the pint—it burned beautifully—and said, "If I had your money, you know what I'd do?"

"Buy yourself a new shirt?"

"You don't like my shirt?"

"I didn't know you had this thing about Hawaii."

"If I had your money, I'd just forget about all this."

"I thought cops were sworn to uphold the right and the true."

"I'm an ex-cop."

"You wear a uniform."

"That's for the American Security Agency."

She sighed. "So I shouldn't have sent the letters?"

"No."

"Well, if they're guilty, they'll show up at Pierce Point tonight."

"Not necessarily."

"Why?"

"Maybe they'll know it's a trap. And not do anything."

She nodded to the school. "You hear that?"

"What?"

"The song."

It was Bobby Vinton's "Roses Are Red."

"I remember one party when we both hated our dates and we ended up dancing to that over and over again. Somebody's basement. "You remember?"

"Sort of, I guess," I said.

"Good. Let's go in the gym and then we can dance to it again." Donna, my lady friend, was out of town attending an advertising convention. I hoped she wasn't going to dance with anybody else because it would sure make me mad.

I started to open the door and she said, "I want to ask you a question."

"What?" I sensed what it was going to be so I kept my eyes on the parking lot.

"Turn around and look at me."

I turned around and looked at her. "Okay."

"Since the time we had dinner a month or so ago I've started receiving brochures from Alcoholics Anonymous in the mail. If you were having them sent to me, would you be honest enough to tell me?"

"Yes, I would."

"Are you having them sent to me?"

"Yes, I am."

"You think I'm a lush?"

"Don't you?"

"I asked you first."

So we went into the gym and danced.

*   *   *

Crepe of red and white, the school colors, draped the ceiling; the stage was a cave of white light on which stood four balding fat guys with spit curls and shimmery gold lamé dinner jackets (could these be the illegitimate sons of Bill Haley?) playing guitars, drum, and saxophone; on the dance floor couples who'd lost hair, teeth, jaw lines, courage, and energy (everything, it seemed, but weight) danced to lame cover versions of "Breaking Up Is Hard To Do" and "Sheila," "Runaround Sue" and "Running Scared" (tonight's lead singer sensibly not even trying Roy Orbison's beautiful falsetto) and then, while I got Karen and myself some no-alcohol punch, they broke into a medley of dance tunes—everything from "Locomotion" to "The Peppermint Twist"—and the place went a little crazy, and I went right along with it.

"Come on," I said.

"Great."

We went out there and we burned ass. We'd both agreed not to dress up for the occasion so we were ready for this. I wore the Hawaiian shirt she found so despicable plus a blue blazer, white socks and cordovan penny-loafers. She wore a salmon-colored Merikani shirt belted at the waist and tan cotton fatigue pants and, sweet Christ, she was so adorable half the guys in the place did the kind of double-takes usually reserved for somebody outrageous or famous.

Over the blasting music, I shouted, "Everybody's watching you!"

She shouted right back, "I know! Isn't it wonderful?"

The medley went twenty minutes and could easily have been confused with an aerobics session. By the end I was sopping and wishing I was carrying ten or fifteen pounds less and sometimes feeling guilty because I was having too much fun (I just hoped Donna, probably having too much fun, too, was feeling equally guilty), and then finally it ended and mate fell into the arms of mate, hanging on to stave off sheer collapse.

Then the head Bill Haley clone said, "Okay, now we're going to do a ballad medley," so then we got everybody from Johnny Mathis to Connie Francis and we couldn't resist that, so I moved her around the floor with clumsy pleasure and she moved me right back with equally clumsy pleasure. "You know something?" I said.

"We're both shitty dancers?"

"Right."

But we kept on, of course, laughing and whirling a few times, and then coming tighter together and just holding each other silently for a time, two human beings getting older and scared about getting older, remembering some things and trying to forget others and trying to make sense of an existence that ultimately made sense to nobody, and then she said, "There's one of them."

I didn't have to ask her what "them" referred to. Until now she'd refused to identify any of the three people she'd sent the letters to.

At first I didn't recognize him. He had almost white hair and a tan so dark it looked fake. He wore a black dinner jacket with a lacy shirt and a black bow tie. He didn't seem to have put on a pound in the quarter century since I'd last seen him.

"Ted Forester?"

"Forester," she said. "He's president of the same savings and loan his father was president of."

"Who are the other two?"

"Why don't we get some punch?"

"The kiddie kind?"

"You could really make me mad with all this lecturing about alcoholism."

"If you're not really a lush then you won't mind getting the kiddie kind."

"My friend, Sigmund Fraud."

We had a couple of pink punches and caught our respective breaths and squinted in the gloom at name tags to see who we were saying hello to and realized all the terrible things you realize at high school reunions, namely that people who thought they were better than you still think that way, and that all the sad little people you feared for—the ones with blackheads and low IQs and lame left legs and walleyes and lisps and every other sort of unfair infirmity people get stuck with—generally turned out to be deserving of your fear, for there was a sadness in their eyes tonight that spoke of failures of every sort, and you wanted to go up and say something to them (I wanted to go up to nervous Karl Carberry, who used to twitch—his whole body twitched—and throw my arm around him and tell him what a neat guy he was, tell him there was no reason whatsoever for his twitching, grant him peace and self-esteem and at least a modicum of hope; if he needed a woman, get him a woman, too), but of course you didn't do that, you didn't go up, you just made edgy jokes and nodded a lot and drifted on to the next piece of human carnage.

"There's number two," Karen whispered.

This one I remembered. And despised. The six-three blond movie-star looks had grown only slightly older. His blue dinner jacket just seemed to enhance his air of malicious superiority. Larry Price. His wife Sally was still perfect, too, though you could see in the lacquered blond hair and maybe a hint of a face lift that she'd had to work at it a little harder. A year out of high school, at a bar that took teenage IDs checked by a guy who must have been legally blind, I'd gotten drunk and told Larry that he was essentially an asshole for beating up a friend of mine who hadn't had a chance against him. I had the street boy's secret belief that I could take anybody whose father was a surgeon and whose house included a swimming pool. I had hatred, bitterness, and rage going, right? Well, Larry and I went out into the parking lot, ringed by a lot of drunken spectators, and before I got off a single punch, Larry hit me with a shot that stood me straight up, giving him a great opportunity to hit me again. He hit me three times before I found his face and sent him a shot hard enough to push him back for a time. Before we could go at it again, the guy who checked IDs got himself between us. He was madder than either Larry or me. He ended the fight by taking us both by the ears (he must have trained with nuns) and dragging us out to the curb and telling neither of us to come back.

"You remember the night you fought him?"

"Yeah."

"You could have taken him, Dwyer. Those three punches he got in were just lucky."

"Yeah, that was my impression, too. Lucky."

She laughed. "I was afraid he was going to kill you."

I was going to say something smart, but then a new group of people came up and we gushed through a little social dance of nostalgia and lies and self-justifications. We talked success (at high school reunions, everybody sounds like Amway representatives at a pep rally) and the old days (nobody seems to remember all the kids who got treated like shit for reasons they had no control over) and didn't so-and-so look great (usually this meant they'd managed to keep their toupees on straight) and introducing new spouses (we all had to explain what happened to our original mates; I said mine had been eaten by alligators in the Amazon, but nobody seemed to find that especially believable) and in the midst of all this, Karen tugged my sleeve and said, "There's the third one."

Him I recognized, too. David Haskins. He didn't look any happier than he ever had. Parent trouble was always the explanation you got for his grief back in high school. His parents had been rich, truly so, his father an importer of some kind, and their arguments so violent that they were as eagerly discussed as who was or who was not pregnant. Apparently David's parents weren't getting along any better today because although the features of his face were open and friendly enough, there was still the sense of some terrible secret stooping his shoulders and keeping his smiles to furtive wretched imitations. He was a paunchy balding little man who might have been a church usher with a sour stomach.

"The Duke of Earl" started up then and there was no way we were going to let that pass so we got out on the floor; but by now, of course, we both watched the three people she'd sent letters to. Her instructions had been to meet the anonymous letter writer at nine-thirty at Pierce Point. If they were going to be there on time, they'd be leaving soon.

"You think they're going to go?"

"I doubt it, Karen."

"You still don't believe that's what I heard them say that night?"

"It was a long time ago and you were drunk."

"It's a good thing I like you because otherwise you'd be a distinct pain in the ass."

Which is when I saw all three of them go stand under one of the glowing red EXIT signs and open a fire door that led to the parking lot.

"They're going!" she said.

"Maybe they're just having a cigarette."

"You know better, Dwyer. You know better."

Her car was in the lot on the opposite side of the gym. "Well, it's worth a drive even if they don't show up. Pierce Point should be nice tonight."

She squeezed against me and said, "Thanks, Dwyer. Really."

So we went and got her Volvo and went out to Pierce Point where twenty-five years ago a shy kid named Michael Brandon had fallen or been pushed to his death.

Apparently, we were about to find out which.

*　　*　　*

The river road wound along a high wall of clay cliffs on the left and a wide expanse of water on the right. The spring night was impossibly beautiful, one of those moments so rich with sweet odor and even sweeter sight you wanted to take your clothes off and run around in some kind of crazed animal circles out of sheer joy.

"You still like jazz," she said, nodding to the radio.

"I hope you didn't mind my turning the station."

"I'm kind of into Country."

"I didn't get the impression you were listening."

She looked over at me. "Actually, I wasn't. I was thinking about you sending me all those AA pamphlets."

"It was arrogant and presumptuous and I apologize."

"No, it wasn't. It was sweet and I appreciate it."

The rest of the ride, I leaned my head back and smelled flowers and grass and river water and watched moonglow through the elms and oaks and birches of this new spring. There was a Dakota Staton song, "Street of Dreams," and I wondered as always where she was and what she was doing, she'd been so fine, maybe the most underappreciated jazz singer of the entire fifties.

Then we were going up a long, twisting gravel road. We pulled up next to a big park pavillion and got out and stood in the wet grass, and she came over and slid her arm around my waist and sort of hugged me in a half-serious way. "This is all probably crazy, isn't it?"

I sort of hugged her back in a half-serious way. "Yeah, but it's a nice night for a walk so what the hell."

"You ready?"

"Yep."

"Let's go then."

So we went up the hill to the Point itself, and first we looked out at the far side of the river where white birches glowed in the gloom and where beyond you could see the horseshoe shape of the city lights. Then we looked down, straight down the drop of two hundred feet, to the road where Michael Brandon had died.

When I heard the car starting up the road to the east, I said, "Let's get in those bushes over there."

A thick line of shrubs and second-growth timber would give us a place to hide, to watch them.

By the time we were in place, ducked down behind a wide elm and a mulberry bush, a new yellow Mercedes sedan swung into sight and stopped several yards from the edge of the Point.

A car radio played loud in the night. A Top 40 song. Three men got out. Dignified Forester, matinee-idol Price, anxiety-tight Haskins.

Forester leaned back into the car and snapped the radio off. But he left the headlights on. Forester and Price each had cans of beer. Haskins bit his nails.

They looked around in the gloom. The headlights made the darkness beyond seem much darker and the grass in its illumination much greener. Price said harshly, "I told you this was just some goddamn prank. Nobody knows squat."

"He's right, he's probably right," Haskins said to Forester. Obviously he was hoping that was the case.

Forester said, "If somebody didn't know something, we would never have gotten those letters."

She moved then and I hadn't expected her to move at all. I'd been under the impression we would just sit there and listen and let them ramble and maybe in so doing reveal something useful.

But she had other ideas.

She pushed through the undergrowth and stumbled a little and got to her feet again and then walked right up to them.

"Karen!" Haskins said.

"So you did kill Michael," she said.

Price moved toward her abruptly, his hand raised. He was drunk and apparently hitting women was something he did without much trouble.

Then I stepped out from our hiding place and said, "Put your hand down, Price."

Forester said, "Dwyer."

"So," Price said, lowering his hand. "I was right, wasn't I?" He was speaking to Forester.

Forester shook his silver head. He seemed genuinely saddened. "Yes, Price, for once your cynicism is justified."

Price said, "Well, you aren't getting a goddamned penny, do you know that?"

He lunged toward me, still a bully. But I was ready for him, wanted it. I also had the advantage of being sober. When he was two steps away, I hit him just once and very hard in his solar plexus. He backed away, eyes startled, and then he turned abruptly away.

We all stood looking at one another, pretending not to hear the sounds of violent vomiting on the other side of the splendid new Mercedes.

Forester said, "When I saw you there, Karen, I wondered if you could do it alone."

"Do what?"

"What?" Forester said. "What? Let's at least stop the games. You two want money."

"Christ," I said to Karen, who looked perplexed, "they think we're trying to shake them down."

"Shake them down?"

"Blackmail them."

"Exactly," Forester said.

Price had come back around. He was wiping his mouth with the back of his hand. In his other hand he carried a silver-plated .45, the sort of weapon professional gamblers favor.

Haskins said, "Larry, Jesus, what is that?"

"What does it look like?"

"Larry, that's how people get killed." Haskins sounded like Price's mother.

Price's eyes were on me. "Yeah, it would be terrible if Dwyer here got killed, wouldn't it?" He waved the gun at me. I didn't really think he'd shoot, but I sure was afraid he'd trip and the damn thing would go off accidentally. "You've been waiting since senior year to do that to me, haven't you, Dwyer?"

I shrugged. "I guess so, yeah."

"Well, why don't I give Forester here the gun and then you and I can try it again."

"Fine with me."

He handed Forester the .45. Forester took it all right, but what he did was toss it somewhere into the gloom surrounding the car. "Larry, if you don't straighten up here, I'll fight you myself. Do you understand me?" Forester had a certain dignity and when he spoke, his voice carried an easy authority. "There will be no more fighting, do you both understand that?"

"I agree with Ted," Karen said.

Forester, like a teacher tired of naughty children, decided to get on with the real business. "You wrote those letters, Dwyer?"

"No."

"No?"

"No. Karen wrote them."

A curious glance was exchanged by Forester and Karen. "I guess I should have known that," Forester said.

"Jesus, Ted," Karen said, "I'm not trying to blackmail you, no matter what you think."

"Then just what exactly are you trying to do?"

She shook her lovely little head. I sensed she regretted ever writing the letters, stirring it all up again. "I just want the truth to come out about what really happened to Michael Brandon that night."

"The truth," Price said. "Isn't that goddamn touching?"

"Shut up, Larry," Haskins said.

Forester said, "You know what happened to Michael Brandon?"

"I've got a good idea," Karen said. "I overheard you three talking at a party one night."

"What did we say?"

"What?"

"What did you overhear us say?"

Karen said, "You said that you hoped nobody looked into what really happened to Michael that night."

A smile touched Forester's lips. "So on that basis you concluded that we murdered him?"

"There wasn't much else to conclude."

Price said, weaving still, leaning on the fender for support, "I don't god-damn believe this."

Forester nodded to me. "Dwyer, I'd like to have a talk with Price and Haskins here, if you don't mind. Just a few minutes." He pointed to the darkness beyond the car. "We'll walk over there. You know we won't try to get away because you'll have our car. All right?"

I looked at Karen.

She shrugged.

They left, back into the gloom, voices receding and fading into the sounds of crickets and a barn owl and a distant roaring train.

"You think they're up to something?"

"I don't know," I said.

We stood with our shoes getting soaked and looked at the green green grass in the headlights.

"What do you think they're doing?" Karen asked.

"Deciding what they want to tell us."

"You're used to this kind of thing, aren't you?"

"I guess."

"It's sort of sad, isn't it?"

"Yeah. It is."

"Except for you getting the chance to punch out Larry Price after all these years."

"Christ, you really think I'm that petty?"

"I know you are. I know you are."

Then we both turned to look back to where they were. There'd been a cry and Forester shouted, "You hit him again, Larry, and I'll break your goddamn jaw." They were arguing about something and it had turned vicious.

I leaned back against the car. She leaned back against me. "You think we'll ever go to bed?"

"I'd sure like to, Karen, but I can't."

"Donna?"

"Yeah. I'm really trying to learn how to be faithful."

"That been a problem?"

"It cost me a marriage."

"Maybe I'll learn how someday, too."

Then they were back. Somebody, presumably Forester, had torn Price's nice lacy shirt into shreds. Haskins looked miserable.

Forester said, "I'm going to tell you what happened that night."

I nodded.

"I've got some beer in the back seat. Would either of you like one?"

Karen said, "Yes, we would."

So he went and got a six pack of Michelob and we all had a beer and just before he started talking he and Karen shared another one of those peculiar glances and then he said, "The four of us—myself, Price, Haskins, and Michael Brandon—had done something we were very ashamed of."

"Afraid of," Haskins said.

"Afraid that, if it came out, our lives would be ruined. Forever," Forester said.

Price said, "Just say it, Forester." He glared at me. "We raped a girl, the four of us."

"Brandon spent two months afterward seeing the girl, bringing her flowers, apologizing to her over and over again, telling her how sorry we were, that we'd been drunk and it wasn't like us to do that and—" Forester sighed, put his eyes to the ground. "In fact we had been drunk; in fact it wasn't like us to do such a thing—"

Haskins said, "It really wasn't. It really wasn't."

For a time there was just the barn owl and the crickets again, no talk, and then gently I said, "What happened to Brandon that night?"

"We were out as we usually were, drinking beer, talking about it, afraid the girl would finally turn us into the police, still trying to figure out why we'd ever done such a thing—"

The hatred was gone from Price's eyes. For the first time the matinee idol looked as melancholy as his friends. "No matter what you think of me, Dwyer, I don't rape women. But that night—" He shrugged, looked away.

"Brandon," I said. "You were going to tell me about Brandon."

"We came up here, had a case of beer or something, and talked about it some more, and that night," Forester said, "that night Brandon just snapped. He couldn't handle how ashamed he was or how afraid he was of being turned in. Right in the middle of talking—"

Haskins took over. "Right in the middle, he just got up and ran out to the Point." He indicated the cliff behind us. "And before we could stop him, he jumped."

"Jesus," Price said, "I can't forget his screaming on the way down. I can't ever forget it."

I looked at Karen. "So what she heard you three talking about outside the party that night was not that you'd killed Brandon but that you were afraid a serious investigation into his suicide might turn up the rape?"

Forester said, "Exactly." He stared at Karen. "We didn't kill Michael, Karen. We loved him. He was our friend."

But by then, completely without warning, she had started to cry and then she began literally sobbing, her entire body shaking with some grief I could neither understand nor assuage.

I nodded to Forester to get back in his car and leave. They stood and watched us a moment and then they got into the Mercedes and went away, taking the burden of years and guilt with them.

This time I drove. I went far out the river road, miles out, where you pick up the piney hills and the deer standing by the side of the road.

From the glove compartment she took a pint of J&B, and I knew better than to try and stop her.

I said, "You were the girl they raped, weren't you?"

"Yes."

"Why didn't you tell the police?"

She smiled at me. "The police weren't exactly going to believe a girl from the Highlands about the sons of rich men."

I sighed. She was right.

"Then Michael started corning around to see me. I can't say I ever forgave him, but I started to feel sorry for him. His fear—" She shook her head, looked out the window. She said, almost to herself, "But I had to write those letters, get them there tonight, know for sure if they killed him." She paused. "You believe them?"

"That they didn't kill him?"

"Right."

"Yes, I believe them."

"So do I."

Then she went back to staring out the window, her small face childlike there in silhouette against the moonsilver river. "Can I ask you a question, Dwyer?"

"Sure."

"You think we're ever going to get out of the Highlands?"

"No," I said, and drove on faster in her fine new expensive car. "No, I don't."

CAROLYN G. HART

Out of the Ashes

DON BROWN, MY FAVORITE HOMICIDE DETECTIVE, lounged against the kitchen counter, watching me with an odd expression.

"I never think of you as a cookie maker, Henrie O."

I squeezed out pink icing to make the final curve of the *e* on a heart-shaped sugar cookie. I tilted my head. The inscription—*Love*—was a bit uneven but readable. "Don't be chauvinist, Don."

His face squeezed in thought. "Yeah. You're right. Sorry."

I let it drop, though I could have ragged on him a bit more. No, after almost fifty years of newspapering and a second career in teaching, I don't fit the stereotype of a dear little grandma whipping up goodies. But I am a grandmother and I do enjoy cooking, although it's definitely not one of my talents—I paused to swipe up some icing that had overshot its mark—but I resent pigeonholing. I like making cookies, hammering nails, outwitting malefactors—don't try to put me in a mold. Anybody's mold.

I studied the last two cookies on the sheet of waxed paper, nodded, and squeezed out a capital *E* on the first. This would be Emily's cookie. Dear Emily. My daughter. God's greatest gift to me. Then I traced a *D* on the last cookie. I folded a napkin, put the cookie on it, and handed it to Don.

"Valentine's Day." Don's tone was morose. He stared at the cookie, the skin of his face stretched tight over the bones.

Don isn't the kind of guy who attracts attention. He's average height and slender, with a carefully blank, unresponsive face, nondescript sandy hair, and an even, uninflected voice. It's easy to miss the sharp intelligence in his weary blue eyes, the dry, wry curve of his mouth, the athletic wiriness of his build.

And something was terribly wrong with my young friend this gray February afternoon.

I got down two mugs, poured coffee, and gestured to the kitchen table.

Don joined me. But he didn't pick up the mug, and he put the heart-shaped cookie down on the table, untasted.

"Henrie O . . ." He looked at me with misery in his eyes.

Now it was my turn to make judgments, but I had no chauvinist intent. The sexes do differ. Markedly. And it's damn hard for men to admit to emotion.

"Tell me what's wrong, Don." My voice was much gentler than usual. I am customarily cool and acerbic.

But not always.

I reached out and touched his arm.

It was such a young arm. Strong. Lean. With—God willing—so many years yet to live. I silently wished him the best of life—and that includes both passion and pain.

"Everything. Nothing." He gripped the coffee mug. "Hell, a cop shouldn't get married anyway."

"Yes, a cop should. Especially this particular cop." I gave his arm a final squeeze, picked up my own cup. "Any woman with taste would know that."

He didn't manage a smile. If anything, his face was even bleaker. "The hell of it is, she loves me. I know she does. But, damn it . . ." He hunched over the table; his anguished blue eyes clung to my face. "Henrie O, you're a natural when it comes to crime. I swear to God, sometimes I think you can smell it, pick it up like a cat sniffing a mouse."

I lifted an eyebrow. "What does crime have to do with love?"

*　　*　　*

He told me.

You don't see many happy faces at the courthouse. You're on reality time here, much as at a hospital. Pain, suffering, and despair mark these faces. I don't know whether it's worse in summer or winter. Now the marble floors were mud scuffed and the smell of wet wool mingled with the occasional whiff of forbidden cigarettes.

The DA's offices were on the third floor. I found the cubbyhole assigned to Assistant DA Kerry O'Keefe at the end of the hall.

I knocked.

"Come in."

She was on the telephone, a slender, quite lovely young woman with blond hair and an expressive, intelligent face. She gestured for me to take a seat.

". . . arraignment is scheduled at ten A.M. tomorrow. We'd be willing to reduce the charge to . . ." Her clear voice was clipped and businesslike.

I sat in the hard wooden chair that faced Assistant DA Kerry O'Keefe's gray metal desk and looked at the young woman who was breaking Don's heart.

Kerry O'Keefe wasn't knockdown gorgeous, but hers was a face with a haunting, unforgettable quality, camellia-smooth skin, almond-shaped hazel eyes flecked with gold, a vulnerable mouth, a determined chin.

". . . see you in court, Counselor." She hung up, looked at me politely. "May I help you?"

"I'm Henrietta O'Dwyer Collins. A friend of Don Brown's."

She had a sudden quick intake of breath, those gold-flecked eyes widened, then her face closed in, smooth, impervious. "I'm terribly busy this morning. I'm due in court." She reached for a brown manila file, grabbed it.

"How do you weigh evidence, Miss O'Keefe?" She pushed back her chair and stood, holding the folder against her as if it were a shield. Anger and misery flickered in those remarkable, pain-filled eyes. "Evidence? In one of my cases?"

I stood, too. "Yes, Miss O'Keefe." The tension eased out of her body. "I don't understand . . . why are you asking me about my work? What does that have to do with Don?"

"Everything."

She shook her head and her honey-bright hair swayed. "I study the record. I look at the physical evidence. I interview witnesses."

"When you interview witnesses, what are you looking for?"

"The truth, of course." Her tone was impatient.

"Yes, of course. The truth. Tell me, Miss O'Keefe, how do you know whether people are telling you the truth?"

She wasn't quite patronizing. "It comes with experience. You can pick up when people are lying. Lots of little tip-offs. They sound too earnest, look at you too directly. Sometimes they'll talk too fast. Sometimes they won't look at you at all."

I smiled. "It takes a lot of intuition."

She tucked the folder under one arm, ready to walk out, terminate this interview. "You can call it that."

"You have to have confidence in your own instincts."

Her eyes blazed with sudden understanding. "Oh. So that's why you're here. Look, I told Don, it's no use. No use at all."

"Please, Miss O'Keefe. Let me finish."

She took a step toward the door, then stopped and stood quite still.

Was it respect for my age? Or was it deeper, a pain-filled heart's desperate reluctance to make an irrevocable decision?

I made my bid. "Don believes in your instinct. He wants you to look at what happened one more time, one last time. And this time, listen to your heart. This time, begin with the premise that Jack O'Keefe was innocent."

"The premise . . ." She began to tremble.

I knew then that no matter how much Kerry had suffered, she'd never questioned the facts as they had appeared—even though every fiber of her being rebelled at acceptance.

Her eyes bored into mine. "But there's no reason to think he was innocent. Is there?"

"Yes. Oh, yes. You, Kerry. Your heart says your dad couldn't have done it. Just as your heart says Don is the man for you. Come on, Kerry, give your heart a chance."

*　　*　　*

The icy wind moaning through the leafless trees sounded like a lost child's cry.

Kerry O'Keefe stood with her hands jammed deep into the pockets of her navy cashmere coat. She didn't wear a scarf. Her cheeks were touched with pink from the cold. She stared at the ruins, her face empty, her eyes as dark and desolate as the blackened remnants of the chimney.

She spoke rapidly, without emotion, as if this were just one more report of one more crime. "The fire was called in at ten past midnight on Friday, January fourteenth, nineteen eighty-three. A three-alarm blaze. It took almost two hours to put it out. The firemen didn't find the bodies until almost dawn. They had to let it cool. Three bodies. My father, Jack O'Keefe. My mother, Elizabeth. My sister, Jenny." She half turned, pointed toward a well-kept two-story Victorian frame house clearly visible through the bare trees. "My grandparents live there. They thought we were all dead, that they hadn't found my body yet." She shivered. "I'd spent the night with a friend. I came home about nine. I saw our house—smoke was still curling up like mist from a river—and I ran up the drive to my grandparents' and burst in. My grandmother screamed. She thought I was a ghost." Kerry once again faced the ruins. "I didn't know what had happened until after the day after the funeral. That's when the story came out in the newspaper saying the fire was set with gasoline and autopsies revealed traces of a narcotic in the bodies." She saw my surprise. "Yes. Percodan. A prescription for my grandmother. For back pain. They said Dad must have dropped by her house, taken the stuff that day. Only a few tablets were missing. But it wouldn't take many. It's very strong stuff. That was in the newspaper. But the rest of it never came out in the paper."

I waited.

She faced me. "But people knew. Everybody knew. The bank examiners found two hundred thousand dollars gone. Dummy loans. Made by my dad."

Kelly turned up the collar of her coat, hunkered down for protection against the bite of the wind. Her voice was as cold as the wind. "I heard my parents quarreling that night. Just before I left. Mother's voice was—I don't know—stern. Determined. She said, 'Jack, you've got to face up to it. You don't have any choice.' And Daddy"—her voice wavered—"Daddy sounded so, so beaten. He said, 'Liz, how can I? How can I?'"

Kelly crossed her arms tight against her body. "I can still hear his voice. But what I don't understand, what I'll never understand, is how could he do it? How could he kill Mother and Jenny?" Her tormented eyes swept from the ruins to my face. "And me. I would have died, too. He must have thought I was in my room, asleep. It was just a last-minute thing, the call from Janet. She asked me to spend the night. I ran down to the kitchen and asked Mother and she said okay and I hurried up to my room and packed my overnight bag and went down the back stairs. Janet picked me up in the alley."

I was familiar with these facts. Don had brought me the fire marshal's report, a copy of the autopsy reports, and the file from homicide.

Because, of course, it was not simply arson, it was murder.

The official conclusion: The bank examiner discovered the dummy loans. Jack O'Keefe, facing disgrace and probable prosecution, drugged his family, waited until they were asleep, then splashed gasoline throughout the downstairs portion of the house. He lighted a candle, wrapped a string around its base. The string led from the kitchen through the dining room to velvet drapes that were also doused with gasoline. O'Keefe hurried upstairs and went to bed. There were traces of Percodan in his body, too.

Was he already groggy when he slipped beneath the covers?

Was he asleep before the blaze erupted in sudden, demonic fury?

Although his body and the bodies of his wife and daughter were badly burned, the cause of death was asphyxiation from the smoke that roiled up from the blaze below.

Now, twelve years later, wind and rain and sun had scoured the ruins, but thick deposits of carbon on the remains of the chimney still glistened purplish black in the pale winter sun.

Despite the tumbled bricks, the occasional poked-out timber, I could discern the outline of the house, imagine the broad sweep of the porch and the jaunty bay windows, estimate the size of the living room and dining room, glimpse a bone-white remnant of the sink in the kitchen.

I looked thoughtfully toward the substantial Victorian house that belonged to Jack O'Keefe's parents.

The ruins would be visible from every window on this side of the house.

I pointed to my left. I could see the roof of a house over a brick wall. "Who lives over there?"

"Uncle Robert and Aunt Louise. My dad's brother." There was no warmth, no fondness in Kerry's voice. "They built the wall a few months after the fire."

I wasn't sure I would blame them for that. Who would want an ever-present reminder of that violent night?

Who did want an ever-present reminder?

"Why are the ruins still here?"

Kerry's face was icily determined. "Grandmother. Then me."

"Why?"

"I don't know what Grandmother thinks. I don't believe anyone's ever known. I remember her, before the fire, as bright and cheerful and fluttery. But she's like a ceramic piece. The color is all on the surface, a surface you can't get past. All I know is she wouldn't let anyone touch any of it—not a piece, not a scrap."

"Didn't the neighbors complain? Don't they now?"

"No. Oh, they might not like it. I suppose a lot of them don't. But it's been so many years now, most people don't even notice. You see, we're the O'Keefes. *The* family in Derry Hills. For good or bad. The richest. The most powerful. Even though Grandad sold the bank a few months after—after the fire. But Uncle Robert's on the board of directors. And so am I. Uncle Robert's president of the country club. Last year he headed up the community drive. And no one would want to talk to Grandmother about the ruins."

"You said the ruins stood because of your grandmother—and then because of you."

"Uncle Robert was the executor of the estate. He did what Grandmother told him to do."

But he built a wall. Brown winter tendrils of ivy clung to it.

I glanced from that wall to Kerry's face. "You own the property now.

Why don't you have the ruins knocked down?"

Her pale face was stubborn. "Then it would be green and grassy—and I might forget."

Abruptly, Kerry turned, headed back toward my car.

I caught up with her.

She slammed into the passenger seat.

I slid behind the wheel.

She glared at me. "This is stupid. Stupid. And it hurts too much. Because I thought my dad loved me, loved all of us. He was my best friend, the greatest guy I ever knew. When he laughed . . ." She swallowed harshly and stared out the winter-grimed window of the car, stared out at ruins and heartbreak. When she spoke again, her voice was dull, exhausted. "I was wrong about my dad. So how can I ever believe in . . . anything."

That was why she'd told Don she wouldn't marry him. That was why these grim ruins stood.

If Jack O'Keefe was not the man she'd believed in, how could Kerry be sure about Don?

About any man?

About any person?

Ever.

Her face streaked with tears, Kerry grabbed the door handle.

"Wait, Kerry. Answer one question. Just one. You spent the night at Janet's. How did you sleep?"

She struggled to control her ragged breathing. "Oh God, I hate to remember. I don't want to remember! We were having so much fun. We stayed up all night and talked and talked and talked. That's why I slept so late—"

"You stayed up all night?" She heard the excitement in my voice. "Yes. You know how it is—"

"You weren't tired? Fighting off sleep?"

Her mouth opened. Her eyes widened. She turned, stared at me. But she wasn't seeing me. "Oh, my God. If I wasn't sleepy—because I should have been, shouldn't I? If Daddy intended for all of us to die, I should have been drugged, too! The police believed Daddy took the Percodan from Grandmother's house and ground it up and put it in our drinks at dinner." Then the eagerness seeped out of her face. Her lips quivered again. "But it could have happened after dinner."

"How?"

"Cocoa." Her lips quivered. "It must have been in the cocoa."

"Cocoa?"

"It was a family thing. In the winter, we always had cocoa at night, sitting around the fire in the living room." She glanced toward the chimney, a sentinel against the pale blue winter sky.

"But you weren't there that night. And, if your dad planned for his family to die, it would be very important to him to be sure you drank the cocoa. But, if he was innocent and you didn't come downstairs for cocoa, it wouldn't matter, would it? He'd simply think you'd already gone to bed. Am I right?"

Kerry's hands came together tight and hard.

She wasn't listening.

She was thinking.

I gave her a moment, then I laid it out.

"If Jack O'Keefe didn't doctor the cocoa, someone else did."

Her eyes locked with mine.

Then I looked back at the ruins of the house, the once-substantial, old, and comfortable house. In a little town, back doors often aren't locked.

It could have been even easier, someone dropping by that winter afternoon. I envisioned a gloved hand lifting the canister lid, dropping in the finely ground powder, giving the canister a shake. Cocoa would better hide the bitter taste, too.

"You see, Kerry, if we're right about your father, then it was terribly, critically important to someone to be sure no one woke up when the fire broke out."

* * *

While I waited to see the president of the Derry Hills National Bank, I considered who might have doctored the cocoa.

Happily for Kerry, I was confident I could exclude several names immediately.

The cocoa wasn't doctored by anyone in the house.

How could I be certain?

Because Kerry lived.

The police had accepted the idea that Jack O'Keefe preferred to die and for his family to die rather than to face disgrace.

But that tortured reasoning made no sense, fulfilled no logic, unless everyone died. The police assumed Jack O'Keefe simply didn't know Kerry was gone for the night.

But on that fateful evening, Kerry's father, mother, and sister knew Kerry had drunk no cocoa.

If one of them were the murderer, he or she could easily have brought a cup of cocoa upstairs to Kerry. Once it was realized that Kerry was absent, the macabre plan would have been delayed until the next night when Kerry, too, would have been home.

So, I didn't put Jack or Elizabeth or Jenny O'Keefe on my list of suspects. If the dead could not be blamed, who could? I intended to find out.

The office door opened and Ray Vickery, the president of the Deny Hills National Bank, walked toward me. An eager smile touched Ray's always-genial face. His handclasp was strong and warm.

"Henrie O, it's good to see you. Always good to see you." His eyes said even more.

I had occasion in the past to be of service to Ray and his wife, Eleanor, and their gratitude continues. I could count on Ray.

He welcomed me into his office, offered me a comfortable red wing chair. He sat in its twin. I came straight to the point.

"Ray, were you with the bank twelve years ago—when Jack O'Keefe and his family died?"

His mobile face was sorrowful. "That was awful. Yes. The bank belonged to the O'Keefes then. I'd been here about seven years when it happened." He shook his head slowly. "I still have trouble believing it."

"Why?"

"Jack O'Keefe—well, he was a fun guy, loud, always joking. A big, good-looking man. Blond, blue eyed, with a grin bigger than Texas. And later, everybody agreed he'd never really settled down, worked like he should, like his father and brother thought he should. Jack was too busy sailing or mountain climbing or building a glider or hiking with his girls or white-water rafting on the Colorado. But he was a fun guy—I couldn't believe it when he set the house on fire. His wife, the girls. And only Kerry left and that just by a stroke of luck. They say it's made Kerry a real loner. Her grandmother worries about it. She won't let anybody get close to her. If Jack had just thought . . ." Ray sighed.

"So Jack was a flake. What made him a crook?"

Ray shrugged. "Who's to know? I mean, it was such a shock. To all of us. But there wasn't any doubt about it. Two hundred thousand missing, and fake loans signed by Jack. The family hushed it up, of course. Old Man O'Keefe made up the losses. But it knocked the stuffing out of him. He sold the bank soon after. It wasn't six months later they found his skiff dumped over in the lake. His body surfaced three days later. He drowned. But I thought he did it on purpose. He was crazy about Jack."

"Who was in the loan department besides Jack?"

"Robert, Jack's brother." He frowned in thought. "And I think Gordon Evans was in loans then, too."

I took my notebook out of my purse. "Ray, some new evidence has turned up. Jack O'Keefe didn't set that fire. And that makes me wonder if he stole the money. Could someone else have signed his name to the fake loans, made him a patsy?"

Ray's mobile face reflected his response: shock, rejection, uncertainty, consideration. He rubbed his cheek thoughtfully. "It would have taken some doing. But, sure, it could have been done. Because Jack was such a loose guy and spent so much time out of the office."

"What happened to the evidence?"

He looked blank.

"The bank examiner found these dummy loans. Where would those papers be?"

It took three hours, and we didn't find the originals. But the yellowed Xerox copies in the dead files in the basement suited my purposes just fine.

Ray Vickery agreed to my plan. I knew he would. "I owe it to Jack," he said simply.

I called Don. He heard me out.

"Henrie O, it could be dangerous."

"I don't think so. But I'll be careful."

"You promise?"

"Yes."

"Henrie O, thanks."

*   *   *

I stopped first in Gordon Evans's office. Evans was a lanky, somber-faced man about ten years younger than I. His handshake was limp and his mustache dispirited.

But he wasn't stupid.

When I finished speaking, he leaned forward, his gray eyes cold. "Anyone in the bank could have used Jack's office. Not I alone. And I resent the implication that I might have been involved." He reached for a sheaf of papers. "Now, I have matters—"

"Of course, there's a simple solution. Mr. Vickery has agreed to make a search of the bank's dead files tomorrow. He will then submit the papers to a document examiner along with samples of Jack O'Keefe's handwriting. If the signature is not that of Jack O'Keefe—if his name is forged on those documents—we will be sure of his innocence." I smiled. "You won't object to providing a sample of your handwriting, will you?"

"I shall do nothing of the kind. Good day, Mrs. Collins."

* * *

Alma Hendricks scooted her chair closer to mine in the bank's employee coffee room. She poked her thick-lensed glasses higher on her beaked nose and glanced uneasily around, then spoke rapidly. "Nothing ever came out in public, but everybody in town knew. I felt so awful for the family."

"You did Jack O'Keefe's secretarial work?"

"Yes. You could have knocked me over with a feather." Her green eyes stared at me earnestly.

"Did you like him?"

Sudden tears filmed her eyes. She swung away, grabbed some Kleenex, swiped under her glasses.

So. "Some new evidence has surfaced, regarding the fire. Now there is some question whether Mr. O'Keefe actually stole that money."

She listened intently as I described the search that would be made of the dead files.

* * *

Antiques, brocaded chairs, and a variety of small tables jammed Iris O'Keefe's living room. The smell of rose potpourri mingled with a violet cologne. But neither could quite mask the sweet thick scent of bourbon.

We were about the same age. An ormolu-framed mirror reflected us. Funny how we often see what we wish in the quick early morning scan of a mirror. Intellectually I know I am old. But it always surprises me—shocks me—to see the lines in my face, the silver in my once raven black hair.

We were a contrast, no doubt about it. I always look impatient. I *am* impatient. My eyes are dark, my face strong boned, my body always poised to move.

Iris O'Keefe's white hair straggled, though it looked as if it had been ineffectually brushed. Her blue eyes peered at me muzzily, but that was alcohol, not age. A heavily veined hand plucked nervously at the unevenly tied white silk bow at the throat of her wrinkled navy dress.

". . . will exonerate your son. We'll know definitely tomorrow when we look at the documents."

Her shoulders sagged. Slowly, wearily, without saying a word, her face drawn, she struggled to her feet and walked unsteadily across the room, habit steering her safely past the bric-a-brac-laden tables.

After a moment, I rose and followed her.

She stood by the one window with the drapes full open.

Not a tree, not a shrub marred the view of the burned-out house.

She shuddered, long, slow, deep shudders.

"Mrs. O'Keefe—"

"Leave. Leave now. Leave me."

*   *   *

"That's all over. Over!" Louise O'Keefe's hair curled in obedient, glistening waves. Her patterned black-and-russet silk dress was stylishly short, but Louise O'Keefe still had the figure to display her legs. She had the glisten of wealth, that unmistakable patina created by fine clothes, expensive cosmetics, superb hairdressing, exquisite jewelry (gold shell earrings and a gold pin crusted with rubies), and the confidence money buys.

Skillfully applied makeup softened the sharpness of her features. Her face was long and thin (thin, of course), her gray eyes remote, her mouth tight.

"No, Mrs. O'Keefe. It isn't over."

"It was twelve years ago." She smoothed back a wisp of hair. "Jack was a thief. And he couldn't face up to it."

I rose, but I kept my eyes on hers. "Whatever he was or wasn't, Mrs. O'Keefe, we're now certain he was not an arsonist—and thereby a murderer. Whether he was a thief will be determined tomorrow, when we study the documents."

She stood by the Adam mantel, one heavily beringed hand clutching it. "We—who is we? What right have you to make these accusations?"

I gave her a cool smile. "There are no accusations yet, Mrs. O'Keefe. But tomorrow . . ."

I waited patiently outside the door to the men's grill. If you want to find sexism alive and thriving, try your nearest country club. The grill was a fitting background for men of wealth: paneled walls, hunting prints, elegant Oriental rugs, and walnut card tables. The cardplayers were sixtyish men in argyle sweaters, fine wool slacks, and Italian loafers.

Often at this time of the day, I was hard at work in my office at the *Clarion*. The newspaper is produced by the journalism department at the college, but it serves the town of Derry Hills. I was op-ed editor this semester. It was strange to contrast the pulsing, scarcely leashed tension of the *Clarion*—of any daily newspaper office—with the muted, relaxed bonhomie here.

The contrast reminded me that life has infinite variations, and it's unwise to assume your pattern is all that exists.

Finally, my quarry laid out his hand, then rose from the table near the fireplace. Robert O'Keefe had thinning blond hair and a petulant face. He might once have been attractive, but his stocky body was flabby with a paunch that even good tailoring didn't quite hide.

When he came through the doorway, I stepped forward. "Mr. O'Keefe, may I speak with you for a moment?"

He took me to a petit-point sofa in an alcove off the main reception area.

His face didn't change as I spoke, but the long slender hands in his lap gripped each other tightly.

". . . sure you'll be delighted if we can clear your brother's name when we find those files tomorrow."

Slowly his hands relaxed. Eyes as shiny and unreadable as blue marbles slid across my face, flicked toward the grandfather clock in the corner.

"Interesting." His voice was bored. "Too bad poor Kerry's going to be disappointed." He pushed back his chair, stood. "Got to get back to the game. Good to talk to you, Mrs. . . . uh—"

"Collins."

"But the truth of it is, Jack took the money."

And he turned and walked away.

*   *   *

The phone call came at six the next morning.

But that was all right. I was already drinking my second cup of Kona.

I picked up the receiver.

"Henrie O, Christ, it worked!" Don was pumped up. "So what do we do now?"

*   *   *

Ray Vickery agreed to loan me the boardroom at the bank.

"I'd say this is bank business." His voice was grim.

"Thank you, Ray." I hung up the phone, made my calls in quick succession. It was an invitation no one quite dared to refuse. I set the meeting for 11 A.M.

I arrived ten minutes early.

Don was waiting in the parking lot.

He opened my car door, his face grim.

"Henrie O, I got word just a few minutes ago. Those signatures on the dummy loans—they're Jack O'Keefe's." Despair etched deep lines in his face. "The examiner's sure."

I'd considered that possibility already. And thought it through. There was nothing to say about it. Now.

Instead I asked briskly, "But you brought the videocassette?"

"It's in the car. But what difference—"

"Get it, Don."

*　　*　　*

Don stood by the oversize television. It was equipped with a videocassette player. He held a cassette in his hand.

I was at the door of the boardroom.

Kerry O'Keefe arrived first. She looked gorgeous in a black-and-white rayon suit with red trim, but her face was pale and strained and the glances she sped at Don alternated between hope and uncertainty.

Don's somber face offered her no encouragement. Gordon Evans walked in, his body stiff, his face resentful. "I am here under protest." The gray pinstripe did little for his sallow coloring. It was a rack suit, the trousers not quite long enough to break.

I raised an eyebrow. "Surely you'd like to know the truth of what happened with those loans—since you worked in that area, too."

"I do know the truth."

"Perhaps. And perhaps, Mr. Evans, you will discover that certitude sometimes does not cover a multitude of sins."

He took a chair in the far corner, crossed one leg over the other, and watched me with distaste. Don shot me a curious, puzzled look. Kerry jumped up from her chair. "Grandmother!"

Iris O'Keefe wavered unsteadily, but with dignity, in the doorway. "Kerry, my dear. You're here, too?"

Kerry took her grandmother's arm and carefully shepherded her to a chair beside her own.

Iris O'Keefe hunched in the chair. Her thin fingers plucked at the pearl necklace at her throat.

Alma Hendricks hesitated in the doorway.

"Come in, Alma. I'm so glad you could join us."

"Good morning, ma'am, Mrs. O'Keefe, Miss O'Keefe." Alma slid into the chair opposite Kerry's. Angry voices rose in the hall. We all looked toward the door. Robert and Louise O'Keefe, their faces flushed, stepped inside and abruptly stopped talking. The instant of silence was full of tension.

"So what are you staring at?" Louise demanded sharply, her angry eyes snapping from face to face.

"If you'll take your seats . . . ," and I motioned to two empty chairs with a direct view of the television set.

Robert O'Keefe glowered at me. Louise tossed her head. But they sat down.

"First, I want to be sure we all know one another." Robert crossed his arms. "Mrs. Collins, certainly we all know—"

Sometimes I don't mind being rude. This was one of those times.

I interrupted. "Yes, of course, you know the family members, the bank staff. But, Mr. O'Keefe, I don't believe you've met Don Brown. Don, I would like for you to meet," and I introduced them, swiftly in turn, "Robert and Louise O'Keefe, Iris O'Keefe, Gordon Evans, and Alma Hendricks, Lieutenant Don Brown of the Derry Hills Police Department homicide unit."

Robert O'Keefe's eyes widened.

Louise O'Keefe drew her breath in sharply. Iris clutched her granddaughter's arm. "Homicide? Homicide? What does that mean?"

I closed the door to the conference room and turned to face my audience. "Ladies and gentlemen, in the public mind, Jack O'Keefe is guilty of theft, murder—by arson—and suicide. I propose to prove that Jack O'Keefe was innocent on all counts."

Kerry leaned forward, her chin cupped in her hands, her heart in her eyes.

"The original police investigation, following the arson, discovered that two hundred thousand dollars was missing through fake loans signed by Jack. When Percodan was discovered in the bodies, the police concluded that Jack stole his mother's prescription, doped his family, then arranged for the fire because he couldn't face disgrace. Kerry O'Keefe's escape was believed to be simply good fortune. While it certainly was that, Kerry's escape was the first proof of Jack's innocence. You see, Kerry wasn't drugged."

Iris pressed trembling hands against her cheeks. "What do you mean? What are you saying?"

"I mean that someone took the pain prescription from your house, ground it into a powder, then dropped by Jack's house and mixed the drug into the top level of the cocoa canister, knowing that the Jack O'Keefe family drank cocoa every night.

"But Kerry drank no cocoa. Jack would have known that, would have had to know it, if he planned to kill his family that night while they slept. So Jack didn't do the drugging. Nor did anyone else in the house because, once again, it would have been a twisted response to disgrace and the intent would be for all to die, and Kerry wasn't there.

"So, someone came by and left without knowing that Kerry would not drink cocoa that night."

"This is absurd." Robert stood.

"Sit down, Mr. O'Keefe. You don't want to miss the main event."

His glance locked with mine. Slowly, he sat down. Louise's face flushed. "This is so insulting. I demand—"

"To know the truth. Good. Don, please begin." Don lifted the remote. The television turned on and then the VCR began to play. Darkness.

I began to speak. "Everything hinges on whether Jack O'Keefe dummied those loans." Nothing but darkness.

"I spoke yesterday with two men who could have arranged the theft to look like Jack's work, Jack's brother Robert and Gordon Evans."

"I object. I object—"

"Quiet, Mr. Evans. I merely said you had the opportunity. I also spoke to Alma Hendricks, both because she could have stolen the money and because she would spread the word of my search to others in the bank, and the fact that the documents would be unearthed today." The video picture was black, but door hinges squeaked. "I alerted Iris O'Keefe and Robert's wife, Louise. And finally I arranged for a video camera to record if anyone came to the basement dead files here in the bank last night."

A light came on. The grainy picture flickered, then came into focus on a row of filing cabinets in the dimly lit room.

A figure dressed in black hurried to the cabinets, pulled out the drawers in quick succession, scanning the folder tabs. It didn't take long. Not quite nine minutes. Then a folder was snatched up, the searcher whirled and hurried to the door, the light went out. The film continued to whir.

Robert O'Keefe jumped to his feet, his face convulsed. He stared down at his wife. "You fool. You stupid fool."

"I had to get them. You—"

"Goddamn it, Jack signed—" He broke off.

"Yes, Mr. O'Keefe? Won't you continue? Please tell us how you persuaded your brother to sign the false loans that you had prepared." Because Robert was right. Handwriting comparisons proved the papers were indeed signed by Jack. But I knew that Jack didn't kill his family. So he must not have been the creator of those dummy loans—even if he did sign them.

"Oh, my God," Louise moaned. "I thought—"

"Shut up, for Christ's sake," her husband ordered.

"Yes, Louise, why don't you tell us about it?" I asked.

"Louise, don't say a goddamn word."

I looked from husband to wife. "Not much communication in your marriage. Right? But Louise knew who would take money—and it wasn't Jack. I don't suppose the two of you ever talked about it. What did you think, Robert? Did you really believe your brother killed himself and his family? Or was it such an enormous stroke of luck for you that you never permitted yourself to think about what really happened?"

Tears slid down Iris's withered cheeks.

"Or why don't you tell us, Iris. You've always known, haven't you? That's why you wouldn't let anyone clear away the ruins from the fire. You wanted Robert to see it day and night. But he built a wall."

"Jack was gone. I couldn't lose Robert, too. But I knew Jack didn't take any money and he'd do whatever Robert asked him to do. I knew that's the way it must have happened, Robert bringing in the loans, spinning Jack a story, asking him to sign the papers. But even knowing it, I couldn't lose Robert, too. I couldn't." She buried her face in her hands.

"Mother, Mother." Robert's voice shook. "Mother, I didn't do it! I swear before God, I didn't do it. Not the fire. I didn't."

Iris's hands fell away. She stared at her older son.

He hurried to her. "Mother, I swear to you."

She looked into his eyes, then she made a noise deep in her throat as her head swung toward her daughter-in-law.

"That's right, Iris." I spoke clearly. "Robert took the money. But Louise drugged the cocoa and set the fire."

*   *   *

It bothers Don a lot that we could never prove murder against Louise O'Keefe. All we had was circumstantial evidence. We were certain, but that isn't enough in a court of law, of course.

She could claim she went after the files because she was trying to protect her husband. Not true, of course. She was trying to protect herself. That was always her goal, to protect the life and social position and security of Louise O'Keefe. And she was willing to destroy a young family to save her husband and her elegant way of life.

Everyone ultimately gets what they deserve. Louise O'Keefe is no exception. And neither is Robert. He has a great capacity for not accepting reality. He should have known that Jack didn't drug the cocoa or set the fire. But he didn't want to think about it, refused to think about it. If he had thought too hard, he would have known the answer.

When he finally knew what had happened, he jettisoned Louise.

And there were no thefts to prove against Robert at this late date, the money long since made good, the statute of limitations long since past.

Louise and Robert are divorced now.

She got quite a nice settlement. She's living in the Canary Islands, a hard-faced, wealthy woman.

But what has her crime gained her?

Oh yes, Louise will get what she deserves, is getting it, has gotten it.

What matters, what really matters, is love.

And love triumphed here.

Kerry and Don's wedding will be in June.

I wouldn't miss it for the world.

Grieving Las Vegas

E D KRAUSE LAY ON HIS BACK, STARING UP at the night sky, his sports jacket surprisingly comfortable as a pillow beneath his head. The desert air in mid-May was still warm, considering how long the sun'd been down. And the stars so bright—Jesus, you could almost understand why they called it the "Milky" Way, account of out here, away from any city lights, more "white" star showed than black background.

At least until Ed turned his head to the east, toward Las Vegas, which glittered on the horizon, like a cut jewel somebody kept turning under a lamp.

Jewel?

Ed coughed, not quite a laugh. Better you stuck with carrying diamonds and jade. But no, this new deal had sounded too good to pass up, especially the final destination and the cash you'd have for enjoying it. From that first day, at Felix. . . .

*   *   *

. . . Wasserman's house. In San Francisco, on one of those crazy fucking hill streets near Fisherman's Wharf that had to be terraced and handrailed before even an ex-paratrooper like Ed Krause could climb up it.

Felix Wasserman was an importer, which is how Ed had met him in the first place, seven—no, more like eight—years ago. Just after Ed had mustered out of the Army and was nosing around for something to do with his life. A buddy from the airborne put him onto being a courier, which at first sounded like the most boring fucking duty Ed could imagine, worse even than KP in the Mess Hall or standing Guard Mount outside some

Godforsaken barracks in the pits of a Southern fort.

Until the buddy also told him how much money could be made for carrying the right kind of stuff. And being able to stop somebody from taking it away from you.

After climbing thirty-five fucking steps, Ed found himself outside Wasserman's house. Or townhouse, maybe, since it shared both its side walls with other structures, what Ed thought was maybe earthquake protection, since he'd seen signs down on more normal streets for stores that were temporarily closed for "seismic retrofitting." Wasserman had his front garden looking like a Caribbean jungle, and Ed had to duck under flowers in every shade of red that grew tall as trees before he could ring the guy's bell.

His door bell, that is, seeing as how Ed Krause was what he liked to call in San Fran' a "confirmed heterosexual."

Wasserman himself answered, turned out in a silk shirt that looked as though his flower trees out front had been spun into cloth for it. Pleated slacks and soft leather loafers that probably cost—in one of the tonier "shoppes" off Union Square—as much as Ed's first car.

"Felix, how you doing?"

"Marvelously, Edward," said Wasserman, elegantly waving him inside. "Simply marvelously."

Give him this: The guy didn't seem to age much. In fact, Wasserman didn't look to Ed any older than he had that day when Ed—working for a legitimate, bonded courier service then—first laid eyes on him. It was after maybe the third or fourth above-board job he'd carried for the gay blade that Wasserman had felt him out—conversationally—on maybe carrying something else for his "import" business. At a commission of ten percent against the value of the parcel involved.

Now Ed just followed the guy up the stairs to a second-floor room with the kind of three-sided window that let you look out over the red-flower trees across to the facing houses and up or down the slope of the hill at other people's front gardens. Only, while there were two easy chairs and a table in the window area, Wasserman never had Ed sit there during business.

Too conspicuous.

Another elegant wave of the hand, this time toward the wet bar set back against one wall. "Drink?"

"Jim and Coke, you got them."

"Edward," Wasserman seeming almost hurt in both voice and expression, "knowing you were coming to see me, of course I stocked Mr. Beam and your mixer."

Ed took his usual seat on one couch while his host first made the simple bourbon and cola cocktail, then fussed over some kind of glass-sided machine with arching tubes that always looked to Ed like a life-support system for wine bottles. Coming away holding a normal glass with brown liquid in it and another like a kid's clear balloon with some kind of red—is this guy predictable or what, colorwise?—Wasserman handed Ed his drink before settling into the opposing couch, a stuffed accordion envelope on the redwood—see?—coffee table between them.

"Edward, to our continued, and mutual, good fortune."

Clinking with the guy, Ed took a slug of his drink, just what the doctor ordered for that forced march up the screwy, terraced street. Wasserman rolled his wine around in his balloon glass about twelve times before sniffing it, then barely wetting his lips with the actual grape juice. Ed wondered sometimes if the wine was that good, or if the dapper gay guy just didn't want to get too smashed too quick.

"So, Felix," gesturing toward the big envelope, "what've we got this time?" Wasserman smiled, and for the first time, Ed wondered if maybe the guy had gone for a face-lift, account of his ears came forward a little. But after putting down the wine glass, Felix used an index finger to just nudge the package an inch toward his guest. "Open it and see."

Ed took a second slug of the Jim and Coke, then set his glass down, too. Sliding the elastic off the bottom of the envelope and lifting the flap, he saw stacks of hundred-dollar bills, probably fifty to the pack.

Ed resisted the urge to whistle through his bottom teeth. "Total?"

"One-quarter-million."

Since they both knew Ed would have to count it out in Wasserman's presence over a second drink, the courier just put the big envelope back on the table, three packs of cash sliding casually over the open flap and onto the redwood.

Ed said, "For?"

A sigh and a frown, as Wasserman delicately retrieved his glass by its stem and settled back into his couch. "I expect you're aware—if only in a general way—of the rather distressing state of the economy?"

"I remember hearing something about it, yeah."

A small smile, not enough to make the ears hunch. "Ah, Edward, both dry and droll. My compliments." Wasserman's lips went back to neutral. "My rather well-heeled clientele hasn't been consuming quite as conspicuously these last few seasons, feeling that fine jewels, no matter the rarity nor brilliance, can't quite replace cash as hedges against the uncertain miasma within which we find ourselves floundering."

Ed just sipped his drink this time, kind of getting off on the way Wasserman made up sentences more elaborate than his garden out front.

"However, the landlord still expects his rent for my shop, and the bank its mortgage payments for my home. And so I've shifted my sights a bit, importwise."

"Meaning?"

Wasserman took an almost normal-person's belt of his wine. "Heroin."

Ed would have bet cocaine. "Let me guess. I take the package of money from here to there, and pick up the powder."

"Precisely. Which, of course, would do me no good, since fine Cabernet," swirling the wine in his glass now, "constitutes my only source of substance abuse. Fortunately, though, I have a business contact in the Lake Tahoe area who will gladly buy said powder from you, as my representative, at . . . twice the price."

Ed did the math. "You're saying my cut of this will be ten percent of five hundred thousand?"

"Precisely so. From Tahoe you'll transport the remainder of the cash involved to Las Vegas."

Christ, even a bonus. Growing up in Cleveland, Ed'd always had an itch to sample the glitzy life, but in all his time in San Fran', he'd never been to Vegas. He'd heard everything there—thanks to the casino action—was bigger and better: spectacular tits and ass on the showgirls, classy singers and magicians, even lion-tamers. Not like the trendy shit that passed for "culture" in the "City by the Bay."

In fact, Ed had also seen—three times, at cineplex prices—that Nick Cage movie, *Leaving Las Vegas*. Got the guy an Oscar, and he fucking well deserved it. I mean, who'd ever believe that anybody'd want to check out of the genuine "City that Never Sleeps."

Felix allowed himself another couple drops of his wine. "When you reach Las Vegas itself, a friend of mine will—shall we say, 'hand-wash?'— the actual bills for his own fee of a mere five percent, after which you shall bring the balance back here to me."

Ed thought about it. A little complicated for his taste, given the number of stops and exchanges. But fifty thousand for what would be maybe three, four days tops of driving? And he didn't give a shit whether his share was laundered or not, since Ed would be passing it in far smaller amounts than Wasserman probably had to pay his creditors.

"Felix, with all this running around, I'm gonna need a cover story, and an advance against expenses."

Now a pursing of the lips. "How much?"

"That'll depend on where I'm picking up the powder to begin with."

Another sigh, but more—what the fuck was the word? Oh, yeah: wistful. "Edward, I actually envy you that, even though the Cabernet varietal, in my humble opinion, doesn't really thrive there. You'll make your first exchange in Healdsburg. Or just outside it."

Ed had noticed the town's name on maps, maybe two hours up U.S. 101 from the Golden Gate, in one of the many parts of the state called "wine country."

He said, "Three thousand, then, upfront, given the cover story I'm thinking about."

"Which is?"

"Bringing a chick along, camouflage for flitting around all these vacation spots like a butterfly."

"A woman." The deepest frown of all from Felix Wasserman. "That I don't envy you, Edward."

*   *   *

"Let me get this straight," said Brandi Willette, trying to size up whether this guy who never plunged for more than three well-drinks at a sitting—but did tip her twenty percent every time he settled a tab—was on the level. "You want to take me—all expenses paid—with you on this whirlwind trip over the next four days?"

A nod from his side of the pub's bar, the guy wearing an honest-to-God, old-fashioned sports jacket. "Maybe even longer, we like it in Vegas enough."

Brandi had been there only once, on the cheap with a girlfriend, splitting every bill down the middle. The girlfriend turned out to be a drag, but Brandi loved the gambling, believing firmly that if she could just sense her luck changing, she'd make a fortune, even from the slot machines. The kind of money that'd let her get out from behind a smelly, tacky bar, listening to offers from guys like this . . . uh, this. . . . "It's 'Eddie,' right?"

"No. Just 'Ed,' like you're 'Brandi' with an 'i'."

She shook her head, then had to blow one of the permed blond curls out of her face. "Okay, Ed. We go together, same room, same bed, but if I don't feel like doing the nasty, we just share the sheets, not stain them?"

"That's the deal."

Brandi gave it a beat. Then, "So, how come you're asking me?"

The guy seemed to squirm a little on his pub stool, which sort of surprised her, since Ed had struck Brandi as the ultra-macho type. Probably six-one, one-ninety, with a military haircut and big, strong-looking hands. Her pre-dick-tion: A fuck-buddy who'd come up skimpy on the foreplay but be a pile-driver during the car chase.

"Well?" she said, wondering if maybe the guy was a little slow in the head.

"It's part of a business transaction."

"What kind of 'transaction'?"

"Just some documents. I exchange what this person gives me for what that person gives me, then I do the same thing a couple more times."

"What, these 'persons' don't trust Federal Express?"

"They trust me more."

"And why is that?" asked Brandi.

"It's confidential."

"Confidential." The curl spilled down over her eye again, and Brandi blew it back away. "You're a spy?"

"No."

"Private eye?"

"No."

Given the guy's limited active vocabulary, Brandi didn't waste her breath on "lawyer," but she did cock her head in a way that she knew guys dug, kind of a "persuade me" angle, like Sarah Jessica Parker did on *Sex and the City*. "So, we're gonna be sleeping together, in the same room, and you can't even share why you're picking me?"

"All right." More squirming. "It's because we don't know each other very well."

Huh, that was sure the truth. On the other hand, Brandi figured she could always just fuck the guy senseless, then while he snored away, search through his stuff, find out what was really going on.

And Vegas would put Brandi one step closer to making her fortune. To attending catered dinner parties at swank homes instead of nuking some frozen muck in the microwave before spending the night surfing the cable channels.

"Okay, Honey," said Brandi, "I want to see your driver's license, and then I'm gonna call three of my girlfriends—who you don't know at all—to tell them I'm going on this grand tour."

Ed seemed to mull that over. "All right."

"And one other thing."

"What?"

Brandi leaned across the pub's bar, used her forearms to push her breasts a smidge higher against her tank-top, give him a little more reason to be nice to her. "You ever eaten at Masa's?"

*　　*　　*

As the slipstream from a passing trailer-truck tried to knock the little Mustang convertible onto the shoulder of U.S. 101, Ed Krause heard Brandi say from the passenger's seat. "I think it's another two exits from here."

He glanced over at the chick, her pouty face buried in a road map from the rent-a-car company, and began to question his own judgment. Not that Brandi with a fucking 'i' wasn't the right type. Just to the "maybe not" side of slutty, with only one nose-stud and six earrings as body piercings, a small tattoo on the left shoulder that looked professional, not homemade. Decent boobs and legs, too, but overall not so smart or good-looking he thought she'd turn down his offer of a free trip.

Or his offer to help her through the night.

But "eating" at Masa's on Bush Street the night before turned out to be at the bar, since they didn't have reservations. Actually, Ed kind of counted his blessings on that one, because the very chi-chi, black-and-chrome restaurant didn't exactly price out as reasonable. He had to admit, though, he'd tried stuff off the "tastings" menu that the bartender suggested, and it was the best fucking food he'd ever eaten. Ed even had wine, served in Felix-like balloons, and Ed could tell that Brandi was impressed by the way he rolled the grape juice around the inside of his glass before sniffing and sipping it.

Not, however, impressed enough to take him to her place or vice-versa to his, for a little "tour preview." No, Brandi begged off, saying she needed to pack something more than the tote bag she'd carried from the pub to the restaurant—"It's Nine West, honey, and only forty-nine-ninety-nine, but the real reason I bought it is how the last three numbers on the price tag all lined up the same, like it was gonna bring me luck?"

Thinking, Vegas at the end will make all this shit worth my while, Ed just picked her up the next morning outside Macy's on Geary Street, thinking too that once he got her hammered on a wine tour and fucked her senseless back in their room, he could always go through the chick's stuff, get a last name and address off her driver's license.

In case you ever want to . . . visit her later.

And Brandi was good enough at navigating, Ed could keep his eyes on the rear and side mirrors, make sure nobody stayed with them as he first did fifty-five for a while, then sixty, then a little over before dropping back down to fifty-five. It was a beautiful day, and frankly the slower speed with the top down was a lot more enjoyable than just putting the pedal to the metal.

There were a bunch of exits for Healdsburg, but give the chick credit: She picked the right one for the Inn on the Plaza. As they were shown to their rooms by a pert brunette younger than Brandi, Ed could tell his "cover story" was watching him to see if he was watching their guide. But all he did was listen to the brunette tell the story of the "bed-and-breakfast," how it had so many skylights because it used to be a "surgery," which Ed took to be where doctors operated before there were hospitals, much less electricity to let them see what they were cutting.

The room was pretty spectacular, even by Ed's images of the Las Vegas glitz to come. For now he could see high ceilings and a king-sized brass bed, a big tiled bathroom and Jacuzzi for two.

If all went according to plan.

Just as Ed was about to tip the brunette and get her out of there, he heard Brandi behind him gush, "Oh, God, he's so cute!"

Which is when Ed noticed the chick grabbing a teddy bear off one of the many throw pillows at the head of the bed and hugging it between her boobs.

Right on cue, the brunette said, "They're even for sale, at our desk downstairs."

As Brandi squealed with delight, Ed Krause hoped that the tab for their dinner the night before wouldn't be an omen for the stuffed animal and everything else on the trip to Vegas, even if Felix Wasserman was fronting expenses.

*　　*　　*

"I still," said Brandi Willette, around a hiccup she thought she stifled pretty well, "don't understand why we couldn't stop at that last winery?"

Driving them, top down, along the nice country lane, Ed—not "Eddie"—seemed to put a little edge on his voice. "Same reason we didn't stop at the other two—of seven, I'm counting right—you wanted to hit: I couldn't see the car from the tasting room."

Brandi swallowed a second hiccup. "Five wineries in one afternoon isn't really enough, I don't think." Then she got an idea. "Is that the same reason you brought your briefcase from the car to the room and then back again?"

"Yes," the edge still there.

The idea turned into a brainstorm. "And how come we have to put the roof and windows up at every stop," she gestured at the beautiful day around them like she'd seen a stage actress do once, "even though there's not a cloud in the sky?"

"That's right." Ed pointed toward the glove compartment. "A little yellow button inside pops the trunk, and I don't want somebody giving it a shot."

"Couldn't—" Brandi tried to stifle yet another hiccup, but it was just not to be denied, "—Oh, excuse me, honey. Couldn't 'somebody' take a knife to the roof, or break one of the windows, or jimmy open one of the doors, and then pop the trunk?"

"They could," Ed's voice getting a little nicer, so when he slid his right hand over and onto her left thigh, Brandi didn't brush it away like she had on the drive up from the city. "But they're not likely to try it when I can see the car, and anyway that'd give me time to get out there and stop them."

Brandi didn't ask Ed how he would stop them, because she'd kind of accidentally stumbled into him at the fourth winery—or maybe the fifth?— and felt something really hard over his right hip.

A gun.

Which, to tell the truth, excited Brandi more than scared her. She figured when he pitched the trip to her back in the pub that something was maybe a little dangerous about the guy, with his overall aura and "confidential transaction."

And besides, Brandi thought—closing her eyes and letting her head just loll against the back-rest, living the moment with the breeze in her hair and the sun on her face and the birds singing around her—what girl doesn't like something . . . hard now and then?

*   *   *

"I still don't see why I can't come in with you?"

Ed Krause just looked at her, sitting in the passenger's seat of the Mustang. He'd left the top down for fresh air, but put Brandi in the shade of a big tree in the circular driveway a large stucco house with orange roof tiles. Let her kind of doze off some of the incredible amount of wine she'd put away, maybe—please, Christ?—even lose the hiccups doing it.

Of course, despite all the "I still don't understand this" and "I still don't see that" bullshit from her, there was no reason to make the chick mad, just as she was letting his non-driving hand, and then his lips, start to soften her up for later, in that brass bed.

Or better, the Jacuzzi.

"Like I told you," he said to Brandi, nice as he could. "This is the business part."

She nodded. Sort of. "The confidential part."

Con-fuh-denture-pah. Ed shook it off with, "Yeah. Just sit tight, enjoy the afternoon, and I'll be back in a few minutes."

Brandi seemed to buy it, slumping deeper into the seat with a sappy grin on her face, so he kissed her once and quickly, slipping his tongue in just enough to know she wouldn't fight more of the same back in their room. Then Ed opened the trunk, took out the briefcase Felix Wasserman had given him to hold the money, and went up to the front entrance, painted the same orange as the roof tiles.

The door swung inward before he could knock or ring, an Asian guy standing there, but more like an owner than a servant. Ed shouldn't have been surprised, since he knew Wasserman dealt with a lot of Chinese guys on the imports, only Ed also thought his gay blade could have prepared him for this by providing more than just a first name.

"Edward?"

"Yeah, though 'Ed' is fine. You're Tommy?"

"The same. Please, come in, though I take it your friend is more comfortable outside?"

"Let's just say I'm more comfortable that way."

A wise smile. "I see."

The guy led Ed into a first-floor living room done up all-Spanish with heavy, dark woods, bullfighting capes and swords, and funny lamps. The guy took one patterned chair and motioned Ed toward its mate.

The courier looked around before sitting down, feeling on his right hip the heft of the Smith & Wesson Combat Masterpiece with its four-inch, extra-heavy barrel—for pistol-whipping, in case he had to discourage some jerk who didn't require actual shooting. "No security?"

Another wise smile. "None evident, shall we say?"

Ed nodded, kind of liking the guy's—what, "subtlety" maybe? "Any reason not to get down to business?"

"As you wish, especially since I don't wish to keep you from your friend."

Tommy clapped his hands twice, and two more Asian guys appeared from around a corner. One carried a briefcase the same make and model as the one Ed had, the other a submachine gun so exotic that even the ex-paratrooper didn't recognize it.

Letting his stomach settle a minute, Ed took his time saying, "And if you clapped just once?"

"Then, regrettably, you'd be dead, and your friend soon thereafter."

Ed trusted himself only to nod this time. They exchanged briefcases—both unlocked, as usual—Ed looking into the one he was given. "Felix told me I didn't have to test the stuff."

"If you did," said Tommy, "he wouldn't be doing business with my family in the first place."

"Good enough." Ed glanced at the guy with the exotic piece. "Okay for me to leave?"

"Of course," said Tommy, standing, "Enjoy your visit to our valleys."

"My friend already has," Ed rising and feeling he could turn his back on these guys as he walked to the door.

*   *   *

"Oh, God," said Brandi Willette, nursing the worst hangover she could remember and afraid to look over the side of the car, because the road just fell away down the steep, piney slope. "I think my ears are popping again."

"The change in altitude," said Ed from behind the wheel. "And that bottle from the last winery you brought back to the room probably isn't helping any."

"Please," Brandi holding her left hand out in a "stop" sign while her right palm went from the teddy bear in her lap to cover her closed eyes. "Don't remind me about last night, all right?"

"Oh, I don't know. I think we both liked what happened next."

Well, you can't disagree with the guy on that one, at least the parts of it you remember.

Which were: Coming back to the room around five-thirty, after hitting the last row of wineries with names like Clos du Bois, Chateau Souverain, and Sausal. Feeling free as could be from all the great stuff she'd tasted, and, although Brandi was still hiccuping, ready for anything. Including letting Ed slip her clothes off, the guy more gentle than she could have hoped. After a quick shower together, him touching her just about everywhere, them getting into the Jacuzzi—the guy must have had it filling up while he was stripping her in the bedroom and soaping her in the stall. And then getting a real good look at that snake he had down there, the head on it big as a cobra's. And Brandi telling him to get in first, sit down, before lowering herself onto his soldier-at-attention. She stayed balanced by resting her palms on his shoulders, her nipples just skimming the surface of the sudsy water as she rocked up and down and back and forth—him laughing, because she still had the hiccups—until she came so violently and thoroughly it was like one long shudder that wasn't a hiccup at all. In fact, took them away.

And then him lifting her up, not even bothering to dry themselves off, and onto the soft mattress of the brass bed—her new teddy bear watching—for another, and another, and. . . .

"Hey," from the driver's side, "you're gonna puke, hold on till I can pull over."

"Yeah, yeah," said Brandi, hoping she'd have better luck controlling her gag reflex than she did with the hiccups.

*   *   *

"Okay," said Ed Krause, nudging the chick on her bicep with his fist, "we're here."

He watched Brandi's head try to find its full and upright position in the passenger's seat. After three hours of complaining about everything under the sun, she'd finally fallen asleep—or passed out—a good ten miles from Tahoe City, and therefore she'd missed some of the best fucking scenery Ed had ever driven through. Snow-capped, purple mountains, sprawling vistas down to pine-green valleys. The whole-nine-yards of America the Beautiful.

And now Lake Tahoe itself.

Brandi said, "I'm cold."

"Like I tried to tell you before, it's the altitude. Walk slow, too, or you'll start to feel sick." Stick in the knife? Sure. "Again."

The chick raised her hand like she had before, reminding him of a school crossing guard, but she managed to get her side door open.

After checking into the Sunnyside Lodge, Ed got them and their luggage to the suite, which had a little balcony off the living room and overlooking the waterfront, more mountains with snowy peaks kind of encircling the lake from high above. Brandi shuffled into the bedroom and flopped face down on the comforter, not even bothering to kick off her shoes. Ed heard snoring before he could secure his briefcase with the heroin behind the couch in the living room, pissed that the key fucking Tommy gave him for the handle lock didn't fucking work, so all Ed could do was click the catch shut.

Leaving the chick to sleep it off, he went back downstairs and did a walkaround, first outside, then in. Big old lodge, dark-log construction, security doors you'd need a computerized room key to open. A moose's head was mounted on a wooden plaque over one fireplace, a bear's over another, a buffalo's over a third.

Ed liked the place. Rugged, with the taxidermy adding just a hint about the history of killing the lodge had seen.

But no pool, and when he asked at the lobby desk, the nice college-looking girl told him it was way too cold to swim in even the lake, because it never got warmer than sixty-eight degrees, "like, ever."

When Ed got back to the room, Brandi was still snoring. But checking how he'd wedged his briefcase behind the bureau, it had turned a few degrees. Ed tilted the briefcase back to its original angle, then stomped his foot a couple of times, harder on the third one.

Brandi's voice trickled out of the bedroom. "What the hell are you doing out there?"

The briefcase never budged. "Testing the floorboards. Be sure they can take us rocking that mattress."

A different tone of voice with, "Wouldn't we be better off doing your testing . . . in here?"

And that's when Ed Krause knew in his bones that Brandi Willette—given how shitty she must still be feeling—had snuck a peek into his unlockable briefcase, just as he'd gone through her "lucky" totebag the night before at the Inn off the Plaza in Healdsburg.

*   *   *

"Honey," said Brandi Willette, in the best seductive/hurt tone she knew, "I still don't understand why I can't come in there with you."

"Keep your voice down."

She watched Ed shut the driver's side door, even almost slam it, in the yard he'd pulled into, a big Swiss-chalet style house on the lakeside in front of them.

Ed turned back to her. "It's like the last time."

"Confidential?"

He glanced into the next yard. "I said, keep your voice down. And stay put."

"All right, all right," Brandi flicking her hand like she couldn't give a damn.

Only she did. After seeing all that "snow" in his briefcase back at the lodge, Brandi could care less about the real thing on the mountaintops and melting in the shaded clumps still on the ground under trees that must block the sun. As they drove, many of the houses—like the one next-door to the chalet—looked like something out of that ancient *Bonanza* TV show with Michael Landon that Brandi caught on the cable sometimes, a program she figured he must have done even before that old show *Little House on the Prairie*, account of how much younger he looked as a son/cowboy instead of a father/farmer.

But the snow in the briefcase? Heroin or cocaine, had to be. Which meant big-time bucks, and maybe an opportunity for her luck really to change, even just riding with Ed.

Or figuring out a way to hijack him. After all, the three friends Brandi called from the pub in the city would go to the police only if she didn't make it back.

Brandi watched Ed move slowly through the yard and toward the chalet. There'd been a wooden privacy fence between it and the road that wound around the lake. On each side of the fence's gate were these totem poles, like Brandi remembered from a Discovery Channel thing on Eskimos—or whatever they were called when they lived more in the deep woods and not so much on icebergs.

And, sure enough, there were three guys doing landscaping in the next yard who could have been Eskimos themselves. Short, blocky guys, with square, copper-colored faces. The oldest of them seemed to be bossing the other two, one gathering up broken limbs and throwing them onto a brushpile, the other sweeping the driveway of huge pine cones from even huger trees looming overhead. Probably getting the neighbor's place ready for the season.

Brandi noticed Ed giving the three Eskimos the eye as he reached the stoop of the chalet. Then the guy knocked and disappeared inside.

Brandi couldn't believe how cold it could be in mid-May nor how her breathing still wasn't back to normal from banging Ed and then just walking downstairs in the lodge and over to the Mustang. In fact, about the only other thing Brandi did notice was how, about five minutes after Ed entered the chalet, the oldest Eskimo in the next yard came strolling toward her side of the car, smiling and taking a piece of paper—no, an envelope?—out of a bulging pocket in his jacket.

And right then, Brandi Willette, even without knowing what was going to happen next, could feel her luck changing, and visions of what that would mean in Vegas—and beyond—began slam-dancing in her head.

*　　*　　*

Natalya, a fat-to-bursting fortysomething who looked like no drug pusher Ed Krause had ever encountered, settled the two of them into over-stuffed chairs that suited her like Felix's red flowers back in San Fran suited him, only different.

She said, "Tell me, do you prefer 'Edward,' 'Ed' . . . ?"

"Just 'Ed,' thanks."

Natalya smiled. Not a bad face, you suck a hundred pounds off the rest of her, let the cheekbones show. She seemed to arrange their seating so he could enjoy the dynamite view of the lake through a wall of windows. Ed was pretty sure the chalet had been designed to be appreciated from the water, not the road.

But the view turned out to be less "enjoyable" and more distracting, as some fucking moron in a scuba wetsuit went water-skiing past, and Ed automatically glanced at all the interior doorways he could see.

The fat lady turned her head toward the skier, then turned back, smiling some more. "There's a rather famous school that teaches that between here and your lodge, though I've always felt it a bit too frosty and . . . strenuous to be diverting."

As soon as he'd entered the room, Ed had seen the sample case on the tiled floor next to the chair Natalya had picked for herself. He'd rather it be at least the same size as his briefcase, but then the two-fifty in hundreds had barely fit in its twin on the way to Healdsburg, and this would be twice as much, maybe some of it in smaller denominations to boot.

Natalya said, "May I offer you refreshment?"

"No, thanks. I gotta be going soon."

"As you wish," the fat lady sighing, as though if he'd said "yes," maybe she could break some kind of weight-watching rule of her own by joining him. "I will be needing to test your product."

A switch from Tommy in wine country. "And I'll be needing to count yours."

"Let us begin, then."

"Before we do," said Ed, leaning forward conversationally but also to free up his right hand to move more fluidly for the revolver under his sports jacket and over his right hip, "any security I should know about, so nobody accidentally gets hurt?"

"Security?" A laugh, the woman's chins and throat wobbling. "No, Tahoe City is a very safe place, Ed."

"Not even those guys next door?"

"'Those guys?'"

"Mexicans maybe, doing yard work."

"Oh," a bigger laugh, shoulders and breasts into it now. "Hardly. And they're Mayans, Ed. They drift up here from the Yucatan to do simple labor—like opening up the houses after the winter's beaten down the foliage? My neighbor's a retired professor of archaeology, and the one who first got them to do landscaping for a lot of us along the lake. In fact, that figurine on the table and the stone statue near the fireplace are both gifts from him." Natalya paused. "I'd have said it was too frigid up here for them, frankly," the fat broad stating something Ed had been thinking from the moment he saw them, "but my neighbor tells me our gorgeous topography reminds them in some ways of their native land."

Ed thought that still didn't ring right: Most people he knew who ever traveled far from home went from colder weather to warmer, not the other way around.

On the other hand, what do you know about Mexicans, period, much less "Mayans" in particular?

Then Natalya opened her hands like a priest doing a blessing. "Shall we?"

Ed brought his briefcase over to her, and he took her sample case back to his chair, accidentally scraping the bottom of the case against the tiles, the thing was that heavy.

*　　*　　*

"This is supposed to be the best restaurant in town."

Brandi Willette heard Ed's comment, but she waited til the waitress at Wolfdale's—who looked like one of the retro-hippies back in the city—took their drink orders and left them before glancing around the old room with exposed ceiling beams and a drop-dead-gorgeous view of the lake, kind of facing down its long side from the middle of its short one. "It better be the best, all the time you spent back there."

Ed just shrugged and read the menu.

Brandi didn't want to push how long it took him inside the chalet, but she did notice he was carrying a different bag coming back to the convertible. The guy wants to keep things "confidential," that's fine. But it didn't take a genius to figure that if what Ed brought in there was drugs, what he brought out was money. Lots of it. And, given the size of the case, lots more than he used in Healdsburg to buy the shit with.

Then Brandi thought about the oldest Eskimo, and what he'd given her while she was waiting for Ed, what was now nestled in her lucky totebag. Plus what that gave her to think about from her side. For her luck, even her fortune, which was a nice fucking change of pace.

The dinner at Wolfdale's turned out to be maybe the best food Brandi had ever eaten in her life—medallions of veal, asparagus, some kind of tricked-out potatoes. And a merlot that made even a lot of the great wines she'd tasted the day before seem weak. A perfect experience.

Just like the catered dinner parties you'll be going to soon.

But, just as they were finishing dessert, Ed said, "How about we take a drive, see the lake by night?"

Remembering the mountains closer to the wine country they'd already gone up and down with her hangover that morning, Brandi said, "I'd rather see our bed by night."

"We can do that, too. Afterwards."

Well, what could a girl say to that? A guy who'd rather drive than get laid, there was just no precedent for dealing with such a situation.

*　　*　　*

"Ohmigod, ohmigod," said Brandi Willette in a tone that made Ed Krause think of the word "shriek."

"What's the matter?" him taking the Mustang through its paces on the ribbon of road—lit only by the moon—switchbacking up one of the mountains on the southwest end of the lake.

"What's the matter?" came out as more what Ed would call a "squeal." The chick pointed over the passenger's side of the car without looking down. "There's no fucking guard-rail here!"

"Highway Department probably thinks it wouldn't help. Either you'd go through it and down, or bounce off it and into a head-on with somebody coming the other way."

"Don't even say that."

Another couple of miles—Brandi now groaning, even shaking—and Ed saw his lights pick up the "SCENIC VISTA" sign that fat Natalya had told him about back at her chalet, after she recommended Wolfdale's for dinner. "Let's give you a break."

He pulled into the otherwise deserted parking area, which seemed, even at night, like just a man-made platform jutting out from the side— nearly the top—of the mountain. They'd passed a few other viewing points—not to mention the entire Nevada town of South Lake Tahoe, but when Brandi had said, "Why don't we stop here for a while, try our luck?" Ed had glanced around at the penny-ante casinos with Harrah's, Trump's and a bunch of other evocative names on them, chintzy motels sprinkled among them, and replied, "Nah, I want to wait for the real thing. In Vegas."

As Ed now came to a stop in one of the vista's parking spaces, Brandi finally opened her eyes. "It's dark out. What're we gonna be able to see?"

He opened his door, came around to hers. "A fat broad told me a story about a guy, said nobody should miss it."

Ed could tell the only reason the chick'd leave the car would be to feel her feet on solid ground again, and that was fine. She got out of the Mustang, leaving her lucky fucking totebag on the floor between her feet, and Ed took her hand, guiding her over to the edge of the vista's platform.

"I don't want to go any closer."

"You have to, appreciate the story I'm gonna tell you."

"Honey, please. I'll do you every which way but loose back in the room—"

"—the suite—"

"—whatever, but please don't. . . ."

"Hey, there it is."

Ed had his hands on the sides of her shoulders now, marching her in front of him, teach her a lesson about going through his briefcase. She was arching over, pushing her butt into his groin, the grinding sensation of their little "dance" making him hard.

"Honey, please. . . ."

"See? Right there, through the tree branches?" Brandi's butt was writhing, like a wet cat trying to get free of the drying towel. "The moon's lighting it up like noon-time."

"It's a . . . all I see is this island—ohmigod, way down there?"

"This fat broad told me that back in the old days—eighteen-hundreds we're talking—there was a care-taker for the house that's on the mainland, back under the trees."

"I don't—"

"Seems this care-taker stayed all winter," said Ed, "but he liked the island more, and his booze the best. Fact is, he'd row all the way from here to where we're staying in Tahoe City—miles and miles through the cold, though the lake doesn't freeze over like you might expect—to hit a saloon, then he'd row all the way back."

"Honey, let's go, huh?"

"But this care-taker, he fell in love with that island, so he built his own tomb on it. For when he died, to be buried there."

"Why are you—"

"Only thing is, the poor old coot was rowing back from town one night with too much of a load on, and he went over into the water. They found his boat, but not him. Not ever. And so he's at the bottom of the lake someplace, and his tomb's just falling apart, empty, down there on that pretty little island."

"Honey, this is too weird for—"

Ed dropped his hands from her shoulders to her biceps, and then lifted her off the ground—swinging her legs straight out—and sat her down, hard, on the ledge overlooking the drop-off.

Brandi lifted her face to the sky and screamed like a baby.

Ed said, "I invited you along on this trip—a complete freebie—and I didn't move on you 'til you let me know you were ready for it."

"Yes, yes," the tears streaming down her cheeks from eyes clenched shut.

"And I don't expect you to help me at all in what I'm doing, just be half the cover story of the nice couple on a vacation."

"Anything, honey, I will."

"But if I ever. . . ." Ed thrust his pelvis forward, into her butt, like Brandi was giving him a lap-dance and he was pounding her doggy-style. She screamed till her voice broke, then began just sobbing and gasping for breath. "Ever . . . ," he banged her harder, nearly over the edge but for him holding her upper arms, Brandi now just choking on her own breaths, ". . . think you're double-crossing me, you're gonna join that fucking care-taker down there, deep at the bottom of the fucking lake. Or worse."

"Don't. . . . Please, don't. . . ."

Ed pulled Brandi with an "i" back off the ledge, almost having to carry her toward the car. He would have done her on the rear seat, too, finish the lesson, but he could smell what she'd already done to herself, and so Ed Krause wanted her back in their suite and cleaned up first.

*   *   *

Standing under the showerhead, the water so hot she almost couldn't bear it, Brandi Willette thought, Girl, nobody does that to you and gets away with it. Nobody.

Fuck Ed, the goddamned homicidal maniac, hanging you over the fuck-ing edge of that fucking cliff. Literally fuck him as soon as you dry off, keep Dickhead happy and his fucking mind off killing you, but really fuck him good tomorrow, just like the Eskimo's note said, just before telling you to tear it up.

Fuck Ed with the other thing that gardener gave you, too.

And, for the first time in hours, Brandi actually smiled, even if only to herself. Feeling the luck changing, guiding her toward the fortune she'd always felt she deserved.

*   *   *

About two hundred miles into the drive that next afternoon, the scenery now pretty much scrub desert on the eastern side of the California mountains, Ed Krause noticed that Brandi wasn't all that interested in small-talk anymore.

Hey, count your blessings, he thought, glancing again to the rearview mirror, not such good viewing with the convertible's top up, but necessary against the withering heat outside: At least today the chick's not complaining every two minutes.

No, their time at the moonlit "vista" over Lake Tahoe seemed to have had the right effect on little Brandi. Or so Ed would have thought, from the way she romped him in bed after her shower back at the lodge. Good thing he'd taken the trouble, though, while she was still in the bathroom, to go through her stuff a second—shit!

Checking the rearview, like always, Ed saw the same vehicle again. Making three times in the same day, even after stopping the Mustang for lunch and once more for gas.

A dark Chevy Suburban, or some other fucking station-wagon-on-steroids, coming around the last turn behind their Mustang along one of the narrow state roads in Nevada that linked together like a poorly designed necklace from Reno to Las Vegas. Between the sun's glare and the Suburban's tinted windshield, though, Ed couldn't make out the driver, much less how many others were in the thing.

"What's the matter?" said Brandi.

Ed thought about how to play it, both with the Suburban and her. "Don't turn around, but we've got somebody tailing us."

Predictably, the stupid bitch started to turn her head, so he reached over and squeezed her thigh like he wanted to break the bones underneath.

"Owwww! That hurt!"

"It was supposed to. I told you, don't turn around. Right now, they've got no reason to think I've spotted them, and I don't want to give them one."

"You didn't have to hurt me for that."

Ed just shook his head, not trusting his voice right then.

"So," said Brandi, "what are we going to do?"

Different tone now, kind of "We're still a team, right?"

He glanced again in his rearview, the Suburban dropping back a little. "Try to lose them."

Ed nailed the accelerator, Brandi making a moaning noise, kind of like when they'd started again in bed back at the lodge the night before. But the Mustang at least didn't give him any trouble, the V-8 he'd insisted on at the rent-a-car agency coming into its own.

Maybe five minutes later, Brandi said, "Aren't you, like, worried about the police or anything?"

"Lesser of two evils," said Ed, noticing nobody behind them now. Problem was, based on his study of the map that morning before heading out from Tahoe City, there were only so many roads you could take to get to Vegas, so the tail could probably find him, and he didn't have the firepower onboard to stage an effective ambush.

At least not until he found a perfect spot, and after dark.

Brandi piped up now with, "Are they gone?"

Ed tried to remember whether he'd ever said "they" in talking about the tail, decided he had. "For now."

"So," the tone growing a little more impatient, "what are we gonna do?"

"Stay ahead of them. At least for a while."

"How long a while?"

"Until sunset."

"Uh-unh, no way, Honey."

"What the fuck do you mean, no way?"

"I gotta pee."

"So, do it in your clothes, like you did last night."

"That's not funny."

Jesus Christ. "Okay. Around this next bend, then."

"No. I want a real bathroom, not . . ." Brandi with a fucking "i" waving her hand ". . . some spot behind a bush in the desert where a snake could get me."

"The desert, or your clothes. You decide how you want to feel, the next hundred miles to Vegas."

"God, I hate you, you know that?"

Checking the rearview again, Ed was beginning to get that impression, yeah.

*   *   *

Brandi Willette, who'd looked forward so much to enjoying this trip to Vegas, now found she'd run out of tissues.

God, she thought, shaking herself dry as best she could before pulling up her panties. I can't wait for this to be over.

Straightening from behind the bush, she looked over to the convertible. Dickhead was slouched in the driver's seat, head back, eyes closed, still wearing that ugly sports jacket to "hide" his gun.

Well, girl, look on the bright side: He doesn't suspect a thing, and that'll make it all the sweeter, once it happens.

"No," said Brandi, out loud but softly as she picked her way back to the car. "When it happens."

*   *   *

Having slowed to fifty-five about twenty minutes before—just after he put the top down to enjoy the clear, crisp night air of the desert—Ed Krause kept one eye on the rearview and the other on the highway in front of him, figuring he didn't have to worry about Brandi trying anything until they came to a stop.

She said, "Is it dark enough yet?"

Right on cue. "Dark enough for what?"

Brandi blew out a breath in the passenger seat next to him, like he noticed she did a lot of times—even during sex—to get the hair out of her face.

Why wouldn't you just get a different 'do, the hair thing bothered you so much?

Brandi said, "Dark . . . enough . . . for whatever you're planning?"

Another thing Ed didn't like about the little bitch: the way she kept hitting her words hard—even just parts of words, like he was some kind of idiot who couldn't get her points otherwise.

Shaking his head, Ed checked the odometer. Thirty miles from Vegas, give or take, its lights just blushing on the horizon. "Yeah, it's dark enough for that."

The Suburban had appeared and disappeared a couple times over the prior two hours, not taking advantage of at least three desolate spots where it could have roared up from behind, tried to force him off the road. Which made Ed pretty sure they were waiting for him to make the first move.

Or, like Brandi, the first "stop."

"Okay," Ed abruptly pulling off the road and onto the sandy shoulder. "Here."

"Honey?"

Ed turned to her. Brandi was leveling a nickel-finish semiautomatic at him in her right hand, a Raven .25 caliber he'd seen only once before.

* * *

Brandi Willette had thought long and hard about how to phrase it to him—even rehearsed some, with the teddy bear as Ed—but decided in the end that less was more. And so she was kind of disappointed that Dickhead didn't look shocked when she said just the one word, and he saw what Brandi had in her hand.

But that was okay. The asshole thought he was so smart, and so macho, and now Ed finds himself trapped and beaten by a girl, one whose luck had finally changed.

"Just what the fuck do you think you're doing?" he said.

Funny, Dickhead didn't sound scared, either, like Brandi also expected. "I'm taking the money. Honey."

Now it seemed like Ed almost laughed, even though she'd worked on that line, too. Make it kind of poignant, even.

"Brandi, Brandi, after all we've meant to each other?"

Okay, now she really didn't get it. "You're going to open the trunk and take out the case with all the money. Then you're going to leave it with me and just drive off."

Brandi saw Dickhead's eyes go to the rearview mirror again, and she thought she caught just a flash of headlights behind them along with the sudden silence of an engine turning off, though Brandi didn't dare look away from Ed, what with that big gun over his right hip.

No problem, though. Her luck was both changing and holding, just like it would in Vegas, when she hit the slots and the tables, or even the—

Dickhead said, "Your friends are here."

That stopped Brandi. "My . . . friends?"

"When we got back to the room at the lodge, after our little talk about the Tahoe caretaker? While you were in the shower, I went through your totebag there and found that gun. I'd done the same thing at the Inn back in Healdsburg, and it wasn't there then. So, I figure the only time you were out of my sight long enough to come up with a piece was when I was inside the chalet, and those Mayans were working in the yard next door."

Mayans? "I thought they were Eskimos?"

Now Ed did laugh, hard. "No, you stupid fucking bitch. The fat broad in the chalet—Natalya—told me they were her neighbor's crew, but I'm guessing they were hers instead, and one of them passed you that gun."

Oh, yeah? "Well, smart guy, that wasn't all he passed me."

"Some kind of instructions, too, right? Like, wait till the courier stops, at night, near Vegas?"

Brandi was beginning to think she hadn't torn up the note in the envelope, though she clearly remembered doing it. Then Brandi let her luck speak for her. "You're the one who's stupid, Honey, you know that? The Eskimo or whatever told me you'd never think to look for the little thingy he put under your bumper."

No laughing now. Just a squint, the eyes going left-right-left.

Good. Finally, Brandi gets her man. The way it hurts him.

Your luck has changed for sure, girl.

Dickhead said, "A homing device, probably based on G.P.S."

Brandi got the first part, at least. "So they could keep track of us, they lost sight of the car."

"Christ, you dense little shit. Don't you understand the deal yet?"

"The deal is that I get ten percent of all the money in the trunk. Because I'm making it easier for them to take it from you."

"No, Brandi." A tired breath. "The deal is that as soon as they see me get out of this vehicle, they're going to charge up here, kill both of us, and take a hundred percent of the money."

"No, that's not what the note said." Brandi kind of used the gun for emphasis. "What it said was, if you don't get out of this car now, I'm supposed to shoot you."

Ed's chin dipped toward his chest. "Good trick, seeing as how I unloaded your little purse piece there."

As Brandi Willette couldn't help looking down at her gun, she felt Dickhead's hand strike like a rattlesnake at her throat, clamping on so tight and yanking her toward him so hard, she barely could register the silver thing—like a Pez dispenser?—in the fingers of his other—

*   *   *

"Christ!" Ed Krause yelled, as Brandi's head exploded next to his, the round carrying enough punch to spider-web the windshield after it came out her right temple, leaving an exit wound like a rotten peach, blood and brains spattered over the dashboard and that fucking teddy bear. Ed ducked as a second round shattered the driver's portion of the windshield, a sound like somebody whistling through water trailing after the impact.

Ed shoved Brandi's rag-doll corpse against the passenger door, then yanked the floorshift back to DRIVE and took off. A second later, he thought the Mustang might be in the clear based on acceleration alone when he first heard and then felt the blow-out of his right rear tire, the convertible wanting to pivot on that wheel rim, send him off the pavement.

Ed wrestled with the steering, finally getting it under some control, and whipped right, over to the shoulder and beyond it. He pictured the three Mayans from the yard next-door to Natalya's chalet, and he hoped he'd put the Mustang's engine block between him and any likely fields of fire from their vehicle. Ed also hoped they didn't have much weaponry beyond the sniper rifle but knew he was probably wrong on that score, the way they'd handled everything else.

And, after their killing Brandi, there was no bargaining with them, no chance of "Take the money and let me live, or I'll nail at least one of you right here."

Nobody leaves a body and a witness behind.

Ed grabbed the little Raven .25 from the floor mat, slapped the magazine back into the butt of its handle, and slid the semiautomatic into the left-side pocket of his sports jacket. Then he slipped out the driver's door, waiting for the Mayans to make their move. They took long enough before starting the Suburban's engine, he was pretty sure one of them did the same thing he'd done: Dropped out of their vehicle and into the desert, to flank him while the others rolled slowly toward him.

Just like Ed learned in Small Unit Tactics, back in the airborne. And just like the big land-yacht was doing now.

Down on his hands and knees, Ed scuttled like a crab across the desert floor, away from the Mustang. And the money, but it was his only chance: Outflank the flanker, and come around behind all of them.

Ed went into the desert fifty or sixty meters at a diagonal to the road, angling slightly toward the direction he'd driven from. Figuring that was far enough, given the superiority of numbers and firepower the Mayans would think they had over him, Ed assumed the prone position to wait.

Listening to the desert sounds. Trying to pick up anything that didn't move like a snake. Or a lizard, even a tarantula.

Or whatever the fuck else there'd be in this kind of desert.

And he did hear some slithering sounds, then a scratching sound, like maybe a mouse's foot would make on wood, then a little squeak that Ed figured was curtains for that particular rodent.

But now, footfalls. Halfway between him and the road, moving parallel to it. Jogging, the guy moving with confidence toward the Mustang.

Ed rose to a sprinter's start, waiting for the Surburban to draw even with him. Then he used the noise of the receding vehicle to cover his own.

The running Mayan stayed on a line with the big vehicle's rear doors. Smart: That way, its headlights wouldn't silhouette him for a shooter still at the Mustang.

Bad luck, though, too: That relative positioning did pinpoint the guy—a pistol of some kind held muzzle up—just right for the angle Ed had from behind.

Closing fast on an interception course, Ed was all over the Mayan—Christ, no more than five-four, max?—before the little guy could have heard him. Ed used the extra-heavy barrel of the Combat Masterpiece to pistol-whip the Mayan across the back of his head, pitching him forward onto the sand with a "whump" sound from his body but nothing from his mouth.

Then Ed planted his left foot on the Mayan's spine, and—with his free hand—hooked under the little guy's chin and snapped his neck.

Scooping up the Mayan's pistol—another semiautomatic, maybe a nine-millimeter but not enough light on it to be sure—Ed put it in his jacket's right side-pocket, kind of balancing off Brandi's Raven .25 in the other. Then he started to run, trying to match the pace of the Mayan he'd just killed.

Thinking: one down, two to go.

The Suburban was now enough ahead of him, he could see it clearly approaching his Mustang. When the driver nailed the gas and kicked in his high-beams, the third Mayan began shooting two-handed from the rear seat, Ed closing his eyes against the blaze from the muzzles, so as not to ruin his night vision. He heard both magazines empty into and around the convertible as they passed—some richochets, some thumps, depending on what the rounds hit. Then, hanging a U-ey, the Suburban came back hard. Ed was already prone again, eyes turned away from the headlights, but his ears picked up the sound of the third Mayan emptying another two magazines into the Mustang from the opposite direction.

Christ, a good thing you left the car. And picked off their flanker, who'd otherwise be standing over you now, capping three rounds through your skull.

Ed turned back toward the Suburban. It hung another U-ey, this time moving back toward the Mustang real slow and weaving a little, let its high beams maybe pick up a dead or wounded courier against the convertible or somewhere near it.

Fuck this.

Ed got into another crouch, then sprang forward, letting Brandi's .25 fill his left hand, since he couldn't waste time fiddling with the maybe-on, maybe-off safety from the first Mayan's semi'. He matched that dead guy's pace again as best he could, let the two Mayans exiting the Suburban—one at the driver's side, of course, the other at the passenger rear door—think their pal was joining up. Until they were clear of the vehicle and fixated on the Mustang, each just forward of the Suburban's front grille, using its high beams to blind anybody left alive to shoot back at them.

After drawing a deep breath and releasing it slowly, Ed emptied both of his weapons into those two Mayans, being careful not to hit their vehicle.

His new transportation, after all.

Ed's targets spazzed out like puppets as his slugs hit them, Ed himself now pulling from his jacket pocket the first guy's semi', to close and finish the fuckers. Then he caught the flash of another muzzle from the rear-passenger's window of the Suburban and simultaneously the impact of two, three rounds spinning him around and down, hard.

Shit: A fourth fucking Mayan?

Hoping the semi' did have its safety off, Ed squeezed the trigger, putting five shots into the rear door. Hearing a scream, he decided to save the remaining slugs, in case the guy was playing possum. But Ed started feeling dizzy, too, knew he was losing too much blood to wait any longer. Levering up on his elbows—Christ, like somebody's hit you in the chest with a battering ram, tough even to breathe shallow—Ed staggered toward the Suburban, keeping the semi' as level as he could. Getting there seemed to take an hour, but when he inhaled as much air as his lungs would hold, he yanked open that rear door, and saw the top half of fat Natalya ooze more than flop onto the pavement, another semiautomatic clattering on the asphalt like it was the tile floor in her chalet.

Fucking bitch didn't trust her Mayans after all.

Then Ed walked around to the front of the Suburban, let its high-beams spotlight his shirt under the sports jacket. He said, "Shit," and, a moment later, the same once more. After that, he didn't see much else to say.

So Ed inched out of the jacket as best he could, found a soft, level spot on the desert floor, and rolled the jacket into sort of a pillow, rest a little easier.

*　　*　　*

Ed Krause opened his eyes, realized he didn't know how long he'd been out, still just lying there on the desert floor. He was starting to feel cold, which he didn't remember from before. And while some of the stars above him seemed to have changed position, there was no sign yet of dawn to the east.

Just the glorious, heavenly effect from the lights of Vegas.

Ed shifted his head on the sports-jacket pillow as best he could, to be able to stare at those lights, the promise of real money and seeing a place he'd always wanted to visit. Last two times he'd coughed, though, blood came up, so right now he wouldn't bet on even seeing morning.

You're gonna bleed out in this fucking desert, you might as well stay focused on the prize, huh? Shows. . . . Lions. . . . Showgirls. . . . Magic acts. . . . Tigers. . . . Casinos.

The Vegas lights started to go funny against Ed's eyes, so he closed them.

Help the imagination, you know?

Slick cars like Maseratis, Ferraris, Rolls-fucking-Royces. Cruising the Strip, just like they did in the movies he'd seen. All the filet mignon and trimmings you could eat, all the Jim and Coke you could drink. Call-girls that'd make Brandi with an "i" look like fucking Spam.

Action of all kinds, non-stop. The genuine "City that Never Sleeps."

Only you're never gonna see it now.

Vegas, Las Vegas. Grieving. . . .

JOAN HESS

The Maggody Files: Hillbilly Cat

I WAS REDUCED TO WHITTLING AWAY the morning, and trying to convince myself that I was in some obscure way whittling away at the length of my sentence in Maggody, Arkansas (pop. 755). Outside the red-bricked PD, the early morning rain came down steadily, and, as Ruby Bee Hanks (proprietress of a bar and grill of the same name, and incidentally, my mother) would say, it was turning a mite crumpy. I figured the local criminal elements would be daunted enough to stay home, presuming they were smart enough to come in out of the rain in the first place. This isn't to say they rampaged when the sun shone. Mostly they ran the stoplight, fussed and cussed at their neighbors, stole such precious commodities as superior huntin' dawgs, and occasionally raced away from the self-service station without paying for gas. There'd been some isolated violence during my tenure, but every last person in town still based their historical perspective on before-or-after Hiram Buchanon's barn burned to the ground.

I suppose I ought to mention that my sentence was self-imposed, in that I scampered home from Manhattan to lick my wounds after a nasty divorce. In that I was the only person stupid enough to apply for the job, I was not only the Chief of Police, but also the entirety of the department. For a while I'd had a deputy, who just happened to be the mayor's cousin, but he'd gotten himself in trouble over his unrequited love for a bosomy barmaid. Now I had a beeper.

That October morning I had a block of balsa wood that was harder than granite, and a pocket knife that was duller than most of the population. I also had some bizarre dreams of converting the wood into something that remotely resembled a duck—a marshland mallard, to be precise. Those loyal souls who're schooled in the local lore know I tried this a while back, with zero success. Same wood, for the record, and thus far, same rate of success.

So I had my feet on the corner of my desk, my cane-bottomed chair propped back against the wall, and an unholy mess of wood shavings scattered all over the place when the door opened. The man who came in wore a black plastic raincoat and was wrestling with a brightly striped umbrella more suited to a swanky golf course (in Maggody, we don't approve of golf— or any other sissified sport in which grown men wear shorts). He appeared to be forty or so, with a good ol' boy belly and the short, wavy hair of a used car salesman.

Strangers come into the PD maybe three times a year, usually to ask directions or to sell me subscriptions to magazines like *Field and Stream* or *Sports Illustrated*. I guess it's never occurred to any of them that some of us backwoods cops might prefer *Cosmopolitan*.

He finally gave up on the umbrella and set it in a corner to drip. Flashing two rows of pearly white teeth at me, he said, "Hey, honey, some weather, isn't it? Is the chief in?"

"It sure is some weather," I said politely, "and the chief is definitely in." I did not add that the chief was mildly insulted, but by no means incensed or inclined to explain further.

This time I got a wink. "Could I have a word with him?"

"You're having a word with *her* at this very moment," I said as I dropped my duck in a drawer and crossed my arms, idly wondering how long it'd take him to work it out. He didn't look downright stupid like the clannish Buchanons, who're obliged to operate solely on animal instinct, but he had squinty eyes, flaccid lips, and minutes earlier had lost a battle to an umbrella.

"Sorry, honey." His shrug indicated he wasn't altogether overwhelmed with remorse. "I'm Nelson Mullein from down near Pine Bluff. The woman at the hardware store said the chief's name was Arly, and I sort of assumed I was looking for a fellow. My mistake."

"How may I help you, Mr. Mullein?" I said.

"Call me Nelson, please. My great-grandaunts live here in Maggody, out on County 102 on the other side of the low-water bridge. Everybody's always called them the Banebury girls, although Miss Columbine is seventy-eight and Miss Larkspur's seventy-six."

"I know who they are."

"Thought you might." He sat down on the chair across from my desk and took out a cigar. When he caught my glare, he replaced it in his pocket, licked his lips, and made a production of grimacing and sighing so I'd appreciate how carefully he was choosing his words. "The thing is," he said slowly, "I'm worried about them. As I said, they're old and they live in that big, ramshackle house by themselves. It ain't in the ghetto, but it's a far cry from suburbia. Neither one of them can see worth a damn. Miss Larkspur took a fall last year while she was climbing out of the tub, and her hip healed so poorly she's still using a walker. Miss Columbine is wheezier than a leaky balloon."

"So I should arrest them for being old and frail?"

"Of course not," he said, massaging his rubbery jowls. "I was hoping you could talk some sense into them, that's all, 'cause I sure as hell can't, even though I'm their only relative. It hurts me to see them living the way they do. They're as poor as church mice. When I went out there yesterday, it was colder inside than it was outside, and the only heat was from a wood fire in a potbelly stove. Seems they couldn't pay the gas bill last month and it was shut off. I took care of that immediately and told the gas company to bill me in the future. If Miss Columbine finds out, she'll have a fit, but I didn't know what else to do."

He sounded so genuinely concerned that I forgave him for calling me "honey," and tried to recall what little I knew about the Banebury girls. They'd been reclusive even when I was a kid, although they occasionally drove through town in a glossy black Lincoln Continental, nodding regally at the peasants. One summer night twenty or so years ago, they'd caught a gang of us skinny-dipping at the far side of the field behind their house. Miss Columbine had been outraged. After she carried on for a good ten minutes, Miss Larkspur persuaded her not to report the incident to our parents and we grabbed our clothes and high-tailed it. We stayed well downstream the rest of the summer. We avoided their house at Halloween, but only because it was isolated and not worth the risk of having to listen to a lecture on hooliganism in exchange for a stale popcorn ball.

"I understand your concern," I said. "I'm afraid I don't know them well enough to have any influence."

"They told me they still drive. Miss Columbine has macular degeneration, which means her peripheral vision's fine but she can't see anything in front of her. Miss Larkspur's legally blind, but that works out just fine—she navigates. I asked them how on earth either had a driver's license, and damned if they didn't show 'em to me. The date was 1974."

I winced. "Maybe once or twice a year, they drive half a mile to church at a speed of no more than ten miles an hour. When they come down the middle of the road, everybody in town knows to pull over, all the way into a ditch if need be, and the children have been taught to do their rubberneckin' from their yards. It's actually kind of a glitzy local event that's discussed for days afterwards. I realize it's illegal, but I'm not about to go out there and tell them they can't drive anymore."

"Yeah, I know," he said, "but I'm going to lose a lot of sleep if I don't do something for them. I'm staying at a motel in Farberville. This morning I got on the phone and found out about a retirement facility for the elderly. I went out and looked at it, and it's more like a boardinghouse than one of those smelly nursing homes. Everybody has a private bedroom, and meals are provided in a nice, warm dining room. There was a domino game going on while I was there, and a couple of the women were watching a soap opera. There's a van to take them shopping or to doctor appointments. It's kind of expensive, but I think I can swing it by using their social security checks and setting up an income from the sale of the house and property. I had a real estate agent drive by it this morning, and he thought he could get eight, maybe ten, thousand dollars."

"And when you presented this, they said . . . ?"

"Miss Columbine's a hardheaded woman, and she liked to scorch my ears," he admitted ruefully. "I felt like I was ten years old and been caught with a toad in the pocket of my choir robe. Miss Larkspur was interested at first, and asked some questions, but when they found out they couldn't take Eppie, the discussion was over, and before I knew what hit me, I was out on the porch shivering like a hound dog in a blizzard."

"Eppie?"

"Their cat. In spite of the sweet-sounding name, it's an obese yellow tomcat with one eye and a tattered ear. It's mangy and mean and moth-eaten, and that's being charitable. But they won't even consider giving it away, and the residence home forbids pets because of a health department regulation. I went ahead and put down a deposit, but the director said she can't hold the rooms for more than a few days and she expects to be filled real soon. I hate to say it, but it's now or never." He spread his hands and gave me a beseeching look. "Do you think you or anybody else in town can talk them into at least taking a look at this place?"

I suspected I would have more luck with my balsa wood than with the Banebury sisters, but I promised Nelson I'd give it a shot and wrote down the telephone number of his motel room. After a display of effusively moist gratitude, he left.

I decided the matter could wait until after lunch. The Banebury sisters had been going about their business nearly four score years, after all, I told myself righteously as I darted through the drizzle to my car and headed for Ruby Bee's Bar & Grill.

*　　*　　*

"So what's this about Miss Columbine and Miss Larkspur being dragged off to an old folks' home?" Ruby Bee demanded as I walked across the tiny dance floor. It was too early for the noon crowd, and only one booth was occupied by a pair of truck drivers working on blue plate specials and a pitcher of beer.

"And who'd pay ten thousand dollars for that old shack?" Estelle Oppers added from her favorite stool at the end of the bar, convenient to the pretzels and the rest room.

I wasn't particularly amazed by the questions. Maggody has a very sturdy grapevine, and it definitely curls through the barroom on its way from one end of town to the other. That was one of the reasons I'd left the day after I graduated, and eventually took refuge in the anonymity of Manhattan, where one can caper in the nude on the street and no one so much as bothers with a second look. In Maggody, you can hear about what you did before you're finished planning to do it.

"To think they'd give up their cat!" Ruby Bee continued, her hands on her hips and her eyes flashing as if I'd suggested we drown dear Eppie in Boone Creek. Beneath her unnaturally blond hair, her face was screwed up with indignation. "It ain't much to look at, but they've had it for fourteen years and some folks just don't understand how attached they are."

I opened my mouth to offer a mild rebuttal, but Estelle leapt in with the agility of a trout going after a mayfly. "Furthermore, I think it's mighty suspicious, him coming to town all of a sudden to disrupt their lives. I always say, when there's old ladies and a cat, the nephew's up to no good. Just last week I read a story about how the nephew tried to trick his aunt so he could steal all her money."

I chose a stool at the opposite end of the bar. "From what Nelson told me, they don't have any money."

"I still say he's up to no good," Estelle said mulishly, which is pretty much the way she said everything.

Ruby Bee took a dishrag and began to wipe the pristine surface of the bar. "I reckon that much is true, but Eula said she happened to see him in the hardware store, and he had a real oily look about him, like a carnival roustabout. She said she wouldn't have been surprised if he had tattoos under his clothes. He was asking all kinds of questions, too."

"Like what?" I said, peering at the pies under glass domes and ascertaining there was a good-sized piece of cherry left.

"Well, he wanted to know where to go to have all their utility bills sent to him, on account of he didn't think they had enough money to pay 'em. He also wanted to know if he could arrange for groceries to be delivered to their house every week, but Eula stepped in and explained that the church auxiliary already sees to that."

I shook my head and made a clucking noise. "The man's clearly a scoundrel, a cad, a veritable devil in disguise. How about meatloaf, mashed potatoes and gravy, and cherry pie with ice cream?"

Ruby Bee was not in her maternal mode. "And wasn't there an old movie about a smarmy nephew trying to put his sweet old aunts in some sort of insane asylum?" she asked Estelle.

"That was because they were poisoning folks. I don't recollect anyone accusing the Banebury girls of anything like that. Miss Columbine's got a sharp tongue, but she's got her wits about her. I wish I could say the same thing about Miss Larkspur. She can be kind of silly and forgetful, but she ain't got a mean bone in her body. Now if the cat was stalking me on a dark street, I'd be looking over my shoulder and fearing for my life. He lost his eye in a fight with old Shep Hume's pit bull. When Shep tried to pull 'em apart, he liked to lose both of his eyes and a couple of fingers, and he said he cain't remember when he heard a gawdawful racket like that night."

"Meatloaf?" I said optimistically. "Mashed potatoes?"

Still wiping the bar, Ruby Bee worked her way towards Estelle. "The real estate agent says he can sell that place for ten thousand dollars?"

"He didn't sound real sure of it, and Eilene said Earl said the fellow didn't think the house was worth a dollar. It was the forty acres he thought might sell." Estelle popped a pretzel in her mouth and chewed it pensively. "I took them a basket of cookies last year just before Christmas, and the house is in such sad shape that I thought to myself, I'm gonna sit right down and cry. The plaster's crumbling off the walls, and there was more than one window taped with cardboard. It's a matter of time before the house falls down on 'em."

Aware I was about to go down for the third time, I said, "Meatloaf?"

Ruby Bee leaned across the bar, and in a melodramatic whisper that most likely was audible in the next county, said, "Do you think they're misers with a fortune buried in jars in the back yard? If this Mullein fellow knows it, then he'd want to get rid of them and have all the time he needs to dig up the yard searching for the money."

"Them?" Estelle cackled. "There was some family money when their daddy owned the feed store, but he lost so much money when that fancy co-op opened in Starley City that he lost the store and upped and died within the year. After that, Miss Larkspur had to take piano students and Miss Columbine did mending until they went on social security. Now how are they supposed to have acquired this fortune? Are you accusing them of putting on ski masks and robbing liquor stores?"

"For pity's sake, I was just thinking out loud," Ruby Bee retorted.

"The next thing, you'll be saying you saw them on that television show about unsolved crimes."

"At least some of us have better things to do than read silly mystery stories about nephews and cats," Ruby Bee said disdainfully. "I wouldn't be surprised if you didn't have a whole book filled with them."

"So what if I do?" Estelle slapped the bar hard enough to dump the pretzels.

It seemed the only thing being served was food for thought. I drove to the Dairee Dee-Lishus and ate a chilidog in my car while I fiddled with the radio in search of anything but whiny country music. I was doing so to avoid thinking about the conversation at Ruby Bee's. Nelson Mullein wasn't my type, but that didn't automatically relegate him to the slime pool. He had good reason to be worried about his great-grandaunts. Hell, now I was worried about them, too.

Then again, I thought as I drove out County 102 and eased across the low-water bridge, Estelle had a point. There was something almost eerie about the combination of old ladies, cats, and ne'er-do-well nephews (although, as far as I knew, Nelson was doing well at whatever he did; I hadn't asked). But we were missing the key element in the plot, and that was the fortune that kicked in the greed factor. Based on what Estelle had said, the Banebury girls were just as poor as Nelson had claimed.

The appearance of the house confirmed it. It was a squatty old farmhouse that had once been white, but was weathered to a lifeless gray. What shingles remained on the roof were mossy, and the chimney had collapsed. A window on the second floor was covered with cardboard; broken glass was scattered on the porch. The detached garage across the weedy yard had fared no better.

Avoiding puddles, I hurried to the front door and knocked, keenly and uncomfortably aware of the icy rain slithering under my collar. I was about to knock a second time when the door opened a few cautious inches.

"I'm Arly Hanks," I said, trying not to let my teeth chatter too loudly. "Do you mind if I come in for a little visit?"

"I reckon you can." Miss Columbine stepped back and gestured for me to enter. To my astonishment, she looked almost exactly the same as she had the night she stood on the bank of Boone Creek and bawled us out. Her hair was white and pinned up in tight braids, her nose was sharp, her cheekbones prominent above concave cheeks. Her head was tilted at an angle, and I remembered what Nelson had said about her vision.

"Thanks," I murmured as I rubbed my hands together.

"Hanks, did you say? You're Ruby Bee's gal," she said in the same steely voice. "Now that you're growed up, are you keeping your clothes on when you take a moonlight swim?"

I was reduced to an adolescent. "Yes, ma'am."

"Do we have a visitor?" Miss Larkspur came into the living room, utilizing an aluminum walker to take each awkward step. "First Nelson and now this girl. I swear, I don't know when we've had so much company, Columbine."

The twenty years had been less compassionate to Miss Larkspur. Her eyes were so clouded and her skin so translucent that she looked as if she'd been embalmed. Her body was bent, one shoulder hunched and the other undefined. The fingers that gripped the walker were swollen and misshapen.

"I'm Arly Hanks," I told her.

"Gracious, girl, I know who you are. I heard about how you came back to Maggody after all those years in the big city. I don't blame you one bit. Columbine and I went to visit kin in Memphis when we were youngsters, and I knew then and there that I'd never be able to live in a place like that. There were so many cars and carriages and streetcars that we feared for our very lives, didn't we?"

"Yes, I seem to recall that we did, Larkspur."

"Shall I put on the tea kettle?"

Miss Columbine smiled sadly. "That's all right, sister; I'll see to it. Why don't you sit down with our company while I fix a tray? Be sure and introduce her to Eppie."

The room was scantily furnished with ugly, battered furniture and a rug worn so badly that the wooden floor was visible. It smelled of decay, and no doubt for a very good reason. Plaster had fallen in several places, exposing the joists and yellowed newspaper that served as insulation. Although it was warmer than outside, it was a good twenty degrees below what I considered comfortable. Both sisters wore shawls. I hoped they had thermal underwear beneath their plain, dark dresses. I waited until Miss Larkspur had made it across the room and was seated on a sofa. I sat across from her and said, "I met Nelson this morning. He seems concerned about you and your sister."

"So he says," she said without interest. She leaned forward and clapped her hands. "Eppie? Are you hiding? It's quite safe to come out. This girl won't hurt you. She'd like the chance to admire you."

An enormous cat stalked from behind the sofa, his single amber eye regarding me malevolently and his tail swishing as if he considered it a weapon. He was everything Nelson had described, and worse. He paused to rake his claws across the carpet, then leapt into Miss Larkspur's lap and settled down to convey to me how very deeply he resented my presence. Had I been a less rational person, I would have wondered if he knew I was there to promote Nelson's plan. Had I been, as I said.

"Isn't he a pretty kitty?" cooed Miss Larkspur. "He acts so big and tough, but him's just a snuggly teddy bear."

"Very pretty," I said, resisting an urge to lapse into baby-talk and tweak Eppie's whiskers. He would have taken my hand off in a flash. Or my arm.

Miss Columbine came into the room, carrying a tray with three cups and saucers and a ceramic teapot. There were more chips than rosebuds, but I was delighted to take a cup of hot tea and cradle it in my hands. "Did Nelson send you?" she said as she served her sister and sat down beside her. Eppie snuggled between them to continue his surly surveillance.

"He came by the PD this morning and asked me to speak to you," I admitted.

"Nelson is a ninny," she said with a tight frown. "Always has been, always will be. When he came during the summers, I had to watch him like a hawk to make sure he wasn't tormenting the cat or stealing pennies from the sugar bowl. His grandmother, our youngest sister, married poor white trash, and although she never said a word against them, we were all of a mind that she regretted it to her dying day." She paused to take a sip of tea, and the cup rattled against the saucer as she replaced it. "I suppose Nelson's riled up on account of our Sunday drives, although it seems to me reporting us to the police is extreme. Did you come out here to arrest us?"

Miss Larkspur giggled. "What would Papa say if he were here to see us being arrested? Can't you imagine the look on his face, Columbine? He'd be fit to be tied, and he'd most likely throw this nice young thing right out the door."

"I didn't come out here to arrest you," I said hastily, "and I didn't come to talk about your driving. As long as you don't run anybody down, stay on this road, and never ever go on the highway, it's okay with me."

"But not with Nelson." Miss Columbine sighed as she finished her tea. "He wants us to give up our home, our car, our beloved Eppie, and go live in a stranger's house with a bunch of old folks. Who knows what other fool rules they'd have in a house where they don't allow pets?"

"But, Columbine," Miss Larkspur said, her face puckering wistfully, "Nelson says they serve nice meals and have tea with sandwiches and pound cake every afternoon. I can't recollect when I last tasted pound cake—unless it was at Mama's last birthday party. She died of influenza back in September of fifty-eight, not three weeks after Papa brought the new car all the way from Memphis, Tennessee." She took a tissue from her cuff and dabbed her eyes. "Papa died the next year, some say on account of losing the store, but I always thought he was heartsick over poor—"

"Larkspur, you're rambling like a wild turkey," Columbine said sternly but with affection. "This girl doesn't want to hear our family history. Frankly, I don't find it that interesting. I think we'd better hear what she has to say so she can be on her way." She stroked Eppie's head, and the cat obligingly growled at yours truly.

"Is Eppie the only reason you won't consider this retirement house?" I asked. I realized it was not such an easy question and plunged ahead. "You don't have to make a decision until you've visited. I'm sure Nelson would be delighted to take you there at tea time."

"Do you think he would?" Miss Larkspur clasped her hands together and her cloudy eyes sparkled briefly.

Miss Columbine shook her head. "We cannot visit under false pretenses, Larkspur, and come what may, we will not abandon Eppie after all these years. When the Good Lord sees fit to take him from us, we'll think about moving to town."

The object of discussion stretched his front legs and squirmed until he was on his back, his claws digging into their legs demandingly. When Miss Columbine rubbed his bloated belly, he purred with all the delicacy of a truck changing gears.

"Thank you for tea," I said, rising. "I'll let myself out." I was almost at the front door when I stopped and turned back to them. "You won't be driving until Easter, will you?"

"Not until Easter," Miss Columbine said firmly.

I returned to the PD, dried myself off with a handful of paper towels, and called Nelson at the motel to report my failure.

"It's the cat, isn't it?" he said. "They're willing to live in squalor because they won't give up that sorry excuse for a cat. You know, honey, I'm beginning to wonder if they haven't wandered too far out in left field to know what's good for them. I guess I'd better talk to a lawyer when I get back to Pine Bluff."

"You're going to force them to move?"

"I feel so bad, honey, but I don't know what else to do and it's for their own good."

"What's in it for you, Nelson?"

"Nothing." He banged down the receiver.

*　　*　　*

"My shoe's full of water," Ruby Bee grumbled as she did her best to avoid getting smacked in the face by a bunch of soggy leaves. It wasn't all that easy, since she had to keep her flashlight trained on the ground in case of snakes or other critters. The worst of it was that Estelle had hustled her out the door on this harebrained mission without giving her a chance to change clothes, and now her best blue dress was splattered with mud and her matching blue suede shoes might as well go straight into the garbage can. "Doncha think it's time to stop acting like overgrown Girl Scouts and just drive up to the door, knock real politely, and ask our questions in the living room?"

Estelle was in the lead, mostly because she had the better flashlight. "At least it's stopped raining, Miss Moanie Mouth. You're carrying on like we had to go miles and miles, but it ain't more than two hundred feet to begin with and we're within spittin' distance already."

"I'd be within spittin' distance of my bed if we'd dropped in and asked them." Ruby Bee stepped over a log and right into a puddle, this time filling her other shoe with cold water and forcing her to bite her tongue to keep from blurting out something unseemly. However, she figured she'd better pay more attention to the job at hand, which was sneaking up on the Banebury girls' garage through the woods behind it.

"I told you so," Estelle said as she flashed her light on the backside of the building. "Now turn out your light and stay real close. If that door's not locked, we'll be inside quicker than a preacher says his prayers at night."

The proverbial preacher would have had time to bless a lot of folks. The door wasn't locked, but it was warped something awful and it took a good five minutes of puffing and grunting to get it open far enough for them to slip inside.

Ruby Bee stopped to catch her breath. "I still don't see why you're so dadburned worried about them seeing us. They're both blind as bats."

"Hush!" Estelle played her light over the black sedan. "Lordy, they made 'em big in those days, didn't they? You could put one of those little Japanese cars in the trunk of this one, and have enough room left for a table and four chairs. And look at all that chrome!"

"This ain't the showroom of a car dealership," Ruby Bee said in the snippety voice that always irritated Estelle, which was exactly what she intended for it to do, what with her ruined shoes and toes nigh onto frozen. "If you want to stand there and admire it all night, that's fine, but I for one have other plans. I'll see if it says the model on the back, and you try the interior."

She was shining her light on the license plate and calculating how many years it had been since it expired when Estelle screamed. Before she could say a word, Estelle dashed out the door, the beam from the flashlight bobbling like a ping-pong ball. Mystified but not willing to linger on her own, Ruby Bee followed as fast as she dared, and only when she caught Estelle halfway through the woods did she learn what had caused the undignified retreat. According to Estelle, there'd been a giant rat right in the front seat of the car, its lone amber eye glaring like the devil's own. Ruby Bee snorted in disbelief, but she didn't go back to have a look for herself.

*   *   *

The next morning, sweet inspiration slapped me up the side of the head like a two by four. It had to be the car. I lunged for the telephone so hastily that my poor duck fell to the floor, and called Plover, a state cop with whom I occasionally went to a movie or had dinner. "What do you know about antique cars?" I demanded, bypassing pleasantries.

"They're old. Some of them are real old."

"Did you forget to jump start your brain this morning? I need to find out the current value of a particular car, and I assumed you were up on something macho like this."

He let out a long-suffering sort of sigh. "I can put gas in one at the self-service pump, and I know how to drive it. That's the extent of my so-called macho knowledge."

"Jesus, Plover," I said with a sigh of my own, "you'd better get your-self a frilly pink shirt and a pair of high heel sneakers. While you're doing that, let me talk to someone in the barracks with balls who knows about cars, okay?"

He hung up on what I thought was a very witty remark. State cops were not renowned for their humor, I told myself as I flipped open the telephone directory and hunted up the number of the Lincoln dealer in Farberville. The man who answered was a helluva lot more congenial, possibly (and mistakenly) in hopes he was dealing with a potential buyer.

Alas, he was no better informed than Plover about the current market value of a '58 Lincoln Continental, but his attitude was much brighter and he promised to call me back as soon as possible.

Rather than waste the time patting myself on the back, I called Plover, apologized for my smart-mouthed remark, and explained what I surmised was going on. "It's the car he's after," I concluded. "The house and land are close to worthless, but this old Lincoln could be a collector's dream."

"Maybe," he said without conviction, "but you can't arrest him for any-thing. I don't know if what he tried to do constitutes fraud, but in any case, he failed. He can't get his hands on the car until they die."

"Or he has them declared incompetent," I said. "I suppose I could let him know that I'm aware of his scheme, and that I'll testify on their behalf if he tries anything further."

We chatted aimlessly for a while, agreed to a dinner date in a few days, and hung up. I was preparing to dial the number of Nelson's motel room when the phone rang.

The dealer had my information. I grabbed a pencil and wrote down a few numbers, thanked him, and replaced the receiver with a scowl of disap-pointment. If the car was in mint condition (aka in its original wrapper), it might bring close to ten thousand dollars. The amounts then plummeted: sixty-five hundred for very good, less than five thousand for good, and on down to four hundred fifty as a source for parts.

It wasn't the car, after all, but simply a case of letting myself listen to the suspicious minds in Ruby Bee's Bar & Grill. I picked up the balsa wood and turned my attention to its little webbed feet.

*　　*　　*

It normally doesn't get dark until five-thirty or so, but the heavy clouds had snuffed out the sunset. I decided to call it a day (not much of one, though) and find out if Ruby Bee was in a more hospitable mood. I had locked the back door and switched off the light when the telephone rang. After a short debate centering around meatloaf versus professional obligations, I reluctantly picked up the receiver.

"Arly! You got to do something! Somebody's gonna get killed if you don't do something!"

"Calm down, Estelle," I said, regretting that I hadn't heeded the plea from my stomach. "What's the problem?"

"I'm so dadburned all shook up I can barely talk!"

I'd had too much experience with her to be overcome with alarm. "Give it your best shot."

"It's the Banebury girls! They just drove by my house, moving real smartly down the middle of the road, and no headlights! I was close enough to my driveway to whip in and get out of their way, but I'm thanking my lucky stars I saw 'em before they ran me over with that bulldozer of a car."

I dropped the receiver, grabbed my car keys, and ran out to the side of the highway. I saw nothing coming from the south, but if they were driving without lights, I wouldn't be the only one not to see them coming . . . relentlessly, in a great black death machine.

"Damn!" I muttered as I got in my car, maneuvered around, and headed down the highway to the turnoff for County 102. Miss Columbine couldn't see anything in front of her, and Miss Larkspur was legally blind. A dynamite duo. I muttered a lot more things, none of them acceptable within my mother's earshot.

It was supper time, and the highway was blessedly empty. I squealed around the corner and stopped, letting my lights shine down the narrow road. The wet pavement glistened like a snakeskin. They had passed Estelle's house at least three or four minutes ago. Presuming they were not in a ditch, they would arrive at the intersection any minute. Maybe Nelson had a justifiable reason to have them declared incompetent, I thought as I gripped the steering wheel and peered into the darkness. I hadn't seen any bunnies hopping outside my window, and if there were chocolate eggs hidden in the PD, I hadn't found them.

It occurred to me that I was in more than minimal danger, parked as I was in their path. However, I couldn't let them go on their merry way. A conscientious cop would have forbidden them to drive and confiscated the keys. I'd practically given them my blessing.

My headlights caught the glint of a massive black hood bearing down on me. With a yelp, I changed the beam to high, fumbled with a switch until the blue light on the roof began to rotate, grabbed a flashlight, and jumped out of my car. I waved the light back and forth as the monster bore down on me, and I had some sharp insights into the last thoughts of potential roadkill.

All I could see was the reflection on the chrome as the car came at me, slowly yet determinedly. The blue light splashed on the windshield, as did my flashlight. "Miss Columbine!" I yelled. "Miss Larkspur! You've got to stop!" I retreated behind my car and continued yelling.

The car shuddered, then, at the last moment, stopped a good six inches from my bumper (and a six-hour session with the mayor, trying to explain the bill from the body shop).

I pried my teeth off my lower lip, switched off the flashlight, and went to the driver's window. Miss Columbine sat rigidly behind the wheel, but Miss Larkspur leaned forward and, with a little wave, said, "It's Arly, isn't it? How are you, dear?"

"Much better than I was a minute ago," I said. "I thought we agreed that you wouldn't be driving until this spring, Miss Columbine. A day later you're not only out, but at night without headlights."

"When you're blind," she said tartly, "darkness is not a factor. This is an emergency. Since we don't have a telephone, we had no choice but to drive for help."

"That's right," said Miss Larkspur. "Eppie has been catnapped. We're beside ourselves with worry. He likes to roam around the yard during the afternoon, but this evening he did not come to the back door to demand his supper. Columbine and I searched as best we could, but poor Eppie has disappeared. It's not like him, not at all."

"Larkspur is correct," Miss Columbine added. Despite her gruff voice and expressionless face, a tear trickled down her cheek. She wiped it away and tilted her head to look at me. "I am loath to go jumping to conclusions, but in this case, it's hard not to."

"I agree," I said, gazing bleakly at the darkness surrounding us. It may not have been a factor for them, but it sure as hell was for me. "Let's go back to your place and I'll try to find Eppie. Maybe he's already on the porch, waiting to be fed. I'll move my car off the road, and then, if you don't object, I think it's safer for me to drive your car back for you."

A few minutes later I was sitting in the cracked leather upholstery of the driver's seat, trying to figure out the controls on the elaborate wooden dashboard. There was ample room for three of us in the front seat, and possibly a hitchhiker or two. Once I'd found first gear, I turned around in the church parking lot, took a deep breath, and let 'er fly.

"This is a daunting machine," I said.

Giggling, Miss Larkspur put her hand on my arm and said, "Papa brought it all the way from Memphis, as I told you. He'd gone there on account of Cousin Pearl being at the hospital, and we were flabbergasted when he drove up a week later in a shiny new car. This was after he'd lost the store, you see, and we didn't even own a car. We felt real badly about him going all the way to Memphis on the bus, but he and Cousin Pearl were kissin' cousins, and she was dying in the Baptist Hospital, so—"

"The Methodist Hospital," Miss Columbine corrected her. "I swear, some days you go on and on like you ain't got a brain in your head. Papa must have told us a hundred times how he met that polite young soldier whose mother was dying in the room right next to Cousin Pearl's."

"I suppose so," Miss Larkspur conceded, "but Cousin Pearl was a Baptist."

I pulled into the rutted driveway beside their house. The garage door was open, so I eased the car inside, turned off the ignition, and leaned back to offer a small prayer. "Why don't you wait in the house? I'll have a look out back."

"I can't believe our own kin would do such a thing," Miss Columbine said as she took Miss Larkspur's arm. I took the other and we moved slowly toward the back porch.

I believed it, and I had a pretty good idea why he'd done it. Once they were inside, I went back to the car, looked at the contents of the glove compartment to confirm my suspicions, and set off across the field. I'd had enough sense to bring my flashlight, but it was still treacherously wet and rough and I wasn't in the mood to end up with my feet in the air and my fanny in the mud. I could think of a much better candidate.

I froze as my light caught a glittery orb moving toward me in an erratic pattern. It came closer, and at last I made out Eppie's silhouette as he bounded past me in the direction of the house. His yowl of rage shattered the silence for a heart-stopping moment, then he was gone and I was once again alone in the field with a twenty-year-old memory of the path that led to Boone Creek.

Long before I arrived at the bank, I heard a stream of curses and expletives way too colorful for my sensitive ears. I followed the sound and stopped at a prudent distance to shine my light on Nelson Mullein. He was not a pretty picture as he futilely attempted to slither up the muddy incline, snatching at clumps of weeds that uprooted in his hands. He was soaked to the skin. His face was distorted not only by a swath of mud across one cheek, but also by angry red scratches, some of which were oozing blood.

"Who is it?" he said, blinking into the light.

"It's traditional to take your clothes off when you skinny-dip in the creek."

"It's you, the lady cop." He snatched at a branch, but it broke and he slid back to the edge of the inky water. "Can you give me a hand, honey? It's like trying to climb an oil slick, and I'm about to freeze to death."

"Oh, my goodness," I said as I scanned the ground with the light until it rested on a shapeless brown mound nearby. "Could that be a gunny sack? Why, I do believe it is. I hope you didn't put Eppie in it in an unsuccessful attempt to drown him in the creek."

"I've never seen that before in my life. I came down here to search for the cat. The damn thing was up in that tree, meowing in a right pitiful fashion, but when I tried to coax him down, I lost my footing and fell into the water. Why don't you try to find a sturdy branch so I can get up the bank?"

I squatted next to the gunny sack. "This ol' thing's nearly ripped to shreds. I guess Eppie didn't take kindly to the idea of being sent to Cat Heaven before his time. By the way, I know about the car, Mr. Mullein."

"That jalopy?" he said uneasily. He stopped skittering in the mud and wiped his face. "I reckoned on getting six, maybe seven thousand for it from an ol' boy what lives in Pine Bluff. That, along with the proceeds from the sale of the property, ought to be more than enough to keep my great-grandaunts from living the way they do, bless their brave souls."

"It ought to be more than enough for them to have the house remodeled and pay for a full-time housekeeper," I said as I rose, the gunny sack dangling between my thumb and forefinger. "I'm taking this along as evidence. If you ever again so much as set one foot in Maggody, I'll tell those brave souls what you tried to do. You may be their only relative, but someone might suggest they leave what's going to be in the range of half a million dollars to a rest home for cats!"

"You can't abandon me like this." He gave me a view of his pearly white teeth, but it was more of a snarl than a smile. "Don't be cruel like that, honey."

"Watch me." Ignoring his sputters, I took my tattered treasure and walked back across the field to the house. Miss Columbine took me into the living room, where her sister had swaddled Eppie in a towel.

"Him was just being a naughty kitty," she said, stroking the cat's remaining ear and nuzzling his head.

I accepted a cup of tea, and once we were settled as before, said, "That polite young soldier gave your papa the car, didn't he?"

Miss Columbine nodded. "Papa didn't know what to think, but the boy was insistent about how he'd gone from rags to riches and how it made him feel good to be able to give folks presents. Papa finally agreed, saying it was only on account of how excited Mama would be."

"It was charity, of course," Miss Larkspur added, "but the boy said he wanted to do it because of Papa's kindness in the waiting room. The boy even told Papa that he was a hillbilly cat himself, and never forgot the little town in Mississippi where he was born."

Eppie growled ominously, but I avoided meeting his hostile eye and said, "He was called the Hillbilly Cat, back in the earliest stage of his career. The original paperwork's in the glove compartment, and his signature is on the bill of sale and registration form." I explained how much the car would bring and agreed to supervise the sale for them. "This means, of course, that you won't be driving anymore," I added.

"But how will we get to church on Easter morning?" Miss Larkspur asked.

Miss Columbine smiled. "I reckon we can afford a limousine, Larkspur. Let's heat up some nice warm milk for Eppie. He's still shivering from his . . . adventure outside."

"Now that we'll be together, will you promise to never run away again?" Miss Larkspur gently scolded the cat.

He looked at her, then at me on the off chance I'd try to pet him and he could express his animosity with his claws.

I waved at him from the doorway, told the ladies I'd be in touch after I talked with the Lincoln dealer, and wished them a pleasant evening. I walked down the road to my car, and I was nearly there before I realized Eppie was a nickname. Once he'd been the Hillbilly Cat, and his death had broken hearts all around the world. But in the Banebury household, Elvis Presley was alive and well—and still the King.

*　　*　　*

"Give me that shovel," Estelle hissed. "All you're doing is poking the dirt like you think this is a mine field."

Ruby Bee eased the blade into the muddy soil, mindful of the splatters on the hem of her coat and the caked mud that made her shoes feel like combat boots. "Hold your horses," she hissed back, "I heard a clink. I don't want to break the jar and ruin the money."

Estelle hurried over and knelt down to dig with her fingers. "Ain't the Banebury girls gonna be excited when we find their Papa's buried treasure! I reckon I could find as much as a thousand dollars before the night is out." She daintily blotted her forehead with her wrist. "It's a darn shame about the car, but if it ain't worth much, then it ain't. It's kinda funny how that man at the Lincoln dealership rattled off the prices like he had 'em written out in front of him and was wishing somebody'd call to inquire. Of course I wasn't expecting to hear anything different. Everybody knows just because a car's old doesn't mean it's valuable."

A lot of responses went through Ruby Bee's mind, none of them kindly. She held them back, though, and it was just as well when Estelle finally produced a chunk of brick, dropped it back in the hole, stood up, and pointed her finger like she thought she was the high and mighty leader of an expedition.

"Start digging over there, Ruby Bee," she said, "and don't worry about them seeing us from inside the house. I told you time and again, they're both blind."

EDWARD D. HOCH

Brothers on the Beach

THE TEMPERATURE WAS IN THE MID-FORTIES on the December day when Ben Snow stepped off the train at Elizabeth City and went about the business of renting a horse and buggy for the remainder of his journey to the shores of the Atlantic.

He often felt there was something contrary about his gradual journey east at a time when the nation had just about completed its western expansion. There were forty-five states now, stretching from coast to coast, and already there was talk that the territories of Oklahoma, New Mexico, and Arizona would soon be admitted to the Union. He'd fought Indians in the West in his younger days, and even journeyed to Mexico on occasion, but now it was the East that drew him. Cities like Buffalo and Savannah and New Orleans.

Rivers like the Mississippi and the Delaware had only been names on a rarely studied map when he was young. Now that he was past forty and the nation had entered the Twentieth Century, things were different. The West didn't need Indian fighters any more, or hired guns whose draw was as fast as Billy the Kid's.

Ben Snow had never been a man to settle down as a ranch hand. He'd considered working for Pinkerton's, putting his crime-solving abilities to some use, but the detective agency's deep involvement in strike-breaking wasn't to his liking. So he drifted, taking jobs where he found them, helping out old friends when he could.

He'd never been as far east as North Carolina before, and he quickly noted that back here men didn't wear gunbelts on the street in 1903. He left his in his suitcase while he dickered for the horse and buggy. "Kitty Hawk," he said to the man at the stable. "How far is it?"

"About thirty-five miles," the man answered. "You take the road east to Barco and then turn south along the coast. It's on a narrow cape that runs all the way down to Hatteras and beyond, but you can get a ferry to take you across. Why'd anyone want to go to Kitty Hawk in December, though? There's nothing there but a beach, and it's too damn cold for swimming. The wind beats across there like a gale most of the time."

"I have to see a man," Ben answered. "How much for the horse and buggy?"

They dickered a bit before Ben finally drove off in the buggy. He'd noticed a few automobiles—as people were starting to call them—on the streets of the city, but he hadn't felt brave enough to try one. Besides, he didn't know what sort of roads awaited him along the coastal sand spit.

It was shortly after he'd passed through Barco and headed south along the coast, getting his first view of the turbulent Atlantic, when a lone horseman overtook him. The man was young and handsome, with curly blond hair, and he sat well in the saddle. "Would you be Ben Snow?" he asked, drawing abreast of the buggy.

"That's me."

He leaned over to offer his hand. "Roderick Claymore. My brother Rudolph hired you, but he had to go to the state capital on business and he asked that I meet you."

They pulled up and Ben swung down from the buggy. "I'm a lot more comfortable on a horse," he admitted, "but with my suitcase, the buggy seemed best."

Claymore took out a cigar and offered Ben one. "How much did my brother tell you?"

"Only that he was hiring me to guard a section of beach at Kitty Hawk for the next week or so. He wanted someone from far away, and that's what he got. He hired me last week in St. Louis."

Roderick Claymore nodded, puffing on the thin cigar. "About three years ago, a pair of brothers from Dayton, the Wrights, started coming here and flying gliders off the dunes at Kitty Hawk. Seems they wrote the Weather Bureau and were told this was the best testing area for gliders because the winds off the ocean blow at a fairly constant twenty miles an hour or better."

"Does this glider-testing bother you?"

"It didn't at first. No one paid much attention to them. But now things are changing. We own some land nearby and it's important that we don't have a lot of trespassers. They're planning something for Monday that could bring the whole country to our door."

"What would that be?"

"Last summer they started shipping in parts for a powered craft they've been constructing there on the beach. They built their own lightweight gasoline engine—four cylinders, watercooled."

"I don't know much about engines," Ben admitted. "It's to drive two eight-foot wooden propellers mounted to the rear of the wings. This craft won't be a glider. It'll take off and fly by itself, with one of the Wrights aboard. That's why we need you."

Ben Snow smiled slightly. "To shoot it down?"

"Hardly."

"Back in '96, out West, there was a fellow billed himself as The Flying Man. He strapped wings to his arms and tried to glide off hilltops. Somebody killed him one day during an exhibition, and I helped solve the murder. I'm just telling you so you'll know which side of the fence I'm on. I've killed plenty of men in my day, but never one who didn't deserve it. I'm not a hired gun, despite what you and your brother might have heard."

"Look here, Snow, we don't want any hired guns. But if those crazy Wrights bring a thousand people to that beach to see their flight on Monday, we want them kept off our property any way that's necessary."

"All right," Ben agreed. "Where am I staying?"

"There's a lady teacher has a house in Kill Devil Hills, just a few miles from Kitty Hawk. We rented a room there for you."

"That'll be just fine."

It seemed ironic to Ben that he'd had to travel east to North Carolina to find the legendary pretty schoolmarm who was supposed to inhabit every western town. Elizabeth Boyers was a dark-haired beauty, probably past thirty but with a fine girlish figure and a smile that could melt the coldest heart. She lived alone in the house across the street from the one-room school building where she taught.

"There aren't many children here," she admitted. "They're mostly from older families who've lived here all their lives. But someone has to teach them. If I left, they'd have to take the ferry to the mainland."

It was Sunday and they were strolling on the beach together, looking over the site where the Wrights would attempt their flight the following day.

"Do you think they'll make it?" he asked.

"Frankly, no. Not after what happened to Langley last Wednesday."

"Who's Langley?"

She laughed. "You don't keep up with the newspapers, Mr. Snow. Samuel Langley, the inventor, had a $50,000 grant from the War Department to develop a flying machine. He spent five years on it, and last Wednesday he tried to launch it from the roof of a houseboat in the Potomac River with boatloads of Washington reporters and government officials looking on. But a wing tip caught on its catapult and the craft broke apart in the air. Langley is secretary of the Smithsonian Institution. If he can't build a proper flying machine, these brothers from a bicycle shop in Dayton can hardly be expected to do it."

"Will there be reporters here tomorrow?"

"Not if the Wrights can help it. They're trying to keep it secret until the flight is successful. Then they'll send a telegram to their father asking that the press be notified."

"Then why is Claymore so worried?"

She hesitated before answering. "Who hired you—Roderick or Rudolph?"

"Rudolph. He's the older one, isn't he? He came to me in St. Louis and offered to pay my expenses and a week's salary if I'd come here to guard his beach. It seemed to me he could have hired someone from here in town for half the money."

"They do own some land down the beach. I've seen them digging there. I kidded them about looking for pirate treasure. These islands along the Atlantic coast have always had pirate legends connected with them."

"Why did you ask which one hired me?"

"Oh," she answered casually, "I've had a little trouble with the younger one, Roderick—the one who brought you here yesterday. I went out with him a few times last year and he asked me to marry him. I said no, but he won't accept that. Now I'm engaged to someone else and he's bothering me. I wouldn't have taken their money for the room if I didn't need it."

"What do they do for a living when they're not digging for buried treasure?"

"They have an ice business. They deliver blocks of ice to homes and businesses in all the towns around here."

"Never had anything like that out where I come from."

She smiled at him. "This is civilization. This is the Twentieth Century."

When they returned to the house after inspecting—at a distance—the Wright brothers' flying machine, Ben found Rudolph Claymore waiting for him. Rudolph was larger and tougher than his younger brother, and while Roderick sat well on a horse Ben couldn't imagine this man ever riding one. In St. Louis, where he'd hired Ben, Rudolph had seemed like a successful businessman. Here, in his home territory, there was something vaguely sinister about him.

"You saw that flying contraption of theirs?" he asked Ben.

Ben nodded. "Looks backwards to me. The tail seems to be in the front. But flying isn't my line."

"If we're in luck, they'll crash tomorrow like that fellow Langley did. But if it's successful and people start pouring in here, I'll need you to guard our beach property for the next week or so."

"Couldn't you have hired someone from one of the towns around here for that purpose?" Elizabeth said. "Why bring Mr. Snow all the way from St. Louis?"

"I want someone who'll be here today and gone tomorrow, not one of the town boys who'll have a few drinks at the bar and get to talking too much. Mr. Snow's got a good reputation out West. When I asked around for someone to hire, he was the one everyone mentioned."

Claymore took Ben aside and gave him a down payment on his fee, along with the travel expenses. "You brought your gun, didn't you?"

"I have it," Ben assured him.

"Wear it tomorrow, but keep it under your coat."

When he'd gone, Ben asked Elizabeth, "What do you think is so valuable about that strip of sand?"

"Besides the pirate treasure?" she answered with a smile. "I have no idea."

Ben slept restlessly that night, wondering what the morning would bring. What it brought was more of the same as far as the weather was concerned. A cool breeze was blowing off the ocean and he found he needed the wool jacket he'd brought with him from the Midwest. He buckled his gunbelt under it, making certain all chambers of the Colt six-shooter were loaded. He wondered vaguely if there were laws back East against carrying concealed weapons. Maybe that's why the Claymore brothers had wanted someone from far away.

"Are you up, Mr. Snow?" Elizabeth called to him through the bedroom door.

"Sure am. I'll be right down."

"Breakfast is ready. My fiancé, Mark Freen, is joining us."

Freen was an agreeable chap with brown hair and a ready smile. Like Elizabeth, he was a teacher, though his school was on the mainland. "I'm playing hooky today," he explained. "We both are. This might be an historic occasion—right here at Kitty Hawk."

Ben was surprised to see that a fair crowd of local residents had gathered along the beach. "Those are the Wright brothers," Elizabeth said, pointing out two men in caps and jackets. They seemed to be in their thirties. "Orville and Wilbur."

"Do you know them personally?"

"I've spoken with them. They've been here since September assembling the *Flyer*. That's the name of it. And last year they made over a thousand controlled glider flights here. Everyone knows them by now."

They were interrupted by the arrival of an older man with thick glasses and a beard. "Oh, Professor—I want you to meet Ben Snow!" Elizabeth Boyers performed the introductions as if they were both her oldest friends. "Ben, this is Professor Minder from the university at Raleigh."

Ben shook hands and asked, "Did you come all this distance for today's flight?"

"Not exactly," the professor replied. "I'm doing research just south of here, on Roanoke Island. You may remember it was the site of Sir Walter Raleigh's lost colony."

Ben nodded and turned up his collar against the chill wind. "I hope they get started soon. It's cold out here."

The *Flyer* had been pulled from its storage shed by the Wrights and five assistants. Ben heard someone in the crowd comment that it weighed over six hundred pounds. They positioned it on a level stretch of sand at the base of a hundred-foot-high dune named Kill Devil Hill. Then the brothers flipped a coin and Wilbur won the toss. After the *Flyer* had been placed aboard a low trolley on the single sixty-foot rail of a greased launching track, he climbed aboard and lay face down in a cradlelike harness across the lower wing, working the wing and rudder controls with his body in a final check before takeoff.

The crowd tensed and Ben glanced around for some sign of the Claymores. There were figures farther down the beach, but he couldn't tell who they were. His attention returned to the *Flyer* as the gasoline engine sputtered into life. The twin propellers started to turn and the machine glided down its greased track. There was the beginning of a roar from the crowd and cameras poised to capture the moment of flight.

Then, unaccountably, the engine stalled at takeoff. The *Flyer* dropped to the sand with a soft thud.

As the crowd groaned, Orville rushed forward to pull his brother from the craft. "It's over," Elizabeth said sadly. "It'll never fly."

"Another Langley," Mark Freen said, summing it all up.

Wilbur stood up, free of the craft, and the brothers began inspecting the damage. Ben turned and noticed Professor Minder sitting on the sand. "Excitement too much for you?" he asked in fun, bending down to offer his hand.

That was when he saw the knife protruding from Minder's back and realized the man he'd just met had been murdered.

The investigation of a murder case was far different in the East than anything Ben had known out West. There a sheriff bothered little with clues or suspects. There he looked for eyewitnesses or the person with the likeliest motive, and if justice came at all it was usually swift and deadly. On that windswept beach in North Carolina, while the Wrights worked to repair their damaged aircraft, justice was slow and plodding. Justice was a pair of State Police officers with notebooks, taking down names and addresses and setting up a camera to take a photograph of the murder scene.

There was general agreement among all witnesses that the brothers Wright couldn't have had a hand in the killing, since all eyes were on them during the entire period. But that did little to narrow the field of suspects. Any one of the dozens of spectators could have been the guilty party, and in the eyes of the State Police that included Ben Snow.

"Private citizens don't wear gunbelts in North Carolina," one of them told him pointedly. "This isn't the wild West."

"Tell that to the dead man," Ben replied.

The officer's name was Rellens, and he eyed Ben as if he'd like to lock him away in a cell. "What are you doing here, anyway?"

"I was hired by the Claymore brothers to guard their strip of beach land. They feared some of the crowd might wander down that way."

"So you're guarding it from up here?"

"I can see it from here. I can see no one's on it."

"Were the Claymores here today?"

"I didn't see them."

"Pretty strange if they missed something like this," Rellens said.

Ben had been thinking the same thing as his eyes traveled over the spectators. Some had started to drift away, but the majority had stayed after giving their names, drawn by the twin spectacles of the murder investigation and the Wrights' efforts to repair their flying machine.

Then he saw Rudolph Claymore striding over the dunes in their direction. He left Rellens and went to meet his employer. "What happened here?" Rudolph demanded. "I just got word there's been a killing—"

"That's right," Ben said. "A professor named Minder."

"Minder! I know the man! He's been working on an island nearby!"

"Someone stabbed him."

"Is my brother here?"

"I haven't seen him all morning."

"He didn't come to work today and I assumed he was down here. I had to cover the entire ice route myself." Rudolph Claymore glanced along the windswept beach. "What about our property?"

"No one's gone near it," Ben assured him.

"Not Minder, before he was killed?"

"Not unless it was early this morning before I got here. You didn't say anything about guarding it day and night."

"No, no. I just thought you might have noticed him wandering down that way."

"I think it's about time you tell me what this is all about," Ben said. "I might be able to help the investigation if I knew all the facts."

"All right," Claymore agreed. "Come to my house tonight. I'll have my brother there, too, if I can find him. Here's the address. It's in the village of Kitty Hawk."

Elizabeth and Freen had been over by the damaged aircraft and were hurrying back. "Orville says the repairs will take a few days, but they hope to try again on Thursday," she said. "Will you be staying that long, Mr. Snow?"

"I expect so. The Claymores hired me for the week."

"I saw that policeman, Rellens, talking to you. Did he ask for your help?"

"Not exactly."

"Does he have any suspects?"

"Right now I may be his prime suspect. He noticed I was wearing a gunbelt."

"That's absurd! We were all standing together."

"But Professor Minder was right behind us. With all eyes on the Wrights and their machine, I suppose I could have reached around and stabbed him. Someone did."

"But why? He was a sweet old man. Why would anyone kill him?"

"What do you know about him? What was he doing here?"

"Mark knows more about him than I do. He went over to see him on

Roanoke Island a few weeks ago."

"He was studying evidence of the so-called Lost Colony," Freen explained. "You know, the colony founded by Sir Walter Raleigh that vanished from that island between 1587 and 1590."

Ben's knowledge of early colonial history was vague at best, but he nodded and urged Freen to continue.

"Well, a colony of some eighty-five men and women remained on the island in 1587 while a ship returned to England for supplies. The war between England and Spain prevented the supplies from reaching Roanoke until 1590, and by that time all that could be found was a deserted, ransacked fortress. None of the settlers was ever found. The name *Croatoan* was carved into a post—apparently the name of an island to the south. They may have gone there, or they may have been killed by Indians. It's one of the mysteries of history."

"And Professor Minder thought he'd found new evidence of what happened," Elizabeth Boyers interjected. "He was over here a few times pursuing his studies."

"Interesting," Ben admitted. "But why should anyone kill him? Why would something that happened over three hundred years ago cost a man his life?"

They returned to the house without an answer. Later that afternoon, while Elizabeth and Freen were alone, Ben walked back up the beach alone. From a distance he watched the Wright brothers and their helpers working on the flying machine. He saw that Rellens was still there, too, pacing back and forth as he examined the trampled sand.

That evening Ben Snow rode over to the address Claymore had given him. It was one of a handful of houses in the tiny village of Kitty Hawk, and Rudolph came out on the porch to greet him as he parked his buggy. "Come in, Snow. My brother's already here."

Ben entered and took a chair in the sparsely furnished parlor. A woman's touch was obviously lacking and it occurred to him for the first time that the elder Claymore was probably not married. He shook hands with Roderick and said, "I didn't see you this morning."

"I had business," Roderick answered. "I hear the flying machine never got off the ground."

"They're repairing it. They plan to try again on Thursday."

Rudolph came in and sat down. "Some of the folks around here are helping them. We got more important things on our minds."

"Tell me about it," Ben suggested. "Tell me why that property of yours is so valuable. Is there really pirate treasure buried there?"

The older brother smiled slightly. "Next best thing, according to Professor Minder. You know about the Lost Colony and that business on Roanoke Island?"

"A little."

"Well, historians have always speculated that the colonists went south to another island, if they weren't killed by Indians. Minder went there and nosed around. He decided they came north instead, right here to the beach at Kitty Hawk. Look at this here map. You can see that the abandoned Fort Raleigh was at the very northern tip of Roanoke, not ten miles across the water from where we are now."

"Minder told you this?"

"Damned right!" Roderick said. "He did a little digging by our property there and came up with evidence of settlement!"

Rudolph showed Ben a bowl with a piece missing from it. "See this? It's not Indian. It's the sort the colonists brought with them from England."

"But you were keeping this a secret?" Ben asked.

"Had to! Other people own some of that beach land, especially near the village here. We started buying it up. An old settlement like that could mean a spot people would pay to see. It could make us rich."

"Who knew about this?" Ben asked.

"Only the two of us and Minder. That's why I went so far away to hire a guard. I didn't want any of the locals getting wind of what we were trying to hide."

"How much land have you bought?"

"Around twenty thousand dollars' worth so far. Minder agreed to act as a middleman so the people wouldn't know we were the buyers."

"And that's what you've been digging for?" Ben asked.

Rudolph nodded. "We uncovered some more things on our own, too—a few trinkets and a sword."

Roderick scratched at his cheek. "We'd better check on those land deeds in the morning. With Minder dead, we could be out twenty grand."

"I've already thought of that," his brother answered sourly.

Ben left them going over their records, trying to establish the extent of their possible losses.

On Tuesday afternoon, the State Police officer, Rellens, showed up at the Boyers' house to see Ben. He sat down heavily and flipped open his notebook. "This case has taken a couple of surprising turns," he said. "I need to interview witnesses again, especially those who were standing closest to the victim."

"Miss Boyers is teaching today," Ben told him.

"You'll do for a beginning. It seems one of the men in that crowd of spectators gave a false name and address. Dick Roer, of Kill Devil Hills. No such person."

"You think you let the murderer walk away?"

"Looks like it," he said glumly. "I seem to remember him vaguely. Had a Teddy Roosevelt mustache and was wearing a wool cap. Of course, the mustache could have been a fake. Do you remember anyone looking like that near you?"

"No," Ben answered honestly. "But I wasn't concentrating on the crowd."

"All right." Rellens closed his notebook, preparing to leave.

"You said the case had taken a couple of surprising turns. What else?"

"The dead man—Minder. It turns out he was a fake, too. There's no Professor Minder connected with any of the universities in Raleigh."

"Interesting," Ben admitted. "Two men with false identities on the beach yesterday—one a murderer and one a victim."

"It looks that way." Rellens nodded.

"But why was Minder using a false name? Who was he?"

"We'll find out," Rellens promised. "You'll be here for the next few days, Mr. Snow?"

"At least till after Thursday's flight."

"That's good," Rellens said and was gone.

On Wednesday Ben Snow sought out Rudolph Claymore on his ice route. He found him lugging fifty-pound blocks into a little cafe in Kill Devil Hills. "I wanted to ask you about your brother," he said.

"He's back at the ice house. You can find him there."

"He was in love with Elizabeth Boyers, wasn't he?"

"Still is, far as I know. But she's sappy over that teacher, Mark Freen. It hit my brother hard."

"Ever hear of someone named Dick Roer around here?"

"Can't say that I have."

"Rellens thinks that was the name the killer used on Monday."

"Never heard of him." Claymore climbed into the back of his wagon and used an ice pick to loosen another fifty-pound block.

"That looks like hard work."

Rudolph shrugged. "It's a living." He flipped the pick into the next block in line. "It pays the bills till something big like that Lost Colony comes along."

"What if the Lost Colony never happens? What if Professor Minder was a fraud?"

Rudolph Claymore blinked and stared at Ben. "What are you saying?"

"Have you and your brother checked on that property yet?"

"He's doing it today."

"I wish you luck," Ben said and started to walk away.

"Wait a minute!" Claymore said, hurrying after him. "What are you trying to tell me?"

"That Minder was a fraud. That wasn't his real name, and chances are those trinkets in the sand were put there by him so you'd find them. Out West we call it salting a mine—putting a few gold nuggets near the surface for the suckers to find."

"But the property—"

"If he was trying to swindle someone, it must have been you. He probably took your twenty thousand and faked some papers, without ever buying the land."

"That—"

Ben left him standing by his ice wagon, still swearing.

The younger Claymore was a bit more difficult to track down. He was gone from the ice house by the time Ben reached it and he had to stop at a couple of nearby bars before he spotted Roderick's horse tethered outside the village stable. He found the young man inside, seeing to the repair of one of his saddle stirrups.

"I had a talk with your brother this morning," Ben told him. "Could I have a few words with you outside?"

Roderick shrugged. "I suppose so. You going to be on guard at the beach again tomorrow?"

"I'll be there. But when you hear what I have to say, you may decide you don't need me." Ben told him quickly what he'd told his brother, about Professor Minder's false identity and the probable swindle. Roderick's reaction wasn't quite as violent as his brother's, but it was obvious he was upset.

"I always wondered about that guy. He didn't seem right for a professor."

"Have you checked on the deeds yet?"

"I was on my way there now."

"There's something else," Ben said.

"What's that?"

"The police think Minder's killer is a man named Dick Roer."

The color drained from Roderick's face.

"That's you, isn't it? Dick Roer is a simple anagram for Roderick."

"I don't know what you mean."

"You were on the beach Monday morning, wearing a wool cap and a false mustache. You killed Professor Minder."

"I didn't! That's not true!"

"Why else would you be there in disguise?"

"That's none of your business. We hired you to guard our property, not to snoop around."

"If you don't answer me, you'll have to answer to the police."

He glowered and started to walk away, then thought better of it. "All right—if you must know. I wanted to see Elizabeth!"

"See her?"

"With him. With that Freen fellow. I wanted to hear what they were talking about."

"You disguised yourself to spy on Elizabeth Boyers?"

"Yes." His voice had dropped and he wouldn't meet Ben's eyes. "I love her."

"You can't accept the fact that she might find pleasure with another man?"

"I just wanted to hear what they talked about, to see for myself if she really cared for him. That's all. I barely realized Minder was there."

"All right," Ben said, not knowing whether he believed him nor not. "Will you be there in the morning?"

"Yes," Roderick answered.

"In disguise?"

"There's no point in it now, is there?"

Thursday morning dawned clear but freezing cold. When Ben reached the beach at Kitty Hawk in the company of Mark Freen and Elizabeth, they were saying the wind off the ocean was blowing at twenty-seven miles an hour. The few spectators were bundled against the cold and some were doubting the Wright brothers would attempt the flight.

But shortly after nine A.M., Wilbur and Orville gathered up their five assistants and once more hauled the machine from its shed. It was lifted onto the trolley at the base of Kill Devil Hill.

In addition to Elizabeth and Freen, who'd taken off another day from their teaching, both Claymore brothers were in attendance. And Ben saw Rellens pacing nearby. The cast was assembled.

Rudolph came up to stand next to Ben. "What did you say to my brother yesterday? Whatever it was, he's been pretty upset by it. He didn't even want to come out here today."

"I notice he's staying clear of Elizabeth Boyers."

"Well, they used to go together. I suppose he's jealous of her friend."

It seemed to take the Wrights forever to make their adjustments to the *Flyer* and the cold wind drove a few of the less hardy souls away. Orville was busy setting up the tripod for his camera, then aiming it at the end of the launching track. If the plane became airborne, he wanted a picture for the ages.

Finally, at 10:30, they were ready.

It was young Orville's turn to be at the controls this time and he glanced around for someone to snap the shutter of his camera. He called to one of the townspeople who'd been helping out and asked him to take the picture if the plane became airborne. Then he climbed aboard the *Flyer* and strapped himself down. Wilbur pulled the cap down more snugly on his head and gripped the lower right wingtip of the biplane.

The engine started and the propellers began to turn. The *Flyer* moved on its track. Wilbur began trotting alongside, holding the wingtip steady.

"He didn't do that on Monday," Rudolph Claymore remarked.

And then Orville opened the throttle more, bringing the engine to full power. The time was 10:35.

"No, he didn't," Ben Snow agreed. "But how did you know if you weren't here?"

The *Flyer* lifted from its track, airborne. Wilbur released the wing as the camera shutter clicked. A cheer went up from the small group of spectators.

The machine wobbled and swooped down, its runner hitting the sand. The flight had lasted only twelve seconds, never more than ten feet off the ground, but it had covered 120 feet.

People were running forward. Rudolph Claymore started to move, but Ben restrained him. "You knew what happened on Monday because you were here. Because you came to murder the man who'd swindled you."

"You think I was this Dick Roer?"

"No, that was your brother, spying on Elizabeth."

"But everyone else in the crowd was accounted for!"

"You never joined the crowd, Rudolph. You hid behind a sand dune, and while all eyes were on the Wrights at the crucial moment, you sneaked up just close enough to *throw* that knife into Minder's back, just like you flipped that ice pick into the cake yesterday. You never came closer than fifteen or twenty feet, and the sand was too trampled to show footprints. No one saw you because we were all looking in the opposite direction."

"But I didn't know he was a swindler until you told me yesterday!" Rudolph argued.

"You put on a very good act, but I think you knew. When your brother met me, he said you'd gone to the state capital on business. That's Raleigh, where Minder claimed to teach. You checked on him while you were there and discovered he was a fake. You came back here and killed him the first chance you had."

Rellens had been overhearing the conversation and now he stepped forward. "Do you have anything to say, Mr. Claymore?"

The fight had gone out of Rudolph. "Only that he deserved to die for swindling us. No jury will convict me."

Ben Snow left town the following morning. The Claymores' land didn't need protection any longer and he never heard what the jury decided. For that matter, it was a few years before he heard the Wright brothers mentioned again. They made four successful flights that December 17th at Kitty Hawk, and their father spread the news, but only two newspapers in the country carried a report the following day.

No crowds came to Kitty Hawk. The Claymores hadn't needed Ben Snow after all.

CLARK HOWARD

Wild Things

TREE O'HARA LAY PRONE ON THE GROUND and peered down at
a little crossroads settlement through twelve-power binoculars. He
was in a stand of tall pines six hundred yards or so up the mountain. The settlement, which did not even have a name, consisted of a
Conoco gas station, a general store, and a roadhouse restaurant, each
occupying a corner where the two mountain highways intersected. The
fourth corner was unimproved and stood vacant except for a roadsign
which read BUTTE 112.

It was Sunday afternoon and both the Conoco station and the general
store were closed. The roadhouse restaurant was open but there was only
one car parked in front of it: a five-year-old Cadillac with California plates.

Tree lowered the binoculars and got to his feet. He was a tall, once lean
man, now beginning to flesh out with his age approaching forty; but still
muscular, still quick. His most striking feature was his eyes—they were
cold, and so black and flat they could have passed as sightless. He wore
denim jeans and a Levi jacket over a faded work shirt; on his feet were lace-
up lumberjack boots.

Leaving the edge of the pines, Tree walked briskly another hundred
yards into the forest where he had left his horse. It was an Appaloosa, the
horse—its foreparts white as a perfect cloud, its loin and shank spotted
with round black markings. A mare, she stood just under fifteen hands
high. When Tree had caught her, wild, in the Nez Perce National Forest
four years earlier she had been a fast and trim thousand or so pounds. Now
he reckoned she weighed around twelve hundred. She had fattened out
from their inactive life in the upper forest. Tree rode her on a regular basis

only twice a month, when he came down to the settlement for supplies. But she was a happy animal—she loved the man who had captured her, and Tree guessed that if he ever had to do any hard riding, she would run her heart out for him.

The mare snorted and dug at the ground with one hoof as Tree approached. "Easy, Elk," he said quietly. Elk City, west of the Bitterroot Range, was where he had roped her, so he had named her Elk. He rubbed her throat now to calm her, then stepped back to the saddle and put his binoculars in a case hanging from the horn. From a blanket roll behind the saddle he removed a pair of telephone-pole climbers and buckled them to the inside of his legs. From one saddlebag, he took a telephone lineman's intercept set—a receiver with a dial built into it and two magnesium clips for tapping into a wire—and hooked it onto his belt. "Keep still," he said to Elk, rubbing her throat again.

Walking fifty feet to a string of telephone poles that went up and over the mountain, Tree put on gloves and climbed one of them to its crossbeam. He hooked one arm around the beam to steady himself. With his free hand he laid the intercept set on the beam, attached the magnesium clips to one of the telephone wires, and got a dial tone in the receiver. He dialed the number of the restaurant at the crossroads. John Grey Sky, the Shoshone owner, answered.

"John," said Tree without preliminary, "who's the Caddy belong to?"

"Oh, Tree, it's you. The Caddy? Nobody, man. A couple of sharpies and some bimbo passing through. They're slopping down beer and arguing about which route to take to Chicago."

"What do they look like?" Tree asked. "The men, I mean."

"Losers," said John. "Small-timers, punks."

"You're sure? They're not just pulling an act?"

"Listen, brother, I know rabble when I see it," John assured him. "You're safe. Come on down. I got your supplies."

"Okay," Tree said. He had hesitated just a beat before answering. He hoped John Grey Sky had not noticed. He and John had been friends for twenty-five years, since attending Caribou Indian School together as young boys. It would never do to insult a friend of such long standing by doubting his judgment. If Grey Sky said he would be safe, Tree had to assume he would be. All the same, when he got back to Elk and put his equipment away, he took a loaded forty-five automatic from the saddlebag, jacked a round into the chamber, thumbed the safety on, and stuck it in his waistband under the Levi jacket where it could not be seen.

Tree led the Appaloosa to the edge of the pines and tied her reins to a buffalobur shrub. The bush had just enough prickly spines on it to discourage Elk from nibbling the reins untied and following him, as she liked to do. "Be a good girl," he said, scratching her ears. "I'll bring you an apple."

Tree made his way down the slope and came onto the highway around the bend from the roadhouse. He approached the crossroads from behind the closed Conoco station, aware with every step of the gun in his waistband. From the side of the station he studied the car with the California plates. The tires were fairly worn, there was some rust on the chrome, and a small dent in the right rear fender had been left unrepaired. It looked like a loser's car, all right, just as Grey Sky had said. All the same, Tree was glad he had the gun.

Hurrying across to the rear of the roadhouse, Tree slipped through the open back door into the kitchen. John Grey Sky was scraping down his fry grill. "Hey, bro," he said.

"Hey, John." Tree's eyes swept the room, looking for anything out of the ordinary. Through the service window he could hear the voices of Grey Sky's three customers.

"Your supplies are there on the meat table," Grey Sky said.

Tree stepped over to a butcher block and examined the contents of a burlap bag: cheese, coffee, tins of meat, dry cereal, powdered milk, beef jerky, magazines, a dozen fresh apples for Elk. "You get my animal food?" he asked the roadhouse owner.

"Under the table."

Tree pulled out a twenty-pound sack of processed dry animal food pellets. Similar to the food sold commercially to feed dogs and cats, it differed in that it contained flavors attractive to wild as opposed to domestic animals.

"You must be feeding half the wild things on that mountain," Grey Sky commented. "They're going to have to learn to scavenge all over again after you're gone."

Tree felt himself tense. "After I'm gone where?"

John Grey Sky shrugged. "Wherever."

Tree stared at his friend's back. Grey Sky could get a lot of money for betraying Tree O'Hara. Tree wondered if his friend was ever tempted.

The voices from the front of the restaurant grew louder. "You're getting a free lift to Chicago," a man's voice said. "Least you could do is be a little more friendly."

"Drop dead," a woman's throaty voice replied. There was a loud cracking noise then—the unmistakable sound of a face being slapped.

Frowning at each other, Tree and Grey Sky walked out from the kitchen. One of the men was standing, half bent over the table. The woman, seated, was staring up at him defiantly, one side of her face turning an angry red.

"You kick dogs, too?" she asked.

He hit her again, backhanded, on the other side of her face.

"Hey, man, no rough stuff in here!" Grey Sky said.

The man raised his hand again.

"Don't do it," Tree said. His voice, like his eyes, was flat and hard. It was clearly an order.

The man at the table turned around, one hand reaching for an empty beer bottle. "Who the hell are you?"

"Don't matter who I am," Tree said. He pulled back one side of his Levi jacket to expose the gun. "Don't hit her again."

"You gonna kill me if I do?" the man challenged with a sneer.

"No, just cripple you," Tree replied matter-of-factly. "I'll put one in your left instep. Blow your foot all to pieces."

The other man at the table intervened. "Hold it, chief," he said with a forced smile. "We don't want no hassle." He took the bottle from his friend's hand and put it down. "Come on, Lou, forget it. It's their patch." Picking up the check Grey Sky had given them, he looked at it and put some money on the table. "You coming?" he asked the woman.

"Not on your life," she said. Both sides of her face were now violently red.

"Please yourself. Come on, Lou."

The two men started to leave.

"Wait a minute, I've got a suitcase in that car!" the woman said urgently.

"Come on," Tree said. He went outside and stood with her while Lou opened the trunk and set her suitcase on the ground. Then the two men got in the Caddy and drove off.

The woman picked up her suitcase and followed Tree back inside. "Thanks," she said.

"Forget it," Tree told her. He studied her for a moment. She was, he guessed, an old twenty-five. There was no telling what her true hair color was—bottle blonde with black roots was what he could see. Too much make-up. A well used but still good body. A bimbo, he thought. Like Grey Sky had said. The kind who'd take a free ride with two losers in a five-year-old Caddy.

"What time's the next bus through here?" she asked uncomfortable under Tree's scrutiny.

"Friday," said Grey Sky.

"Friday! This is only Sunday. Are you kidding me?"

"I never kid about anything as serious as bus service. Just once a week the bus comes over the mountain. Rest of the time it follows the Interstate around the mountain." Grey Sky looked over at his friend. Tree was staring at him, the realization having just dawned on him that the roadhouse owner was right. "Didn't think about that, did you, Galahad?" asked Grey Sky.

"Where the hell am I going to stay until Friday?" the woman asked in a half whine. "I don't have money for a motel."

"That works out just fine," Grey Sky said, "cause there's no motel anyway."

"Well, what am I gonna do!" she shrieked.

Tree looked at his friend. Grey Sky held both hands up, palms out.

"Not me, bro. I got my wife, four kids, my wife's mother, my unemployed brother-in-law and *his* wife and two kids—all in a two-bedroom, one-bath house. Sorry."

"Could you let her sleep here, put a cot in the kitchen—?"

Grey Sky shook his head. "My insurance don't allow overnight occupation of the premises. If she accidentally burned the place down, I couldn't collect a nickel. You're going to have to handle this good deed yourself, Galahad."

Tree glared at his friend. Grey Sky was obviously enjoying himself.

* * *

He could hear the woman panting as she trudged along behind him, lugging her suitcase with both hands. "How—much farther—is it?" she gasped.

"Not far." Carrying the burlap bag of supplies on one shoulder, the sack of animal food on the other, Tree deliberately kept his pace slow to allow her to keep up with him. But when he saw that she was falling too far behind anyway, he stopped to let her rest.

"How come you live up in the mountains anyway?" she demanded. "You antisocial? Don't you like people?"

"As a matter of fact, I don't," he said, "very much."

Now it was her turn to study him. She was not sure whether she liked what she saw. Those eyes of his didn't seem to have even a degree of warmth in them. "What'd that fellow down there say your name was? Galahad?"

"He was just trying to be funny. My name's Tree O'Hara."

"Tree? How'd you get a name like that?"

"My mother's family name. She was Indian. I'm one-quarter Minnetonka."

"Oh. Well, my name's Violet. I was named after a flower. *You* can call me Vi."

He nodded. "Come on," he said, "let's go on."

After one more rest stop, they came to the edge of the pines where Elk waited. As they approached, the mare snorted and pawed the ground edgily. "She smells you," Tree said. "She knows you're a woman. She's jealous. Come on—easy, baby," he said to Elk, putting an arm under her neck.

"Sure is a funny-looking horse," Vi said. "Looks like the front of one and the back of another, stuck together."

Tree threw her an irritated glance. "This happens to be an Appaloosa. It's one of the most intelligent breeds of horse in the world, as well as one of the fastest. This horse has more stamina and endurance than any other breed you can name. It is the best stock horse, the best show horse—"

"All's I said was it was funny-looking," she interrupted. "I'm sorry, but that's my opinion. Personally, I like Palaminos. Like Trigger, you know?"

Tree turned away in disgust. *Trigger!* A Hollywood horse. Great spirits!

Tree lashed the two sacks one on top of each other just behind the blanket roll, then helped Vi into the saddle. She had to hike her skirt far up on her thighs in order to straddle the horse's back, but it didn't seem to bother her. Tree noticed that her legs were well rounded, fleshy—in fact, all of her was well rounded and fleshy; she wasn't skinny anywhere, a fact that Tree approved of. He didn't care for overly slim women—they always looked too fragile, like stickwood. Elk was of a different mind, however; the mare did not like the woman at all, and showed it by shuffling around skittishly and snorting loudly through flared nostrils. Tree finally had to cut up an apple and feed it to her so they could be on their way.

The trip to the cabin took another two hours, Tree leading the horse and rider while carrying Vi's suitcase in his free hand. He didn't mind the walk—in fact, he was glad to get the exercise because he knew he was about ten pounds overweight. For the first couple of years after he had gone into hiding he had made a point of exercising five days a week—calisthenics, weight-lifting, jogging through the woods. That, along with chopping wood and pumping water out of his cistern, had kept him nicely in shape. But for the past three or four years he had grown lazy: sleeping late, not watching his diet, lying around like a much older man. He had become complacent in his mountain hideaway. He felt safe there; only rarely did he feel threatened any more. After six years, he figured they had stopped looking for him.

Probably.

Maybe.

*　　*　　*

Tree and the woman arrived at the cabin just at twilight. It sat on a small clearing at the six-thousand-foot level in the Beaverhead Forest, just east of the Continental Divide. When the clouds were high, Chief Joseph Pass could be seen from the porch. If they were very high, one could regularly see the moon and the sun at the same time, in different parts of the sky. The natural beauty of the place was indelible. The woman didn't notice the scenery, however—she was too acutely aware of how isolated it was.

"Look, before we go in," Vi said, "I think we ought to get something straight. I had a falling-out with those other two guys because they had some weird ideas about how I should pay for my ride. I hope you're not thinking along those same lines as far as room-and-board goes."

"I'm not," Tree told her.

He said it a little too quickly to suit her. With a little too much determination. She hesitated on the porch, not following him into the cabin.

"Listen, no offense, you understand," she said, "but you're not—well, *peculiar* or anything, are you? I mean, living up here all alone—"

Tree returned to the doorway and faced her. "Why don't you lighten up?" he said. "You'll be safe here. But if you don't believe me, hike on back down the mountain and make other arrangements."

"A girl can't be too careful, is all I mean. I have this problem in that men usually find me very attractive—"

"I don't," Tree assured her. "My taste runs to darker women. When I get lonely, I ride down to the Salmon River Reservation. Lots of nice Nez Perce and Shoshone women down there. They like me because my skin's light. I stay for a few days and then come back home. I was just down to the reservation last week, so I'm settled for about a month now. Like I said, you're safe."

Turning, he walked away. When she finally came into the cabin several minutes later, she found her suitcase on the bed in the tiny bedroom. Tree had decided, he told her, to sleep on the couch. Not because he was such a gentleman—he just didn't like the idea of leaving her out in the main room alone all night. The main room—which was a kitchen-living room—was where he had the television, shortwave receiver, his books, magazines, guns, ammunition: things he didn't want her fooling with. Sleeping on the couch, he could keep an eye on everything.

After Tree took care of Elk, rubbing her down briskly and putting her in the one-horse lean-to stable he had built onto the rear of the cabin, he came back into the cabin just in time to hear Vi, in the bedroom, say, "Damn!"

"What's the trouble?" he asked.

"My cosmetics bag! It was in the back seat of the car! I don't have any makeup!"

"Tough break," he said indifferently.

He went into the kitchen, unpacked his supplies, and began preparing supper. Presently Vi came in.

"Listen, I can cook," she said. "Why don't you let me fix supper?"

"I'll do it," he replied. "I know how I like things."

Vi shrugged. Strolling, she looked the place over. "You've got enough books," she commented. "All the comforts of home, too—radio, TV everything. How do you manage it way up here?"

"I manage," Tree said. He was not about to share any confidences with her. For electrical power he had illegally tapped into a main power line running across the mountain. For water he had a cistern next to the cabin. For television, a microwave dish he had assembled on the roof, which stole signals from the sky. For shortwave, a simple antenna wire strung up a high tree. For backup, a battery-operated generator, constantly charging off the tapped electricity.

"Okay if I look at these old magazines?" she asked, standing in front of the bookcase where he kept them.

"Sure. But do me a favor first. Step around back and make sure I closed the lean-to door, will you? I don't want Elk to be in a draft."

While she was out of the cabin, he went quickly to the bookcase, took a small scrapbook from one of the shelves, and put it on top of the bookcase out of her sight and reach. Then he returned to the kitchen.

They shared an uneasy supper, both telling whatever lies they felt necessary to project or protect their respective images. Tree told Vi he had originally come to live in the mountains to avoid the Vietnam draft, and had not gone back because he didn't relish the idea of steady employment. He said he worked down at the roadhouse restaurant during tourist season to earn enough to live on the rest of the year. Vi told Tree that she was a model on her way to Chicago for a job at Marshall Field's. Because she wasn't due there for another week, she had accepted a ride with the two guys in the Cadillac. She had thought, she said, that they were legitimate businessmen, traveling salesmen or something, and had been very surprised to learn they were just a couple of petty hustlers.

Because each of them was lying, neither Tree or the woman asked any questions of the other. They kept conversation to a minimum. After supper, Vi found that she was extremely tired. It was the climb and the altitude, Tree told her. "Your blood's thinned out. Better go to bed." She did, and fell into an immediate deep sleep.

When he was sure she was sleeping soundly, Tree slipped into the bedroom and got her purse. He brought it into the main room and searched it. There was an expired Illinois driver's license, a faded Social Security card, an address book containing no names that Tree recognized, a blank, unmailed postcard with a photo on it of Harold's Club in Reno, and twelve dollars.

A loser's purse for sure, Tree thought. He put it back in the bedroom.

Later, Tree fed Elk, opened his nightly bottle of beer, chewed a little peyote, and watched an old John Garfield movie on some channel he was pulling in from a satellite. When the movie was over, he spread his sleeping bag on the couch, stripped, climbed in, and went to sleep, the forty-five lying loaded and cocked on the floor just inches away.

*   *   *

The next morning, Vi found him out back of the cabin with his wild things. She stood out of sight around a corner of the cabin and watched him feed them from the sack of pellet food he had brought back. She was amazed at the number and variety of the animals. Some of them she couldn't even identify—others, like the rabbits, squirrels, and small deer she knew. Tree knelt right in their midst and fed them from his open hand. The sight of it was a wonder to her.

"You can come around and watch if you want to," he told her without looking around. "Just don't make any sudden moves."

Vi eased around the corner but stayed well back from the menagerie. "How'd you know I was there?" she asked curiously.

"This little mule deer told me," he said, scratching the middle forehead of a somewhat scroungy, unattractive deer. "I saw its nostrils flare—that meant a new scent was close by. Mule deer have very poor eyesight; they have to depend on their sense of smell for survival." He looked at her over his shoulder and grinned. "Plus which, I saw your shadow."

"Oh, you!" She moved a little closer. "What in the world are all of them? What's that reddish one with the yellow belly?"

"Ermine weasel. Turns pure white in the winter. That's when the trappers go after them."

"And that one, by the deer?"

"Pronghorn. It's a kind of bastard antelope." He stood up and started pointing. "That's a wolverine over there: baby wolf. This big guy with the white mark on his forehead is a badger. My mother's people named him. They called the white mark a badge. I bet you didn't know 'badge' was an Indian word."

She shook her head. "No."

Tree smiled. "Most cops don't, either."

"What's that one, with the partly webbed feet?"

"That's the one the ladies like: she's a mink. Next to her there—that big shiny grey animal—that's a marten."

From a nearby limb came a clipped, scolding bird call. Tree looked over at a long-tailed black-and-white bird chattering noisily.

"All right," he said. He stepped out of the center of the wild things, closing the bag, and came over to where Vi stood. From a wooden storage box, he removed another bag and scooped out a handful of its contents. "Bird seed," he said. He took her hand. It felt good. "Come on."

She let him lead her over to a low aspen and watched him hold out his open hand to feed the bird. "It's a magpie," he told her. "Biggest nag in the woods. Never gives you a minute's peace if he's hungry."

After a couple of minutes, he closed his hand. "That's enough, Porky. I named him Porky 'cause he's such a pig."

He bobbed his chin toward another tree, a spruce. "Want to see an owl?" They walked over to a low, heavily leafed limb where a small, unpleasant-looking owl was hunched. Its oversized head seemed to comprise half of its body, and its big direct eyes and hooked beak gave it a definite aura of hostility.

"Is it mad?" Vi asked, holding back tentatively.

"No," said Tree, "just sleepy. He'll burrow down into the leaves and go to sleep in a bit." Tree fed the owl, as he had the magpie, from his palm. "Mostly he eats forest mice, but he likes these seeds, too." With the last of the seed, he led Vi to a small flat boulder jutting up from the ground like a fist. He sprinkled the rest of the seed on the flat of the rock and drew Vi a few feet away from it. "Now you'll see my favorite wild thing," he said quietly.

As they watched, a glossy black bird with wild yellow eyes swooped gracefully onto the rock and, after a cautious look around, began eating. As it ate, it honed its already razor-sharp talons on the rock.

"That's Midnight," Tree told her. "A raven."

"Won't it eat out of your hand like the others?"

"Not yet. He doesn't trust me enough yet. Someday he will. In another few years."

They walked back to the rear of the cabin. A few of the wild things were still there. Vi shook her head in wonder. "I didn't know animals were that friendly."

"They aren't, as a rule," Tree said. "That wolverine there, she's a natural enemy to the mink, the rabbit, and the marten. They're usually her prey. And the badger generally goes after the ermine weasel when he sees one. But they know I don't allow any fighting here in the clearing. I chase them off if they start fighting. It doesn't take long for them to learn that not fighting is best. Animals are a lot smarter than people."

"You really love them, don't you? These animals?"

"Yeah, I guess I do," Tree admitted. "It makes me feel good when I bring two natural enemies together and get them both to eat out of my hand at the same time."

"Too bad that can't be done with people," Vi remarked. "It would stop all the war and killing in the world."

"No, it wouldn't," Tree said quietly. "People would still kill, for sport. Man is the only animal that kills for sport, you'd never stop that. Man will always have to kill. It's his nature."

Vi stared at him. As he spoke, his eyes seemed to grow colder.

The next morning when Vi came out of the bedroom, Tree was at his shortwave set listening to an English-language broadcast from Moscow. "Don't look at me," she said. "I'm totally out of makeup and I look awful."

Tree did look at her, and liked what he saw. "You look fine to me," he said.

"Nice and scrubbed." He switched off the radio. "Want to go fishing with me?" he asked. He didn't want to leave her alone in the cabin.

"I don't know how to fish."

"I'll teach you. Or you can just watch. We can take some food and have a picnic."

Vi consented and together they packed a knapsack with lunch. Tree got his lines and bait, and they trudged up-mountain several hundred yards toward a narrow stream of cold snow-water coming from high up.

"How come everything's always uphill?" Vi complained, taking his hand so he could help her. "Isn't anything ever downhill?"

"Nothing worthwhile," Tree replied matter-of-factly.

They walked along the stream and Tree showed her how to set fish lines without poles or other apparatus. "Poles scare fish off," he explained. "They cast a shadow over the water."

When he had the lines set, they walked on to a point where the stream bed dropped six feet, creating a low waterfall. There the water rushed and formed whitecaps, and occasionally they could see a mountain trout swimming upstream, actually jumping up the falling water. They found a place to open the knapsack and eat. While they were there, Vi told him about herself.

"I was one of those young girls with stars in her eyes who went out to California to get into the movies. Or TV Or modeling—*anything*, you know, except the nine-to-five office bit. It took me a while to realize I wasn't the only one with big ideas. There were hundreds of others just like me. We were all pilgrims who made it to Mecca—only Mecca turned out to be Hustle City. I was lucky—I ended up waiting tables at a Hamburger Hamlet. A lot of others weren't lucky. They ended up on drugs or selling themselves on Hollywood Boulevard for some pimp, or even worse. That's why when the two sports in the Cadillac asked if I wanted a ride east, I took it."

"No modeling job at Marshall Field's?"

Vi shook her head. "The most I've got to look forward to is a monotonous job in some dull office."

"That's more than some people have got," Tree commented darkly.

*   *   *

That night, her third night at the cabin, Tree let her cook for him. She made breaded pork chops from his freezer and managed to whip up some decent mashed potatoes from his dehydrated food stock.

"Not bad," he said. "Where'd you learn to cook?"

"Marshall High School, on the west side of Chicago. Home Ec was required. Where'd you go to school?"

"A reservation in Idaho."

"What was it like living on a reservation?"

"Poor," he said quietly. "Cold poor. Hungry poor. Hard-knock poor."

"How'd you get away from it?"

"I joined the Army." He realized the slip at once.

"You told me you came up here to evade the draft," she reminded him.

Tree looked down at the table for a long, silent moment. Finally he met her eyes. "That was a lie. But I can't tell you the truth. Let's just leave it alone for the rest of the time you're here, okay?"

They resumed eating, with no further conversation for several minutes. Finally Vi put her fork down and rose.

"I told you the truth about me," she said. It was clearly an accusation. She left the table and went outside.

Tree finished his supper, cleared off the table, and washed the dishes. Then he got an apple out of the food locker for Elk and went outside. Vi was sitting on the porch looking up at a sky full of stars that looked close enough to touch.

"Want to feed this apple to Elk?" Tree asked.

"Elk doesn't like me," Vi said.

"She's just not used to you. Come, you can feed her." Vi did not move. Tree coaxed her. "Come on. I'll show you how. It's easy. Come on."

Finally Vi got up and went with him around to the lean-to. Tree cut the apple into sixths and showed Vi how to hold her hand out straight, palm up, so that the horse could take the food with its lips and not hurt Vi's hand with its powerful teeth. Vi was nervous, but Elk, whose affections could always be bought with fresh apples, played the perfect lady and ate properly.

"Go ahead, scratch her neck," Tree said. "She likes that."

"Don't we all," Vi replied mostly to herself

Vi petted the Appaloosa for awhile, then Tree closed the stall and they returned to the porch.

"I'll let you help me feed the wild things in the morning if you like," he offered.

"You don't have to."

"I don't want you to be mad."

"I'm not. I don't blame you for not trusting me."

"It's not that I don't trust you. It's just something I don't talk about. Not to anybody."

She was sitting in a shaft of light from the window and Tree saw her shrug. "Okay," she said.

"I'm sorry."

Another shrug. "Sure."

They sat without speaking for ten minutes, listening to the night sounds of the cool, high-mountain evening. Finally Vi stood up. "I think I'll go to bed. Goodnight."

"Goodnight."

Tree remained on the porch for a long time, thinking about things—the vivid dangerous past, the nebulous, unsure future, and the clear, demanding present. He admitted to himself that he wanted the woman, then told himself in definite, forceful language that he could not have her. Alone is safest, he reminded himself. Alone is smartest. Alone is best.

He grunted softly. Alone was also loneliest.

It was midnight when he finally went inside, stripped down, and slid into his sleeping bag. But he couldn't sleep. It was as if he was waiting for something.

He was still awake when she came to him in the darkness.

*　　*　　*

At first they were skittish about her, made nervous by the sight and scent of her so close. But because they trusted Tree so completely they gradually eased their way up to her. Soon she was kneeling in their midst just as Tree did, and they were nuzzling her hands, putting front paws up on her legs, making their individual little noises to get her attention. She learned that the mule deer and the pronghorn would nibble at her ears with their lips if she paid too much attention to the ground animals and not enough to them. Feeding the wild things was a decided thrill for Vi—she couldn't wait for the next day to feed them again.

"I want to feed them every morning!" she said with delight. Tree looked curiously at her and Vi's smile faded. "I forgot," she said. "I've only got two more mornings, haven't I? The bus comes over the mountain on Friday."

Tree nodded. "Yes. On Friday."

They went swimming that afternoon, in the same stream in which they'd fished the previous day. Vi thought she was going to freeze.

"It's like ice water!" she shrieked.

"It is ice water," Tree said, laughing. "It's melted snow from way up. Move around—you'll get warm."

She did move around, but she did not warm up. After five minutes she had to get out. Tree wrapped her in a blanket and left her on the bank while he swam for another quarter hour. When he came out, his tan body shone like the coats of the wild things who were his friends.

After their swim, they walked arm-in-arm back to the cabin and Tree built a fire. They stretched out on a Navajo blanket in front of the fireplace, chewed some peyote, slept, woke up and made love, and slept again.

That night, Tree said, "You don't want to leave, do you?"

Vi shrugged. "I don't want to mess with your life, Tree. You got everything you want up here. The one thing you haven't got—well, it's available down on the Salmon River Reservation when you want it, and you don't have to bring it home with you." She looked away from him. "I think it would be bad for both of us if I stayed."

They didn't discuss it any further that night, each retreating into silence.

On Thursday morning, Tree was sick.

"My cooking," Vi said lightly. "Now you know why I've never married."

"Probably the peyote," he told her. "It gives you a great feeling but sometimes it raises hell with the digestive system. How's your stomach?"

"Fine. Let me *mix* you some cold powdered milk—that'll probably settle it."

The milk helped some, but later in the day he had severe nausea and a bad headache.

"Do you have any medicine up here at all?" Vi asked. He directed her to a cabinet in the kitchen where he had aspirin, codeine, and Valium tablets. She gave him two of each and made him take a nap in the bedroom.

While he was sleeping, she went to the bookcase and took down the scrapbook he had hidden on top of it. She had watched through the window the night he had put it there. Opening it on the table, she read the newspaper clippings he had saved. The stories they told were different, but they all had common headlines:

LABOR LEADER SLAIN, one read.

GANGLAND BOSS FOUND DEAD, read another.

WITNESS MURDERED IN HOTEL.

RACKETS INFORMER EXECUTED.

GAMBLER KILLED IN MIAMI.

The clippings had datelines covering a five-year period. The last one was dated six years earlier.

Tree came out of the bedroom while she still had the scrapbook open in front of her. He was very pale, but his eyes were still dark and dangerous. He was fully dressed and Vi couldn't tell whether he had his gun or not.

He sat down heavily across from her. "You enjoy my press notices?" he asked.

Vi closed the scrapbook. "They ended six years ago. That was when you came to live up here. What happened?"

"They wanted me to hit a woman," he said. "A young woman with a brace on one leg, who was going into a convent of handicapped nuns who taught handicapped children. She was heir to a lot of money, but she was going to take a vow of poverty and give it all to the order she was joining. A cousin who was her only living relative bought the hit. Prior to then, I had never hit anybody but gangsters and punks—a stoolie now and then, a gambler who welshed on somebody. Now they wanted me to do a crippled young woman who never hurt nobody. They wanted me to run her down in the street so it'd look like a hit-and-run, an accident." Tree shook his head. "I couldn't do it. So I took off."

"And now there's a contract on you," Vi concluded.

"A big one," Tree confirmed. "And it keeps getting bigger every year." Suddenly he buried his face in his hands. "I'm sick, Vi—" he said weakly.

She helped him back to bed, mixed him some more powdered milk and made him eat a few soda crackers to see if that would help calm his stomach.

Sitting on the bed beside him, she felt his forehead. "No fever," she reported.

"Maybe it's the flu," he said. "My muscles and joints ache like hell."

After he ate, she massaged him where he hurt and gave him more aspirin and Valium. Then she tucked him in and stroked his cheek.

"How'd you get to be a—you know," she asked curiously.

"A paid killer?" Tree smiled wanly. "In the Army. I was a P.O.W. I did time with a Ranger captain who had mob connections. When we were exchanged and went home, he asked me to work for him. It sounded better than going back to the reservation." He reached up and touched her hand. "You won't go tomorrow, will you?"

"No. I won't leave you while you're sick."

He had a miserable night. Between bouts of diarrhea and vomiting, he was left weak and shaky. She helped him to and from bed, gave him more medication, more milk, more crackers. His muscle and joint aches agonized him all through the night—even codeine tablets failed to curb the pain.

Toward morning he still had no fever, but his pulse had become very weak and his eyes no longer looked threatening. When Vi took his gun from under his pillow where she had noticed it, he didn't complain—he knew he did not have the strength to fire it, anyway. Still, he was relieved to see her merely lay it on the nearby bureau and leave it there.

Two hours after sunup, he was breathing very lightly and was extremely pale. She was holding his head up, feeding him a little warm oatmeal.

"Feed them," he said feebly.

"I will," she assured him. "After I feed you. "You're sick, they're not."

When he had eaten as much as she thought he could, she let his head back down and wiped his face with a damp cloth. She opened a window for him to get some fresh air and cleaned up the dishes they had used during the night. When she came back in to check on him he was barely awake. Just enough to say faintly, "The wild things—"

"All right," she said. "I'll do it right now."

He gave her a faint smile. She bent and kissed him lightly on the lips.

Out back, Vi got a bucket of pellet food from the storage locker and went over to where the animals waited. She held out her hand to them, but they would not come. They merely stared at her. She tossed a handful of food to them, but they didn't touch it. Maybe they smell the arsenic on my hands, she thought.

She shrugged, poured the bucket of food on the ground, and went back inside to see if Tree was in a coma yet.

DOROTHY B. HUGHES

That Summer at Quichiquois

TIME AND PLACE DO NOT MATTER. They are happenings. Simply happenings.

There are other happenings. Some you don't or won't remember. Some you will. Deliberately. It is not that you remember the important and don't remember the unimportant. Often it's the other way around. Like dancing with Voss.

Sometimes I think of Voss and I cry. Tears. Wet tears. I don't cry easily. I don't make myself cry. It's just a happening.

I didn't actually know him. He was just someone I danced with. When I was fourteen years old. By the accident of him being there and me being there when the music changed. Does anyone remember the "Paul Jones"? Sort of like a grand march only gentlemen going one way and ladies another. Touching hands but not clasping, touching in passing. Until the music changes. Without warning. Like in "Going to Jerusalem." Musical chairs.

And that happening was when the music changed. I was right beside Voss. So I danced with Voss. Close tight, chest to chest, feeling him surrounding me. Engulfing me. Almost as if I were an integral part of his body. For those few moments.

I was nothing to him. Not a happening to him. It was simply the way he danced. To him that was the happening. To dance. As if dancing were created by him, for him.

Except Elektra. When he danced with Elektra they were one person. Not two dancing. One. Transformed. Two become one. Tightly together. Never again one and one. Two melded. Like by flame. The flame of movement and music.

My cousin Katty was sixteen going on seventeen. She and her very best friends—four or five of them—would have none of Voss. He wasn't privileged. Their cant word of the summer. He worked in a *butcher shop*! Henschel's Butcher Shop. His uncle Gus. Underprivileged. As if Voss had blood spattered all over his clothes. Like Uncle Gus had on his white apron when he waited on my aunt Georgie. In those days in a small town, meat didn't come prepackaged and iced by Armour or Swift. It came from a nearby farm. The farmer butchered and brought the haunch to the butcher shop. It was hung in an icebox room out back. The butcher cut from the haunch what the customer wanted. Sometimes blood would spatter on his white apron.

Voss worked mostly at the front counter. By the cash register. By the big front window.

But the girls shrieked "underprivileged" when I asked about him. The girls accepted only the privileged. Like Katty's choice for the summer, Roddy Rockefeller. No, not the rich Rockefellers with the wizened old golfer who gave a dime-a-day tip to his caddy. Rockefeller is a common name in upstate New York.

"What's Claude?" I asked them. Deliberately to provoke them. Claude had to be privileged. He was a Clark. Founders of Clarksvale back in Revolutionary days. His father was owner and president of the bank. The one where Aunt Georgie used to work and now owned a big piece of.

Of course they shouted with laughter at my question. "Whey-face?" I did not ever understand "Whey-face." He had a round doughy face. Something about curds and whey.

They added their other names for him. "Toady." "Cipher." And one daring friend of Katty's who considered herself sophisticated, "Faggotty."

Voss let Claude hang around. That was about all. Voss was a loner. He didn't have friends. Didn't want them.

We went back to the village every other summer. We—my mother, the children—my eight-year-old brother and six-year-old sister, and me. My father wanted us to know his people. He didn't come with us. He had his business as excuse. He had had enough of villages before he walked away from them to make his mark in the city. And did, all the way to California.

Every other summer we took the train—there were trains in those days—from California to New York, upstate New York. Change at Chicago to the N.Y. Central. Disembark at Albany. But not for the local train. Met there by Aunt Georgie and her chauffeur Fred. He was one of the garage men in a chauffeur cap. We stayed with Aunt Priscilla. George was the younger sister by two years. She was the businesswoman. She owned half the town by now. Aunt Priscilla was the stay-at-home who took care of her kinfolk's children.

Katherine—Katty—had always lived with Aunt Pris. Her mother died in childbirth and her father was in the air corps, a captain or something. He wasn't on land very often.

This summer Aunt Pris also had the Tompkin boys. Their father, a nephew, was an archaeology professor at one of the universities, and so was his wife. They were off to some big dig deep in South America. No place to take little boys. The boys were around my brother's age.

I shared Katty's room in summer and we didn't see much of the children. Not if we could help it.

The village itself was a happening. For a girl born and raised in a big city, it was like a storybook holiday. Walking around town. No traffic. No streetcars. No buses. A post office with its walls of neat little golden boxes. An ice cream parlor with tables and chairs.

And every Saturday night there was dancing on the pavilion in the town park. Which was how a fourteen-year-old came to dance with an older young man. That summer at Quichiquois. That summer of Elektra.

An open pavilion up a flight of steps to raise it above the park benches and the paths below. The pavilion was also the bandstand. The band played there in summer every night. Except Saturday. On Saturday night there was an orchestra, a real orchestra. Live music, it is called today. Miss Estelle had for some twenty-five years taught classical piano to all the children of the village whose parents were music minded, but on Saturday night in summer she played mean jazz. Deacon Raven of some local church played violin for the service. For dancing at the pavilion, he played a jazz fiddle. The drummer was the owner of the local hay-and-feed store. He was in the National Guard band. On special occasions, the city fathers would enlist a clarinet player, a young farmer up the road a piece who played in his college band. Musicians who aren't professionals have a certain spirit. They play for the love of it, certainly not for the pittance they are paid.

Everyone danced. Little children capered with one another. Or now and again politely waltzed with their mums or dads. Even the grampaws and gramaws sashayed around the floor.

And I danced with Voss. A happening only that once. Although after that night the older girls taught me how to lag. Without appearing to lag. No one would know you were looking for one specific partner. When you saw him you would lag a step here or there until he was almost beside you. Katty and I would practice it at night in her bedroom. But I never had a chance to try it out for real.

Because Aunt George decided. She made all the decisions in the family. Aunt Priscilla acquiesced or did not. If she did not, it was the end of that happening. Aunt Pris was a woman of few words. Quietly spoken. Aunt Georgie was the talker. Emphatic. Accurate. Almost always. A business-woman, accustomed to dealing with men. With yea and nay. No palavering.

She decided that the children should have three weeks at Lake Quichiquois. There are myriad small lakes all through the Berkshires. This was nearest to Clarksvale, about twenty miles. No resort. Just summer cottages. Friends of Aunt George offered theirs as they were going north to visit family for several weeks. The cottages were in the woods above the lake. Each was surrounded by woods, land was not costly, everyone had privacy. Just comfortably set far enough apart.

Aunt Priscilla acquiesced. My mother, being company, had no yea or nay. My mother preferred the busiest city street to the beauties of the woods. Not to the beauty but to the creatures that came with it, flies and spiders and bees and creepy crawlers. But my mother was company. Polite. Company was expected to acquiesce.

Of course, Aunt Georgie wasn't going. Shut up for three weeks surrounded by children? Like my father, she had business excuses.

After her decision, Aunt Georgie said, "I have a hired girl to go along. No sense of you and Elizabeth [my mother] turning your holiday into a wash and iron and cook for six children."

Aunt Priscilla was wary. "Who is the hired girl?"

"I hired Elektra." Aunt Georgie slid the name off her tongue as if she just recalled it.

A look. From one to another of the aunts. And returned the other to the one. Aunt Pris decided, half-reluctantly, "Well, she's as good as we could hope for this late in the summer."

Imperceptible. Aunt George had been apprehensive. Priscilla could have said no. She hadn't. Now Aunt Georgie could resume her position as head of the family. In name. She paid the bills.

"She's strong," Aunt George said. "Remember how she took up all your rugs last spring—beat them like a man would, the air was grimy."

"And laid them all again," Aunt Priscilla mentioned. "And she would carry the whole laundry in one load up the stairs."

There were twenty-three steps up from the living room to the second floor. I had counted them. I always count steps. Another eighteen up to the attic bedrooms where the boys slept, and live-in help when Aunt Priscilla tolerated it I don't know how many steps to the basement. I didn't go to the basement. The furnace was there and the storage. Years of the *Saturday Evening Post* and the *Geographic,* and old trunks filled with old clothes.

Elektra was strong. Elektra didn't natter. She was scrub clean. The aunts ticked off her good points. Nothing said of the bad. Of the cause for apprehension one to the other. Somehow I didn't want to ask Katty. Katty had a way of embroidering words to make a bland story an exciting one. If not exactly a true one.

I'd seen Elektra, of course. Someone must have said, "There's Elektra." Walking on Main Street. Or going into the post office. Or sitting at a soda table at the soda fountain. "There's Elektra." I could describe her as if I'd seen a snapshot of her. Tall. Man tall. Lean. Man lean. Straight black hair, held back by a barrette. Hanging to her waist. Not when she was working. Then piled in braids or in loops. High ruddy cheekbones. Straight nose. Like on an Iroquois.

I'd seen her. She delivered the ironing that Aunt Priscilla sent to Gammer Goodwife. Gammer lived in that big square yellow rooming house on the terrace you passed walking to town. The townsfolk called it the "Poor House." Elektra lived there too. She was kin to Gammer.

I'd seen Elektra. Dancing with Voss.

I couldn't but wonder if Katty had put the idea of Lake Quichiquois into Aunt Georgie's head. Linda, her best friend, was going up there for the rest of the summer. Her family owned a summer cottage there. There was a boys' camp across the lake. For little boys, but the counselors were privileged!

And so we went to Lake Quichiquois. Aunt George's chauffeur, Fred in the chauffeur's cap, drove us up there in the seven-seater. The ladies in the backseat. My younger sister squeezed in by my mother. Katty and I on the jump seats. The three little boys in front with Fred.

Elektra would be up the next day. Fred was borrowing a pickup truck from the garage to carry our trunks. The aunts always took trunks, even for a short stay. Elektra would ride with Fred in the cab of the pickup.

Time goes quickly by the water. Too quickly. We are water people. Quichiquois was a dream happening. Elektra would have the breakfast cooked and served before eight o'clock every morning. She'd red up the kitchen while we waited out the dictum: "Do not go in the water until one hour after eating." We wouldn't. But we would go down to our dock before the hour was up and the children would splash through the shore water.

Elektra would get our rowboat turned over, ready to row out for anyone in trouble. Elektra was a strong swimmer. She cleaved the water as beautifully as a dolphin.

Dover Camp, a long established one, was just across the lake. The little boys and our boys could and did exchange taunts across the water.

And of the three counselors, two were already in college, lordly sophomores the coming year. The other was a senior in prep school. Katty and Linda were in rhapsodies. New boys—or as they called them, men—and these girls were practiced at making boyfriends. The boys were at Brown, and the girls' college was just across the Massachusetts line. The talk became all about football games and weekend soirees. And house parties in the spring.

Across the lake was also Mr. Gruen's general store and soda fountain. The meeting place for all lakers. He had a year ago built on a room for the soda fountain. He had old-fashioned tables and chairs in there during the week, but they were moved out on Saturday and there was dancing to a juke box. No Paul Jones.

The Dover Camp boys only had to walk downhill a short way to the soda fountain. On our side it was a quarter-mile walk, after we reached the lane from the cottage, down to the bend that led to the store. It was much shorter to get into the rowboat and row right across to the store dock. If you knew how to row. We didn't. Elektra did. She tried to teach us. It isn't easy to learn to row. The boat goes around and around in circles. Unless you have a very strong arm. Muscles. Like Elektra. The children, Katty, and I were allowed to go with Elektra in the boat on Saturdays. My mother and Aunt Pris would walk over later to fetch the little children home early. Katty and I were allowed to stay until the eleven-fifteen closing. With Elektra.

Until our first Saturday evening, I had not known Voss was also working at the camp. Three afternoons a week. Instructing the young campers on the fine points of sailing.

And I couldn't help but wonder which one of them had decided to find a job up at the lake, when the other had been already hired.

The cottagers danced. Katty and Linda and the counselors danced. The little boys and girls tried to dance. Voss and Elektra danced together. I watched from the sidelines. So did Whey-face.

I never did find out why he was called Whey-face. The girls would simply explode into "curds and whey" when I asked. He was sort of doughlike, not fat but a bit puffy; he would always be a little off side. No matter how fine an education he would have. No matter that when he grew up he would take over the president's chair at the bank and his father would retire to chairman of the board.

Both Claude and I just sat on the bench in the corner and watched the dancers. Sometimes I'd get him up on his feet and would try to show him how to move to the music. But he never understood rhythm or timing or movement. Two left feet. He always came out to the lake on dance nights to drive Voss back to town. On weeknights Voss hopped a ride to Clarksvale with workers at the camp. Once—just once at Quichiquois—I danced again with Voss. He walked over to where Claude and I were sitting to ask Claude something or other. I think he recognized how my feet were in rhythm even while sitting down there on the bench. He would understand because he was a dancer. Not a professional, but bred in the bone, roiling in the blood. Without warning, he took my hand and pulled me up from the bench, said, "Come on," and we danced out onto the floor. Entirely different from the Paul Jones. A jazz jazzy. Exhilarating.

When Elektra came back from powdering her nose or whatever, Voss sat me down. He winked at me as they went off. But ours had been the best jazzy of the evening. It even led to my having some dances with Katty's older boys. Yes, I too have dance in my blood and bones.

It was that same night that I asked Claude how Voss could know so much about sailing to be able to teach the boys. Claude looked at me aghast. How could I know Voss and not know that? I tried to explain that I didn't know Voss. It was our hired girl who knew Voss. I'd just happened to dance with him once in the Paul Jones at the pavilion.

So Claude told me, "He's going to join the coast guard. He's been studying all this year to pass their tests or whatever you have to do to get in. He used to sail when he was a boy and lived up the coast. His father was a sailor. On a cargo boat. His father sailed all the way to China." It could be so. Or a sailor's yarn to a small hero-worshiping boy. It didn't matter. Voss would be a sailor if that was what he wanted.

I remember so well everything about that last dance night. It was getting on to eleven thirty, and I didn't see Elektra anywhere. I excused myself to Claude and walked across to where Katty was whooping it up with her current favorite boyfriend. Katty didn't shoo me away. Maybe I looked that worried. "Where's Elektra?" I asked her.

She surveyed the dancers on the floor. "She's probably down at the boat-house," she said.

"What's she doing down there?" I asked. Innocence. Too young. For a beat Katty and her friends just looked at me. And Linda started laughing.

Katty joined in. The boys were politely inexpressive. They were sophisticates.

After she'd stopped laughing, Linda said, as if everyone knew that, "It's where couples go."

Katty added, "When they want to be alone."

"Smooching," Linda said.

I caught on. I wasn't that innocent. Necking, they called it at my school.

"She'll be here after the music stops," Katty said. "She wouldn't dare not," she explained to her friends. "She knows Aunt Priscilla is waiting up."

Truly true. Aunt Priscilla wasn't as sharp-tongued as Aunt George. But you could bully Aunt George by a temper tantrum. Katty explained it to me early in the summer. Aunt Priscilla was immovable.

When Mr. Gruen dimmed the colored lights and set the juke box for the last dance, always "Three O'Clock in the Morning," I saw them. Elektra and Voss. Dancing. Two become one. I watched through the whole record. Daydreaming. Why call it "day" when it's at night? Someday I'd grow up and have a boyfriend who danced like Voss.

Voss and Claude said good night and walked off. Elektra rowed us home. Aunt Pris glanced at her watch. "It will be midnight before you get to sleep." This was a nudge to go to bed, not stay up talking. "And we have to start packing up tomorrow. Aunt George and Fred will be here Monday morning."

Katty and I didn't talk much. Too tired. Too much, each of us, to remember. From the beginning of summer through this our final night of the boys' farewell across the water. "Good Night, Ladies . . ."

We had to miss Sunday morning church when at the lake. The nearest was in Clarksvale, too far to walk. Aunt Priscilla read her Bible. The children were kept quiet, and Katty and I usually slept until noon. In the afternoon we were allowed to swim and splash by our dock.

This Sunday was different. I woke—it wasn't eight o'clock—to the children gabbling in loud voices. Loud voices. Like on a weekday. My mother and Aunt Pris were ahead of me to the kitchen. Mother with her hair still in kid curlers, Aunt Pris with her gray hair in a plait down her back. Both in their nightgowns and robes. Aunt Pris was asking, "Whatever is the matter?" and my mother saying to her two, "Quiet. Quiet now. What's wrong?"

The children all talked at once. Emerged, one question. "Where's Elektra?"

Aunt Pris was dubious. "She isn't here?"

"No. She isn't here," all talking again at once. Almost shouting. "She's not here. There's no breakfast."

"Perhaps she overslept," Aunt Pris said. She hesitated. Then made her way to the back of the house, past my room, sleepy-eyed Katty just emerging, saying, "What's wrong?"

On to Elektra's bedroom beyond. Aunt Priscilla proper. Knocking on the door. Calling gently, careful not to startle a sleeper. "Elektra . . . Elektra . . . it's Miss Priscilla."

No response. She tried it again, a bit louder. Again no response. Aunt Priscilla took hold of the doorknob. Reluctantly. It was against all the principles of good manners. To open another's bedroom door. Even a servant's. But with no sound within, she did open the door, one small slant. Enough to peep inside. Then wider. And she said, "She isn't here."

"She must be around someplace." Katty and I had followed into the room. Katty said, "She can't have left. She hasn't taken her things." The hairbrush was on the bureau. The box of powder and the puff also there. Her nightdress still folded neatly over the back of a chair. The bed already made up. Or was it used last night?

"She'll be back," Aunt Priscilla decided. "I'll dress and then I'll cook breakfast."

Mother said, "I'll give the children some cornflakes and milk to tide them over." She had already put the kettle on for Aunt Priscilla's morning tea.

Aunt George came up in the afternoon. She said the same as Aunt Priscilla. "She'll be back." Her reasoning was different. "I owe her five dollars. For last week. She won't leave without her pay."

But she didn't come back. Not that day.

Not the next day. My small suitcase was packed. All else was confusion. Katty trying to curl her hair before closing her suitcase. Aunt Priscilla had packed all of Elektra's belongings into her own trunk. There wasn't much. The skirt and shirt she wore to work in, the few cosmetics, even her toothbrush and toothpaste had been left behind, and her undergarments (one to wear, one to wash, one to dry), her bedroom slippers, and an old night-robe that Aunt Pris had given her. Of course she'd taken her purse with her; the one she carried last night wasn't in the room. There'd be a comb and lipstick and powder compact in it.

Aunt Priscilla was trying to get everything shipshape, as it had been when we arrived. Mother was trying to get her children ready to leave. Aunt George arrived and added to the confusion while insisting, "Of course Elektra's gone back to Clarksvale. For reasons of her own." She finally took the Tompkin boys out to Fred, let him keep them busy out by the truck.

I managed to slip out the side door at a propitious moment when all the others were in the house or in front by the cars. I skulked rapidly through the trees until I was on the path that led to High Peak. It wasn't a real path. Just bumpy earth, pebbles and rocks, bits of green that wasn't weeds or wild grass, just green stuff. I zigzagged up the path to the promontory at the top. High above the shore. Elektra's special place. One afternoon when Katty and Linda were being exceptionally boy-crazies, Elektra had let me go with her to the peak. This was her time off from children and chores—why would she take me with her? Maybe because Voss danced with me once in the Paul Jones.

She didn't talk about him. She didn't talk when we were there. She just stood on the promontory and looked at the sky or down at the water. Under the promontory but still high on the slope there was a shelf. Not far below the peak. No way to get to it except by zigzagging down the slope and stooping your way under the protruding upper slope. She didn't take me there. She didn't go there either. Just pointed it out to me as we leaned over the tip. Scary.

I didn't want to go there now. She wasn't there. But she had been here last night. With Voss? A farewell? In each other's arms. Two into one. "Stop dreaming," Katty would say. Or my mother. Or anyone if I spoke of it. But I knew. Before I saw the bead, the red glass bead on the green stuff scattered on the earth. She wore those beads to the dance last night. She always wore them with her summer dress, her white dress with the little roses sprinkled across the pattern. The beads almost looked like crystals. Not really. They were pretend, cut like crystals, but made of glass. They were a little handful of beauty to her. She must have searched for them when the strand was broken. Caught on a tree branch, or the button on a man's jacket. Too dark to find all of them. I looked. There was one out on the tip, but I didn't go there. I scruffed through the green and found another. And another, with leaf mold patterning it. No more. I hadn't time to search for more. I ran until the cottage was in sight. Then I just hurried, the beads tight in my left fist. Fred was loading the last of the suitcases.

My mother came to me with, "Emmy, where have you been?" and as she looked into my face, softly, "Saying good-bye?"

She understood the need to say good-bye. To the woods and the water. To some of summer memories. In some secret place you had marked as your own.

*   *   *

Another week and the end of August. Of summer. My mother and the children off for California and school days again. Long good-byes until Christmas. Behind the scenes it had been decided that I would enter Mount

Academy this year, the school where the women of my father's family had all attended to be finished. Katty had graduated there this spring. My mother approved though as a Californian she had been finished there. I would stay on with Aunt Priscilla until school started. Aunt George had assured me that with a diploma from Mount Academy I could attend any college of my choice. Such was its academic standing. Even Cambridge? Yes, even Cambridge. I doubted. Cambridge wasn't exclusively female, and Aunt Georgie with all her modern ideas and bold businesss maneuvers did not hold with coeducation. It was all right for primary students. Although better for the girls to go to Miss Mastersons and the boys to Albany Cadet. No hanky-panky.

It was one of those last nights before Katty would depart for college. Aunt Pris, Katty, and I had had early supper and cleanup and were relaxing in the living room. Until Aunt Georgie came by. She was again all het up about Elektra. She'd been at some meeting and none of the women knew anything about the disappearance of Elektra. No one had seen her since she went to the lake with us. They seemed to think Aunt Priscilla and Aunt George were to blame.

Aunt Priscilla said, "Stop worrying your head about the five dollars. I was going to have to let her go anyway. She was beginning to show."

They exchanged a few of their wise looks and dropped the subject.

Later when Katty and I went up to our room, I asked her. "What did Aunt Pris mean? Beginning to show."

Katty just looked at me. Stared. Finally she said, "You know."

"I don't know. If I knew, why would I ask you? 'Beginning to show'? Do you know?"

"Of course I do. Everybody knows. That she's going to have a baby. That's what it means."

"She's married!" I could not believe it. But if she and Voss were married . . .

"No. She's not married," Katty stated.

But if she's not married, how can she—I didn't ask that question out loud. Some people did. We just didn't know people who did. I sighed to Katty. "How do you know all these things?"

"Emmy," she told me, "you find out a lot living with the aunts. You keep quiet and listen and they forget you're there. And you learn a lot."

I figured for myself. In a small town you learned things that city girls didn't know about. Small towns were evolved from farm country. Where life and death were the beginning and end, and in between were all manner of happenings.

Another week of flurry and then we drove with Katty to Albany to put her on the train for New York. Three of her friends were also going to the college on the Hudson. Linda, of course, and Willa and Maleen. The college proctors would meet the train with the school bus.

When we returned to the house late that afternoon, we collapsed into chairs, even Aunt Georgie. I would be the next to go. But only as far as Hudson, where I'd be met by the school bus.

I'd stopped listening to the aunts long before they were talked out. It became tiresome listening to all the memories of Aunt A and Uncle B and Cousins C, D, E, etc. When I didn't know any of them. They were reminiscing to each other, remembering their own college days.

Finally Aunt Georgie gathered her gloves and string bag and high-stepped to the front door. She'd sent Fred and the car home; she'd be walking. Of course she carried her umbrella as always, to ward off sun or rain.

She said to me, "You be ready in the morning, Emmy. I'll come by for you about ten o'clock."

Aunt Priscilla showed mild surprise. "You're taking Emmy along?"

"I certainly am." Evidently I'd missed something in their long conversation. "She's the last to see Elektra."

"I saw her," Aunt Pris corrected.

"You weren't with her all evening. Or in the boat."

I could have told them I knew no more than Aunt Pris. Elektra never talked. She spoke necessary words, but she never talked. Not even phrases like "Is my lipstick on straight?" "Does my petticoat show?" Things all females say to each other.

Instead I asked, "Where are we going?"

"We're going looking for Elektra. Find out where she is. Find out why she hasn't been around for her five dollars. You think of some questions yourself, Emmy. We'll both ask questions."

I reacted in my veins. In my bones. I was to be a Miss Paul Pry. I could ask a dozen questions. I could ask Voss: "Where did she spend the night? How did she get back to Clarksvale? How did she break her strand of red glass beads?" But I wouldn't. It was none of my business. Just the same, I carried the three red glass beads along in my party handkerchief deep in my little purse, where I had tucked them away while we were still at the cottage. While no one was looking at me. Before I got into the car and shared a jump seat with Katty.

I was ready for Aunt George when she arrived next morning. She had walked over. "No sense in taking the car. More trouble than it's worth."

She was thinking out loud. "We have to prowl."

We prowled along Town Street, which carried you into Main Street. But we stopped before then. We stopped at the big yellow boarding house where Elektra had lived. A flight of wooden steps led up to the porch. Aunt George didn't ring or knock on the door, she opened it. She knew her way around here. I followed her. She walked past the staircase that mounted to a second floor, and strode down the uncarpeted corridor, all the way to a door near the back of the house. She knocked a ratatat on that door. And again, stronger. From within now came a voice shouting, "Who's that come knocking at my door?" Aunt George shouted back, "Just Aunt George, Gammer, that's who." Everyone in town called her Aunt George or Georgie.

Came another shout: "George Fanshawe?"

"What other George do you know, Gammer?"

Sometime along the years I'd heard, just like an aside from someone in the family, that Aunt George had been married once on a time. Not for long. That's why she wasn't a Davenport like Aunt Priscilla and my father and his family.

"Well, don't stand out there yammering, Georgie. Come on inside."

My aunt opened the unlocked door and went in, me following behind her.

"Gammer," she said, "this is my niece Emmy."

I managed to stammer a "How d'you do" to the diminutive old woman in the big rocker with varnish peeling from it. This was Gammer Goodwife, supposed to be kin of Elektra. Half-toothless, a browned corncob pipe clutched by the few remaining teeth. A squawky voice like something was caught in her throat. The ironing woman. Hard to believe that those rheumatic cramped fingers could iron ruffles until they rippled. Could iron linen napkins down to the very edge of the hand hem. Could iron lace as delicately as if she'd spun it. She took one look at me out of her spiteful black eyes and dismissed me as without interest.

She had three different ironing boards set up in her large untidy room. One, oversize, for sheets, tablecloths and such; a middle-size one for the usual clothes wash, and a baby one, a sleeve board it was called. Probably for the ruffles and laces. A screen closed off a corner of the room. Behind it, Aunt Georgie told me later, was the bed and washbasin. An old-fashioned rooming house with the bathroom down the hall.

"I don't have your laundry done," Gammer spat.

"I didn't come for my laundry," Aunt George informed her. "I didn't bring any this week."

"Then what you doing here?"

"I'm looking for Elektra."

"Well, you can see she an't here." Gammer set the rocker rocking hard again. "She's up at the lake with your sister."

"She isn't up at the lake. We've all left the lake."

"Did you bring her back here?"

"We couldn't," stated Aunt George. "She left before we packed out."

"Why did she leave?"

"That's what I want to know. I want to ask her."

"Well, she an't here."

"Where's her room?"

"She an't in her room."

"How do you know she isn't up in her room?"

Gammer cackled. A cackle laugh. I'd read of them. But I didn't know there was really such a sound.

She dug her fist into a voluminous pocket in her skirt. "Because I got her key." She unreeled a long chain attached inside the pocket. On the end of it was a large ring of keys. "She leaves it with me when she's out of town. So nobody gets into her things." She beetled suspiciously at Aunt George.

"You haven't seen her since she came back? You haven't had any message from her?"

Gammer kept humming "Nnnnoooo" and rocking harder. Like little boys do to make it go faster.

"Then where is she?" Aunt George said. Not exactly to Gammer. At her own frustration.

But Gammer responded. "She's a Canuck. I told you that before. A Canuck witch." She restarted the rocker. "She flew away—up high—way up high . . ."

"On your broomstick," Aunt George bristled. She'd had enough of Gammer's antics. She stood up and brushed the dust off her skirt, although the chair she'd sat on had been brushed by her handkerchief before she sat down on it. "If you do see her or hear from her," Aunt George instructed, "tell her I'm looking for her. To pay her the money I owe her."

The rocking stopped like that. "You can pay me. I'll give it to her."

"I'll pay her. No one else."

"You think I'd spend it on myself."

"I pay what I owe to the one I owe." With that she stalked out while Gammer was still embroidering her role as a caretaker of Electra's money as well as her room. I sidled out beside Aunt George. I didn't want to be left alone in that room with Gammer.

All the way to Main Street Aunt George kept talking to herself, not to me, about the perfidious Gammer and her grandniece. I managed to keep up with her fast walk by saving my breath. Only three blocks to Main Street.

Waiting to cross the street, I could ask, "Now where do we go?"

"We'll go to Gus Henschel's. I understand his nephew, Voss, and that girl were what we used to call an item."

"Did everybody know?" Somehow I'd thought it was a private affair, known only to Katty and her friends who saw them dancing together.

"It's the talk of this town the way she went after him." She was opening the door of the butcher shop before I could think of some excuse to keep from going in there. I didn't want Voss to see me and think I'd talked about him and Elektra.

Voss wasn't up front today. His uncle was. He was arranging steaks for his display case. "Morning, Miss Georgie," he said, but it was a glum morning from his expression. "What can I do for you today?"

"You can let me talk to that nephew of yours."

"Voss?"

"I understand that is the name."

He peered over the counter at me. I was too young to be a friend of Voss so he dismissed me from his answer. To Aunt George he growled, "I'd like to talk to him myself. That javel never come back from the lake. That camp has been calling and calling him. He hasn't been around there either."

Aunt George was only temporarily speechless. "You haven't seen Elektra?"

"That the pawky girl been hanging around him all summer?"

"She hasn't been around lately?"

"Not since she went up to the lake with your sister. Leastways that was what she told him."

Both of them gone. Together. But she wouldn't go without taking her belongings. Yes, she might. If he was in a hurry. He'd have some money with two jobs. He'd buy her a new hairbrush and nightgown.

"Good riddance to bad rubbish," Uncle Gus was saying. "But he'll be around once he runs out of money. I paid him before he went off to the lake that Saturday. He'll be back."

"I owe Elektra some money. I don't like to owe money. If either of them turns up, you let me know. Right off. Hear?"

"I ain't deaf, Aunt George. I hear."

And she stomped away, me trailing. Again talking to herself. "They'll turn up when they want money."

I could have told her they weren't coming back. They had each other. But she wouldn't have believed me.

II

Ten years ago. Eleven come summer. High school and college over and done. Two years assistant women's editor on a medium-small-town newspaper. You want to know what an assistant women's club editor covers? Women's club meetings. Women's club social teas. Women's club holiday occasions. Washington's birthday cardboard hatchets. Cotton Easter bunnies in straw bonnets. Fourth of July crepe paper firecrackers. September, miniature grandmothers' school slates. October, take your pick, witches, brooms, jack-o'-lanterns. November, yam turkeys. No need to illustrate December and January. How often can you write that the decorations were so charming, unique, attractive, amusing—add your own adjectives.

I couldn't get out of the groove. The editor wanted me where I was. I could spell.

On a September morning, I read on the AP tape, DATELINE CLARKSVALE. HUMAN BONES FOUND AT LAKE QUICHIQUOIS.

I didn't have to read on. I knew exactly where, and, without knowing, I knew who. And a chance to break from my shackles. I knocked on Editor Briar's door. His office is a square of window glass, but we observed the courtesy of a knock. He was chewing his pencil. Obviously working on his weekend editorial. Yes, he uses a pencil. A yellow wooden pencil with very black lead.

"Mr. Briar," I said, "I'd like to leave now. My page has gone to press."

"Who's going to read proof?"

"You are," I told him. "Or one of those callow youths you call reporters." I'd known Mr. Briar a long time. Since I was subeditor on the college paper. I knew how to give him just enough information to whet his news appetite. "I have a story that takes investigative reporting, and I want to get at it ahead of the pack."

He stuttered and glowered and called anathema on my head. A hot story was for callow Quentin, the one he was training to be a star metropolitan reporter. Like he'd always wanted to be.

He was wasting my time. I interrupted him. "It just came over AP. Finding bones upstate. Human bones."

His pink face glistened. "I'll send Quent—"

"Indeed you won't," I countered. "I have the inside track. I was there." Stress on there. "When that girl disappeared. I can beat the city slickers.

They'll be coming around. But I know these folks. See you Monday."

With which I was out the door, leaving him to his blood pressure.

I retrieved my car from our parking lot and took off for Clarksvale. Ninety miles upstate. I didn't stop to pack up anything. I could buy a toothbrush. Borrow everything else from Aunt Priscilla or Aunt George.

I stopped at Aunt Priscilla's house—it was on the way into town. After ejaculations of surprise, I told her, "I'm here to cover the big story. Finding human bones at Quichiquois."

"I'll call George. She'll want to hear about this."

Aunt George was over to Aunt Priscilla's in a trice. She must be well in her sixties now and just as spry and as domineering as ever. As that summer of Elektra.

"You think it's Elektra," she said after I'd given her a rundown on the news story.

I did think so. I'd always thought that she had never left the lake. But couldn't let myself say it back then. Didn't want it to be so.

"Aunt George, you come uptown with me," I invited. "You know all these local officials. In case they try to freeze me out. I want the story."

"You'll get it." She did not doubt. She was too accustomed to getting what she wanted from the town fathers.

As we came out on Aunt Priscilla's porch she asked, "Is that your car?" nodding to where it stood in the driveway.

"We'll walk," she told me, just as she always said ten, almost eleven, years ago. "Easier than trying to park. Talk to more people anyhow."

And there were plenty of people out on Main Street. Gossiping. Gawking. And there was Claude, near the bank, his father's bank. Also Aunt Georgie's.

He greeted us Claude-like. "Good morning, Aunt George. Hello, Emmy. You haven't been to Clarksvale for a long time." He was still a whey-face, but he had some assurance now. He had been appointed an attorney with the county. Aunt Priscilla had kept me informed of all Clarksvale news. She wrote me every week.

Claude and I shook hands. As visitors do.

Aunt Georgie said to us, "I'm going on down to the courthouse." Where she could gather information.

Claude said, "You're here about the bones."

I showed him my newspaper card. "It was on the AP wire this morning."

"We sent the bones to the lab in Albany. Two weeks ago. They're on the way back here now. With the report."

I was reluctant but I asked. "Do you know . . ."

"Yes." He said almost to himself, "The director informed me. I inquired . . ." It took a moment or so before he could continue. But he said it without inflection. "They are male bones. The bones of a young man probably in his twenties. The skull has been bashed."

I only half asked. "They were found under the promontory, the one called High Peak."

"There is a ledge, an open cave. The bones were there. Nothing left of clothing."

"No leather? A belt? A wallet?"

"Not after ten years. Pumas take refuge there if a winter storm interrupts their hunting. Sometimes there are bears."

I didn't want to say it but I had to. "She killed him."

"We don't know that."

"She loved him. He was going away. She couldn't let him go."

"If she did, we will never know," Claude said. "She cannot be brought back to trial. Not without evidence. Even if she is found."

"She was carrying his child. He was leaving her and their child."

Somewhere there is a little girl, near ten years old. Straight as a lance. Long dark hair hanging down her back. Or a sandy little boy. Agile. Scrawny but muscular. Strong.

"She loved him." I kept repeating it. Not for Claude. For myself.

Claude said, "I don't think she planned it. I don't think she intended it. I think it was by accident."

In a rage, she struck him. There were some sizable rocks on the promontory. There would be some in the cave. And kept striking him until he was gone. Before she knew what she was doing.

He broke the strand of beads trying to get away from her. She must have had a rock. He was stronger. If it had been possible to get away from her, he could have stopped her.

"I hope you won't mention her in your story. Why torment her further? She'll always live with this. An agony of loss."

He had loved Voss. The way he'd never love anyone else. Nothing homosexual about it. A teenage boy's hero-worship of his hero.

"I won't. There may be gossip but it will come to nothing. There aren't many who really knew her." And I hesitated. "Gammer . . ."

"Everyone knows Gammer makes up tall tales."

We were left with a pause of silence, each in his own thoughts. Then Claude said, "Shall we go down to the courthouse? It's time for them to get here with the report. You can call your paper from my office."

Together we walked the half block. On the way he said, "I'm going to be married this spring. To Willa. Do you remember Willa?"

"She was one of Katty's very best friends."

"We'll have a church wedding. Bridesmaids, attendants. All the frills. Willa wants it. We'll send you an invitation. I hope you'll be able to come. Katty's coming from Maryland."

Katty's husband is in government.

It occurred to him. "You're not married?"

"Not yet. I'm a career woman. I'm younger than Katty and her friends."

"That's right," he recalled. "You were just a little girl. You sat on the bench with me and we watched Voss."

"That's right," I echoed. I closed my eyes and I could see him. "He was a wonderful dancer."

Maybe to keep from tears, he laughed. "You tried to teach me to dance."

I laughed for the same reason. "You had two left feet."

So we went into the courthouse to hear the full report on the bones. Just another happening.

But I did not tell Claude that I would give up the story. I wouldn't mention Elektra. Not unless someone else did. But I would try to find her. I'm an investigative reporter. I have to know the entire story.

J. A. JANCE

Oil and Water

I WAS HEADED INTO THE PRECINCT briefing room when Captain Waldron stopped me. "You're up, Detective Lanier. We've just had a 9-1-1 call reporting a homicide out in May Valley. Detective Barry's gassing up the car. He'll pick you up out front."

Of all the detectives who work for the King County Police Department, Detective James Joseph Barry was my least favorite possible partner. A recent transfer from Chicago PD, Detective Barry shared his reactionary views with all concerned. Although barely thirty-five, his unbearably tedious monologues made Mike Royko's curmudgeonly rumblings sound like those of a lily-livered liberal.

But newly appointed to the Detective Division, I didn't dare question the captain when it came to handing out assignments. I shut my mouth, kept my opinions to myself, and headed for the door.

Moments after I stepped outside, the unmarked car skidded to a stop beside me. As I slipped into the rider's seat, Detective Barry made a big deal of checking out my legs. He was obvious as hell, but I ignored it.

"So," he said, ramming the car into gear and careening through the rain-slicked parking lot, "how come a great-looking babe like you isn't married?"

"Homicide dicks aren't much good in the marriage department," I told him evenly. "A fact of life your wife must have figured out all on her own."

Touché! The fleeting grimace on his face told me my remark had hit the intended target. "Shut up and drive, will you?" I said.

He did, for the time being. Meanwhile, I got on the horn to ask Records what they knew about where we were headed and what we'd be up against. From the radio I gathered that patrol officers were already on the scene. The victim was dead and the crime scene secure, so there was no need for either flashing lights or siren. Detective Barry made liberal use of both.

It was a chilly October night. After a delightful Indian-summer September, this was winter's first real rainstorm. The pavement was glassy and dangerously slick with mixed accumulations of oil and water. Instead of telling him to slow down, I made sure my seatbelt was securely fastened and thanked God for airbags.

Over the rhythmic slap of the windshield wipers, Barry launched off into one of his interminable stories about the good old days back in Chicago, this one featuring his late, unlamented, bowling partner—the beady-eyed Beady Dodgson.

"So I says to him, I says, 'Beady, you old billy goat. For chrissakes, when you gonna wash that damn shirt of yours?' And he says back, he says, 'Barry, you stupid mick, after the damn tournament. Whaddaya tink? You want I should wash away my luck?'"

Detective Barry liked nothing better than the sound of his own voice. However, boring tales of reminiscence were far preferable to questions about my current marital status which seemed to surface every time the two of us had any joint dealings. Detective Barry made no secret of the fact that he thought I should be home taking care of a husband and kids. He didn't approve of what he called *girl* detectives. Which is no doubt why Captain Waldron made sure he was stuck with me. Or vice versa.

"Turn here," I said. "Take the first right up the hill."

As we turned off the May Valley Highway and headed up a steep, winding incline, the headlights cut through sheets of slanting raindrops illuminating a yellow "Livestock" warning sign along the road. Detective Barry slowed the car to a bare crawl.

City born and bred, Detective Barry was in his element and totally at home when confronting a group of urbanized, street-toughened teenagers. It was strange to realize that he was petrified of encountering stray cattle or horses on one of King County's numerous rural roads.

At last the radio crackled back to life and the harried Records clerk's voice came over the air to deliver what scanty information was then available. The victim's name was de Gasteneau, Renee Denise de Gasteneau. A computer check of the de Gasteneau address in the 18500 block of Rainier Vista had turned up six priors in the previous six weeks—two domestics, one civil disturbance, and the rest noise complaints. Chances were Renee de Gasteneau was probably none too popular with her neighbors.

"One other thing," the operator from Records added. "Her husband's there on the scene right now. Emile de Gasteneau."

The name was one I had seen in local society columns from time to time but most recently in the police blotter. "Is that as in Dr. de Gasteneau, the plastic surgeon?" I asked.

"That's the one. When officers responded to the first domestic, they let him go. The second time they picked him up. He's out on bail for that one."

"Three's the charm," I muttered.

Domestic disturbances are tough calls for all cops. For me personally they were especially disturbing. "Why do women stay with men like that?" I demanded. "Why the hell don't they get out while there's still time?"

Detective Barry shrugged. "Maybe they stay because they don't have anywhere else to go."

"That's no excuse," I said. And I meant it with every ounce of my being.

I left the very first time Mark hit me—the only time Mark hit me—and I never went back. It was less than six weeks after our wedding—a three-ring circus, storybook, church, and country-club affair with all the necessary trimmings. I came back to the Park and Ride after work late one Friday afternoon and discovered that someone had broken into my little Fiat and stolen both the stereo and the steering wheel.

That Fiat was my baby. It was the first car I had chosen, bought, and paid for all on my own. When I told Mark about it, I expected some sympathy. Instead, he lit into me. He said I should have had better sense than to leave it at the Park and Ride in the first place. The argument got totally out of hand, and before I knew what was happening, he hit me—knocked me out cold.

Once I picked myself up off the kitchen floor, I called the cops. I remember trying to keep the blood from my loosened teeth from dripping into the telephone receiver. The two patrol officers who responded were wonderful. One of them kept Mark out of the room while the other one stuck with me. He followed me around the house while I threw my clothes and makeup into suitcases and plastic trash bags. He helped amass an odd assortment of hastily collected household goods—dishes, silverware, pots, and pans. I made off with Aunt Mindy's wedding present waffle iron, one of the two popcorn poppers, and every single set of matching towels and washcloths I could lay hands on.

The two cops were more than happy to help me drag my collection of stuff downstairs and out the door where they obligingly loaded it into a waiting yellow cab. Now that I'm a police officer myself, I know why they were so eager to help me. I was the exception, not the rule. Most women don't leave. Ever.

By then our car was rounding a tight curve on the winding foothills road called Rainier Vista, although any view of Mount Rainier was totally shrouded in clouds. Ahead of us the narrow right-of-way and the lowering clouds were brightly lit by the orange glow of flashing lights from numerous emergency vehicles—several patrol cars and what was evidently a now totally unnecessary ambulance.

The figure of a rain-slickered patrol officer emerged out of the darkness. The cop motioned for us to park directly behind one of the medical examiner's somber gray vans.

"How the hell did the meat wagon beat us?" Detective Barry demanded irritably.

"Believe me," I said, "it wasn't because you didn't try."

The uniformed deputy hurried over to our car. Detective Barry lowered his window. "What's up?"

"The husband's waiting out back. I let him know detectives were on the way; told him you'd probably want to talk to him."

Barry nodded. "I'm sure we do."

"That's his Jaguar over there in the driveway," the deputy added.

A Jag, I thought. That figured. Mark loved his Corvette more than life itself. Certainly more than he loved me. He beat the crap out of me, but as far as I know, he never damaged so much as a fender on that precious car of his.

By the time Detective Barry rolled his window back up, I was already out of the car and headed up the sidewalk. He caught me before I made it to the front porch.

"Let me handle the guy, Detective Lanier," Barry said. "I know where he's coming from."

"I don't give a damn where he's coming from," I returned. "Just as long as he goes to jail."

"Jumping to conclusions, aren't we?" Barry taunted.

His patronizing attitude bugged the hell out of me. Yes, he had been a cop a whole lot longer than I had, transferring out to Washington State after years of being a detective in Chicago. But as a transferring officer, he had been cycled through King County's training program all the same, and he had spent his obligatory time in Patrol right along with the new hires. When it was time to make the move from Patrol to Detective Division, the two of us did it at almost the same time. Since scores on training exams are posted, I knew I had outscored him on every written exam we'd been given.

I shoved my clenched fists out of sight in the pockets of my already dripping raincoat. "Cram it, Barry," I told him. "I'll do my best to keep an open mind."

Looking at it from the outside, the house was one of those you expect to find featured on the pages of *House Beautiful* or *Architectural Digest*—vast expanses of clear glass and straight up-and-downs punctuated here and there by unexpectedly sharp angles. The place was lit up like the proverbial Christmas tree with warmly inviting lights glowing through every window. Appearances can be deceiving. Once inside, it was clear the entire house was a shambles.

Even in the well-appointed entryway, every available surface—including the burled maple entryway table—was covered with an accumulation of junk and debris. There were dirty dishes and glasses everywhere, along with a collection of empty beer and soda cans, overflowing ashtrays, and unopened mail. Under the table was a mound of at least a month's worth of yellowed, unread newspapers, still rolled up and encircled by rubber bands.

The human mind is an amazing device. One glance at that hopeless disarray threw me back ten years to the weeks and months just after I left Mark. Once beyond the initial blast of hurt and anger, I closeted myself away in a tiny, two-room apartment and drifted into a miasma of despair and self-loathing. It was a time when I didn't do the dishes, answer the phone, open the mail, pay the bills, or take messages off the machine. Even the simplest tasks became impossibilities, the smallest decisions unthinkable.

If it hadn't been for Aunt Mindy and Uncle Ed, I might be there still. The telephone company had already disconnected my phone for lack of payment when Aunt Mindy and Uncle Ed showed up on my doorstep early one Saturday morning. They knocked and knocked. When I wouldn't open the door, Uncle Ed literally broke it down. They packed me up, cleaned out the place, and took me home with them. One piece at a time, they helped me start gluing my life back together. Six months later I found myself down at the county courthouse, filling out an application to become a police officer.

Thrusting that sudden series of painful memories aside, I took a deep breath and focused my attention on the dead woman lying naked in the middle of the parquet entryway floor. Her pale skin was spotlit by the soft light of a huge crystal chandelier that hung down from the soaring ceiling some three stories above us.

Careful to disturb nothing, I stepped near enough to examine her more closely. Renee Denise de Gasteneau was white, blonde, and probably not much more than thirty. She lay sprawled in an awkward position. One knee was drawn up and thrust forward—as though she had been struck down in mid-stride.

While I bent over the body, Detective James Barry moved farther into the entryway and glanced into the living room.

"I'll tell you one thing," he announced. "This broad was almost as shitty a housekeeper as my ex-wife."

"Believe me," I returned coldly, "housekeeping is the least of this woman's problems."

Tom Hammond, an assistant from the Medical Examiner's office, was standing off to one side, watching us quizzically. "What do you think, Tom?" I asked.

"I've seen worse—housekeeping, that is."

"Forget the damn housekeeping, for godssake! What do you think killed her?"

"Too soon to tell," he replied. "I can see some bruising on the back of the neck, right there where her hair is parted. Could be from a blow to the back of the head. Could be she was strangled. We won't know for sure until we get her downtown."

"How long's she been dead?" Barry asked.

"Hard to say. Ten to twelve hours at least. Maybe longer."

About that time one of the county's crime-scene techs showed up with their photography equipment as well as the Alternate Light Source box that can be used to locate all kinds of trace evidence from latent fingerprints to stray strands of hair or thread or carpet fuzz. What crime techs need more than anything is for people to get the hell out of the way and leave them alone.

"Let's go talk to her husband," I said.

"Suits me," Detective Barry said.

We found Dr. Emile de Gasteneau sitting in an Adirondack chair on a covered deck at the rear of the house. He sat there, sobbing quietly, his face buried in his hands. When he glanced up at our approach, his cheeks were wet with tears. "Are you the detectives?" he croaked.

I nodded and flashed my badge in front of him, but he barely noticed. "I didn't mean for it to end this way," he groaned.

"What way is that, Dr. de Gasteneau?" I asked.

"With her dead like this," he answered hopelessly. "I just wanted to get on with my life. I never meant to hurt her."

My initial reaction was to Mirandize the guy on the spot. It sounded to me as though he was ready to blurt out a full-blown confession, and I didn't want it disqualified in a court of law on some stupid technicality.

Evidently Detective Barry didn't agree. He stepped forward and moved me aside. "How's that, Dr. de Gasteneau? How'd you hurt your wife?"

"I left her," the seemingly distraught man answered. "I just couldn't go on living a lie. I told her I wanted out, but I offered her a good settlement, a fair settlement. I told her she could have the entire equity from the house on the condition she sell it as soon as possible. I thought she'd take the money and run—find someplace less expensive to live and keep the change.

"Instead, she just let the place go to ruin. You can see it's a mess. There's a For Sale sign out front, but as far as I know, no one's even been out here to look at it. I think the real estate agent is ashamed to bring any-one by. I don't blame her. Who would want to buy a $750,000 pigsty—"

"Excuse me, Dr. de Gasteneau," I interrupted. "It sounds to me as though you're more upset by the fact that your wife was a poor housekeep-er than you are by the fact she's dead."

The widower stiffened and glared at me. "That was rude."

"So is murder," I countered.

Giving up on any possibility of a voluntary confession, I took my notepad out of my pocket. "Are you the one who called 9-1-1?"

De Gasteneau nodded. "Yes."

"What time?"

He glanced at his watch—an expensive jewel-encrusted timepiece the size of a doorknob, with luminous hands that glowed in the dim light of the porch. "Right after I got here," he answered. "About an hour ago now."

Without a word, Detective Barry stepped off the porch and moved pur-posefully toward the Jaguar parked a few feet away in the driveway. He put his hand on the hood, checking for residual warmth, and then nodded in my direction.

"Since you and your wife were separated, why did you come here?"

"Mrs. Wilbur called me."

"Who's she?"

"A neighbor from just across the road. She was worried about Renee. She called my office and asked me to come check on her—on Renee."

"Why?"

"I don't know. She was worried about her, I guess. I told her I'd come over right after work."

"Why was she worried? Had she seen strange cars, heard noises, what?"

"I don't know. She didn't say, and I didn't ask. I came out as soon as I could. I had an engagement."

I was about to ask him what kind of engagement when Detective Barry sauntered back up onto the porch. "That's a pretty slick Jagwire you've got out there. Always wanted to get me one of those. What kind of gas mileage does that thing get?"

"It's not that good on gas," de Gasteneau admitted.

Jagwire! The man sounded like he'd just crawled out from under a rock. Renee de Gasteneau was dead, and here was this jerk of a Detective Barry sounding like a hick out kicking the tires at some exotic car dealership. How the hell did Captain Waldron expect me to work with a creep like that?

"How about if we step inside, Dr. de Gasteneau?" I said. "Maybe you can tell us whether or not anything is missing from your wife's house."

What I really wanted to do was to get inside where the light was better. I wanted to check out Emile de Gasteneau's arms and wrists and the backs of his hands to see if there were any scratches, any signs of a life-and-death struggle that might have left telltale marks on the living flesh of Renee de Gasteneau's killer.

Without a word the good doctor de Gasteneau stood up and went inside. "Just wait," Detective Barry whispered over my shoulder as we followed him into the house. "Next thing you know, he's going to try telling us a one-armed man did it. You know—like in *The Fugitive.*"

"Please," I sighed. "I got it. You don't have to explain." As we trailed Dr. de Gasteneau from one impossibly messy room to another, I stole several discreet glances in the direction of his hands and arms. I was more disappointed than I should have been when there was nothing to see.

Checking throughout the house, it was difficult to tell whether or not anything was missing. Several television sets and VCRs were in their proper places as were two very expensive stereo systems. The jewelry was a tougher call, but as far as de Gasteneau could tell, none of that was missing, either.

"When's the last time you saw your wife?" I asked as we left the upstairs master bedroom and headed back toward the main level of the house.

He paused before he answered. "Two weeks ago," he answered guardedly. "But you probably already know about that."

"You mean the time when you were arrested for hitting her?"

"Yes."

"And you haven't seen her since then?"

"No."

"What time do you get off work?"

"Between four and four-thirty. I'm my own boss. I come and go when I damn well please."

"But you told the neighbor, Mrs. Wilbur, that you'd come here as soon as you could after work. The 9-1-1 call didn't come in until a little after eight. Where were you between four and eight?"

"I already told you. I had an engagement."

"With whom?"

"I don't have to tell you that."

"Phyllis—" Detective Barry interjected, but I silenced him with a single hard-edged stare. I was on track, and I wasn't about to let him pull me away.

"You're right," I said easily. "You don't have to tell us anything at all. But if you don't, I guarantee you we'll find out anyway—one way or the other."

It was nothing more than an empty threat, but de Gasteneau fell for it all the same. "I was seeing my friend," he conceded angrily. "We met for a drink."

Just the way he answered triggered a warning signal in my mind, made me wonder if we were dealing with a lover's triangle. "What kind of friend?" I asked. "Male or female?"

"A male friend," he answered.

So much for the lover theory, I thought. I said, "What's his name?"

De Gasteneau looked at Detective Barry in a blatant appeal for help, but I wasn't about to be derailed. "What's his name?" I insisted.

"Garth," de Gasteneau answered flatly. "His name's Garth Homewood. But please don't call him. Believe me, he's got nothing to do with all this."

"Why would we think he did?" I asked.

We were descending the broad, carpeted stairway when, suddenly, de Gasteneau sank down on the bottom step.

"Garth and I are lovers," he answered unexpectedly. "He's the whole reason I left Renee in the first place. I guess that's one of the reasons she was so upset about it. Maybe if I'd left her for another woman, it wouldn't have bothered her so much."

These are the nineties. Detective Barry and I are both adults and we are both cops. I guess de Gasteneau's admission shouldn't have shocked or surprised either one of us, but it did. My partner looked stunned. I felt like someone who pokes something he thinks is a dead twig only to have it turn out to be a quick brown snake. Once again I was struck by an incredible feeling of kinship toward the dead woman. Poor Renee de Gasteneau. It occurred to me that learning her husband was gay was probably as much a blow to her self-esteem as Mark Lanier's punishing balled fist had been to mine.

"Why?" I said. Not why did you leave her? That much was clear. But why did you marry her in the first place?

The last question as well as the unspoken ones that followed were more reflex than anything else. I didn't really expect Emile de Gasteneau to answer, but he did.

"I tricked her," he admitted, somberly. "I wanted an heir, a child. Someone to leave all this to." His despairing glance encompassed the whole house and everything in it. "Except it didn't work out. I picked the wrong woman. Renee loved me, I guess, but I didn't care about her. Not the same way she did for me. And when it turned out she couldn't get pregnant, it was too much. After a while, I couldn't bring myself to try anymore. It was too dishonest. Now she's dead. Although I didn't kill her, I know it's my fault."

The tears came again. While Emile de Gasteneau sat sobbing on the bottom stair, Detective Barry tapped me on the shoulder.

"Come on," he said, jerking his head toward the door. "Leave the guy alone. Let's go talk to the woman across the street."

I thought it was uncharacteristically nice of Barry to want to give the poor man some privacy, but outside and safely out of earshot, James Joseph Barry, ex-Chicago cop, let go with an amazing string of oaths.

"The guy's a frigging queer!" he raged. "For all we know, he's probably dying of AIDS. Jesus Christ! Did he breathe on us? You got a breath spray on you?"

Detective Barry's only obvious concession toward society's current mania for political correctness was refraining from use of the N-word in racially mixed company. The word "gay" had neither entered his vocabulary nor penetrated his consciousness. I, too, had been shocked by Emile de Gasteneau's revelation, but not for the same reason my partner was.

We walked across the road together and made our way down a steeply pitched driveway to the house we had been told belonged to a family named Wilbur. This one was somewhat older than Renee de Gasteneau's had been, and slightly less showy, but it was still a very expensive piece of suburban real estate.

Detective Barry continued to mutter under his breath as he rang the doorbell. An attractive woman in her late sixties or early seventies answered the door and switched on the porch light. "Yes?" she said guardedly. "Can I help you?" I moved forward and showed her my badge. "We're Detectives Barry and Lanier," I explained. "We're investigating the incident across the street. Are you Mrs. Wilbur?"

She nodded but without opening the door any wider. "Inez," she said, "what do you want?"

"I understand you were the person who called Dr. de Gasteneau. Is that true?"

"Yes."

"Why did you call him? Did you hear something unusual? See something out of the ordinary?"

"Well, yes. I mean no. It's just that Renee was always on the go, rushing off this way or that. When her car didn't move all day long, I was worried."

I looked back over my shoulder. From where I stood on the front step of Inez Wilbur's porch, only the topmost gable of the de Gasteneau roof was visible over the crest of the hill. Inez Wilbur seemed to follow both my movements as well as my train of thought.

"You're right," she put in quickly, "it's not easy to see from where you are, but I can see her house from upstairs, from my room . . ."

"Mama," a man's voice said from somewhere behind her. "Who is it?"

"It's nothing, Carl. Go back to your program. I'll be done here in a minute."

"But it's a boring program, Mama," he replied. "I don't like it."

The voice had the basso timbre of an adult, but the words were the whining complaints of a dissatisfied child.

"Please, Carl," Inez Wilbur said, with a tight frown. "Change channels then. I'll be done in a minute."

"Who's Carl?" I asked.

"He's my son," she answered. "He's not a child, but he's like a child, if you know what I mean. All this would upset him terribly."

"All what would upset him terribly?" I asked.

A look of anguished confusion washed over Inez Wilbur's delicately made-up face. "About Mrs. de Gasteneau."

"What about her?"

"She's dead, isn't she?"

"Mama," Carl said behind her, "who is it? Is it company? Are we going to have dessert now?"

Inez let go of the doorknob and covered her face with her hands. Slowly, as though being pushed by the wind, the heavy wooden door swung open.

A large, open-faced man with a wild headful of slightly graying hair stood illuminated in the vestibule behind her. He was wearing a short-sleeved shirt and expertly playing with a yo-yo. His muscular forearms were raked with long deep parallel scratches—a last desperate message from a dying woman.

"Hello, Carl," I said quietly. "My name's Detective Lanier and this is Detective Barry. We'd like to talk to you for a few minutes if you don't mind."

Inez stepped aside and let us into the house while Carl Wilbur's mouth broke into a broad, gap-toothed grin. "Detectives? Really? Do you hear that,

Mama? They're cops, and they want to talk to me!"

Inez Wilbur's face collapsed like a shattered teacup, and she began to cry.

Detective Barry pulled his Miranda card out of his wallet. "I'll bet you've seen this on *TV,* Carl. It's called reading you your rights. "You have the right to remain silent..."

*   *   *

It was six o'clock the next morning before we finally finished our paper. Inez Wilbur had tried to explain to Renee de Gasteneau that Carl was watching her, that she should always pull her curtains and be more careful about walking around the house without any clothes on. But Renee had ignored the warnings just as she had ignored Carl himself.

In the aftermath of Emile's defection, Renee de Gasteneau had searched for validation of her womanhood by taking on all comers. Carl Wilbur, her curious neighbor, had watched all the proceedings with rapt fascination, learning as he did so that there was more to life than he had previously suspected, that there were some interesting things that he wanted to try for himself. And when those things were denied him, he had responded with unthinking but lethal rage. He had thrown a lifeless Renee de Gasteneau to the floor, like a discarded and broken doll.

I was dragging myself out to the parking lot when Captain Waldron caught me by the front door. He hurried up to me, his kind face etched with concern.

"Are you all right?" he asked.

"Just tired. Worn out."

Detective Barry drove by out in the parking lot. He tapped on his horn and waved. I waved back.

"Tough case," Captain Waldron said, "but you handled it like a pair of champs. How do you like working with Detective Barry?"

"He's okay," I said.

Waldron nodded. "Good. I was worried about whether or not you two could get along."

I laughed. "Why? Because Barry's an asshole?"

"No, because of his divorce."

"What about his divorce?"

"You mean you don't know about that? It's common knowledge. I thought everyone knew. His wife left him because he beat her up and she turned him in. That's why he transferred out here from Chicago. Her father's a captain on the Berwyn P.D. somewhere outside of Chicago. I guess things got pretty sticky for a while, but with his track record for cracking serial-killer cases, the sheriff was willing to take him on."

"No questions asked?" I demanded.

Waldron shrugged. "I think he had to complete one of those anger-management courses."

"Did he?"

"As far as I know. I just wanted to let you know how glad I was that the two of you were able to get along."

"We got along, all right," I said. "Just like oil and water."

STUART M. KAMINSKY

Blowout in Little Man Flats

THE LAST MURDER IN LITTLE MAN FLATS was back in, let me see, 1963, before Kennedy was shot by who knows how or why," Sheriff George Fingerhurt told his prime suspect. "Want some tea? Do you good in this heat."

"No . . . thanks."

"Suit yourself."

Fingerhurt sat back drinking his herbal peppermint tea from the Rhett Butler cup his daughter had brought him from Atlanta. George Fingerhurt liked Rhett Butler and herbal tea. Rhett was cool, never mind the temperature—like today, pushing a hundred in the shade.

"Got a theory about tea, got it from my grandfather Ocean Fingerhurt who was half Apache. Grandpa Ocean said hot tea cooled you off. Since Grandpa Ocean had got lost and wound up in Little Man Flats, New Mexico, back in 1930, when he thought he was in southern California, he was hardly a man to trust, at least not about directions. He was better about tea. Sure you don't want to change your mind?"

"Okay," said the suspect. "I'll have some tea."

"Gets dry out here," said the sheriff, pouring a cup of dark-green tea into a Scarlett O'Hara cup and handing it to the truckdriver, whose name, as he had told the sheriff, was Tector (Teck) Gorch. "Careful—hot."

"Obliged," said Teck.

They drank for about a minute, and Teck looked out the window.

"Quite a crowd," the sheriff said.

"Umm," Teck grunted.

There were eight people outside the one-story adobe town hall and sheriff's office. One of them was Ollie Twilly, from the feed store, wide-brimmed Stetson shading his eyes as he leaned back against the front fend-er of his '88 Ford pickup. Ollie had reason to be there. His brother Stan was one of the three people who had been killed, probably by the trucker sitting across from George drinking herbal tea.

The trucker was, George figured, maybe thirty-five, forty. One of those solid mailbox types. Curly hair cut a little long, could use a shave, but con-sidering what had happened, made sense he hadn't considered the social graces. Teck the trucker was wearing slightly washed-out blood-specked jeans and a bloody T-shirt with the words I'M HAVING A BAD DAY writ-ten across the front in black. Amen to that sentiment, George thought.

"Last murder, back when I was a boy," George explained after a careful sip. "Indian named Double Eagle out of Gallup on a motorcycle went ravin' down 66 and plowed into Andrew Carpenter. Jury figured it was on pur-pose. Not much point to it. Andrew was near ninety. Am I getting too folksy for you? I haven't had much practice with murder cases. Haven't had any, really."

Teck shrugged and tried to think. The tea was making him feel a little cooler, but the sheriff was making him nervous. Fingerhurt was wearing matching khaki trousers and short-sleeved shirt. His black hair was freshly cut, combed straight back, and he looked a hell of a lot like the crying Indian in the TV commercials about polluting the rivers.

A sweat-stained khaki cowboy hat sat on the empty desk.

"Hey," said Fingerhurt, pointing out the window. "Crowd's growing. Those two are Mr. and Mrs. Barcheck, what passes for society in Little Man Flats. Own a lot of the town, including the Navajo Fill-up."

Teck looked out the window for the first time.

"Nice-lookin' woman," the sheriff said. "Not enough meat for me, but we're not in Santa Fe, so one's voyeuristic choices are limited. You wanna just tell your story? State police'll be here in a half hour, maybe less, to pick you up. Won't have a good report on what it looks like up there till Red comes in." Teck held his cup in two hands, feeling warm moisture seep into his palms.

"Red's my deputy, one you saw out at the Fill-up."

"His hair isn't red," said Teck.

"Never was. His father had red hair, was called Red. Deputy was Little Red. When his daddy died, deputy was just plain Red."

"Interesting," said Teck.

It was the sheriff's turn to shrug.

"Say, listen, information like that counts for lore in Little Man Flats."

He looked out the window and observed, "Crowd's getting bigger. I'd say twenty out there, coming to take a look at you. Four, five more people, and practically the whole town'll have turned out. State troopers are gonna be here soon, asking if I found anything. You want to tell your story? I'll take notes."

"I'm arrested? I need a lawyer?"

"You're here for questioning in the murder of Miss Rose Bryant Fernandez, Mr. Stanley Twilly, and a man who had a wallet in his back pocket strongly suggesting he was Lincoln Smart. You know the man?"

"Trucker, like me," said Teck. "Knew him to say hello. Where's my rig?"

"Safe, gathering dust out at the Fill-up, where you parked it. Wanna tell me what happened out there?"

"Someone cut your population almost in half," said Teck without a smile.

Sheriff Fingerhurt shook his head. He put down his Rhett Butler cup and folded his hands, looking unblinking at the trucker. "Educated?"

"A little too much," said Teck. "Almost finished college. Almost a lot of things."

"Feeling a little sorry for yourself?"

"Considering, I think I've got a right."

"Maybe so. Story?"

Teck sat back, looked out the window at the gathered crowd, focused on a little boy about nine, who was looking directly back at him and covering his eyes to shade out the sun.

"Came thundering in a little before four in the morning," Teck began, nodding his agreement to the sheriff, who had pulled a tape recorder out of a desk drawer. Fingerhurt pushed the button and sat back.

"Came thundering in before four in the morning," Teck repeated. "Wanted to make Gallup, usually do. Never stopped at the Navajo Fill-up overnight before. One bad tire out of sixteen didn't stop me. I'd have even tried outlasting the knock in the diesel, even with nothing but desert for fifty more miles. Rain and backache did me in. Learned enough in eleven years in the high cab to know that when the back says stop, you stop, or you will have one hell of a tomorrow."

Sheriff Fingerhurt nodded and shook his head.

"Grit and sand on my neck, air conditioner gone lazy, shirt sticking to my chest, back, and deep down into my behind," Teck continued. "I was a sorry mess by one in the A.M. I never stopped in your town before last night except for diesel. I don't know the two locals who got killed, and I barely knew Line."

"Lincoln Smart, the other driver?" asked the sheriff.

"There was only one rig in the opening beyond the pumps. Linc's big silver-and-blue, bigger than mine. I own my truck out there, and I've got a load of furniture from a factory just outside of Baines, Arkansas. Taking it to a pair of stores in Bakersfield."

"Where you from, Teck?"

"Tupelo. Tupelo, Mississippi."

"Elvis's town?"

"Yeah."

"You ever see the King himself?"

"He was long gone when I was growing up."

Sheriff Fingerhurt sat back, shaking his head.

"Well," Teck went on, "I—"

"Married?" asked the sheriff.

"Divorced. One kid. A boy, about seven or eight."

"You don't know?"

"Seven. His birthday's February 11. I just forget the year. Haven't seen him for three years. My ex-wife won't let me."

"Sorry," said Fingerhurt.

"I got bigger things to worry about today," Teck said, putting down his now empty cup.

"Yeah," said the sheriff.

"Got out of my rig, with my rain poncho over my head, duffel in my hand, locked up, and went inside the cafe. Woman behind the counter was reading a paperback."

"Remember what it was?"

"Make a difference?"

"Who knows?" said Fingerhurt.

"Woman behind the counter looked up at me like I was a surprise she could have done without," Teck went on. "People tend not to be overjoyed when I walk in, but this woman—"

"Rosie Fernandez," Fingerhurt supplied.

"I guess," Teck said with a shrug, looking out the window.

The small crowd had grown. There were more men now, and they were talking, arguing.

"You ever have a lynching in this town?" Teck said, his eyes meeting those of Ollie Twilly, whose Stetson was now tilted back on his head. Ollie either had a very high forehead or he was bald. Bald or balding, he was clearly in one hell of a bad mood.

"Not a white man," said the sheriff. "Last Indian was shot in 1928 by a mob for drunk talk to a white woman."

"Your grandfather picked one hell of a town to settle in," Teck said.

"He was lost."

"We keep this up, I won't get my story told before the troopers get here," Teck said.

"Go on. Rose Fernandez was behind the counter, reading a paperback."

"Dean Koontz. It was Dean Koontz."

"Read one by him," said Fingerhurt. "People turned into machines in a small town. Scared shit out of me."

"I asked her for a room and something to eat," Teck went on. "I wasn't particular as long as it wasn't trout. I'm allergic."

"We don't have much call for trout in New Mexico," the sheriff said.

Outside the window, the crowd was getting louder, and there was, the sheriff noted, a very bad sign even a white man could read. The children were being sent off, as if there might be something the adults didn't want them to see.

"I think they're working themselves up to come here and lynch me," said Teck, following the sheriff's line of vision.

"Closest yucca that'll hold your weight is two miles out of town," said the sheriff, reaching for his hat. "Shoot you is what I'm thinking."

"Like the Indian in 1928?"

"Something like that," George Fingerhurt agreed. "But we'll stop 'em."

"We?"

"Me and Red. He's pulling up."

About twenty-five yards beyond the window where the crowd had gathered, a dust-covered pickup pulled in and a man in jeans, a khaki shirt, and a hat climbed out.

People flocked around him as he strode forward, shaking his head.

"He found something," the sheriff said.

"How can you tell? Your Indian blood?"

"Got the look. Known Red for almost forty years. You know things like that about people you know."

The door behind Teck flew open, and voices from outside came in, full of fear and anger. Red closed the door and stepped in. He was thinner and, considering the mood of the mob, less formidable than Teck would have liked. Red looked at the sheriff and then at Teck.

"Wanna talk in the other room, George?"

"What'd you find?" asked the sheriff.

"You sure you—"

"You found what, Red?"

"Troopers came with a truck. All over the place. Told me I could go. They'd be here quick. Said we shoulda held Gorch at the murder site. Found this under Rosie's body. Said you should have a look at it."

Red stepped to the sheriff's desk, avoiding Teck's eyes, pulled a crumpled paper bag out of his jeans pocket, and handed it to George Fingerhurt. The sheriff held the bag open behind the desk, looked into it and then out the window and then at Red.

"Damn," said Fingerhurt.

"Damn right, damn," said Red.

"Sheriff. . . ." Teck tried, but the door behind him opened with a jolt. He turned and found himself facing Ollie Twilly, both Barchecks, and a variety of others, mostly with the look and matching intellect of bewildered cattle. Twilly was carrying a shotgun.

"We want him," said Ollie, pointing his shotgun barrel at Teck, who jumped up and stood with his back to the wall behind the still seated sheriff.

"You all want him? You too, Mrs. Barcheck?" Fingerhurt asked.

"Yes," she said.

She was, indeed, a fine-looking woman, freckled brown with yellow hair tied back, could have been any age from thirty to fifty, Teck thought, and wondered how he could do such thinking with a shotgun cocked and aimed in the general area of his gut.

"And what'll you do with him?" asked the sheriff.

"Take him out. Shoot him," said Twilly. "Shoot him through the brains like the dog he is."

The shotgun came up toward Teck Gorch's face, and Ollie Twilly continued with:

"You shot my brother like a dog, and I'm—"

"How'd you know Stan was shot, Mr. Twilly?" the sheriff asked, as two of the more oxlike men stepped toward Teck.

"Red told us," said Andrew Barcheck, who was decidedly a slouching Saint Bernard to his wife's well-groomed poodle.

The sheriff closed his eyes and shook his head before he looked up at Red, whose left cheek twitched.

"George, you and Red go out for a shake at Veronica's," said Ollie Twilly. "When you come back—"

"No, Mr. Twilly," said the sheriff.

"We'll have your goddamn job, George," Twilly said through gritted teeth.

"You couldn't live on my salary, Mr. Twilly You take him. You shoot him. Red and I arrest you for murder," said the sheriff. "Is it worth going to jail for, Mr. Twilly?"

"Yes."

The two bovine men were now about three feet in front of Teck, who had sucked in his stomach, feeling more than a little sick.

"Rest of you feel the same way?" the sheriff asked. "You got murder looking at you, conspiracy, impeding a lawman in the dispatching of his duty. Hell, folks, you're looking at a lot of bleak years in the state house."

"No jury will convict us. Not after what he did."

"Act your age, Ollie," Mrs. Barcheck said. "There isn't a jury that wouldn't convict us."

"Then by shit and a wild pig," shouted Twilly, "I don't give a crap. I'll shoot him right here."

The two bulls in front of Teck jumped out of the line of fire.

"Man was telling his side when you came in," said the sheriff. "Think you can hold off till he finishes? Give him that?"

"Let him speak, Ollie," Mr. Barcheck said.

Someone behind the front line let out a groan and an "Oh, shit."

"Miguel, that you?" the sheriff called.

A heavy, hard-breathing dark man with bad skin worked his way forward through the crowd.

"Let him say," Miguel said.

"No," said Twilly, the gun now firmly against the chest of Miguel.

"My sister got killed last night too," Miguel Fernandez said. "We can listen. Who knows what Leon Harvey Oswald would have said if the Jew guy hadn't shot him?"

"Lee. Oswald's name was Lee," Mrs. Barcheck corrected.

"And the man who shot him was Jack Ruby."

"This isn't goddamn Trivial Pursuit," screamed Twilly. "Can't you see Fingerhurt's stalling till the state police get here?"

"I'll look out the window," said Miguel. "We see them coming, and you can shoot."

Defeated for the moment, Ollie Twilly let the shotgun point toward the floor.

"Finish your story, Tector," the sheriff said.

Teck, back to the wall, looked at the faces of anger, hate, and confusion around the room.

"I don't think I . . . " Teck began, and then said, "I walked in, soaking wet, told the woman I needed a room for the night and a mechanic in the morning. She said . . ."

Teck's eyes met Miguel's and then went to the sheriff.

"I don't . . ."

"Tector," said the sheriff, "I don't see a hell of a lot of choice here, do you?"

"She said all she had was eggs any way I wanted 'em, and if I wanted company in bed for a couple of hours, she could handle that too, for a reasonable fee."

Teck's eyes were watching Miguel Fernandez. Fernandez betrayed nothing but heavy breathing.

"I said I'd think on it," Teck went on.

"A fine-looking woman, Rosie," said the sheriff. "Some meat on her bones. Nothing to hold back here, Teck. Rosie was the town—begging your pardon, Mrs. Barcheck—lady of the afternoon and evening."

"She was a whore, yes," said Miguel, "but she was a good person. Anybody in this room say anything else?"

No one in the room had anything else to say relating to Rosie Fernandez's behavior, so the sheriff nodded at Teck, who went on.

"She said she'd make me two over-easy sandwiches with mayo and onions and figured from the onion order that I wasn't interested in company. I said I wanted to change into something dry, and she told me to go up the stairs off in the corner and go into room three, where I could shower and get decent and dry."

"What else?" the sheriff said.

"Jukebox in the corner near the window was playing Patsy Cline," Teck said hopefully.

"She was reading Dean Koontz and listening to Patsy Cline," the sheriff said.

"Stairs were dark. I started up. This guy passed me coming down."

"Guy?" asked Fingerhurt. "What'd he look like?"

"Don't know. Wasn't really looking. About my height, weight. Maybe."

"Met himself coming and going," said Twilly. "We heard enough here yet?"

"Wait," Teck said. "He had a big silver belt buckle."

"Every man in this room and a few of the women are wearing big silver belt buckles," the sheriff said. "Even me and Red."

"I'm telling you what I remember," Teck pleaded. "I'm telling the truth."

"Okay. Sha-hair-a-zadie," said Ollie Twilly. "Keep going."

"Not much more to tell. I went to room three, got my clean jeans, socks, and the shirt I'm wearing out of my bag, took a quick shower, got dressed, and headed back down. Patsy Cline was still singing, eggs were burning bad, and Miss Fernandez was laying there in the middle of the room, dead and bloody. I tried to help her, but she was—"

"And you were covered in her blood," the sheriff said.

"Yes."

"And then?"

"I called for help. No one answered. The rain was harder. It was pushing dawn. I ran back up the stairs and knocked at doors and yelled. No answer. One of the doors was open. Line Smart was naked, bloody, and dead. I kept opening doors. One was an office. Bald man was laying across the desk, dead."

"That was my brother. That was Stan," cried Ollie. "You lying son of a bitch and a half."

"No," said Teck, holding up his hands to ward off the anticipated shotgun blast. "No lie. I found the phone, called the operator, told her that someone had murdered who knows how many people at the Navajo Fill-up. And that was it."

The sheriff's eyes met Teck's and then moved for an instant to the running tape recorder before returning to Teck's face.

"Question, Mr. Gorch," the sheriff said. "You didn't hear gunshots when you drove up to the Fill-up and walked in?"

"No. It was raining hard. Whoever it was must have shot Line and the other guy before I got to the door."

"How many times were they shot, Red?" the sheriff asked.

"The trucker three times, Mr. Stanley Twilly twice. Then Miss Rosie twice."

"Why," the sheriff asked, "did Miss Rosie sit there reading a Dean Koontz and offer you eggs and companionship if she just heard five shots?"

"Yes," said Miguel, turning angrily toward Teck.

"I don't know," said Teck.

"And why didn't you hear Rosie getting shot?" the sheriff went on.

"I was in the shower. It was raining hard. I don't know."

"This is the stupidest damn story," Ollie said. "Everybody step back. Fairy tale's over."

The shotgun came up toward Teck again.

"Why would I kill those people?" Teck said.

"You thought Rose was alone," said Ollie. "You went for her behind the counter. She fought you, threatened to call the sheriff. You shot her. Then you panicked and went to look for any witnesses who might have seen you. You shot that truckdriver and my brother."

"And then I called the police?" Teck cried.

"Maybe you were trying to be tricky," Miguel Fernandez said. "Maybe you just got damned confused, decided you couldn't get away, tire tracks, whatever. So you made up your story."

"No," cried Teck. "Sheriff."

"What'd he do with the gun?" Sheriff Fingerhurt asked.

"Threw it away, maybe buried it couple hundred yards off in the desert," said Barcheck. "What's the difference?"

"Troopers are coming down the street," said Miguel softly, turning his eyes to Teck's frightened face.

"That does it," said Ollie. "Everybody stand back. We in this together?"

The two bulls who had approached Teck grunted something. The rest of the crowd was shuffling, silent now that the troopers were a minute or two away.

"I've got one thing I can't figure," said the sheriff. "If his story is true, why didn't Rose call me and Red, or go upstairs to see what was happening? Why did she sit there reading a book?"

"He made up a dumb story," said Miguel.

"Miguel," said the sheriff, "how long I know you?"

"Your whole life."

"What if Rose did hear the shots? What if Rose knew Stan and the trucker were dead when Gorch came in looking for a warm room and meal? What if he surprised her, she picked up a book, looked as if she didn't want company, and then, to keep him from getting suspicious, offered to bed down with him for the night, not forgetting to say it wasn't free. Gorch goes upstairs. Killer comes down. Rose tells him about Gorch. Killer gets the idea of blaming everything on the dumb trucker. Sorry, Tector."

"No offense," said Teck.

"Why would anyone want to kill my brother?" Ollie said.

"Property, money's my guess," said Sheriff Fingerhurt. "Killer probably considered burying Stan and the dead trucker and having Rose say Stan just got fed up, grabbed some cash, and took off for northern California."

The troopers' car door opened and then slammed shut a beat later. All eyes turned to the window. Two troopers were walking toward the Little

Man Flats municipal building, where most of the adult population was gathered in the sheriff's office.

"That's crazy," shouted Ollie.

The sheriff lifted his right hand and displayed a crinkled brown paper bag.

"Red found this on the floor under Rose's body," he said, pulling a bright silver buckle out of the bag and holding it up for the congregation to see. The silver was hammered into the shape of a buffalo, with huge horns in relief.

"So," said Miguel, "everybody around here has a belt buckle like that, something like that. It could be this guy's, this truckdriver's."

"Right," said the sheriff, "but he's got a buckle on his belt, and he had time to look for it if Rose pulled it off in a struggle with him. But the killer, the killer heard the shower go off, made a decision not to kill the trucker, and ran without finding the buckle. Hell, maybe he didn't even notice till he got home or too far to turn back."

The door behind the crowd opened, and a deep voice said: "What the hell is going on in here?"

"I'm not interested in who has a buffalo-head silver buckle," said Fingerhurt, ignoring the troopers who were muscling their way forward through the gathering. "I'm interested in who *doesn't* have one anymore. With the cooperation of the troopers who have just arrived, I'm going to ask a few of you who I know have buffalo buckles to go back to their houses with me and show me the buckle. Miguel, Dan Sullivan, Mr. Barcheck, and you, Ollie."

The troopers were in front now, near twins, well built, unwrinkled uniforms, hats flat on their heads and brims perfectly parallel to the ground.

"What's going on, George?" the older of the two said.

The sheriff held up a finger to show that he needed only a minute more.

"All right with me," said Barcheck.

"Me too," said Miguel.

"I'm wearing mine," said Danny Sullivan, stepping forward to show the buckle in question.

"Mr. Twilly?" Sheriff Fingerhurt asked.

"Lost," he said defiantly. "I looked for it a few days ago. Someone stole it."

"You wore it yesterday, Oliver," Mrs. Barcheck said.

"Hey, that's right," said Danny Sullivan. "You sat next to me at Veronica's for lunch. You were wearing the buckle. You had the meat loaf with chilies, and I had . . . who the hell cares what I had?"

"Is there a punch line here, George?" the older trooper said, doing a magnificent job of hiding his complete confusion.

"I think Mr. Twilly here has some questions to answer," the sheriff said.

The shotgun was coming up again, but before Twilly could level it at anyone, Teck Gorch pushed himself from the wall with a rebel yell and threw himself at the armed man. The shotgun barrel was still coming up toward Teck's face when Miguel Fernandez punched Twilly in the gut. Twilly went down with Teck on top of him, and the shotgun spun around in the air like the bone at the beginning of *2001*.

Three people made it out the door. Some went for the floor. Barcheck pushed his wife against the wall. The troopers and Red dived behind the desk, where Sheriff George Fingerhurt sat shaking his head.

The gun hit the ceiling, dropped quickly to the floor with a clatter-clack, and didn't discharge.

It took Red about twenty seconds to clear everyone but the troopers, the sheriff, Teck, and Ollie out of the room.

It took Ollie Twilly two minutes and some resuscitation from the younger trooper to revive enough to deny everything, from his affair with Rose to the murder of his brother. He even managed to deny a variety of crimes, including felonies of which no one had yet accused him.

Within four minutes, the troopers were being led by Red, with Ollie in tow, for a tour of Ollie's home and office.

"Can I go now?" Teck asked when he was alone with the sheriff again.

"Nope," said Fingerhurt. "You're our key witness."

"But . . ."

"Up to the troopers now," the sheriff said. "They can let you go when they take you off my hands, but who knows. Maybe they'll get a statement and let you deliver your furniture to Bakersfield."

"Okay if I go back to my rig and pick up some clean clothes?"

"Sure," said the sheriff "I'll give you a lift."

George Fingerhurt backed his wheelchair from behind the desk and carefully maneuvered it through the space between it and the window. From that point, it was out the door, down the ramp, and another day starting.

HARRY KEMELMAN

Time and Time Again

LTHOUGH IT WAS MORE THAN TWO YEARS since I had left the Law Faculty to become County Attorney, I still maintained some connection with the university. I still had the privileges of the gymnasium and the library and I still kept up my membership in the Faculty Club. I dropped in there occasionally for a game of billiards, and about once a month I dined there, usually with Nichols Welt.

We had finished dinner, Nicky and I, and had repaired to the Commons Room for a game of chess, only to find that all the tables were in use. So we joined the group in front of the fire where there was always interminable talk about such highly scholarly matters as to whether there was any likelihood of favorable action by the trustees on an increase in salary schedules—there wasn't—or whether you got more miles per gallon with a Chevrolet than you got with a Ford.

This evening as we joined the group, the talk was about Professor Rollins' paper in the Quarterly Journal of Psychic Research, which no one had read but on which everyone had an opinion. The title of the paper was something like "Modifications in the Sprague Method of Analysis of Extra-Sensory Experimentation Data," but the academic mind with its faculty for generalization had quickly gone beyond the paper and Rollins' theories to a discussion on whether there was anything in "this business of the supernatural," with burly professor Lionel Graham, Associate in Physics, asserting that "of course, there couldn't be when you considered the type of people who went in for it, gypsies and whatnot." And gentle, absentminded Roscoe Summers, Professor of Archaeology, maintaining doggedly that you couldn't always tell by that and that he had heard stories from people whose judgment he respected that made you pause and think a bit.

To which Professor Graham retorted, "That's just the trouble. It's always something that happened to somebody else. Or better still, something that somebody told you that happened to somebody he knew." Then catching sight of us, he said, "Isn't that right, Nicky? Did you ever hear about anything supernatural as having happened to somebody you yourself knew well and whose word and opinion you could rely on?"

Nicky's lined, gnomelike face relaxed in a frosty little smile. "I'm afraid that's how I get most of my information," he said. "I mean through hearing about it at third or fourth hand."

Dr. Chisholm, the young instructor in English Composition, had been trying to get a word in and now he succeeded. "I had a case last summer. I mean I was there and witnessed something that was either supernatural or was a most remarkable coincidence."

"Something on the stage, or was it a séance in a dark room?" asked Graham with a sneer.

"Neither," said Chisholm defiantly. "I saw a man cursed and he died of it." He caught sight of a pompous little man with a shining bald head and he called out, "Professor Rollins, won't you join us? I'm sure you'd be interested in a little incident I was about to tell."

Professor Rollins, the author of the paper in the Quarterly, approached and the men sitting on the red leather divan moved over respectfully to make room for him. But he seemed to sense that he was being asked to listen as an expert and he selected a straight-backed chair as being more in keeping with the judicial role he was to play.

*   *   *

I spent my summer vacation (Chisholm began) in a little village on the Maine coast. It was not a regular summer resort and there was little to do all day long except sit on the rocks and watch the gulls as they swooped above the water. But I had worked hard all year and it was precisely what I wanted.

The center of the town was inland, clustered about the little railroad depot, and I was fortunate in getting a room way out at the end of town near the water. My host was a man named Doble, a widower in his forties, a decent quiet man who was good company when I wanted company and who did not obtrude when I just wanted to sit and daydream. He did a little farming and had some chickens; he had a boat and some lobster pots; and for the rest, he'd make a little money at various odd jobs. He didn't work by the day but would contract for the whole job, which put him a cut above the ordinary odd jobman, I suppose.

Ours was the last house on the road and our nearest neighbor was about a hundred yards away. It was a large nineteenth-century mansion, set back from the road, and decorated with the traditional fretsaw trim and numerous turrets and gables. It was owned and occupied by Cyrus Cartwright, the president of the local bank and the richest man in town.

He was a brisk, eager sort of man, like the advertisement for a correspondence course in salesmanship, the type of man who carries two watches and is always glancing at his wristwatch and then checking it against his pocket watch.

(Chisholm warmed as he described Cyrus Cartwright, the result of the natural antipathy of a man who spends his summer watching sea gulls for the type of man who weighs out his life in small minutes. Now he smiled disarmingly and shrugged his shoulders.)

I saw him only once. I had come in town with Doble and before going home, he stopped in at the bank to see if Cartwright was still interested in making some change in the electric wiring system in his house, which they had talked about some months ago. It was typical of Doble that he should only now be coming around to make further inquiry about it.

Cartwright glanced at the radium dial of his wristwatch and then tugged at his watch chain and drew out his pocket watch, squeezing it out of its protective chamois covering. He mistook my interest in the ritual for interest in the watch itself and held it out so that I could see it, explaining with some condescension that it was a repeater, a five-minute repeater he was at some pains to point out, and then proceeded to demonstrate it by pressing a catch so that I could hear it tinkle the hour and then in a different key tinkle once for every five-minute interval after the hour.

I made some comparison between the man who carries two watches and the man who wears both a belt and suspenders. But though he realized I was joking, he said with some severity, "Time is money, sir, and I like to know just where I am with both. So I keep accurate books and accurate watches."

Having put me in my place, he turned to Doble and said crisply, "I don't think I'll bother with it, Doble. It was Jack's idea having the extra light and switch in the hallway and now that he's gone into the service, I don't think I'll need it. When it gets dark, I go to bed."

Once again he glanced at his wristwatch, checked its accuracy against his pocket watch as before, and then he smiled at us, a short, meaningless, businessman's smile of dismissal.

As I say, I saw him only that once, but I heard a great deal about him. You know how it is, you hear a man's name mentioned for the first time and then it seems to pop up again and again in the next few days.

According to Doble, Cartwright was a tight-fisted old skinflint who had remained a bachelor, probably to save the expense of supporting a wife.

When I pointed out that paying a housekeeper to come in every day was almost as expensive as keeping a wife, and that in addition he had brought up his nephew Jack, Doble retorted that nobody but Mrs. Knox would take the job of Cartwright's housekeeper and that she took it only because no one else would take her. She was almost stone deaf and general opinion was that her wages were small indeed.

"As for Jack," he went on, "the old man never let him see a penny more than he actually needed. He never had a dime in his pocket, and when he'd go into town of an evening, he'd just have to hang around—usually didn't even have the price of a movie. Nice young fellow, too," he added reflectively.

"He could have got a job and left," I suggested.

"I suppose he could've," Doble said slowly, "but he's the old man's heir, you see, and I guess he figured it was kind of politic, as you might say, to hang around doing any little jobs at the bank that the old man might ask of him."

I was not too favorably impressed with the young man's character from Doble's description, but I changed my mind when he came down a few days later on furlough.

He turned out to be a decent chap, quiet and reserved, but with a quick and imaginative mind. We grew quite close in those few days and saw a great deal of each other. We went fishing off the rocks, or lazed around in the sun a good deal talking of all sorts of things, or shot at chips in the water with an old rifle that he had.

He kept his gun and fishing rod over at our house. And that gives some indication of the character of Cyrus Cartwright and of Jack's relations with him. He explained that his uncle knew that he wasn't doing anything during this week of furlough and didn't really expect him to, but if he saw him with the fishing rod, that traditional symbol of idleness, it would seem as though he were flaunting his indolence in his face. As for the gun, Cyrus Cartwright considered shooting at any target that could not subsequently be eaten as an extravagant waste of money for shells.

Jack came over every evening to play cribbage or perhaps to sit on the porch and sip at a glass of beer and argue about some book he had read at my suggestion. Sometimes he spoke about his uncle and in discussing him, he was not bitter—ironic, rather.

On one occasion he explained, "My uncle is a good man according to his lights. He likes money because it gives him a sense of accomplishment to have more than anyone else in town. But that alone doesn't make him a hard person to live with. What does make him difficult is that everything is set in a rigid routine, a senseless routine, and his household has to conform to it. After dinner, he sits and reads his paper until it gets dark. Then he looks at his wristwatch and shakes his head a little as though he didn't believe it was that late. Then he takes his pocket watch out and checks the wristwatch against it. But, of course, even that doesn't satisfy him. So he goes into the dining room where he has an electric clock and he sets both watches by that.

"When he's got all timepieces perfectly synchronized, he says, 'Well, it's getting late,' and he goes upstairs to his room. In about fifteen minutes he calls to me and I go up to find him already in bed.

"'I forgot to fix the windows,' he says. So I open them an inch at the top and an inch at the bottom. It takes a bit of doing because if I should open them a quarter of an inch too wide, he says he'll catch his death of cold, and if it is short of an inch, he's sure he'll smother. But finally I get them adjusted just right and he says, 'My watch, would you mind, Jack?' So I get his pocket watch that he had put on the bureau while undressing and I put it on the night table near his bed.

"As far back as I can remember, I've had to do that little chore. I am sure he insists on it so as to fix our relations in my mind. While I was away, he must have remembered to do it for himself, but the first day I got back I had to do it."

(Chisholm looked from one to the other of us as if to make sure that we all understood the characters and their relations with each other. I nodded encouragingly and he continued.)

Jack was scheduled to leave Sunday morning and naturally we expected to see him Saturday, but he did not show up during the day. He came over in the evening after dinner, however, and he was hot and angry.

"The hottest day of the summer," he exclaimed, "and today of all days my uncle suddenly finds a bunch of errands for me to do. I've been all over the county and I couldn't even take the car. I'll bet you fellows were lying out on the beach all day. How about going in for a dip right now?"

Well, of course, we had been in and out of the water all day long, but it was still hot and muggy, and besides we could see that he wanted very much to go, so we agreed. We took some beer down and we didn't bother with bathing suits since it was already quite dark. After a while, however, it began to get chilly. It had clouded up and the air was oppressive as though a storm were impending. So we got dressed again and went back to our house.

The atmosphere had a charged, electric quality about it, and whether it was that or because he was leaving the following day, Jack was unusually quiet and conversation lagged. Around half past eleven, he rose and stretched and said he thought he ought to be going.

"It's been good meeting you," he said. "I don't look forward to this furlough particularly, but now I'm sure I'm going to look back on it."

We shook hands and he started for the door. Then he remembered about his fishing rod and his rifle and came back for them. He seemed reluctant to leave us, and Doble, understanding, said, "We might as well walk down with you, Jack."

He nodded gratefully and all three of us strolled out into the darkness. We walked along slowly, Jack with his fishing rod over one shoulder and his gun over the other.

I offered to carry the gun, but he shook his head and handed me the rod instead. I took it and walked on in silence until we reached the gate of his uncle's house. Perhaps he misinterpreted my silence and felt that he had been ungracious, for he said, "I'm a lot more used to carrying a rifle than you are." And then lest I take his remark as a reflection on my not being in the service, he hurried on with, "I'm kind of fond of this gun. I've had it a long time and had a lot of fun with it."

He patted the stock affectionately like a boy with a dog and then he nestled the butt against his shoulder and sighted along the barrel.

"Better not, Jack," said Doble with a grin. "You'll wake your uncle."

"Damn my uncle," he retorted lightly, and before we could stop him, he pulled the trigger.

In that silence, the crack of the rifle was like a thunderclap. I suppose we all expected one of the windows to fly up and the irate voice of old Cartwright to demand what was going on. In any case, instinctively, like three small boys, we all ducked down behind the fence where we could not be seen. We waited several minutes, afraid to talk lest we be overheard. But when nothing happened, we straightened up slowly and Doble said, "You better get to bed, Jack. I think maybe you've had a little too much beer."

"Maybe I ought at that," Jack answered and eased the gate open.

Then he turned and whispered, "Say, do you fellows mind waiting a minute? I think I may have locked the door and I haven't a key."

We nodded and watched as he hurried down the path to the house. Just before he reached the door, however, he hesitated, stopped, and then turned and came hurrying back to us.

"Could you put me up for the night, Doble?" he asked in a whisper.

"Why sure, Jack. Was the door locked?"

He didn't answer immediately and we started down the road to our house. We had gone about halfway when he said, "I didn't check to see if the door was locked or not."

"I noticed that," I remarked.

There was another silence and then as we mounted the porch steps, the moon, which had been hidden by clouds, suddenly broke through and I saw that he was deathly pale.

"What's the matter, Jack?" I asked quickly.

He shook his head and did not answer. I put my hand on his arm and asked again, "Are you all right?"

He nodded and tried to smile,

"I've—I've—Something funny happened to me," he said. "Did you mean what you said the other day about believing in spirits?"

At first I could not think what he was referring to, and then I remembered having argued—not too seriously—for belief in the supernatural during a discussion of William Blake's Marriage of Heaven and Hell, which I had lent him.

I shrugged my shoulders noncommittally, wondering what he was getting at.

He smiled wanly. "I didn't really have too much beer," he said and looked at me for confirmation.

"No, I don't think you did," I said quietly.

"Look," he went on, "I'm cold sober. And I was sober a few minutes ago when I started for my uncle's house. But as I came near the door, I felt something like a cushion of air building up against me to block my progress. And then, just before I reached the door, it became so strong that I could not go on. It was like a wall in front of me. But it was something more than an inanimate wall. It did not merely block me, but seemed to be pushing me back as though it had a will and intelligence like a strong man. It frightened me and I turned back. I'm still frightened." "Your uncle—" I began.

"Damn my uncle!" he said vehemently. "I hope he falls and breaks his neck."

Just then Doble's kitchen clock chimed twelve. The brassy ring, coming just as he finished, seemed to stamp the curse with fateful approval.

It made us all a little uncomfortable. We didn't seem to feel like talking, and after a while we went to bed.

We were awakened the next morning early by someone pounding on the door. Doble slipped his trousers on and I managed to get into my bathrobe. We reached the front door about the same time. It was Mrs. Knox, Cartwright's housekeeper, and she was in a state of considerable excitement.

"Mister Cartwright's dead!" she shouted to us. "There's been an accident."

Since she was deaf, it was no use to question her. We motioned her to wait while we put on our shoes. Then we followed her back to the house. The front door was open as she had left it when she had hurried over to us. And from the doorway we could see the figure of Cyrus Cartwright in an old-fashioned nightgown, lying at the foot of the stairs, his head in a sticky pool of blood.

He was dead all right, and looking up we could see the bit of rumpled carpeting at the head of the stairs which had probably tripped him up and catapulted him down the long staircase.

He had died as he had lived, for in his right hand he still clutched his precious pocket watch. The watch he was wearing on his wrist, however, had smashed when he fell and it gave us the time of his death. The hands pointed to just before twelve, the exact time as near as I could judge, that Jack had uttered his curse!

There was a minute of appreciative silence after Chisholm finished. I could see that no one's opinion had been changed materially by the story. Those who had been skeptical were scornful now and those who were inclined to believe were triumphant, but we all turned to Professor Rollins to see what he thought and he was nodding his head portentously.

Nicky, however, was the first to speak. "And the pocket watch," he said, "had that stopped, too?"

"No, that was ticking away merrily," Chisholm replied. "I guess his hand must have cushioned it when he fell. It had probably been badly jarred though, because it was running almost an hour ahead."

Nicky nodded grimly.

"What about Jack? How did he take it?" I asked.

Chisholm considered for a moment. "He was upset naturally, not so much over his uncle's death, I fancy, since he did not care for him very much, but because of the fact that it confirmed his fears of the night before that some supernatural influence was present." He smiled sadly. "I did not see him much after that. He had got his leave extended, but he was busy with his uncle's affairs. When finally he went back to the army, he promised to write, but he never did. Just last week, however, I got a letter from Doble. He writes me occasionally—just the usual gossip of the town. In his letter he mentions that Jack Cartwright crashed in his first solo flight."

"Ah." Professor Rollins showed interest. "I don't mind admitting that I rather expected something like that."

"You expected Jack to die?" Chisholm asked in amazement.

Rollins nodded vigorously. "This was truly a supernatural manifestation. I haven't the slightest doubt about it. For one thing, Jack felt the supernatural forces. And the curse, followed almost immediately by its fulfillment even to the manner of death, that is most significant. Now, of course, we know very little of these things, but we suspect that they follow a definite pattern. Certain types of supernatural forces have what might be called an ironic bent, a sort of perverted sense of humor. To be sure, when Jack uttered his fervent wish that his uncle fall and break his neck, he was speaking as a result of a momentary exasperation, but it is the nature of evil or mischievous forces to grant just such wishes. We meet with it again and again in folklore and fairy tales, which are probably the cryptic or symbolic expression of the wisdom of the folk. The pattern is familiar to you all, I am sure, from the stories of your childhood. The wicked character is granted three wishes by a fairy, only to waste them through wishes that are just such common expressions of exasperation as Jack used. You see, when supernatural forces are present, a mere wish, fervently expressed, may serve to focus them, as it were. And that is what happened at the Cartwright house that fateful evening."

He held up a forefinger to ward off the questions that leaped to our minds.

"There is another element in the pattern," he went on soberly, "And that is that whenever a person does profit materially through the use of evil supernatural forces, even though unintentionally on his part, sooner or later, they turn on him and destroy him. I have no doubt that Jack's death was just as much the result of supernatural forces as was the death of his uncle."

Professor Graham muttered something that sounded like "rubbish."

Dana Rollins, who could have gone on indefinitely I suppose, stopped abruptly and glared.

But Professor Graham was not one to be silenced by a look. "The young man died as a result of a plane crash. Well, so did thousands of others. Had they all been granted three wishes by a wicked fairy? Poppycock! The young man died because he went up in a plane. That's reason enough. As for the old man, he tumbled down the stairs and cracked his skull or broke his neck, whichever it was. You say his nephew's curse must have been uttered about the same time. Well, even granting that by some miracle Doble's kitchen clock was synchronized to Cartwright's watches, that would still be nothing more than a coincidence. The chances are that the young man uttered that same wish hundreds of times. It was only natural: he was his heir and besides, he didn't like him. Now on one of those hundreds of times, it actually happened. There's nothing supernatural in that—not even anything out of the ordinary. It makes a good story, young man, but it doesn't prove anything."

"And Jack's sensing of a supernatural force," asked Chisholm icily, "is that just another coincidence?"

Graham shrugged his massive shoulders. "That was probably just an excuse not to go home. He was probably afraid he'd get a dressing down from his uncle for shooting off his rifle in the middle of the night. What do you think, Nicky?"

Nicky's little blue eyes glittered. "I rather think," he said, "that the young man was not so much afraid of his uncle asking him about the rifle as he was that he would ask him what time it was."

We all laughed at Nicky's joke. But Professor Graham was not to be put off.

"Seriously, Nicky," he urged.

"Well, then, seriously," said Nicky with a smile as though he were indulging a bright but impetuous freshman, "I think you're quite right in calling the young man's death an accident. Parenthetically, I might point out that Dr. Chisholm did not suggest that it was anything else. As for the uncle's death, I cannot agree with you that it was merely coincidence."

Professor Rollins pursed his lips and appeared to be considering Nicky's cavalier dismissal of half his theory, but it was obvious that he was pleased at his support for the other half. I could not help reflecting how Nicky automatically assumed control over any group that he found himself in. He had a way of treating people, even his colleagues on the faculty, as though they were immature schoolboys. And curiously, people fell into this role that he assigned to them.

Professor Graham, however, was not yet satisfied. "But dammit all, Nicky," he insisted, "a man trips on a bit of carpet and falls downstairs. What is there unusual about that?"

"In the first place, I think it is unusual that he should go downstairs at all," said Nicky. "Why do you suppose he did?"

Professor Graham looked at him in aggrieved surprise like a student who has just been asked what he considers an unfair question.

"How should I know why he went downstairs?" he said. "I suppose he couldn't sleep and wanted a snack, or maybe a book to read."

"And took his pocket watch with him?"

"Well, according to Chisholm he was always checking his wrist-watch against it."

Nicky shook his head. "When you're wearing two watches, it's almost impossible not to check the other after you've glanced at the one, just as we automatically glance at our watches when we pass the clock in the jeweler's window even though we might have set it by the radio only a minute or two before. But for Cyrus Cartwright to take his pocket watch downstairs with him when he had a watch on his wrist is something else again. I can think of only one reason for it."

"And what's that?" asked Chisholm curiously.

"To see what time it was on the electric clock."

I could understand something of Graham's exasperation as he exclaimed, "But dammit, Nicky, the man had two watches. Why would he want to go downstairs to see the time?"

"Because in this case, two watches were not as good as one," said Nicky quietly.

I tried to understand. Did he mean that the supernatural force that had manifested itself to Jack Cartwright that night and had prevented him from entering the house had somehow tampered with the watches?

"What was wrong with them?" I asked.

"They disagreed."

Then he leaned back in his chair and looked about him with an air of having explained everything. There was a short silence and as he scanned our faces, his expression of satisfaction changed to one of annoyance.

"Don't you see yet what happened?" he demanded. "When you wake up in the middle of the night, the first thing you do is look at the clock on the mantelpiece or your watch on the night table in order to orient yourself. That's precisely what Cyrus Cartwright did. He woke up and glancing at his wristwatch he saw that it was quarter to twelve, say. Then quite automatically he reached for his pocket watch on the night table. He pressed the catch and the chiming mechanism tinkled twelve and then went on to tinkle half or three quarters past. He had set the watches only a few hours before and both of them were going, and yet one was about an hour faster than the other. Which was right? What time was it? I fancy he tried the repeater again and again and then tried to dismiss the problem from his mind until morning. But after tossing about for a few minutes, he realized that if he hoped to get back to sleep that night, he would have to go downstairs to see what time it really was." Nicky turned to Chisholm. "You see, the jar from the fall would not have moved the watch ahead. A blow will either stop the movement or it might speed up or slow down the escapement for a few seconds. But a watch with hands so loose that a jar will move them would be useless as a timepiece. Hence, the watch must have been moved ahead sometime before the fall. Cyrus Cartwright would not do it, which means that his nephew must have, probably while transferring the watch from the bureau to the night table."

"You mean accidentally?" asked Chisholm. "Or to annoy his uncle?"

Nicky's little blue eyes glittered. "Not to annoy him," he said, "to murder him!"

He smiled pleasantly at our stupefaction. "Oh yes, no doubt about it," he assured us. "After arranging the windows to his uncle's satisfaction and placing the watch on the night table, Jack bade his uncle a courteous good night. And on his way out, he stopped just long enough to rumple or double over the bit of carpet at the head of the stairs. There was no light in the hallway remember."

"But—but I don't understand. I don't see—I mean, how did he know that his uncle was going to wake up in the middle of the night?" Chisholm finally managed.

"Firing off his rifle under his uncle's windows insured that, I fancy," Nicky replied. He smiled. "And now you can understand, I trust, why he could not enter his uncle's house that night. He was afraid that his uncle, awake now, would hear him come in and instead of venturing downstairs, would simply call down to him to ask what time it was."

This time we did not laugh.

The silence that followed was suddenly broken by the chiming of the chapel clock. Subconsciously, we glanced at our watches, and then realizing what we were doing, we all laughed.

"Quite," said Nicky.

JOHN LUTZ

Ride the Lightning

A SLANTED SHEET OF RAIN SWEPT LIKE A scythe across Placid
Cove Trailer Park. For an instant, an intricate web of lightning illu-
mined the park. The rows of mobile homes loomed square and still
and pale against the night, reminding Nudger of tombs with awnings and
TV antennas. He held his umbrella at a sharp angle to the wind as he
walked, putting a hand in his pocket to pull out a scrap of paper and dou-
ble-check the address he was trying to find in the maze of trailers. Finally,
at the end of Tranquility Lane, he found Number 307 and knocked on its
metal door.

"I'm Nudger," he said when the door opened.

For several seconds the woman in the doorway stood staring out at him,
rain blowing in beneath the metal awning to spot her cornflower-colored
dress and ruffle her straw blond hair. She was tall but very thin, fragile-look-
ing, and appeared at first glance to be about twelve years old. Second glance
revealed her to be in her mid-twenties. She had slight crow's feet at the corners of her luminous blue eyes when she winced as a raindrop struck her
face, a knowing cast to her oversized, girlish, full-lipped mouth, and slightly buck teeth. Her looks were hers alone. There was no one who could look
much like her, no middle ground with her; men would consider her
scrawny and homely, or they would see her as uniquely sensuous. Nudger
liked coltish girl-women; he catalogued her as attractive.

"Whoeee!" she said at last, as if seeing for the first time beyond Nudger.
"Ain't it raining something terrible?"

"It is," Nudger agreed. "And on me."

Her entire thin body gave a quick, nervous kind of jerk as she smiled apologetically. "I'm Holly Ann Adams, Mr. Nudger. And you are getting wet, all right. Come on in."

She moved aside and Nudger stepped up into the trailer. He expected it to be surprisingly spacious; he'd once lived in a trailer and remembered them as such. This one was cramped and confining. The furniture was cheap and its upholstery was threadbare; a portable black and white TV on a tiny table near the Scotch-plaid sofa was blaring shouts of ecstasy emitted by "The Price is Right" contestants. The air was thick with the smell of something greasy that had been fried too long.

Holly Ann cleared a stack of *People* magazines from a vinyl chair and motioned for Nudger to sit down. He folded his umbrella, left it by the door, and sat. Holly Ann started to say something, then jerked her body in that peculiar way of hers, almost a twitch, as if she'd just remembered something not only with her mind but with her blood and muscle, and walked over and switched off the noisy television. In the abrupt silence, the rain seemed to beat on the metal roof with added fury. "Now we can talk," Holly Ann proclaimed, sitting opposite Nudger on the undersized sofa. "You a sure-enough private investigator?"

"I'm that," Nudger said. "Did someone recommend me to you, Miss Adams?"

"Gotcha out of the Yellow Pages. And if you're gonna work for me, it might as well be Holly Ann without the Adams."

"Except on the check," Nudger said.

She grinned a devilish twelve-year-old's grin. "Oh, sure, don't worry none about that. I wrote you out a check already, just gotta fill in the amount. That is, if you agree to take the job. "You might not."

"Why not?"

"It has to do with my fiance, Curtis Colt."

Nudger listened for a few seconds to the rain crashing on the roof. "The Curtis Colt who's going to be executed next week?"

"That's the one. Only he didn't kill that liquor store woman; I know it for a fact. It ain't right he should have to ride the lightning."

"Ride the lightning?"

"That's what convicts call dying in the electric chair, Mr. Nudger. They call that chair lotsa things: Old Sparky . . . The Lord's Frying Pan. But Curtis don't belong sitting in it wired up, and I can prove it."

"It's a little late for that kind of talk," Nudger said. "Or did you testify for Curtis in court?"

"Nope. Couldn't testify. You'll see why. All them lawyers and the judge and jury don't even know about me. Curtis didn't want them to know, so he never told them." She crossed her legs and swung her right calf jauntily. She was smiling as if trying to flirt him into wanting to know more about the job so he could free Curtis Colt by a governor's reprieve at the last minute, as in an old movie.

Nudger looked at her gauntly pretty, country-girl face and said, "Tell me about Curtis Colt, Holly Ann."

"You mean you didn't read about him in the newspapers or see him on the television?"

"I only scan the media for misinformation. Give me the details."

"Well, they say Curtis was inside the liquor store, sticking it up—him and his partner had done three other places that night, all of 'em gas stations, though—when the old man that owned the place came out of a back room and seen his wife behind the counter with her hands up and Curtis holding the gun on her. So the old man lost his head and ran at Curtis, and Curtis had to shoot him. Then the woman got mad when she seen that and ran at Curtis, and Curtis shot her. She's the one that died. The old man, he'll live, but he can't talk nor think nor even feed himself."

Nudger remembered more about the case now. Curtis Colt had been found guilty of first degree murder, and because of a debate in the legislature over the merits of cyanide gas versus electricity, the state was breaking out the electric chair to make him its first killer executed by electricity in over a quarter of a century. Those of the back-to-basics school considered that progress.

"They're gonna shoot Curtis full of electricity next Saturday, Mr. Nudger," Holly Ann said plaintively. She sounded like a little girl complaining that the grade on her report card wasn't fair.

"I know," Nudger said. "But I don't see how I can help you. Or, more specifically, help Curtis."

"You know what they say thoughts really are, Mr. Nudger?" Holly Ann said, ignoring his professed helplessness. Her wide blue eyes were vague as she searched for words. "Thoughts ain't really nothing but tiny electrical impulses in the brain. I read that somewheres or other. What I can't help wondering is, when they shoot all that electricity into Curtis, what's it gonna be like to his thinking? How long will it seem like to him before he finally dies? Will there be a big burst of crazy thoughts along with the pain? I know it sounds loony, but I can't help laying awake nights thinking about that, and I feel I just gotta do whatever's left to try and help Curtis."

There was a sort of checkout-line tabloid logic in that, Nudger conceded; if thoughts were actually weak electrical impulses, then high-voltage electrical impulses could become exaggerated, horrible thoughts. Anyway, try to disprove it to Holly Ann.

"They never did catch Curtis's buddy, the driver who sped away and left him in that service station, did they?" Nudger asked.

"Nope. Curtis never told who the driver was, neither, no matter how much he was threatened. Curtis is a stubborn man."

Nudger was getting the idea.

"But you know who was driving the car."

"Yep. And he told me him and Curtis was miles away from that liquor store at the time it was robbed. When he seen the police closing in on Curtis in that gas station where Curtis was buying cigarettes, he hit the accelerator and got out of the parking lot before they could catch him. The police did- n't even get the car's license plate number."

Nudger rubbed a hand across his chin, watching Holly Ann swing her leg as if it were a shapely metronome. She was barefoot and wearing no nylon hose. "The jury thought Curtis not only was at the liquor store, but that he shot the old man and woman in cold blood."

"That ain't true, though. Not according to—" she caught herself before uttering the man's name.

"Curtis's friend," Nudger finished.

"That's right. And he ought to know," Holly Ann said righteously, as if that piece of information were the trump card and the argument was over.

"None of this means anything unless the driver comes forward and sub- stantiates that he was with Curtis somewhere other than at the liquor store when it was robbed."

Holly Ann nodded and stopped swinging her leg. "I know. But he won't. He can't. That's where you come in."

"My profession might enjoy a reputation a notch lower than dog-nap- per," Nudger said, "but I don't hire out to do anything illegal."

"What I want you to do is legal," Holly Ann said in a hurt little voice. Nudger looked past her into the dollhouse kitchen and saw an empty gin bottle. He wondered if she might be slightly drunk. "It's the eyewitness accounts that got Curtis convicted," she went on. "And those people are wrong. I want you to figure out some way to convince them it wasn't Curtis they saw that night."

"Four people, two of them customers in the store, picked Curtis out of a police lineup."

"So what? Ain't eyewitnesses often mistaken?"

Nudger had to admit that they were, though he didn't see how they could be in this case. There were, after all, four of them. And yet, Holly Ann was right; it was amazing how people could sometimes be so certain that the wrong man had committed a crime just five feet in front of them.

"I want you to talk to them witnesses," Holly Ann said. "Find out *why* they think Curtis was the killer. Then show them how they might be wrong and get them to change what they said. We got the truth on our side, Mr. Nudger. At least one witness will change his story when he's made to think about it, because Curtis wasn't where they said he was."

"Curtis has exhausted all his appeals," Nudger said. "Even if all the witnesses changed their stories, it wouldn't necessarily mean he'd get a new trial."

"Maybe not, but I betcha they wouldn't kill him. They couldn't stand the publicity if enough witnesses said they was wrong, it was somebody else killed the old woman. Then, just maybe, eventually, he'd get another trial and get out of prison."

Nudger was awed. Here was foolish optimism that transcended even his own. He had to admire Holly Ann.

The leg started pumping again beneath the cornflower-colored dress. When Nudger lowered his gaze to stare at it, Holly Ann said, "So will you help me, Mr. Nudger?"

"Sure. It sounds easy."

*   *   *

"Why should I worry about it anymore?" Randy Gantner asked Nudger, leaning on his shovel. He didn't mind talking to Nudger; it meant a break from his construction job on the new Interstate 170 cloverleaf. "Colt's been found guilty and he's going to the chair, ain't he?"

The afternoon sun was hammering down on Nudger, warming the back of his neck and making his stomach queasy. He thumbed an antacid tablet off the roll he kept in his shirt pocket and popped one of the white disks into his mouth. With his other hand, he was holding up a photograph of Curtis Colt for Gantner to see. It was a snapshot Holly Ann had given him of the wiry, shirtless Colt leaning on a fence post and holding a beer can high in a mock toast: this one's for Death!

"This is a photograph you never saw in court. I just want you to look at it closely and tell me again if you're sure the man you saw in the liquor store was Colt. Even if it makes no difference in whether he's executed, it will help ease the mind of somebody who loves him."

"I'd be a fool to change my story about what happened now that the trial's over," Gantner said logically.

"You'd be a murderer if you really weren't sure."

Gantner sighed, dragged a dirty red handkerchief from his jeans pocket, and wiped his beefy, perspiring face. He peered at the photo, then shrugged. "It's him, Colt, the guy I seen shoot the man and woman when I was standing in the back aisle of the liquor store. If he'd known me and Sanders was back there, he'd have probably zapped us along with them old folks."

"You're positive it's the same man?"

Gantner spat off to the side and frowned; Nudger was becoming a pest, and the foreman was staring. "I said it to the police and the jury, Nudger; that little twerp Colt did the old lady in. Ask me, he deserves what he's gonna get."

"Did you actually see the shots fired?"

"Nope. Me and Sanders was in the back aisle looking for some reasonable-priced bourbon when we heard the shots, then looked around to see Curtis Colt back away, turn, and run out to the car. Looked like a black or dark green old Ford. Colt fired another shot as it drove away."

"Did you see the driver?"

"Sort of. Skinny dude with curly black hair and mustache. That's what I told the cops. That's all I seen. That's all I know."

And that was the end of the conversation. The foreman was walking toward them, glaring. *Thunk!* Gantner's shovel sliced deep into the earth, speeding the day when there'd be another place for traffic to get backed up. Nudger thanked him and advised him not to work too hard in the hot sun.

"You wanna help?" Gantner asked, grinning sweatily.

"I'm already doing some digging of my own," Nudger said, walking away before the foreman arrived.

The other witnesses also stood by their identifications. The fourth and last one Nudger talked with, an elderly woman named Iris Lange-neckert, who had been walking her dog near the liquor store and had seen Curtis Colt dash out the door and into the getaway car, said something that Gantner had touched on. When she'd described the getaway car driver, like Gantner she said he was a thin man with curly black hair and a beard or mustache, then she had added, "Like Curtis Colt's hair and mustache."

Nudger looked again at the snapshot Holly Ann had given him. Curtis Colt was about five foot nine, skinny, and mean-looking, with a broad bandito mustache and a mop of curly, greasy black hair. Nudger wondered if it was possible that the getaway car driver had been Curtis Colt himself, and his accomplice had killed the shopkeeper. Even Nudger found that one hard to believe.

He drove to his second-floor office in the near suburb of Maple-wood and sat behind his desk in the blast of cold air from the window unit, sipping the complimentary paper cup of iced tea he'd brought up from Danny's Donuts directly below. The sweet smell of the doughnuts was heavier than usual in the office; Nudger had never quite gotten used to it and what it did to his sensitive stomach.

When he was cool enough to think clearly again, he decided he needed more information on the holdup, and on Curtis Colt, from a more objective source than Holly Ann Adams. He phoned Lieutenant Jack Hammersmith at home and was told by Hammersmith's son Jed that Hammersmith had just driven away to go to work on the afternoon shift, so it would be awhile before he got to his office.

Nudger checked his answering machine, proving that hope did indeed spring eternal in a fool's breast. There was a terse message from his former wife Eileen demanding last month's alimony payment; a solemn-voiced young man reading an address where Nudger could send a check to help pay to form a watchdog committee that would stop the utilities from continually raising their rates; and a cheerful man informing Nudger that with the labels from ten packages of a brand name hot dog he could get a Cardinals' ballgame ticket at half price. (That meant eating over eighty hot dogs. Nudger calculated that baseball season would be over by the time he did that.) Everyone seemed to want some of Nudger's money. No one wanted to pay Nudger any money. Except for Holly Ann Adams. Nudger decided he'd better step up his efforts on the Curtis Colt case.

He tilted back his head, downed the last dribble of iced tea, then tried to eat what was left of the crushed ice. But the ice clung stubbornly to the bottom of the cup, taunting him. Nudger's life was like that.

He crumpled up the paper cup and tossed it, ice and all, into the wastebasket. Then he went downstairs where his Volkswagen was parked in the shade behind the building and drove east on Manchester, toward downtown and the Third District station house.

*　　*　　*

Police Lieutenant Jack Hammersmith was in his Third District office, sleek, obese, and cool-looking behind his wide metal desk. He was pounds and years away from the handsome cop who'd been Nudger's partner a decade ago in a two-man patrol car. Nudger could still see traces of a dashing quality in the flesh-upholstered Hammersmith, but he wondered if that was only because he'd known Hammersmith ten years ago.

"Sit down, Nudge," Hammersmith invited, his lips smiling but his slate gray, cop's eyes unreadable. If eyes were the windows to the soul, his shades were always down.

Nudger sat in one of the straight-backed chairs in front of Hammersmith's desk. "I need some help," he said.

"Sure," Hammersmith said, "you never come see me just to trade recipes or to sit and rock." Hammersmith was partial to irony; it was a good thing, in his line of work.

"I need to know more about Curtis Colt," Nudger said. Hammersmith got one of his vile greenish cigars out of his shirt pocket and stared intently at it, as if its paper ring label might reveal some secret of life and death. "Colt, eh? The guy who's going to ride the lightning?"

"That's the second time in the past few days I've heard that expression. The first time was from Colt's fiancée. She thinks he's innocent."

"Fiancées think along those lines. Is she your client?"

Nudger nodded but didn't volunteer Holly Ann's name.

"Gullibility makes the world go round," Hammersmith said. "I was in charge of the Homicide investigation on that one. There's not a chance Colt is innocent, Nudge."

"Four eyewitness I.D.'s is compelling evidence," Nudger admitted. "What about the getaway car driver? His description is a lot like Colt's. Maybe he's the one who did the shooting and Colt was the driver."

"Colt's lawyer hit on that. The jury didn't buy it. Neither do I. The man is guilty, Nudge."

"You know how inaccurate eyewitness accounts can be," Nudger persisted.

That seemed to get Hammersmith mad. He lit the cigar. The office immediately fogged up.

Nudger made his tone more amicable. "Mind if I look at the file on the Colt case?"

Hammersmith gazed thoughtfully at Nudger through a dense greenish haze. He inhaled, exhaled; the haze became a cloud. "How come this fiancée didn't turn up at the trial to testify for Colt? She could have at least lied and said he was with her that night."

"Colt apparently didn't want her subjected to taking the stand."

"How noble," Hammersmith said. "What makes this fiancée think her prince charming is innocent?"

"She knows he was somewhere else when the shopkeepers were shot."

"But not with her?"

"Nope."

"Well, that's refreshing."

Maybe it was refreshing enough to make up Hammersmith's mind. He picked up the phone and asked for the Colt file. Nudger could barely make out what he was saying around the fat cigar, but apparently everyone at the Third was used to Hammersmith and could interpret cigarese.

The file didn't reveal much that Nudger didn't know. Fifteen minutes after the liquor store shooting, officers from a two-man patrol car, acting on the broadcast description of the gunman, approached Curtis Colt inside a service station where he was buying a pack of cigarettes from a vending machine. A car that had been parked near the end of the dimly lighted lot had sped away as they'd entered the station office. The officers had gotten only a glimpse of a dark green old Ford; they hadn't made out the license plate number but thought it might start with the letter "L."

Colt had surrendered without a struggle, and that night at the Third District Station the four eyewitnesses had picked him out of a lineup. Their description of the getaway car matched that of the car the police had seen speeding from the service station. The loot from the holdup, and several gas station holdups committed earlier that night, wasn't on Colt, but probably it was in the car.

"Colt's innocence just jumps out of the file at you, doesn't it, Nudge?" Hammersmith said. He was grinning a fat grin around the fat cigar.

"What about the murder weapon?"

"Colt was unarmed when we picked him up."

"Seems odd."

"Not really," Hammersmith said. "He was planning to pay for the cigarettes. And maybe the gun was still too hot to touch so he left it in the car. Maybe it's still hot; it got a lot of use for one night."

Closing the file folder and laying it on a corner of Hammersmith's desk, Nudger stood up. "Thanks, Jack. I'll keep you tapped in if I learn anything interesting."

"Don't bother keeping me informed on this one, Nudge. It's over. I don't see how even a fiancée can doubt Colt's guilt."

Nudger shrugged, trying not to breathe too deeply in the smoke-hazed office. "Maybe it's an emotional thing. She thinks that because thought waves are tiny electrical impulses, Colt might experience time warp and all sorts of grotesque thoughts when all that voltage shoots through him. She has bad dreams."

"I'll bet she does," Hammersmith said. "I'll bet Colt has bad dreams, too. Only he deserves his. And maybe she's right."

"About what?"

"About all that voltage distorting thought and time. Who's to say?"

"Not Curtis Colt," Nudger said. "Not after they throw the switch."

"It's a nice theory, though," Hammersmith said. "I'll remember it. It might be a comforting thing to tell the murder victim's family."

"Sometimes," Nudger said, "you think just like a cop who's seen too much."

"Any of it's too much, Nudge," Hammersmith said with surprising sadness. He let more greenish smoke drift from his nostrils and the corners of his mouth; he looked like a stone Buddha seated behind the desk, one in which incense burned.

Nudger coughed and said goodbye.

*   *   *

"Only two eyewitnesses are needed to convict," Nudger said to Holly Ann the next day in her trailer, "and in this case there are four. None of them is at all in doubt about their identification of Curtis Colt as the killer. I have to be honest; it's time you should face the fact that Colt is guilty and that you're wasting your money on my services."

"All them witnesses know what's going to happen to Curtis," Holly Ann said. "They'd never want to live with the notion they might have made a mistake, killed an innocent man, so they've got themselves convinced that they're positive it was Curtis they saw that night."

"Your observation on human psychology is sound," Nudger said, "but I don't think it will help us. The witnesses were just as certain three months ago at the trial. I took the time to read the court manuscript; the jury had no choice but to find Colt guilty, and the evidence hasn't changed."

Holly Ann drew her legs up and clasped her knees to her chest with both arms. Her little-girl posture matched her little-girl faith in her lover's innocence. She believed the white knight must arrive at any moment and snatch Curtis Colt from the electrical jaws of death. She believed hard. Nudger could almost hear his armor clank when he walked.

She wanted him to believe just as hard. "I see you need to be convinced of Curtis's innocence," she said wistfully. There was no doubt he'd forced her into some kind of corner. "If you come here tonight at eight, Mr.

Nudger, I'll convince you."

"How?"

"I can't say. "You'll understand why tonight."

"Why do we have to wait till tonight?"

"Oh, you'll see."

Nudger looked at the waiflike creature curled in the corner of the sofa. He felt as if they were playing a childhood guessing game while Curtis Colt waited his turn in the electric chair. Nudger had never seen an execution; he'd heard it took longer than most people thought for the condemned to die. His stomach actually twitched.

"Can't we do this now with twenty questions?" he asked.

Holly Ann shook her head. "No, Mr. Nudger."

Nudger sighed and stood up, feeling as if he were about to bump his head on the trailer's low ceiling even though he was barely six feet tall.

"Make sure you're on time tonight, Mr. Nudger," Holly Ann said as he went out the door. "It's important."

*   *   *

At eight on the nose that evening Nudger was sitting at the tiny table in Holly Ann's kitchenette. Across from him was a thin, nervous man in his late twenties or early thirties, dressed in a long-sleeved shirt despite the heat, and wearing sunglasses with silver mirror lenses. Holly Ann introduced the man as "Len, but that's not his real name," and said he was Curtis Colt's accomplice and the driver of their getaway car on the night of the murder.

"But me and Curtis was nowhere near the liquor store when them folks got shot," Len said vehemently.

Nudger assumed the sunglasses were so he couldn't effectively identify Len if it came to a showdown in court. Len had lank, dark brown hair that fell to below his shoulders, and when he moved his arm Nudger caught sight of something blue and red on his briefly exposed wrist. A tattoo. Which explained the long-sleeved shirt.

"You can understand why Len couldn't come forth and testify for Curtis in court," Holly Ann said.

Nudger said he could understand that. Len would have had to incriminate himself

"We was way on the other side of town," Len said, "casing another service station, when that liquor store killing went down. Heck, we never held up nothing but service stations. They was our specialty."

Which was true, Nudger had to admit. Colt had done time for armed robbery six years ago after sticking up half a dozen service stations within a week. And all the other holdups he'd been tied to this time around were of service stations. The liquor store was definitely a departure in his M.O, not one noted in court during Curtis Colt's rush to judgment.

"Your hair is in your favor," Nudger said to Len.

"Huh?"

"Your hair didn't grow that long in the three months since the liquor store killing. The witnesses described the getaway car driver as having shorter, curlier hair, like Colt's, and a mustache."

Len shrugged. "I'll be honest with you—it don't help me at all. Me and Curtis was kinda the same type. So to confuse any witnesses, in case we got caught, we made each other look even more alike. I'd tuck up my long hair and wear a wig that looked like Curtis's hair. My mustache was real, like Curtis's. I shaved it off a month ago. We did look alike at a glance; sorta like brothers."

Nudger bought that explanation; it wasn't uncommon for a team of holdup men to play tricks to confuse witnesses and the police. Too many lawyers had gotten in the game; the robbers, like the cops, were taking the advice of their attorneys and thinking about a potential trial even before the crime was committed.

"Is there any way, then, to prove you were across town at the time of the murder?" Nudger asked, looking at the two small Nudgers staring back at him from the mirror lenses.

"There's just my word," Len said, rather haughtily.

Nudger didn't bother telling him what that was worth. Why antagonize him?

"I just want you to believe Curtis is innocent," Len said with desperation. "Because he is! And so am I!"

And Nudger understood why Len was here, taking the risk. If Colt was guilty of murder, Len was guilty of being an accessory to the crime. Once Curtis Colt had ridden the lightning, Len would have hanging over him the possibility of an almost certain life sentence, and perhaps even his own ride on the lightning, if he were ever caught. It wasn't necessary to actually squeeze the trigger to be convicted of murder.

"I need for you to try extra hard to prove Curtis is innocent," Len said. His thin lips quivered; he was near tears.

"Are you giving Holly Ann the money to pay me?" Nudger asked.

"Some of it, yeah. From what Curtis and me stole. And I gave Curtis's share to Holly Ann, too. Me and her are fifty-fifty on this."

Dirty money, Nudger thought. Dirty job. Still, if Curtis Colt happened to be innocent, trying against the clock to prove it was a job that needed to be done.

"Okay. I'll stay on the case."

"Thanks," Len said. His narrow hand moved impulsively across the table and squeezed Nudger's arm in gratitude. Len had the look of an addict; Nudger wondered if the long-sleeved shirt was to hide needle tracks as well as the tattoo.

Len stood up. "Stay here with Holly Ann for ten minutes while I make myself scarce. I gotta know I wasn't followed. You understand it ain't that I don't trust you; a man in my position has gotta be sure, is all."

"I understand. Go."

Len gave a spooked smile and went out the door. Nudger heard his running footfalls on the gravel outside the trailer. Nudger was forty-three years old and ten pounds overweight; lean and speedy Len needed a ten minute head start like Sinatra needed singing lessons.

"Is Len a user?" Nudger asked Holly Ann.

"Sometimes. But my Curtis never touched no dope."

"You know I have to tell the police about this conversation, don't you?"

Holly Ann nodded. "That's why we arranged it this way. They won't be any closer to Len than before."

"They might want to talk to you, Holly Ann."

She shrugged. "It don't matter. I don't know where Len is, nor even his real name nor how to get in touch with him. He'll find out all he needs to know about Curtis by reading the papers."

"You have a deceptively devious mind," Nudger told her, "considering that you look like Barbie Doll's country kid cousin."

Holly Ann smiled, surprised and pleased. "Do you find me attractive, Mr. Nudger?"

"Yes. And painfully young."

For just a moment Nudger almost thought of Curtis Colt as a lucky man. Then he looked at his watch, saw that his ten minutes were about up, and said goodbye. If Barbie had a kid cousin, Ken probably had one somewhere, too. And time was something you couldn't deny. Ask Curtis Colt.

*   *   *

"It doesn't wash with me," Hammersmith said from behind his desk, puffing angrily on his cigar. Angrily because it did wash a little bit; he didn't like the possibility, however remote, of sending an innocent man to his death. That was every good homicide cop's nightmare. "This Len character is just trying to keep himself in the clear on a murder charge."

"You could read it that way," Nudger admitted.

"It would help if you gave us a better description of Len," Hammersmith said gruffly, as if Nudger were to blame for Curtis Colt's accomplice still walking around free.

"I gave you what I could," Nudger said. "Len didn't give me much to pass on. He's streetwise and scared and knows what's at stake." Hammersmith nodded, his fit of pique past. But the glint of weary frustration remained in his eyes.

"Are you going to question Holly Ann?" Nudger said.

"Sure, but it won't do any good. She's probably telling the truth. Len would figure we'd talk to her; he wouldn't tell her how to find him."

"You could stake out her trailer."

"Do you think Holly Ann and Len might be lovers?"

"No."

Hammersmith shook his head. "Then they'll probably never see each other again. Watching her trailer would be a waste of manpower."

Nudger knew Hammersmith was right. He stood up to go.

"What are you going to do now?" Hammersmith asked.

"I'll talk to the witnesses again. I'll read the court transcript again. And I'd like to talk with Curtis Colt."

"They don't allow visitors on Death Row, Nudge, only temporary boarders."

"This case is an exception," Nudger said. "Will you try to arrange it?"

Hammersmith chewed thoughtfully on his cigar. Since he'd been the officer in charge of the murder investigation, he'd been the one who'd nailed Curtis Colt. That carried an obligation.

"I'll phone you soon," he said, "let you know."

Nudger thanked Hammersmith and walked down the hall into the clear, breathable air of the booking area.

That day he managed to talk again to all four eyewitnesses. Two of them got mad at Nudger for badgering them. They all stuck to their stories. Nudger reported this to Holly Ann at the Right-Steer Steak-house, where she worked as a waitress. Several customers that afternoon got tears with their baked potatoes.

Hammersmith phoned Nudger that evening.

"I managed to get permission for you to talk to Colt," he said, "but don't get excited. Colt won't talk to you. He won't talk to anyone, not even a clergyman. He'll change his mind about the clergyman, but not about you."

"Did you tell him I was working for Holly Ann?"

"I had that information conveyed to him. He wasn't impressed. He's one of the stoic ones on Death Row."

Nudger's stomach kicked up, growled something that sounded like a hopeless obscenity. If even Curtis Colt wouldn't cooperate, how could he be helped? Absently Nudger peeled back the aluminum foil on a roll of antacid tablets and slipped two chalky white disks into his mouth. Hammersmith knew about his nervous stomach and must have heard him chomping the tablets. "Take it easy, Nudge. This isn't your fault."

"Then why do I feel like it is?"

"Because you feel too much of everything. That's why you had to quit the department."

"We've got another day before the execution," Nudger said. "I'm going to go through it all again. I'm going to talk to each of those witnesses even if they try to run when they see me coming. Maybe somebody will say something that will let in some light."

"There's no light out there, Nudge. You're wasting your time. Give up on this one and move on."

"Not yet," Nudger said. "There's something elusive here that I can't quite grab."

"And never will," Hammersmith said. "Forget it, Nudge. Live your life and let Curtis Colt lose his."

Hammersmith was right. Nothing Nudger did helped Curtis Colt in the slightest. At eight o'clock Saturday morning, while Nudger was preparing breakfast in his apartment, Colt was put to death in the electric chair. He'd offered no last words before two thousand volts had turned him from something into nothing.

Nudger heard the news of Colt's death on his kitchen radio. He went ahead and ate his eggs, but he skipped the toast.

That afternoon he consoled a numbed and frequently sobbing Holly Ann and apologized for being powerless to stop her true love's execution. She was polite, trying to be brave. She preferred to suffer alone. Her boss at the Right-Steer gave her the rest of the day off, and Nudger drove her home.

Nudger slept a total of four hours during the next two nights. On Monday, he felt compelled to attend Curtis Colt's funeral. There were about a dozen people clustered around the grave, including the state-appointed clergyman and pallbearers. Nudger stood off to one side during the brief service. Holly Ann, looking like a child playing dress-up in black, stood well off to the other side. They didn't exchange words, only glances.

As the coffin was lowered into the earth, Nudger watched Holly Ann walk to where a taxi was waiting by a weathered stone angel. The cab wound its way slowly along the snaking narrow cemetery road to tall iron gates and the busy street. Holly Ann never looked back.

That night Nudger realized what was bothering him, and for the first time since Curtis Colt's death, he slept well.

In the morning he began watching Holly Ann's trailer.

At seven-thirty she emerged, dressed in her yellow waitress uniform, and got into another taxi. Nudger followed in his battered Volkswagen Beetle as the cab drove her the four miles to her job at the Right-Steer Steakhouse. She didn't look around as she paid the driver and walked inside through the molded plastic Old-West-saloon swinging doors.

At six that evening another cab drove her home, making a brief stop at a grocery store.

It went that way for the rest of the week, trailer to work to trailer. Holly Ann had no visitors other than the plain brown paper bag she took home every night.

The temperature got up to around ninety-five and the humidity rose right along with it. It was one of St. Louis's legendary summer heat waves. Sitting melting in the Volkswagen, Nudger wondered if what he was doing was really worthwhile. Curtis Colt was, after all, dead, and had never been his client. Still, there were responsibilities that went beyond the job. Or perhaps they were actually the essence of the job.

The next Monday, after Holly Ann had left for work, Nudger used his Visa card to slip the flimsy lock on her trailer door, and let himself in.

It took him over an hour to find what he was searching for. It had been well hidden, in a cardboard box inside the access panel to the bathroom plumbing. After looking at the box's contents—almost seven hundred dollars in loot from Curtis Colt's brief life of crime, and another object Nudger wasn't surprised to see—Nudger resealed the box and replaced the access panel.

He continued to watch and follow Holly Ann, more confident now.

Two weeks after the funeral, when she left work one evening, she didn't go home.

Instead her taxi turned the opposite way and drove east on Watson Road. Nudger followed the cab along a series of side streets in South St. Louis, then part way down a dead-end alley to a large garage, above the door of which was lettered "Clifford's Auto Body."

Nudger backed out quickly onto the street, then parked the Volkswagen near the mouth of the alley. A few minutes later the cab drove by without a passenger. Within ten minutes, Holly Ann drove past in a shiny red Ford. Its license plate number began with an L.

When Nudger reached Placid Cove Trailer Park, he saw the Ford nosed in next to Holly Ann's trailer.

On the way to the trailer door, he paused and scratched the Ford's hood with a key. Even in the lowering evening light he could see that beneath the new red paint the car's color was dark green.

Holly Ann answered the door right away when he knocked. She tried a smile when she saw it was him, but she couldn't quite manage her facial muscles, as if they'd become rigid and uncoordinated. She appeared ten years older. The little-girl look had deserted her; now she was an emaciated, grief-eroded woman, a country Barbie doll whose features some evil child had lined with dark crayon. The shaded crescents beneath her eyes completely took away their innocence. She was holding a glass that had once been a jelly jar. In it were two fingers of a clear liquid. Behind her on the table was a crumpled brown paper bag and a half-empty bottle of gin.

"I figured it out," Nudger told her.

Now she did smile, but it was fleeting, a sickly bluish shadow crossing her taut features. "You're like a dog with a rag, Mr. Nudger. You surely don't know when to let go." She stepped back and he followed her into the trailer. It was warm in there; something was wrong with the air conditioner. "Hot as hell, ain't it," Holly Ann commented. Nudger thought that was apropos.

He sat down across from her at the tiny Formica table, just as he and Len had sat facing each other two weeks ago. She offered him a drink. He declined. She downed the contents of the jelly jar glass and poured herself another, clumsily striking the neck of the bottle on the glass. It made a sharp, flinty sound, as if sparks might fly.

"Now, what's this you've got figured out, Mr. Nudger?" She didn't want to, but she had to hear it. Had to share it.

"It's almost four miles to the Right-Steer Steakhouse," Nudger told her. "The waitresses there make little more than minimum wage, so cab fare to and from work has to eat a big hole in your salary. But then you seem to go everywhere by cab."

"My car's been in the shop."

"I figured it might be, after I found the money and the wig."

She bowed her head slightly and took a sip of gin. "Wig?"

"In the cardboard box inside the bathroom wall."

"You been snooping, Mr. Nudger." There was more resignation than outrage in her voice.

"You're sort of skinny, but not a short girl," Nudger went on. "With a dark curly wig and a fake mustache, sitting in a car, you'd resemble Curtis Colt enough to fool a dozen eyewitnesses who just caught a glimpse of you. It was a smart precaution for the two of you to take."

Holly Ann looked astounded.

"Are you saying I was driving the getaway car at the liquor store holdup?"

"Maybe. Then maybe you hired someone to play Len and convince me he was Colt's accomplice and that they were far away from the murder scene when the trigger was pulled. After I found the wig, I talked to some of your neighbors, who told me that until recently you'd driven a green Ford sedan."

Holly Ann ran her tongue along the edges of her protruding teeth.

"So Curtis and Len used my car for their holdups."

"I doubt if Len ever met Curtis. He's somebody you paid in stolen money or drugs to sit there where you're sitting now and lie to me."

"If I was driving that getaway car, Mr. Nudger, and *knew* Curtis was guilty, why would I have hired a private investigator to try to find a hole in the eyewitnesses' stories?"

"That's what bothered me at first," Nudger said, "until I realized you weren't interested in clearing Curtis. What you were really worried about was Curtis Colt talking in prison. You didn't want those witnesses' stories changed, you wanted them verified. And you wanted the police to learn about not-his-right-name Len."

Holly Ann raised her head to look directly at him with eyes that begged and dreaded. She asked simply, "Why would I want that?"

"Because you were Curtis Colt's accomplice in all of his robberies. And when you hit the liquor store, he stayed in the car to drive. *You* fired the shot that killed the old woman. He was the one who fired the wild shot from the speeding car. Colt kept quiet about it because he loved you. He never talked, not to the police, not to his lawyer, not even to a priest. Now that he's dead you can trust him forever, but I have a feeling you could have anyway. He loved you more than you loved him, and you'll have to live knowing he didn't deserve to die."

She looked down into her glass as if for answers and didn't say anything for a long time. Nudger felt a bead of perspiration trickle crazily down the back of his neck. Then she said, "I didn't want to shoot that old man, but he didn't leave me no choice. Then the old woman came at me." She looked up at Nudger and smiled ever so slightly. It was a smile Nudger hadn't seen on her before, one he didn't like. "God help me, Mr. Nudger, I can't quit thinking about shooting that old woman."

"You murdered her," Nudger said, "and you murdered Curtis Colt by keeping silent and letting him die for you."

"You can't prove nothing," Holly Ann said, still with her ancient-eyed, eerie smile that had nothing to do with amusement.

"You're right," Nudger told her, "I can't. But I don't think legally proving it is necessary, Holly Ann. You said it: thoughts are actually tiny electrical impulses in the brain. Curtis Colt rode the lightning all at once. With you, it will take years, but the destination is the same. I think you'll come to agree that his way was easier."

She sat very still. She didn't answer. Wasn't going to.

Nudger stood up and wiped his damp forehead with the back of his hand. He felt sticky, dirty, confined by the low ceiling and near walls of the tiny, stifling trailer. He had to get out of there to escape the sensation of being trapped.

He didn't say goodbye to Holly Ann when he walked out. She didn't say goodbye to him. The last sound Nudger heard as he left the trailer was the clink of the bottle on the glass.

CHARLOTTE MACLEOD

It Was an Awful Shame

"The Coddies gave a party just about a week ago.
Everything was plentiful, the Coddies they're not slow."

With an ever-so-knowing wink, Exalted Chowderhead Jeremy Kelling of the Beacon Hill Kellings raised his foaming flagon and quaffed. In accordance with time-honoured ritual, the other Comrades of the Convivial Codfish gulped in unison, then slapped their own tankards down on the emerald green tablecloth with one great, unanimous thwack.

"They treated us like gentlemen, we tried to act the same,
And only for what happened, sure it was an awful shame."

Again the tankards were raised, this time in gallant toast to the plump and pleasing person in kelly green who sailed into the room bearing the Ceremonial Cauldron. Behind her in single file marched the Highmost, Midmost, and Leastmost Hod-carriers.

As Mrs. Coddie, for such was her title, set the Cauldron in front of Jeremy Kelling, the three Hod-carriers clicked the poles of their hods smartly together, then stepped back in order of precedence to form a guard of honor behind their Exalted Chowderhead. Jem tied an oversize green linen napkin under his bottom chin, then went on with the incantation:

"When Mistress Coddie dished the chowder out, she fainted on the spot.
She found a pair of overalls in the bottom of the pot."

The Comrades had engaged many Mistress Coddies in their long and sometimes glorious history, but never one who swooned with more elan or finesse. As they rose in admiration of their recumbent hostess of the day, Comrade Bardwell voiced the consensus.

"By gad, this Mistress Coddie is a ring-tailed doozy with a snood on."

"Any objections or abstentions?" said the Exalted Chowderhead.

There being none, he raised the Ancient and Timeworn Overalls which had occasioned Mrs. Coddie's well-feigned swoon slowly from the cauldron.

"Fluke Flounder he got fighting mad, his eyes were bulging out.
He jumped upon the pi-an-o and loudly he did shout."

This year, Comrade Archer of the real estate Archers was Fluke Rounder. Despite his fourscore years and then some, despite the fact that he had to be boosted to the top of the Steinway by a dozen comradely hands, right loudly did Comrade Archer in good sooth manage to shout.

"Who threw the overalls in Mistress Coddie's chowder?
Nobody spoke, so he hollered all the louder."

And, by George, he did. So did they all. In reasonably close harmony, making up in volume for what they lacked in tone, the Comrades bellowed their way through the ballad composed in 1899 by George Geifer and bastardized in 1923 by Jeremy's late uncle Serapis Kelling.

At the end of the first chorus, Mistress Coddie (actually Mistress Cholmondely of the Perkins Square Cholmondelys) recovered her senses with fine dramatic effect and rose to take away the Ceremonial Cauldron, into which the Exalted Chowderhead had again lowered the Ancient and Timeworn Overalls with due ceremony and pomp. Escorted again by the Highmost, Midmost, and Leastmost Hod-carriers, she bore away the sacred relics and returned with a tureen full of genuine codfish chowder.

Excellent chowder it was, and full justice did the Comrades do it. Not until the tureen was bone dry did they quit baling. And not until Jeremy Kelling had untied his green napkin from beneath his nethermost jowl did he realize he was no longer wearing his insignia of office.

"The Codfish," he gasped. "It's gone!"

"It fell into the Cauldron, you jackass," said Comrade Archer, who'd got his wind back after a bellyful of chowder and several more restorative flagons.

"I didn't hear it clink."

"Of course you didn't. You're deaf as a haddock and drunk as a skunk."

This was the kind of after-dinner speaking in which the Comrades delighted. They kept it up with variations and embellishments while their leader commanded the Keeper of the Cauldron to go get the goddamn thing and bring it back. This done, the Exalted Chowderhead personally shook out the overalls, fished in the pockets and down the mortar-crusted legs to the accompaniment of ribaldries most uncouth, and finally stuck his head into the empty pot.

"It's not there," he wailed.

"Then it's under the table, where you generally wind up, you old souse," shouted Archer the wit.

It was not. It wasn't anywhere. That cumbrous chain of heavy silver with its dependent silver codfish, so recently ornamenting Jeremy Kelling's neat little paunch, was now vanished like the chowders of yesteryear.

"You forgot to put it on," sneered the Highmost Hod-carrier. "Softening of the brain, that's all. Nothing to worry about. Let's have our Codly coffee."

All hailed this sage counsel except the Exalted Chowderhead. A relative infant among the Comrades of the Convivial Codfish, being yet on the sunny side of seventy, Jeremy Kelling had labored long to achieve high office. He'd worked his way up from Journeyman Bouncer to Leastmost Hod-carrier. He'd been Fluke Flounder for one halcyon term, during which he'd pulled a calf muscle leaping to the piano and strained a tonsil putting too much fortissimo into his shouts.

At every meeting and frequently in between, he'd dreamed of the day when he would wear the Great Chain, sit behind the Ceremonial Cauldron, and show these clods how to run a meeting. His installation had taken place only last month. This was the first time he'd got to officiate. How breathtaking had been the moment when the Great Chain was withdrawn from its secret hiding place by the Opener of the Shell and hung around his palpitating neck. At the end of the meeting, the Chain was supposed to be returned to its hiding place with the Secret Valedictory Chant. How the hell could he conduct the concluding ceremonies without the blasted Codfish?

Where, Jeremy asked himself as he sipped with less than usual relish at his whiskey-laden coffee under its cargo of whipped cream, had the damn thing got to? The Great Chain couldn't have fallen off. Its overlapping links had been clinched together forever and aye by an old-time artisan, there was no clasp to come undone. The only way to get it away from him would have been to lift it over his head.

Quod erat absurdem. An experienced toper like Jeremy Kelling could never have got drunk enough on a paltry few schooners of special dark to be oblivious to any such trick as that. Furthermore, he'd been in full view of all the Comrades ever since he'd donned the Chain, and there was not such unanimity of spirit among them that somebody wouldn't have ratted on anybody else who made so free with the revered relic.

As the Codly coffee mugs were replenished, speculation about the Chain's disappearance grew more imaginative. Everybody naturally accused everybody else of codnapping. They took to visiting the men's room in squads to make sure nobody was trying to sneak the Codfish off in his codpiece.

Mrs. Coddie, of course, was exonerated, firstly because she'd been under escort by the three Hod-carriers all the time, secondly because she'd been in her swoon during the time when the fell deed was most likely to have befallen, and thirdly because she proved to be somebody's mother.

At last a thorough search of the room was conducted, with all the members crawling around on their knees, barking like a pack of foxhounds, but finding nothing. For the first time in the club's history, they had to close the meeting without the Valedictory Chant, though a few Comrades gave it anyway either because they were too befuddled not to or because they always had before and they damn well would now if they damn well felt like it.

Most appeared to regard the Great Chain's disappearance as a jolly jape and to be confident it would turn up at the April meeting pinned to the seat of the Ancient and Time worn Overalls. Jeremy Kelling was not so sanguine. His first act on returning to his Beacon Hill apartment was to fight off the ministrations of his faithful henchman Egbert, who took it for granted Mr. Jem must be sick because he'd come home sober and perturbed instead of sloshed and merry. His second was to put in an emergency call to his nephew-in-law, Max Bittersohn. "Max, I've lost the Codfish!"

"I knew a man once who lost a stuffed muskellunge," Max replied helpfully.

"Dash it, man, cease your persiflage. The Great Chain of the Convivial Codfish is a sacred relic. Like the grasshopper on top of Faneuil Hall," he added to emphasize the gravity of the situation. "It disappeared while I was removing the Ancient and Timeworn Overalls from the Ceremonial Cauldron."

"That was probably as good a time as any," said Max. "The Chain didn't fall into the pot, by any chance?"

"How the hell could it? I looked. Anyway, the thing was around my neck. I'd have had to fall in, too. Which," Jem added, "I did not. I'd have remembered. I'm not drunk. Egbert can testify to that."

"Put him on," said Bittersohn.

Egbert, to their mutual amazement, was able to vouch for his employer's unprecedented sobriety.

"It's very worrisome, Mr. Max. I've never seen him like this before. Except sometimes on the morning after," he qualified, for Egbert was a truthful man when circumstances didn't require him to be otherwise. "I think he might be described as shaken to the core."

"To the core, eh? Okay, let me talk to him again."

Max Bittersohn was a professional tracker-down of valuables that had been stolen, pawned by spuses faced with private financial emergencies, or otherwise detached from their rightful owners. Thanks to his expertise, he was able to extract from Jem a complete and perhaps even reasonably accurate account of what had happened. He offered words of cheer and comfort, then went back to his Sarah, who did not want to hear about her uncle's missing Codfish, she being a recent bride with other things on her mind.

In truth, Bittersohn himself gave little thought to Jeremy Kelling's dilemma until the following evening when Egbert dropped by to break the tidings that Mr. Jem had fallen downstairs and broken his hip. Sarah was horrified. Max was intrigued.

"Fell downstairs? How the hell did he manage that? Jem hates stairs."

"The elevator appears to have been stuck on the top floor, Mr. Max."

That was credible enough. The building where Jem and Egbert lived had an antique elevator about the size of a telephone booth, that wouldn't work unless it had been tightly latched by the last person who got out of it, which frequently didn't happen.

Jem's usual procedure in such cases was to bellow up the elevator shaft until somebody was goaded into going out and shutting the door properly. In desperate circumstances, however, such as when it was Egbert's day off and he'd run out of gin, Jem had been known to walk down the one flight of stairs from his second-floor apartment. This had been one of those times. Now he was over at Phillips House with a brand-new stainless steel ball where the hip end of his left femur used to be. Egbert thought Mrs. Sarah and Mr. Max would want to know.

"Of course we do," cried Sarah. "How ghastly! Bad enough for Uncle Jem, of course, but think of those poor nurses. What happened, do you know?"

"All I know is, I got home about five o'clock and found him sprawled on the floor of the vestibule, yowling his head off. He said Fuzzly's had called to say his whiskers were ready and they'd be closing soon, so he'd rushed out, found the elevator stuck, and gone cavorting down the stairs. There was no darn need of it, you know. I could perfectly well have gone and got them tomorrow morning but you know Mr. Jem. He wanted those whiskers."

"What for?" asked Max.

"The Tooters' railroad party," Sarah told him. "Uncle Jem was going to dress up in Dundreary whiskers and Grandfather Kelling's old frock coat, and impersonate Jay Gould."

"Did Jay Gould have Dundrearies?"

"Who knows? Anyway Uncle Jem was all in a dither about the party. He's an old railroad buff like Tom Tooter."

"Do you mean model trains?"

"No, that's Tom's brother Wouter. Tom collects real trains. He has his own steam locomotive and a parlor car with velvet-covered settees and fringed lampshades. Also a dining car and a caboose."

"Any particular reason?"

Sarah shrugged. "I suppose he got them cheap. The Tooters have always been in railroads. Anyway, Tom and his wife are having an anniversary and Tom's rented the B&M tracks for the evening. They're going to have a string ensemble playing Strauss waltzes and a fountain spouting champagne."

"My God," said Bittersohn. "Jem will have apoplexy at missing a bash like that."

"He was in a highly aggravated state of profanity when I left him," Egbert agreed. "They were about to administer a sedative."

"I don't wonder." Sarah poured Egbert a tot of their best brandy, for he was an old and beloved friend. "Here, have one yourself, then Max will walk you home. Go to bed early, you're going to need your rest."

"Truer words were never spoken, Mrs. Sarah."

"At least a broken hip ought to take his mind *off* that silly Codfish for a while. He's been phoning every hour on the hour to see whether Max has found it yet."

"As a matter of fact, his parting bellow was that I—er—call the matter to Mr. Max's attention."

Max grinned. "In precisely those words?"

"Not precisely, Mr. Max."

"Tell him I'm hot on the trail. More brandy?"

"Thanks, but I ought to be getting along."

"Come on, then."

The two men set out to walk the short distance from Tulip Street to Pinckney. "Who else is going to the party?" Max asked. "The whole Codfish crowd?"

"No, I believe Mr. Jem was the only Comrade invited, except for the

Tooters themselves, of course, and Mr. Wripp, who's recently had a cataract operation. Mrs. Tooter felt the outing would do Mr. Wripp good."

"No doubt," said Bittersohn. "What office does Mr. Wripp hold?"

"Mr. Wripp is a Formerly Grand Exalted Chowderhead. Being by now ninety-two years of age, he appears content to rest on past laurels. Oh yes, and Mr. Obed Ogham will be among those present. So maybe it's all for the best that Mr. Jem won't."

"Why? Don't he and Ogham get along?"

"None of the Kellings get along with Obed Ogham, Mr. Max. He's the bird who sued Mr. Percy Kelling for two dollars and forty-seven cents he claimed Mr. Percy overcharged him. That was after Mr. Percy's accounting firm had helped Ogham recover the five and a half million dollars Ogham's comptroller had been swindling him out of."

"Oh yes, the King of the Crumbs. How come he and Jem both belong to the same club?"

"There have always been Kellings and Oghams among the Codfish," Egbert explained. "Neither is willing to cede his ancestral right. Noblesse oblige, as you might say."

"But don't the Tooters know Jem and Ogham are feuding?"

"They're not exactly feuding, Mr. Max. I believe it's more a matter of maintaining a haughty silence in each other's presence."

Max found his mind boggling at the notion of Jem's maintaining a haughty silence in anybody's presence, but he was kind enough not to say so.

"Besides," Egbert went on, "Mr. Ogham and Mr. Wouter Tooter are this year's Highmost and Leastmost Hod-carriers respectively. It's not the done thing for one Hod-carrier to exclude a Comrade of the Hod from any of his routs and junkets, personal feelings notwithstanding. Comrade White, the Midmost Hod-carrier, would normally have been included, too, but he's just left for Nairobi on a business trip. Mr. Jem was to have escorted Mrs. White."

"Mrs. White's a good-looking, well-dressed woman somewhat on the buxom side and fond of a good time in a nonthreatening sort of way, right?"

"You know the lady, Mr. Max?"

"No, but I know Jem. And the rest, I suppose would be friends of the Tooters?"

"I expect they'll be mostly railroad buffs and members of Mr. Wouter Tooter's model railroad club. It won't be a large party, since the parlor car can't accommodate more than thirty or forty people comfortably."

"That sounds like a lot of money to spend on a relatively small affair, wouldn't you say?"

"Between you and me, Mr. Max. I think it's partly what they call public relations. Somebody's been spreading a rumor that the Tooter enterprises are in financial difficulties. I shouldn't be surprised if making a splash now is their way of squashing the rumor before their stock starts to drop."

"Very interesting. Well, here's the old homestead. Mind if I come up with you?"

"Thanks, Mr. Max, but you mustn't feel obliged."

"I want to see where it happened."

"Just a second till I find my keys. Ah, here we are. There's the staircase, you see, and Mr. Jem was on the floor at the foot."

"Marble floor, I see. Damn good thing he didn't go down head first. Who uses the stairs as a rule?"

"Nobody, unless the elevator gets stuck. I used to, but I have to say I find them more of a climb than I like nowadays."

"Did Jem say how he happened to use them today?"

"He said there was a power outage just as he received the phone call from the shop. The lights were out and the radio went off. That meant the elevator wouldn't be working either, of course. A very unfortunate coincidence. My mother always claimed bad luck came in threes. First the Codfish, and now this. What next, is what I'm wondering. Do you think we can count Mr. Jem's having to miss the party as the third piece of bad luck, Mr. Max?"

"I'm not sure we should count any of it as just luck. What happened to the clothes he was wearing when he fell?"

"I brought them home from the hospital and dropped them off before going on to your place."

"Good. Let's have a look."

The tiny elevator was sitting in the lobby, its folding brass gates meticulously fastened. Word of Jem's accident must have got around. Max and Egbert squeezed in together and rode to the second floor. Egbert fetched the clothes and Max pulled out a magnifying glass.

"Aha! See that, Egbert?"

"A grease spot on his pantleg? Mr. Max, you don't think I'd have let Mr. Jem go around looking like that? He must have done it when he fell."

"My thought exactly. There's grease on his shoe sole, too. Got a good flashlight?"

"Oh yes, I always keep one handy."

"Come on then, let's see which stair got buttered."

It was Egbert who first noticed the brownish glob under the fifth tread from the landing. "Would this be what you're looking for, Mr. Max?"

Bittersohn rubbed a little on his finger and sniffed. "It sure as hell would. Bowling alley wax, I'd say. It's been cleaned off the step with some kind of solvent, but whoever did it forgot to wipe underneath, probably because he was in a hurry to get away. I'll bet he was hiding in the cellar while they were lugging Jem off. Let's go call on the neighbors."

The first-floor people were away. On the third floor lived an elderly lady, her cook and her maid. The lady was out playing bridge with her maid in attendance because Herself didn't like going out alone at night, the cook explained. "Can I give you a cup of tea in the kitchen, now?"

The two men were happy to accept. "I see your electric clock's right on the dot," Max remarked as they sat down.

"Has to be," said the cook. "Herself likes her meals prompt to the second."

"You haven't had to reset it lately?"

"No, I haven't touched it in ages, except to dust it now and then when the spirit moves me."

Cook was plainly glad of company and ready to talk, but she didn't have much to tell. The first-floor people were in Palm Beach, and had been for the past two months. Her own household hadn't known about Jeremy Kelling's fall until they heard him being taken away in the ambulance. Herself considered him to have been struck down by a Mighty Hand in retribution for his ungodly and riotous ways. Cook personally thought Mr. Kelling was a lovely man, always so kind-spoken when they happened to meet, which wasn't often because Herself was of the old school and believed in servants using the back stairway. This very night, Mary the maid had been required to go down the back way, around the alley, and walk back up to the front door while Herself used the elevator in lone elegance. Mary might get to ride up after Herself when they got back, it being so late and good maids hard to come by.

"That's nice," said Max. "Thanks for the pleasure of your company. The cake was delicious."

"Would you be a wanting a piece to take to Mr. Kelling, now?" Egbert expressed the opinion that Mr. Jem would prefer a cake that had a bottle of Old Grandad baked into it, and they parted on a merry note.

Going back to Jem's flat, Max asked, "Egbert, would you have a recent picture of that Codfish crowd?"

"Scads of them, Mr. Max. Mr. Jem keeps an album of all the doings since he joined the club."

"Great. Where is it?"

New Englanders love to look at photograph albums, for some reason.

They spent quite a while over this one. Jem had each photograph neatly labeled. He himself appeared in most of them wearing various appurtenances of office. The latest showed the Great Chain of the Convivial Codfish adorning his well-padded front. "I'll take this," said Max.

Egbert was alarmed. "Mr. Max, if anything should happen to that album, Mr. Jem would have a stroke."

"I'll guard it with my life. Where's his invitation to that ungodly revel he was supposed to go on?"

"It's a ticket. Mr. Tooter had them printed up special. Can't ride the train without a ticket, you know." Egbert produced the precious oblong. "Is it a clue, do you think?"

"Who knows? Anyway, Jem won't be needing it now. Sleep tight, Egbert. Sarah will be over to the hospital at crack of dawn, I expect, so take your time in the morning."

Max took his leave, pondering deeply. The next day, leaving Sarah to comfort the afflicted, he first collected Jem's whiskers from Fuzzly's, dropped in on some pals at the Fraud Squad, lunched with a prominent member of the Securities and Exchange Commission who owed him a favor, had a chat with his Uncle Jake the lawyer, paid a call on a fair and buxom matron who was mystified, gratified, and eager to cooperate; and finally went home to placate his wife.

"Sorry I can't have dinner with you tonight, sweetie-pumpkin."

"And where are you off to, pray tell? What are you getting all pressed up for?"

"A train ride," he replied from the depths of a starched shirt. "Seen my studs lately?"

"You might try your stud box. Uncle Jem wants to know when in blazes you're going to catch his Codfish."

"Anon, I hope. One kiss, my bonny sweetheart, I'm off for a prize tonight. With the voluptuous Mrs. White, in case some kind friend thinks you ought to know."

"In that disgusting clawhammer coat? Where on earth did you get it?"

"Same place I got these." He put on Jem's Dundreary whiskers. "How do I look?"

"Don't ask. I'm going next door and cry on Cousin Theonia's shoulder. Mrs. White, indeed! I hope she singes your whiskers."

Mrs. White was ready and waiting when he went to pick her up. They had some trouble stowing her into the taxi on account of her bustle, feather boa, and a hat freighted with a whole stuffed pheasant; but at last they were able to proceed.

On Track Four at North Station, business was booming. A conductor in a stiff cap and brass-buttoned uniform was joyfully clipping tickets. Max recognized him from Jem's album as Tom Tooter, their host. Up ahead in the engine cab, a melancholy individual wearing a high-rise cap of striped ticking, greasy striped overalls, and a tremendous scrubbing-brush mustache leaned out to survey the throng flocking aboard. This could be none other than Wouter Tooter, throwing himself into his role.

Max himself received some puzzled glances as Mrs. White introduced him right and left as her dear, dear friend Mr. Jay Gould. People must either be putting him down as somebody they'd met before but couldn't place, or else making mental notes to have a quiet chat with Mr. White when he got back from Nairobi.

Mrs. Tom Tooter was doing the honours inside the parlor car, wearing silver lace over a straight-front corset, with white gloves up to her armpits and strings of pearls down to her knees. She looked a trifle nonplussed when Max made his bow, but pleased to have such a good-looking man aboard even if his ginger side whiskers did clash rather j ferociously with his wavy dark hair. Luckily, Mr. Wripp tottered in just behind him and had to be fussed over, so Max escaped without a grilling.

The lights were dim enough to make all the ladies look charming and all the men distinguished. There was no fountain splashing champagne, but they did have a swan carved out of ice to chill the caviar, and a bartender wearing red arm garters and a black toupee neatly parted down the middle. Max got Mrs. White a white lady, which seemed appropriate, then turned her over to her friends and went prospecting.

Tom Tooter was in his glory. He'd changed his conductor's cap and coat for a Prince Albert. He bagged at the knees and bulged at the shoulders, but what did he care? Kings might be blest, but Tom was glorious, o'er all the ills of life victorious. He couldn't possibly be the man Max was looking for.

Mrs. Tooter kept glancing at her husband with fond wifely indulgence and brushing imaginary specks off his lapels as women do in public places where decorum forbids more overt displays of affection. Max indulged himself for a moment in thinking that if Sarah were here, she might be brushing specks off his lapels, then got on with his job. Obed Ogham was easy to spot and would no doubt be a pleasure to dislike. He was one of those loud, beefy men who trap people in corners and tell them a lot of stuff they don't want to hear. Max stayed well clear of him. He'd be the sort to ask personal questions of strangers.

Wouter Tooter was not in the parlor car. Various guests were asking for him; no doubt cronies from his model railroad club as they wore trainmen's caps with their false whiskers and old-fashioned clothes. Tom said he was around somewhere and why didn't they come into the dining car?

This was an excellent suggestion, Max found. Rows of tables with snowy napery and genuine old railroad cutlery were set out around a long center buffet laden with hams, roasts of beef, whole turkeys, hot dishes under metal covers the size of igloos, cold platters of every description, and epergnes dripping with fruits, sweets, and exotic flowers. Edward VII would have found it adequate.

Waiters hovered ready to fetch and carry. A wine steward wearing a silver corkscrew on a heavy silver sommelier's chain circulated among the tables murmuring recommendations through a well-trimmed but all-covering beard. He sounded as if he had a marble in his mouth. Max took one long, earnest look at the wine steward, then slipped out into the vestibule. When the man came through, Max tackled him.

"Mr. Wouter Tooter, I believe? Changed your overalls, I see."

"Who the hell are you?" mumbled the man.

"You'd better take that marble out of your mouth, Mr. Tooter. You might swallow it. To respond to your question, my name's Bittersohn and I'm a private detective sent by the Securities and Exchange Commission to guard Mr. Obed Ogham. They don't want anything to happen to him before he's indicted."

"Indicted? What for?"

"You don't really have to ask, do you? You know damn well Ogham's trying by highly illegal methods to scuttle your brother's firm so he can make a killing on the stock market. That's why you're playing wine steward tonight with the Great Chain of the Convivial Codfish."

Wouter looked down at his chest as if he thought it might possibly belong to someone else, and said nothing.

"That's why you deliberately disabled Jeremy Kelling, so that he couldn't come tonight and catch you wearing the chain. Your brother's too busy with the guests to notice, and old Mr. Wripp's too bleary-eyed from his cataract operation. Ogham might catch on, but he's not supposed to live long enough to rat on you, is he?"

"I don't know what you're talking about."

"Like hell you don't. You cut off the electricity in Jem's apartment yesterday afternoon and waxed the stairs. Then you put in a fake phone call from Fuzzly's, knowing that would send Jem charging out to get his whiskers. He'd find the elevator inoperative, gallop down the stairs, and take a toss, which he did. And you've got some kind of muck in your pocket right now that you're planning to drop into Ogham's wine as soon as he's drunk enough not to notice. You needn't bother. He's on his way to jail, though he doesn't know it yet. Your brother's business is safe and so are you, on two conditions."

"What conditions?" said Wouter sulkily.

"You leave Ogham alone and you show me how the hell you got that chain off Jem's neck."

"Oh." Light dawned on what little Max could see of Wouter's lavishly disguised countenance. "I know you now. You're the bird who married Jem's niece. The pretty one who's always getting murdered."

"Right. And you're the wise guy who landed your buddy in the hospital with a broken hip."

"Well, hell, what was a man to do? I couldn't make Tom listen to reason. He simply refused to believe even that reptile Ogham would scuttle a Comrade. Jem won't mind once he knows I did it for Tom. I knew the old sculpin would land on his feet, he always does. This time he bounced on his backside first. Too bad, but it was in good cause. Surely you must realize that."

"Couldn't you just have asked Jem to stay away from the party?"

"Jem Kelling miss a bash like this? You must be out of your mind. I'd have had to explain why, then all Jem would have done was swagger in here, waltz up to Obed, and paste him straight in the mouth. He'd have to stand on a chair to reach that high, I expect, but he'd do it. You know Jem."

Max did know Jem, and he could not dispute Wouter's logic. "Okay, if you can make that sound sane to Jem, more power to you. What were you planning to fix Ogham's wagon with?"

"Just a Mickey Finn. I thought I'd make believe he'd passed out from too much booze, drag him to the observation platform supposedly to sober up, and shove him overboard. Then I'd take off my disguise and go back to being me."

"While Ogham was found suffering from minor contusions and rushed to the nearest hospital, where the doctors would start wondering how he got bunged full of chloral hydrate and your nice family train ride would turn into a major scandal. Nice going, Tooter."

"Well, damn it, I never committed a murder before. This seemed like a good idea."

"Take it from me, it stinks. Hand me the chloral and show me how you worked the Chain."

"Oh well, there's nothing to that." Wouter gave Max the little bottle, then took off the Chain. "You see, last year I was Opener of the Shell, which meant I had custody of the Great Chain. Just for fun, I split one of the links and inserted a tiny magnetic coupling to hold it together. You'd need a magnifying glass to see it."

"No problem." Max had one, of course. Wouter's craftsmanship was indeed masterful.

"It's worked by a remote-control switch. I meant to open it as a joke sometime, but when this foul business with Ogham came up, I got I the idea of wearing the Chain and posing as a wine steward. No sense in going out and buying one when I'd never use it again, was there?"

"Hardly," said Max. He was feeling a trifle dizzy by now.

"You see, I'm Leastmost Hod-carrier this year. That means I get to stand behind Jem when he pulls the Ancient and Timeworn Overalls out of the Cauldron. This is all highly confidential, top-secret stuff, of course, so don't breathe a word to a soul. So anyway, then Mrs. Coddie swoons. I knew they'd all be watching her, so I released the Chain, grabbed it as it fell, and slid it down inside my own overalls. As soon as I could, I slipped into the men's room, put the Chain around my own neck under my clothes, and wore it home."

"Not bad," said Max. "How were you planning to get it back?"

"Frankly, I hadn't thought that far ahead. Maybe I could write old Jem a ransom note and deliver it myself. I could slink in wearing all this face fungus."

Wouter started peeling off false eyebrows and chin whiskers. "Might as well get my money's worth out of it. Fuzzly's aren't expecting it back till tomorrow afternoon. In the meantime, I can put the Codfish back on the Chain. Had to switch it for a corkscrew, you know. I mean, without the Codfish, the Chain's just a chain."

"That did occur to me," said Max. "Also, since you fiddle around with model railroads, I thought you might be pretty good at midget switches and convenient power failures. If I may make a suggestion, you'd do better to send Jem the corkscrew and a bottle of something by way of penance."

"Damn good idea. I'll make it a case of burgundy. Speaking of which, now that I've resigned as wine steward, let's you and I go put on the feedbag. Then we can go up to the engine. Maybe the fireman will let us shovel some coal."

Small Homicide

H ER FACE WAS SMALL AND CHUBBY, the eyes blue and inno-cently rounded, but seeing nothing. Her body rested on the seat of the wooden bench, one arm twisted awkwardly beneath her.

The candles near the altar flickered and cast their dancing shadows on her face. There was a faded, pink blanket wrapped around her, and against the whiteness of her throat were the purple bruises that told us she'd been strangled.

Her mouth was open, exposing two small teeth and the beginnings of a third.

She was no more than eight months old.

The church was quiet and immense, with early-morning sunlight light-ing the stained-glass windows. Dust motes filtered down the long, slanting columns of sunlight, and Father Barren stood tall and darkly somber at the end of the pew, the sun touching his hair like an angel's kiss.

"This is the way you found her, Father?" I asked.

"Yes. Just that way." The priest's eyes were a deep brown against the chalky whiteness of his face. "I didn't touch her."

Pat Travers scratched his jaw and stood up, reaching for the pad in his back pocket. His mouth was set in a tight, angry line. Pat had three children of his own. "What time was this, Father?"

"At about five-thirty. We have a six o'clock mass, and I came out to see that the altar was prepared. Our altar boys go to school, you understand, and they usually arrive at the last moment. I generally attend to the altar myself."

"No sexton?" Pat asked.

"Yes, we have a sexton, but he doesn't arrive until about eight every morning. He comes earlier on Sundays."

I nodded while Pat jotted the information in his pad. "How did you happen to see her, Father?"

"I was walking to the back of the church to open the doors. I saw something in the pew, and I . . . well, at first I thought it was just a package someone had forgotten. When I came closer, I saw it was . . . was a baby." He sighed deeply and shook his head.

"The doors were locked, Father?"

"No. No, they're never locked. This is God's house, you know. They were simply closed. I was walking back to open them. I usually open them before the first mass in the morning."

"They were unlocked all night?"

"Yes, of course."

"I see." I looked down at the baby again. "You . . . you wouldn't know who she is, would you, Father?"

Father Barron shook his head again. "I'm afraid not. She may have been baptized here, but infants all look alike, you know. It would be different if I saw her every Sunday. But . . . " He spread his hands wide in a helpless gesture.

Pat nodded, and kept looking at the dead child. "We'll have to send some of the boys to take pictures and prints, Father. I hope you don't mind. And we'll have to chalk up the pew. It shouldn't take too long, and we'll have the body out as soon as possible."

Father Barron looked down at the dead baby. He crossed himself then and said, "God have mercy on her soul."

I was sipping my hot coffee when the buzzer on my desk sounded. I pushed down the toggle and said, "Levine here."

"Dave, want to come into my office a minute? This is the lieutenant."

"Sure thing," I told him. I put down the cup and said, "Be right back," to Pat, and headed for the Skipper's office.

He was sitting behind his desk with our report in his hands. He glanced up when I came in and said, "Sit down, Dave. Hell of a thing, isn't it?"

"Yes," I said.

"I'm holding it back from the papers, Dave. If this breaks, we'll have every mother in the city telephoning us. You know what that means?"

"You want it fast."

"I want it damned fast. I'm pulling six men from other jobs to help you and Pat. I don't want to go to another precinct for help because the bigger this gets, the better its chances of breaking print are. I want it quiet and small, and I want it fast." He stopped and shook his head, and then muttered, "Goddamn thing."

"We're waiting for the autopsy report now," I said. "As soon as we get it, we may be able to—"

"What did it look like to you?"

"Strangulation. It's there in our report."

The lieutenant glanced at the typewritten sheet in his hands, mumbled, "Uhm," and then said, "While you're waiting, you'd better start checking the Missing Persons calls."

"Pat's doing that now, sir."

"Good, good. You know what to do, Dave. Just get me an answer to it fast."

"We'll do our best, sir."

He leaned back in his leather chair, "A little girl, huh?" He shook his head. "Damn shame. Damn shame." He kept shaking his head and looking at the report, and then he dropped the report on his desk and said, "Here're the boys you've got to work with." He handed me a typewritten list of names. "All good, Dave. Get me results."

"I'll try, sir."

Pat had a list of calls on his desk when I went outside again. I picked it up and glanced through it rapidly. A few older kids were lost, and there had been the usual frantic pleas from frantic mothers who should have watched their kids more carefully in the first place.

"What's this?" I asked. I put my forefinger alongside a call clocked in at eight-fifteen. A Mrs. Wilkes had phoned to say she'd left her baby outside in the carriage, and the carriage was gone.

"They found the kid," Pat said. "Her older daughter had simply taken the kid for a walk. There's nothing there, Dave."

"The Skipper wants action, Pat. The photos come in yet?"

"Over there." He indicated a pile of glossy photographs on his desk. I picked up the stack and thumbed through it. They'd shot the baby from every conceivable angle, and there were two good close-ups of her face. I fanned the pictures out on my desk top and phoned the lab. I recognized Caputo's voice at once.

"Any luck, Cappy?"

"That you, Dave?"

"Yep."

"You mean on the baby?"

"Yeah."

"The boys brought in a whole slew of stuff. A pew collects a lot of prints, Dave."

"Anything we can use?"

"I'm running them through now. If we get anything, I'll let you know."

"Fine. I want the baby's footprints taken and a stat sent to every hospital in the state."

"Okay. It's going to be tough if the baby was born outside, though."

"Maybe we'll be lucky. Put the stat on the machine, will you? And tell them we want immediate replies."

"I'll have it taken care of, Dave."

"Good. Cappy, we're going to need all the help we can get on this one. So . . ."

"I'll do all I can."

"Thanks. Let me know if you get anything."

"I will. So long, Dave. I've got work."

He clicked off, and I leaned back and lighted a cigarette. Pat picked up one of the baby's photos and glumly studied it.

"When they get him, they should cut off his . . ."

"He'll get the chair," I said. "That's for sure."

"I'll pull the switch. Personally. Just ask me. Just ask me and I'll do it."

The baby was stretched out on the long white table when I went down to see Doc Edwards. A sheet covered the corpse, and Doc was busy typing up a report. I looked over his shoulder:

The McBain Brief

POLICE DEPARTMENT

City of New York

Date: June 12, 1953

From: Commanding Officer, Charles R. Brandon, 77th Pct.

To: Chief Medical Examiner

SUBJECT: DEATH OF Baby girl (unidentified)

Please furnish information on items checked below in connection with the death of the above named. Body was found on June 12, 1953 at Church of the Holy Mother, 1220 Benson Avenue, Bronx, New York

Autopsy performed or examination made? Yes

By Dr James L. Edwards, Fordham Hospital Mortuary

Date: June 12, 1953 Where? Bronx County

Cause of death: Broken neck

Doc Edwards looked up from the typewriter.

"Not nice, Dave."

"No, not nice at all." I saw that he was ready to type in the *Result of chemical analysis* space. "Anything else on her?"

"Not much. Dried tears on her face. Urine on her abdomen, buttocks, and genitals. Traces of Desitin and petroleum jelly there, too. That's about it."

"Time of death?"

"I'd put it at about three A.M. last night."

"Uh-huh."

"You want a guess?"

"Sure."

"Somebody doesn't like his sleep to be disturbed by a crying kid. That's my guess."

"Nobody likes his sleep disturbed," I said. "What's the Desitin and petroleum jelly for? That normal?"

"Yeah, sure. Lots of mothers use it. Mostly for minor irritations. Urine burn, diaper rash, that sort of thing."

"I see."

"This shouldn't be too tough, Dave. You know who the kid is yet?"

"We're working on that now."

"Well, good luck."

"Thanks."

I turned to go, and Doc Edwards began pecking at the typewriter again, completing the autopsy report on a dead girl.

There was good news waiting for me back at the office. Pat rushed over with a smile on his face and a thick sheet of paper in his hands. "Here's the ticket," he said.

I took the paper and looked at it. It was the photostat of a birth certificate.

U.S. NAVAL HOSPITAL St. Albans, N.Y. Birth Certificate

This certifies that Louise Ann Dreiser was born to Alice Dreiser in this hospital at 4:15 P.M. on the tenth day of November, 1952 Weight 7 lbs. 6 _ozs.

In witness whereof, the said hospital has caused this certificate to be issued, properly signed and the seal of the hospital hereunto affixed.

Gregory Freeman, LTJG MC USN
Attending Physician
Frederick L. Mann, CAPTAIN MC
Commanding Officer USN

"Here's how they got it," Pat said, handing me another stat. I looked at it quickly. It was obviously the reverse side of the birth certificate.

The McBain Brief
Baby's Footprint (Permanent Evidence of Identity)
Left foot
Right foot
  Sex of child Female
  Weight at birth _7_ lbs.
  _6_ ozs.

Certificate of birth should be carefully preserved as record of value for future use:
  1. To identify relationship
  2. To establish age to enter school

There were several more good reasons why a birth certificate should be kept in the sugar bowl, and then below that:
  Official registration at 148-15 Archer Avenue, Jamaica, L.I., N.Y.

==

===================================

  Mother's left thumb
Mother's right thumb

"Alice Dreiser," I said.

"That's the mother. Prints and all. I've already sent a copy down to Cappy to check against the ones they lifted from the pew."

"Fine. Pick one of the boys from the list the Skipper gave us, Pat. Tell him to get whatever he can on Alice Dreiser and her husband. They have to be sailors or relations to get admitted to a naval hospital, don't they?"

"Yeah. You've got to prove dependency."

"Fine. Get the guy's last address, and we'll try to run down the woman, or him, or both. Get whoever you pick to call right away, will you?"

"Right. Why pick anyone? I'll make the call myself."

"No, I want you to check the phone book for any Alice Dreisers. In the meantime, I'll be looking over the baby's garments."

"You'll be down at the lab?"

"Yeah. Phone me, Pat."

"Right."

Caputo had the garments separated and tagged when I got there. "You're not going to get much out of these," he told me.

"No luck, huh?"

He held out the pink blanket. "Black River Mills. A big trade name. You can probably buy it in any retail shop in the city." He picked up the small pink sweater with the pearl buttons. "Toddlers, Inc., ditto. The socks have no markings at all. The undershirt came from Gilman's here in the city. It's the largest department store in the world, so you can imagine how many of these they sell every day. The cotton pajamas were bought there, too."

"No shoes?"

"No shoes."

"What about the diaper?"

"What about it? It's a plain diaper. No label. You got any kids, Dave?"

"One."

"You ever see a diaper with a label?"

"I don't recall."

"If you did, it wasn't in it long. Diapers take a hell of a beating."

"Maybe this one came from a diaper service."

"Maybe. You can check that."

"Safety pins?"

"Two. No identifying marks. Look like five-and-dime stuff."

"Any prints?"

"Yeah. There are smudged prints on the pins, but there's a good partial thumbprint on one of the pajama snaps."

"Whose?"

"It matches the right thumbprint on the stat you sent down. Mrs. Dreiser's."

"Uh-huh. Did you check her prints against the ones from the pew?"

"Nothing, Dave. None of her, anyway."

"Okay, Cappy. Thanks a lot."

Cappy shrugged. "I get paid," he said. He grinned and waved as I walked out and headed upstairs again. I met Pat in the hallway, coming down to the lab after me.

"What's up?" I asked.

"I called the Naval Hospital. They gave me the last address they had for the guy. His name is Carl Dreiser, lived at 831 East 217th Street, Bronx, when the baby was born."

"How come?"

"He was a yeoman, working downtown on Church Street. Lived with his wife uptown, got an allotment. You know the story."

"Yeah. So?"

"I sent Artie to check at that address. He should be calling in soon now."

"What about the sailor?"

"I called the Church Street office, spoke to the commanding officer, Captain"—he consulted a slip of paper—"Captain Thibet. This Dreiser was working there back in November. He got orders in January, reported aboard the U.S.S. Hanfield, DD 981, at the Brooklyn Navy Yard on January fifth of this year."

"Where is he now?"

"That's the problem, Dave."

"What kind of problem?"

"The Hanfield was sunk off Pyongyang in March."

"Oh."

"Dreiser is listed as missing in action."

I didn't say anything. I nodded, and waited.

"A telegram was sent to Mrs. Dreiser at the Bronx address. The Navy says the telegram was delivered and signed for by Alice Dreiser."

"Let's wait for Artie to call in," I said.

We ordered more coffee and waited. Pat had checked the phone book, and there'd been no listing for either Carl or Alice Dreiser. He'd had a list typed of every Dreiser in the city, and it ran longer than my arm.

"Why didn't you ask the Navy what his parents' names are?" I said.

"I did. Both parents are dead."

"Who does he list as next of kin?"

"His wife. Alice Dreiser."

"Great."

In a half hour, Artie called in. There was no Alice Dreiser living at the Bronx address. The landlady said she'd lived there until April and had left without giving a forwarding address. Yes, she'd had a baby daughter. I told Artie to keep the place staked out, and then buzzed George Tabin and told him to check the Post Office Department for any forwarding address.

When he buzzed back in twenty minutes, he said, "Nothing, Dave. Nothing at all."

We split the available force of men, and I managed to wangle four more men from the lieutenant. Half of us began checking on the Dreisers listed in the phone directory, and the rest of us began checking the diaper services.

The first diaper place I called on had a manager who needed only a beard to look like Santa Claus. He greeted me affably and offered all his assistance.

Unfortunately, they'd never had a customer named Alice Dreiser.

At my fourth stop, I got what looked like a lead.

I spoke directly to the vice-president, and he listened intently.

"Perhaps," he said, "perhaps." He was a big man, with a wide waist, a gold watch chain straddling it. He leaned over and pushed down on his intercom buzzer.

"Yes, sir?"

"Bring in a list of our customers. Starting with November of 1952."

"Sir?"

"Starting with November of 1952."

"Yes, sir."

We chatted about the diaper business in general until the list came, and then he handed it to me and I began checking off the names. There were a hell of a lot of names on it. For the month of December, I found a listing for Alice Dreiser. The address given was the one we'd checked in the Bronx.

"Here she is," I said. "Can you get her records?"

The vice-president looked at the name. "Certainly, just a moment." He buzzed his secretary again, told her what he wanted, and she brought the yellow file cards in a few minutes later. The cards told me that Alice Dreiser had continued the diaper service through February. She'd been late on her February payment, and had cancelled service in March. She'd had the diapers delivered for the first week in March but had not paid for them. She did not notify the company that she was moving. She had not returned the diapers they'd sent her that first week in March. The company did not know where she was.

"If you find her," the vice-president told me, "I'd like to know. She owes us money."

"I'll keep that in mind," I said.

The reports on the Dreisers were waiting for me back at the precinct. George had found a couple who claimed to be Carl's aunt and uncle. They knew he was married. They gave Alice's maiden name as Grant. They said she lived somewhere on Walton Avenue in the Bronx, or at least *had* lived there when Carl first met her, they hadn't seen either her or Carl for months. Yes, they knew the Dreisers had had a daughter. They'd received an announcement card. They had never seen the baby.

Pat and I looked up the Grants on Walton Avenue, found a listing for Peter Grant, and went there together.

A bald man in his undershirt, his suspenders hanging over his trousers, opened the door. "What is it?" he asked.

"Police officers," I said. "We'd like to ask a few questions."

"What about? Let me see your badges."

Pat and I flashed our buzzers and the bald man studied them.

"What kind of questions do you want to ask?"

"Are you Peter Grant?"

"Yeah, that's right. What's this all about?"

"May we come in?"

"Sure, come on in." We followed him into the apartment, and he motioned us to chairs in the small living room. "Now, what is it?" he asked.

"Your daughter is Alice Dreiser?"

"Yes," he said.

"Do you know where she lives?"

"No."

"Come on, mister," Pat said. "You know where your daughter lives."

"I don't," Grant snapped, "and I don't give a damn, either."

"Why? What's wrong, mister?"

"Nothing. Nothing's wrong. It's none of your business, anyway."

"Her daughter had her neck broken," I said. "It is our business."

"I don't give a . . ." he started to say. He stopped then and looked straight ahead of him, his brows pulled together into a tight frown. "I'm sorry. I still don't know where she lives."

"Did you know she was married?"

"To that sailor. Yes, I knew."

"And you knew she had a daughter?"

"Don't make me laugh," Grant said.

"What's funny, mister?" Pat said.

"Did I know she had a daughter? Why the hell do you think she married the sailor? Don't make me laugh!"

"When was your daughter married, Mr. Grant?"

"Last September." He saw the look on my face, and added, "Go ahead, you count it. The kid was born in November."

"Have you seen her since the marriage?"

"No."

"Have you ever seen the baby?"

"No."

"Do you have a picture of your daughter?"

"I think so. Is she in trouble? Do you think she did it?"

"We don't know who did it yet."

"Maybe she did," Grant said softly. "She just maybe did. I'll get you the picture."

He came back in a few minutes with a picture of a plain girl wearing a cap and gown. She had light eyes and straight hair, and her face was intently serious.

"She favors her mother," Grant said, "God rest her soul."

"Your wife is dead?"

"Yes. That picture was taken when Alice graduated high school. She graduated in June and married the sailor in September. She's . . . she's only just nineteen now, you know."

"May we have this?" He hesitated and said, "It's the only one I've got. She . . . she didn't take many pictures. She wasn't a very . . . pretty kid."

"We'll return it."

"All right," he said. His eyes began to blink. "She . . . If she's in trouble, you'll . . . you'll let me know, won't you?"

"We'll let you know."

"Kids . . . kids make mistakes sometimes." He stood up abruptly. "Let me know."

We had copies of the photo made, and then we staked out every church in the neighborhood in which the baby was found. Pat and I covered the Church of the Holy Mother, because we figured the suspect was most likely to come back there.

We didn't talk much. There is something about a church of any denomination that makes a man think rather than talk. Pat and I knocked off at about seven every night, and the night boys took over then. We were back on the job at seven in the morning, every morning.

It was a week before she came in.

She was a thin girl, with the body of a child and a pinched, tired face. She stopped at the font in the rear of the church, dipped her hand in the holy water, and crossed herself. Then she walked to the altar, stopped before an idol of the Virgin Mary, lighted a candle, and knelt before it.

"That's her," I said.

"Let's go," Pat answered.

"Not here. Outside."

Pat's eyes locked with mine for an instant. "Sure," he said.

She knelt before the idol for a long time, and then got to her feet slowly, drying her eyes. She walked up the aisle, stopped at the font, crossed herself, and then walked outside.

We followed her out, catching up with her at the corner. I pulled up on one side of her and Pat on the other.

"Mrs. Dreiser?" I asked.

She stopped walking. "Yes?"

I showed my buzzer. "Police officers," I said. "We'd like to ask some questions."

She stared at my face for a long time. She drew a trembling breath then, and said, "I killed her. I . . . Carl was dead, you see. I . . . I guess that was it. It wasn't right—his getting killed, I mean. And she was crying." She nodded blankly. "Yes, that was it. She just cried all the time, not knowing that I was crying inside. You don't know how I cried inside. Carl . . . he was all I had. I . . . I couldn't stand it anymore. I told her to shut up and when she didn't I . . . I . . . "

"Come on now, ma'm," I said.

"I brought her to the church." She nodded, remembering it all now. "She was innocent, you know. So I brought her to the church. Did you find her there?"

"Yes, ma'm," I said. "That's where we found her."

She seemed pleased. A small smile covered her mouth and she said, "I'm glad you found her."

She told the story again to the lieutenant. Pat and I checked out and on the way to the subway, I asked him, "Do you still want to pull the switch, Pat?"

He didn't answer.

SHARYN MCCRUMB

A Wee Doch and Doris

H E STOOD FOR A LONG WHILE STARING UP at the house, but
all was quiet. There was one light on in an upstairs window, but
he saw no shadows flickering on the shades. Not a creature was
stirring, not even a mouse, Louis smirked to himself. Christmas wasn't so
hot if you were in his line of work. People tended to stay home with the family one night a year when everybody wishes they were The Waltons. But all
that togetherness wore off in a week. By now everybody had cabin fever, and
they were dying to get away from the in-laws and the rug rats. That's how it
was in his family, anyway. By New Year's Eve his ma had recovered from the
thrill of receiving candy from Anthony, bubble bath from Michael, and a
bottle of perfume from Louis, and she had started nagging again. Louis
always gave her a bottle of perfume. He preferred small, lightweight gifts
that could be slipped easily and unobtrusively into one's pocket.

He also preferred not to have endless discussions with his nearest and
dearest over whether he was going to get a job or enroll in the auto mechanics program at the community college. Neither idea appealed to Louis. He
liked his schedule: sleeping until eleven, a quick burger for brunch, and a
few hours of volunteer work at the animal shelter.

Nobody at the shelter thought Louis was lazy or unmotivated. He was
their star helper. He didn't mind hosing down the pens and cleaning the
food dishes, but what he really enjoyed was playing with the dogs and
brushing down the shaggy ones. They didn't have a lot of money at the shelter, so they couldn't afford to pay him. It took all their funds to keep the animals fed and healthy; the shelter refused to put a healthy animal to sleep.
Louis heartily approved of this policy, and thus he didn't mind working for

free; in fact, sometimes when the shelter's funds were low, he gave them a donation from the proceeds of his night's work. Louis thought that rich people should support local charities; he saw himself as the middleman, except that his share of the take was ninety percent. Louis also believed that charity begins at home.

Christmas was good for the shelter. Lots of people high on the Christmas spirit adopted kittens and puppies, or gave them as gifts, and the shelter saw to it that they got a donation for each adoptee. So their budget was doing okay, but Louis's personal funds were running short. Christmas is not a good time of year for a burglar. Sometimes he'd find an empty house whose occupants were spending Christmas out of town, but usually the neighborhood was packed with nosy people, eyeballing every car that went by. You'd think they were looking for Santa Claus.

If Christmas was bad for business, New Year's Eve made up for it. Lots of people went out to parties that night, and did not plan on coming home until well after midnight. Being out for just the evening made them less security conscious the Christmas people who went out of town: New Year's party-goers were less likely to hide valuables, activate alarms, or ask the police to keep an eye on the premises. Louis had had a busy evening. He'd started around nine o'clock, when even the tardiest guests would have left for the party, and he had hit four houses, passing on one because of a Doberman Pinscher in the backyard. Louis had nothing against the breed, but he found them very unreasonable, and not inclined to give strangers the benefit of the doubt.

The other four houses had been satisfactory, though first one was "guarded" by a haughty white Persian whose owners had forgotten to feed it. Louis put down some canned mackerel for the cat, and charged its owners one portable television, one 35mm camera, three pairs of earrings, a player, and a collection of compact discs. The other houses had been equally rewarding. After a day's visit to various flea markets and pawn shops, his financial standing should be greatly improved. This was much better than auto mechanics. Louis realized that larceny and auto mechanics are almost never mutually exclusive, but he felt that in free-lance burglary the hours were better.

He glanced at his watch. A little after midnight, would be his last job of the evening. Louis wanted to be before the drunks got out on the highway. His New Year's resolution was to campaign for gun control and for tougher drunk driving laws. He turned his attention back to the white house with the boxwood hedge and the garden gnome next to the birdbath. No danger of Louis stealing *that*. He thought people ought to have to pay to have garden gnomes stolen. A promising sideline—he would have to consider it. But now to the business at hand.

The hedge seemed high enough to prevent the neighbors from seeing into the yard. The house across the street was vacant, with a big yellow For Sale sign stuck in the yard. The brick split-level next door was dark, but they had a chain link fence, and their front yard was floodlit like the exercise yard of a penitentiary. Louis shook his head: paranoia *and* bad taste.

There was no car in the driveway, a promising sign that no one was home. He liked the look of the rectangular kitchen window. It was partly hidden by a big azalea bush, and it looked like the kind of window that opened out at the bottom, with a catch to keep it from opening too far. It was about six feet off the ground. Louis was tempted to look under the garden gnome for a spare house key, but he decided to have a look at the window instead. Using a key was unsporting; besides, the exercise would be good for him. If you are a burglar, your physique is your fortune.

He walked a lot, too. Tonight Louis had parked his old Volkswagen a couple of streets away, not so much for the exercise as for the fact that later no one would remember seeing a strange car in the vicinity. The long walk back to the car limited Louis's take to the contents of a pillowcase or two, also from the burgled home, but he felt that most worthwhile burglary items were small and lightweight, anyway. The pillowcases he gave as baby gifts to new parents of his acquaintance, explaining that they were the perfect size to use as a cover for a bassinet mattress. Even better than a fitted crib sheet, he insisted, because after the kid grows up, you can use the pillowcases yourself. Louis was nothing if not resourceful.

He stayed close to the boxwood hedge as he edged closer to the house. With a final glance to see that no one was driving past, he darted for the azalea bush, and ended up crouched behind it, just under the rectangular window. Perfect. Fortunately it wasn't too cold tonight—temperature in the mid-thirties, about average for the Virginia Christmas season. When it got colder than that, his dexterity was impaired, making it hard to jimmy locks and tamper windows. It was an occupational hazard. Tonight would be no problem, though, unless the window had some kind of inside lock.

It didn't. He was able to chin himself on the windowsill and pull the window outward enough to get a hand inside and slip the catch. With that accomplished, another twenty seconds of wriggling got him through the window and onto the Formica countertop next to the sink. There had been a plant on the windowsill, but he managed to ease that onto the counter, before sliding himself all the way through. The sound he made was a slight thump as he went countertop to floor; no problem if the house was unoccupied.

Taking out his pen-sized flashlight, Louis checked out the kitchen. It was squeaky clean. He could even smell the lemon floor cleaner. He shone the light on the gleaming white refrigerator. Some people actually put their valuables in the freezer compartment. He always checked that last, though. In the corner next to the back door was a small washing machine and an electric dryer, with clean clothes stacked neatly o top. Louis eased his way across the room, and inspected the laundry. Women's clothes—small sizes—towels, cloths . . . ah, there they were! Pillowcases. He helped himself to the two linen cases, sniffing them appreciatively. Fabric softener. *Very* nice. Now he was all set. Time to shop around.

He slipped into the dining room and flashed the light on the round oak table and the ladderback chairs. Two place laid for breakfast. Weren't they the early birds, though? The and pepper shakers looked silver. They were in the shape of pheasants. Louis slid them into his pillowcase and examined the rest of the room. The glass of the china cabinet flashed his light back at him. Bunch of flowery plates. No chance he'd be taking those. He looked around for a silver chest, but didn't see one. He'd check on it later. He wanted to examine the living room first.

Louis flashed an exploratory light at the fireplace, the chintz couch covered in throw pillows, and the glass-fronted bookcase. There were some candlesticks on the mantelpiece that looked promising. As he crept forward to inspect them, the room was flooded with light.

Squinting at the sudden brightness, Louis turned toward the stairs and saw that he wasn't alone. The overhead lights had been switched on by a sweet-faced old woman in a green velvet bathrobe. Louis braced himself for the scream, but the old lady was smiling. She kept coming daintily down the stairs. Smiling. Louis stared, trying to think up a plausible story. She couldn't have been more than five feet tall, and her blue eyes sparkled from a wrinkled but pleasant face. She patted her white permed hair into place. She looked delighted. Probably senile, Louis thought.

"Well, I'm that glad to see you!" the woman said brightly. "I was afraid it was going to be my daughter Doris."

Definitely senile, thought Louis. "No, it's just me," he said, deciding to play along. He held the pillowcase behind his back.

"Just after midnight, too, isn't it? That's grand, that is. Otherwise I'd have to ask you to go out and come in again, you know."

Louis noticed her accent now. It was sort of English, he thought. But she wasn't making any sense. "Come in again?"

"Ah, well, being an American you wouldn't know the custom, would you? Well, you're welcome all the same. Now, what can I get for you?"

Louis realized just in time that she meant food or drink, rather than jewelry and savings bonds. "Nothing for me, thanks," he said, giving her a little wave and trying to edge for the front door.

Her face fell. "Oh, no. Please! You must let me fix you something. Otherwise, you'll be taking the luck away with you. How about a piece of cake? I made it today. And a bit of strong drink? It's New Year's, after all."

She stilt didn't look in the least perturbed. And she wasn't trying to get to the telephone or to trip an alarm. Louis decided that he could definitely use a drink.

The old lady beamed happily up at him and motioned him to follow her into the kitchen. "I've been baking for two days," she confided. "Now, let's see, what will you have?"

She rummaged around in a cupboard, bringing out an assortment of baked goods on glass plates, which she proceeded to spread out on the kitchen table. She handed Louis a blue-flowered plate and motioned for him to sit down. When she went in the dining room to get some napkins, Louis stuffed the pillowcase under his coat, making sure that the salt and pepper shakers didn't clink together. Finally, he decided that the least suspicious thing to do would be to play along. He sat.

"Now," she announced, "we have Dundee cake with dried fruit, black bun with almonds, shortbread, petticoat tails . . ."

Louis picked up a flat yellow cookie and nibbled at it hostess babbled on.

"When I was a girl in Dundee—"

"Where?"

"Dundee. Scotland. My mother used to bake a bannock—you know, a wee cake—for each one of us children. The bannocks had a hole in the middle, and they were nipped in about the edges for decorations. She flavored them with carvey—carroway seed. And we ate them or Year's morning. They used to say that if your bannock while it was baking, you'd be taken ill or die in the new year. So I never baked one for my daughter Doris. Oh, but they were good!"

Louis blinked. "You're from Scotland?"

She was at the stove now, putting a large open pot on the burner and stirring it with a wooden spoon. "Yes, that's right," she said. "We've been in this country since Doris was five, though. My husband wanted to come over, and did. I've often thought of going home, now that he's passed on, but Doris won't hear of it."

"Doris is your daughter," said Louis. He wondered if he ought to bolt before she showed up, in case she turned out to be sane.

"Yes. She's all grown up now. She works very hard, does Doris. Can you imagine having to work on Hogmanay?"

"On what?"

"*Hogmanay*. New Year's Eve. She's out right now, poor dear, finishing up her shift. That's why I was so glad to see you tonight. We could use a bit of luck this year, starting with a promotion for Doris. Try a bit of the Dundee cake. It's awfully rich, but you can stand the calories, from the look of you."

Louis reached for another pastry, still trying to grasp a thread of sense in the conversation. He wanted to know why he was so welcome. Apparently she hadn't mistaken him for anyone else. And she didn't seem to wonder what he was doing in her house in the middle of the night. He kept trying to think of a way to frame the question without incriminating himself.

Steam was rising in white spirals from the pot on the stove. The old lady took a deep breath over the fumes and nodded briskly. "Right. That should be done now. Tell me, lad, are you old enough to take spirits?"

After a moment's hesitation, Louis realized that he was being offered a drink and not a seance. "I'm twenty-two," he mumbled.

"Right enough, then." She ladled the steaming liquid into two cups and set one in front of him.

Louis sniffed it and frowned.

"It's called a het pint," said the old lady, without waiting for him to ask. "It's an old drink given to first footers. Spirits, sugar, beer, and eggs. When I was a girl, they used to carry it round door to door in a kettle. Back in Dundee. Not that I drink much myself, of course. Doris is always on about my blood pressure. But tonight *is* Hogmanay, and I said to myself: Flora, why don't you stir up the het pint. You never know who may drop in. And, you see, I was right. Here you are!"

"Here I am," Louis agreed, taking a swig of his drink tasted a little like eggnog. Not bad. At least it was alcoholic. He wouldn't have more than a cup, though. He still had to drive home.

The old lady—Flora—sat down beside Louis and lifted her cup. "Well, here's to us, then. What's your name, lad?"

"Louis," he said, before he thought better of it.

"Well, Louis, here's to us! And not forgetting a promotion for Doris!" They clinked their cups together and drank to the new year.

Flora dabbed at the corners of her mouth with a linen napkin and reached for a piece of shortbread. "I must remember to eat fewer of these during the coming year," she remarked. "Else Doris will have me out jogging."

Louis took another piece to keep her company. It tasted pretty good. Sort of like a sugar cookie with delusion of grandeur. "Did you have a nice Christmas?" he asked politely.

Flora smiled. "Perhaps not by American standards. Doris had the day off, and we went to church in the morning, and then had our roast beef for dinner. She gave me bath powder and I gave her a new umbrella. She's always losing umbrellas. I suppose that's a rather subdued holiday by your lights, but when I was a girl, Christmas wasn't such a big festival in Scotland. The shops didn't even close for it. We considered it a religious occasion for most folk, and a lark for children. The holiday for grown people was New Year's."

"Good idea," grunted Louis. "Over here, we get used to high expectations when we're kids, and then as adults, we get depressed every year because Christmas is just necktie boredom."

Flora nodded. "Oh, but you should have seen Hogmanay when I was a girl! No matter what the weather, people in Dundee would gather in the City Square to wait out the old year's end. And there'd be a great time of singing all the old songs . . ."

"'Auld Lang Syne'?" asked Louis.

"That's a Scottish song, of course," nodded Flora. "But we sang a lot of the other old tunes as well. And there was country dancing. And then just when the new year was minutes away, everyone would lapse into silence. Waiting. There you'd be in the dark square, with your breath frosting the air, and the stars shining down on the world like snowflakes on velvet. And it was so quiet you could hear the ticking of the gentlemen's pocket watches."

"Sounds like Times Square," said Louis, inspecting the bottom of his cup.

Flora took the cup and ladled another het pint for each of them. "After the carrying on to welcome in the new year, everyone would go about visiting and first footing their neighbors. My father was always in great demand for that, being tall and dark as he was. And he used to carry lumps of coal in his overcoat to be sure of his welcome."

"What," said Louis, "is *first footing*?"

"Well, it's an old superstition," said Flora thoughtfully. "Quite pagan, I expect, if the truth were told, but then, you never can be sure, can you? You don't have a lump of coal about you, by any chance?"

Louis shook his head.

"Ah, well. First footing, you asked." She took a deep breath, as if to warn him that there was a long explanation to follow. "In Scotland the tradition is that the first person to cross your threshold after midnight on Hogmanay symbolizes your luck in the year to come. *The first foot* to enter your house, you see."

Louis nodded. *It's lucky to be burgled?* he was thinking.

"The best luck of all comes if you're first footed by a tall, dark stranger carrying a lump of coal. Sometimes family friends would send round a tall, dark houseguest that our family had not met, so that we could be first footed by a stranger. The rest of the party would catch up with him a few minutes later."

"I guess I fit the bill all right," Louis remarked. He just over six feet and looked more Italian than Tony Bennett. His uncles called him *Luigi*.

"So you do," smiled Flora. "Now the worst luck for the new year is to be first footed by a short blond woman who comes in empty-handed."

Louis remembered the first thing the old woman had to him. "So Doris is a short blond?"

"She is that. Gets her height from me. Or the lack of it. And she can never remember to hunt up a lump of coal or bring some wee gift home with her to help the luck. Ever since Colin passed away, Doris has been first foot in house, and where has it got us? Her with long hours precious little time off, and me with rheumatism and a fixed income—while prices go up every year. We could a change of luck. Maybe a sweepstakes win."

Louis leaned back in his chair, struggling between courtesy and common sense. "You really believe in all this stuff?" he asked her.

A sad smile. "Where's the harm? When you get older, it's hard to let go of the customs you knew when you young. You'll see."

Louis couldn't think of any family customs, except eating in front of the TV set and never taking the last ice cube—so you wouldn't have to refill the tray. Other than that, he didn't think he had much in common with the people he lived with He thought about telling Flora about his work at the animal shelter, but he decided that it would be a dangerous thing to do. She already knew his name. Any further information would enable her and the police to locate him in a matter of hours. If she ever cottoned on to the fact that she had been robbed, that is.

"Do you have any pets?" he asked.

Flora shook her head. "We used to have a wee dog, but he got old and died a few years back. I haven't wanted to get another one, and Doris is too busy with her work to help in taking care of one."

"I could get you a nice puppy, from—" He stopped himself just in time. "Well, never mind. You're right. Dogs are more work than most people think. Or they *ought* to be."

Flora beamed. "What a nice young man you are!"

He smiled back nervously.

Louis nibbled another piece of shortbread while he considered his dilemma. He had been caught breaking into a house, and the evidence from the rest of the evening's burglaries was in the trunk of his Volkswagen. The logical thing to do would be to kill the old dear, so that he wouldn't have to worry about getting caught. Logical, yes, but distasteful. Louis was not a killer. The old lady reminded him of one of the sad-eyed cocker spaniels down at the shelter. Sometimes people brought in pets because they didn't want them anymore or were moving. Or because the kid was allergic to them. Often these people asked that the animal be destroyed, which annoyed Louis no end. Did they think that if they didn't want the pet, no one else should have it? Suppose divorce worked like that? Louis could see putting an old dog to sleep if it was feeble and suffering, but not just because the owners found it inconvenient to have it around. He supposed that his philosophy would have to apply to his hostess as well, even if she were a danger to his career. After all, Flora was old, but she was not weak or in pain. She seemed quite spry and happy, in fact, and Louis couldn't see doing away with her just for expedience. After all, people had rights, too, just like animals.

He wondered what he ought to do about her. It seemed to boil down to two choices: He could tie her up, finish robbing the house, and make his getaway, or he could finish his tea and leave, just as if he had been an ordinary—what was it?—*first footer.*

He leaned back in his chair, considering the situation, and felt a sharp jab in his side. A moment's reflection told him what it had been: the tail of the pheasant salt shaker. He had stashed the pair in the pillowcase, now concealed under his coat. He couldn't think of any way to get rid of his loot without attracting suspicion. *Then* she might realize that he was a burglar; *then* she might panic and try to call the police; *then* he would have to hit her to keep himself from being captured. It was not an appealing scenario. Louis decided that the kindest thing to do would be to tie her up, finish his job, and leave.

Flora was prattling on about Scottish cakes and homemade icing, but he hadn't been listening. He thought it would be rather rude to begin threatening his hostess while he still had a mouthful of cake, but he told himself that she had been rather rude, too. After all, she hadn't asked him anything about himself. That was thoughtless of her. A good host ought to express a polite interest in her guests.

Flora's interminable story seemed to have wound down at last. She looked up at the kitchen clock. It was after one. "Well," she said, beaming happily at Louis. "It's getting late. Can I get you a *wee doch and dorris?*"

Louis blinked. "A what?"

"A drink, lad. *Wee doch and dorris* is a Scottish expression for the last drink of the evening. One for the road, as you say over here. Scotch, perhaps?"

He shook his head. "I'm afraid not," he said. "I do need to be going, but I'm afraid I will have to tie you up now."

He braced himself for tears, or, even worse, a scream, but the old lady simply took another sip of her drink and waited. She wasn't smiling anymore, but she didn't look terrified, either. Louis felt his cheeks grow hot, wishing he could just get out of there. Burglars weren't supposed to have to interact with people; it wasn't part of the job description. If you emotional scenes, you became an armed robber. Louis hated confrontations.

"I hope this won't change your luck for the New Year or anything," he mumbled, "but the reason I came in here tonight was to rob the house. You see, I'm a burglar."

Flora nodded, still watching him closely. Not a flicker of surprise had registered on her face.

"I really enjoyed the cakes and all, but after all, business is business."

"In Scotland, it's considered unlucky to do evil after you've accepted the hospitality of the house," the old lady said calmly.

Louis shrugged. "In America it's unlucky to miss car payments."

She made no reply to this remark, but continued to gaze up at him impassively. At least she wasn't being hysterical. He almost wished that he had given up the whole idea.

Louis cleared his throat and continued. "The reason I have to tie you up is that I have to finish getting the stuff, and I have to make sure you can't call for help until I'm long gone. But I won't beat you up or anything."

"Kind of you," she said dryly. "There is some spare clothesline in the bottom drawer of the left-hand cabinet."

He looked at her suspiciously. "Don't *try* anything, okay? I don't want to have to do anything rough." He didn't carry a gun (nobody was *supposed* to be home), but they both knew that a strong young man like Louis could do considerable damage to a frail old lady like Flora with his fists—a candlestick—almost anything could be a weapon.

Keeping his eyes on her, he edged toward the cabinet, squatting down to pull out the drawer. She watched him steadily, making no move to leave her seat. As he eased the drawer open, he saw the white rope clothesline neatly bundled above a stack of paper bags. With considerable relief at the ease of it all, he picked up the rope and turned back to the old lady.

"Okay," he said, a little nervously. "I'm going to tie you up. Just relax. I don't want to make it so tight it cuts off circulation, but I'm not, like, experienced, you know? Just sit in the chair with your feet flat on the floor in front of you."

She did as she was told, and he knelt and began winding the clothesline around her feet, anchoring it to the legs of the chair. He hoped it wasn't going to be too painful, but he couldn't risk her being able to escape. To cover his uneasiness at the silent reproach from his hostess, Louis began to whistle nervously as he worked. That was probably why didn't hear anything suspicious.

His first inkling that anything was wrong was that Flora suddenly relaxed in her chair. He looked up quickly, thinking, *"Oh, God! The old girl's had a heart attack!"* But her eyes were open, and she was smiling. She seemed gazing at something just behind him.

Slowly Louis turned his head in the direction of the back door. There was a short blond woman of about thirty standing just inside the door. She was wearing a dark blue uniform and a positively menacing expression. But what bothered the most about the intruder was the fact that her knees were bent, and she was holding a service revolver in both hands, its barrel aimed precisely at Louis's head.

Louis looked from the blond woman to Flora and again, just beginning to make the connection. A jerk of the gun barrel made him move slowly away from the chair and put his hands up.

"This is my daughter Doris," said Flora calmly. "She's a policewoman. You see, you were lucky for us, Louis. I'm sure she'll get her promotion after this!"

Craps

JUST WHEN I THOUGHT HE'D DRIFTED OFF to sleep, his head heavy and warm on my shoulder, Hughie says, What's that story you were going to tell me about Vegas? And I tell him quickly, There's lots of stories about Vegas.

Late Sunday morning I'm lying on top of the bed half dressed with Hughie, my ex-husband, sort of cradled in my arms—he'd dropped by earlier just wanting to talk, he said, in one of his moods where he needs consolation and some signs of affection—and lying together like this, just lying still and drowsy, is an old habit of ours but it's Hughie who always requires it, these days. We fit together like a hand and a glove—Hughie's head on my right shoulder and my arm under his neck (where, sometimes, it goes to sleep, gets so numb I can't feel it there), his right arm cradling my breasts from beneath, and his right foot tucked between mine. There are these old habits you slip into no matter how you actually feel about each other, or anything else. Or where your mind drifts, late Sunday morning.

I was seventeen when I met Hughie, who is twenty-two years older than me. I was twenty-seven when I asked him please to leave. The divorce came through in about eighteen months but we're still friends; you could say we are like brother and sister if it was qualified to mean not always getting along with each other but always there; in a small town like this where's there to go? After the divorce, last year, we have actually gotten along better. Hughie is always changing jobs and changing woman friends and stopping drinking (and starting again) and none of what he does is my problem now, though naturally, being the way I am, I take an interest. But I don't let it hurt me, now.

He's away for months and doesn't call and I'm busy with my own life; then suddenly he'll drop by, lonely, depressed, three days' beard and bloodshot eyes and I won't lend him money if that's what he wants (sometimes I think he's just testing me, anyway) but I'll make him supper, or sometimes he has brought something special to eat, or a bottle of wine, sometimes even flowers. Flowers! I can't help laughing when he holds them out to me like a guilty little boy. He was always ready to spend our money on things we didn't need and I saw through that long ago but here's the same Hughie; they don't change. All other things change but they don't change, men like him.

So what's this story about Vegas? Hughie says. I'm waiting.

It isn't any story, I tell him. What's Lynn been telling you behind my back? Some guy you met at craps. Some millionaire Texan.

I didn't meet him at craps and he wasn't any millionaire Texan and why don't you stay quiet, if you're going to stay here at all. You said you just wanted to nap.

So Hughie draws this long deep breath and burrows his face in my neck and lies very still. You've been to Vegas yourself, I say, you know what it's like. Hughie doesn't answer but I can tell he's waiting for me to go on. Of course it was a real surprise to *me*, I say, walking into the casino with Lynn and already at 9 A.M. there's so many people gambling, at these machines that look like video games. Almost the first people I saw, I swear they looked like your parents: this elderly couple playing the slots side by side, and she's winning some, a few quarters, and he doesn't care to be interrupted, just keeps on playing, leaning real close to the machine like he can't see too well, dropping in a quarter and pulling the lever, dropping in a quarter and pulling the lever, over and over the way they do, and it *is* fascinating, sort of, you can see how people get hooked. Lynn and I spent the morning on the machines and won some, lost some, the way you do. We saw some people Lynn said were probably retired to Vegas just for the slots and some of them, their right hands were actually deformed, like with arthritis, shaped like claws, pulling the lever a thousand times a day. But you could see they were happy, doing what they want to do.

There's lots of Vegas stories we heard just in the brief time we were there, and new ones every day. A man drives across the desert with two suitcases in the car, one empty and one filled with five-hundred-dollar bills; he's got five hundred thousand dollars and places a bet on some heavyweight boxer that the odds are six to one against—and he wins! And they fill the second suitcase for him with thousand-dollar bills and he drives off again and nobody even knows his name. That's a true story, supposed to have happened just a few weeks before. Then there are these millionaire, I mean billionaire, Arab sheiks that fly in for the poker games, these special poker games at some club not open to the general public where there's no limit on bets. I saw some of them, I think, just caught a glimpse. Up at the Sands some man died at blackjack, he'd been at the table for a long time they said and had a coronary for no special reason—I mean, not because he'd won a lot of money, or lost. We were in Vegas at the time but not in that casino, thank God! One thing that did occur, in the Rainbow Casino, it's sort of disgusting, a woman lost control of her bladder, playing the slots and not wanting to take time off, I suppose; people all started walking away fast, as Lynn and I did. Can you imagine! And she wasn't all that old either, around fifty, but a drinker—they must be the worst kind, hooked in with the slots on top of drinking.

Lynn's crazy about the slots but she said we should set ourselves a limit, make it seventy-five apiece, and see how far that would go, which is the only sensible way to approach gambling, and I wasn't playing ten minutes before I won a hundred and sixty dollars, which was one third of a jackpot for that machine. I was excited as a kid, jumping up and down; if it'd been me alone I would have quit right there and gone off and celebrated with a drink and something rich and fancy like a chocolate eclair, but Lynn just laughed and kissed me and said to calm down. Wait till you win a real jackpot, she said. That'll be time to celebrate, then.

I forgot to mention all the conventions being held in the big hotels, and people drinking too much and acting like kids: the National Association of Morticians was one of them, the Fred Astaire Dance Association was another, a bunch of hypnotists, veterinarians—you name it! A lot of them fattish bald guys wearing badges with a look like they're running loose, no wives to crimp their style. I mean *a lot.*

I did see one sight that scared me, a little: that night, late, we were walking with these guys we'd met through Caesar's Palace—you know what that place is like, my God!—and there's this nice-looking woman about my age playing the slots, all alone evidently, with her cigarettes and her drink and one of those waxy paper buckets half filled with coins, and all of a sudden she hits the jackpot and it's one of the big jackpots, one thousand silver dollars, and the machine lights up, you know, the way they do, and plays some honkeytonk music, and people come over to watch, especially tourists who've never seen a big jackpot, and all she does is light up a cigarette, her hands are shaking and she doesn't even look at the coins spilling out, she's half turned away from the machine, her face so sad you'd think she was about to cry, and all the while the silver coins are tumbling out and filling the trough and spilling onto the floor and on and on and on! I mean, it keeps *on*, one thousand coins! It's just such a happy sight, the machine lighting up, and the silly music like cartoon music, but she isn't taking the least bit of happiness from it—just tired-looking and so sad it was painful to look at her. This man I was with, Sonny, he said, She's waiting for the jackpot to finish so she can keep on playing. That's all she wants, to keep on playing. A jackpot like that gets in the way.

And that turned out to be the case. At least with that woman—we stood off a ways and watched.

OK, Hughie says. Now tell me about Sonny.

*   *   *

What I was needing, I thought, was a new life. Not a new *life*, that sounds sort of extreme, but some new outlook on *this* life. Some new surprise, a set of new feelings. I want a baby but that's not it; I been wanting a baby for a long time. (Which was one of the reasons Hughie and I broke up. He has kids from his first marriage and definitely doesn't want any more.) That might be part of it but that's not it. Some nights, after work, thinking how there's nobody prominent in my affections any longer and nobody I even know of I'd like to be prominent, not in this town at least, where everybody knows everybody else's business and some of them, the men, have the idea I'm still married to Hughie or belong to him at least—some nights I'd start in crying for no reason I could name. Or, not even crying, just my throat closing up, that feeling of some old hurt returning.

So Lynn, my crazy friend Lynn, she comes over and shows me this charter-airline stuff, these brochures about Vegas, how cheap it is to fly there and how the hotels, some of them, aren't really that expensive, considering where you are—the big-name stars playing out there, the quality entertainment. Lynn has been to Vegas a half-dozen times and always enjoyed herself, and she told me if I was feeling bad this was the time to go—mid-January and the holiday season dead and gone and anybody's spirits just naturally need picking up. It didn't matter whether you were sad or not, Lynn said, this time of year would do it.

So I said no, then I heard myself say yes—you know how Lynn is with me. She just winds me around her little finger.

Hughie stirs and says, Oh, yes? And who wants to be wound?

I give him a pinch and tell him to be quiet. Does he want to hear this or doesn't he?

Go on, he says. I'm waiting for Sonny, the millionaire Texan.

Anyway, as you know, it was my first time in Vegas. The first time flying over the Rockies like that, and the Grand Canyon—my God, that's beautiful; the whole time in the air was beautiful, sort of like a dream—Lynn hates window seats so I was sitting next to the window and we're flying at thirty thousand feet or whatever the pilot said, over these mountains, these snowy peaks, then over clouds like snow crust—miles and miles of it, I mean *hundreds* of miles of it—and I guess I got sort of hypnotized looking out. It's a funny feeling you have, flying over a big stretch of cloud, like a field piled with snow, but there are people living below it not able to guess how big the field is and how there's other people flying above it. How they're down there hidden and you're up above, flying over.

Hughie is lying heavy against me with his chin sort of sharp on my shoulder. He's breathing hard and steady so I think he might be dropping off to sleep. But he says, a little too loud in my ear to suit me, OK, OK, I'm waiting for the high roller. So I tell *him* OK: this guy, Sonny Drexel as he introduced himself, from Oklahoma City, a rancher he said he was, him and his buddy were watching Lynn and me at blackjack, where we hadn't any luck—all those damn games go fast, the serious ones; you put your chip down and Christ it's gone before you know what happened. (Which is why some people prefer the slots—you go at your own speed and never lose much.) So these two, Sonny and Brady, said they'd stake us just to keep us in the game, and we all played for a while and got along pretty well, though Lynn and I never did get any luck, me especially. The strange thing is, Sonny said I was luck for him, wearing my turquoise dress, you know that one, and a black velvet ribbon in my hair, that makes me look ten years younger than I am—that's what caught his eye, he told me afterward, the ribbon, reminded him of his little girl. That is, when she was actually little. I guess she's all grown up, now, and then some.

How old was he? Hughie asks.

He *looked* like middle forties, maybe fifty, but I calculated later on he was around sixty—

Sixty!

—but didn't act it at all, good-looking in this cowboy style you see out in Vegas, a suede hat with silver studs, and snakeskin boots, designer jeans, jeweled bracelet on one wrist and wristwatch on the other, even some rings—the rings all had special meanings. Like one was a birth-stone, one used to belong to his great-grandfather, that sort of thing. Lynn says the serious gamblers are all superstitious, they don't do anything by chance. What Sonny reminded me of was one of these cigarette billboard ads, an older man I mean, with pale hair you can't tell is blond or silver, and longish sideburns, and a creased, kindly, slightly puzzled face as if he'd been looking too long into the sun. His voice was higher-pitched than you'd expect. Brady was younger, heavier, with a coarser skin. What the connection was between them I never did learn.

The two of them were taking a break from craps; I got the idea they'd done pretty well judging from the good mood they were in, especially Sonny, buying drinks for Lynn and me and some Japanese tourists we got to talking with at the bar in the Tropicana, then this expensive supper they bought us at the Barbary Coast where we saw some of the floor show, a kind of Ice Capades with singing and rainbow lights and acrobatics—it was beautiful to see, and Lynn and I loved it, but Sonny got restless so we had to leave. Brady was ragging him about not being able to stay away from the craps table for more than an hour or two like he needs his oxygen replenished, and Sonny laughs but you can tell he's annoyed. That kind of a man, you can get intimate with him to a degree and think you know him, but the least hint of familiarity he draws back and chills you out. I picked up on that right away.

Another thing Brady ragged him about was going to the john all the time and washing his hands. He's afraid of germs, Brady said, and Sonny said, You'd be too if you could see them with the naked eye, and we all laughed and Brady said, Can *you* see them with the naked eye? and Sonny laughed too but said in this serious voice, Sometimes. And I don't like it.

And I did notice, the short period of time I was in the man's company, he must have excused himself a dozen times to go to the lavatory. Only when he was shooting craps he didn't, of course—it was like he was another person then. When he was hot, I mean. Really rolling high and nothing could have stopped him.

So we went back to the Dunes and Sonny and Brady got into a game and Sonny was shooting and almost right away got hot. Won eighteen hundred dollars in less time than it takes me to say it! He had me stand on his left-hand side, told me not to move an inch if I could help it. At first he didn't want me to bet, thinking that might go against his own luck, but after a while, when he kept winning and so many other people were betting on the game, he said it might be all right so I started placing little bets on what they called the pass line—the easiest bet. And naturally I won too, though it didn't seem real or right, betting with chips he'd given me and following what he did.

Craps isn't my favorite game, it's so fast and nervous and wild, and so complicated, Christ—like some game that was invented to keep ordinary minds at a distance. All Lynn and I did was bet on the pass line and later on the come line—we wouldn't have wanted to bet no pass and go against Sonny—but these other gamblers got involved, and of course Brady was doing all kinds of things, special bets we couldn't follow. And the smart thing about Sonny was, he knew when to quit for awhile—with this big pile of chips he'd built up in half an hour—and let somebody else shoot, so he could bet or not bet, depending. He told me what to do and I did it and most of the time I won, but if I lost he told me to stop for a while till my luck returned; he said you can feel your luck in you like a pressure in the chest and head but not a cruel pressure, a feeling that's highwired and happy, and you can feel it drain away, sudden, he said, as water draining out of a sink. A gambler moves by instinct, he said, like a man dousing for water.

I had a granddaddy who could douse for water, I said.

We'll talk about it some other time, he said.

So after Brady shot for awhile and did OK, Sonny took over again and you could tell something would happen: this feeling all around the table, like the air's charged up. Of course we'd all been drinking this while, I don't know how long, Lynn and me excited and giggling like high school girls, arms around each other's waist, saying, This is something different, isn't it! This is something different from the old home routine! And Sonny started his roll and I placed bets on the pass line, which is the only bet I ever felt easy with, that I understood: before the shooter rolls the dice, you place your bet, and if he rolls seven or eleven you and him both win and he keeps the dice to roll again. If he hits two, three, or ten the bet is lost but he keeps his point and goes on rolling until either he makes his point and you both win or he shoots seven and the bet is lost. I *think* that's how the game goes.

That's how it goes, Hughie says. He's wider awake than I thought he would be, which is flattering. Except it's two, three, or twelve on that first roll.

And anyway I won my bets. But like I say it didn't seem real, or exactly right.

Around 4:30 A.M. Sonny quit for the night. He'd been playing in all about fifteen hours, he estimated, in the past twenty-four and needed some rest. As far as I could calculate—they didn't like to talk about these things, like it was in bad taste—he'd won about twenty-five thousand just the time I was with him.

Called me his good luck talisman, said he'd always want me by his side. All the time he was shooting he hadn't touched me, but now he put his arm around me so tight it was hard to walk and sort of leaned on me, calling me pretty girl, pretty Irene, Irene-y, I'll see you in my dreams. He was drunk I guess but not so you'd really notice. Had a way of talking that was a combination of a high-class gentleman and a country boy—a sort of twangy accent, warm and rich like Johnny Cash.

He *was* sweet. Next day down in the promenade—we were staying in the big Hilton, there's all these boutiques and special stores there—he bought me a Japanese kimono, the most beautiful thing, turquoise with a brocade design like a sunburst, gold, red, green: just so beautiful. And some black silk pants to go with the kimono, and some gold lame sandals with spike heels. And some gold teardrop earrings, and a bottle of perfume. And—

Uh-huh, says Hughie, his leg muscles twitching the way they do when he's asleep but he isn't asleep now, I get the drift of it.

It wasn't *that,* I tell Hughie, I liked him for himself. He was a fine, sweet, generous, thoughtful man. And a gentleman.

Hughie keeps quiet, not wanting to pick a fight and get kicked out of here on his ass as he's in danger of being. My heart's beating hard just at that one thing he said, his sly innuendo that I don't have to swallow any more than I swallowed any of his shit and he knows it—he's the boy who knows it no matter what he goes around town telling his buddies.

He was a gentleman, I say. There aren't many of that kind around.

Hughie doesn't say a word but I know he's fully awake and listening.

I *will* say, though, when we first got to his room—a real nice room in the Hilton Tower, nothing like what Lynn and I were sharing at our motel—I started in feeling very strange and wanted to just say good night and leave. Before, you know, it was too late and Sonny got the wrong idea. I'm just standing there, afraid if I sit down I'll fall asleep—I was more exhausted all of a sudden than I've ever been in my life—and my eyes weren't focusing right, everything sort of swimmy and blurry. I was drunk but that wasn't the only thing. There's this man I don't even know whistling to himself and taking off his shirt and his chest is covered in what looks like actual fur: gray-grizzled, silvery, matted. And his nipples dark as a woman's. And fat loose around his waist though his ribs were showing. And some sort of scar, or burn, on his back that looked just terrible. It's like him and me were married and had been married a long time, he's tossing his things around, whistling loud and happy, has me help him with his boots—these snakeskin boots like nothing you've ever seen, Lynn says something like that would go for five hundred dollars if not a thousand. You don't even see them in any store around here.

So I'm feeling very, very strange, this sickish feeling in my stomach, and Sonny's in the bathroom running the water loud and still whistling. He's happier now than down in the casino, like it was all held in, down there, and now it's coming out—just how happy he is, and how powerful it is, that kind of happiness!—like it would be too much for an ordinary person.

Sonny comes out of the bathroom drying his hands on a towel and when he sees me it's like he's almost forgotten I was there: this big smile comes over his face that looks as if it could stretch his face out of shape. Kisses me, and stands back staring at me, tells me how much I mean to him, how pretty I am, will I be his pretty pretty girl forever, and he takes the velvet bow out of my hair and kisses it solemn and serious and I'm thinking to myself, God, am I doing this? This is me? In a hotel room with some guy who, nice as he is, I don't know, just met? And I'm laughing too, giggling and scared, 'cause it's so easy, you could see doing this every night, I don't mean for the money or even for the man but just—the fact of how easy it is, once it starts.

Hughie stirs. Irene, he says, and it's the first time I have heard him call me Irene in a long time, this is a hard story to hear.

I told you, be quiet. Or don't you want to hear it?

I *want* to hear it, Hughie says, but I guess I want some parts of it to go by fast.

There's nothing to go by fast, I say, since all that happens is I sort of pass out on one of the beds and Sonny loosens my clothes and takes off my shoes and that's all—he sleeps in his own bed like a gentleman. And that's all.

Then the next morning I wake up pretty late, around eleven, and already he's in the shower, he orders us breakfast from room service which neither one of us can stomach, except for the Bloody Marys, and we go downstairs and pick out those nice things—which were a surprise to me, I swear, completely unexpected. Where Brady and Lynn are, I don't know, and I didn't like to make any inquiries.

Later on we drove over to Vegas World in this special car of Sonny's, Italian, hand-built, he said, like a custom-made suit, some sort of Ferrari with a long name, bright red like lipstick and capable Sonny said of doing 175 miles an hour under the right road conditions. How'd I like to go for a drive in the desert maybe the next day? Sonny asked. Out to Death Valley maybe. I told him I'd like that a lot, but I seemed to know we'd never get there, that something was due to happen; it was like a movie where things are going so well you know they can't last. Also, it was only a few blocks to Vegas World but the sunlight hurt our eyes, even with dark sunglasses. What the actual desert would be like I didn't want to think.

(It's kind of a startling thing, leaving the inside world and going to the outside, that you've sort of forgotten is still there. This ordinary sunshine and ordinary sidewalks and traffic lights and things, and people in it that didn't seem to have anything to do with all that was happening in the casinos. It made me feel sort of sickish, I told Sonny, and he said yes but you get used to it.)

At Vegas World it's sort of like a circus for adults but Sonny wasn't interested in any of it, just headed straight for the casino. And what a crowd packed in! Not just every slot machine taken, but people waiting for some to open up. Sonny staked me to some blackjack again, but I didn't do too well, then for a few turns at roulette, ditto; he didn't play because as he said you get to know which game is yours and which isn't.

Also, he said, the games were too simple. Didn't command his fullest concentration.

So it was back at craps, and he had me stand close beside him, on his left, wearing my new outfit, including the shoes, and the black velvet ribbon in my hair. And again Sonny got on a roll, couldn't seem to make a mistake; he doubled his bet, and won, and doubled, and won, and there was this feeling of—it's hard to explain—a kind of excitement at the table, happiness so strong it's scary. That it could go through you like electricity, and kill you, bend your skull out of shape. Some of it's because other people get caught up in the betting, strangers that a few minutes ago didn't know one another but suddenly they're all united, close as old friends or something deeper, sisters and brothers—the exact same blood.

So he did real well again but never allowed himself to show what he was feeling. I could never be like that, I guess; I could never be a real gambler! All my feelings show on my face.

So we went back to the Hilton, this is maybe 6 P.M. that day, and Sonny's in a state like I don't believe I have ever seen any person in, giving off heat like a radiator, I swear I could almost feel the waves of it, and I was pretty high too, and we're kissing a little, sort of fooling around, but more like kids, or puppies, than, you know—like he's too worked up for anything to actually happen. His skin is burning like fever, but without sweat. And his eyes, this tawny cat color, the eyeball and the iris or whatever it's called sort of run together, like a man with jaundice, and I notice he's breathing hard, and loud, but don't make much of it. Whatever we're doing he stops all of a sudden and goes into the bathroom to wash his hands—I mean, I guess that's what he was doing—then he comes back and looks at me and says, Get dressed, honey, let's go back to the casino. And I can't believe it.

So we go back out again, this time down to the Sands, and in the car he's talking a mile a minute, to me you'd naturally think but really to himself. I listened hard but I can't remember much of it now. He did want me to marry him, that's for sure—come back with him to Oklahoma City to this new house he planned to build. He didn't ask me anything about myself, such as did I have any children, let alone did I want any children, so I sat there nodding and agreeing but thinking he probably wasn't serious, really. What he said, he meant, but only while he was saying it.

Then at the Sands his luck turned on him after about an hour, I don't know why. I mean—I don't know why he didn't know it was going to turn, the way he'd said he always did. Right in the middle of one of these red-hot rolls—what you would think was a red-hot roll—when he'd made, I calculated, about twenty-two thousand in not much more time than it's taking me to say so, he rolled the wrong numbers and lost the bet; and that was the beginning of the end. The two or three guys that'd been betting don't come won really big, and Sonny just stood there like he couldn't believe he was seeing what he was seeing. And the terrible thing is, the girl just raked in the chips like nothing had gone wrong, or even changed. Not the slightest understanding in her face of what had happened.

Now, *I* seemed to know that poor man should quit right then but he didn't pay the least heed to me, and when I put my hand on his arm he pushed away like I was something nasty. Don't touch! he said.

And this feeling came over me like the floor was tilting, and I thought, I know the truth of why we're here on earth, human beings here on earth: it's to love one another if we can, but if we can't—if we try, but can't—we're here to show kindness and gentleness and mercy and respect to one another, and to protect one another. I don't know how I knew but I *knew.*

But would he pay any attention to me? He wouldn't. Saying he wanted to marry me one minute and telling me to go to hell, calling me cunt, the next. For all the good I meant to do him.

So his luck ran out, and I don't know how much he lost, but people made big money betting against him, and in the end nobody wanted to look at him. I should mention he was wearing the suede cowboy hat and the same black silk shirt with one of these little string neckties he'd been wearing the day before, and the fancy boots. And a leather belt with a big silver buckle. And hot as he was he wasn't sweating much. (I was the one that was sweating now!)

I recall one final sight: the girl in her costume with *Sands* stitched in gold on the back, black jumpsuit and tight belt and black spike heels, hair blonder and puffier than mine, she took this little Plexiglas rake of hers and just raked Sonny's chips away, and took a crumpled-up five-hundred-dollar bill from him the same way except that she pushed it down a little slot in the table like a mail slot. And it just disappeared.

So finally Sonny turned away, his face like paper that's been burnt though but hasn't burst into actual flames yet. Finish up your drink, Blondie, he says to me, smiling. I'm hurt to think the man has forgotten my name.

*   *   *

We went back to the Hilton and he made some calls, then went out, saying he'd be gone awhile. I watched some television and washed my hair and finished this champagne we'd got the night before, and it got late but I was too worked up to sleep. I had the drapes open looking over at Vegas World— that's the tallest building, all colored lights like fireworks. But everywhere on the Strip there's lights: the Sahara, the Oasis, the Golden Nugget, Caesar's Palace, all the rest. Off in the distance the mountains you can't see and I never did get to see except from the air and going to and from the airport in the cab.

Around 4 A.M. when I was actually asleep a little, with all the lights on, Sonny came back to the room. He had that look so drunk it might be said to be sober. He sat on the edge of the bed and kneaded his chest with both hands like it hurt him inside. In this calm voice he said, I have led the wrong life. I have done wrong things. At the very time of doing them I knew they were wrong, but I did them nonetheless. I did them *nonetheless*—this word drawn out slow, in a whisper.

He started to cry so it was painful to watch. Begging me not to leave him now his luck had run temporarily out.

I was crying too. I told him I'd stay with him as long as he wanted.

He said, I'm not from where I said. I'm from a different place. Not even Oklahoma. I've been a bad husband and father. There's people back home loved me and gave me their trust, and I let them down. I let them down a lot of times. Rjght now they don't even know where I am.

I was sort of cradling his head, stooping over him. I said, Don't think about that now, Sonny, and he shot back, Don't think about it *now!* When the fuck *am* I supposed to think about it, then?

But right away he changed his tone back. Said, Dolly, I'm a dead man. What? I asked.

I'm dying, I'm a dying man, he said. I'm next thing to dead.

Are you serious? Should I call a—

You can't leave me just yet, he said, gripping my arm hard. *You* know I'm crazy about you; I'd love you if I could.

That didn't make any sense so I said, You *can* love me, why can't you love me? And he says right away, in this voice like we've been quarreling, Dolly, if I *could,* I *would.*

He grabs me around the hips so hard it hurts and pulls me down onto the bed. Then he's on me pawing and grunting and making this terrible hoarse sobbing noise, and I'm there not helping him much but just waiting for it to get over. I think, He can't do it, he's too drunk, or too sick, or too old, and that's more or less the way it was, I guess, but I wasn't paying close attention, shutting my eyes tight and seeing all kinds of things that had nothing to do with him or what was going on. I could see the wheat field out behind here, the way the wind makes it look like waves. And the Grand Canyon, when the pilot turned the plane for us, explained some things to us, those natural rock formations, what a canyon actually is.

And other things too. Lying there with my eyes shut like they are now, my mind taking me far away from where I was.

Afterward I couldn't wake him. It was almost noon and he was lying on his back with his mouth open and saliva on the pillow and I seemed to know he wasn't just sleeping or even blacked out but something more serious. I tried to wake him, slapped his face and got a washcloth soaked in cold water, and that didn't help; oh, Christ, I'm thinking, the man is in a coma, he's going to die. The loud wheezing breath in a rhythm not like a normal breath: he's going to die. No matter what I do, shaking him, shouting in his ear, *I can't wake him up.*

I remembered something I'd read about brain death, a coma caused by too much alcohol and pills—did I mention Sonny'd been taking some kind of pills, just popping them now and then, not too many, and I didn't know if they were for his health, or what, like my daddy has to take heart pills every day of his life and glycerine if he gets pains in his chest—but I didn't want to ask Sonny; I figured it was too personal a question.

I got so scared, I guess I panicked. Thinking if he's going to die I will be involved. I would be a witness, and maybe arrested. Called to testify. Or charged with murder like that woman, that actress, who gave John Belushi a shot of heroin and he died. And she was tried and found guilty of murder!

So I got dressed and left. I left the kimono behind, and the jewelry, and even the perfume, and the shoes—it was the only decent thing to do. I wasn't thinking too clearly but I thought he could sell them back, maybe, to the stores. Or pawn them. I found some hundred-dollar bills loose in my purse and left them too, on the bedside table where he couldn't miss them.

So I went downstairs to the lobby, and in the lobby I called the house physician and told him Sonny's room number and hung up quick before he could ask any questions. I went back to our motel and nobody was there, thank God, and I took a long bath and tried to keep myself from thinking. I fell asleep in the bath and sometime that afternoon Lynn helped me out and dried me and seeing my face she just said, Don't tell me, so I didn't tell her. I never did tell her much of it.

*   *   *

Before we left Vegas I called Sonny's room but the phone just rang and rang. I asked at the desk was Sonny Drexel still registered and the girl said there wasn't any Sonny Drexel listed and had not been, and I said, That can't be right, and the girl repeated what she'd said, and I asked who was registered in 2023 up in the tower and she said, in the snottiest voice possible, The Hilton does not give out such information.

And that was the end of that. Like that—it was the end of that.

Hughie? Are you listening?

But Hughie's asleep by now. Warm moist breath against my neck like a baby's. Pressing heavy against me, foot twitching between mine, like always. He's here, then he's gone.

SARA PARETSKY

At the Old Swimming Hole

I

THE GYM WAS DANK—CHLORINE AND sweat combined in a hot, sticky mass. Shouts from the trainers, from the swimmers, from the spectators, bounced from the high metal ceilings and back and forth from the benches lining the pool on two sides. The cacophony set up an unpleasant buzzing in my head.

I was not enjoying myself. My shirt was soaked through with sweat. Anyway, I was too old to sit cheering on a bleacher for two hours. But Alicia had been insistent—I had to be there in person for her to get points on her sponsor card.

Alicia Alonso Dauphine and I went to high school together. Her parents had bestowed a prima ballerina's name on her, but Alicia showed no aptitude for fine arts. From her earliest years, all she wanted was to muck around with engines. At eighteen, off she went to the University of Illinois to study aeronautics.

Despite her lack of interest in dance, Alicia was very athletic. Next to airplanes, the only thing she really cared about was competitive swimming. I used to cheer her when she was NCAA swimming champ, always with a bit of irritation about being locked in a dank, noisy gym for hours at a time—swimming is not a great spectator sport. But after all, what are friends for?

When Alicia joined Berman Aircraft as an associate engineer, we drifted our separate ways. We met occasionally at weddings, confirmations, bar mitzvahs (my, how our friends were aging! Childlessness seemed to suspend us in time, but each new ceremony in their lives marked a new milestone toward old age for the women we had played with in high school).

Then last week I'd gotten a call from Alicia. Berman was mounting a team for a citywide corporate competition—money would be raised through sponsors for the American Cancer Society. Both Alicia's mother and mine had died of cancer—would I sponsor her for so many meters? Doubling my contribution if she won? It was only after I'd made the pledge that I realized she expected me there in person. One of her sponsors had to show up to testify that she'd done it, and all the others were busy with their homes and children, and come on, V.I., what do you do all day long? I need you.

How can you know you're being manipulated and still let it happen? I hunched an impatient shoulder and turned back to the starting blocks.

From where I sat, Alicia was just another bathing-suited body with a cap. Her distinctive cheekbones were softened and flattened by the dim fluorescence. Not a wisp of her thick black hair trailed around her face. She was wearing a bright red tank suit—no extra straps or flounces to slow her down in the water.

The swimmers had been wandering around the side of the pool, swinging their arms to stretch out the muscles, not talking much while the timers argued some inaudible point with the referee. Now a police whistle shrilled faintly in the din and the competitors snapped to attention, moving toward the starting blocks at the far end of the pool.

We were about to watch the fifty-meter freestyle. I looked at the hand-scribbled card Alicia had given me before the meet. After the fifty-meter, she was in a 4 x 50 relay. Then I could leave.

The swimmers were mounting the blocks when someone began complaining again. The woman from the Ajax insurance team seemed to be having a problem with the lane marker on the inside of her lane. The referee reshuffled the swimmers, leaving the offending lane empty. The swimmers finally mounted the blocks again. Timers got into position.

Standing to see the start of the race, I was no longer certain which of the women was Alicia. Two of the other six contenders also wore red tank suits; with their features smoothed by caps and dimmed lighting, they all became anonymous. One red suit was in lane two, one in lane three, one in lane six.

The referee raised the starting gun. Swimmers got set. Arms swung back for the dive. Then the gun, and seven bodies flung themselves into the water. Perfect dive in lane six—had to be Alicia, surfacing, pulling away from all but one other swimmer, a fast little woman from the brokerage house of Feldstein, Holtz and Woods.

Problems for the red-suited woman in lane two. I hadn't seen her dive, but she was having trouble righting herself, couldn't seem to make headway in the lane. Now everyone was noticing her. Whistles were blowing; the man on the loudspeaker tried ineffectually to call for silence.

I pushed my way through the crowds on the benches and vaulted over the barrier dividing the spectators from the water. Useless over the din to order someone into the pool for her. Useless to point out the growing circle of red. I kicked off running shoes and dove from the side. Swimming underwater to the second lane. Not Alicia. Surely not. Seeing the water turn red around me. Find the woman. Surface. Drag her to the edge where, finally, a few galvanized hands pulled her out.

I scrambled from the pool and picked out someone in a striped referee's shirt. "Get a fire department ambulance as fast as you can." He stared at me with a stupid gape to his jaw. "Dial 911, damn it. Do it now!" I pushed him toward the door, hard, and he suddenly broke into a trot.

I knelt beside the woman. She was breathing, but shallowly. I felt her gently. Hard to find the source of bleeding with the wet suit, but I thought it came from the upper back. Demanding help from one of the bystanders, I carefully turned her to her side. Blood was oozing now, not pouring, from a wound below her left shoulder. Pack it with towels, elevate her feet, keep the crowd back. Wait. Wait. Watch the shallow breathing turn to choking. Mouth-to-mouth does no good. Who knows cardiopulmonary resuscitation? A muscular young man in skimpy bikini shorts comes forward and works at her chest. By the time the paramedics hustle in with stretcher and equipment, the shallow, choking breath has stopped. They take her to the hospital, but we all know it's no good.

As the stretcher-bearers trotted away, the rest of the room came back into focus. Alicia was standing at my side, black hair hanging damply to her shoulders, watching me with fierce concentration. Everyone else seemed to be shrieking in unison; the sound re-echoing from the rafters was more unbearable than ever.

I stood up, put my mouth close to Alicia's ear, and asked her to take me to whoever was in charge. She pointed to a man in an Izod T-shirt standing on the other side of the hole left by the dead swimmer's body. I went to him immediately. "I'm V. I. Warshawski. I'm a private detective. That woman was murdered—shot through the back. Whoever shot her probably left during the confusion. But you'd better get the cops here now. And tell everyone over your megaphone that no one leaves until the police have seen them."

He looked contemptuously at my dripping jeans and shirt. "Do you have anything to back up this preposterous statement?"

I held out my hands. "Blood," I said briefly, then grabbed the microphone from him. "May I have your attention, please." My voice bounced around the hollow room. "My name is V.I. Warshawski; I am a detective. There has been a serious accident in the pool. Until the police have been here and talked to us, none of us must leave this area. I am asking the six timers who were at the far end of the pool to come here now."

There was silence for a minute, then renewed clamor. A handful of people picked their way along the edge of the pool toward me. The man in the Izod shirt was fulminating but lacked the guts to try to grab the mike.

When the timers came up to me, I said, "You six are the only ones who definitely could not have killed the woman. I want you to stand at the exits." I tapped each in turn and sent them to a post—two to the doors on the second floor at the top of the bleachers, two to the ground-floor exits, and one each to the doors leading to the men's and women's dressing rooms.

"Don't let anyone, regardless of *anything* he or she says, leave. If they have to use the bathroom, tough—hold it until the cops get here. Anyone tries to leave, keep them here. If they want to fight, let them go but get as complete a description as you can."

They trotted off to their stations. I gave Izod back his mike, made my way to a pay phone in the corner, and dialed the Eleventh Street homicide number.

II

Sergeant McGonnigal was not fighting sarcasm as hard as he might have. "You sent the guy to guard the upstairs exit and he waltzed away, probably taking the gun with him. He must be on his knees in some church right now thanking God for sending a pushy private investigator to this race."

I bit my lips. He couldn't be angrier with me than I was with myself. I sneezed and shivered in my damp, clammy clothes. "You're right, Sergeant. I wish you'd been at the meet instead of me. You'd probably have had ten uniformed officers with you who could've taken charge as soon as the starting gun was fired and avoided this mess. Do any of the timers know who the man was?"

We were in an office that the school athletic department had given the police for their investigation-scene headquarters. McGonnigal had been questioning all the timers, figuring their closeness to the pool gave them the best angle on what had happened. One was missing, the man I'd sent to the upper balcony exit.

The sergeant grudgingly told me he'd been over that ground with the other timers. None of them knew who the missing man was. Each of the companies in the meet had supplied volunteers to do the timing and other odd jobs. Everyone just assumed this man was from someone else's firm. No one had noticed him that closely; their attention was focused on the action in the pool. My brief glance at him gave the police their best description: medium height, light, short brown hair, wearing a pale green T-shirt and faded white denim shorts. Yes, baggy enough for a gun to fit in a pocket unnoticed.

"You know, Sergeant, I asked for the six timers at the far end of the pool because they were facing the swimmers, so none of them could have shot the dead woman in the back. This guy came forward. That means there's a timer missing—either the person actually down at the far end was in collusion, or you're missing a body."

McGonnigal made an angry gesture—not at me. Himself for not having thought of it before. He detailed two uniformed cops to round up all the volunteers and find out who the errant timer was.

"Any more information on the dead woman?"

McGonnigal picked up a pad from the paper-littered desk in front of him. "Her name was Louise Carmody. You know that. She was twenty-four. She worked for the Ft. Dearborn Bank and Trust as a junior lending officer. You know that. Her boss is very shocked—you probably could guess that. And she has no enemies. No dead person ever does."

"Was she working on anything sensitive?"

He gave me a withering glance. "What twenty-four-year-old junior loan officer works on anything sensitive?"

"Lots," I said firmly. "No senior person ever does the grubby work. A junior officer crunches numbers or gathers basic data for crunching. Was she working on any project that someone might not want her to get data for?"

McGonnigal shrugged wearily but made a note on a second pad—the closest he would come to recognizing that I might have a good suggestion.

I sneezed again. "Do you need me for anything else? I'd like to get home and dry off."

"No, go. I'd just as soon you weren't around when Lieutenant Mallory arrives, anyway."

Bobby Mallory was McGonnigal's boss. He was also an old friend of my father, who had been a beat sergeant until his death fifteen years earlier. Bobby did not like women on the crime scene in any capacity—victim, perpetrator, or investigator—and he especially did not like his old friend Tony's daughter on the scene. I appreciated McGonnigal's unwillingness to witness any acrimony between his boss and me, and was getting up to leave when the uniformed cops came back.

The sixth timer had been found in a supply closet behind the men's lockers. He was concussed and groggy from a head wound and couldn't remember how he got to where he was. Couldn't remember anything past lunchtime. I waited long enough to hear that and slid from the room.

Alicia was waiting for me at the far end of the hall. She had changed from her suit into jeans and a pullover and was squatting on her heels, staring fiercely at nothing. When she saw me coming, she stood up and pushed her black hair out of her eyes.

"You look a mess, V.I."

"Thanks. I'm glad to get help and support from my friends after they've dragged me into a murder investigation."

"Oh, don't get angry—I didn't mean it that way. I'm sorry I dragged you into a murder investigation. No, I'm not, actually. I'm glad you were on hand. Can we talk?"

"After I put some dry clothes on and stop looking a mess."

She offered me her jacket. Since I'm five-eight to her five-four, it wasn't much of a cover, but I draped it gratefully over my shoulders to protect myself from the chilly October evening.

At my apartment Alicia followed me into the bathroom while I turned on the hot water. "Do you know who the dead woman was? The police wouldn't tell us."

"Yes," I responded irritably. "And if you'll give me twenty minutes to warm up, I'll tell you. Bathing is not a group sport in this apartment."

She trailed back out of the bathroom, her face set in tense lines. When I joined her in the living room some twenty minutes later, a towel around my damp hair, she was sitting in front of the television set changing channels.

"No news yet," she said briefly. "Who was the dead girl?"

"Louise Carmody. Junior loan officer at the Ft. Dearborn. You know her?"

Alicia shook her head. "Do the police know why she was shot?"

"They're just starting to investigate. What do you know about it?"

"Nothing. Are they going to put her name on the news?"

"Probably, if the family's been notified. Why is this important?"

"No reason. It just seems so ghoulish, reporters hovering around her dead body and everything."

"Could I have the truth, please?"

She sprang to her feet and glared at me. "It is the truth."

"Screw that. You don't know her name, you spin the TV dials to see the reports, and now you think it's ghoulish for the reporters to hover around? . . . Tell you what I think, Alicia. I think you know who did the shooting. They shuffled the swimmers, nobody knew who was in which lane. You started out in lane two, and you'd be dead if the woman from Ajax hadn't complained. Who wants to kill you?"

Her black eyes glittered in her white face. "No one. Why don't you have a little empathy, Vic? I might have been killed. There was a madman out there who shot a woman. Why don't you give me some sympathy?"

"I jumped into a pool to pull that woman out. I sat around in wet clothes for two hours talking to the cops. I'm beat. You want sympathy, go someplace else. The little I have is reserved for myself tonight.

"I'd really like to know why I had to be at the pool, if it wasn't to ward off a potential attacker. And if you'd told me the real reason, Louise Carmody might still be alive."

"Damn you, Vic, stop doubting every word I say. I told you why I needed you there—someone had to sign the card. Millie works during the day. So does Fredda. Katie has a new baby. Elene is becoming a grandmother for the first time. Get off my goddamn back."

"If you're not going to tell me the truth, and if you're going to scream at me about it, I'd just as soon you left."

She stood silent for a minute. "Sorry, Vic. I'll get a better grip on myself."

"Great. You do that. I'm fixing some supper—want any?" She shook her head. When I returned with a plate of pasta and olives, Joan Druggen was just announcing the top local story. Alicia sat with her hands clenched as they stated the dead woman's name. After that, she didn't say much. Just asked if she could crash for the night—she lived in Warrenville, a good hour's drive from town, near Berman's aeronautic engineering labs.

I gave her pillows and a blanket for the couch and went to bed. I was pretty angry; I figured she wanted to sleep over because she was scared, and it infuriated me that she wouldn't talk about it.

When the phone woke me at 2:30, my throat was raw, the start of a cold brought on by sitting around in wet clothes for so long. A heavy voice asked for Alicia.

"I don't know who you're talking about," I said hoarsely.

"Be your age, Warshawski. She brought you to the gym. She isn't at her own place. She's gotta be with you. You don't want to wake her up, give her a message. She was lucky tonight. We want the money by noon, or she won't be so lucky a second time."

He hung up. I held the receiver a second longer and heard another click. The living room extension. I pulled on a dressing gown and padded down the hallway. The apartment door shut just as I got to the living room. I ran to the top of the stairs; Alicia's footsteps were echoing up and down the stairwell.

"Alicia! Alicia—you can't go out there alone. Come back here!" The slamming of the entryway door was my only answer.

III

I didn't sleep well, my cold mixing with worry and anger over Alicia. At eight I hoisted my aching body out of bed and sat sneezing over some steaming fruit juice while I tried to focus my brain on possible action. Alicia owed somebody money. That somebody was pissed off enough to kill because he didn't have it. Bankers do not kill wayward loan customers. Loan sharks do, but what could Alicia have done to rack up so much indebtedness? Berman probably paid her seventy or eighty thousand a year for the special kinds of designs she did on aircraft wings. And she was the kind of client a bank usually values. So what did she need money for that only a shark would provide?

The clock was ticking. I called her office. She'd phoned in sick; the secretary didn't know where she was calling from but had assumed home. On a dim chance I tried her phone. No answer. Alicia had one brother, Tom, an insurance agent on the far south side. After a few tries I located his office in Flossmoor. He hadn't heard from Alicia for weeks. And no, he didn't know who she might owe money to.

Reluctantly Tom gave me their father's phone number in Florida. Mr. Dauphine hadn't heard from his daughter, either.

"If she calls you, or if she shows up, *please* let me know. She's in trouble up here, and the only way I can help her is by knowing where she is." I gave him the number without much expectation of hearing from him again.

I did know someone who might be able to give me a line on her debts. A year or so earlier, I'd done a major favor for Don Pasquale, a local mob leader. If she owed him money, he might listen to my intercession. If not, he might be able to tell me whom she had borrowed from.

Torfino's, an Elmwood Park restaurant where the don had a part-time office, put me through to his chief assistant, Ernesto. A well-remembered gravel voice told me I sounded awful.

"Thank you, Ernesto," I snuffled. "Did you hear about the death of Louise Carmody at the University of Illinois gym last night? She was probably shot by mistake, poor thing. The intended victim was a woman named Alicia Dauphine. We grew up together, so I feel a little solicitous on her behalf. She owes a lot of money to someone: I wondered if you know who."

"Name isn't familiar, Warshawski. I'll check around and call you back."

My cold made me feel as though I was at the bottom of a fish tank. I couldn't think fast enough or hard enough to imagine where Alicia might have gone to ground. Perhaps at her house, believing if she didn't answer the phone no one would think she was home? It wasn't a very clever idea, but it was the best I could do in my muffled, snuffled state.

The old farmhouse in Warrenville that Alicia had modernized lay behind the local high school. The boys were out practicing football. They were wearing light jerseys. I had on my winter coat—even though the day was warm, my cold made me shiver and want to be bundled up. Although we were close enough that I could see their mouthpieces, they didn't notice me as I walked around the house looking for signs of life.

Alicia's car was in the garage, but the house looked cold and unoccupied. As I made my way to the back, a black-and-white cat darted out from the bushes and began weaving itself around my ankles, mewing piteously. Alicia had three cats. This one wanted something to eat.

Alicia had installed a sophisticated burglar alarm system—she had an office in her home and often worked on preliminary designs there. An expert had gotten through the system into the pantry—some kind of epoxy had been sprayed on the wires to freeze them. Then, somehow disabling the phone link, the intruder had cut through the wires.

My stomach muscles tightened, and I wished futilely for the Smith & Wesson locked in my safe at home. My cold really had addled my brains for me not to take it on such an errand. Still, where burglars lead shall P.I.s hesitate? I opened the window, slid a leg over, and landed on the pantry floor. My feline friend followed more gracefully. She promptly abandoned me to start sniffing at the pantry walls.

Cautiously opening the door I slid into the kitchen. It was deserted, the refrigerator and clock motors humming gently, a dry dishcloth draped over the sink. In the living room another cat joined me and followed me into the electronic wonderland of Alicia's study. She had used built-in bookcases to house her computers and other gadgets. The printers were tucked along a side wall, and wires ran everywhere. Whoever had broken in was not interested in merchandise—the street value of her study contents would have brought in a nice return, but they stood unharmed.

By now I was dreading the trek upstairs. The second cat, a tabby, trotted briskly ahead of me, tail waving like a flag. Alicia's bedroom door was shut. I kicked it open with my right leg and pressed myself against the wall. Nothing. Dropping to my knees I looked in. The bed, tidily covered with an old-fashioned white spread, was empty. So was the bathroom. So was the guest room and an old sun porch glassed in and converted to a solarium.

The person who broke in had not come to steal—everything was preternaturally tidy. So he (she?) had come to attack Alicia. The hair stood up on the nape of my neck. Where was he? Not in the house. Hiding outside?

I started down the stairs again when I heard a noise, a heavy scraping. I froze, trying to locate the source. A movement caught my eye at the line of vision. The hatch to the crawl space had been shoved open; an arm swung down. For a split second only I stared at the arm and the gun in its grip, then leaped down the stairs two at a time.

A heavy thud—the man jumping onto the upper landing. The crack as the gun fired. A jolt in my left shoulder, and I gasped with shock and fell the last few steps to the bottom. Righted myself. Reached for the deadlock on the front door. Heard an outraged squawk, loud swearing, and a crash that sounded like a man falling downstairs. Then I had the door open and was staggering outside while an angry bundle of fur poured past me. One of the cats, a heroine, tripping my assailant and saving my life.

IV

I never really lost consciousness. The football players saw me stagger down the sidewalk and came trooping over. In their concern for me they failed to tackle the gunman, but they got me to a hospital, where a young intern eagerly set about removing the slug from my shoulder; the winter coat had protected me from major damage. Between my cold and the gunshot, I was just as happy to let him incarcerate me for a few days.

They tucked me into bed, and I fell into a heavy, uneasy sleep. I had jumped into the black waters of Lake Michigan in search of Alicia, trying to reach her ahead of a shark. She was lurking just out of reach. She didn't know that her oxygen tank ran out at noon.

When I woke finally, soaked with sweat, it was dark outside. The room was lit faintly by a fluorescent light over the sink. A lean man in a brown wool business suit was sitting next to the bed. When he saw me looking at him, he reached into his coat.

If he was going to shoot me, there wasn't a thing I could do about it—

I was too limp from my heavy sleep to move. Instead of a gun, though, he pulled out an ID case.

"Miss Warshawski? Peter Carlton, Federal Bureau of Investigation. I know you're not feeling well, but I need to talk to you about Alicia Dauphine."

"So the shark ate her," I said.

"What?" he demanded sharply. "What does that mean?"

"Nothing. Where is she?"

"We don't know. That's what we want to talk to you about. She went home with you after the swimming meet yesterday. Correct?"

"Gosh, Mr. Carlton, I love watching my tax dollars at work. If you've been following her, you must have a better fix on her whereabouts than I do. I last saw her around 2:30 this morning. If it's still today, that is."

"What did she talk to you about?"

My mind was starting to unfog. "Why is the Bureau interested in Miss Dauphine?"

He didn't want to tell me. All he wanted was every word Alicia had said to me. When I wouldn't budge, he started in on why I was in her house and what I had noticed there.

Finally I said, "Mr. Carlton, if you can't tell me why you're interested in Miss Dauphine, there's no way I can respond to your questions. I don't believe the Bureau—or the police—or anyone, come to that—has any right to pry into the affairs of citizens in the hopes of turning up some scandal. *You* tell me why you're interested, and I'll tell you if I know anything relevant to that interest."

With an ill grace he said, "We believe she has been selling Defense Department secrets to the Russians."

"No," I said flatly. "She wouldn't."

"Some wing designs she was working on have disappeared. She's disappeared. And a Soviet functionary in St. Charles has disappeared."

"Sounds pretty circumstantial to me. The wing designs might be in her home. They could easily be on a disk someplace—she did all her drafting on computer."

They'd been through her computer files at home and at work and found nothing. Her boss did not have copies of the latest design, only of the early stuff. I thought about the heavy voice on the phone demanding money, but loyalty to Alicia made me keep it to myself—give her a chance to tell her story first.

I did give him everything Alicia had said, her nervousness and her sudden departure. That I was worried about her and went to see if she was in her house. And was shot by an intruder hiding in the crawl space. Who might have taken her designs. Although nothing looked pilfered.

He didn't believe me. I don't know if he thought I knew something I wasn't telling, or if he thought I had joined Alicia in selling secrets to the Russians. But he kept at me for so long that I finally pushed my call button. When the nurse arrived, I explained that I was worn out and could she please show my visitor out? He left but promised me that he would return.

Cursing my weakness, I fell asleep again. When I next woke it was morning, and both my cold and my shoulder were much improved. When the doctors came by on their morning visit, I got their agreement to a discharge. Before I bathed and left, the Warrenville police sent out a man who took a detailed statement.

I called my answering service from a phone in the lobby. Ernesto had been in touch. I reached him at Torfino's.

"Saw about your accident in the papers, Warshawski. How you feeling? ... About Dauphine. Apparently she's signed a note for $750,000 to Art Smollensk. Can't do anything to help you out. The don sends his best wishes for your recovery."

Art Smollensk, gambling king. When I worked for the public defender, I'd had to defend some of his small-time employees—people at the level of smashing someone's fingers in his car door. The ones who did hits and arson usually could afford their own attorneys.

Alicia as a gambler made no sense to me—but we hadn't been close for over a decade. There were lots of things I didn't know about her.

At home for a change of clothes I stopped in the basement, where I store useless mementos in a locked stall. After fifteen minutes of shifting boxes around, I was sweating and my left shoulder was throbbing and oozing stickily, but I'd located my high school yearbook. I took it upstairs with me and thumbed through it, trying to gain inspiration on where on earth Alicia might have gone.

None came. I was about to leave again when the phone rang. It was Alicia, talking against a background of noise. "Thank God you're safe, Vic. I saw about the shooting in the paper. Please don't worry about me. I'm okay. Stay away and don't worry."

She hung up before I could ask her anything. I concentrated, not on what she'd said, but what had been in the background. Metal doors banging open and shut. Lots of loud, wild talking. Not an airport—the talking was too loud for that, and there weren't any intercom announcements in the background. I knew what it was. If I'd just let my mind relax, it would come to me.

Idly flipping through the yearbook, I looked for faces Alicia might trust. I found my own staring from a group photo of the girls' basketball team. I'd been a guard—Victoria the protectress from way back. On the next page, Alicia smiled fiercely, holding a swimming trophy.

Her coach, who also taught Latin, had desperately wanted Alicia to train for the Olympics, but Alicia had had her heart set on the U of I and engineering.

Suddenly I knew what the clanking was, where Alicia was. No other sound like that exists anywhere on earth.

V

Alicia and I grew up under the shadow of the steel mills in South Chicago. Nowhere else has the deterioration of American industry shown up more clearly. Wisconsin Steel is padlocked shut. The South Works are a fragment of their former monstrous grandeur. Unemployment is over thirty percent, and the number of jobless youths lounging in the bars and on the streets had grown from the days when I hurried past them to the safety of my mother's house.

The high school was more derelict than I remembered. Many windows were boarded over. The asphalt playground was cracked and covered with litter, and the bleachers around the football field were badly weathered.

The guard at the doorway demanded my business. I showed her my P.I. license and said I needed to talk to the women's gym teacher on confidential business. After some dickering—hostile on her side, snuffly on mine—she gave me a pass. I didn't need directions down the scuffled corridors, past the battered lockers, past the smell of rancid oil coming from the cafeteria, to the noise and life of the gym.

Teenage girls in blue shirts and white shorts—the school colors—were shrieking, jumping, wailing in pursuit of volleyballs. I watched the pandemonium until the buzzer ended the period, then walked up to the instructor.

She was panting and sweating and gave me an incurious glance, looking only briefly at the pass I held out for her. "Yes?"

"You have a new swimming coach, don't you?"

"Just a volunteer. Are you from the union? She isn't drawing a paycheck. But Miss Finley, the coach, is desperately shorthanded—she teaches Latin, you know—and this woman is a big help."

"I'm not from the union. I'm her trainer. I need to talk to her—find out why she's dropped out and whether she plans to compete in any of her meets this fall."

The teacher gave me the hard look of someone used to sizing up fabricated excuses. I didn't think she believed me, but she told me I could go into the pool area and talk to the swim coach.

The pool dated to the time when this high school served an affluent neighborhood. It was twenty-five yards long, built with skylights along the outer wall. You reached it through the changing rooms, separate ones with showers for girls and boys. It didn't have an outside hallway entrance.

Alicia was perched alone on the high dive. A few students, boys and girls, were splashing about in the pool, but no organized training was in progress. Alicia was staring at nothing.

I cupped my hands and called up to her, "Do you want me to climb up, or are you going to come down?"

At that she turned and recognized me. "Vic!" Her cry was enough to stop the splashing in the pool. "How—Are you alone?"

"I'm alone. Come down. I took a slug in the shoulder—I'm not climbing up after you."

She shot off the board in a perfect arc, barely rippling the surface of the water. The kids watched with envy. I was pretty jealous, myself—nothing I do is done with that much grace.

She surfaced near me but looked at the students. "I want you guys swimming laps," she said sharply. "What do you think this is—summer camp?"

They left us reluctantly and began swimming.

"How did you find me?"

"It was easy. I was looking through the yearbook, trying to think of someone you would trust. Miss Finley was the simple answer—I remembered how you practically lived in her house for two years. You liked to read *Jane Eyre* together, and she adored you.

"You are in deep trouble. Smollensk is after you, and so is the FBI. You can't hide here forever. You'd better talk to the Bureau guys. They won't love you, but at least they're not going to shoot you."

"The FBI? Whatever for?"

"Your designs, sweetie pie. Your designs and the Russians. The FBI are the people who look into that kind of thing."

"Vic. I don't know what you're talking about." The words were said with such slow deliberateness that I was almost persuaded.

"The $750,000 you owe Art Smollensk."

She shook her head, then said, "Oh. Yes. That."

"Yes, that. I guess it seems like more money to me than it does to you.

Or had you forgotten Louise Carmody getting shot? . . . Anyway, a known Russian spy left Fermilab yesterday or the day before, and you're gone, and some of your wing designs are gone, and the FBI thinks you've sold them overseas and maybe gone East yourself. I didn't tell them about Art, but they'll probably get there before too long."

"How sure are they that the designs are gone?"

"Your boss can't find them. Maybe you have a duplicate set at home nobody knows about."

She shook her head again. "I don't leave that kind of thing at home. I had them last Saturday, working, but I took the diskettes back. . . ." Her voice trailed off as a look of horror washed across her face. "Oh, no. This is worse than I thought." She hoisted herself out of the pool. "I've got to go. Got to get away before someone else figures out I'm here."

"Alicia, for Christ's sake. What has happened?" She stopped and looked at me, tears swimming in her black eyes. "If I could tell anyone, it would be you, Vic." Then she was jogging into the girls' changing room, leaving the students in the pool swimming laps.

I stuck with her. "Where are you going? The Feds have a hook on any place you have friends or relations. Smollensk does, too."

That stopped her. "Tom, too?"

"Tom first, last, and foremost. He's the only relative you have in Chicago." She was starting to shiver in the bare corridor. I grabbed her and shook her. "Tell me the truth, Alicia. I can't fly blind. I already took a bullet in the shoulder."

Suddenly she was sobbing on my chest. "Oh, Vic. It's been so awful. You can't know . . . you can't understand . . . you won't believe . . ." She was hiccupping.

I led her into the shower room and found a towel. Rubbing her down, I got the story in choking bits and pieces.

Tom was the gambler. He'd gotten into it in a small way in high school and college. After he went into business for himself, the habit grew. He'd mortgaged his insurance agency assets, taken out a second mortgage on the house, but couldn't stop.

"He came to me two weeks ago. Told me he was going to start filing false claims with his companies, collect the money." She gave a twisted smile. "He didn't have to put that kind of pressure on—I can't help helping him."

"But Alicia, why? And how does Art Smollensk have your name?"

"Is that the man Tom owes money to? I think he uses my name— Alonso, my middle name—I know he does; I just don't like to think about it. Someone came around threatening me three years ago. I told Tom never to use my name again, and he didn't for a long time, but now I guess he was desperate—$750,000 you know. . . .

"As to why I help him . . . You never had any brothers or sisters, so maybe you can't understand. When Mom died, I was thirteen, he was six. I looked after him. Got him out of trouble. All kinds of stuff. It gets to be a habit, I guess. Or an obligation. That's why I've never married, you know, never had any children of my own. I don't want any more responsibilities like this one."

"And the designs?"

She looked horrified again. "He came over for dinner on Saturday. I'd been working all day on the things, and he came into the study when I was logging off. I didn't tell him it was Defense Department work, but it's not too hard to figure out what I do is defense-related—after all, that's all Berman does; we don't make commercial aircraft. I haven't had a chance to look at the designs since—I worked out all day Sunday getting ready for that damned meet Monday. Tom must have taken my diskettes and swapped the labels with some others—I've got tons of them lying around."

She gave a twisted smile. "It was a gamble: a gamble that there'd be something valuable on them and a gamble I wouldn't discover the switch before he got rid of them. But he's a gambler."

"I see. . . . Look, Alicia. You can only be responsible for Tom so far. Even if you could bail him out this time—and I don't see how you possibly can—there'll be a next time. And you may not survive this one to help him again. Let's call the FBI."

She squeezed her eyes shut. "You don't understand, Vic. You can't possibly understand."

While I was trying to reason her into phoning the Bureau, Miss Finley, swim coach-cum-romantic-Latin-teacher, came briskly into the locker room. "Allie! One of the girls came to get me. Are you all—" She did a double-take. "Victoria! Good to see you. Have you come to help Allie? I told her she could count on you."

"Have you told her what's going on?" I demanded of Alicia.

Yes, Miss Finley knew most of the story. Agreed that it was very worrying but said Allie could not possibly turn in her own brother. She had given Allie a gym mat and some bedding to sleep on—she could just stay at the gym until the furor died down and they could think of something else to do.

I sat helplessly as Miss Finley led Alicia off to get some dry clothes. At last, when they didn't rejoin me, I sought them out, poking through half-remembered halls and doors until I found the staff coaching office. Alicia was alone, looking about fifteen in an old cheerleader's uniform Miss Finley had dug up for her.

"Miss Finley teaching?" I asked sharply.

Alicia looked guilty but defiant. "Yes. Two-thirty class. Look. The critical thing is to get those diskettes back. I called Tom, explained it to him. Told him I'd try to help him raise the money but that we couldn't let the Russians have those things. He agreed, so he's bringing them out here."

The room rocked slightly around me. "No. I know you don't have much of a sense of humor, but this is a joke, isn't it?"

She didn't understand. Wouldn't understand that if the Russian had already left the country, Tom no longer had the material. That if Tom was coming here, she was the scapegoat. At last, despairing, I said, "Where is he meeting you? Here?"

"I told him I'd be at the pool."

"Will you do one thing my way? Will you go to Miss Finley's class and conjugate verbs for forty-five minutes and let me meet him at the pool? Please?"

At last, her jaw set stubbornly, she agreed. She still wouldn't let me call the Bureau, though. "Not until I've talked to Tom myself. It may all be a mistake, you know."

We both knew it wasn't, but I saw her into the Latin class without making the phone call I knew it was my duty to make and returned to the pool. Driving out the two students still splashing in the water, I put signs on the locker room doors saying the water was contaminated and there would be no swimming until further notice.

I turned out the lights and settled in a corner of the room remote from the outside windows to wait. And go over and over in my mind the story. I believed it. Was I fooling myself? Was that why she wouldn't call the Feds?

At last Tom came in through the men's locker room entrance. "Allie? Allie?" His voice bounced off the high rafters and echoed around me. I was well back in the shadows, my Smith & Wesson in hand; he didn't see me.

After half a minute or so another man joined him. I didn't recognize the stranger, but his baggy clothes marked him as part of Smollensk's group, not the Bureau. He talked softly to Tom for a minute. Then they went into the girl's locker room together.

When they returned, I had moved part way up the side of the pool, ready to follow them if they went back into the main part of the high school looking for Alicia.

"Tom!" I called. "It's V.I. Warshawski. I know the whole story. Give me the diskettes."

"Warshawski!" he yelled. "What the hell are you doing here?"

I sensed rather than saw the movement his friend made. I shot at him and dived into the water. His bullet zipped as it hit the tiles where I'd been standing. My wet clothes and my sore shoulder made it hard to move. Another bullet hit the water by my head, and I went under again, fumbling with my heavy jacket, getting it free, surfacing, hearing Alicia's sharp, "Tom, why are you shooting at Vic? Stop it now. Stop it and give me back the diskettes."

Another flurry of shots, this time away from me, giving me a chance to get to the side of the pool, to climb out. Alicia lay on the floor near the door to the girls' locker room. Tom stood silently by. The gunman was jamming more bullets into his gun.

As fast as I could in my sodden clothes I lumbered to the hitman, grabbing his arm, squeezing, feeling blood start to seep from my shoulder, stepping on his instep, putting all the force of my body into my leg. Tom, though, Tom was taking the gun from him. Tom was going to shoot me.

"Drop that gun, Tom Dauphine." It was Miss Finley. Years of teaching in a tough school gave creditable authority to her; Tom dropped the gun.

VI

Alicia lived long enough to tell the truth to the FBI. It was small comfort to me. Small consolation to see Tom's statement. He hoped he could get Smollensk to kill his sister before she said anything. If that happened, he had a good gamble on her dying a traitor in their eyes—after all, her designs were gone, and her name was in Smollensk's files. Maybe the truth never would have come out. Worth a gamble to a betting man.

The Feds arrived about five minutes after the shooting stopped. They'd been watching Tom, just not closely enough. They were sore that they'd let Alicia get shot. So they dumped some charges on me—obstructing federal authorities, not telling them where Alicia was, not calling as soon as I had the truth from her, God knows what else. I spent several days in jail. It seemed like a suitable penance, just not enough of one.

ANNE PERRY

Rearrangements

G OOD FRIDAY, 1964, WAS A DAY I SHALL never forget, for a lot
of reasons, good and bad. It was the first anniversary of my mother's death. My two brothers live in the east, but we three sisters,
Mary, Jean and I, decided to spend the time together at my home in Seward,
Alaska.

I drove over to meet Jean off her flight from Seattle, picking Mary up in
Juneau on the way. We were a little on the late side, as is usual where Mary
is concerned, because she was busy fetching or carrying for some neighbor
or other.

I am the middle sister, Kate—middle in every way, usually at the center
of the battles, and the reconciliations, whether I mean to be or not.

Jean was feeling a little emotional, remembering what day it was. She
had been the closest to Mother, by a long way, always the favorite, although
I don't think she was as aware of that as Mary and I were. It was kind of a
sore subject.

For once she forbore from making any criticism about having to stand
around the airport for twenty minutes in the cold waiting for us. We greeted her, put her luggage in the trunk of the car, and started back on the long
drive, me at the wheel as always. It was my car, and anyway, I hate being
driven by anyone else, in fact I won't put up with it. Another thing I won't
put up with is Jean's backseat instructions.

We made small talk most of the time, asking about each other's families, especially children. I was divorced, Mary widowed. We both knew and
liked Jean's husband, but there was nothing particular to be said about him.
As usual there were all the little edges to any remark. We had done it all so

often I could have predicted them, but still we went through the motions. Silence would have grown too obvious.

The scenery was magnificent, winding through the razor-edged mountains, still white with snow right down to the shoulders of the road where the traffic had cleared most of it. The valleys opened out and by half past five we were running along the coast road only a couple of miles from home.

All the way Jean had done her usual telling me what to do. I had largely ignored her. I daresay she was only concerned for our safety. Maybe she thought she was helping, but in spite of all my resolutions, it nearly drove me crazy. But since she had done it for the last thirty years, I should not have let it bother me.

"You're going too fast!" she said as I reached a straight stretch.

I said nothing, but increased the pressure of my foot on the gas.

Her voice rose sharply. "You'll hit something!"

"You've got that right!" I snapped back. "And if you tell me one more time how to drive my car, it'll be you!"

"I'm only trying to stop an accident!" she said with great reasonableness.

"It won't be an accident," I retorted. I looked at the speedometer. I wasn't doing more than fifty-five.

"You're too far to the left!" she said with a note of alarm rising to real fear.

I put my foot down further, and the car shot forward and veered into the middle of the road, then right out of my control it went off the other way. It was as if the steering had broken. We went first one way and then slithered back again, all over the road.

I fought with the wheel, wrenching my shoulders in my efforts, and it made no difference at all. I could feel the sweat break out on my body. I was clinging on, fighting it with all my strength, but it was as if the road were fighting back, heaving and twisting under me.

Jean was shrieking. Beside me Mary sat white-knuckled and rigid.

I tried to slow up, but we were still reeling all over the place. The mountains, fields, fences, roadway al swung in front of me, not to mention the better part of my whole life!

"I told you!" Jean yelled. "You're going much too fast!"

I had the brakes on as hard as I dared. We skewed around crazily, and the next moment there was a terrible jolt and I was thrown forward hard against my seatbelt, and then back again so violently it all but knocked the wind out of me. When I opened my eyes and focused, we were facefirst into the ditch, motionless, the hood buckled and steam rising in a thin, hissing column.

Beside me, Mary was ashen white, but her eyes were open and she seemed to be more or less all right. I swung around to look at Jean the best I could over my shoulder. I was dimly conscious of my knee hurting.

Jean stared back at me, shivering with terror. Then I realized why. We were wedged in the ditch, but everything was still moving! It was shuddering, swaying and jolting all at once, and there was a dull roaring sound that had nothing to do with the engine, which had stopped.

Earthquake! Bigger than anything I'd ever imagined and still going on . . . and on . . . and on! The ground itself was reeling, buckling like a carpet someone had shaken, and odd bits here and there seemed to quiver like boiling oatmeal.

This is an earthquake area, especially close to the sea, so I know something about them. You can get rockfalls, landslides, and infinitely worse than that—tidal waves—great tsunamis that roll in fifteen or twenty feet high—or thirty—or more!

"Get out," I shouted as loudly as I could, trying not to sound hysterical and at the same time feeling for the handle of the door beside me, forcing it open.

I could hear Jan scrambling around in the back, trying to open her door. "Are we going to catch fire?" Her voice soared in panic.

"No," I answered, with no idea whether that was true or not. "It's an earthquake! Did you think that was just my driving? Thank you very much!" I don't know what made me try to be funny, perhaps to hide from her how scared I was. My vivid imagination already had waves roaring in on us like walls of death. "It'll be okay—just get out!" I yelled. "We need to be away from here. Maybe climb up that ridge inland a bit." I waved my free hand in the general direction of the nearest spur out from the mountains. "Mary! Come on . . . move!"

Mary came to life at last and fumbled for the door handle, finding it and heaving it open about two feet before it got stuck in the earth. She is quite a bit shorter than I am, and definitely more than a bit wider.

"You'll just have to do it!" I said fiercely. "We can't stay here!"

Whether she caught the urgency in my voice, or realized for herself what I was thinking, she threw her weight against it and made not more than an inch or two's difference, but it was enough. She squeezed her body through, gasping and grunting, and landed awkwardly on the snow just as Jean did the same from the back.

"Come on!" Jean called at me impatiently. "If it's going to catch fire, get out! I'll stand here. Someone's bound to come past. We'll get a lift." As she spoke she moved into the middle of the highway just as another violent heave of the ground cracked the tarmac, and a sheet of water shot up eight or ten feet into the air not a dozen yards in front of us.

I think we all screamed. I certainly felt as if I did. I stopped even trying to open my door, and clawed my way across, never mind the gear lever jabbing at me, and fell out of the passenger door, rolled over and stood up. I was bruised and twisted but did that matter? "Get our anoraks," I ordered. "And the blankets and torch out of the trunk."

Mary moved to obey.

The water was still shooting out of the ground, and half a mile ahead there was another geyser like a burst main.

Mary banged the trunk shut, her arms full of clothes, and looked toward the spur of land I'd pointed to.

"We've got to stay here!" Jean told her roughly. "There may not be anybody living up there." She took her anorak from Mary and struggled into it. "I can't see any houses. Anyway, why should they drive us home when someone'll come along any time now. Don't go wandering off, that's just stupid."

I saw Mary's face tighten. For years Jean had been telling her what to do, it's a habit, and for years Mary had been going her own way, building up her temper, but promising one day she'd tell Jean what she thought of her. But family history runs deep. We can't even recall where some of the memories came from: Mary looking after me while Mother was out, which, looking back, seemed to be most of the time, or else she was ill. Me a sickly baby, and stubborn as all get-out. The boys off working as soon as they were old enough. And Jean, generous, funny and spoiled, Mother's favorite, who could do no wrong. Mary promised that one day she'd retaliate, and she never did. And Jean probably never knew she wanted to.

But that was Mary, not me. "It's an earthquake!" I swung around on Jean. "That means there are going to be landslides! Hell! Can't you hear the water sloshing around underneath us now?" I took my anorak too and put it on. It was going to be cold.

Jean swallowed, gulping air. "Then the farther away we are from the hills and any landslides, the better!" she pointed out. "And off the soil. The road's about as firm as anything." She made a move to drag Mary from the shoulder onto the tarmac beside her "And you!" she said to me sharply.

There was a gurgling, sucking sound, and a pool of water gushed out of what had looked like solid ground a moment ago.

"We're only a hundred yards from the sea," I replied, trying to sound sane and as if I knew what was talking about, although my heart was going like a trip-hammer. I had not wanted to tell her. Like me she had a terror of drowning. I don't know where it comes from. "Earthquakes cause tidal waves, Jean."

She stared at me as if I'd spoken to her in Greek.

"Come on," I said more gently. "We've got to get to higher ground; it's not far. We should start moving. It's cold and we'll do a lot better if we stay dry. That was a magnificent understatement. Dry was definitely better than under a twenty foot wall of water. "Come on."

We started to walk, carrying the blanket and torch, and reluctantly, white-faced, Jean caught up with us and we pushed steadily, side by side, up the slope until it became steeper. I was out of breath and so was Mary. I could see her gasping. Only then did I realize how united all three of us were, and for an instant it was as if we were children again, us against the world, and I found myself smiling, all the resentments forgotten.

Mary turned and smiled at me, tears in her eyes.

Then we heard them, loud popping sounds, way over toward the town, and a moment later black smoke billowed against the sky, and then gouts of flame, brilliant yellow and orange.

"What's that?" Jean's voice all but choked in her throat. "Earthquakes don't have lava . . . do they? Oh, God, help us!"

"No!" I said quickly. "No!" I put my arm around her. She was stiff as a tree. "It's the Chevron oil tanks over in Seward. Don't worry, nothing will reach us out here."

"Nothing?" she demanded with a note of hysteria. "What sort of nothing? You mean like fire?"

"Nothing like anything!" I said impatiently. "Except water. Come on, don't stand there, keep moving!"

We started up again, walking more separately now, each looking back at the skyline of the town every now and again as the dark cloud expanded and the flames seemed to get bigger. It was not easy going. The ground was rough, caked in snow in patches, with coarse grass spiking through and we kept slipping. I don't know whether it was clumsiness or fear, or if there were still tremors that threw us off balance.

Over toward the left, water sprayed yards high in the air, up out of a new crack in the earth, and a shower of stones rattled above the slope ahead of us.

Mary plodded on at one side of me, her face set, eyes fixed wide. I wished there was something I could do to reach her, but the invisible barrier between us was as solid as ever. She disapproved of me. She always would. I had run off when I was seventeen. Mother had said I deserted the family and she had never forgiven me for it. I kept on trying to bridge the gulf and finally succeeded, at least a little. We had made some kind of accommodation in the last few years of her life. She had taken back the "disowning" bit, but she had not forgotten it. I had still "betrayed" them all. The price of that was that I could never belong again, even though it was I who sat with Mother at the end when Mary was too hurt and too angry, and Jean was too upset. She had taker Mother's death terribly hard. Unlike for Mary or me in life nothing had broken the bond between them and for her the loss was raw and new. I had learned to accept it a while ago and finally Mary had too.

I looked at her now, struggling up the hill beside me in the growing dusk, stubborn, sad, angry with the loneliness inside herself, but still cherishing all the old wounds that I could not reach.

Another oil tank burst with a distant thud and another flame joined the wall of fire. God only knew what was happening to the people over there, but there was nothing we could do to help.

A creek to the right of us roared through a ravine in the rocks, twice its usual size. A loose rock crashed down, bounced, and disappeared, followed by a dozen more.

The ground under my feet gave and suddenly I was in a quagmire up to my ankles, then almost to my knees. I shrieked and Mary froze, then slithered back, holding out her hands toward me. Jean was closer and threw herself onto her stomach as I grasped at her arms, heaving at me for what seemed like an endless time. Every muscle ached and I felt as if my shoulders were coming out of their sockets. Then the next moment we were all three lying in a heap on the shale, sodden wet, shuddering with cold and relief.

"Thank you," I said numbly, and by heaven I meant it.

No one answered.

A few stones bounced and clattered from above us, and rolled down to the grass below.

"I don't know what we're climbing up here for!" Jean said angrily. "You always think you know everything!" That was directed at me. "We should have waited on the road. Someone would have found us! Nobody in their senses is going to look for us here!"

"Nobody's going to be looking for us anywhere," Mary pointed out. "Apart from the fact that they'll all be too busy trying to put the fires out, and attending to burst mains and things like that. And maybe find people trapped under rubble."

She pushed her hands up over her face, unintentionally smearing it with mud. "I wonder how widespread it is? If s possibly hit lots of places. Juneau could be worse than this."

"Or better," I said, trying to comfort her. "Anyway, we're all right. We'll be cold, but we'll survive that." I knew she was thinking of her son and daughters and their families, but there was no way we could find out about them, still less do anything to help.

"We should have stayed by the road!" Jean said yet again. "We . . ." She saw it even before she finished speaking, a wall of water heaving out of the sea, crashing over, roaring toward us, engulfing the land, tearing away trees and sweeping everything in front of it, wild, curling, pale spume-edged in the fading light.

For a moment we were paralyzed.

Then as one we shot to our feet and flung ourselves forward up the incline, scrambling, clawing over every yard of ground as if hell had opened up behind us. My skin was torn and bleeding, nails shredded, clothes ripped before I realized that the wave had broken and stopped short of us. My legs collapsed and I fell into the snow and mud, trying to fill my lungs with the cold air, shuddering and sobbing with relief.

I swiveled around and heard the sucking sound as the water tore the earth away about twenty feet below us, retreating filthy, hungry for debris, grasping after us like a great tongue, then arching back into itself and sliding away again.

The flames on the horizon were brighter. How much oil was there to burn? I had no idea.

"We've got to go higher!" I said, straightening up awkwardly. "The next one could be bigger."

"Why should it be?" Jean demanded. "You're only guessing."

"You want to stay and argue, you do it!" I snapped back at her. She was just perverse enough to stop, and I was afraid she would. It was getting darker and the ground was very rough. Every now and then the earth trembled and more rocks and stones came rattling down. There seemed to be water everywhere, oozing up out of the soil, squelching under our feet, crashing down the hillside in the swollen creek, breaking off chunks of the bank as it went. Nothing was fixed, nothing certain. I put my foot on something, and it gave way, pitching me forward to land on bruised hands and knees.

And there were strange noises, sucking and grinding, as if the earth were gathering its strength for another attempt to throw us off.

Mary was on my left, toiling upward a step at a time, glaring at me occasionally, but never at Jean. This was still the anniversary of Mother's death, and it would take more than an earthquake to cover the rift between them. It was all life deep. Mary could remember the time when Mother and Dad had been happy. Like me, sometimes she had taken Dad's side in the endless fights. For Mother and Jean there was no forgiving that.

On the other side Jean was panting, her face pale in the dying light. She too had never accepted that I had had the right to go. It was my turn to look after things, to stand by my sick mother, and instead I had run off to get married, putting myself first. At least that was how she saw it, and had never let me forget. It wasn't actually spoken of, but it was there underneath the surface, in the little needling remarks.

Sometimes I wondered if I really was as bad as they said. It had seemed to me at the time just a matter of survival. Mother was always going to be ill when she wanted somebody else to do something. She'd been dying every day since I'd been old enough to understand it. She'd been better than ninety when it actually happened. I guess when we talked about our childhood we were like blind men describing an elephant; we each perceived something completely different.

In a way I was as alone struggling up that hill as if there'd been no one else closer than Seward a couple of miles away, burning on the horizon under its pall of smoke, the oil flames still bright.

Then there was another wave, bigger than the last. It came roaring and crashing out of the dusk as if it would never stop. I felt the spray of it sting my face, and its wet, icy breath all around me.

When it retreated we were huddled together on a spur that jutted out over broken scree, and as Jean stood up the ground gave way under her and she teetered for a moment on the edge, her arms waving. Then with a shout of terror she overbalanced and fell flailing over the rim and down, down into the mud, still crying out.

I wasn't prepared for the horror I felt, the engulfing sense of loss, not as if it were my sister who had gone, but a part of me. I went after her without even thinking of how or if I could get back, or even of the next wave!

The ground seemed to cling onto me one moment, and to throw me off the next, but Jean was still below me, and that was all I could think of, all that mattered. Drowning never entered my head.

Mary was beside me, and even without being able to see her face in the gloom, I knew that she felt exactly as I did. For once we acted as one person, scrabbling, pulling and shouting together as we reached Jean and hauled her out of the mud and rubble, talking all the time, nonsense most of it, trying to reassure her, and I suppose ourselves, that she was all right and that we would all get above the waterline before the next wave hit.

We pulled her out, without any help from her, and it was only when we were almost level with the spur that had collapsed that we both realized at the same moment that Jean had not spoken a word, or really moved other than as we had dragged her.

I reached to feel for a pulse at the same moment that Mary did, and our hands collided over Jean's wrist. Was the pulse I felt Jean's or my own? My heart was beating so wildly it could have been either.

"She's alive," Mary said quietly, but there was confidence in it, and I felt myself steadying, breathing more calmly. We sat there together, holding Jean, trying to warm her, to rub a little life back into her arms and hands.

I wanted to say something, to retrieve some of all that we'd lost, but I didn't know how to begin. I was not sorry for having left all those years ago, but I was sorry for what it had done to Mary and Jean. And I was sorry for the gulf between them that I couldn't help to heal.

"She'll be all right," I said, because I had to believe it.

"I know," Mary replied, but there was more hope in her voice than conviction. "Do you think there'll be another wave?"

I had no idea. "Probably. We'd better be prepared."

Mary smiled at me, I could just make it out in the last of the light.

"I'm sorry I left you," I said suddenly.

She looked surprised, then she shook her head.

"I know you're still angry," I went on hurriedly. "But I paid for it. For half my life I've felt as if I didn't belong, I had no family—and I've missed you!"

Over in the distance, across the floodwater of the last wave, something like a rocket sped over the surface, trailing fire. I nearly missed what Mary said.

"I know you did," her voice was soft in the darkness. "But I still wish I'd made it when I tried. I'm not angry with you, but I'm angry with myself, because I hadn't the guts to do it. I envied you."

There was such honesty in her I couldn't disbelieve it, and yet it astonished me. I'd always thought Mary had all she wanted . . . except Mother's approval, of course. Jean was the only one of us who ever had that.

"You envied me?" I said incredulously, still rubbing Jean's arms with my hands.

Another loose propane gas tank went screaming across the water, spewing fire.

"Yes—but I had nowhere to go," she explained. "I came creeping back, feeling such a failure. But you managed it and you stayed."

I thought of the first few years of happiness, and then all the years afterward when I would have given so much to have had my family back, my sisters. "Too stubborn," I admitted.

She laughed, but it ended in something like a sob. "I'd have called you a liar if you'd said anything else," she answered. "Do you think she'll be all right?" There was fear in her now and she was not trying to hide it anymore. For all the rift between them, she loved Jean, in her own way, and she desperately wanted Jean to love her, to approve of her, just once to say she admired her and that she understood that our world was different from hers, the time when Mother and Dad had been happy, but it was just as real. Jean was not as strong as Mary, not as calm inside with her own belief. There was some hurt in her we'd never been able to reach. Perhaps it hadn't been so easy being the favorite after all.

"Of course she will," I said, forcing myself to believe it. "Rescuers will be out. This is Alaska. We're tough! National disasters are our heritage. And think of all our good Highland ancestors . . ."

She laughed, a trifle hollowly. "Who spent most of our history trying to kill each other."

"Sounds about right," I agreed. "So those of us who made it are pretty tough. Anyway, Jean's too stubborn to give up and die." I knew I should not have said that the moment it was out of my mouth. She wasn't tough and we both knew it. Neither of us wanted to speak of the dreadful time when she had run away, and been found in such deep unhappiness we were afraid she would just will herself dead. We never referred to it, and she never told us what had happened. There are some things too private ever to be touched.

I knew then as I held her limp body in my arms that something in it was still unhealed. All my anger, the rejection, the remembered slights evaporated. They were only words, like spots of blood on the outside. They were not scars, not really, and it was time they were washed off.

There was another wave, screaming out of the darkness, its pale foam hissing, luminous, pink-touched by the fires on the horizon. It curled over and crashed about fifteen feet below us, but I felt the shudder and aftershock of its bruising force. About a mile away I saw more propane tanks whizz by, trailing plumes of flame like rockets.

I'm not sure how long we sat there shivering in silence, even though we were so close we were touching each other. But it was a silence of peace. All kinds of things I had thought I needed to say I now realized that I didn't. We had all traveled the same path in the ways we thought divided us. The differences—Mary's widowhood, Jean's quiet, gentle, frustrating marriage, and my divorce—were not as wildly different either, just turns of events that we could all of us have understood.

Why had we traveled alone when we had not needed to? I should have tried sooner, and much harder. Suddenly I was glad we decided to get together on Mother's anniversary. It was no longer a duty I was performing to try to help Jean, knowing she was the one who would find it most painful.

Anyway, perhaps she wasn't? Maybe Mary was hurting just as much, for the acceptance she would never achieve now. It would be too obvious to thank her in words for all the times she had filled my mother's place when I was a child, but I resolved to let her know some other way.

I don't know how long it was until Jean stirred at last, but I never felt anything that mattered more to me. She coughed and began to move.

Mary tightened her grip. "Jean!" she said urgently. "Are you all right? Don't sit up too quickly. Where do you hurt?"

"Everywhere," Jean said ruefully, but the words didn't matter, it was the strength in her voice and the fact that she was struggling to rise. "What's happened?"

"More waves," I said, but I sounded as if that were a triumph, not a totally predictable disaster. "We're well above them."

She didn't answer, but I felt her relax against me.

We sat close together. I was too cold to sleep, but it was only on the outside. More waves came and went, I didn't count them. We talked now and then, all on the lines of "Do you remember?" But we chose only the good things: picnics—Joe putting a blanket over his head and pretending to be a radio, every time we touched him changing stations and giving us snatches of news, stories, music; skinny-dipping in the creek in the summer; picking wild berries and "borrowing" apples from the neighbors' trees. Mr. Campbell pretended to be mad, but actually he'd have been disappointed if we hadn't tried—and succeeded.

The bitterness was gone. At last we could choose what to remember, and what to let slip away into forgetting.

When dawn came finally, still smudged dark with smoke over the town, we saw the devastation: trees uprooted, land torn away, oil drums and tanks, the shards of buildings, two or three cars strewn over the fields. The water had gone away, leaving mud and debris behind, but the road gleamed like a pale, torn ribbon in the distance, and it was only a matter of climbing down to it and waiting until someone passed. By now all Alaska would know what had happened and there would be people pouring in to help, to search for the lost, to heal the wounds, filled with strength to rebuild.

I wished more than anything else to be part of that.

Good Friday was a day when a lot of things were broken, and Easter was the beginning of things that were better. Mary says the same thing every year, in her own way, and so does Jean.

Engines

W HEN GEENA MOVED OUT AND FILED for divorce, the first two things I did were to put the house up for sale and to quit Unidyne, a job I'd hated from the beginning. Then I loaded the Jeep and drove straight to Death Valley.

I told no one where I was going. Not that there was anybody to tell, really; we had no close friends, or at least I didn't, and my folks were both dead. Geena could have guessed, of course. She knew me that well, though not nearly well enough to understand my motives.

I did not go to Death Valley because something in my life had died.

I went there to start living again.

October is one of the Valley's best months. All months in the Monument are good, as far as I'm concerned, even July and August, when the midday temperatures sometimes exceed 120 degrees Fahrenheit and Death Valley justifies its Paiute Indian name, *Tomesha*—ground afire. If a sere desert climate holds no terrors for you, if you respect it and accept it on its terms, survival is not a problem and the attractions far outweigh the drawbacks. Still, I'm partial to October, the early part of the month. The beginning of the tourist season is still a month away, temperatures seldom reach 100 degrees, and the constantly changing light show created by sun and wind and clouds is at its most spectacular. You can stay in one place all day, from dawn to dark—Zabriskie Point, say, or the sand dunes near Stovepipe Wells—and with each ten-degree rise and fall of the sun the colors of rock and sand hills change from dark rose to burnished gold, from chocolate brown to purple and indigo and gray-black, with dozens of subtler shades in between.

It had been almost a year since I'd last been to the Valley. Much too long, but it had been a difficult year. I'd been alone on that last visit, as I was alone now; alone the last dozen or so trips, since Geena refused to come with me anymore five years ago. I preferred it that way. The Valley is a place to be shared only with someone who views it in the same perspective, not as endless miles of coarse, dead landscape but as a vast, almost mystical place—a *living* place—of majestic vistas and stark natural beauty. Deciding where to go first hadn't been easy. It has more than three thousand square miles, second only among national parks to Yellowstone, and all sorts of terrain: the great trough of the valley floor, with its miles of salt pan two hundred feet and more below sea level, its dunes and alluvial fans, its borate deposits and old borax works, its barren fields of gravel and broken rock; and five enclosing mountain ranges full of hidden canyons, petroglyphs, played-out gold and silver mines, ghost towns. I'd spent an entire evening with my topos—topographical maps put out by the U.S. Geological Survey—and finally settled on the Funeral Mountains and the Chloride Cliffs topo. The Funerals form one of the eastern boundaries, and their foothills and crest not only are laden with a variety of canyons but contain the ruins of the Keane Wonder Mill and mine and the gold boom-town of Chloride City.

I left the Jeep north of Scotty's Castle, near Hells Gate, packed in, and stayed for three days and two nights. The first day was a little rough; even though I'm in good shape, it takes a while to refamiliarize yourself with desert mountain terrain after a year away. The second day was easier. I spent that one exploring Echo Canyon and then tramping among the thick-timbered tramways of the Keane, the decaying mill a mile below it which in the 1890s had twenty stamps processing eighteen hundred tons of ore a month. On the third day I went on up to the Funerals' sheer heights and Chloride City, and the climb neither strained nor winded me.

It was a fine three days. I saw no other people except at a long distance. I reestablished kinship with the Valley, as only a person who truly loves it can, and all the tension and restless dissatisfaction built up over the past year slowly bled out of me. I could literally feel my spirit reviving, starting to soar again.

I thought about Geena only once, on the morning of the third day as I stood atop one of the crags looking out toward Needles Eye. There was no wind, and the stillness, the utter absence of sound, was so acute it created an almost painful pressure against the eardrums. Of all the things Geena hated about Death Valley, its silence—"void of silence," an early explorer had termed it—topped the list. It terrified her. On our last trip together, when she'd caught me listening, she'd said, "What are you listening to? There's nothing to hear in this godforsaken place. It's as if everything has shut down. Not just here; everywhere. As if all the engines have quit working."

She was right, exactly right: as if all the engines have quit working. And that perception, more than anything else, summed up the differences between us. To her, the good things in life, the essence of life itself, were people, cities, constant scurrying activity. She needed to hear the steady, throbbing engines of civilization in order to feel safe, secure, alive. And I needed none of those things; needed *not* to hear the engines.

I remembered something else she'd said to me once, not so long ago. "You're a dreamer, Scott, an unfocused dreamer. Drifting through life looking for something that might not even exist." Well, maybe there was truth in that too. But if I was looking for something, I had already found part of it right here in Death Valley. And now I could come here as often as I wanted, without restrictions; resigning from Unidyne had seen to that. I couldn't live in the Monument—permanent residence is limited to a small band of Paiutes and Park Service employees—but I could live nearby, in Beatty or Shoshone or one of the other little towns over in the Nevada desert. After the L.A. house sold, I'd be well fixed. And when the money finally did run out I could hire out as a guide, do odd jobs—whatever it took to support myself. Dreamer with a focus at last.

For a little time, thinking about Geena made me sad. But the Valley is not a place where I can feel sad for long. I had loved her very much at first, when we were both students at UCLA, but over our eleven years together the love had eroded and seeped away, and now what I felt mainly was relief. I was free and Geena was free. Endings don't have to be painful, not if you look at them as beginnings instead.

Late that third afternoon I hiked back to where I'd left the Jeep. No one had bothered it; I had never had any trouble with thieves or vandals out here. Before I crawled into my sleeping bag I sifted through the topos again to pick my next spot. I don't know why I chose the Manly Peak topo. Maybe because I hadn't been in the southern Panamints, through Warm Springs Canyon, in better than three years. Still, it was an odd choice to make. That region was not one of my favorite parts of the Valley. Also, a large portion of the area is under private claim, and the owners of the talc mines along the canyon take a dim view of trespassing; you have to be extra careful to keep to public lands when you pack in there.

In the morning, just before dawn, I ate a couple of nutrition bars for breakfast and then pointed the Jeep down Highway 178. The sun was out by the time I reached the Warm Springs Canyon turnoff. The main road in is unpaved, rutted and talc-covered, and primarily the domain of eighteen-wheelers passing to and from the mines. You need at least a four-wheel-drive vehicle to negotiate it and the even rougher trails that branch off it. I would not take a passenger car over one inch of that terrain. Neither would anyone else who knows the area or pays attention to the Park Service brochures, guidebooks, and posted signs.

That was why I was amazed when I came on the Ford Taurus.

I had turned off the main canyon road ten miles in, onto the trail into Butte Valley, and when I rounded a turn on the washboard surface there it was, pulled off into the shadow of a limestone shelf. The left rear tire was flat, and a stain that had spread out from underneath told me the oil pan was ruptured. No one was visible inside or anywhere in the immediate vicinity.

I brought the Jeep up behind and went to have a look. The Ford had been there awhile—that was clear. At least two days. The look and feel of the oil stain proved that. I had to be the first to come by since its abandonment, or it wouldn't still be sitting here like this. Not many hikers or offroaders venture out this way in the off-season, the big ore trucks use the main canyon road, and there aren't enough park rangers for daily backcountry patrols.

The Ford's side windows were so dust- and talc-caked that I could barely see through them. I tried the driver's door; it was unlocked. The interior was empty except for two things on the front seat. One was a woman's purse, open, the edge of a wallet poking out. The other was a piece of lined notepaper with writing on it in felt-tip pen, held down by the weight of the purse.

I slid the paper free. Date on top—two days ago—and below that, "To Frank Spicer," followed by several lines of shaky backhand printing. I sensed what it was even before I finished reading the words.

I have no hope left. You and Conners have seen to that. I can't fight you anymore and I can't go on not knowing if Kevin is safe, how you must be poisoning his mind even if you haven't hurt him physically. Someday he'll find out what kind of man you really are. Someday he will find out. And I pray to God he makes you pay for what you've done.

I love you, Kevin. God forgive me.

I couldn't quite decipher the scrawled signature. Christine or Christina something—not Spicer. I opened the wallet and fanned through the card section until I found her driver's license. The Ford had California plates, and the license had also been issued in this state. Christina Dunbar. Age 32. San Diego address. The face in the ID photo was slender and fair-haired and unsmiling.

The wallet contained one other photo, of a nice-looking boy eight or nine years old—a candid shot taken at a lake or large river. Kevin? Nothing else in the wallet told me anything. One credit card was all she owned. And twelve dollars in fives and singles.

I returned the wallet to the purse, folded the note in there with it. In my mouth was a dryness that had nothing to do with the day's gathering heat. And in my mind was a feeling of urgency much more intense than the situation called for. If she'd brought along a gun or pills or some other lethal device, she was long dead by now. If she'd wanted the Valley to do the job for her, plenty enough time had elapsed for that too, given the perilous terrain and the proliferation of sidewinders and daytime temperatures in the mid nineties and no water and improper clothing. Yet there was a chance she was still alive. A chance I could keep her that way if I could find her.

I tossed her purse into the Jeep, uncased my 7 x 50 Zeiss binoculars, and climbed up on the hood to scan the surrounding terrain. The valley floor here was flattish, mostly fields of fractured rock slashed by shallow washes. Clumps of low-growing creosote bush and turtleback were the only vegetation. I had a fairly good look over a radius of several hundred yards: no sign of her.

Some distance ahead there was higher ground. I drove too fast on the rough road, had to force myself to slow down. At the top of a rise I stopped again, climbed a jut of limestone to a notch in its crest. From there I had a much wider view, all the way to Striped Butte and the lower reaches of the Panamints.

The odds were against me spotting her, even with the powerful Zeiss glasses. The topography's rumpled irregularity created too many hidden places; she might have wandered miles in any direction. But I did locate her, and in less than ten minutes, and when I did I felt no surprise. It was as if, at some deep level, I'd been certain all along that I would.

She was a quarter of a mile away, to the southwest, at the bottom of a salt-streaked wash. Lying on her side, motionless, knees drawn up to her chest, face and part of her blond head hidden in the crook of one bare arm. It was impossible to tell at this distance if she was alive or dead.

The wash ran down out of the foothills like a long, twisted scar, close to the trail for some distance, then hooking away from it in a gradual snake-track curve. Where she lay was at least four hundred yards from the four-wheel track. I picked out a trail landmark roughly opposite, then scrambled back down to the Jeep.

It took me more than an hour to get to her: drive to the landmark, load my pack with two extra soft-plastic water bottles and the first-aid kit, strap the pack on, and then hike across humps and flats of broken rock as loose and treacherous as talus. Even though the prenoon temperature was still in the eighties, I was sweating heavily—and I'd used up a pint of water to replace the sweat loss—by the time I reached the wash.

She still lay in the same drawn-up position. And she didn't stir at the noises I made, the clatter of dislodged rocks, as I slid down the wash's bank. I went to one knee beside her, groped for a sunburned wrist. Pulse, faint and irregular. I did not realize until then that I had been holding my breath; I let it out thin and hissing between my teeth.

She wore only a thin, short-sleeved shirt, a pair of Levis, and tattered Reeboks. The exposed areas of her skin were burned raw, coated with salt from dried sweat that was as gritty as fine sand; the top of her scalp was flecked with dried blood from ruptured blisters. I saw no snake or scorpion bites, no limb fractures or swellings. But she was badly dehydrated. At somewhere between 15 percent and 22 percent dehydration, a human being will die, and she was at or near the danger zone.

Gently I took hold of her shoulders, eased her over onto her back. Her limbs twitched; she made a little whimpering sound. She was on the edge of consciousness, more submerged than not.

The sun's white glare hurt her eyes even through the tightly closed lids. She turned her head, lifted an arm painfully across the bridge of her nose.

I freed one of the foil-wrapped water bottles, slipped off the attached cap. Her lips were cracked, split deeply in a couple of places; I dribbled water on them, to get her to open them. Then I eased the spout into her mouth and squeezed out a few more drops.

At first she struggled, twisting her head, moaning deep in her throat: the part of her that wanted death rebelling against revival and awareness. But her will to live hadn't completely deserted her, and her thirst was too acute. She swallowed some of the warm liquid, swallowed more when I lifted her head and held it cushioned against my knee. Before long she was sucking greedily at the spout, like an infant at its mother's nipple. Her hands came up and clutched at the bottle; I let her take it away from me, let her drain it. The idea of parceling out water to a dehydration victim is a fallacy. You have to saturate the parched tissues as fast as possible to accelerate the restoration of normal functions.

I opened another bottle, raised her into a sitting position, and then gave it to her. Shelter was the next most important thing. I took the lightweight space blanket from my pack, unfolded it, and shook it out. A space blanket is five by seven feet, coated on one side with a filler of silver insulating material and reflective surface. Near where she lay, behind her to the east, I hand-scraped a sandy area free of rocks. Then I set up the blanket into a lean-to, using takedown tent poles to support the front edge and tying them off with nylon cord to rocks placed at a forty-five-degree angle from the shelter corners. I secured the ground side of the lean-to with more rocks and sand atop the blanket's edge.

Christina Dunbar was sitting slumped forward when I finished, her head cradled in her hands. The second water bottle, as empty as the first, lay beside her. I gripped her shoulders again, and this time she stiffened, fought me weakly as I drew her backward and pressed her down into the lean-to's shade. The struggles stopped when I pillowed her head with the pack. She lay still, half on her side, her eyes still squeezed tight shut. Conscious now but not ready to face either me or the fact that she was still alive.

The first-aid kit contained a tube of Neosporin. I said as I uncapped it, "I've got some burn medicine here. I'm going to rub it on your face and scalp first."

She made a throat sound that might have been a protest. But when I squeezed out some of the ointment and began to smooth it over her blistered skin, she remained passive. Lay there silent and rigid as I ministered to her.

I used the entire tube of Neosporin, most of it on her face and arms. None of the cuts and abrasions she'd suffered was serious; the medicine would disinfect those too. There was nothing I could do for the bruises on her upper arms, along her jaw, and on the left temple. I wondered where she'd got them. Not stumbling around in the desert: they were more than two days old, already fading.

When I was done I opened another quart of water, took a nutrition bar from my pack. Her eyes were open when I looked at her again. Gray-blue, dull with pain and exhaustion, staring fixedly at me without blinking. Hating me a little, I thought.

I said, "Take some more water," and extended the bottle to her.

"No."

"Still thirsty, aren't you?"

"No."

"We both know you are."

"Who're you?" Her voice was as dry and cracked as her lips, but strong enough. "How'd you find me?"

"Scott Davis. I was lucky. So are you."

"Lucky," she said.

"Drink the water, Christina."

"How do you know . . . ? Oh."

"That's right. I read the note."

"Why couldn't you just let me die? Why did you have to come along and find me?"

"Drink."

I held the bottle out close to her face. Her eyes shifted to it; the tip of her tongue flicked out, snakelike, as if she were tasting the water. Then, grimacing, she lifted onto an elbow and took the bottle with an angry, swiping gesture—anger directed at herself, not me, as if for an act of self-betrayal. She drank almost half of it, coughed and then lowered the bottle.

"Go a little slower with the rest of it."

"Leave me alone."

"I can't do that, Christina."

"I want to sleep."

"No, you don't." I unwrapped the nutrition bar. "Eat as much of this as you can get down. Slowly, little bites."

She shook her head, holding her arms stiff and tight against her sides.

"Please," I said.

"I don't want any food."

"Your body needs the nourishment."

"No."

"I'll force-feed you if I have to."

She held out a little longer, but her eyes were on the bar the entire time. When she finally took it, it was with the same gesture of self-loathing. Her first few bites were nibbles, but the honey taste revived her hunger, and she went at the bar the way she had at the water bottle. She almost choked on the first big chunk she tried to swallow. I made her slow down, sip water between each bite.

"How do you feel?" I asked when she was finished.

"Like I'm going to live, damn you."

"Good. We'll stay here for a while, until you're strong enough to walk."

"Walk where?"

"My Jeep, over on the trail. Four hundred yards or so, and the terrain is pretty rough. I don't want to have to carry you, at least not the whole way."

"Then what?"

"You need medical attention. There's an infirmary at Furnace Creek."

"And after that, the psycho ward," she said, but not as if she cared. "Where's the nearest one?"

I let that pass. "If you feel up to talking," I said, "I'm a good listener."

"About what?"

"Why you did this to yourself."

"Tried to kill myself, you mean. Commit suicide."

"All right. Why, Christina?"

"You read my note."

"It's pretty vague. Is Kevin your son?"

She winced when I spoke the name. Turned her head away without answering.

I didn't press it. Instead I shifted around and lay back on my elbows, with my upper body in the lean-to's shade. I was careful not to touch her. It was another windless day, and the near-noon stillness was as complete as it had been the other morning in the Funerals. For a time nothing moved anywhere; then a chuckwalla lizard scurried up the bank of the wash, followed a few seconds later by a horned toad. It looked as though the toad were chasing the lizard, but like so many things in the Valley, that was illusion. Toads and lizards are not enemies.

It was not long before Christina stirred and said, "Is there any more water?" Her tone had changed; there was resignation in it now, as if she had accepted, at least for the time being, the burden of remaining alive.

I sat up, took one of the last two full quarts from my pack. "Make this last until we're ready to leave," I said as I handed it to her. "It's a long walk to the Jeep, and we'll have to share the last bottle."

She nodded, drank less thirstily, and lowered the bottle with it still two-thirds full. That was a good sign. Her body was responding, its movements stronger and giving her less pain.

I let her have another energy bar. She took it without argument, ate it slowly with sips of water. Then she lifted herself into a sitting position, her head not quite touching the slant of the blanket. She was just a few inches over five feet, thin but wiry. The kind of body she had and the fact that she'd taken care of it was a major reason for her survival and swift recovery.

She said, "I guess you might as well know."

"If you want to tell me."

"Kevin's my son. Kevin Andrew Spicer. He'll be ten years old in December."

"Frank Spicer is your ex-husband?"

"Yes, and I hope his soul rots in hell."

"Custody battle?"

"Oh, yes, there was a custody battle. But I won. I had full legal custody of my son."

"Had?"

"Frank kidnapped him."

"You mean literally?"

"Literally."

"When?"

"A year and a half ago," Christina said. "He had visitation rights, every other weekend. He picked Kevin up one Friday afternoon and never brought him back. I haven't seen either of them since."

"The authorities couldn't find them?"

"Nobody could find them. Not the police, not the FBI, not any of the three private detectives I hired. I think they're still somewhere in the southwest—Nevada or Arizona or New Mexico. But I don't know. I don't know."

"How could they vanish so completely?"

"Money. Everything comes down to money."

"Not everything."

"He was a successful commercial artist. And bitter because he felt he was prostituting his great talent. Even after the settlement he had a net worth of more than two hundred thousand dollars."

"He liquidated all his assets before he took Kevin?"

"Every penny."

"He must've wanted the boy very badly."

"He did, but not because he loves him."

"To get back at you?"

"To hurt me. He hates me."

"Why? The custody battle?"

"That, and because I divorced him. He can't stand to lose any of his possessions."

"He sounds unstable."

"Unstable is a polite term for it. Frank Spicer is a paranoid sociopath with delusions of grandeur. That's what a psychiatrist I talked to called him."

"Abusive?"

"Not at first. Not until he started believing I was sleeping with everybody from the mayor to the mailman. I was never unfaithful to him, not once."

"Did he abuse Kevin too?"

"No, thank God. He never touched Kevin. At least . . . not before he took him away from me."

"You think he may have harmed the boy since?"

"He's capable of it. He's capable of anything. There's no doubt of that now." Headshake. She drank more water.

"Conners," I said. "Who's he?"

She winced again. "The last straw."

I waited, but she didn't go on. She was not ready to talk about Conners yet. "Christina, why did you come here?"

"I don't know. I was on the main road, and there was a sign—"

"I mean Death Valley itself. All the way from San Diego, nearly four hundred miles."

"I didn't drive here from San Diego."

"Isn't that where you live?"

"Yes, but I was in Las Vegas. I came from there."

"Why were you in Vegas?"

"Fool's errand," she said bitterly.

"Something happened there. What was it?" She didn't answer. For more than a minute she sat stiffly, squinting in the direction of Striped Butte; the sun, on its anamorphic conglomeration of ribbons of crinoid limestone, jasper, and mother minerals, was dazzling. Then—

"A man called me a few days ago. He said his name was Conners and he knew where Frank and Kevin were living, but he wanted a thousand dollars for the information. In cash, delivered to him in Vegas."

"Did you know him?"

"No."

"But you believed him."

"I wanted to believe him," she said. "He claimed to've known Frank years ago, to've had business dealings with him; he mentioned the names of people I knew. And the last detective I hired . . . he traced Frank and Kevin to a Vegas suburb six weeks ago. They disappeared again the day after he found out where they'd been staying."

"Why didn't you send the detective to meet with Conners?"

"He stopped working for me a month ago, when I couldn't pay him anymore. All the settlement money was gone, and I had nothing left to sell. And no friends left to borrow from."

"Then you couldn't raise the thousand Conners demanded?"

"No, I couldn't raise it. So I stole it."

I didn't say anything.

"I was desperate," she said. "Desperate and crazy."

"Where did you steal it?"

"From the hardware supply company where I work . . . worked. My boss is a nice guy. He loaned me money twice before, he was supportive and sympathetic, but he just couldn't loan me any more, he said. So I paid him back by taking a thousand dollars out of the company account. Easy; I was the office manager. Then I drove to Vegas and gave it to Conners."

"And it was all just a scam," I said. "He didn't know where Spicer and Kevin are."

"Oh, he knew, all right. He knew because Frank had set the whole thing up. That was part of the message Conners delivered afterward."

"Afterward?"

"After he beat me up and raped me."

"Jesus," I said.

"Frank is tired of being dogged by detectives. Frank says I'd better leave him and Kevin alone from now on. Frank says if I don't, there'll be more of the same, only next time he'll do it himself, and it won't just be rape and a beating—he'll kill me. End of message."

"Did you call the police?"

"What for? Conners isn't his real name, and he doesn't live in Vegas. What could the police have done except maybe arrest me and send me back to San Diego to stand trial for theft? No. No. I stayed in the motel room where it happened until I felt well enough to leave, and then I started driving. By the time the car quit on me I was way out here in the middle of nowhere and I didn't care anymore. I just didn't want to go on living."

"You still feel that way?"

"What do you think?"

I said, "There are a lot of miles between Vegas and Death Valley. And a lot of remote desert. Why did you come this far?"

"I don't know. I just kept driving, that's all."

"Have you ever been to the Valley before?"

"No."

"Was it on your mind? Death Valley, dead place, place to go and die?"

"No. I didn't even know where I was until I saw a sign. What difference does it make?"

"It makes a difference. I think it does."

"Well, I don't. The only thing that matters is that you found me before it was too late."

She picked up the water bottle, sat holding it in brooding silence without drinking. I gave my attention to the Panamints, Manly Peak and the taller, hazy escarpments of Telescope Peak to the north. To some they were silent and brooding—bare monoliths of dark-gray basalt and limestone, like tombstones towering above a vast graveyard. But not to me. I saw them as old and benevolent guardians, comforting in their size and age and austerity. Nurturing. The Paiutes believe that little mountain spirits, *Kai-nu-suvs,* live deep in their rock recesses—kindly spirits, as beautiful as sunset clouds and as pure as fresh snow. When clouds mass above the peaks, the *Kai-nu-suvs* ride deer and bighorn sheep, driving their charges in wild rides among the crags. For such joyous celebrations of life, the Paiutes cherish them.

Time passed. I sat looking and listening. Mostly listening, until I grew aware of heat rays against my hands where they rested flat on my thighs. The sun had reached and passed its zenith, was robbing the shelter of its shade. If we didn't leave soon, I would have to reset the position of the lean-to.

"How do you feel?" I asked Christina. "Strong enough to try walking?"

She was still resigned. "I can try," she said.

"Stay where you are for a couple of minutes, while I get ready. I'll work around you."

I gathered and stowed the empty water bottles, took down the lean-to and stowed the stakes and then strapped on the pack. When I helped Christina to her feet she seemed able to stand all right without leaning on me. I shook out the blanket, draped it over her head and shoulders so that her arms were covered, showed her how to hold it in place under her chin. Then I slipped an arm around her thin body and we set out.

It was a long, slow trek to the Jeep. And a painful one for her, though she didn't complain, didn't speak the entire time. We stayed in the wash most of the way, despite the fact that it added a third as much distance, because the footing was easier for her. I stopped frequently so she could rest; and I let her have almost all the remaining water. Still, by the time we reached the trail her legs were wobbly and most of her new-gained strength was gone.

I had to swing her up and carry her the last two hundred yards. But it was not much of a strain. She was like a child in my arms.

I eased her into the passenger seat, took the blanket, and put it and my pack into the rear. There were two quarts of water left back there. I drank from one, two long swallows, before I slid in under the wheel. She had slumped down limply in the other seat, with her head back and her eyes shut. Her breath came and went in ragged little pants.

"Christina?"

"I'm awake," she said.

"Here. More water."

She drank without opening her eyes.

I said, "There are some things I want to say before we go. Something important that needs to be settled."

"What would that be?"

"When we get to Furnace Creek, I'm not going to report you as an attempted suicide. We'll say you made the mistake of driving out here in a passenger car, and when it broke down you tried to walk out and lost your sense of direction. That sort of thing happens a dozen times a year in the Valley. The rangers won't think anything of it."

"Why bother? It doesn't matter if you report me as a psycho case."

"You're not a psycho case. And it does matter. I want to keep on helping you."

"There's nothing you can do for me."

"I can help you find your son."

Her head jerked up; she opened her eyes to stare at me. "What're you talking about?"

"Just what I said. I want to help you find your son and take him back from his father."

"You can't be serious."

"I've never been more serious."

"But why would you . . . ?"

"A lot of reasons. Because you're still alive and I'd like you to stay that way. Because I don't want Frank Spicer to get away with kidnapping Kevin or with having you raped and beaten. Because it's right. Because I can."

She shook her head: trying to shake away disbelief so she could cling to hope again. "The heat must have made you crazy. I told you, I'm a fugitive; I stole money from my boss in San Diego—"

"You also told me he was supportive and sympathetic. Chances are he still is, or will be if he gets his thousand dollars back. I'll call him tonight, explain the situation, offer to send him the money right away if he drops any charges he may have filed. With interest, if he asks for it."

"My God, you'd do that?"

"You can pay me back after we find Kevin. Money's not a problem, Christina. I have more than enough for both of us."

"But Frank . . . you don't know him. He meant what he said about killing me. He'd kill you too."

"He won't harm either of us, I'll see to that. Or Kevin, if I can help it.

I'm not afraid of men like Frank Spicer. He may be disturbed, but he's also a coward. Sending Conners proves that."

Another headshake. "How could we hope to find them? The FBI couldn't in a year and a half, the detectives couldn't. . . . "

"They didn't spend all their time looking," I said. "You and I can, as long as it takes. Time's not a problem, either. Before I came out here my wife filed for divorce and I quit my job. That part of my life is over. There's nothing to keep me from spending the rest of it any way I see fit."

"Why *this* way? Why would you do so much for a stranger? What do you expect to get out of it?"

"Nothing from you, Christina. It's as much for myself as it is for you."

"I want to believe you, but I just . . . I don't understand. Are you trying to be some kind of hero?"

"There's nothing heroic about me. My wife once called me an unfocused dreamer, drifting through life looking for something that might not even exist. She was half right. What I've been looking for I've had all along without realizing it—Death Valley, and my relationship to it. I've been coming here ever since I was a kid, more than twenty years, and I've always felt that it's a living place, not a dead one. Now . . . it seems almost sentient to me. As if it were responsible for bringing us together. I could have gone anywhere in three thousand square miles today, and I came to the exact spot you did two days ago; I could easily have missed finding you, but I didn't. The feeling of sentience is illusion, I suppose, but that doesn't make it any less important. If I don't finish saving your life—help you find your son, give you a reason to go on living—then none of what's happened today will mean anything. And my relationship with the Valley will never be the same again. Does that make any sense to you?"

"Maybe," she said slowly. "Maybe it does."

"Will you let me finish what's been started, then? For your son's sake, if not for yours or mine?"

She had no words yet. Her head turned away from me, and at first I thought she was staring out through the windshield. Then some of the hurt smoothed out of her ravaged face, and her expression grew almost rapt, and I knew she wasn't looking at anything. Knew, too, what her answer would be. And that there was a closer bond between us than I'd thought.

She was listening.

What are you listening to? There's nothing to hear in this godforsaken place.

Yes, there was. Geena just hadn't been able to hear it.

It's as if everything has shut down. Not just here; everywhere. As if all the engines have quit working.

No, not all. There was still one engine you could hear if you tried hard enough. The engine I'd been listening to out in the wash, when I'd been making up my mind about Christina and Kevin and Frank Spicer. The engine she was listening to now. One engine clear and steady in the void of silence, the only one that really counts.

Your own.

ELLERY QUEEN

The Adventure of the One-Penny Black

"**A**CH!" SAID OLD UNEKER. "It iss a terrible t'ing, Mr. Quveen, a terrible t'ing, like I vass saying. Vat iss New York coming to? Dey come into my store—polizei, undt bleedings, undt whackings on de headt. . . . Diss iss vunuff my oldest customers, Mr. Quveen. He too hass hadt exberiences. . . . Mr. Hazlitt, Mr. Quveen. . . . Mr. Quveen iss dot famous detectiff feller you read aboudt in de papers, Mr. Hazlitt. Inspector Richardt Quveen's son."

Ellery Queen laughed, uncoiled his length from old Uneker's counter, and shook the man's hand. "Another victim of our crime wave, Mr. Hazlitt? Unky's been regaling me with a feast of a whopping bloody tale."

"So you're Ellery Queen," said the frail little fellow; he wore a pair of thick-lensed goggles and there was a smell of suburbs about him. "This *is* luck! Yes, I've been robbed."

Ellery looked incredulously about old Uneker's bookshop. "Not *here?*" Uneker was tucked away on a side street in mid-Manhattan, squeezed between the British Bootery and Mme. Carolyne's, and it was just about the last place in the world you would have expected thieves to choose as the scene of a crime.

"Nah," said Hazlitt. "Might have saved the price of a book if it had. No, it happened last night about ten o'clock. I'd just left my office on Forty-fifth Street—I'd worked late—and I was walking crosstown. Chap stopped me on the street and asked for a light. The street was pretty dark and deserted, and I didn't like the fellow's manner, but I saw no harm in lending him a packet of matches. While I was digging it out, though, I noticed he was eyeing the book under my arm. Sort of trying to read the title."

"What book was it?" asked Ellery eagerly. Books were his private passion.

Hazlitt shrugged. "Nothing remarkable. That best-selling nonfiction thing, *Europe in Chaos*; I'm in the export line I like to keep up to date on international conditions. Anyway, this chap lit his cigarette, returned the matches, mumbled thanks, and I began to walk on. Next thing I knew something walloped me on the back of my head and everything went black. I seem to remember falling. When I came to, I lying in the gutter, my hat and glasses were on the stones, my head felt like a baked potato. Naturally thought I'd been robbed; I had a lot of cash about me, and I was wearing a of diamond cuff links. But—"

"But, of course," said Ellery with a grin, "the only thing that was taken was *Europe in Chaos*. Perfect, Mr. Hazlitt! A fascinating little problem. Can you describe your assailant?"

"He had a heavy mustache and dark-tinted glasses of some kind. That's all. I—"

"He? He can describe not'ing," said old Uneker sourly. "He iss like all you Americans—blindt, a *dummkopf*. B book, Mr. Quveen—de book! Vhy should any von vant to steal a book like dot?"

"And that isn't all," said Hazlitt. "When I got home last night—I live in East Orange, New Jersey—I found my home broken into! And what do you think had been stolen, Mr. Queen?"

Ellery's lean face beamed. "I'm no crystal-gazer; but if there's any consistency in crime, I should imagine another book had been stolen."

"Right! And it was my second copy of *Europe in Chaos*!"

"Now you do interest me," said Ellery, in quite a different tone. "How did you come to have two, Mr. Hazlitt?"

"I bought another copy from Uneker two days ago to give to a friend of mine. I'd left it on top of my bookcase. It's gone. Window was open—it had been forced; and there were smudges of hands on the sill. Plain case of housebreaking. And although there's plenty of valuable stuff in my place— silver and things—nothing else had been taken. I reported it at once to the East Orange police, but they just tramped about the| place, gave me funny looks, and finally went away. I suppose they thought I was crazy."

"Were any other books missing?"

"No, just that one."

"I really don't see . . ." Ellery took off his *pince-nez* eye-glasses and began to polish the lenses thoughtfully. "Could it have been the same man?

Would he have had time to get out to East Orange and burglarize your house before you got there last night?"

"Yes. When I picked myself out of the gutter I reported the assault to a cop, and he took me down to a nearby station-house, and they asked me a lot of questions. He would have had plenty of time—I didn't get home until one o'clock in the morning."

"I think, Unky," said Ellery, "that the story *you* told me begins to have point. If you'll excuse me, Mr. Hazlitt, I'll be on my way. *Auf wiedersehen!*"

Ellery left old Uneker's little shop and went downtown to Centre Street. He climbed the steps of Police Headquarters, nodded amiably to a desk lieutenant, and made for his father's office. The Inspector was out. Ellery twiddled with an ebony figurine of Bertillon on his father's desk, mused deeply, then went out and began to hunt for Sergeant Velie, the Inspector's chief of operations. He found the mammoth in the Press Room, bawling curses at a reporter.

"Velie," said Ellery, "stop playing bad man and get me some information. Two days ago there was an unsuccessful manhunt on Forty-ninth Street, between Fifth and Sixth Avenues. The chase ended in a little bookshop owned by a friend of mine named Uneker. Local officer was in on it. Uneker told me the story, but I want less colored details. Get me the precinct port like a good fellow, will you?"

Sergeant Velie waggled his big black jaws, glared at the reporter, and thundered off. Ten mintues later he came back with a sheet of paper, and Ellery read it with absorption.

The facts seemed bald enough. Two days before, at the noon hour, a hatless, coatless man with a bloody face had rushed out of the office building three doors from old Uneker's bookshop, shouting: "Help! Police!" Patrolman McCallum had run up, and the man yelled that he had been robbed of a valuable postage stamp—"My one-penny black!" he kept shouting, "my one-penny black!"—and that the thief, black-mustached and wearing heavy blue-tinted spectacles, had just escaped. McCallum had noticed a man of this description a few minutes before, acting peculiarly, enter the nearby bookshop. Follow by the screaming stamp dealer, he dashed into old Uneker's place with drawn revolver. Had a man with black mustache and blue-tinted spectacles come into the shop within the past few minutes? "*Ja*—he?" said old Uneker. "Sure, he iss still here." Where? In the back room looking at some books. McCallum and the bleeding man rushed into Uneker's back room; it was empty. A door leading to the alley from the back room was open; the man had escaped, apparently having been scared off by the noisy entrance of the policeman and the victim a moment before. McCallum had immediately searched neighborhood; the thief had vanished.

The officer then took the complainant's statement. He was, he said, Friederich Ulm, dealer in rare postage stamps. His office was in a tenth-floor room in the building three doors away—the office of his brother Albert, his partner, and himself. He had been exhibiting some valuable items to an invited group of three stamp collectors. Two of them had gone away. Ulm happened to turn his back; and the third, the man with the black mustache and blue-tinted glasses, who had introduced himself as A very Beninson, had swooped on him swiftly from behind and struck at his head with a short iron bar as Ulm twisted back. The blow had cut open Ulm's cheekbone and felled him, half-stunned; and then with the utmost coolness thief had used the same iron bar (which, said the report, from its description was probably a "jimmy") to pry open the lid of a glass-topped cabinet in which a choice collection of stamps was kept. He had snatched from a leather box in the cabinet an extremely high-priced item—"the Queen Victoria one-penny black"—and had then dashed out, locking the door behind him. It had taken the assaulted dealer several minutes to open the door and follow. McCallum went with Ulm to the office, examined the rifled cabinet, took the names and addresses of the three collectors who had been present that morning—with particular note of "Avery Beninson"—scribbled his report, and departed.

The names of the other two collectors were John Hinchman and J. S. Peters. A detective attached to the precinct had visited each in turn, and had then gone to the address of Beninson. Beninson, who presumably had been the man with black mustaches and blue-tinted spectacles, was ignorant of the entire affair; and his physical appearance did not tally with the description of Ulm's assailant. He had received no invitation from the Ulm brothers, he said, to attend the private sale. Yes, he had had an employee, a man with black mustaches and tinted glasses, for two weeks—this man had answered Beninson's advertisement for an assistant to take charge of the collector's private stamp albums, had proved satisfactory, and had suddenly, without explanation or notice, disappeared after two weeks' service. He had disappeared, the detective noted, on the morning of the Ulms's sale.

All attempts to trace this mysterious assistant, who had called himself William Planck, were unsuccessful. The man had vanished among New York City's millions.

Nor was this the end of the story. For the day after the theft old Uneker himself had reported to the precinct detective a queer tale. The previous night—the night of the Ulm theft—said Uneker, he had left his shop for a late dinner; his night clerk had remained on duty. A man had entered the shop, had asked to see *Europe in Chaos,* and had then to the night clerk's astonishment purchased all copies of the book in stock—seven. The man who had made this extraordinary purchase wore black mustaches and blue-tinted spectacles!

"Sort of nuts, ain't it?" growled Sergeant Velie.

"Not at all," smiled Ellery. "In fact, I believe it has a very simple explanation."

"And that ain't the half of it. One of the boys told me just now of a new angle on the case. Two minor robberies were reported from local precincts last night. One was uptown in the Bronx; a man named Hornell said his apartment was broken into during the night, and what do you think? Copy of *Europe in Chaos* which Hornell had bought in this guy Uneker's store was stolen! Nothin' else. Bought it two days ago. Then a dame: named Janet Meakins from Greenwich Village had *her* flat robbed the same night. Thief had taken her copy of *Europe in Chaos*—she'd bought it from Uneker the afternoon before. Screwy, hey?"

"Not at all, Velie. Use your wits." Ellery clapped his hat on his head. "Come along, you Colossus; I want to speak to old Unky again."

They left Headquarters and went uptown.

"Unky," said Ellery, patting the little old bookseller's bald pate affectionately, "how many copies of *Europe in Chaos* you have in stock at the time the thief escaped from your back room?"

"Eleffen."

"Yet only seven were in stock that same evening when thief returned to buy them," murmured Ellery. "Therefore, four copies had been sold between the noon hour two days ago and the dinner hour. So! Unky, do you keep a record of your customers?"

"*Ach*, yes! De few who buy," said old Uneker sadly, "I addt to my mailing lisdt. You vant to see?"

"There is nothing I crave more ardently at the moment."

Uneker led them to the rear of the shop and through a door into the musty back room from whose alley door the thief had escaped two days before. Off this room there was a partitioned cubicle littered with papers, files, and old books. The old bookseller opened a ponderous ledger and, wetting his ancient forefinger, began to slap pages over. "You vant to know de f who boughdt *Europe in Chaos* dot afternoon?"

"*Ja.*"

Uneker hooked a pair of greenish-silver spectacles over his ears and began to read in a singsong voice. "Mr. Hazlit dot's the gentleman you met, Mr. Quveen. *He* bought the second copy, de vun dot vass robbed from his house... Den dere vass Mr. Hornell, an oldt customer. Den a Miss Janet Meakins—*ach!* dese Anglo-Saxon names. *Schrecklich!* Undt de fourt' vun vass Mr. Chester Singermann, uff t'ree-tvelf E Siggsty-fift' Street. Und dot's all."

"Bless your orderly old Teutonic soul," said Ellery. "Velie, cast those Cyclopean peepers of yours this way." There was a door from the cubicle which, from its location, led out into the alley at the rear, like the door in the back room. Ellery bent over the lock; it was splintered away from the wood. He opened the door; the outer piece was scratched and mutilated. Velie nodded. "Forced," he growled. "This guy's a regular Houdini."

Old Uneker was goggle-eyed. "Broken!" he shrilled. "Budt dot door is neffer used! I didn't notice not'ing, undt de detectiff—"

"Shocking work, Velie, on the part of the local man," said Ellery. "Unky, has anything been stolen?" Old Uneker flew to an antiquated bookcase; it was neatly tiered with volumes. He unlocked the case with anguished fingers, rummaging like an aged terrier. Then he heaved a vast sigh. "*Nein,*" he said. "Dose rare vons . . . Not'ing stole."

"I congratulate you. One thing more," said Ellery briskly. "Your mailing list—does it have the business as well as private addresses of your customers?" Uneker nodded. "Better and better. Ta-ta, Unky. You may have a finished story to relate to your other customers after all. Come along, Velie; we're going to visit Mr. Chester Singermann."

They left the bookshop, walked over to Fifth Avenue, and turned north, heading uptown. "Plain as the nose on your face," said Ellery, stretching his long stride to match Velie's. "And that's pretty plain, Sergeant."

"Still looks nutty to me, Mr. Queen."

"On the contrary, we are faced with a strictly logical set of facts. Our thief stole a valuable stamp. He dodged into Uneker's bookshop, contrived to get into the back room. He heard the officer and Friederich Ulm enter, and got busy thinking. If he were caught with the stamp on his person. . . . You see, Velie, the only explanation that will make consistent the business of the subsequent thefts of the same book—a book not valuable in itself—is that the thief, Planck, slipped the stamp between the pages of one of the volumes on a shelf while he was in the back room—it happened by accident to be a copy of *Europe in Chaos*, one of a number kept in stock on the shelf—and made his escape immediately thereafter. But he still had the problem of regaining possession of the stamp—what did Ulm call it?—the 'one-penny black,' whatever *that* may be. So that night he came back, watched for old Uneker to leave the shop, then went in and bought from the clerk all copies of *Europe in Chaos* in the place. He got seven. The stamp was not in any; one of the seven he purchased, otherwise why did he later steal the others which had been bought that afternoon? So far, so good.

Not finding the stamp in any of the seven, then, he returned, broke into Unky's little office during the night—witness the shattered lock—from the alley, and looked up in Unky's Dickensian ledger the names and addresses of those who had bought copies of the book during that afternoon. The next night he robbed Hazlitt; Planck evidently followed him from his office. Planck saw at once that he had made a mistake; the condition of the weeks-old book would have told him that this wasn't the book purchased only the day before. So he hurried out to East Orange, knowing Hazlitt's private as well as business address, and stole Hazlitt's recently purchased copy. No luck there either, so he feloniously visited Hornell and Janet Meakins, steal-ing their copies. Now, there is still one purchaser unaccounted for, which is why we are calling upon Singermann. Planck was unsuccessful in his theft of Homell's and Meakins's books, he will inevitably visit Singermann, and we will want to beat our wily thief to it if possible."

Chester Singermann, they found, was a young student living with his parents in a battered old apartment-house flat. Yes, he still had his copy of *Europe in Chaos*—needed it for plementary reading in political economy—and he produced it. Ellery went through it carefully, page for page; there was trace of the missing stamp.

"Mr. Singermann, did you find an old postage stamp tween the leaves of this volume?" asked Ellery.

The student shook his head. "I haven't even opened it Stamp? What issue? I've got a little collection of my own, you know."

"It doesn't matter," said Ellery hastily, who had heard the maniacal enthusiasm of stamp collectors, and he and Velie beat a precipitate retreat.

"It's quite evident," explained Ellery to the Sergeant, "that our slippery Planck found the stamp in either Hornell's or Miss Meakins's. Which rob-bery was first in point of time, Velie?"

"Seem to remember that this Meakins woman was robbed second."

"Then the one-penny black was in her copy. . . . Here's that office build-ing. Let's pay a little visit to Mr. Friederick Ulm."

Number 1026 on the tenth floor of the building bore a black legend on its frosted-glass door:

ULM
Dealers in
Old & Rare Stamps

Ellery and Sergeant Velie went in and found themselves in a large office. The walls were covered with glass cases in which, separately mounted, could be seen hundreds of canceled and uncanceled postage stamps. Several special cabinets on tables contained, evidently, more valuable items. The place was cluttered; it had a musty air astonishingly like that of old Uneker's bookshop.

Three men looked up. One, from a crisscrossed plaster on his cheekbone, was apparently Friederich Ulm himself, a tall gaunt old German with sparse hair and the fanatic look of the confirmed collector. The second man was just as tall and gaunt and old; he wore a green eyeshade and bore a striking resemblance to Ulm, although from his nervous movements and shaky hands he must have been much older. The third man was a little fellow, quite stout, with an expressionless face.

Ellery introduced himself and Sergeant Velie; and the third man picked up his ears. "Not *the* Ellery Queen?" he said, waddling forward. "I'm Heffley, investigator for the insurance people. Glad to meet you." He pumped Ellery's hand with vigor. "These gentlemen are the Ulm brothers, who own this place. Friederich and Albert. Mr. Albert Ulm was out of the office at the time of the sale and robbery. Too bad; might have nabbed the thief."

Friederich Ulm broke into an excited gabble of German. Ellery listened with a smile, nodding at every fourth word. "I see, Mr. Ulm. The situation, then, was this: you sent invitations by mail to three well-known collectors to attend a special exhibition of rare stamps—object, sale. Three men called on you two mornings ago, purporting to be Messrs. Hinchman, Peters, and Beninson. Hinchman and Peters you knew by sight, but Beninson you did not. Very well. Several items were purchased by the first two collectors. The man you thought was Beninson lingered behind, struck you—yes, yes, I know all that. Let me see the rifled cabinet, please."

The brothers led him to a table in the center of the office. On it there was a flat cabinet, with a lid of ordinary thin glass framed by a narrow rectangle of wood. Under the glass reposed a number of mounted stamps, lying nakedly on a field of black satin. In the center of the satin lay a leather case, open; its white lining had been denuded of its stamp. Where the lid of the cabinet had been wrenched open there were the unmistakable marks of a "jimmy," four in number. The catch snapped and broken.

"Amatchoor," said Sergeant Velie with a snort. "You could damn' near force that locked lid up with your fingers."

Ellery's sharp eyes were absorbed in what lay before him. "Mr. Ulm," he said, turning to the wounded dealer, "the stamp you call 'the one-penny black' was in this open leather box?"

"Yes, Mr. Queen. But the leather box was closed when the thief forced open the cabinet."

"Then how did he know so unerringly what to steal?" Fi erich Ulm touched his cheek tenderly. "The stamps in cabinet were not for sale; they're the cream of our collection; every stamp in this case is worth hundreds. But when the three men were here we naturally talked about the rarer items, and I opened this cabinet to show them our very valuable stamps. So the thief saw the one-penny black. He was a collector, Queen, or he wouldn't have chosen that particular stamp to steal. It has a funny history."

"Heavens!" said Ellery. "Do these things have histories?"

Heffley, the man from the insurance company, laughed. "And how! Mr. Friederich and Mr. Albert Ulm are well kn to the trade for owning two of the most unique stamps issued, both identical. The one-penny black, as it is called by collectors, is a British stamp first issued in 1840; there arelots of them around, and even an uncanceled one is worth seventeen and a half dollars in American money. But the in the possession of these gentlemen are worth thirty thousand dollars a piece, Mr. Queen—that's what makes the theft dog-gone serious. In fact, my company is heavily involved, since the stamps are both insured for their full value."

"Thirty thousand dollars!" groaned Ellery. "That's a lot money for a little piece of dirty paper. Why are they so valuable?"

Albert Ulm nervously pulled his green shade lower lower over his eyes. "Because both of ours were actually initialed by Queen Victoria, that's why. Sir Rowland Hill, the man who created and founded the standard penny-postage system in England in 1839, was responsible for the issue of the one-penny black. Her Majesty was so delighted—England, like other countries, had had a great deal of trouble working out a successful postage system—that she autographed the first two stamps off the press and gave them to the designer—I don't recall his name. Her autograph made them immensely valuable. My brother and I were lucky to get our hands on the only two in existence."

"Where's the twin? I'd like to take a peep at a stamp worth a queen's ransom."

The brothers bustled to a large safe looming in a corner of the office. They came back, Albert carrying a leather case as if it were a consignment of golden bullion, and Friederich anxiously holding his elbow, as if he were a squad of armed guards detailed to protect the consignment. Ellery turned the thing over in his fingers; it felt thick and stiff. It was an average-sized stamp rectangle, imperforate, bordered with a black design, and containing an engraving in profile view of Queen Victoria's head—all done in tones of black. On the lighter portion of the face appeared two tiny initials in faded black ink—V. R.

"They're both exactly alike," said Friederich Ulm. "Even to the initials."

"Very interesting," said Ellery, returning the case. The brothers scurried back, placed the stamp in a drawer of the safe, and locked the safe with painful care. "You closed the cabinet, of course, after your three visitors looked over the stamps inside?"

"Oh, yes," said Friederich Ulm. "I closed the case of the one-penny black itself, and then I locked the cabinet."

"And did you send the three invitations yourself? I noticed you have no typewriter here."

"We use a public stenographer in Room 1102 for all our correspondence, Mr. Queen."

Ellery thanked the dealers gravely, waved to the insurance man, nudged Sergeant Velie's meaty ribs, and the two men left the office. In Room 1102 they found a sharp-featured young woman. Sergeant Velie flashed his badge, and Ellery was soon reading carbon copies of the three Ulm invitations. He took note of the names and addresses, and the two men left.

*   *   *

They visited the collector named John Hinchman first. Hinchman was a thick-set old man with white hair and gimlet eyes. He was brusque and uncommunicative. Yes, he had been present in the Ulms's office two mornings before. Yes, he knew Peters. No, he'd never met Beninson before. The one-penny black? Of course. Every collector knew of the valuable stamps owned by the Ulm brothers; those little scraps of paper bearing the initials of a queen were famous in stampdom. Theft? Bosh! He, Hinchman, knew nothing of Beninson, or whoever it was that impersonated Beninson. He, Hinchman, had left before the thief. He, Hinchman, furthermore didn't care two raps in Hades who stole the stamp; all he wanted was to be let strictly alone.

Sergeant Velie exhibited certain animal signs of hostility; but Ellery grinned, sank his strong fingers into the muscle of the Sergeant's arm, and herded him out of Hinchman's house They took the subway uptown.

J. S. Peters, they found, was a middle-aged man, tall and thin and yellow as Chinese sealing wax. He seemed anxious to be of assistance. Yes, he and Hinchman had left the Ulms's office together, before the third man. He had never seen third man before, although he had heard of Beninson from other collectors. Yes, he knew all about the one-penny blacks, had even tried to buy one of them from Friederich Ulm years before; but the Ulms had refused to sell.

"Philately," said Ellery outside to Sergeant Velie, whose honest face looked pained at the word, "is a curious hobby. It seems to afflict its victims with a species of mania. I doubt these stamp-collecting fellows would murder each other for one of the things."

The Sergeant was wrinkling his nose. "How's she look now?" he asked rather anxiously.

"Velie," replied Ellery, "she looks swell—and different."

They found Avery Beninson in an old brownstone near the River; he was a mild-mannered and courteous host.

"No, I never did see that invitation," Beninson said, see, I hired this man who called himself William Planck, and he took care of my collection and the bulky mail all serious collectors have. The man knew stamps, all right. For two weeks he was invaluable to me. He must have intercepted the Ulms's invitation. He saw his chance to get into their office, went there, said he was Avery Beninson . . ." The collector shrugged "It was quite simple, I suppose, for an unscrupulous man."

"Of course, you haven't had word from him since the morning of the theft?"

"Naturally not. He made his haul and lit out."

"Just what did he do for you, Mr. Beninson?"

"The ordinary routine of the philatelic assistant—assorting, cataloguing, mounting, answering correspondence. He lived here with me for the two weeks he was in my employ." Beninson grinned deprecatingly. "You see, I'm a bachelor—live in this big shack all alone. I was really glad of his company, although he *was* a queer one."

"A queer one?"

"Well," said Beninson, "he was a retiring sort of creature. Had very few personal belongings, and I found those gone two days ago. He didn't seem to like people, either. He always went to his own room when friends of mine or collectors called, as if he didn't want to mix with company."

"Then there isn't anyone else who might be able to supplement your description of him?"

"Unfortunately, no. He was a fairly tall man, well advanced in age, I should say. But then his dark glasses and heavy black mustache would make him stand out anywhere."

Ellery sprawled his long figure over the chair, slumping on his spine. "I'm most interested in the man's habits, Mr. Beninson. Individual idiosyncrasies are often the innocent means by which criminals are apprehended, as the good Sergeant here will tell you. Please think hard. Didn't the man exhibit any oddities of habit?"

Beninson pursed his lips with anxious concentration. His face brightened. "By George, yes! He was a snuff taker."

Ellery and Sergeant Velie looked at each other. "That's interesting," said Ellery with a smile. "So is my father—Inspector Queen, you know—and I've had the dubious pleasure of watching a snuff taker's gyrations ever since my childhood. Planck inhaled snuff regularly?"

"I shouldn't say that exactly, Mr. Queen," replied Beninson with a frown. "In fact, in the two weeks he was with me I saw him take snuff only once, and I invariably spent all day with him working in this room. It was last week; I happened to go out for a few moments, and when I returned I saw him holding a carved little box, sniffing from a pinch of something between his fingers. He put the box away quickly, as if he didn't want me to see it—although I didn't care, lord knows, so long as he didn't smoke in here. I've had one fire from a careless assistant's cigarette, and I don't want another."

Ellery's face had come alive. He sat up straight and began to finger his *pince-nez* eyeglasses studiously. "You didn't know the man's address, I suppose?" he asked slowly.

"No, I did not. I'm afraid I took him on without the proper precautions." The collector sighed. "I'm fortunate that he d steal anything from me. My collection is worth a lot of money."

"No doubt," said Ellery in a pleasant voice. He rose." May I use your telephone, Mr. Beninson?"

"Surely."

Ellery consulted a telephone directory and made several calls, speaking in tones so low that neither Beninson nor Sargeant Velie could hear what he was saying. When he put down the instrument he said: "If you can spare a half-hour, Beninson, I'd like to have you take a little jaunt with us downtown."

Beninson seemed astonished; but he smiled, said: "I'd be delighted," and reached for his coat.

Ellery commandeered a taxicab outside, and the three were driven to Forty-ninth Street. He excused himself they got out before the little bookshop, hurried inside came out after a moment with old Uneker, who locked his with shaking fingers.

In the Ulm brothers' office they found Heffley, the insurance man, and Hazlitt, Uneker's customer, waiting for them. "Glad you could come," said Ellery cheerfully to both men. "Good afternoon, Mr. Ulm. A little conference, and I think we'll this business cleared up to the Queen's taste. Ha, ha!"

Friederich Ulm scratched his head; Albert Ulm, sitting a corner with his hatchet knees jack-knifed, his green shade over his eyes, nodded.

"We'll have to wait," said Ellery. "I've asked Mr. Peters and Mr. Hinchman to come, too. Suppose we sit down."

They were silent for the most part, and not a little uneasy. No one spoke as Ellery strolled about the office, examining the rare stamps in their wall cases with open curiosity, whistling softly to himself. Sergeant Velie eyed him doubtfully. Then the door opened, and Hinchman and Peters appeared together. They stopped short at the threshold, looked at each other, shrugged, and walked in. Hinchman was scowling.

"What's the idea, Mr. Queen?" he said. "I'm a busy man."

"A not unique condition," smiled Ellery. "Ah, Mr. Peters, good day. Introductions, I think, are not entirely called for . . . Sit down, gentlemen!" he said in a sharper voice, and they sat down.

The door opened and a small, gray, birdlike little man peered in at them. Sergeant Velie looked astounded, and Ellery nodded gaily. "Come in, Dad, come in! You're just in time for the first act."

Inspector Richard Queen cocked his little squirrel's head, looked at the assembled company shrewdly, and closed the door behind him. "What the devil is the idea of the call, son?"

"Nothing very exciting. Not a murder, or anything in your line. But it may interest you. Gentlemen, Inspector Queen." The Inspector grunted, sat down, took out his old brown snuff box, and inhaled with the voluptuous gasp of long practice.

Ellery stood serenely in the hub of the circle of chairs, looking down at curious faces. "The theft of the one-penny black, as you inveterate stamp fiends call it," he began, "presented a not uninteresting problem. I say 'presented' advisedly. For the case is solved."

"Is this that business of the stamp robbery I was hearing about down at Headquarters?" asked the Inspector.

"Yes."

"Solved?" asked Beninson. "I don't think I understand, Mr. Queen. Have you found Planck?"

Ellery waved his arm negligently. "I was never too sanguine of catching Mr. William Planck, as such. You see, he wore tinted spectacles and black mustachios. Now, anyone familiar with the science of crime detection will tell you that the average person identifies faces by superficial details. A black mustache catches the eye. Tinted glasses impress the memory. In fact, Mr. Hazlitt here, who from Uneker's description is a man of poor observational powers, recalled even after seeing his assailant in dim street light that the man wore a black mustache and tinted glasses. But this is all fundamental and not even particularly smart. It was reasonable to assume that Planck wanted these special facial characteristics to be remembered. I was convinced that he had disguised himself, that the mustache was probably a false one, and that ordinarily he does not wear tinted glasses."

They all nodded.

This was the first and simplest of the three psychological sign posts to the culprit," Ellery smiled and turned suddenly to the Inspector. "Dad, you're an old snuff addict. How many times a day do you stuff that unholy brown dust up your nostrils?"

The Inspector blinked. "Oh, every half-hour or so. Sometimes as often as you smoke cigarettes."

"Precisely. Now, Mr. Beninson told me that in the weeks during which Planck stayed at his house, and despite the fact that Mr. Beninson worked side by side with the every day, he saw Planck take snuff only *once.* Please observe that here we have a most enlightening and suggestive fact."

From the blankness of their faces it was apparent that, far from seeing light, their minds on this point were in total darkness. There was one exception—the Inspector; he nodded, shifted in his chair, and coolly began to study the faces about him.

Ellery lit a cigarette. "Very well," he said, expelling little puffs of smoke, "there you have the second psychological factor. The third was this: Planck, in a fairly public place, bashes Mr. Friederich Ulm over the face with the robust intention of stealing a valuable stamp. Any thief under the circumstances would desire speed above all things. Mr. Ulm was only half-stunned—he might come to and make an outcry; a customer might walk in; Mr. Albert Ulm might return unexpectedly—"

"Just a moment, son," said the Inspector. "I unders there are two of the stamp thingamajigs in existence. I'd to see the one that's still here."

Ellery nodded. "Would one of you gentlemen please get the stamp?"

Friederich Ulm rose, pottered over to the safe, tinkered with the dials, opened the steel door, fussed about the interior a moment, and came back with the leather case containing the second one-penny black. The Inspector examined the thick little scrap curiously; a thirty-thousand-dollar bit of old paper as awesome to him as to Ellery.

He almost dropped it when he heard Ellery say to Sergeant Velie: "Sergeant, may I borrow your revolver?"

Velie's massive jaw seesawed as he fumbled in his hip pocket and produced a long-barreled police revolver. Ellery took it and hefted it thoughtfully. Then his fingers closed about the butt and he walked over to the rifled cabinet in the middle of the room.

"Please observe, gentlemen—to expand my third point—that in order to open this cabinet Planck used an iron bar; and that in prying up the lid he found it necessary to insert the bar between the lid and the front wall four times, as the four marks under the lid indicate.

"Now, as you can see, the cabinet is covered with thin glass. Moreover, it was locked, and the one-penny black was in this closed leather case inside. Planck stood about here, I should judge, and mark that the iron bar was in his hand. What would you gentlemen expect a thief, working against time, to do under these circumstances?"

They stared. The Inspector's mouth tightened, and a grin began to spread over the expanse of Sergeant Velie's face.

"But it's so clear," said Ellery. "Visualize it. I'm Planck. The revolver in my hand is an iron 'jimmy.' I'm standing over the cabinet . . ." His eyes gleamed behind the *pince-nez*, and he raised the revolver high over his head. And then, deliberately, he began to bring the steel barrel down on the thin sheeting of glass atop the cabinet. There was a scream from Albert Ulm, and Friederich Ulm half-rose, glaring. Ellery's hand stopped a half-inch from the glass.

"Don't break that glass, you fool!" shouted the green-shaded dealer. "You'll only—"

He leaped forward and stood before the cabinet, trembling arms outspread as if to protect the case and its contents. Ellery grinned and prodded the man's palpitating belly with the muzzle of the revolver. "I'm glad you stopped me, Mr. Ulm. Put your hands up. Quickly!"

"Why—why, what do you mean?" gasped Albert Ulm, raising his arms with frantic rapidity.

"I mean," said Ellery gently, "that you're William Planck, and that brother Friederich is your accomplice!"

The brothers Ulm sat trembling in their chairs, and Sergeant Velie stood over them with a nasty smile. Albert Ulm had gone to pieces; he was quivering like an aspen leaf in high wind.

"A very simple, almost an elementary, series of deductions," Ellery was saying. "Point three first. Why did the thief, instead of taking the most logical course of smashing the glass with the iron bar, choose to waste precious minutes using a 'jimmy' four times to force open the lid? *Obviously to protect the other stamps in the cabinet which lay open to possible injury,* as Mr. Albert Ulm has just graphically pointed out. And who had the greatest concern in protecting these other stamps? Hinchman, Peter, Beninson, even the mythical Planck himself? Of course not. Only the Ulm brothers, owners of the stamp."

Old Uneker began to chuckle; he nudged the Inspector "See? Didn't I say he vass smardt? Now me—me, I'd nei t'ink of dot."

"And why didn't Planck steal these other stamps in the cabinet? You would expect a thief to do that. Planck did not But if the *Herren* Ulm were the thieves, the theft of the other stamps became pointless."

"How about that snuff business, Mr. Queen?" asked Peters.

"Yes. The conclusion is plain from the fact that Planck apparently indulged only once during the days he worked with Mr. Beninson. Since snuff addicts partake freely and often, Planck wasn't a snuff addict. Then it wasn't snuff he inhaled that day. What else is sniffed in a similar manner? Well—drugs in powder form—heroin! What are the characteristics of a heroin addict? Nervous, drawn appearance; gauntness, almost emaciation; and most important, telltale eyes, the pupils of which contract under influence of the drug. Then here another explanation for the tinted glasses Planck wore. I served a double purpose—as an easily recognizable disguise and also to conceal his eyes, which would give his vice addiction away! But when I observed that Mr. Albert Ulm"—Ellery went over to the cowering man and ripped the gray eyeshade away, revealing two stark, pinpoint pupils—"wore this shade, it was a psychological confirmation of his identity as Planck."

"Yes, but that business of stealing all those books," said Hazlitt.

"Part of a very pretty and rather far-fetched plot," said Ellery. "With Albert Ulm the disguised thief, Friederich Ulm, who exhibited the wound on his cheek, must have been an accomplice. Then with the Ulm brothers the thieves, the entire business of the books was a blind. The attack on Friederich the ruse of the bookstore escape, the trail of the minor robbery of copies of *Europe in Chaos*—a cleverly planned series incidents to authenticate the fact that there was an outside thief, to convince the police and the insurance company that the stamp actually was stolen when it was not. Object, of course, to collect the insurance without parting with the stamp. These men are fanatical collectors."

Heffley wriggled his fat little body uncomfortably. "That's all very nice, Mr. Queen, but where the deuce is that stamp they stole from themselves? Where'd they hide it?"

"I thought long and earnestly about that, Heffley. For while my trio of deductions were psychological indications of guilt, the discovery of the stolen stamp in the Ulms's possession would be evidential proof." The Inspector was turning the second stamp over mechanically. "I said to myself," Ellery went on, "in a reconsideration of the problem: what would be the most likely hiding place for the stamp? And then I remembered that the two stamps were identical, even the initials of the good Queen being in the same place. So I said to myself: if I were Messrs Ulm, I should hide that stamp—like the character in Edgar Allan Poe's famous tale—in the most obvious place. And what is the most obvious place?"

Ellery sighed and returned the unused revolver to Sergeant Velie. "Dad," he remarked to the Inspector, who started guiltily, "I think that if you allow one of the philatelists in our company to examine the second one-penny black in your fingers, you'll find that the *first* has been pasted with noninjurious rubber cement precisely over the second!"

BRUCE HOLLAND ROGERS

Enduring as Dust

I DRIVE PAST THE DEPARTMENT OF AGRICULTURE every morning
on my way to work, and every morning I slow to a crawl so that I can
absorb the safe and solid feel of that building as I go by. The north side
of Agriculture stretches for two uninterrupted city blocks. The massive
walls look as thick as any castle's. Inside, the place is a warren of offices and
suboffices, a cozy organizational hierarchy set in stone. I've often thought
to myself that if an H-bomb went off right over the Mall, then the White
House, the Capitol, the memorials and the reflecting pools would all be
blown to ash and steam, but in the midst of the wreckage and the settling
dust, there would stand the Department of Agriculture, and the work inside
its walls would go securely on.

I don't have that kind of security. The building that houses the
Coordinating Administration for Productivity is smaller than our agency's
name. The roof leaks. The walls are thin and haven't been painted since the
Great Depression.

That I am here is my own fault. Twenty years ago, when I worked for
the Bureau of Reclamation, I realized that the glory days of public dam
building were over. I imagined that a big RIF wave was coming to the
bureau, and I was afraid that I'd be one of those drowned in the Reduction
In Force. So I went looking for another agency.

When I found the Coordinating Administration for Productivity, I
thought I had found the safest place in Washington to park my career. I'd
ask CAP staffers what their agency did.

"We advise other agencies," they would say.

"We coordinate private and public concerns."

"We review productivity."

"We revise strategies."

"We provide oversight."

"But clearly, clearly, we could always do more."

In other words, nobody knew. From the top down, no one could tell me precisely what the administrative mission was. And I thought to myself, I want to be a part of this. No one will ever be able to suggest that we are no longer needed, that it's time for all of us to clear out our desks, that our job is done, because no one knows what our job *is*.

But I was wrong about the Bureau of Reclamation. It hasn't had a major project for two decades, doesn't have any planned, and yet endures, and will continue to endure, through fiscal year after fiscal year, time without end. It is too big to die.

The Coordinating Administration for Productivity, on the other hand, employs just thirty civil servants. We're always on the bubble. With a stroke of the pen, we could vanish from next year's budget. All it would take is for someone to notice us long enough to erase us. And so, as I soon learned, there was an administrative mission statement after all: Don't Get Noticed.

That's why we never complained to GSA about the condition of our building, why we turned the other cheek when FDA employees started parking in our lot and eventually took it over. That's also why no one ever confronted the secretaries about the cats named Dust. And above all, that is why I was so nervous on the morning that our chief administrator called an "urgent meeting."

I sat waiting outside of the administrator's office with Susana de Vega, the assistant administrator, and Tom Willis, Susana's deputy. "I don't like this," Tom said. "I don't like this one damn bit."

Susana hissed at him and looked at the administrator's secretary. But Roxie wasn't listening to us. She was talking, through an open window, to the cat on the fire escape. The cat was a gray torn with the tattered ears of a streetfighter. He backed up warily as Roxie put the food bowl down. "Relax, Dust," she said. "I'm not going to hurt you."

It was January, a few days before the presidential inauguration, and the air coming in through the window was cold, but nobody asked Roxie to close it.

"When has Cooper ever called an *urgent* meeting?" Tom continued in a lower voice. "Hell, how many times has he called a meeting of any damn kind? He's up to something. He's got to throw his goddam Schedule-C weight around while he still has it to throw."

Throwing his weight around didn't sound like Bill Cooper, but I didn't bother to say so. After all, Cooper was a political appointee on his way out, so whether he threw his weight around or not, Tom's underlying point was correct: Cooper was a loose cannon. He had nothing to lose. Intentionally or not, he might blow us up.

Roxie waited to see if the cat would consent to having his chin scratched, but Dust held his ground until the window was closed. Even then, he approached the food warily, as if checking for booby traps.

Susana told Tom to relax. "Two weeks," she reminded him. "Three at the outside."

"And then God only knows what we'll be getting," Tom said, pulling at his chin. "I hate politics."

Roxie's intercom buzzed, and without turning away from the cat she told us, "You can go in now."

I followed Susana and Tom in, and found Cooper nestled deeply in his executive chair, looking as friendly and harmless as he ever had. His slightly drooping eyelids made him seem, as always, half asleep. He waved us into our seats, and as I sat down, I realized how little he had done to personalize his office in the twelve years of his tenure. Everything in the room was government issue. There weren't any family pictures or the usual paperweights made by children or grandchildren. In fact, there wasn't anything on the surface of his desk at all. It was as if Cooper had been anticipating, from the day he moved in, the day when he would have to move out.

There was *some* decoration in the room, a pen and ink drawing on the wall behind Cooper, but that had been there for as long as I had been with the CAP. It showed an Oriental-looking wooden building next to a plot of empty ground, and I knew from having looked once, maybe fifteen years ago, that the drawing wasn't just hung on the wall. The frame had been nailed into the paneling, making it a permanent installation.

"People," Cooper said from deep inside his chair, "we have a problem." He let that last word hang in the air as he searched for what to say next.

Susana, Tom and I leaned forward in our chairs. "An impropriety," he went on. We leaned a little more. "A mystery."

We watched expectantly as Cooper opened his desk drawer and took out a sheet of paper. He studied it for a long time, and then said, "You people know my management style. I've been hands-off. I've always let you people handle the details," by which he meant that he didn't know what we did all day and didn't care, so long as we told him that everything was running smoothly. He tapped the sheet of paper and said, "But here is something that demands my attention, and I want it cleared up while I'm still in charge."

And then he read from the letter in his hand. The writer represented something called the Five-State Cotton Consortium, and he had come to Washington to get advice on federal funding for his organization. He had taken an employee of the Coordinating Administration for Productivity to lunch, picking her brain about the special appropriations process as well as various grant sources. The woman had been very helpful, and the letter writer just wanted Cooper to know that at least one member of his staff was really on the ball. The helpful staffer's name was Kim Semper.

At the sound of that name, I felt ice form in the pit of my stomach. I stared straight ahead, keeping my expression as plain as I could manage. I knew some of what Cooper was going to say next, but I tried to look genuinely surprised when he told us what had happened after he received the letter.

"I wanted to touch base with Ms. Semper and make sure that the citizen hadn't actually paid for her lunch. You people know as well as I do that we don't want any conflict of interest cases."

"Of course not," said Susana. "But I don't see how there could be any such conflict. We don't actually make funding decisions."

"We don't?" Cooper said, and then recovered to say, "No, of course not. But you people will agree that we wouldn't want even the *appearance* of impropriety. And anyway, that doesn't matter. What matters is that in my search for Kim Semper, I came up empty. We don't have an employee by that name."

Trying to sound more convincing than I felt, I said, "Maybe it's a mistake, Bill. Maybe the letter writer had the name wrong, or sent the letter to the wrong agency."

"Hell, yes!" Tom said with too much enthusiasm. "It's just some damn case of mistaken identity!"

But Cooper wasn't going to be turned easily. "I called the citizen," he told us. "No mistake. Someone is posing as an officer of our agency, a criminal offense."

I said, "Doesn't there have to be intent to defraud for this to be a crime?"

Cooper frowned. "The citizen did buy lunch for this Kim Semper. She benefited materially." He shook the letter at me. "This is a serious matter."

"And one we'll get to the bottom of," Susana promised.

"I want it done before my departure," Cooper said. "I don't want to saddle my successor with any difficulties," by which he meant that he didn't want to leave behind any dirty laundry that might embarrass him when he was no longer in a position to have it covered up.

Susana said again, "We'll get to the bottom of it."

Cooper nodded at Tom. "I want a single point of responsibility on this, so the personnel director will head up the investigation."

With Cooper still looking at him, Tom looked at me expectantly, and I felt compelled to speak up. "That would be me," I said. "Tom's your deputy assistant."

"Of course," Cooper said, covering. He turned to me. "And you'll report to him." Then he added, "You aren't too busy to take care of this matter, I assume."

"It'll be tight," I said, thinking of the Russian novel I'd been wading through for the last week, "but I'll squeeze it in."

Outside of Cooper's office, Susana patted Tom's shoulder, then mine, and said with complete ambiguity, "You know what to do." Then she disappeared down the hall, into her own office.

Roxie's cat was gone, but Roxie had something else to distract her now. She was reading a GPO publication called, *Small Business Administration Seed Projects: Program Announcement and Guidelines.* She didn't even look up when Tom hissed at me, "Sit on it!"

"What?"

"You know damn well what I mean," Tom said through his teeth. "I don't know what this Kim Semper thing is all about, and I don't want to know! This is just the kind of problem that could blow us out of the goddam water!"

I said, "Are you telling me to ignore an assignment from the chief administrator?"

I could see in Tom's eyes the recognition that he had already been too specific. "Not at all," he said in a normal voice, loud enough for Roxie to overhear if she were listening. "I'm telling you to handle this in the most appropriate fashion." Then he, too, bailed out, heading for his own office.

I found my secretary, Vera, trying to type with a calico cat in her lap. The cat was purring and affectionately digging its claws into Vera's knee.

"Damn it, Vera," I said, surprising myself, "the memo specifies feeding only. Everybody knows that. You are not supposed to have the cat inside the building!"

"You hear that, Dust?" Vera said as she rubbed behind the cat's ears. "It's back out into the cold with you." But she made no move to get up.

"Hold my calls," I growled. I went into my office and closed the door, wishing that I had a copy of the legendary memo so that I could read chapter and verse to Vera. It was bad enough that the secretaries had distorted the wording of the memo, issued well over twenty years ago, that had allowed them to feed a stray cat named Dust, "and only a cat named Dust." It seemed like every so often, they had to push beyond even the most liberal limits of that allowance, and no manager was willing to make an issue of it, lest it turn into a civil service grievance that would bring an OPM investigation crashing down around our ears.

I didn't stew about the cat for long. I still had Kim Semper on my mind. It took me a few minutes to find the key to my file cabinet, but once I had the drawer open, there weren't many folders to search through before I found what I wanted. I untaped the file folder marked PRIVATE and pulled out the letter. It was addressed to me and sported an eleven-year-old date. "After failing to determine just who her supervisor is," the text began, "I have decided to write to you, the Director of Personnel, to commend one of your administrators, Miss Kim Semper." The story from there was pretty much the same: a citizen had come to Washington looking for information, had stumbled across the Coordinating Administration for Productivity, and had ended up buying Semper's lunch in exchange for her insights on the intricacies of doing business in the Beltway. Though he had been unable to contact her subsequently, her advice had been a big help to him.

After checking the personnel files, I had called the letter writer to tell him that he'd been mistaken, that there was no Kim Semper here at the CAP. Maybe, I suggested, he had gone to some other agency and confused the names? But he was sure that it was the CAP that he had consulted, and he described our building right down to the tiny, nearly unreadable gray lettering that announced the agency's name on the front door.

In a government agency, a mystery, any mystery, is a potential bomb. If you're not sure of what something is, then you assume that it's going to blow up in your face if you mess with it. At the CAP, where everything was uncertain and shaky to begin with, the unknown seemed even more dangerous. So I had buried the letter.

Now maybe it was coming back to haunt me. I wondered if I should cover my tail by Xeroxing my letter and bringing Cooper a copy right now. "Hey, Bill. I had to check my files on this, to make sure, but would you believe . . ." Maybe that would be good damage control.

But maybe not. After all, Cooper seemed to think this was an urgent matter. I had known about it for eleven years and done nothing. And my letter was so old that I probably didn't have to worry about it hurting me if I didn't bring up its existence. By now, the writer himself might not even remember sending it to me. Perhaps the man was even dead. If I kept my mouth shut, it was just possible that no one would ever know about my Kim Semper letter. And if that was what I wanted, then it would help my cause to do just what Tom had urged: To sit on the investigation, to ignore Kim Semper until the executive branch resignations worked their way down, layer by layer, from the new president's cabinet to our agency, and Cooper was on his way.

Either option, hiding the letter or revealing it, had its dangers. No matter how I played it out in my mind, I couldn't see the safe bet. I returned to what I'd been doing before the meeting with Cooper, and I should have been able to concentrate on it. Napoleon was watching this Polish general, who wanted to impress him, trying to swim some cavalry across a Russian river, but the horses were drowning and everything was a mess. It was exciting, but it didn't hold my attention. I read the same page over and over, distracted with worry.

At the end of the day, there was no cat in Vera's lap, but there was a skinny little tabby begging on the fire escape. At her desk, Vera was pouring some cat food into a bowl labeled, "Dust."

"Sorry I snapped earlier," I said.

"Bad day?" Vera said, opening the window.

"The worst," I told her, noticing the stack of outgoing mail on her desk. "Is that something I asked you to do?"

"Oh, I'm just getting some information for the staff library," she said.

I nodded, trying to think of something managerial to say. "You're self-directed, Vera. I like to see that."

"Oh, I've always been that way," she told me. "I can't stand to be idle." She opened the window to feed the cat and said, "Here you go, Dust."

Cooper called another meeting for Thursday of the next week. It was the day after the inauguration, and he must have felt the ticking clock. Before the meeting, Tom called me.

"How's your investigation coming?" he said.

"Slowly."

"Good. That's damn good. See you in the old man's office."

For once there wasn't a cat on Roxie's fire escape. Cooper's door was open, and I walked right in. Susana and Tom were already there, and Cooper motioned me to a seat. Cooper didn't waste any time.

"What have you got?"

I opened my notebook. "First, I double-checked the personnel files, not just the current ones, but going back twenty-five years." I looked at Cooper grimly. "No one by the name of Kim Semper has *ever* worked for the Coordinating Administration for Productivity."

"Yes, yes," Cooper said. "What else?"

"I called over to the Office of Personnel Management. There is not now, nor has there ever been, anywhere in the civil service system, an employee named Kim Semper." I closed the notebook and put on the face of a man who has done his job well.

Cooper stared at me. I pretended to look back at him earnestly, but my focus was actually on the framed pen and ink behind him. If I had to give it a title, I decided, it would be, "Japanese Shed With Empty Lot."

At last Cooper said, "Is that all?"

"Well, Bill, I haven't been able to give this my full attention."

"It's been a week, a *week* since I brought this up to you people."

"And a hellish week it's been," I said, looking to Tom for help.

"That's true," Tom jumped in. "The inauguration has stirred things up. We've had an unusually, ah, unusually heavy run of requests." Cooper frowned, and I could see Tom's hands tighten on the side of his chair. He was hoping, I knew, that Cooper wouldn't say, "Requests for what? From whom?"

Susana saved us both by saying, "I'm ashamed of the two of you! Don't you have any sense of priorities? And, Tom, you're supposed to be supervising this investigation. That means staying on top of it, making sure it's progressing." She turned to Cooper. "We'll have something substantial next week, Bill."

"I don't know, people," Cooper said. "Realistically, something like this is out of your purview. Maybe it calls for an outside investigator."

Cooper was almost certainly bluffing. Any dirt at the bottom of this would cling to him like tar if we brought in the consul general's office. He wanted to keep this internal as much as we did.

Even so, Susana paled. She played it cool, but it was a strain on her. "Why don't you see what we come up with in seven working days? Then you can decide."

Minutes later, in the hallway, Tom said, "So what now?"

"Don't look at me," Susana told him without breaking stride. "I pulled your bacon out of the fire, boys. Don't ask me to think for you, too." Then over her shoulder, she added, "You'd just better appear to be making progress by our next little get-together."

Before he left me standing alone in the hallway, Tom said, "You heard the lady, Ace. Let's see some goddam action."

In my office, with the door closed behind me, I finished another chapter of the Russian novel and then got right on the case. I cleared space on the floor and laid out the personnel files for the last eleven years. It made

sense to assume that "Kim Semper" was an insider, or had an inside con-
federate who could arrange her lunchtime meetings. And I knew that Ms.
Semper had been working this free-lunch scam since at least the date of my
letter. I figured that I could at least narrow down my suspect pool by weed-
ing out anyone who hadn't been with the CAP for that long.

Unfortunately, this didn't narrow things much. Even Cooper, by virtue
of three straight presidential victories for his party, had been with the CAP
for longer than that.

So what did I really have to go on? Just two letters of praise for Kim
Semper, dated eleven years apart. The letter writers themselves had met
Kim Semper, but there were good reasons for not calling them for more
information. After all, I wanted to keep my letter buried to preserve my
plausible deniability. And Cooper's letter writer had already been con-
tacted once about Kim Semper. If I called again and grilled him, he
might resent it, and I could use up his good will before I even knew what
questions to ask. Also, he might get the impression that the
Coordinating Administration for Productivity didn't have its act together,
and who knew where that could lead? I didn't want a citizen complaining
to his congressional rep.

What I needed was another source, but there wasn't one.

Or was there?

I arranged the personnel files on the floor to look like an organizational hierarchy. If someone were to send a letter praising an employee of the
CAP, where might that letter go?

To the top, of course. That was Cooper.

And to the Director of Personnel. That was me.

But what about the space between these two? What about the Assistant
Administrator and her Deputy? That is, what about Susana and Tom?

Outside of Susana's office, her administrative assistant, Peter, was
preparing to feed a black cat on the fire escape. Almost as soon as he opened
the window, Peter sneezed.

"Susana in?"

"Yes," Peter said, "but she's unavailable." He set the cat bowl down and
closed the window. Then he sneezed again.

"If you're so allergic," I said, "how come you're feeding the kitty?"

"Oh, I like cats, even if they do make my eyes swell shut." He laughed.
"Anyway, feeding Dust is the corporate culture around here, right? When in
Rome . . ."

From the other side of Susana's door, I could hear the steady beat of music.

I watched the stray cat as it ate. "I'm surprised, with all the cats on our fire escapes, that it isn't just one continuous cat fight out there."

"They're smart animals," Peter said. "Once they have a routine, they stay out of each other's way."

I nodded, but I wasn't really paying attention. Over the beat of the music, I could hear a female voice that wasn't Susana's counting *one-and-two-and-three-and—*

I went to her door and put my hand on the knob.

"I told you," Peter said. "Susana's unavailable. If you want to make an appointment . . ."

"This can't wait," I said. I opened the door.

Susana was in a leotard, and I caught her in the middle of a leg lift. She froze while the three women on the workout tape kept on exercising and counting without her.

"I told Peter I wasn't to be disturbed," she said, still holding her leg up like some varicolored flamingo.

"This won't take but a minute," I said. "In fact, you can go right on with your important government business while we talk."

She stopped the tape and glared at me. "What do you want?"

"To get to the bottom of this Kim Semper thing. And if that's what you really want too, then you can't be throwing me curve balls."

"What are you talking about?" She pushed the audiovisual cart between two file cabinets and threw a dust cover over it.

"I'm talking, Susana, about sitting on information. Or call it withholding evidence. I want your correspondence file on Kim Semper."

Susana circled behind her desk and sat down. Ordinarily, that would have been a good gesture, a way of reminding me that she was, after all, the assistant admin, and this was her turf I had invaded. But it was a hard move to pull off in a leotard. "Just what makes you think I even have such a file?"

That was practically a confession. I fought down a smile. "I'm on your side," I reminded her. "But we've got to show some progress on this. Cooper is on his last official breath. Dying men are unpredictable. But if we hold all the cards, how dangerous can he be?"

She stared over my head, no doubt thinking the same thoughts I had about my own Kim Semper letter. How would Cooper react to knowing that she'd had these letters in her files all along?

"You've got the file where, Susana? In your desk? In one of those cabinets? If I close my eyes," I said, closing them, "then I'll be able to honestly tell Cooper that I don't know *exactly* where my information came from. It was just sort of dropped into my lap."

It took her a minute of rummaging, and then a folder fell into my hands. I opened my eyes. The three letters ranged from two to ten years old.

"Read them in your own office," she said. "And next time, knock."

On my way out, I noticed that Peter was reading something called *America's Industrial Future: A Report of the Presidential Colloquium on U.S. Manufacturing Productivity for the Year 2020 and Beyond.* A thing like that wouldn't ordinarily stick in my mind, except that Tom's secretary, Janet, was reading the same report. She was also holding a mottled white and tan cat in her lap. I didn't bother to confront her about it—that was Tom's fight, if he wanted to fight it. I just knocked on Tom's door and stepped into his office.

He swept a magazine from his desk and into a drawer, but he wasn't fast enough to keep me from noting the cover feature: THE GIRLS OF THE PAC TEN. "What the hell do you want?" he growled.

"A hell of a lot more than I'm getting," I barked back. "Damn little you've done to help this investigation along, Willis. Enough bullshit. I'm up to here with bullshit. I want your goddam Kim Semper correspondence file."

"Like hell." Tom glowered, but a little quiver of uncertainty ran across his lowered eyebrows. He wasn't used to being on the receiving end of such bluster.

"Cut the crap, Tom. This goddam Semper bullshit will toss us all on our asses if we don't give Cooper something to chew on. So give."

A little timidly, he said, "I don't know what you're . . ."

"Like hell," I said, waving de Vega's letters. "Susana came across, and I'd sure as hell hate to tell Cooper that you're the one stalling his goddam investigation."

He bit his lip and took a file cabinet key from his desk drawer. "Jesus," he said. "I've never seen you like this."

"You better hope like hell you never see it again," I said, which was probably overdoing things, but I was on a roll.

As I read it in my office, the first of Tom's letters cheered me considerably. One was twenty years old, which altered my suspect list quite a bit. From my array of files on the floor, I removed anyone who hadn't been with the CAP for the last two decades. That left just myself, Tom Willis, and Tom's secretary Janet. I picked up Janet's file and smiled. Kim Semper, I thought, you have met your match.

And then I read Tom's other letter, the most recent one of all, excepting Cooper's. It praised Mr. Kim Semper, for *his* dedication to public service.

No, I thought. This can't be right.

Unless there was more than one Kim Semper.

I sat down behind my desk. Hard. And I thought about the cat named Dust, who came in a dozen variations, but who, by long tradition, was always Dust, was always considered to be the same cat, because the ancient memo had allowed for the feeding of a cat named Dust, "and only a cat named Dust."

I picked up the phone and dialed the number of the man who had written to praise Mr. Semper. "Mr. Davis," I said when I had him on the line, "one of our employees is in line for a service award, and I just want to make sure it's going to the right person. You wrote a letter to us about a Mr. Kim Semper. Now, we've got a Kim Semple on our staff, and a Tim Kemper, but no Kim Semper. Could you do me the favor of describing the man who was so helpful?"

As lame stories go, this one worked pretty well. It sounded plausible, and it didn't make the CAP look bad. And it brought results. Davis was only happy to make sure Semper or Semple or Kemper got his due. The description fit Peter to a T.

I tried the next most recent letter, but the number had been disconnected. The next one back from that—I changed Tim Kemper to Lynn— brought me a good description of Roxie. The third call, the one that cinched it, paid off with a description that could only be my own Vera.

That's when I buzzed Vera into my office.

"I want a copy of the cat memo," I told her.

"The cat memo?"

"Don't fence with me. If you don't have a copy of it yourself, you know how to get one. I want it within the hour." Then I lowered my voice conspiratorially. "Vera, I don't have anything against cats. Trust me on that."

She had a copy in my hands in five minutes. When I looked at the date, I whistled. Dust the cat had been on this officially sanctioned meal ticket for more than forty years, much longer than I had supposed. The memo also named the secretary who had first started feeding Dust. After a phone call to OPM, I was on my way to Silver Spring, Maryland.

The house I stopped in front of was modest, but nonetheless stood out from all the other clapboard houses on that street. There were abstract, Oriental-looking sculptures in the garden. The white stones around the plum trees had been raked into tidy rows, and there was a fountain bubbling near the walkway to the front door.

A white-haired woman holding a gravel rake came around the side of the house, moving with a grace that belied her eighty years.

"Mrs. Taida?" I said. She looked up and waved me impatiently into the garden. As I opened the gate, I said, "I'm the one who called you, Mrs. Taida. From the Coordinating Administration for Productivity?"

"*Yes,* of course," she said. As I approached, she riveted me with her gaze. Her eyes were blue as arctic ice.

"You are Janet Taida, yes?"

"You expected me to look more Japanese," she said. "Taida was my husband's name. Sakutaro Taida. The artist." She waved at the sculptures.

"I see," I said, then reached into my pocket for the photocopied memo. "Mrs. Taida, I want to talk to you about the cat named Dust."

"Of course you do," she said. "Come inside and I'll make some tea."

The house was furnished in the traditional Japanese style, with furniture that was close to the floor. While Mrs. Taida started the water boiling in the kitchen, I looked at the artwork hanging on the walls. There were paintings and drawings that seemed vaguely familiar, somehow, but it wasn't until I saw the big pen and ink on the far wall that I knew what I was looking for.

"There's a drawing like this in the administrator's office," I said when Mrs. Taida came into the room with the teapot.

"A drawing *almost* like that one," Mrs. Taida said. She waved toward a cushion. "Won't you sit down?" she commanded. She poured the tea. "That's a Shinto temple. It has two parts, two buildings. But only one stands at a time. Every twenty years, one is torn down and the other is rebuilt. They are both present, always. But the manifestation changes."

"The drawing at work shows the other phase," I said, "when the other building is standing and this one has been torn down."

Mrs. Taida nodded. A white long-haired cat padded into the room.

"Dust?" I said.

Taking up her teacup, Mrs. Taida shook her head. "No, there's only one Dust."

I laughed. "But like the temple, many manifestations." I unfolded the memo. "This memo, the Dust memo, mentions you by name, Mrs. Taida. You started it, didn't you? You were the administrator's secretary when the secretaries received their sanction to keep caring for, as it says here, a cat named Dust."

"Once we began to feed one, it was very hard to turn the others away. So I read the memo very carefully."

"Mrs. Taida, cats are one thing, but . . ."

"I know. Cats are one thing, but Kim Semper is far more serious, right?" She lowered her teacup. "Let me explain something to you," she said. "The Coordinating Administration for Productivity was commissioned over fifty years ago. They had a clear wartime purpose, which they completed, and then the agency began to drift. Your tea is getting cold."

She waited until I had picked it up and taken a sip.

"A government agency develops a culture, and it attracts people who are comfortable with that culture. After its wartime years the CAP attracted ostriches."

I opened my mouth, but she held up her hand.

"You can't deny it," she said. "For forty years, the CAP has been managed by men and women who wanted to rule over a quiet little fiefdom where nothing much happened."

She sipped her own tea.

"Do you have any idea what it's like to be a secretary under conditions like that?" She shook her head. "Nothing happens. There's too little to do, and the day just crawls by. You can't have any idea how hard it was, at the end of the war and with a Japanese husband, to get a government job. And then to have to sit on my hands all day, doing nothing . . ."

"Mrs. Taida . . ."

"I am not finished speaking," she said with authority, and I felt my face flush. "As I was saying, working at the CAP was like being a sailor on a rudderless ship. Have some more tea."

I held out my cup, as commanded.

"What endures in a government agency?" she asked as she poured again. "The management? The support staff? Job titles shift. Duties change. But the culture remains. It's like the tradition of a secretary feeding a stray cat at ten in the morning. The secretary may retire, but another will come, and if there's a tradition of feeding the stray cat at ten, then the person who takes the job will likely be someone who likes cats anyway. The cat may die or move on, but another will appear before long. The feeding goes on, even if who is fed and by whom changes over time."

She put the teapot down. "Administrators come and go, but the culture endures. And Kim Semper endures. When a citizen calls the agency for help, he isn't referred to management. No one at that level knows anything. No, the citizen is referred to Kim Semper. And for the pleasure of the work itself, of knowing things and being helpful, the secretaries do the job of the Coordinating Administration for Productivity. And they do a very good job. How many of those people who are helped by Kim Semper bother to write letters, do you suppose? And how many of the letters that are written actually end up in the hands of CAP administrators? Kim Semper provides good answers to hard questions about productivity and legislative action. I gave the CAP a rudder, you see. It operates from the galley, not the bridge."

"There's the question of ethics," I said. "There's the matter of lunches paid for by citizens, of benefit derived by fraud."

She looked at me long and hard. It was a look that said everything there was to say about collecting a GS-13 salary working for an agency where the managers were fuzzy about how they should fill their days. She didn't have to say a word.

"Well, what am I supposed to do then?" I said. "Now that I know the truth, what do I say when the administrator asks for my report?"

"You didn't get to where you are today without knowing how to stall," Mrs. Taida said. "You do what you do best, and let the secretaries do what *they* do best."

"What about *after* Cooper is gone?" I said. "This is a bomb just waiting to go off. This is the kind of thing that can sink a little agency like ours."

"The Coordinating Administration for Productivity is a fifty-year-old bureaucracy," Mrs. Taida said, "with a little secret that no one has discovered for forty years. You're the only one who threatens the status quo." She picked up our teacups and the pot. "If you don't rock the boat, I'm sure the CAP, along with Dust and Kim Semper, will endure for time without end. And now, if you don't mind, I have things to do."

I drove back to the office slowly. I knew what I had to do, but I didn't know exactly how to get it done. At least, not until I got as far as the Department of Agriculture. There, I pulled into the right lane and slowed to a crawl.

Size, I thought. The thing that comforts me about the Department of Agriculture is its size. It is big and white and easy to get lost in. That's what safety is.

I drove back and got right to work. It was a big job. I enlisted Vera and Roxie, along with Janet, Peter, and some of the secretaries from downstairs. I didn't explain in great detail what we were doing or why it was important. They understood. In a week, we had generated the very thing that Bill Cooper had called for.

"Results," I announced, shouldering between Susana and Tom to drop my report onto Cooper's desk. It landed with a thud. Cooper blinked slowly, then opened the heavy white binding to the first page. *A Report on Personnel and Operational Dislocation at the Coordinating Administration for Productivity,* it read. "Everything you need to know about Kim Semper is in there."

Cooper nodded. "It's, ah, impressive. You people really knocked yourselves out."

"Yes, sir," I said. "I can't take all the credit. Susana and Tom were instrumental, really."

Neither of them looked up. They were still staring at the report.

Cooper began to scan the executive summary, but his eyes began to glaze when he got to the paragraph about operational location as a time- and institution-based function not contingent upon the identity of the individual operator. "So can you summarize the contents for me?"

"Well," I said, "it's a bit involved. But you can get the gist of it in the summary that you're reading."

Cooper kept thumbing through the summary. It went on for ninety-three pages.

"To really get a complete sense of the situation," I said, "you'll need to read the complete report. Right, Susana?"

She nodded. "Of course."

"Tom?"

"You bet your ass. It's all there, though. Every damn bit of it." He said it with pride, as though he really had made some contribution.

"It took a thousand pages to get it said, Bill. And it really takes a thousand to make sense of it all. So, you see, I can't just give it to you in a sentence."

"I see," Cooper said, nodding, and he was still nodding, still looking at the four-inch volume, when Susana and Tom and I left the room.

"You're a goddam genius is what you are," Tom said. And Susana told me, "Good work."

And when Cooper cleared out for good, he left the report behind. It's there still, taking up space on his successor's desk. Sometimes when I see it sitting there, I think to myself that a bomb could go off in that room, and everything would be blown to hell but that plastic-bound, metal-spined, ten-pound volume of unreadable prose. It wouldn't suffer so much as a singed page.

It gives me a safe and solid feeling.

REX STOUT

Murder Is No Joke

I

I WAS A LITTLE DISAPPOINTED IN FLORA GALLANT when she arrived that Tuesday morning for her eleven-o'clock appointment with Nero Wolfe. Her getup was a letdown. One of my functions as Wolfe's factotum is checking on people who phone for an appointment with him, and when I had learned that Flora Gallant was one of the staff of her brother Alec's establishment on East Fifty-fourth Street, and remembered remarks a friend of mine named Lily Rowan had made about Alec Gallant, I had phoned Lily for particulars.

And got them. Gallant was crowding two others for top ranking in the world of high fashion. He thumbed his nose at Paris and sneered at Rome, and was getting away with it. He had refused to finish three dresses for the Duchess of Harwynd because she postponed flying over from London for fittings.

He declined to make anything whatever for a certain famous movie actress because he didn't like the way she handled her hips when she walked. He had been known to charge as little as eight hundred dollars for an afternoon frock, but it had been for a favorite customer so he practically gave it away.

And so forth. Therefore when I opened the door to admit his sister Flora that Tuesday morning it was a letdown to see a dumpy middle-aged female in a dark gray suit that was anything but spectacular. It needed pressing, and the shoulders were too tight, and her waist wasn't where it thought it was. As I ushered her down the hall to the office and introduced her to Wolfe, I was thinking that if the shoemaker's son went barefoot I supposed his sister could too, but all the same I felt cheated.

Her conversation was no more impressive than her costume, at least at the beginning. Seated on the edge of the red leather chair beyond the end of Wolfe's desk, the fingers of both hands gripping the rim of the gray leather bag on her lap, she apologized, in a low meek mumble with just a trace of a foreign accent, for asking such an important man as Nero Wolfe to give any of his valuable time to her and her troubles. That didn't sound promising, indicating as it did that she was looking for a bargain. As she went on with it Wolfe started a frown going, and soon he cut her off by saying that it would take less of his time if she would tell him what her troubles were.

She nodded. "I know. I just wanted you to understand that I don't expect anything for myself. I'm not anybody, myself, but you know who my brother is? My brother Alec?"

"Yes. Mr. Goodwin has informed me. An illustrious dressmaker."

"He is not merely a dressmaker. He is an artist, a great artist." She wasn't arguing, just stating a fact. "This trouble is about him, and that's why I must be careful with it. That's why I come to you, and also"—she sent me a glance and then back to Wolfe—"also Mr. Archie Goodwin, because I know that although you are private detectives, you are gentlemen. I know you are worthy of confidence."

She stopped, apparently for acknowledgment. Wolfe obliged her. "Umph."

"Then it is understood I am trusting you?"

"Yes. You may."

She looked at me. "Mr. Goodwin?"

"Right. Whatever Mr. Wolfe says. I only work here."

She hesitated, seeming to consider if that was satisfactory, decided it was, and returned to Wolfe. "So I'll tell you. I must explain that in France, where my brother and I were born and brought up, our name was not 'Gallant.' What it was doesn't matter. I came to this country in nineteen-thirty-seven, when I was twenty-five years old, and Alec only came in nineteen-forty-five, after the war was over. He had changed his name to Gallant and entered legally under that name. Within seven years he had made a reputation as a designer, and then—Perhaps you remember his fall collection in nineteen-fifty-three?"

Wolfe grunted no.

Her right hand abandoned its grip on the bag to gesture. "But of course you are not married, and you have no mistress, feeling as you do about women. That collection showed what my brother was—an artist, a true creator. He got financial backing, more than he needed, and opened his place on Fifty-fourth Street. I had quit my job four years earlier—my job as a governess—in order to work with him and help him, and had changed my name to have it the same as his. From nineteen-fifty-three on it has been all a triumph, many triumphs. I will not say I had a hand in them, but I have been trying to help in my little way. The glory of great success has been my brother's, but I have been with him, and so have others. But now trouble has come."

Both hands were gripping the bag again. "'The trouble," she said, "is a woman. A woman named Bianca Voss."

Wolfe made a face. She saw it and responded to it. "No, not an *affaire d'amour*, I'm sure it's not that. Though my brother has never married, he is by no means insensible to women, he is very healthy about women, but since you are worthy of confidence I may tell you that he has an *amie intime*, a young woman who is of importance in his establishment. It is impossible that Bianca Voss has attracted him that way. She first came there a little more than a year ago. My brother had told us to expect her, so he had met her somewhere. He designed a dress and a suit for her, and they were made there in the shop, but no bill was ever sent her. Then he gave her one of the rooms, the offices, on the third floor, and she started to come every day, and then the trouble began. My brother never told us she had any authority, but she took it and he allowed her to. Sometimes she interferes directly, and sometimes through him. She pokes her nose into everything. She got my brother to discharge a fitter, a very capable woman, who had been with him for years. She has a private telephone line in her office upstairs, but no one else has. About two months ago some of the others persuaded me to try to find out about her, what her standing is, and I asked my brother, but he wouldn't tell me. I begged him to, but he wouldn't."

"It sounds," Wolfe said, "as if she owns the business. Perhaps she bought it."

Flora Gallant shook her head. "No, she hasn't. I'm sure she hasn't. She wasn't one of the financial backers in nineteen-fifty-three, and since then there have been good profits, and anyway my brother has control. But now she's going to ruin it and he's going to let her, we don't know why. She wants him to design a factory line to be promoted by a chain of department stores using his name. She wants him to sponsor a line of Alec Gallant cosmetics on a royalty basis. And other things. We're against all of them, and my brother is too, really, but we think he's going to give in to her, and that will ruin it."

Her fingers tightened on the bag. "Mr. Wolfe, I want you to ruin *her*."

Wolfe grunted. "By wiggling a finger?"

"No, but you can. I'm sure you can. I'm sure she has some hold on him, but I don't know what. I don't know who she is or where she came from. I don't know what her real name is. She speaks with an accent, but not French; I'm not sure what it is. I don't know when she came to America; she may be here illegally. She may have known my brother in France, during the war. You can find out. If she has a hold on my brother you can find out what it is. If she is blackmailing him, isn't that against the law? Wouldn't that ruin her?"

"It might. It might ruin him too."

"Not unless you betrayed him." She swallowed that and added hastily, "I don't mean that, I only mean I am trusting you, you said I could, and you could make her stop and that's all you would have to do. Couldn't you just do that?"

"Conceivably." Wolfe wasn't enthusiastic. "I fear, madam, that you're biting off more than you can chew. The procedure you suggest would be prolonged, laborious, and extremely expensive. It would probably require elaborate investigation abroad. Aside from my fee, which would not be modest, the outlay would be considerable and the outcome highly uncertain. Are you in a position to undertake it?"

"I am not rich myself, Mr. Wolfe. I have some savings. But my brother—if you get her away, if you release him from her—he is truly *généreux*—excuse me—he is a generous man. He is not stingy."

"But he isn't hiring me, and your assumption that she is galling him may be groundless." Wolfe shook his head. "No. Not a reasonable venture. Unless, of course, your brother himself consults me. If you care to bring him? Or send him?"

"Oh, I couldn't!" She gestured again. "You must see that isn't possible! When I asked him about her, I told you, he wouldn't tell me anything. He was annoyed. He is never abrupt with me, but he was then. I assure you, Mr. Wolfe, she is a villain. You are *sagace*—excuse me—you are an acute man. You would know it if you saw her, spoke with her."

"Perhaps." Wolfe was getting impatient. "Even so, my perception of her villainy wouldn't avail. No, madam."

"But you would know I am right." She opened her bag, fingered in it with both hands, came out with something, left her chair to step to Wolfe's desk, and put the something on his desk pad in front of him. "There," she said, "that is one hundred dollars. For you that is nothing, but it shows how I am in earnest. I can't ask her to come so you can speak with her, she would merely laugh at me, but you can. You can tell her you have been asked in confidence to discuss a matter with her and ask her to come to see you. You will not tell her what it is. She will come, she will be afraid not to, and that alone will show you she has a secret, perhaps many secrets. Then when she comes you will ask her whatever occurs to you. For that you do not need my suggestions. You are an acute man."

Wolfe grunted. "Everybody has secrets."

"Yes," she agreed, "but not secrets that would make them afraid not to come to see Nero Wolfe. When she comes and you have spoken with her, we shall see. That may be all or it may not. We shall see."

I do not say that the hundred bucks there on his desk in used twenties was no factor in Wolfe's decision. Even though income tax would reduce it to sixteen dollars, that would buy four days' supply of beer. Another factor was plain curiosity: would she come or wouldn't she? Still another was the chance that it might develop into a decent fee. But what really settled it was her saying, "We shall see" instead of "We'll see" or "We will see." He will always stretch a point, within reason, for people who use words as he thinks they should be used. So he muttered at her, "Where is she?"

"At my brother's place. She always is."

"Give Mr. Goodwin the phone number."

"I'll get it. She may be downstairs." She started a hand for the phone on Wolfe's desk, but I told her to use mine and left my chair, and she came and sat, lifted the receiver, and dialed. In a moment she spoke. "Doris? Flora. Is Miss Voss around? . . . Oh. I thought she might have come down No, don't bother, I'll ring her there."

She pushed the button down, told us, "She's up in her office," waited a moment, released the button, and dialed again. When she spoke it was another voice, as she barely moved her lips and brought it out through her nose: "Miss Bianca Voss? Hold the line, please. Mr. Nero Wolfe wishes to speak with you . . . Mr. Nero Wolfe, the private detective."

She looked at Wolfe and he got at his phone. Having my own share of curiosity, I extended a hand for my receiver, and she let me take it and left my chair. As I sat and got it to my ear Wolfe was speaking.

"This is Nero Wolfe. Is this Miss Bianca Voss?"

"Yes." It was more like "yiss." "What do you want?" The "wh" and the "w" were off.

"If my name is unknown to you, I should explain—"

"I know your name. What do you want?" "I want to invite you to call on me at my office. I have been asked to discuss certain matters with you, and—"

"Who asked you?"

"I am not at liberty to say. I shall—"

"What matters?" The "wh" was more off.

"If you will let me finish. The matters are personal and confidential, and concern you closely. That's all I can say on the telephone. I am sure you—"

A snort stopped him, a snort that might be spelled "Tzchaahh!" followed by: "I know your name, yes! You are scum, I know, in your stinking sewer! Your slimy little ego in your big gob of fat! And you dare to— *owulggh!*"

That's the best I can do at spelling it. It was part scream, part groan, and part just noise. It was followed immediately by another noise, a mixture of crash and clatter, then others, faint rustlings, and then nothing. I looked at Wolfe and he looked at me. I spoke to my transmitter. "Hello hello hello. *Hello!* Hello?"

I cradled it and so did Wolfe. Flora Gallant was asking, "What is it? She hung up?"

We ignored her. Wolfe said, "Archie? You heard."

"Yes, sir. If you want a guess, something hit her and she dragged the phone along as she went down and it struck the floor. The other noises, not even a guess, except that at the end either she put the receiver back on and cut the connection or someone else did. I don't—Okay, Miss Gallant. Take it easy." She had grabbed my arm with both hands and was jabbering, "What is it? What happened?" I put a hand on her shoulder and made it emphatic. "Take a breath and let go. You heard what I told Mr. Wolfe. Apparently something fell on her and then hung up the phone."

"But it couldn't! It is not possible!"

"That's what it sounded like. What's the number? The one downstairs?"

She just gawked at me. I looked at Wolfe and he gave me a nod, and I jerked my arm loose, sat at my desk, got the Manhattan book, flipped to the Gs and got the number, PL2 0330, and dialed it.

A cultured female voice came. "Alec Gallant Incorporated."

"This is a friend of Miss Voss," I told her. "I was just speaking to her on the phone, in her office, and from the sounds I got I think something may have happened to her. Will you send someone up to see? Right away. I'll hold the wire."

"Who is this speaking, please?"

"Never mind that. Step on it. She may be hurt."

I heard her calling to someone, then apparently she covered the transmitter. I sat and waited. Wolfe sat and scowled at me. Flora Gallant stood for a good five minutes at my elbow, staring down at me, then turned and went to the red leather chair and lowered herself onto its edge. I looked at my wristwatch: 11:40. It had said 11:31 when the connection with Bianca Voss had been cut. More waiting, and then a male voice came.

"Hello?"

"Hello."

"This is Carl Drew. What is your name, please?"

"My name is Watson, John H. Watson. Is Miss Voss all right?"

"May I have your address, Mr. Watson, please?"

"What for? Miss Voss knows my address. Is she all right?"

"I must have your address, Mr. Watson. I must insist. You will understand the necessity when I tell you that Miss Voss is dead. She was assaulted in her office and is dead. Apparently, from what you said, the assault came while she was on the phone with you, and I want your address. I must insist."

I hung up, gently not to be rude, swiveled, and asked Flora Gallant, "Who is Carl Drew?"

"He's the business manager. What happened?"

I went to Wolfe. "My guess was close. Miss Voss is dead. In her office. He said she was assaulted, but he didn't say with what or by whom."

He glowered at me, then turned to let her have it. She was coming up from the chair, slow and stiff. When she was erect she said, "No. No. It isn't possible."

"I'm only quoting Carl Drew," I told her.

"It isn't possible. He said that?"

"Distinctly."

"But how—" She let it hang. She said, "But how—" stopped again, turned, was going. When Wolfe called to her, "Here, Miss Gallant, your money," she paid no attention but kept on, and he poked it at me, and I took it and headed for the hall. I caught up with her halfway to the front door, but when I offered it she just kept going, so I blocked her off, took her bag and opened it and dropped the bills in and closed it, handed it back, and went and pulled the door open. She hadn't said a word. I stood on the sill and watched, thinking she might stumble going down the seven steps of the stoop, but she made it to the sidewalk and turned east, toward Ninth Avenue. When I got back to the office Wolfe was sitting with his eyes closed, breathing down to his big round middle. I went to my desk and put the phone book away.

"She is so stunned with joy," I remarked, "that she'll probably get run over. I should have gone and put her in a taxi."

He grunted.

"One thing," I remarked, "Miss Voss's last words weren't exactly *généreux*. I would call them catty."

He grunted.

"Another thing," I remarked, "in spite of the fact that I was John H. Watson on the phone, we'll certainly be called on by either Sergeant Stebbins or Inspector Cramer or both. When they go into whereabouts Flora will have to cough it up for her own protection. And we actually heard it. Also we'll have the honor of being summoned to the stand. Star witnesses."

He opened his eyes. "I'm quite aware of it," he growled. "Confound it. Bring me the records on *Laelia gouldiana*."

No orchid ever called a genius a slimy little ego in a big gob of fat. I remarked that too, but to myself.

II

"Sure I appreciate it," Cramer declared. "Why shouldn't I? Very thoughtful of you. Saves me time and trouble. So it was eleven-thirty-one when you heard the blow?"

Inspector Cramer, big and brawny with a round red face and all his hair, half of it gray, had nothing to be sarcastic about as he sat in the red leather chair at six-thirty that Tuesday afternoon, and he knew it, but he couldn't help it. It was his reaction, not to the present circumstances, but to his memory of other occasions, other experiences he had undergone in that room. He had to admit that we had saved him time and trouble when I had anticipated his visit by typing out a complete report of the session with Flora Gallant that morning, including the dialogue verbatim, and having it ready for him in duplicate, signed by both Wolfe and me. He had skimmed through it first, and then read it slowly and carefully.

"We heard no blow, identifiably," Wolfe objected. His bulk was comfortably arranged in his oversize chair back of his desk. "Mr. Goodwin wrote that statement, but I read it, and it does not say that we heard a blow."

Cramer found the place on page four and consulted it. "Okay. You heard a groan and a crash and rustles. But there *was* a blow. She was hit in the back of the head with a chunk of marble, a paperweight, and then a scarf was tied around her throat to stop her breathing. You say here at eleven-thirty-one."

"Not when we heard the groan," I corrected. "After that there were the other noises, then the connection went, and I said hello a few times, which was human but dumb. It was when I hung up that I looked at my watch and saw eleven-thirty-one. The groan had been maybe a minute earlier. Say eleven-thirty. If a minute is important."

"It isn't. But you didn't hear the blow?"

"Not to recognize it, no."

He went back to the statement, frowning at it, reading the whole first page and glancing at the others. He looked up, at Wolfe. "I know how good you are at arranging words. This implies that Flora Gallant was a complete stranger to you, that you had never had anything to do with her or her brother or any of the people at that place, but it doesn't say so in so many words. I'd like to know."

"The implication is valid," Wolfe told him. "Except as related in that statement, I have never had any association with Miss Gallant or her brother, or, to my knowledge, with any of their colleagues. Nor has Mr. Goodwin. Archie?"

"Right," I agreed.

"Okay." Cramer folded the statement and put it in his pocket. "Then you had never heard Bianca Voss's voice before and you couldn't recognize it on the phone."

"Of course not."

"And you can't hear it now, since she's dead. So you can't swear it was her talking to you."

"Obviously."

"And that raises a point. If it was her talking to you, she was killed at exactly half-past eleven. Now there are four important people in that organization who had it in for Bianca Voss. They have admitted it. Besides Flora Gallant, there is Anita Prince, fitter and designer, been with Gallant eight years; Emmy Thorne, in charge of contacts and promotion, been with him four years; and Carl Drew, business manager, been with him five years. None of them killed Bianca Voss at half-past eleven. From eleven-fifteen on, until the call came from a man who said he was John H. Watson, Carl Drew was down on the main floor, constantly in view of four people, two of them customers. From eleven o'clock on Anita Prince was on the top floor, the workshop, with Alec Gallant and two models and a dozen employees. At eleven-twenty Emmy Thorne called on a man by appointment at his office on Forty-sixth Street, and was with him and two other men until a quarter to twelve. And Flora Gallant was here with you. All airtight."

"Very neat," Wolfe agreed.

"Yeah. Too damn neat. Of course there may be others who wanted Bianca Voss out of the way, but as it stands now those four are out in front. And they're all—"

"Why not five? Alec Gallant himself?"

"All right, five. They're all in the clear, including him, if she was killed at eleven-thirty. So suppose she wasn't. Suppose she was killed earlier, half an hour or so earlier. Suppose when Flora Gallant phoned her from here and put you on to talk with her, it wasn't her at all, it was someone else imitating her voice, and she pulled that stunt, the groan and the other noises, to make you think you had heard the murder at that time."

Wolfe's brows were up. "With the corpse there on the floor."

"Certainly."

"Then you're not much better off. Who did the impersonation? Their alibis still hold for eleven-thirty."

"I realize that. But there were nineteen women around there altogether, and a woman who wouldn't commit a murder might be willing to help cover up after it had been committed. You know that."

Wolfe wasn't impressed. "It's very tricky, Mr. Cramer. If you are supposing Flora Gallant killed her, it was elaborately planned. Miss Gallant phoned here yesterday morning to make an appointment for eleven this morning. Did she kill Miss Voss, station someone there beside the corpse to answer the phone, rush down here, and maneuver me into ringing Miss Voss's number? It seems a little far-fetched."

"I didn't say it was Flora Gallant." Cramer hung on. "It could have been any of them. He or she didn't have to know you were going to ring that number. He might have intended to call it himself, before witnesses, to establish the time of the murder, and when your call came, whoever it was there by the phone got rattled and went ahead with the act. There are a dozen different ways it could have happened. Hell, I know it's tricky. I'm not asking you to work your brain on it. You must know why I brought it up."

Wolfe nodded. "Yes, I think I do. You want me to consider what I heard—and Mr. Goodwin. You want to know if we are satisfied that those sounds were authentic. You want to know if we will concede that they might have been bogus."

"That's it. Exactly."

Wolfe rubbed his nose with a knuckle, closing his eyes. In moment he opened them. "I'm afraid I can't help you, Mr. Cramer. If they were bogus they were well executed. At the time, hearing them, I had no suspicion that it was flummery. Naturally, as soon as I learned that they served to fix the precise moment of a murder, I knew they were open to question, but I can't challenge them intrinsically. Archie?"

I shook my head. "I pass." To Cramer: "You've read the statement, so you know that right after I heard it my guess was that something hit her and she dragged the phone along as she went down and it struck the floor. I'm not going to go back on my guess now. As for our not hearing the blow, read the statement. It says that it started out as if it was going to be a scream but then it was a groan. She might have seen the blow coming and was going to scream, but it landed and turned it into a groan, and in that case we wouldn't hear the blow. A chunk of marble hitting a skull wouldn't make much noise. As for supposing she was killed half an hour or so earlier, I phoned within three minutes, or John H. Watson did, and in another six or seven minutes Carl Drew was talking to me, so he must have seen the body, or someone did, not more than five minutes after we heard the groan. Was she twitching?"

"No. You don't twitch long with a scarf as tight as that around your throat."

"What about the M.E.?"

"He got there a little after twelve. With blood he might have timed it pretty close, but there wasn't any. That's out."

"What about the setup? Someone left that room quick after we heard the sounds. If it was the murderer, he or she had to cradle the phone and tie the scarf, but that wouldn't take long. If it was a fill-in, as you want to suppose, all she had to do was cradle the phone. Whichever it was, wasn't there anyone else around?"

"No. If there was, they're saving it. As you know, Bianca Voss wasn't popular around there. Anyway, that place is a mess, with three different elevators, one in the store, one at the back for service and deliveries, and one in an outside hall with a separate entrance so they can go up to the offices without going through the store."

"That makes it nice. Then it's wide open."

"As wide as a barn door." Cramer stood up. To Wolfe: "So that's the best you can do. You thought the sounds were open to question."

"Not intrinsically. Circumstantially, of course."

"Yeah. Much obliged." He was going. After two steps he turned. "I don't like gags about homicide, murder is no joke, but I can mention that Bianca Voss had you wrong. Scum. Stinking sewer. Orchids don't smell." He went.

Apparently he hadn't really swallowed it that she was already dead when we heard the sounds.

III

The next morning, Wednesday, eating breakfast in the kitchen with the *Times* propped up in front of me, which is routine, of course I read the account of the Bianca Voss murder. There were various details that were news to me, but nothing startling or even helpful. It included the phone call from John H. Watson, but didn't add that he had been identified as Archie Goodwin, and there was no mention of Nero Wolfe. I admit that the cops and the D.A. have a right to save something for themselves, but it never hurts to have your name in the paper, and I had a notion to phone Lon Cohen at the *Gazette* and give him an exclusive. However, I would have to mention it to Wolfe first, so it would have to wait until eleven o'clock.

As a matter of fact, another item in the *Times* came closer to me. Sarah Yare had committed suicide. Her body had been found Tuesday evening in her little walk-up apartment on East Thirteenth Street. I had never written a fan letter to an actress, but I had been tempted to a couple of years back when I had seen Sarah Yare in *Thumb a Ride.* The first time I saw it I had a companion, but the next three times I was alone. The reason for repeating was that I had the impression I was infatuated and I wanted to wear it down, but when the impression still stuck after three tries' I quit. Actresses should be seen and heard, but not touched. At that, I might have given the impression another test in a year or two if there had been an opportunity, but there wasn't. She quit *Thumb a Ride* abruptly some months later, and the talk was that she was an alco and done for.

So I read that item twice. It didn't say that it had been pronounced suicide officially and finally, since she had left no note, but a nearly empty bourbon bottle had been there on a table, and on the floor by the couch she had died on there had been a glass with enough left in it to identify the cyanide. The picture of her was as she had been when I had got my impression. I asked Fritz if he had ever seen Sarah Yare, and he asked what movies she had been in, and I said none, she was much too good for a movie.

I didn't get to suggest phoning Lon Cohen to Wolfe because when he came down from the plant rooms at eleven o'clock I wasn't there. As I was finishing my second cup of coffee a phone call came from the District Attorney's office inviting me to drop in, and I went and spent a couple of hours at Leonard Street with an assistant D.A. named Brill. When we got through I knew slightly more than I had when we started, but he didn't. He had a copy of our statement on his desk, and what could I add to that? He had a lot of fun, though. He would pop a question at me and then spend nine minutes studying the statement to see if I had tripped.

Getting home a little before noon, I was prepared to find Wolfe grumpy. He likes me to be there when he comes down from the plant rooms to the office, and while he can't very well complain when the D.A. calls me on business that concerns us, this wasn't our affair. We had no client and no case and no fee in prospect. But I got a surprise. He wasn't grumpy; he was busy. He had the phone book open before him on his desk. He had actually gone to my desk, stooped to get the book, lifted it, and carried it around to his chair. Unheard of.

"Good morning," I said. "What's the emergency?"

"No emergency. I needed to know a number."

"Can I help?"

"Yes. I have instructions."

I sat. He wants you at his level because it's too much trouble to tilt his head back. "Nothing new," I said, "at the D.A.'s office. Do you want a report?"

"No. You will go to Alec Gallant's place on Fifty-fourth Street and speak with Mr. Gallant, his sister, Miss Prince, Miss Thorne, and Mr. Drew. Separately if possible. You will tell each of them—You read the *Times* this morning as usual?"

"Certainly."

"You will tell each of them that I have been engaged to make certain inquiries about Miss Sarah Yare, and that I shall be grateful for any information they may be able and willing to furnish. I would like to see any communications they may have received from her, say in the past month. Don't raise one brow like that. You know it disconcerts me."

"I've never seen you disconcerted yet." I let the brow down a little. "If they ask me who engaged you what do I say?"

"That you don't know. You are merely following instructions,"

"If I ask you who engaged you what do you say?"

"I tell you the truth. No one. Or more accurately, I have engaged myself. I think I may have been hoodwinked and I intend to find out. You may be fishing where there are no fish. They may all say they have never had any association with Sarah Yare, and they may be telling the truth or they may not. You will have that in mind and form your conclusions. If any of them acknowledge association with her, pursue it enough to learn the degree of intimacy, but don't labor it. That can wait until we bait a hook. You are only to discover if there are any fish."

"Now?"

"Yes. The sooner the better."

I stood up. "It may take a while if the cops and the D.A. are working on them, and they probably are. How urgent is it? Do you want progress reports by phone?"

"Not unless you think it necessary. You must get all five of them."

"Right. Don't wait dinner for me." I went.

On the way uptown in the taxi I was using my brain. I will not explain at this point why Wolfe wanted to know if any of the subjects had known Sarah Yare, and if so how well, for two reasons: first, you have certainly spotted it yourself; and second, since I am not as smart as you are, I had not yet come up with the answer. It was underneath. On top, what I was using my brain for, was the phone book. Unquestionably it was connected with his being hoodwinked, since that was what was biting him, and therefore it probably had some bearing on the call that had been made from his office to Bianca Voss, but what could he accomplish by consulting the phone book? For that I had no decent guess, let alone an answer, by the time I paid the hackie at Fifty-fourth and Fifth Avenue.

Alec Gallant Incorporated, on the north side of the street near Madison Avenue, was no palace, either outside or in. The front was maybe thirty feet, and five feet of that was taken by the separate entrance to the side hall. The show window, all dark green, had just one exhibit: a couple of yards of plain black fabric, silk or rayon or nylon or Orion or Dacron or cottonon or linenon, draped on a little rack. Inside, nothing whatever was in sight—that is, nothing to buy. The wall-to-wall carpet was the same dark green as the show window. There were mirrors and screens and tables and ashtrays, and a dozen or more chairs, not fancy, more to sit in than to look at. I had taken three steps on the carpet when a woman standing with a man by a table left him to come to meet me. I told her my name and said I would like to see Mr. Gallant. The man, approaching, spoke.

"Mr. Gallant is not available. What do you want?"

That didn't strike me as a very tactful greeting to a man who, for all he knew, might be set to pay eight hundred dollars for an afternoon frock, but of course he had had a tough twenty-four hours, so I kept it pleasant. "I'm not a reporter," I assured him, "or a cop, or a lawyer drumming up trade. I'm a private detective named Archie Goodwin, sent by a private detective named Nero Wolfe to ask Mr. Gallant a couple of harmless questions—not connected with the death of Bianca Voss."

"Mr. Gallant is not available."

I hadn't heard his voice in person before, only on the phone, but I recognized it. Also he looked like a business manager, with his neat well-arranged face, his neat well-made dark suit, and his neat shadow-stripe four-in-hand. He was a little puffy around the eyes, but the city and county employees had probably kept him from getting much sleep.

"May I ask," I asked, "if you are Mr. Carl Drew?"

"Yes. I am."

"Then I'm in luck. I was instructed to see five different people here—Mr. Gallant, Miss Gallant, Miss Prince, Miss Thorne, and Mr. Carl Drew. Perhaps we could sit down?"

He ignored that. "See us about what?"

The woman had left us. She was in earshot if her hearing was good, but this was certainly no secret mission, with five of them on the list. "To get information," I told him, "if you have any, about a woman who died yesterday. Not Bianca Voss. Miss Sarah Yare."

"Oh." He blinked. "Yes. That was tragic. Information? What kind of information?"

"I don't exactly know." I was apologetic. "All I know is that someone has engaged Mr. Wolfe to make inquiries about her, and he sent me to ask you people if you had any messages or letters from her in the past month or so, and if so will you let him see them."

"Messages or letters?"

"Right."

"That seems a little— Who engaged him?"

"I don't know." I was not permitting my face or voice to show that I had caught sight of a fish. "If you have had messages or letters, and would like to know who wants to see them before you produce them, I suppose Mr. Wolfe would tell you. He would have to."

"I have no messages or letters."

I was disappointed. "None at all? I said the past month or so, but before that would help. Any time."

He shook his head. "I never have had any. I doubt if she ever wrote a letter—that is, to anyone here—or any messages, except phone messages. She always did everything by telephone. And for the past month, longer than that, more than a year, she hasn't been—uh—she hasn't been around."

"I know." I was sympathetic, and I meant it, though not for him. "Anyway, I don't think Mr. Wolfe would be interested in letters about clothes. I think it's personal letters he wants, and he thought you might have known her well enough personally to have some."

"Well, I haven't. I can't say I didn't know her personally—she was a very fine customer here for two years, and she was a very personal person. But I never had a personal letter from her."

I had to resist temptation. I had him talking, and there was no telling if or when I would get at the others. But Wolfe had said not to labor it, and I disobey instructions only when I have reason to think I know more about it than he does, and at that moment I didn't even know why he had been consulting the phone book. So I didn't press. I thanked him and said I would appreciate it if he would tell me when Mr. Gallant would be available. He said he would find out, and left me, going to the rear and disappearing around the end of a screen, and soon I heard his voice, but too faint to get any words. There was no other voice, so, being a detective, I figured it out that he was on a phone. That accomplished, I decided to detect whether the woman, who was seated at a table going through a portfolio, was either Anita Prince or Emmy Thorne. I voted no, arriving at it by a process so subtle and complicated that I won't go into it.

Drew reappeared, and I met him in the middle of the room. He said that Mr. Gallant was in his office with Miss Prince and could let me have five minutes. Another fish. Certainly Drew had told Gallant what my line was, and why did I rate even five seconds? As Drew led me to an elevator and entered with me, and pushed the button marked "2," I had to remember to look hopeful instead of smug.

The second-floor hall was narrow, with bare walls, and not carpeted. As I said, not a palace. After following Drew down six paces and through a door, I found myself in a pin-up paradise. All available space on all four walls was covered with women, drawings and prints and photographs, both black-and-white and color, all sizes, and in one respect they were all alike: none of them had a stitch on. It hadn't occurred to me that a designer of women's clothes should understand female anatomy, but I admit it might help. The effect was so striking that it took me four or five seconds to focus on the man and woman seated at a table. By that time Drew had pronounced my name and gone.

Though the man and woman were fully clothed, they were striking too. He reminded me of someone, but I didn't remember who until later: Lord Byron—a picture of Lord Byron in a book in my father's library that had impressed me at an early age. It was chiefly Gallant's dark curly hair backing up a wide sweeping forehead, but the nose and chin were in it too. The necktie was all wrong; instead of Byron's choker he was sporting a narrow ribbon tied in a bow with long ends hanging.

The woman didn't go with him. She was small and trim, in a tailored suit that had been fitted by an expert, and her face was all eyes. Not that they popped, but they ran the show. In spite of Alec Gallant's lordly presence, as I approached the table I found myself aiming at Anita Prince's eyes.

Gallant was speaking. "What's this? About Sarah Yare?"

"Just a couple of questions." He had eyes too, when you looked at them. "It shouldn't take even five minutes. I suppose Mr. Drew told you?"

"He said Nero Wolfe is making an inquiry and sent you. What about? About how she died?"

"I don't think so, but I'm not sure. The fact is, Mr. Gallant, on this I'm just an errand boy. My instructions were to ask if you got any messages or letters from her in the past month or so, and if so will you let Mr. Wolfe see them."

"My God." He closed his eyes, tilted his head back, and shook it—a lion pestered by a fly. He looked at the woman. "This is too much. Too much!" He looked at me. "You must know a woman was assassinated here yesterday. Of course you do!" He pointed at the door. "There!" His hand dropped to the desk like a dead bird. "And after that calamity, now this, the death of my old and valued friend. Miss Yare was not only my friend; in mold and frame she was perfection, in movement she was music, as a mannequin she would have been divine. My delight in her was completely pure. I never had a letter from her." His head jerked to Anita Prince. "Send him away," he muttered.

She put fingers on his arm. "You gave him five minutes, Alec, and he has only had two." Her voice was smooth and sure. The eyes came to me. "So you don't know the purpose of Mr. Wolfe's inquiry?"

"No, Miss Prince, I don't. He only tells me what he thinks I need to know."

"Nor who hired him to make it?"

So Drew had covered the ground. "No. Not that either. He'll probably tell you, if you have what he wants, letters from her, and you want to know why he wants to see them."

"I have no letters from her. I never had any. I had no personal relations with Miss Yare." Her lips smiled, but the eyes didn't. "Though I saw her many times, my contact with her was never close. Mr. Gallant preferred to fit her himself. ɪ just looked on. It seems—" She stopped for a word, and found it. "It seems odd that Nero Wolfe should be starting an inquiry immediately after her death. Or did he start it before?"

"I couldn't say. The first I knew, he gave me this errand this morning. This noon."

"You don't know much, do you?"

"No, I just take orders."

"Of course you do know that Miss Yare committed suicide?"

I didn't get an answer in. Gallant, rutting the table with a palm, suddenly shouted at her, "Name of God! Must you? Send him away!"

"I'm sorry, Mr. Gallant," I told him. "I guess my time's up. If you'll tell me where to find your sister and Miss Thorne, that will—"

I stopped because his hand had darted to an ashtray, a big metal one that looked heavy, and since he wasn't smoking he was presumably going to let fly with it. Anita Prince beat him to it. With her left hand she got his wrist, and with her right she got the ashtray and moved it out of reach. It was very quick and deft. Then she spoke, to me. "Miss Gallant is not here. Miss Thorne is busy, but you can ask Mr. Drew downstairs. You had better go."

I went. In more favorable circumstances I might have spared another five minutes for a survey of the pin-ups, but not then, not if I had to dodge ashtrays.

In the hall, having pulled the door shut, the indicated procedure, indicated both by the situation and by Miss Prince's suggestion, was to take the elevator down and see Drew again, but a detective is supposed to have initiative. So when I heard a voice, female, floating out through an open door, I went on past the elevator, to the door, for a look. Not only did I see, I was seen, and a voice, anything but female, came at me.

"You. Huh?"

I could have kicked myself. While, as I said, my mission couldn't be called secret with five people on the list, certainly Wolfe had intended it to be private, and there was Sergeant Purley Stebbins of Homicide West, glaring at me.

"Sightseeing?" he asked. Purley's idea of humor is a little primitive. "The scene of the crime?"

I descended to his level. "Just morbid," I told him, crossing the sill, "Compulsion neurosis. Is this it?"

Evidently it was. The room was about the same size as Alec Gallant's, but while his had been dominated by women without clothes, this one ran to clothes without women. There were coats, suits, dresses, everything. They were on dummies, scattered around; on hangers, strung on a pole along a wall; and piled on a table. At my right one dummy, wearing a skirt, was bare from the waist up; she might have blushed if she had had a face to blush with. There was one exception: a well-made tan wool dress standing by a corner of a desk contained a woman—a very attractive specimen in mold and frame, and in movement she could have been music. Standing beside her was Carl Drew. Seated at the desk was Sergeant Purley Stebbins, with a paper in his hand and other papers on the desk. Also on the desk, at his left, was a telephone—the one, presumably, that Wolfe and I had heard hit the floor.

What I had stumbled into was obvious. Purley was examining the effects, including papers, probably the second time over, of Bianca Voss, deceased, under surveillance on behalf of Alec Gallant Incorporated.

"Actually," I said, advancing past the immodest dummy, "this is one homicide I have no finger in. I'm on a fishing trip." I moved my eyes. "Would you tell me, Mr. Drew, where I can find Miss Thome?"

"Right here," the tan wool dress said. "I am Miss Thorne."

"I'm Archie Goodwin of Nero Wolfe's office. May I have a word with you?"

She exchanged glances with Carl Drew. Her glance told me that Drew had told her about me; and his, if I am half as bright as I ought to be, told me that if he was not on a more personal basis with her than he had been with Sarah Yare it wasn't his fault. If he wasn't he would like to be.

"Go ahead," Drew told her. "I'll stick around." She moved toward the door, and I was following when Purley pronounced my name, my last name. He has on occasion called me Archie, but not when I suddenly appeared, uninvited, when he was working on a homicide. I turned.

"Who are you fishing for?" he demanded.

"If I knew," I said, "I might tell you, but don't hold your breath." There was no point in trying to sugar him. The damage, if any, had been done the second he saw me. "See you in court."

Emmy Thorne led me down the hall to a door, the next one, and opened it. Walking, she could have been music at that, if her heels had had any purchase. She held the door for me to enter, shut it, went to a chair behind a desk, and sat. The room was less than half the size of the others and displayed neither women nor clothes.

"Sit down," she said. "What is this nonsense about letters from Sarah Yare?"

I took the chair at the end of her desk. "You know," I said, "my tie must be crooked or I've got a grease spot. Mr. Drew resented me, and Mr. Gallant was going to throw an ashtray at rne. Now you. Why is it nonsense to ask a simple question politely and respectfully?"

"Maybe 'nonsense' isn't the word. Maybe I should have said 'gall.' What right have you to march in here and ask questions at all? Polite or not."

"None. It's not a right, it's a liberty. I have no right to ask you to have dinner with me this evening, which might not be a bad idea, but I'm at liberty to, and you're at liberty to tell me you'd rather dine at the automat with a baboon, only that wouldn't be very polite. Also when I ask if you have any letters from Sarah Yare you're at liberty to tell me to go climb a tree if you find the question ticklish. I might add that I would be at liberty to climb a pole instead of a tree. Have you any letters from Sarah Yare?"

She laughed. She had fine teeth. She stopped laughing abruptly. "Good Lord," she said, "I didn't think I would laugh for a year. This mess, what happened here yesterday, and then Sarah. No, I have no letters from her. You don't have to climb a tree." The laughter was all gone, and her gray eyes, straight at me, were cool and keen. "What else?"

Again I had to resist temptation. With Drew the temptation had been purely professional; with her it was only partly professional and only partly pure. Cramer had said she was in charge of contacts, and one more might be good for her.

Having resisted, I shook my head. "Nothing else, unless you know of something. For instance, if you know of anyone who might have letters."

"I don't." She regarded me. "Of course I'm curious, if you want to call it that. I was very fond of Sarah, and this coming after all her trouble, naturally I'm wondering why you came here. You say Nero Wolfe is making an inquiry?"

"Yes, he sent me. I don't know who his client is, but my guess would be that it's some friend of Miss Yare's." I stood up. "Someone else may be curious. Thank you, Miss Thorne, I'm glad I don't have to climb a tree."

She got up and offered her hand. "You might tell me who it is."

"I might if I knew." Her hand was cool and firm and I kept it for a second. "I'm sorry I interrupted you in there." That was absolutely true. "By the way, one more liberty: is Miss Gallant around?"

She said no and came with me to the hall and left me, heading for the scene of the crime. I went the other way, to the elevator. Down on the main floor the woman was there alone, at a table with a portfolio. Not at all like Macy's main floor. Emerging I turned left, found a phone booth on Madison Avenue, dialed the number I knew best, got Fritz, and asked for Wolfe.

His voice came. "Yes, Archie?"

"It's full of fish. Swarming. Sarah Yare bought her clothes there for two years and they all loved her. I'm phoning to ask about Flora Gallant. I've seen all the others, but Flora isn't around. My guess is that she's at the D. A.'s office. Do I stick until she comes?"

"No. Satisfactory."

"Any further instructions?"

"No. Come home."

IV

In the office, after a late lunch of corned-beef hash with mushrooms, chicken livers, white wine, and grated cheese, which Fritz apologized for because he had had to keep it warm too long, I gave Wolfe a full report of the fishing trip, including all dialogue. When I had finished he nodded, took in air through his nose all the way down, and let it out through his mouth.

"Very well," he said, "that settles it. You will now go—"

"Just a minute," I cut in. "It doesn't settle it for me. It was bad enough up there, not knowing the score, and before I do any more going I want a little light. Why did you pick on Sarah Yare, and where did the phone book come in?"

"I have an errand for you."

"Yeah. Will it keep for ten minutes?"

"I suppose so."

"Then why?"

He leaned back. "As I told you this morning, I thought I might have been hoodwinked and I intended to find out. It was quite possible that that performance here yesterday—getting us on the phone just in time to hear a murder committed—was flummery. Indeed, it was more than possible. Must I expound that?"

"No. Even Cramer suspected it."

"So he did. But his theory that Bianca Voss had been killed earlier and that another woman, not the murderer, was there beside the corpse waiting for a phone call, was patently ridiculous. Must I expound that?"

"No, unless it was a lunatic. Anyone who would do that, even the murderer, with the chance that someone might come in any second, would be batty."

"Of course. But if she wasn't killed at the time we heard those sounds she must have been killed earlier, since you phoned almost immediately and sent someone to that room. Therefore the sounds didn't come from there. Miss Gallant did not dial that number. She dialed the number of some other person whom she had persuaded to perform that hocus-pocus."

He turned a hand over. "I had come to that conclusion, or call it surmise, before I went to bed last night, and I had found it intolerable. I will not be mistaken for a jackass. Reading the *Times* at breakfast this morning, the item about the death of Sarah Yare, my attention was caught by the fact that she had been an actress. An actress can act a part. Also she had been in distress. Also she had died. If she had been persuaded to act *that* part, it would be extremely convenient—for the one who persuaded her—for her to die before she learned that a murder had been committed and she had been an accessory after the fact. Certainly that was mere speculation, but it was not idle, and when I came down to the office I looked in the phone book to see if Sarah Yare was listed, found that she was, and dialed her number. Algonquin nine, one-eight-four-seven."

"What for? She was dead."

"I didn't lift the receiver. I merely dialed it, to hear it. Before doing so I strained my memory. I had to recall an experience that was filed somewhere in my brain, having reached it through my ears. As you know, I am trained to attend, to observe, and to register. So are you. That same experience is filed in your brain. Close your eyes and find it. Take your ears back to yesterday, when you were standing there, having surrendered your chair to Miss Gallant, and she was at the phone, dialing. Not the first number she dialed; you dialed that one yourself later. The second one, when, according to her, she was dialing the number of the direct line to Bianca Voss's office. Close your eyes and let your ears and brain take you back. Insist on it."

I did so. I got up and stood where I had stood while she was dialing, shut my eyes, and brought it back. In ten seconds I said, "Okay."

"Keep your eyes closed. I'm going to dial it. Compare."

The sound came of his dialing. I held my breath till the end, then opened my eyes and said positively, "No. Wrong. The first and third and fourth were wrong. The second might—"

"Close your eyes and try it again. This will be another number. Say when."

I shut my eyes and took five seconds. "Go."

The dialing sound came, the seven units. I opened my eyes. "That's more like it. That was it, anyway the first four. Beyond that I'm a little lost. But in that case—"

"Satisfactory. The first four were enough. The first number, which you rejected, as I did this morning, was Plaza two, nine-oh-two-two, the number which Miss Gallant pretended to be dialing. The second was Sarah Yare's number, Algonquin nine, one-eight-four-seven."

"Well." I sat down. "I'll be damned."

"So it was still a plausible surmise, somewhat strengthened, but no more than that. If those people, especially Miss Gallant, could not be shown to have had some association with Sarah Yare, it was untenable. So I sent you to explore, and what you found promoted the surmise to an assumption, and a weighty one. What time is it?"

He would have had to twist his neck a whole quarter-turn to look at the wall clock, whereas I had only to lower my eyes to see my wrist. I obliged. "Five to four."

"Then instructions for your errand must be brief, and they can be. You will go to Sarah Yare's address on Thirteenth Street and look at her apartment. Her phone might have been discontinued since that book was issued. I need to know that the instrument is still there and operable before I proceed. If I intend to see that whoever tried to make a fool of me regrets it, I must take care not to make a fool of myself. Have I furnished the light you wanted?"

I told him it was at least a glimmer and departed on the errand. If you think I might have shown fuller appreciation of his dialing display, I beg to differ. There is no point in assuring a man that he is a genius when he already knows it. Besides, I was too busy being sore at me. I should have thought of it myself. I certainly should have caught on when I saw him with the phone book.

It was not my day. At the address of the late Sarah Yare on East Thirteenth Street I stubbed my toe again. One thing I think I'm good at is sizing up people, and I was dead wrong about the janitor of that old walk-up. He looked as if anything would go, so I merely told him to let me into Sarah Yare's apartment to check the telephone, and the bum insisted on seeing my credentials. So I misjudged him again. I offered him a sawbuck and told him I only wanted two minutes for a look at the phone with him at my elbow, and when he turned me down I showed him a twenty. He just sneered at it. By that time we were bitter enemies, and if I had showed him a C he would probably have spit on it. The upshot was that I went back home for an assortment of keys, returned, posted myself across the street, waited nearly an hour to be sure the enemy was not peeking, and broke and entered, technically.

I won't describe it; it was too painful. It was a hell of a dump for a Sarah Yare, even for a down-and-outer who had once been Sarah Yare. But the telephone was there, and it was working. I dialed to make sure, and got Fritz, and told him I just wanted to say hello and would be home in fifteen minutes, and he said that would please Mr. Wolfe because Inspector Cramer was there.

"No," I said.

"Yes," he said.

"When did he come?"

"Ten minutes ago. At six o'clock. Mr. Wolfe said to admit him and is with him in the office. Hurry home, Archie."

I did so.

I got a hackie who liked to take advantages, and it took a little less than the fifteen minutes. I ascended the stoop and let myself in, not banging the door, and tiptoed down the hall and stopped short of the office door, thinking to get a sniff of the atmosphere before entering. I got it. Wolfe's voice came.

". . . and I didn't say I have never known you to be wrong, Mr. Cramer. I said I have never known you to be more wrong. That is putting it charitably, under provocation. You have accused me of duplicity. Pfui!"

"Nuts." Cramer had worked up to his grittiest rasp. "I have accused you of nothing. I have merely stated facts. The time of the murder was supposed to be established by you and Goodwin hearing it on the phone. Is that a fact? Those five people all have alibis for that time. One of them was here with you. Is that a fact? When I put it to you yesterday that that phone business might have been faked, that she might have been killed earlier, all I got was a run-around. You could challenge it circumstantially but not intrinsically, whatever the hell that means. Is that a fact? So that if you and Goodwin got to the witness stand you might both swear that you were absolutely satisfied that you had heard her get it at exactly half-past eleven. Is that a fact? Giving me to understand that you weren't interested, you weren't concerned, you had no—"

"No," Wolfe objected. "That was not broached."

"Nuts. You know damn well it was implied. You said you had never had any association with any of those people besides what was in your state-ment, so how could you be concerned, with Bianca Voss dead? Tell me this, did any of them approach you, directly or indirectly, between seven o'clock yesterday and noon today?"

"No."

"But—" He bore down on the *but.* "*But* you sent Goodwin there today. He told Stebbins he was on a fishing trip. He talked with Drew, and Gallant, and Miss Prince, and he actually took Miss Thome from under Stebbins's nose, took her out to talk with her. Is that a fact? And they all refuse to tell what Goodwin said to them or what they said to him. That is a fact. They say it was a private matter and had nothing to do with the murder of Bianca Voss. And when I come and ask you what you sent Goodwin there for, ask you plainly and politely, you say that you will—What are you laughing at?"

It wasn't a laugh, I just barely caught it, it was hardly even a chuckle, but all the same it could get under your skin. I knew.

"It escaped me, Mr. Cramer. Your choice of adverbs. Your conception of politeness. Pray continue."

"All right, I asked you. And you said you will probably be ready to tell me within twenty-four hours. And what I said was absolutely justified. I did not accuse you of duplicity. You know what I said."

"I do indeed, Mr. Cramer." I couldn't see Wolfe, but I knew he had upturned a palm. "This is childish and futile. If a connection is established between your murder investigation and the topic of Mr. Goodwin's talks with those people today, it will be only because I formed a conjecture and acted on it. I hope to establish it within twenty-four hours, and meanwhile it will do no harm to give you a hint. Have you any information on the death of a woman named Sarah Yare?"

"Some, yes. Presumed a suicide, but it's being checked. I have two men on it. What about it?"

"I suggest that you assign more men to it, good ones, and explore it thoroughly. I think we will both find it helpful. I may soon have a more concrete suggestion, but for the present that should serve. You know quite well—"

The doorbell rang. I about-faced and looked through the one-way glass panel of the front door. It wasn't a visitor on the stoop, it was a mob. All five of them were there: Gallant, his sister, Anita Prince, Emmy Thorne, and Carl Drew. Fritz appeared from the kitchen, saw me, and stopped. I got my notebook and pen from pockets and wrote:

That phone works. The five subjects are outside wanting in.
AG

I told Fritz to stand by, tore out the sheet, entered the office and crossed to Wolfe's desk, and handed it to him.

Wolfe read it, frowned at it for three seconds, turned his head and called, "Fritz!"

Fritz appeared at the door. "Yes, sir?"

"Put the chain-bolt on and tell those people they will be admitted shortly. Stay there."

"Yes, sir." Fritz went.

Wolfe looked at Cramer. "Mr. Gallant, his sister, Miss Prince, Miss Thorne, and Mr. Drew have arrived, uninvited and unexpected. You'll have to leave without being seen. In the front room until they have entered. I'll communicate with you later."

"Like hell I'll leave." Cramer was on his feet. "Like hell they're unexpected." He was moving, toward the hall, his intention plain—taking over as receptionist.

"Mr. Cramer!" It snapped at his back, turning him. "Would I lie so clumsily? If they had been expected would I have let you in? Would I have sat here bickering with you? Either you leave or I do. If you admit them you'll have them to yourself, and I wish you luck."

Cramer was glaring. "You think I'm going to sneak out and sit on your goddam stoop until you whistle?"

"That *would* be unseemly," Wolfe conceded. "Very well." He pointed at a picture on the wall to his left behind him—a pretty waterfall. "You know about that. You may take that station, but only if you engage not to disclose yourself unless you are invited. Unequivocally."

The waterfall covered a hole in the wall. On the other side, in a wing of the hall across from the kitchen, the hole was covered by nothing, and you could not only see through but also hear through. Cramer had used it once before, a couple of years ago.

Cramer stood, considering. Wolfe demanded, "Well? They're waiting. For you or for me?"

Cramer said, "Okay, we'll try it your way," turned and marched to the hall, and turned left.

Wolfe told me, "All right, Archie. Bring them in."

V

Lord Byron, alias Alec Gallant, and the red leather chair went together fine. He sat well back, unlike most people I have seen there. Usually they are either too mad or too upset. Any of the other four probably would have been; they looked it. They were on yellow chairs that I had moved up to make a row facing Wolfe, with Emmy Thorne nearest me, then Anita Prince, then Carl Drew, then Flora Gallant. That put Flora nearest her brother, which seemed appropriate.

Wolfe was turned to Gallant. "You ask me, sir, why I sent Mr. Goodwin to ask you people about Sarah Yare. Of course I'm under no compulsion to reply, and I'm not sure that I am prepared to. Instead, I may ask why his questions, certainly not provocative, so disturbed you. Apparently they have even impelled you to call on me in a body. Why?"

"Talk," Gallant said. "*Vent.* Wind." There was an ashtray on the little table at his elbow, but not a heavy one.

Anita Prince put in, "The police have insisted on knowing why he was there, what he wanted."

Wolfe nodded. "And you refused to say. Why?"

"Because," Emmy Thorne declared, "it was none of their business. And we have a right to know why you sent him, whether his questions were provocative or not." That girl was strong on rights.

Wolfe's eyes went from right to left and back again. "There's no point," he said, "in dragging this out. I'll grant your question priority and we'll go on from there. I sent Mr. Goodwin to see you because I suspected I had been gulled and wanted to find out; and further, because I had guessed that there was a connection between Sarah Yare, and her death, and the murder of Bianca Voss. By coming here en masse you have made that guess a conviction, if any doubt had remained."

"I knew it," Flora Gallant mumbled.

"Tais-toi," her brother commanded her. To Wolfe: "I'll tell you why we came here. We came for an explanation. We came—"

"For an understanding," Carl Drew cut in. "We're in trouble, all of us, you know that, and we need your help, and we're ready to pay for it. First we have to know what the connection is between Sarah Yare and what happened to Bianca Voss."

Wolfe shook his head. "You don't mean that. You mean you have to know whether I have established the connection, and if so, how. I'm willing to tell you, but before I do so I must clarify matters. There must be no misunderstanding. For instance, I understand that all of you thought yourselves gravely endangered by Miss Voss's presence. You, Miss Prince, you, Miss Thorne, and you, Mr. Drew—your dearest ambitions were threatened. Your future was committed to the success and glory of that enterprise, and you were convinced that Miss Voss was going to cheapen it, and perhaps destroy it. Do you challenge that?"

"Of course not." Emmy Thorne was scornful. "Everybody knew it."

"Then that's understood. That applies equally to you, Miss Gallant, but with special emphasis. You also had a more intimate concern, for your brother. You told me so. As for you, Mr. Gallant, you are not a man to truckle, yet you let that woman prevail. Presumably you were under severe constraint. Were you?"

Gallant opened his mouth and closed it. He looked at his sister, returned to Wolfe, and again opened his mouth and closed it. He was under constraint now, no doubt about that.

He forced it out. "I was under her heel." He clamped his jaw. He unclamped it. "The police know. They found out enough, and I have told them the rest. She was a bad woman. I met her in France, during the war. We were in the Resistance together when I married her. Only afterward I learned that she was *perfide*. She had been a traitor to France—I couldn't prove it, but I knew it. I left her and changed my name and came to America—and then last year she found me and made demands. I was under her heel."

Wolfe grunted. "That won't do, Mr. Gallant. I doubt if it has satisfied the police, and it certainly doesn't satisfy me. In that situation you might have killed her, but surely you wouldn't have let her take charge of your business and your life. What else was there?"

"Nothing. Nothing!"

"Pfui. Of course there was. And if the investigation is prolonged the police will discover it. I advise you to disclose it and let me get on and settle this affair. Didn't her death remove her heel?"

"Yes. Thank God, it did." Gallant hit the arms of the chair with his palms. "With her gone there is no evidence to fear. She had two brothers, and they, like her, were traitors, and I killed them. I would have killed her too, but she escaped me. During the war it would have been merely an episode, but it was later, much later, when I found out about them, and by then it was a crime. With her evidence I was an *assassin,* and I was doomed. Now she is gone, thank God, but I did not kill her. You know I did not. At half-past eleven yesterday morning I was in my workshop with Miss Prince and many others, and you can swear that she was killed at that moment. That is why we came to see you, to arrange to pay—"

"Hold it, Alec." Anita Prince headed him off. "Mr. Wolfe wants to clarify matters. Let him."

"The cat's head is out," Wolfe told her, "but I had already heard it scratch. Let's get on. I cannot swear that Bianca Voss was killed 'at that moment.' On the contrary, I'm sure she wasn't, for a variety of reasons. There are such minor ones as the extraordinary billingsgate she spat at me on the phone, quite gratuitous; and her calling "me a gob of fat. A woman who still spoke the language with so marked an accent would not have the word 'gob' so ready, and probably wouldn't have it at all."

He waved "gob" away. "But the major reasons are more cogent. In the first place, it was too pat. Since the complexities of nature permit a myriad of coincidences we cannot reject one offhand, but we can discriminate. That one—that the attack had come just at the moment when Miss Gallant had got Mr. Goodwin and me on the phone with her—was highly suspect. Besides, it was indiscreet to strike just then. Why not wait until she had hung up? Whoever was talking with her would certainly hear the sounds and take alarm. As I told Mr. Cramer, it was open to challenge circumstantially, though not intrinsically. However, there was another challenge, on surer ground. Miss Gallant did not dial Plaza two, nine-oh-two-two, Miss Voss's number, as she pretended. She dialed Algonquin nine, one-eight-four-seven, Sarah Yare's number." A noise, a sort of low growl, came from the waterfall. I was farthest away, and I heard it distinctly, so it must have reached their ears too, but Wolfe's last words had so riveted their attention that it didn't register.

It did with Wolfe, and he added hastily, "I didn't know that yesterday. I became certain of it only after you rang my doorbell, when Mr. Goodwin handed me this note." He tapped it, there on his desk. "Its first words are 'That phone works.' I had sent him to learn if Sarah Yare's phone was in operation. Obviously, Miss Gallant had arranged with Miss Yare to impersonate Bianca Voss, and it is a reasonable—"

"Wait a minute." Gallant had come forward in the red leather chair. "You can't prove that."

"Directly, no. Inferentially, yes."

"And how do you know she dialed Sarah Yare's number? You weren't where you could see the dial, and neither was Goodwin."

Wolfe nodded. "Evidently you have discussed it with her. You're quite right, Mr. Gallant; we couldn't see the dial. Nevertheless, we can supply evidence, and we think it will be persuasive. I am not—"

"What kind of evidence?"

"That's no good, Alec." It was Emmy Thorne, the contact girl. "You can't push Nero Wolfe. He has his teeth in it, you can see that. You know what we decided."

"I'm not sure," Anita Prince objected, "that we decided right."

"I am. Carl?"

"Yes." Drew was chewing his lip. "I think so. Yes."

"Flora? It's up to you."

"I guess so." Flora's voice was cracked, and she tried again. "I guess so." A little better.

Emmy nodded. "Go ahead, Alec. You can't push him."

"My God." Gallant looked at his sister, and back at Wolfe. "All right. We will pay you to help us. I will pay you. My sister is innocent and she must not suffer. It would be an offense against nature, against God Himself. She has told me all about it, and she was stupid, but she is innocent. She did arrange with Sarah Yare, as you said, but only to move you. She had read much about you and had a great opinion of your abilities. She was desperate about Bianca Voss. She knew you demanded high fees, much beyond her resources, so she conceived a plan. She would persuade you to talk with Bianca Voss on the phone, and she would get Sarah instead, and Sarah would abuse you with such violence that you would be offended and resent it, and you would be moved to act against Bianca Voss. It was stupid, yes, very stupid, but it was not criminal."

Wolfe's eyes, at him, were half closed. "And you want to pay me to help her."

"Yes. When I told her you had sent your man to inquire about Sarah Yare I saw she was frightened and asked her why, and she told me. I consulted the others, and it was apparent that you knew something, and that was dangerous. We decided to come and ask you to help. My sister must not suffer."

Wolfe's eyes moved. "Miss Gallant. You heard your brother. Did he quote you correctly?"

"Yes!" That time it was too loud.

"You did those things? As he related them?"

"Yes!"

Wolfe returned to Gallant. "I agree with you, sir, that your sister was stupid, but you are not the one to proclaim it. You say that she arranged with Sarah Yare to abuse me on the phone, but Miss Yare didn't stop at that. She ended by making noises indicating that she had been violently attacked, and jerked the phone off onto the floor, and made other noises, and then hung up the phone and cut the connection. Was that on her own initiative? Her own idea? Your sister's stupidity can bow to fours if you expected me to overlook that point—or worse, if you missed it yourself."

"I am not stupid, Mr. Wolfe."

"Then you are devious beyond my experience."

"Devious?"

"*Ruse. Subtil.*"

"No. I am not." Gallant clamped his jaw. He released it. "*Bien.* Suppose, only to suppose, she arranged that too, that comedy. Suppose even that she killed Bianca Voss. Was that a crime? No; it was justice; it was the hand of God. Bianca Voss was an evil woman. She was *vilaine.* Are you so virtuous that you must crucify my sister? Are you a paragon? For she is in your hands, at your mercy. You know about Sarah Yare, but the police do not. You know she dialed that number, but the police do not, and they will not unless you tell them. By your word it can be that my sister was here with you at the time that Bianca Voss was killed. As I have said, I will pay you. It will be a great service from you, and it deserves payment. I will trust you. I will pay you now."

Wolfe grunted. "That was quite a speech."

"It was not a speech. I do not make speeches. It was an appeal to your charity. From my heart."

"And to my cupidity." Wolfe shook his head. "No. I am not a paragon. I am not even a steward of the law. But you have ignored two important factors: one, my self-esteem. Even if Bianca Voss deserved to die, I will not permit a murderer to take me for a simpleton. Two, another woman died too. Was Sarah Yare also evil? Was she *vilaine?*"

"But she—Sarah killed herself!"

"No. I don't believe it. That's another coincidence. Granted that she may have been wretched enough for that extreme, why did she choose that particular moment? Again too pat. According to the published account, she died between ten o'clock yesterday morning and two in the afternoon, but I can narrow it a little. Since she spoke with me on the phone at eleven-thirty, she died between that hour and two o'clock. I believe that the person who killed Bianca Voss at some time prior to eleven-thirty, and arranged with Sarah Yare to enact that comedy, as you call it, went to Sarah Yare's apartment later and killed her. Indeed, prudence demanded it. So you ask too much of my charity. If only Bianca Voss had died—"

"No!" Gallant exploded. "Impossible! Totally impossible! My sister loved Sarah! She killed her? Insane!"

"But you believe she killed Bianca Voss. You came here believing that. That was stupid too. She didn't."

Gallant gawked at him. Lord Byron shouldn't gawk, but he did. So did the others. Also they made noises. Carl Drew demanded, "Didn't? You say she *didn't?*" Emmy Thorne asked coolly, "What's this, Mr. Wolfe? A game?"

"No, madam, not a game. Nor a comedy—Mr. Gallant's word. As a man I know said yesterday, murder is no joke." Wolfe's eyes went to Flora. "There was much against you, Miss Gallant, especially the fact that you dialed that other number before you dialed Sarah Yare's, and asked someone you called Doris if Miss Voss was around. Are you too rattled to remember that?"

"No." She was clutching the rim of her bag with both hands. "I remember."

"Of course the reason for it was obvious, if you had killed Bianca Voss before you came here; you had to know that the body had not been found before you proceeded with your strategem. Since you had *not* killed Bianca Voss, why did you make that call?"

"I wanted to make sure that she hadn't gone out. That she was there in her office. You might call her again after I left and find out she hadn't been there. I didn't care if you called her and she denied she had talked to you like that. I thought you would think she was lying. I suppose that was stupid." Her mouth worked. "How did you know I didn't kill her?"

"You told me. You showed me. If you had devised that elaborate humbug, certainly you would have decided how to act at the moment of crisis. You would have decided to be alarmed, and shocked, and even perhaps a little dazed. But it wasn't like that. You were utterly stunned with bewilderment. When Mr. Goodwin told us what Mr. Drew had said, what did you say? You said, 'But how—' And repeated it, 'But how—' If you had killed Bianca Voss you would have had to be a master dramatist to write such a line, and an actress of genius to deliver it as you did; and you are neither."

Wolfe waved it away. "But that was for me. For others, for a judge and jury, I must do better, and think I can. If you are innocent, someone else is guilty. Someone else learned of the arrangement you had made with Sarah Yare, either from you or from her, and persuaded her to add a dramatic climax. Someone else killed Bianca Voss and then established an invulnerable alibi for the crucial period. Someone else had secured the required amount of cyanide—it doesn't take much. Someone else, having established the alibi, went to Sarah Yare's apartment and poisoned her glass of whisky. That was done before two o'clock, and that should make it simple. Indeed, it *has* made it simple. Shortly before you came I learned from Mr. Cramer of the police that you arrived at your brother's place yesterday a few minutes after noon. Since you left here at a quarter of twelve, you hadn't had time to go. first to Thirteenth Street and dispose of Sarah Yare; and you were continuously under the eyes of policemen the rest of the afternoon. That is correct?"

"Yes." Flora's eyes were wet but she hadn't used a handkerchief. "I wanted to go and see what had happened to Sarah, but I was afraid—I didn't know—"

"It's a good thing you didn't, madam. I also learned from Mr. Cramer that you, Mr. Gallant, you, Mr. Drew, and you, Miss Prince, were also constantly under surveillance, for hours, from the time the police arrived. That leaves you, Miss Thorne." His eyes were narrowed at her. "You were with three men in an office on Forty-sixth Street from eleven-twenty until a quarter to twelve. You arrived at Mr. Gallant's place, and found the police there, shortly before three o'clock. You may be able to account for the interim satisfactorily. Do you want to try?"

"I don't have to try." Emmy Thorne's gray eyes were not as cool and keen as they had been when she had told me I didn't have to climb a tree. She had to blink to keep them at Wolfe. "So it *is* a game."

"Not one you'll enjoy, I fear. Nor will I; I'm out of it. To disclose your acquisition of the cyanide you would need for Sarah Yare; to show that you entered Bianca Voss's room yesterday morning, or could have, before you left for your business appointment; to find evidence of your visit to Thirteenth Street after your business appointment; to decide which homicide you will be put on trial for—all that is for others. You must see now that it was a mistake—*Archie!*"

I was up and moving, but halted. Gallant, out of his chair and advancing, wasn't going to touch her. His fists were doubled, but not to swing; they were pressed against his chest. He stopped square in front of her and commanded, "Look at me, Emmy."

To do so she would have had to move her head, tilt it back, and she moved nothing.

"I have loved you," he said. "Did you kill Sarah?"

Her lips moved but no sound came.

His fists opened for his fingers to spread on his chest. "So you heard us that day, and you knew I couldn't marry you because I was married to her, and you killed her. That I can understand, for I loved you. But that you killed Sarah, no. No! And even that is not the worst! Today, when I told you and the others what Flora had told me, you accepted it, you allowed us to accept it, that she had killed Bianca. You would have let her suffer for it. Look at me! You would have let my sister—"

Flora was there, tugging at his sleeve, sputtering at him, "You love her, Alec, don't hurt her now, don't—"

Gallant jerked loose, backed up, folded his arms, and breathed; and Emmy Thorne moved. She came up out of her chair, stood rigid long enough to give Gallant a straight, hard look, shook her head, spun away from him, and headed for the door, brushing against Flora. Her route took her past Anita Prince, who tilted her head back to look up at her, and past Carl Drew, who had to pull his feet back not to trip her.

I didn't budge, thinking I wasn't needed, and I was right. In movement she might have been music, but if so, the music got stopped. As she made the hall and turned toward the front a hand gripped her arm—a hand that had had plenty of practice gripping arms.

"Take it easy, Miss Thorne," Cramer said. "We'll have to have a talk."

"Grand Dieu," Gallant groaned, and covered his face with his hands.

DONALD E. WESTLAKE

Never Shake a Family Tree

A CTUALLY, I HAVE NEVER BEEN SO SHOCKED in all my born days, and I am seventy-three my last birthday and eleven times a grandmother and twice a great-grandmother. But never in all my born days did I see the like, and that's the truth.

Actually, it all began with my interest in genealogy, which I got from Mrs. Ernestine Simpson, a lady I met at Bay Arbor, in Florida, when I went there three summers ago. I certainly didn't like Florida—far too expensive, if you ask me, and far too bright, and with just too many mosquitoes and other insects to be believed—but I wouldn't say the trip was a total loss, since it did interest me in genealogical research, which is certainly a wonderful hobby, as well as being very valuable, what with one thing and another.

Actually, my genealogical researches had been valuable in more ways than one, since they have also been instrumental in my meeting some very pleasant ladies and gentlemen, although some of them only by postal, and of course it was through this hobby that I met Mr. Gerald Fowlkes in the first place.

But I'm getting far ahead of my story, and ought to begin at the beginning, except that I'm blessed if I know where the beginning actually is. In one way of looking at things, the beginning is my introduction to genealogy through Mrs. Ernestine Simpson, who has since passed on, but in another way the beginning is really almost two hundred years ago, and in still another way the story doesn't really begin until the first time I came across the name of Euphemia Barber.

Well. Actually, I suppose, I really ought to begin by explaining just what genealogical research is. It is the study of one's family tree. One checks marriage and birth and death records, searches old family Bibles and talks to various members of one's family, and one gradually builds up a family tree, showing who fathered whom and what year, and when so-and-so died, and so on. It's really a fascinating work, and there are any number of amateur genealogical societies throughout the country, and when one has one's family tree built up for as far as one wants—seven generations, or nine generations, or however long one wants—then it is possible to write this all up in a folder and bequeath it to the local library, and then there is a *record* of one's family for all time to come, and I for one think that's important and valuable to have even if my youngest boy Tom does laugh at it and say it's just a silly hobby. Well, it *isn't* a silly hobby. After all, I found evidence of murder that way, didn't I?

So, actually, I suppose the whole thing really begins when I first came across the name of Euphemia Barber. Euphemia Barber was John Anderson's second wife. John Anderson was born in Goochland County, Virginia, in 1754. He married Ethel Rita Mary Rayborn in 1777, just around the time of the Revolution, and they had seven children, which wasn't at all strange for that time, though large families have, I notice, gone out of style today, and I for one think it's a shame.

At any rate, it was John and Ethel Anderson's third child, a girl named Prudence, who is in my direct line on my mother's father's side, so of course I had them in my family tree. But then, in going through Appomattox County records—Goochland County being now a part of Appomattox, and no longer a separate county of its own—I came across the name of Euphemia Barber. It seems that Ethel Anderson died in 1793, in giving birth to her eighth child—who also died—and three years later, 1796, John Anderson remarried, this time marrying a widow named Euphemia Barber. At that time, he was forty-two years of age, and her age was given as thirty-nine.

Of course, Euphemia Barber was not at all in my direct line, being John Anderson's second wife, but I was interested to some extent in her pedigree as well, wanting to add her parents' names and her place of birth to my family chart, and also because there were some Barbers fairly distantly related on my father's mother's side, and I was wondering if this Euphemia might be kin to them. But the records were very incomplete, and all I could learn was that Euphemia Barber was not a native of Virginia, and had apparently only been in the area for a year or two when she had married John Anderson. Shortly after John's death in 1798, two years after their marriage, she had sold the Anderson farm, which was apparently a somewhat prosperous location, and had moved away again. So that I had neither birth nor death records on her, nor any record of her first husband, whose last name had apparently been Barber, but only the one lone record of her marriage to my great-great-great-great-great-grandfather on my mother's father's side.

Actually, there was no reason for me to pursue the question further, since Euphemia Barber wasn't in my direct line anyway, but I had worked diligently and, I think, well, on my family tree, and had it almost complete back nine generations, and there was really very little left to do with it, so I was glad to do some tracking down.

Which is why I included Euphemia Barber in my next entry in the Genealogical Exchange. Now, I suppose I ought to explain what the Genealogical Exchange is. There are any number of people throughout the country who are amateur genealogists, concerned primarily with their own family trees, but of course family trees do interlock, and any one of these people is liable to know about just the one record which has been eluding some other searcher for months. And so there are magazines devoted to the exchanging of some information, for nominal fees. In the last few years, I had picked up all sorts of valuable leads in this way. And so my entry in the summer issue of the Genealogical Exchange read:

BUCKLEY, Mrs. Henrietta Rhodes, 119A Newbury St., Boston, Mass. Xch data on *Rhodes, Anderson, Richards, Pryor, Marshall, Lord.* Want any info Euphemia *Barber,* m. John Anderson, Va. 1796.

Well. The Genealogical Exchange had been helpful to me in the past, but I never received anywhere near the response caused by Euphemia Barber. And the first response of all came from Mr. Gerald Fowlkes.

It was a scant two days after I received my own copy of the summer issue of the Exchange. I was still poring over it myself, looking for people who might be linked to various branches of my family tree, when the telephone rang. Actually, I suppose I was somewhat irked at being taken from my studies, and perhaps I sounded a bit impatient when I answered.

If so, the gentleman at the other end gave no sign of it. His voice was most pleasant, quite deep and masculine, and he said, "May I speak, please, with Mrs. Henrietta Buckley?"

"This is Mrs. Buckley," I told him.

"Ah," he said. "Forgive my telephoning, please, Mrs. Buckley. We have never met. But I noticed your entry in the current issue of the Genealogical Exchange—"

"Oh?"

I was immediately excited, all thought of impatience gone. This was surely the fastest reply I'd ever had to date!

"Yes," he said. "I noticed the reference to Euphemia Barber. I do believe that may be the Euphemia Stover who married Jason Barber in Savannah, Georgia, in 1791. Jason Barber is in my direct line, on my mother's side. Jason and Euphemia had only the one child, Abner, and I am descended from him."

"Well," I said. "You certainly do seem to have complete information."

"Oh, yes," he said. "My own family chart is almost complete. For twelve generations, that is. I'm not sure whether I'll try to go back farther than that or not. The English records before 1600 are so incomplete, you know."

"Yes, of course," I said. I was, I admit, taken aback. Twelve generations! Surely that was the most ambitious family tree I had ever heard of, though I had read sometimes of people who had carried particular branches back as many as fifteen generations. But to actually be speaking to a person who had traced his entire family back twelve generations!

"Perhaps," he said, "it would be possible for us to meet, and I could give you the information I have on Euphemia Barber. There are also some Marshalls in one branch of my family; perhaps I can be of help to you there, as well." He laughed, a deep and pleasant sound, which reminded me of my late husband, Edward, when he was most particularly pleased. "And, of course," he said, "there is always the chance that you may have some information on the Marshalls which can help me."

"I think that would be very nice," I said, and so I invited him to come to the apartment the very next afternoon.

At one point the next day, perhaps half an hour before Gerald Fowlkes was to arrive, I stopped my fluttering around to take stock of myself and to realize that if ever there were an indication of second childhood taking over, my thoughts and actions preparatory to Mr. Fowlkes' arrival were certainly it. I had been rushing hither and thither, dusting, rearranging, polishing, pausing incessantly to look in the mirror and touch my hair with fluttering fingers, all as though I were a flighty teenager before her very first date. "Henrietta," I told myself sharply, "you are seventy-three years old, and all that nonsense is well behind you now. Eleven times a grandmother, and just look at how you carry on!"

But poor Edward had been dead and gone these past nine years, my brothers and sisters were all in their graves, and as for my children, all but Tom, the youngest, were thousands of miles away, living their own lives— as of course they should—and only occasionally remembering to write a

duty letter to Mother. And I am much too aware of the dangers of the clinging mother to force my presence too often upon Tom and his family. So I
am very much alone, except of course for my friends in the various church
activities and for those I have met, albeit only by postal, through my
genealogical research.

So it *was* pleasant to be visited by a charming gentleman caller, and particularly so when that gentleman shared my own particular interests. And
Mr. Gerald Fowlkes, on his arrival, was surely no disappointment. He
looked to be no more than fifty-five years of age, though he swore to sixty-
two, and had a fine shock of gray hair above a strong and kindly face. He
dressed very well, with that combination of expense and breeding so little
found these days, when the well-bred seem invariably to be poor and the
well-to-do seem invariably to be horribly plebeian. His manner was refined
and gentlemanly, what we used to call courtly, and he had some very nice
things to say about the appearance of my living room. Actually, I make no
unusual claims as a housekeeper. Living alone, and with quite a comfortable
income having been left me by Edward, it is no problem at all to choose
tasteful furnishings and keep them neat. (Besides, I had scrubbed the apartment from top to bottom in preparation for Mr. Fowlkes' visit.)

He had brought his pedigree along, and what a really beautiful job he
had done. Pedigree charts, photostats of all sorts of records, a running history typed very neatly on bond paper and inserted in a looseleaf notebook—
all in all, the kind of careful, planned, well-thought-out perfection so unsuc-
cessfully striven for by all amateur genealogists.

From Mr. Fowlkes, I got the missing information on Euphemia Barber.
She was born in 1765, in Salem, Massachusetts, the fourth child of seven
born to John and Alicia Stover. She married Jason Barber in Savannah in
1791. Jason, a well-to-do merchant, passed on in 1794, shortly after the birth
of their first child, Abner. Abner was brought up by his paternal grandparents, and Euphemia moved away from Savannah. As I already knew, she
had then gone to Virginia, where she had married John Anderson. After
that, Mr. Fowlkes had no record of her, until her death in Cincinnati, Ohio,
in 1852. She was buried as Euphemia Stover Barber, apparently not having
used the Anderson name after John Anderson's death.

This done, we went on to compare family histories and discover an Alan
Marshall of Liverpool, England, around 1680, common to both trees. I was
able to give Mr. Fowlkes Alan Marshall's birth date. And then the specific purpose of our meeting was finished. I offered tea and cakes, it then being four-
thirty in the afternoon, and Mr. Fowlkes graciously accepted my offering.

And so began the strangest three months of my entire life. Before leaving, Mr. Fowlkes asked me to accompany him to a concert on Friday evening, and I very readily agreed. Then, and afterward, he was a perfect gentleman.

It didn't take me long to realize that I was being courted. Actually, I couldn't believe it at first. After all, at *my* age! But I myself did know some very nice couples who had married late in life—a widow and a widower, both lonely, sharing interests, and deciding to lighten their remaining years together—and looked at in that light it wasn't at all as ridiculous as it might appear at first.

Actually, I had expected my son Tom to laugh at the idea, and to dislike Mr. Fowlkes instantly upon meeting him. I suppose various fictional works that I have read had given me this expectation. So I was most pleasantly surprised when Tom and Mr. Fowlkes got along famously together from their very first meeting, and even more surprised when Tom came to me and told me Mr. Fowlkes had asked him if he would have any objection to his, Mr. Fowlkes', asking for my hand in matrimony. Tom said he had no objection at all, but actually thought it a wonderful idea, for he knew that both Mr. Fowlkes and myself were rather lonely, with nothing but our genealogical hobbies to occupy our minds.

As to Mr. Fowlkes' background, he very early gave me his entire history. He came from a fairly well-to-do family in upstate New York, and was himself now retired from his business, which had been a stock brokerage in Albany. He was a widower these last six years, and his first marriage had not been blessed with any children, so that he was completely alone in the world.

The next three months were certainly active ones. Mr. Fowlkes—Gerald—squired me everywhere, to concerts and to museums and even, after we had come to know one another well enough, to the theater. He was at all times most polite and thoughtful, and there was scarcely a day went by but what we were together.

During this entire time, of course, my own genealogical researches came to an absolute standstill. I was much too busy, and my mind was much too full of Gerald, for me to concern myself with family members who were long since gone to their rewards. Promising leads from the Genealogical Exchange were not followed up, for I didn't write a single letter. And though I did receive many in the Exchange, they all went unopened into a cubbyhole in my desk. And so the matter stayed, while the courtship progressed.

After three months, Gerald at last proposed. "I am not a young man, Henrietta," he said. "Nor a particularly handsome man" —though he most certainly was very handsome, indeed—"nor even a very rich man, although I do have sufficient for my declining years. And I have little to offer you, Henrietta, save my own self, whatever poor companionship I can give you, and the assurance that I will be ever at your side."

What a beautiful proposal! After being nine years a widow, and never expecting even in fanciful daydreams to be once more a wife, what a beautiful proposal and from what a charming gentleman!

I agreed at once, of course, and telephoned Tom the good news that very minute. Tom and his wife, Estelle, had a dinner party for us, and then we made our plans. We would be married three weeks hence. A short time? Yes, of course, it was, but there was really no reason to wait. And we would honeymoon in Washington, D.C., where my oldest boy, Roger, has quite a responsible position with the State Department. After which, we would return to Boston and take up our residence in a lovely old home on Beacon Hill, which was then for sale and which we would jointly purchase.

Ah, the plans! The preparations! How newly filled were my so-recently empty days!

I spent most of the last week closing my apartment on Newbury Street. The furnishings would be moved to our new home by Tom, while Gerald and I were in Washington. But, of course, there was ever so much packing to be done, and I got at it with a will.

And so at last I came to my desk, and my genealogical researches lying as I had left them. I sat down at the desk, somewhat weary, for it was late afternoon and I had been hard at work since sunup, and I decided to spend a short while getting my papers into order before packing them away. And so I opened the mail which had accumulated over the last three months.

There were twenty-three letters. Twelve asked for information on various family names mentioned in my entry in the Exchange, five offered to give me information, and six concerned Euphemia Barber. It was, after all, Euphemia Barber who had brought Gerald and me together in the first place, and so I took time out to read these letters.

And so came the shock. I read the six letters, and then I simply sat limp at the desk, staring into space, and watched the monstrous pattern as it grew in my mind. For there was no question of the truth, no question at all.

Consider: Before starting the letters, this is what I knew of Euphemia Barber: She had been born Euphemia Stover in Salem, Massachusetts, in 1765. In 1791, she married Jason Barber, a widower of Savannah, Georgia.

Jason died two years later, in 1793, of a stomach upset. Three years later, Euphemia appeared in Virginia and married John Anderson, also a widower. John died two years thereafter, in 1798, of stomach upset. In both cases, Euphemia sold her late husband's property and moved on.

And here is what the letters added to that, in chronological order:

From Mrs. Winnie Mae Cuthbert, Dallas, Texas: Euphemia Barber, in 1800, two years after John Anderson's death, appeared in Harrisburg, Pennsylvania, and married one Andrew Cuthbert, a widower and a prosperous feed merchant. Andrew died in 1801, of a stomach upset. The widow sold his store, and moved on.

From Miss Ethel Sutton, Louisville, Kentucky: Euphemia Barber, in 1804, married Samuel Nicholson of Louisville, a widower and a well-to-do tobacco farmer. Samuel Nicholson passed on in 1807, of a stomach upset. The widow sold his farm, and moved on.

From Mrs. Isabelle Padgett, Concord, California: in 1808, Euphemia Barber married Thomas Norton, then Mayor of Dover, New Jersey, and a widower. In 1809, Thomas Norton died of a stomach upset.

From Mrs. Luella Miller, Bicknell, Utah: Euphemia Barber married Jonas Miller, a wealthy shipowner of Portsmouth, New Hampshire, a widower, in 1811. The same year, Jonas Miller died of a stomach upset. The widow sold his property and moved on.

From Mrs. Lola Hopkins, Vancouver, Washington: In 1813, in southern Indiana, Euphemia Barber married Edward Hopkins, a widower and a farmer. Edward Hopkins died in 1816, of a stomach upset. The widow sold the farm, and moved on.

From Mr. Roy Cumbie, Kansas City, Missouri: In 1819, Euphemia Barber married Stanley Thatcher of Kansas City, Missouri, a river barge owner and a widower. Stanley Thatcher died, of a stomach upset, in 1821. The widow sold his property, and moved on.

The evidence was clear, and complete. The intervals of time without dates could mean that there had been other widowers who had succumbed to Euphemia Barber's fatal charms, and whose descendants did not number among themselves an amateur genealogist. Who could tell just how many husbands Euphemia had murdered? For murder it quite clearly was, brutal murder, for profit. I had evidence of eight murders, and who knew but what there were eight more, or eighteen more? Who could tell, at this late date, just how many times Euphemia Barber had murdered for profit, and had never been caught?

Such a woman is inconceivable. Her husbands were always widowers, sure to be lonely, sure to be susceptible to a wily woman. She preyed on widowers, and left them all a widow.

Gerald.

The thought came to me, and I pushed it firmly away. It couldn't possibly be true; it couldn't possibly have a single grain of truth.

But what did I know of Gerald Fowlkes, other than what he had told me? And wasn't I a widow, lonely and susceptible? And wasn't I financially well off?

Like father, like son, they say. Could it be also, like great-great-great-great-great-grandmother, like great-great-great-great-great-grandson?

What a thought! It came to me that there must be any number of widows in the country, like myself, who were interested in tracing their family trees. Women who had a bit of money and leisure, whose children were grown and gone out into the world to live their own lives, and who filled some of the empty hours with the hobby of genealogy. An unscrupulous man, preying on well-to-do widows, could find no better introduction than a common interest in genealogy.

What a terrible thought to have about Gerald! And yet, I couldn't push it from my mind, and at last I decided that the only thing I could possibly do was try to substantiate the autobiography he had given me, for if he had told the truth about himself, then he could surely not be a beast of the type I was imagining.

A stockbroker, he had claimed to have been, in Albany, New York. I at once telephoned an old friend of my first husband's, who was himself a Boston stockbroker, and asked him if it would be possible for him to find out if there had been, at any time in the last fifteen or twenty years, an Albany stockbroker named Gerald Fowlkes. He said he could do so with ease, using some sort of directory he had, and would call me back. He did so, with the shattering news that no such individual was listed!

Still I refused to believe. Donning my coat and hat, I left the apartment at once and went directly to the telephone company, where, after an incredible number of white lies concerning genealogical research, I at last persuaded someone to search for an old Albany, New York, telephone book. I knew that the main office of the company kept books for other major cities, as a convenience for the public, but I wasn't sure they would have any from past years. Nor was the clerk I talked to, but at last she did go and search, and came back finally with the 1946 telephone book from Albany, dusty and somewhat ripped, but still intact, with both the normal listings and the yellow pages.

No Gerald Fowlkes was listed in the white pages, or in the yellow pages under Stocks & Bonds.

So. It was true. And I could see exactly what Gerald's method was. Whenever he was ready to find another victim, he searched one or another of the genealogical magazines until he found someone who shared one of his own past relations. He then proceeded to effect a meeting with that person, found out quickly enough whether or not the intended victim was a widow, of the proper age range, and with the properly large bank account, and then the courtship began.

I imagined that this was the first time he had made the mistake of using Euphemia Barber as the go-between. And I doubted that he even realized he was following in Euphemia's footsteps. Certainly, none of the six people who had written to me about Euphemia could possibly guess, knowing only of one marriage and death, what Euphemia's role in life had actually been.

And what was I to do now? In the taxi, on the way back to my apartment, I sat huddled in a corner, and tried to think.

For this *was* a severe shock, and a terrible disappointment. And could I face Tom, or my other children, or any one of my friends, to whom I had already written the glad news of my impending marriage? And how could I return to the drabness of my days before Gerald had come to bring gaiety and companionship and courtly grace to my days?

Could I even call the police? I was sufficiently convinced myself, but could I possibly convince anyone else?

All at once, I made my decision. And, having made it, I immediately felt ten years younger, ten pounds lighter, and quite a bit less foolish. For, I might as well admit, in addition to everything else, this had been a terrible blow to my pride.

But the decision was made, and I returned to my apartment cheerful and happy.

*   *   *

And so we were married.

Married? Of course. Why not?

Because he will try to murder me? Well, of course he will try to murder me. As a matter of fact, he has already tried, half a dozen times.

But Gerald is working at a terrible disadvantage. For he cannot murder me in any way that looks like murder. It must appear to be a natural death, or, at the very worst, an accident. Which means that he must be devious, and he must plot and plan, and never come at me openly to do me in.

And there is the source of his disadvantage. For I am forewarned, and forewarned is forearmed.

But what, really, do I have to lose? At seventy-three, how many days on this earth do I have left? And how *rich* life is these days! How rich compared to my life before Gerald came into it! Spiced with the thrill of danger, the excitement of cat and mouse, the intricate moves and countermoves of the most fascinating game of all.

And, of course, a pleasant and charming husband. Gerald *has* to be pleasant and charming. He can never disagree with me, at least not very forcefully, for he can't afford the danger of my leaving him. Nor can he afford to believe that I suspect him. I have never spoken of the matter to him, and so far as he is concerned I know nothing. We go to concerts and museums and the theater together. Gerald is attentive and gentlemanly, quite the best sort of companion at all times.

Of course, I can't allow him to feed me breakfast in bed, as he would so love to do. No, I told him I was an old-fashioned woman, and believed that cooking was a woman's job, and so I won't let him near the kitchen. Poor Gerald!

And we don't take trips, no matter how much he suggests them.

And we've closed off the second story of our home, since I pointed out that the first floor was certainly spacious enough for just the two of us, and I felt I was getting a little old for climbing stairs. He could do nothing, of course, but agree.

And, in the meantime, I have found another hobby, though of course Gerald knows nothing of it. Through discreet inquiries, and careful perusal of past issues of the various genealogical magazines, the use of the family names in Gerald's family tree, I am gradually compiling another sort of tree. Not a family tree, no. One might facetiously call it a hanging tree. It is a list of Gerald's wives. It is in with my genealogical files, which I have willed to the Boston library. Should Gerald manage to catch me after all, what a surprise is in store for the librarian who sorts out those files of mine! Not as big a surprise as the one in store for Gerald, of course.

Ah, here comes Gerald now, in the automobile he bought last week. He's going to ask me again to go for a ride with him.

But I shan't go.

CAROLYN WHEAT

Ghost Station

*I*F THERE'S ONE THING *I* CAN'T STAND, IT'S A WOMAN DRUNK. The words burned my memory the way Irish whiskey used to burn my throat, only there was no pleasant haze of alcohol to follow. Just bitter heartburn pain.

It was my first night back on the job, back to being Sergeant Maureen Gallagher instead of "the patient." Wasn't it hard enough being a transit cop, hurtling beneath the streets of Manhattan on a subway train that should have been in the Transit Museum? Wasn't it enough that after four weeks of detox I felt empty instead of clean and sober? Did I *have* to have some rookie's casually cruel words ricocheting in my brain like a wild-card bullet?

Why couldn't I remember the good stuff? Why couldn't I think about O'Hara's beefy handshake, Greenspan's "Glad to see ya, Mo," Ianuzzo's smiling welcome? Why did I have to run the tape in my head of Manny Delgado asking Captain Lomax for a different partner?

"Hey, I got nothing against a lady sarge, Cap," he'd said. "Don't get me wrong. It's just that if there's one thing I can't stand . . ." Et cetera.

Lomax had done what any standup captain would—kicked Delgado's ass and told him the assignment stood. What he hadn't known was that I'd heard the words and couldn't erase them from my mind.

Even without Delgado, the night hadn't gotten off to a great start. Swinging in at midnight for a twelve-to-eight, I'd been greeted with the news that I was on Graffiti Patrol, the dirtiest, most mind-numbing assignment in the whole transit police duty roster. I was a sergeant, damn it, on my way to a gold shield, and I wasn't going to earn it dodging rats in tunnels or going after twelve-year-olds armed with spray paint.

Especially when the rest of the cop world, both under- and above-ground, was working overtime on the torch murders of homeless people. There'd been four human bonfires in the past six weeks, and the cops were determined there wouldn't be a fifth.

Was Lomax punishing me, or was this assignment his subtle way of easing my entry back into the world? Either way, I resented it. I wanted to be a real cop again, back with Sal Minucci, my old partner. He was assigned to the big one, in the thick of the action, where both of us belonged. I should have been with him. I was Anti-Crime, for God's sake, I should have been assigned—

Or should I? Did I really want to spend my work nights prowling New York's underground skid row, trying to get information from men and women too zonked out to take care of legs gone gangrenous, whose lives stretched from one bottle of Cool Breeze to another?

Hell, yes. If it would bring me one step closer to that gold shield, I'd interview all the devils in hell. On my day off.

If there's one thing I can't stand, it's a woman drunk.

What did Lomax think—that mingling with winos would topple me off the wagon? That I'd ask for a hit from some guy's short dog and pass out in the Bleecker Street station? Was that why he'd kept me off the big one and had me walking a rookie through routine Graffiti Patrol?

Was I getting paranoid, or was lack of alcohol rotting my brain?

Manny and I had gone to our respective locker rooms to suit up. Plain clothes—and I do mean plain. Long Johns first; damp winter had a way of seeping down into the tunnels and into your very blood. Then a pair of denims the Goodwill would have turned down. Thick wool socks, fisherman's duck boots, a black turtleneck, and a photographer's vest with lots of pockets. A black knit hat pulled tight over my red hair.

Then the gear: flashlight, more important than a gun on this assignment, handcuffs, ticket book, radio, gun, knife. A slapper, an oversize blackjack, hidden in the rear pouch of the vest. They were against regulations; I'd get at least a command discipline if caught with it, but experience told me I'd rather have it than a gun going against a pack of kids.

I'd forgotten how heavy the stuff was; I felt like a telephone lineman.

I looked like a cat burglar.

Delgado and I met at the door. It was obvious he'd never done vandal duty before. His tan chinos were immaculate, and his hiking boots didn't look waterproof. His red plaid flannel shirt was neither warm enough nor the right dark color. With his Latin good looks, he would have been stunning in an L. L Bean catalog, but after ten minutes in a subway tunnel, he'd pass for a chimney sweep.

"Where are we going?" he asked, his tone a shade short of sullen. And there was no respectful "Sergeant" at the end of the question, either. This boy needed a lesson in manners.

I took a malicious delight in describing our destination. "The Black Hole of Calcutta," I replied cheerfully, explaining that I meant the unused lower platform of the City Hall station downtown. The oldest, darkest, dankest spot in all Manhattan. If there were any subway alligators, they definitely lurked in the Black Hole.

The expression on Probationary Transit Police Officer Manuel Delgado's face was all I could have hoped for. I almost—but not quite—took pity on the kid when I added, "And after that, we'll try one or two of the ghost stations."

"Ghost stations?" Now he looked really worried. "What are those?"

This kid wasn't just a rookie; he was a suburbanite. Every New Yorker knew about ghost stations, abandoned platforms where trains no longer stopped. They were still lit, though, and showed up in the windows of passing trains like ghost towns on the prairie. They were ideal canvases for the aspiring artists of the underground city.

I explained on the subway, heading downtown. The car, which rattled under the city streets like a tin lizzie, was nearly riderless at 1:00 A.M. A typical Monday late hour.

The passengers were one Orthodox Jewish man falling asleep over his Hebrew Bible, two black women, both reading thick paperback romances, the obligatory pair of teenagers making out in the last seat, and an old Chinese woman.

I didn't want to look at Delgado. More than once I'd seen a fleeting smirk on his face when I glanced his way. It wasn't enough for insubordination; the best policy was to ignore it.

I let the rhythm of the subway car lull me into a litany of the AA slogans I was trying to work into my life: EASY DOES IT. KEEP IT SIMPLE, SWEETHEART. ONE DAY AT A TIME. I saw them in my mind the way they appeared on the walls at meetings, illuminated, like old Celtic manuscripts.

This night I had to take one hour at a time. Maybe even one minute at a time. My legs felt wobbly. I was a sailor too long from the sea. I'd lost my subway legs. I felt white and thin, as though I'd had several major organs removed.

Then the drunk got on. One of the black women got off, the other one looked up at the station sign and went back to her book, and the drunk got on.

If there's one thing I can't stand, it's a woman drunk.

ONE DAY AT A TIME. EASY DOES IT.

I stiffened. The last thing I wanted was to react in front of Delgado, but I couldn't help it. The sight of an obviously intoxicated man stumbling into our subway car brought the knowing smirk back to his face.

There was one at every AA meeting. No matter how nice the neighborhood, how well dressed most people attending the meeting were, there was always a drunk. A real drunk, still reeling, still reeking of cheap booze. My sponsor, Margie, said they were there for a reason, to let us middle-class, recovery-oriented types remember that "there but for the grace of God . . ."

I cringed whenever I saw them, especially if the object lesson for the day was a woman.

"Hey, kid," the drunk called out to Delgado, in a voice as inappropriately loud as a deaf man's, "how old are you?" The doors closed and the car lurched forward; the drunk all but fell into his seat.

"Old enough," Manny replied, flashing the polite smile a well-brought-up kid saves for his maiden aunt.

The undertone wasn't so pretty. Little sidelong glances at me that said, *See how nice I am to this old fart. See what a good boy I am. I like drunks, Sergeant Gallagher.*

To avoid my partner's face, I concentrated on the subway ads as though they contained all the wisdom of the Big Book. "Here's to birth defects," proclaimed a pregnant woman about to down a glass of beer. Two monks looked to heaven, thanking God in Spanish for the fine quality of their brandy.

Weren't there any signs on this damn train that didn't involve booze? Finally an ad I could smile at: the moon in black space; on it, someone had scrawled, "Alice Kramden was here, 1959."

My smile faded as I remembered Sal Minucci's raised fist, his Jackie Gleason growl. "One of these days, Gallagher, you're goin' to the moon. To the *moon!*"

It wasn't just the murder case I missed. It was Sal. The easy partnership of the man who'd put up with my hangovers, my depressions, my wild nights out with the boys.

"Y'know how old I am?" the drunk shouted, almost falling over in his seat. He righted himself. "Fifty-four in September," he announced, an expectant look on his face.

After a quick smirk in my direction, Manny gave the guy what he wanted. "You don't look it," he said. No trace of irony appeared on his Spanish altar boy's face. It was as though he'd never said the words that were eating into me like battery-acid AA coffee.

The sudden jab of anger that stabbed through me took me by surprise, especially since it wasn't directed at Delgado. *No, you don't look it,* I thought. *You look more like seventy.* White wisps of hair over a bright pink scalp. The face more than pink; a slab of raw calves' liver. Road maps of broken blood vessels on his nose and cheeks. Thin white arms and matchstick legs under too-big trousers. When he lifted his hand, ropy with bulging blue veins, it fluttered like a pennant in the breeze.

Like Uncle Paul's hands.

I turned away sharply. I couldn't look at the old guy anymore. The constant visual digs Delgado kept throwing in my direction were nothing compared to the pain of looking at a man dying before my eyes. I didn't want to see blue eyes in that near-dead face. *As blue as the lakes of Killarney,* Uncle Paul used to say in his mock-Irish brogue.

I focused on the teenagers making out in the rear of the car. A couple of Spanish kids, wearing identical pink T-shirts and black leather jackets. If I stared at them long enough, would they stop groping and kissing, or would an audience spur their passion?

Uncle Paul. After Daddy left us, he was my special friend, and I was his best girl.

I squeezed my eyes shut, but the memories came anyway. The red bike Uncle Paul gave me for my tenth birthday. The first really big new thing, bought just for me, that I'd ever had. The best part was showing it off to cousin Tommy. For once I didn't need his hand-me-downs, or Aunt Bridget's clucking over me for being poor. *God bless the child who's got her own.*

I opened my eyes just as the Lex passed through the ghost station at Worth Street. Closed off to the public for maybe fifteen years, it seemed a mirage, dimly seen through the dirty windows of the subway car. Bright color on the white tile walls told me graffiti bombers had been there. A good place to check, but not until after City Hall. I owed Manny Delgado a trip to the Black Hole.

"Uh, Sergeant?"

I turned; a patronizing smile played on Delgado's lips. He'd apparently been trying to get my attention. "Sorry," I said, feigning a yawn. "Just a little tired."

Yeah, sure, his look remarked. "We're coming to Brooklyn Bridge. Shouldn't we get off the train?"

"Right." *Leave Uncle Paul where he belongs.*

At the Brooklyn Bridge stop, we climbed up the steps to the upper platform, showed our ID to the woman token clerk, and told her we were going into the tunnel toward City Hall. Then we went back downstairs, heading for the south end of the downtown platform.

As we were about to go past the gate marked NO UNAUTHORIZED PERSONNEL BEYOND THIS POINT, I looked back at the lighted platform, which made a crescent-shaped curve behind us. Almost in a mirror image, the old drunk was about to pass the forbidden gate and descend into the tunnel heading uptown.

He stepped carefully, holding on to the white, bathroom-tile walls, edging himself around the waist-high gate. He lowered himself down the stone steps, the exact replica of the ones Manny and I were about to descend, then disappeared into the blackness.

I couldn't let him go. There were too many dangers in the subway, dangers beyond the torch killer everyone was on the hunt for. How many frozen bodies had I stumbled over on the catwalks between tunnels? How many huddled victims had been hit by trains as they lay in sodden sleep? And yet, I had to be careful. My friend Kathy Denzer had gone after a bum sleeping on the catwalk, only to have the man stab her in the arm for trying to save his life.

I couldn't let him go. Turning to Delgado, I said, "Let's save City Hall for later. I saw some graffiti at Worth Street on the way here. Let's check that out first."

He shrugged. At least he was being spared the Black Hole, his expression said.

Entering the tunnel's blackness, leaving behind the brightly lit world of sleepy riders, a tiny rush of adrenaline, like MSG after a Chinese dinner, coursed through my bloodstream. Part of it was pure reversion to childhood's fears. Hansel and Gretel. Snow White. Lost in dark woods, with enemies all around. In this case, rats. Their scuffling sent shivers up my spine as we balanced our way along the catwalk above the tracks.

The other part was elation. This was my job. I was good at it. I could put aside my fears and step boldly down into murky depths where few New Yorkers ever went.

Our flashlights shone dim as fireflies. I surveyed the gloomy underground world I'd spent my professional life in.

My imagination often took over in the tunnels. They became caves of doom. Or an evil wood, out of *Lord of the Rings*. The square columns holding up the tunnel roof were leafless trees, the constant trickle of foul water between the tracks a poisonous stream from which no one drank and lived.

Jones Beach. Uncle Paul's huge hand cradling my foot, then lifting me high in the air and flinging me backward, laughing with delight, into the cool water. Droplets clinging to his red beard, and Uncle Paul shaking them off into the sunlight like a wet Irish setter.

Me and Mo, we're the only true Gallaghers. The only redheads. I got straight A's in English; nobody's grammar was safe from me—except Uncle Paul's.

I thought all men smelled like him: whiskey and tobacco.

As Manny and I plodded along the four-block tunnel between the live station and the dead one, we exchanged no words. The acrid stench of an old track fire filled my nostrils the way memories flooded my mind. Trying to push Uncle Paul away, I bent all my concentration on stepping carefully around the foul-smelling water, the burned debris I didn't want to identify.

I suspected Delgado's silence was due to fear; he wouldn't want a shaking voice to betray his tension. I knew how he felt. The first nighttime tunnel trek was a landmark in a young transit cop's life.

When the downtown express thundered past, we ducked into the coffin-sized alcoves set aside for transit workers. My heart pounded as the wind wake of the train pulled at my clothes; the fear of falling forward, landing under those relentless steel wheels, never left me, no matter how many times I stood in the well. I always thought of Anna Karenina; once in a while, in my drinking days, I'd wondered how it would feel to edge forward, to let the train's undertow pull me toward death.

I could never do it. I'd seen too much blood on the tracks.

Light at the end of the tunnel. The Worth Street station sent rays of hope into the spidery blackness. My step quickened; Delgado's pace matched mine. Soon we were almost running toward the light, like cavemen coming from the hunt to sit by the fire of safety.

We were almost at the edge of the platform when I motioned Delgado to stop. My hunger to bathe in the light was as great as his, but our post was in the shadows, watching.

A moment of panic. I'd lost the drunk. Had he fallen on the tracks, the electrified third rail roasting him like a pig at a barbecue? Not possible; we'd have heard, and smelled.

I had to admit, the graffiti painting wasn't a mindless scrawl. It was a picture, full of color and life. Humanlike figures in bright primary shades, grass green, royal blue, orange, sun yellow, and carnation pink—colors unknown in the black-and-gray tunnels—stood in a line, waiting to go through a subway turnstile. Sexless, they were cookie-cutter replicas of one another, the only difference among them the color inside the black edges.

A rhythmic clicking sound made Delgado jump. "What the hell—?"

"Relax, Manny," I whispered. "It's the ball bearing in the spray-paint can. The vandals are here. As soon as the paint hits the tiles, we jump out and bust them."

Four rowdy teenagers, ranging in color from light brown to ebony, laughed raucously and punched one another with a theatrical style that said *We bad. We* real *bad.* They bounded up the steps from the other side of the platform and surveyed their artwork, playful as puppies, pointing out choice bits they had added to their mural.

It should have been simple. Two armed cops, with the advantage of surprise, against four kids armed with Day-Glo spray paint. Two things kept it from being simple: the drunk, wherever the hell he was, and the fact that one of the kids said, "Hey, bro, when Cool and Jo-Jo gettin' here?"

A very black kid with a nylon stocking on his head answered, "Jo-Jo be comin' with Pinto. Cool say he might be bringin' Slasher and T. P."

Great. Instead of two against four, it sounded like all the graffiti artists in New York City were planning a convention in the Worth Street ghost station.

"Sarge?" Delgado's voice was urgent. "We've gotta—"

"I know," I whispered back. "Get on the radio and call for backup."

Then I remembered. Worth Street was a dead spot. Lead in the ceiling above our heads turned our radios into worthless toys.

"Stop," I said wearily as Manny pulled the antenna up on his handheld radio. "It won't work. You'll have to go back to Brooklyn Bridge. Alert Booth Robert two-twenty-one. Have them call Operations. Just ask for backup, don't make it a ten thirteen." A 10-13 meant "officer in trouble," and I didn't want to be the sergeant who cried wolf.

"Try the radio along the way," I went on. "You never know when it will come to life. I'm not sure where the lead ends."

Watching Delgado trudge back along the catwalk, I felt lonely, helpless, and stupid. No one knew we'd gone to Worth Street instead of the Black Hole, and that was my fault.

"Hey," one of the kids called, pointing to a pile of old clothes in the corner of the platform, "what this dude be doin' in our crib?"

Dude? What dude? Then the old clothes began to rise; it was the drunk from the train. He was huddled into a fetal ball, hoping not to be noticed by the graffiti gang.

Nylon Stocking boogied over to the old drunk, sticking a finger in his ribs. "What you be doin' here, ol' man? Huh? Answer me."

A fat kid with a flat top walked over, sat down next to the drunk, reached into the old man's jacket pocket, and pulled out a half-empty pint bottle.

A lighter-skinned, thinner boy slapped the drunk around, first lifting him by the scruff of the neck, then laughing as he flopped back to the floor. The old guy tried to rise, only to be kicked in the ribs by Nylon Stocking.

The old guy was bleeding at the mouth. Fat Boy held the pint of booze aloft, teasing the drunk the way you tease a dog with a bone. The worst part was that the drunk was reaching for it, hands flapping wildly, begging. He'd have barked if they'd asked him to.

I was shaking, my stomach starting to heave. God, where was Manny? Where was my backup? I had to stop the kids before their friends got there, but I felt too sick to move. *If there's one thing I can't stand, it's a woman drunk.* It was as though every taunt, every kick, was aimed at me, not just at the old man.

I reached into my belt for my gun, then opened my vest's back pouch and pulled out the slapper. Ready to charge, I stopped cold when Nylon Stocking said, "Yo, y'all want to do him like we done the others?"

Fat Boy's face lit up. "Yeah," he agreed. "Feel like a cold night. We needs a little fire."

"You right, bro," the light-skinned kid chimed in. "I got the kerosene. Done took it from my momma's heater."

"What he deserve, man," the fourth member of the gang said, his voice a low growl. "Comin' into our crib, pissin' on the art, smellin' up the place. This here *our* turf, dig?" He prodded the old man in the chest.

"I—I didn't mean nothing," the old man whimpered. "I just wanted a place to sleep."

Uncle Paul, sleeping on our couch when he was too drunk for Aunt Rose to put up with him. He was never too drunk for Mom to take him in. Never too drunk to give me one of his sweet Irish smiles and call me his best girl.

The light-skinned kid opened the bottle—ironically, it looked as if it once contained whiskey—and sprinkled the old man the way my mother sprinkled clothes before ironing them. Nylon Stocking pulled out a book of matches.

By the time Delgado came back, with or without backup, there'd be one more bonfire if I didn't do something. Fast.

Surprise was my only hope. Four of them, young and strong. One of me, out of shape and shaky.

I shot out a light. I cracked the bulb on the first shot. Target shooting was my best asset as a cop, and I used it to give the kids the impression they were surrounded.

The kids jumped away from the drunk, moving in all directions. "Shit," one said, "who shootin'?"

I shot out the second and last bulb. In the dark, I had the advantage. They wouldn't know, at least at first, that only one cop was coming after them.

"Let's book," another cried. "Ain't worth stayin' here to get shot."

I ran up the steps, onto the platform lit only by the moonlike rays from the other side of the tracks. Yelling "Stop, police," I waded into the kids, swinging my illegal slapper.

Thump into the ribs of the kid holding the kerosene bottle. He dropped it, clutching his chest and howling. I felt the breath whoosh out of him, heard the snap of rib cracking. I wheeled and slapped Nylon Stocking across the knee, earning another satisfying howl.

My breath came in gasps, curses pouring out of me. Blood pounded in my temples, a thumping noise that sounded louder than the express train.

The advantage of surprise was over. The other two kids jumped me, one riding my back, the other going for my stomach with hard little fists. All I could see was a maddened teenage tornado circling me with blows. My arm felt light as I thrust my gun deep into the kid's stomach. He doubled, groaning.

It was like chugging beer at a cop racket. Every hit, every satisfying *whack* of blackjack against flesh made me hungry for the next. I whirled and socked. The kids kept coming, and I kept knocking them down like bowling pins.

The adrenaline rush was stupendous, filling me with elation. I was a real cop again. There was life after detox.

At last they stopped. Panting, I stood among the fallen, exhausted. My hair had escaped from my knit hat and hung in matted tangles over a face red-hot as a griddle.

I pulled out my cuffs and chained the kids together, wrist to wrist, wishing I had enough sets to do each individually. Together, even cuffed, they could overpower me. Especially since they were beginning to realize I was alone.

I felt weak, spent. As though I'd just made love.

I sat down on the platform, panting, my gun pointed at Nylon Stocking. "You have the right to remain silent," I began.

As I finished the last Miranda warning on the last kid, I heard the cavalry coming over the hill. Manny Delgado, with four reinforcements.

As the new officers took the collars, I motioned Manny aside, taking him to where the drunk lay sprawled in the corner, still shaking and whimpering.

"Do you smell anything?" I asked.

Manny wrinkled his nose. I looked down at the drunk.

A trickle of water seeped from underneath him; his crotch was soaked.

Uncle Paul, weaving his way home, singing off-key, stopping to take a piss under the lamppost. Nothing unusual in that, except that this time Julie Ann Mackinnon, my eighth-grade rival, watched from across the street. My cheeks burned as I recalled how she'd told the other kids what she'd seen, her hand cupped over her giggling mouth.

"Not that," I said, my tone sharp, my face reddening. "The kerosene. These kids are the torch killers. They were going to roast this guy. That's why I had to take them on alone."

Delgado's face registered the skepticism I'd seen lurking in his eyes all night. Could he trust me? He'd been suitably impressed at my chain gang of prisoners, but now I was talking about solving the crime that had every cop in the city on overtime.

"Look, just go back to Brooklyn Bridge and radio"—I was going to say Captain Lomax, when I thought better—"Sal Minucci in Anti-Crime. He'll want to have the guy's coat analyzed. And make sure somebody takes good care of that bottle." I pointed to the now-empty whiskey bottle the light-skinned boy had poured kerosene from.

"Isn't that his?" Manny indicated the drunk.

"No, his is a short dog," I said, then turned away as I realized the term was not widely known in nondrunk circles.

Just go, kid, I prayed. *Get the hell out of here before—*

He turned, following the backup officers with their chain gang. "And send for Emergency Medical for this guy," I added. "I'll stay here till they come."

I looked down at the drunk. His eyes were blue, a watery, no-color blue with all the life washed out of them. Uncle Paul's eyes.

Uncle Paul, blurry-faced and maudlin, too blitzed to care that I'd come home from school with a medal for the best English composition. I'd put my master-piece by his chair, so he could read it after dinner. He spilled whiskey on it; the blue-black ink ran like tears and blotted out my carefully chosen words.

Uncle Paul, old, sick, and dying, just like this one. Living by that time more on the street than at home, though there were people who would take him in. His eyes more red than blue, his big frame wasted. I felt a sob rising, like death squeezing my lungs. I heaved, grabbing for air. My face was wet with tears I didn't recall shedding.

I hate you, Uncle Paul. I'll never be like you. Never.

I walked over to the drunk, still sprawled on the platform. I was a sleep-walker; my arm lifted itself. I jabbed the butt of my gun into old, thin ribs, feeling it bump against bone. It would be a baseball-size bruise. First a raw red-purple, then blue-violet, finally a sickly yellow-gray.

I lifted my foot, just high enough to land with a thud near the kidneys. The old drunk grunted, his mouth falling open. A drizzle of saliva fell to the ground. He put shaking hands to his face and squeezed his eyes shut. I lifted my foot again. I wanted to kick and kick and kick.

Uncle Paul, a frozen lump of meat found by some transit cop on the aboveground platform at 161st Street. The Yankee Stadium stop, where he took me when the Yanks played home games. We'd eat at the Yankee Tavern, me wolfing down a corned beef on rye and cream soda, Uncle Paul putting away draft beer after draft beer.

Before he died, Uncle Paul had taken all the coins out of his pocket, stacking them in neat little piles beside him. Quarters, dimes, nickels, pennies. An inventory of his worldly goods.

I took a deep, shuddering breath, looked down at the sad old man I'd brutalized. A hot rush of shame washed over me.

I knelt down, gently moving the frail, blue-white hands away from the near-transparent face. The fear I saw in the liquid blue eyes sent a piercing ray of self-hatred through me.

If there's anything I can't stand, it's a woman drunk. Me too, Manny, I can't stand women drunks either.

The old man's lips trembled; tears filled his eyes and rolled down his thin cheeks. He shook his head from side to side, as though trying to wake himself from a bad dream.

"Why?" he asked, his voice a raven's croak.

"Because I loved you so much." The words weren't in my head anymore, they were slipping out into the silent, empty world of the ghost station. As though Uncle Paul weren't buried in Calvary Cemetery but could hear me with the ears of this old man who looked too damn much like him. "Because I wanted to be just like you. And I am." My voice broke. "I'm just like you, Uncle Paul. I'm a drunk." I put my head on my knee and sobbed like a child. All the shame of my drinking days welled up in my chest. The stupid things I'd said and done, the times I'd had to be taken home and put to bed, the times I'd thrown up in the street outside the bar. *If there's one thing I can't stand . . .*

"Oh, God, I wish I were dead."

The bony hand on mine felt like a talon. I started, then looked into the old man's watery eyes. I sat in the ghost station and saw in this stranger the ghost that had been my dying uncle.

"Why should you wish a thing like that?" the old man asked. His voice was clear, no booze-blurred slurring, no groping for words burned out of the brain by alcohol. "You're a young girl. You've got your whole life ahead of you."

My whole life. To be continued . . .

One day at a time. One night at a time.

When I got back to the District, changed out of my work clothes, showered, would there be a meeting waiting for me? Damn right; in the city that never sleeps, AA never sleeps either.

I reached out to the old man. My fingers brushed his silver stubble.

"I'm sorry, Uncle Paul," I said. "I'm sorry."